M·O·N·T·A·N·A

A Legacy of Faith and Love in Four Complete Novels

Ann Bell

BARBOUR
PUBLISHING, INC.
Uhrichsville, Ohio

Autumn Love © 1994 by Ann Bell.
Contagious Love © 1994 by Ann Bell.
Inspired Love © 1995 by Ann Bell.
Distant Love © 1995 by Ann Bell.

ISBN 1-57748-794-X

Published by Barbour Publishing, Inc., P.O. Box 719, Uhrichsville, Ohio 44683 http://www.barbourbooks.com

 Member of the
Evangelical Christian
Publishers Association

Printed in the United States of America.

ANN BELL is a librarian by profession and lives in Iowa with her husband Jim, who is her biggest supporter. Ann has worked as a librarian and teacher in Iowa, Oregon, Guam, and Montana. She has been honored in the top three picks of **Heartsong Presents** members' favorite authors. Her eight **Heartsong** books all center around a fictional town in Montana called Rocky Bluff. She has also written numerous articles for Christian magazines and a book titled *Proving Yourself: A Study of James.*

Autumn Love

For my mother, Frances Hartman, of Stuart, Iowa,
who proofread this manuscript at age eighty-four;
my children, Philip and Teresa Orr, who did not say,
"But you're too old, Mother;"
and my husband's children,
Elizabeth Guimont, Pamela and Frances Bell, and Patricia Mishler,
who did not say,
"But not at your age, Dad."

Chapter 1

Biting March winds howled around the one-story high school building in central Montana. Yet the brick walls of Rocky Bluff High offered little protection from a more sinister threat as a loud, sharp report echoed down the lonely corridors. Edith Harkness ran from the teachers' lounge toward the principal's office as fast as her sixty-four-year-old legs could carry her. Montana born and bred, Edith was no stranger to guns and was an excellent shot herself. From the quickness of the resounding noise, she believed the offending weapon was a small-caliber handgun.

As she flung the office door open, the scene that greeted her filled her heart with terror. Her principal, Grady Walker, lay on the floor bleeding from a head wound. Viola Tomkins, his secretary, huddled in a corner crying hysterically. Edith instantly recognized the young man holding the .38 police special as Larry Reynolds, a tall, husky member of the senior class.

Edith felt her heart pound and blood rush to her face as though someone had slapped her on the cheek. She had to act quickly. Grady might survive if he could get to a hospital immediately.

First, however, she transferred her attention to Larry. He seemed detached from himself. Even though he was looking directly at her, he didn't show any recognition. *He's in a catatonic state,* she thought thankfully.

"Give me the gun, Larry." The confidence in her voice surprised her, and she hoped Larry wouldn't see how frightened she was. The six-foot, two-inch quarterback of the Rocky Bluff football team, Larry was also the greatest center its basketball team had ever produced.

He pointed the gun at her chest.

"Larry," she said, taking a few steps toward him, "give me the gun and no one else will get hurt."

The young man's arm went limp. Gradually he relaxed his grip until the weapon fell into Edith's trembling hand. Within seconds she became aware of the crowd milling in the hallway outside the office door. Basketball coach Todd Watson pushed his way into the room.

"Todd, take Larry to your office. Hold him there until the police arrive."

"Come with me, Larry. Everything will be all right," the coach said soothingly as he led his player away. The crowd parted in shocked silence.

"Get the school nurse up here," Edith yelled to no one in particular. Yanking the telephone from its cradle, she dialed 911. "There has been a shooting at Rocky Bluff High School. We need an ambulance and the police immediately."

As Edith hung up the telephone, Amy Wallace, the school nurse, ran into the room. She immediately began to apply pressure to the principal's head in an effort to stop the bleeding.

Edith suddenly noticed she still had Larry's gun in her hand. Fighting the urge to fling it away, she took a deep breath and laid the weapon on the principal's desk. A boost of adrenaline seemed to surge through her as she pulled the trembling secretary to her feet. Still sobbing, Viola laid her head on Edith's shoulder.

"Amy, can you handle Grady by yourself?" Edith questioned anxiously as she supported most of Viola's weight against her body.

"Yes. Get Viola out of here."

Edith turned Viola over to the physical education teacher, who took her to the teachers' lounge. She then quietly made her way to her own classroom past a curious crowd of onlooking faculty and students. She fell into her chair, buried her head into her hands, and cried. Her heart continued to pound uncontrollably and she was having trouble breathing. As the ambulance sirens became louder, she fought to compose herself. Help was on the way!

A short time later Amy burst into the room accompanied by two police officers. "Edith, are you all right?"

"Yes, I think so. How is Grady?"

"He's one lucky man. The bullet grazed his temple and caused a lot of bleeding, but he'll be fine in a few days. They're taking him to the hospital for observation. Edith, this is Officer Phil Mooney and Officer Scott Packwood. They would like to ask you some questions and afterward I want to check you over."

Edith spoke into Officer Mooney's pocket-sized tape recorder, trying to describe exactly what happened. She agonized over every detail of those terrifying moments. In retelling the story she was surprised at how fast it had happened. She was in the office no more than two minutes, but those moments had seemed like an eternity.

After the officers left Edith walked down the corridor to the nurse's office where Amy waited. "Lie down on the cot," Amy directed as Edith nearly collapsed onto the clean sheets. "I want to check your pulse and blood pressure."

A worried frown spread across Amy's face. "Do you have a history of heart trouble, Edith?"

"No, I rarely even have a cold."

"Any member of your family ever had heart trouble?"

"Not that I know of. I lost my husband to a heart attack ten years ago, but there was no history of heart trouble in his family, either. Why do you ask?"

"Well, your pulse rate is sky high and your blood pressure is almost off the charts. This is most likely a reaction to the horrible experience you had today, but to be on the safe side, I'd like a doctor to examine you."

"I'm sure I'll be okay, but if you think it's necessary, I'll go."

"I'll call Dr. Brewer and tell him it's an emergency. Classes are dismissed for the rest of the day. See the doctor and then go straight home. Better yet, take several days off work. I'll call you tomorrow."

Edith returned to her classroom and mechanically took her purse from the top left-hand drawer and her coat from the closet. The bitter cold wind didn't bother her as she walked across the parking lot. She was already numb with shock.

Cautiously she steered the car down Grove Street to Dr. Brewer's office. The nurse quickly ushered her into an examining room, bypassing patients already waiting in the reception area.

"Edith, you have the heart of a twenty year old," the dark-haired, middle-aged doctor assured her after he completed a few minutes of routine examination. "Your elevated blood pressure is merely due to the crisis you experienced. I'll write a prescription for a tranquilizer to help you rest tonight."

"Dr. Brewer, I've never taken a tranquilizer in my life and I'm not about to start now," Edith stated firmly. "If it is all right with you, I'd just as soon take a couple aspirin and have a cup of herbal tea to help me relax. It has worked for me before, I don't know why it wouldn't work tonight."

The doctor considered a moment. "Go ahead, try the aspirin and tea, but be sure and call me if you have any problems. I do want you to take a few days off work, though."

That evening Edith's daughter-in-law Nancy came to visit. The two women relaxed in the living room. Nancy curled her long, slender legs under her on the sofa while Edith leaned back in her recliner by the window.

"Bob would be here, but he's in Billings buying inventory for the store," Nancy said. "Jay and Dawn send their love. They wanted to come, but I didn't want them out late on a school night."

"I can't erase those few horrible moments from my mind," Edith confessed with her hand still trembling as she took a sip of tea. "I keep asking myself why. Why Larry Reynolds? Why here in Rocky Bluff?"

9

"Mom, the Reynoldses are good customers at the store, but all I know about Larry is that he's the community sports hero."

Edith lifted her shoulders helplessly. "Larry is more than a good athlete. As the kids say, he's a megastar. He was quarterback of the football team, but his greatest talent was on the basketball floor. Everybody admired him. Larry has had more press coverage than anyone else in the history of Rocky Bluff."

"Sounds like he earned it."

"Yes, he has," Edith explained. "For two years running he was named center on the all-state basketball team. To top off his outstanding high school career, last month he received a basketball scholarship to Montana A & M."

"He had everything going for him. Why would he throw it all away now?"

"Actually he threw it away two weeks ago. Remember when half the town went to Billings to see the class A state basketball championship? I yelled myself hoarse. I was proud of our school and even prouder of our basketball team, especially Larry. He did an outstanding job."

"Bob listened to the game on the radio," Nancy recalled with an amused grin. "I've never heard him get that excited over a simple ball game. The next day there were rumors around town that some of the team got in trouble after the game. What happened?"

"As I understand it, after the game the team went out to celebrate, and a few of the boys had a little too much to drink, Larry among them. On the way back to the motel, Larry was stopped by the Billings police for running a red light and was given a breathalyzer test. He was well over the legal limit. To make matters worse, at his booking the police found three marijuana cigarettes in his shirt pocket."

Nancy's mouth dropped open with surprise. "I've heard of drug problems in Great Falls and Billings but not here in Rocky Bluff."

"We've been fortunate until now," Edith explained. "As far as I know this was the first time any of our students were involved with drugs. Rocky Bluff could have forgiven him for the DUI, but not for the marijuana. Grady had no choice but to suspend him for the remainder of the school year."

"But isn't Larry a senior? Wouldn't that affect his graduation in June?"

"Worse than that, he not only won't graduate in June, but Montana A & M cancelled his basketball scholarship. His parents can't afford to send him to college without that scholarship. Larry blamed Grady for all his problems and vowed revenge."

"It sounds like he just snapped under the pressure," Nancy observed.

Edith hesitated a moment. "That is the sad commentary on small town athletics. We put too much pressure on our young people to perform well and entertain us. Larry simply could not handle it."

"The ones I feel sorry for are Larry's parents. They are in the store nearly every week picking up supplies for their ranch. They appear to be such hard-working people who would sacrifice anything for their children. They also have a son in the third grade with Jay. All he can talk about is his big brother."

"Bob gave me cause for many sleepless nights during his high school days. But he outgrew his rebellious nature," Edith confessed to her daughter-in-law. "During his school days alcohol was the biggest temptation to the students, and that was generally limited to an occasional Saturday night beer party."

"Oh, look at the time," Nancy groaned, glancing at her watch. "If I don't do a load of laundry tonight the family won't have any clothes to wear tomorrow. I'll stop by in the morning and see how you're doing. Have a good night's sleep."

Nancy leaned over and kissed her mother-in-law on the forehead before slipping out the door into the late winter evening.

Edith sat in silence for a few minutes trying to calm her racing heart. She reached for her Bible on the coffee table beside her and turned to her favorite passage, the Twenty-third Psalm.

"The Lord is my shepherd; I shall not want.
"He maketh me to lie down in green pastures: he leadeth me
    beside the still waters.
"He restoreth my soul: he leadeth me in the paths of righteous-
    ness for his name's sake.
"Yea, though I walk through the valley of the shadow of death, I
    will fear no evil: for thou art with me; thy rod and thy staff
    they comfort me.
"Thou preparest a table before me in the presence of mine ene-
    mies: thou anointest my head with oil; my cup runneth over.
"Surely goodness and mercy shall follow me all the days of my
    life: and I will dwell in the house of the Lord for ever."

Edith tried to pray but words escaped her. Surely the Lord heard her heartfelt cry, for Grady. . .for Larry. . .for herself. She laid her Bible on the coffee table and walked slowly to the kitchen phone. If ever she needed a human voice to talk to it was now.

She dialed the familiar number in Chamberland, Idaho, and waited for her daughter Jean to answer. Upon hearing the familiar "Hello," Edith broke down and sobbed.

"Mother, what's wrong?"

Edith regained her composure. "Honey, the most terrible thing happened today. One of our students shot the principal, and I happened to be the one to take the loaded gun away from him. I was absolutely terrified and I still haven't stopped shaking."

"Mother! Tell me exactly what happened."

Edith retold the story. As the words tumbled out, her heart raced.

"I wish I could be there with you tonight," Jean moaned. "You shouldn't be alone after such an experience."

"I'll be fine," Edith tried to assure her with false sincerity. "I've already decided what I am going to do."

"What's that?"

"Tomorrow I'm going to turn in my resignation effective at the end of this school year. I will be sixty-five in a few weeks and I have an ample income from the store. I need to get away from the school, away from Rocky Bluff. What kind of world is it where schoolchildren try to kill their principals or even their teachers? I survived a terrible ordeal and I don't ever want another experience like that."

"Mom, why don't you wait a few days before deciding something so important? Things may look better in a few days."

"No, Jean, my mind is made up. I want to retire to Arizona, where many of my friends are. I can still maintain controlling interest in the hardware store from there. Bob is doing a good job managing its daily affairs. In fact, he appears to resent anything I do regarding the store. He seems to have forgotten that his father and I ran that store successfully for over thirty years."

"I know you've worked hard all your life and deserve a rest, but I wish you would wait awhile before you make definite plans."

"I appreciate your concern, but I know what I have to do." Edith was too tired to argue and steered the conversation to the antics of Jay and Dawn. They chatted aimlessly for a full ten minutes before hanging up.

Extremely tired now, Edith went into her bedroom and laid out her nightgown. She then went to the bathroom and filled the tub. As she was undressing, the telephone rang.

"Oh, no!" she groaned. "Who could that be at this hour?"

"Mom!" Bob's rapid-fire delivery followed, the trademark of this consummate business professional. "I'm still in Billings. Nancy called and told me what happened. Are you sure you're all right?"

"I'm fine. Just very tired. I'm getting ready to take a bath and go to bed."

"It must have been a frightening day. You don't need any more experiences like that."

"That's the understatement of the year," Edith sighed as she sank into the chair beside the phone.

"You know, Mom, you've worked hard all your life. Why not think about retiring? The Millers and several of your other friends have moved to Arizona. Why don't you join them?"

"I've been thinking about doing that very thing. In fact, I'm going to turn in my resignation to the assistant principal tomorrow. If I move to Sun City, I can still be in telephone contact with you as to the operation of the store."

"Mom, I don't think you even need the worry of the store. Why don't you turn the operation completely over to Nancy and me and save yourself the worries?"

"The business arrangement we have right now is working very well. You run the day-to-day routine and I'll make the major decisions. Your father and I started that store from scratch thirty years ago, and it wouldn't be what it is today if it hadn't been for your father's hard work."

"But things are changing so rapidly. It will be hard for you to keep up from the sidelines. You deserve a rest."

Edith's irritation rose. "If I leave teaching, I'll have even more time to devote to the store, not less."

"Mother, why do you want that extra worry?" Bob persisted. "You will have enough income to live comfortably wherever you choose. You deserve a break after all you've been through. You're almost sixty-five. You don't need to be working with deranged youth who run around using guns on their teachers. There are plenty of younger teachers to handle the misfits of today."

"That was the conclusion I was coming to myself. I was very disappointed with the younger teachers today. They all just stood there frozen with fear. It seemed like none of them knew what to do. I was never so glad to see a familiar face over fifty as I was to see Coach Watson."

"Today you were competent, but you're getting too old to keep up with all the changes in the *business* world."

Edith's eyes fired with rage. "Bob, soon I may be too old to handle deranged young people, but I'm not too old to handle my own business affairs. That is not open for further discussion."

"I didn't mean to upset you, Mother," Bob stated with an air of condescension. "You are tired and need to get some rest. I'll see you in a couple days."

13

Edith hung up the phone and took a deep breath. The crisis of the day had been more than she wanted to deal with. She didn't want to end it with a conflict with her son. The tub of warm water filled with soothing bath oils was inviting.

He maketh me to lie down in green pastures, he leadeth me beside the still waters, Edith recited to herself as she relaxed in the bath. As the tensions of the day began to leave her body, she was able to put her future plans—and her disagreement with Bob—into perspective. I want to retire from teaching. . .but I'm not too old to be a contributing member of society!

Chapter 2

"But Grady, isn't there any way I can get my teaching position back?" Edith protested as she surveyed the handsome, dark-haired principal. "It's only been three weeks since I turned in my resignation and left for a vacation in Arizona. Resigning was the most foolish thing I've ever done."

"I questioned the wisdom of it at the time. But you were so shaken over the episode with Larry Reynolds that nothing would change your mind."

"My daughter tried to discourage me from acting so quickly, but back then I was determined to get as far away from here as possible."

"I'm sorry it turned out this way, but it is out of my hands now," Grady Walker explained as apologetically as he could. "Two days after you submitted your resignation to the school board, they received an application from a home economics teacher in Vermont who wanted to relocate to Montana. She has her master's degree and twelve years of experience. The school board was so impressed with her credentials and her enthusiasm that they offered her a contract on the spot."

"I was so sure before I left for spring break that I wanted to retire and move. But I should never have submitted my resignation prematurely. I didn't know how much the people of Rocky Bluff meant to me until I was away and realized that I would be giving up everything I cherished the most."

"I sympathize with your situation," the principal tried to assure her, "but I'm sure in a few months you'll be glad you retired when you did. You're still strong and healthy enough to do all the things you have wanted to do for years."

Edith thanked him and walked gloomily back to her classroom. She had assumed her position would still be open and she could continue teaching for a couple more years. She wasn't ready to retire.

Rocky Bluff High School had been good to her. Few school districts would have been willing to hire a fifty-five-year-old widow who was returning to teaching after a twenty-five-year layoff. Because of their confidence in her potential, Edith had worked hard not to disappoint them. However, now faced with the finality of her resignation letter, a sense of fear kept tugging at the back of her brain. All her life she had been needed; she did not feel ready to join her older friends in Sun City.

She felt she had to share her frustrations with someone. Even though her relationship with Bob was strained, Edith decided to confide in him when he got off work at the family hardware store that evening.

"But Mom," Bob protested as Edith explained her decision not to retire to Sun City after all. "I thought you had it all worked out to turn complete ownership and control of the store over to me and retire south. Why would you want to stay in Rocky Bluff, especially when the school board has already hired a replacement for you?"

"At your age I know it's hard to understand, but I don't feel sixty-five. Seeing my retired friends passing their days by playing golf, bridge, and chess I knew I could never resign myself to that kind of life. I thought maybe I could help part-time at the store by keeping the books. I know your present bookkeeper wants more time off to spend with her family."

"Things have changed since you were the primary bookkeeper for Dad. You know we've completely computerized our bookkeeping system. It's a totally different world today."

"Bob, I can always learn new skills. Every quarter they offer computer classes at the community college. Many people my age have been taking them. Besides, Nancy said she would teach me your particular system."

Edith was becoming more and more frustrated as the conversation progressed. Little had she realized when she turned the actual management of the store over to Bob after George's death that she would be frozen out even though she was still the legal owner of the business. Bob did not want her back at the store in any capacity and the conversation was going nowhere. She turned and walked away. Tension filled the room.

"Mother, don't go away angry," Bob called after her. "I'm sure there are other things you can do to pass your time in Rocky Bluff."

Edith did not respond and let the door slam behind her as she left.

⁊

Seeing no immediate solution to her imminent retirement, Edith resolved to ignore the pressure from her son and continue her normal routine. The last few weeks of school flew by with the usual end-of-the-year activities. As senior class sponsor, she was busy planning the senior picnic, senior-parent brunch, and graduation.

The reality of her retirement hit her on the last day of school.

"Good-bye, have a good summer," Edith responded to her last student's farewell. Edith shuffled restlessly to her desk. This was not the end of a typical school year, this was the end of her teaching career. *I wish I hadn't submitted my resignation so early,* she lamented for the thousandth time. *I have only myself to blame. I should have waited.*

"Your end-of-the-year reports seem in order, Edith," Grady Walker observed, glancing over the attendance and grade sheets. "I realize it must be extremely difficult to hand me the key to the home economics room for the last time. You've invested ten years of your life developing an outstanding program and the school is extremely grateful for your contributions."

Edith's mind began to roam as the principal expounded about her accomplishments and the many students who entered the working world better prepared because of her dedication. *"Difficult to hand in the key" is the biggest understatement of the year,* she thought. *I now have nothing to do with my time and am no longer needed anywhere. Even my own son doesn't want me to work at the very store his father and I founded.*

"As interested as you've been in all aspects of community affairs, you must have some exciting retirement plans," Grady continued, bringing Edith's wandering mind back to the present.

"Not really," Edith replied, trying to shove her inner feelings into the background. "I plan to get my garden planted right away and then spend a couple weeks in Idaho with my daughter Jean."

"I wish you the very best," he declared, rising from his vinyl padded office chair and escorting her to the door. "Do stop back and see us from time to time."

No mention was made of the encounter with Larry Reynolds and the gun. The situation was still too painful for both of them to discuss.

"Thank you" was all Edith could utter through the lump building in her throat. She hurried down the hallway for the last time, tears cascading down her cheeks.

The hot May sun beat down on the cement parking lot as Edith blindly found her way to her Ford Escort. Fumbling in her black leather purse, she took out her sunglasses and keys and dabbed her eyes and face with a lone tissue. Solemnly inserting the key into the lock, she opened the door and slid mechanically behind the wheel. All her habits of the last ten years were about to end. The drive onto Grove Street and then Main took on a strange new meaning. Ever since she had come to Rocky Bluff as a new bride she had felt a part of the lifeblood of the community. Today that part of her life was over.

In front of the county courthouse Edith's serious face relaxed and the corners of her mouth turned up. Skipping down the sidewalk was her six-year-old granddaughter. Carefully, Edith pulled into a vacant parking stall as Dawn came darting toward the familiar car.

"Hi, Grandma, are you glad that school's out?" Dawn shouted. "I am," she continued without waiting for a response.

"Hello, sweetie," Edith replied as she quickly joined her granddaughter on the sidewalk. "I'm sad that school is over," she explained, putting her arm around the child's slim shoulders. "I'll never be going back like you will be."

"I wish I didn't have to. Can I come home with you instead of going to the baby-sitter's?"

Later that night as Edith was curled up in her favorite chair reading the current *Better Homes and Gardens* the phone rang.

"Mom, do you have your garden in yet?" Jean questioned with characteristic eagerness as Edith greeted her. "When are you coming to visit us?"

"Jean, you haven't changed in the least. You never forget a 'maybe' promise," Edith teased. "I just finished teaching school six hours ago and my superhuman abilities do not lend themselves to planting the garden today."

"Since you've confessed your mortality, I'll give you until a week from Friday to get your garden in order and then Jim and I will meet the seven P.M. bus from Rocky Bluff."

"Seriously, Jean, are you sure I won't be in the way? You and Jim both work and have been so busy lately."

"Mother, don't be silly. Of course you won't be in the way. I know it will be rather lonesome during the daytime, but we'll make up for it in the evenings and on weekends," Jean replied, ignoring her mother's weak protests. As a hospital nurse she had developed a sensitivity to both the spoken and the unspoken needs of others. "Once you get here I know you'll find more than enough things to do. I might even give you some mending."

"You've convinced me," Edith said enthusiastically. "But please, no more hemming cheerleader skirts. I gave that up the day you graduated."

"I promise," Jean replied. Then a note of seriousness entered her voice. "In fact, I thought we'd do some sightseeing next Saturday and go to the symphony that night. There is a lot of beautiful country to see, and a symphonic orchestra from Seattle will be in town for that weekend."

"That sounds great," Edith readily agreed. She switched the phone to the other ear, pushing aside wisps of her gray-flecked black hair. She enjoyed classical music and professional symphonies rarely toured in Rocky Bluff, Montana.

Friday morning Edith boarded the Trailways bus. Although she was eager to see her daughter and son-in-law, who hadn't been home to Rocky Bluff in nearly a year, a sense of fear and doubt began to plague her. *Will I be able to develop an independent lifestyle, or will I become a dependent old woman?* she pondered. *Does Jean really miss those talks we used to have or is she just patronizing me? After all, she's a grown, married woman now, more capable than I to deal with the problems of life.*

As the bus turned off the interstate and headed toward the business section of Chamberland, Edith fell into a peaceful silence, lost in her own thoughts.

A block from the Chamberland station, she spied Jean and Jim standing outside the depot. The young couple's fingers were entwined in simple unity. How often she and George had enjoyed that same sense of oneness! Immersing herself in the lives of high school students had not replaced the empty place at the dinner table or the gentle snoring in her bed. Rarely could she look upon a happily married couple without feeling a twinge of emptiness, but it was even more acute when she saw the shared love of her own daughter and son-in-law. *Was it time to pass the torch of happiness and usefulness on to the next generation?* she thought as she gathered her packages around her.

"Mom, I'm glad you could come," Jean exclaimed as she gave her mother a warm embrace. "Jim will get your luggage for you. How was your trip? Have you had dinner yet?"

"No, we didn't have a long enough stop at any of the towns along the way, and I'm famished." Edith handed Jim her claim check, relieved to have a man around to help with the heavy suitcases.

"There's a new Chinese restaurant at the edge of town. Let's go there for dinner. We have so much visiting to catch up on." Jean happily led the way through the maze of cars in the parking lot.

A petite, dark-haired hostess dressed in a Chinese-style embroidered robe and slippers led the party of three to a private back table. A few minutes later after perusing the menu, the only item they all understood was the eggroll. Their confused expressions summoned the waitress, who patiently described each dish on the menu. After much deliberation Edith chose chow mai fon with pork while Jean and Jim decided upon Szechwan beef with scallions.

They barely had time to discuss the recent events of the sawmill that Jim managed when the waitress returned with the meal and chopsticks. After several hilarious attempts, the chopsticks were abandoned for the knife and fork. The food and atmosphere complemented the family news each wanted to share.

"Mother, have you thought about how you're going to spend your time now that you have more of it?" Jim asked, taking a sip of orange pekoe tea. "I don't mean to pry, but more than anything I want to see you happy."

"I'm not sure yet," Edith responded hesitantly. "My garden will keep me busy most of the summer. Then the house will need plenty of tender loving care. It hasn't had a thorough cleaning since your father passed away. I piled all his tools and personal belongings in the storage room in the basement and have rarely opened the door since then. I've been so busy with the young people at school that I've kept putting off that job."

"All your work projects might keep you busy until Christmas, but then what? Have you thought about working part-time at the hardware store with Bob?"

Edith's eyes became distant. *Is this a good time to explain the hurtful truth? Should I let Jean know that all is not well between her brother and me?* She took a sip of tea before she answered.

"Jean, you don't know how much I'd like to work at the store. I'd enjoy taking computer classes at the community college to learn to use the new business computer software," Edith explained, laying her fork on her plate and concentrating on every word, "but I'm afraid that Bob would resent my presence."

"But why, Mom?" Jean had a look of bewilderment in her eyes. "What's happened to my easy-going, fun-loving brother?"

"I don't fully understand myself. Bob seems to think when a person reaches age sixty-five both the mind and body cease to function."

"That kind of thinking has forced society to change its policy toward a retirement based solely on chronological age," Jim said with irritation in his voice. "Mom, that brings us back to the first question. Despite what Bob thinks, you deserve a meaningful retirement life. What are you going to do with your time? You're not ready to settle back in your rocking chair all day long."

"That's something I'm still working on." Edith's suppressed restlessness was beginning to surface. "I didn't think retirement would affect me this way. I enjoy stopping at the senior citizens center for a cup of coffee now and then and visiting with friends, but I can't spend all my time doing that. I can't get interested in playing bridge or canasta or cribbage, and I'd rather curl up with a good book than play bingo. If others enjoy that sort of recreation, that's fine, but it's just not for me."

⁂

The days with Jean and Jim passed swiftly. Each new day brought long walks in the park and time to enjoy one another's company. There were visits over the back fence with Jean's neighbor and time to read the top three books on the nonfiction best-seller list. Edith never had another twinge of not being needed, but after two weeks she was ready to return to her own home and garden.

Edith's period of mental escape ended as she boarded the morning bus bound for Rocky Bluff the last Friday of June. One concern weighed heavily on her mind, one that would not be resolved in a few hours. How could she convince her son that Harkness Hardware was a *family* business and not solely *his* business? What would she do with herself for the rest of her life?

Chapter 3

"Welcome home, Grandma," Jay and Dawn shouted as Edith stepped off the bus at the Rocky Bluff station. "We missed you a lot."

Edith grabbed both grandchildren and pulled them against her. "I missed you, too. As soon as we get my suitcases, I have some special surprises for each of you."

"Mom, you certainly have a way of spoiling those kids," Nancy teased as she gave her mother-in-law a warm hug. "It's good to have you home."

"I'm glad to be back. But for the record, my grandchildren are not spoiled, they're just well loved."

Nancy giggled while Edith's eyes scanned the bus terminal. "Didn't Bob come with you?" she queried with a note of disappointment in her voice.

"I've afraid not. He's busy working on the books at the store. He said he'd be by to see you Sunday afternoon."

"Well, this is Friday night, our traditional family night," Edith sighed as she took Dawn's hand and walked toward the baggage counter. Not wanting her grandchildren to be suspicious of the tension between their father and his mother, she quickly changed the subject. "But the four of us can still make it a special occasion. Let's stop at the Dairy Queen for ice cream on our way home."

❧

The Thursday before school started passed with the usual late summer flurry of activities. Edith paused a moment at the basement window. Jay and Dawn were happily constructing what they called a clubhouse from the pile of scrap lumber George had left stacked behind the garage. Suddenly an idea flashed through her mind. "Jay, Dawn, put your tools away and come with me. I need your help."

"Where are we going, Grandma?" Jay wondered, his sandy hair in its usual disarray as a cool breeze whistled through the trees. Without waiting for an answer, Dawn and Jay hurriedly gathered up the hammers and nails and piled them on the workbench in the garage and came running to the house as fast as their legs would carry them.

"I've decided to paint my house and I need your help in picking out the colors. Let's surprise your parents and go to the store as ordinary customers."

As she drove her grandchildren down the tree-lined streets of Rocky Bluff, Edith's countenance changed. *What colors do I want in my bedroom or in my kitchen and living room?* she pondered. Instead of a future vagueness concerning her day-to-day routine after the children returned to school, she now knew what Monday morning would bring. Dressed in her faded blue jeans, she would be wielding a paintbrush, thankful that she still had the physical strength to maintain her own home.

Edith's feelings of anticipation were momentarily dampened when her son learned of her plans. "Now, Mother, are you sure you can paint the inside of the house by yourself? I've a good friend who could use the work, and he'll be finished with his construction site job sometime next month," Bob volunteered as Edith and the children thumbed through the sample cards of available paint.

"No, Bob, I want to get it done right away," she insisted, angered at the subtle questioning of her abilities. "The last time the walls were painted was when your father did it fifteen years ago, and I'm ready for a change. Why should I pay someone else to do it when I have the time and can probably do as good a job as they?"

"I still think you should call Ron Brown. You've worked hard all your life and deserve a rest."

"You don't seem to understand. This is something I want to do myself. It may take me a little longer, but at least I'll have the satisfaction of accomplishment."

"Well, if you insist, Mother, I won't stand in your way. Just remember you aren't as young as you used to be."

"But I'm not ready for a rocking chair, either," Edith replied stubbornly.

"What color are you going to paint your living room, Grandma?" Jay interrupted as he glanced through the pile of paint samples. "I like the lime green."

"You have good taste, Jay. Maybe if we paint it one shade darker, it will match the carpet better. Then we can paint the ceiling white to add more light to the room."

Edith turned her attention back to her overbearing son standing behind the counter. A mixture of anger and pity engulfed her. If only he would try to understand her situation. In a brisk, businesslike manner she instructed, "Just have your delivery person bring the sample number 24 green paint and sample number 5 white paint along with two rollers, two brushes for the trim, two paint pans, and three sheets of plastic to the house before the store closes tomorrow. I want to begin in the living room as soon as possible."

Edith didn't let her son's words and attitude dishearten her for long. The next morning the children helped Edith move the furniture, and together they began putting masking tape around the windows and the trim in the living room. Dawn was proud of the way she covered the carpeting with newspapers. When the painting materials arrived later in the day, they had finished preparing the room.

"I'm ready to start painting and you're both ready to go back to school, so let's celebrate," Edith said to her grandchildren as they surveyed their hard work. "Let's go out for banana splits. It's my treat for a job well done. I wouldn't have been done until late tonight if you both hadn't helped."

"I wish I didn't have to go to school tomorrow so I could help you paint. It looks like a lot of fun," Jay declared as he reached for his baseball cap and followed his sister out the door.

"I'm sorry you won't be able to help, but school comes first. However, as soon as I'm finished, I'm going to invite you to my celebration party."

By ten the next evening Edith had completed the first coat of paint on the living room wall and fell into bed exhausted. *When I finish painting in the living room, maybe I'll shampoo the carpeting,* she thought as her eyes closed. Edith drifted into a deep sleep and did not stir until the morning sun shone directly into her bedroom.

The next few days followed the same basic pattern. The former home economics teacher budgeted her strength and maintained a steady work pattern. By late the following Friday the furniture, pictures, and knick-knacks were back in place. Edith picked up the telephone and called Harkness Hardware.

"Hello, Nancy," she greeted. "I've finished painting the downstairs and shampooing the carpeting and I figure it's time for a celebration. How about you and Bob bring the children over for Sunday dinner? I'll be sure and make your favorite dishes."

"We'd love to, Mom. Is there anything I can bring?"

"This is entirely my treat. Just bring your appetites and nothing more."

On Sunday Edith hurried home from church in order to put the finishing touches on dinner before her guests arrived. Soon she heard familiar footsteps on the porch.

"Mom, this is beautiful," Nancy admired as she stepped into the freshly painted living room. "You've done an excellent job. It's as good as any professional could have done."

Edith smiled to herself as she intentionally avoided looking her son in the eye. She had learned long ago never to say I told you so.

"Thanks, dear. After painting the walls and cleaning the carpet, don't you think the drapes look a bit shabby?" Edith asked as she critically surveyed her windows. "How about taking a couple hours off work Monday to help me pick out new drapes?"

"That sounds like fun. I'll meet you at one at Herman's Drapery."

Bob didn't want his mother's momentary victory to go unchecked. He walked around the living room, then cleared his throat. "I must admit, Mother, that you did a good job, but I still think you'll need help with the upstairs bedrooms. Those high, slanting ceilings could be dangerous. You'll need more than a stepladder to do the job safely. I'll call Ron Brown in the morning, that is, if you'd like."

"You'll do nothing of the sort. Beverly Short from next door said she'd come over and help me when I get to the hard part. She even has some scaffolding from her husband's old carpentry business."

"But Beverly is nearly seventy," Bob protested, speaking to his mother the way he did to his own children. "What if one of you falls off the ladder and breaks a leg? I'd never forgive myself for letting you do your own painting."

"We could break a leg walking down our front steps, too. Neither situation has anything to do with you. The subject is closed. I'll finish the painting myself." Edith placed her hands firmly on her hips and stomped into the kitchen. Nancy shot a look of annoyance at her husband, who was shaking his head in frustration. Without a word, she followed her mother-in-law into the kitchen.

The subject of who was to paint the house was not discussed again. Despite how old and feeble she might become, Edith never wanted to be mothered by her own children. Whenever she needed more supplies from the hardware store she waited until Nancy was free to help her.

The week before Thanksgiving Edith completed painting the interior of her house. For several minutes after the last paint can was carried to the garage, she wandered throughout her home admiring the change of tone and mood. In a sense it was symbolic of a change of direction she wanted her life to take. Yet it would take more than a can of paint to change her unsettled future. As she took a cup of coffee and relaxed on her living room couch, a sense of loneliness swept over her.

If only George were here to share my moment of triumph. . . . Now Edith, she scolded herself, *there's no reason to sit here sulking. You are surrounded by a host of friends and neighbors. Invite them over to share your happiness.*

The next Wednesday afternoon the Harkness home was a hive of activity as a dozen neighbors noisily approved Edith's and Bev's hard work.

After a tour of the house, some visiting, and coffee, punch, and strawberry rhubarb dessert, one by one the guests asked for their coats and bade the hostess farewell. As the door closed behind the last group, only one neighbor remained.

"Edith, now that you're not working full time, would you be interested in joining our ladies aid group?" Grace Blair, a friend who lived in the next block, asked hesitantly. "We meet the first and third Tuesdays of every month and we'd love to have you join us."

"I'd be delighted to."

"Great, I'll pick you up Tuesday at one-fifteen," Grace said breezily as she reached for her coat. "I'm sure you'll enjoy it. We are quite an active group of women."

Tuesday afternoon Edith was standing at the window as Grace pulled her Chevy Citation to the curb in front of the house. She grabbed her coat and hurried to the waiting car. After exchanging greetings, Edith was full of questions concerning the group's activities. In her heart Edith was hoping that the rumors about the center of community gossip were unfounded.

When Grace hesitated before answering, Edith sensed she was caught off-balance. "Every Christmas we send a basket of goodies to the nursing home," Grace began, evidently surprised that someone as active in the church as Edith didn't know about the activities of the ladies aid.

Not satisfied, Edith persisted. "Do you run the nursery? Serve church dinners? Support the missionaries? Help at the rescue mission? Have Bible study groups?"

Grace again hesitated, then cleared her throat. "It's kind of hard to explain," she replied as she slowed for the stoplight. "We're a pretty small group to make much of an impact on the needs of the community. Basically we just enjoy getting together and sharing each other's company."

Imagine a church group not having a purpose, Edith pondered as Grace parked the car in the church parking lot. *Maybe Grace is so involved in the group that she no longer realizes how ineffective it is.*

Grace and Edith descended the stairs to the basement and quietly slipped into the waiting chairs as the chairwoman finished the opening prayer. Ellen Watson then read Hebrews 11 and asked if there were any discussion over the chapter. The room was silent as each of the eight women looked at one another and then at the floor.

"If there is no discussion, let's go on with the business meeting," Ellen continued. "Is there any old business?"

Again the room fell silent, except for the chiming of the wall clock in the background. "Is there any new business?" Ellen's voice again echoed against the blank walls as everyone looked at the floor. The leader's eyes swept the room. "I'd like to welcome our guest, Edith Harkness. I hope she'll be able to join us on a regular basis."

Edith smiled as each woman in turn gave her a warm greeting. When the room was again quiet, Ellen continued. "If there is no business, who will be responsible for refreshments for the next meeting, when we'll be assembling our Christmas baskets?"

At that point the group seemed to come alive. "Oh, I'll be glad to do that," Betty volunteered, before anyone else had a chance to respond. "I found an excellent recipe for cherry turnovers in my mother's old cookbook."

"That sounds delicious. Does it use the regular pie crust recipe?" Grace inquired, adjusting her wire-framed glasses on her nose.

"Not quite. It calls for a half-cup more flour and a little more salt than what I use for my pumpkin pies." Cooking had long been Betty's favorite pastime, a skill advertised by her own ample figure.

"Not to change the subject," Joy piped in with her high twangy voice, "but did you taste Hilda's pie at the last potluck supper? I don't know what she did to it, but I would've been embarrassed to have brought anything like that to a church dinner."

"Yes, I did notice the bland flavor and lack of spices. But maybe we shouldn't judge Hilda too severely," Ellen protested, trying to regain her authority. "You know that her husband has divorced her to marry Kay Bly. It must've been very traumatic for her and she's just not up to her normal self."

"Oh, poor dear," Helen cooed, her eyes shining with interest. "I never did think much of him. He never stayed home with Hilda and the children. She had to raise their family almost entirely by herself."

"Well, maybe we should all pray for them instead of discussing their personal problems," Ellen tried to remind them.

"I didn't know all this was happening to poor Hilda," Grace inserted. "I really don't know how to pray for her. Maybe you can share more of the details so I can pray intelligently."

With each added comment Edith became more and more withdrawn and angered. She did not want to participate or spend her time in idle gossip disguised as Christian concern. Maybe someday she could help start a more meaningful group, but she had had enough for now.

※

During Thanksgiving vacation Edith decided to attack her long overdue task of sorting through the basement storage room. At least her time in the cluttered basement would accomplish more than watching morning soap operas. Besides, Jay and Dawn were coming that afternoon and they could help her load the boxes into the car.

As she cautiously opened the door of the storage room, a flood of memories engulfed her and she was enveloped by a wave of guilt for her own procrastination. George would have wanted this done long ago so that others could make use of his things. With a deep breath and a sudden surge of determination, Edith began sorting through the boxes.

When the children arrived that afternoon, Edith led them to the basement. "Would you help carry these things to the car for me? They were your grandfather's and I want to take them to the Salvation Army so that others may use them."

As soon as the door opened, Dawn spied her grandfather's old golf clubs in the corner. "Did Grandpa play golf?"

"Oh, yes. For many years every Sunday afternoon your grandpa and I would tee off in a foursome with the Millers. They moved to Arizona soon after your grandpa died, and I haven't touched a golf club since."

"Do you want this old shovel carried to the car, too?" Jay asked, picking up the rusty tool leaning against the wall.

"I don't have any use for it now. Your grandfather used that a great deal when he was helping level the ground for the city park. The young people who play there today will never know all the sweat and toil that went into building that park."

Dawn continued exploring the once forbidden room. "What did Grandpa do to earn this trophy?" she asked, picking the brass statue from the top of a pasteboard box.

Edith smiled with satisfaction as she remembered how George was honored as the outstanding businessman of 1968. The children were learning more about their grandfather by helping clean the storage room than by all the stories their father had told them. "I was very proud of your grandfather as he walked across the stage to receive that award. The president of the Rocky Bluff Rotary Club acknowledged his contributions to many community affairs."

Taking the treasured trophy from Dawn, Edith placed it in a box she was saving and picked up George's black leather Bible. The edges were tattered and torn and the binding was broken. Gently she flipped the pages. Edith paused long enough to read some of the passages he had underlined in red ink. One by one the children came to look over her shoulder.

"See all the words underlined in red? Your grandfather wanted to indicate every verse that meant something to him. He loved God and he left his family with a name that you can be proud to carry on."

Dawn wrapped her arms around her grandmother's neck. "If Grandpa was anything like you, he must've really been great."

Edith quickly wiped her eyes, a gesture unnoticed by her two scavenging grandchildren. "Honey, your grandpa was a great man and for years we made a great team. Now I've got to be strong all by myself. . . ." As Edith's voice trailed off, her thoughts completed the sentence, *and find my bearings again.*

Chapter 4

"Grandma, this has been the best Christmas ever," Jay exclaimed as he lay on the floor of Edith's living room trying to figure out the rules of his newest computer game.

"Every Christmas is special to me," she assured him. "Especially when I am surrounded by such a loving family. I only wish that Jean and Jim were here to share the holidays with us."

"I like Christmas because Daddy spends the day with us instead of always leaving to go back to the store," Dawn interjected as she hugged her father, who was busy reading the *Wall Street Journal*.

To Edith the day had been truly delightful, but that euphoric feeling was short-lived. While Nancy was helping Edith prepare evening sandwiches from ham left over from dinner, the younger woman laid the knife on the counter and sank into a nearby kitchen chair.

"Mom, this is a hard subject to bring up, but I just have to talk to someone," she confided with tears beginning to build in her eyes. "I know you're Bob's mother, but you've been like a mother to me, especially after my own mother passed away." Nancy paused for a moment and then blurted out, "Do you think it's possible that Bob is being unfaithful to me?"

Edith felt her hands turn cold and clammy. She seated herself on a nearby chair. "Whatever gave you that idea?"

"Well, nothing specifically, but he's become so distant lately. He seems to be spending every waking hour at the store."

"Have you seen any signs that might suggest another woman?" Edith asked. Nancy shook her head.

"Have you found letters, perhaps lipstick on his clothes, or received any unexplained phone calls?"

Nancy continued to shake her head. "Well, no, but there has to be something going on. We aren't nearly as close as we used to be. When we were first married Bob would tell me every detail of his life and we would spend a lot of time together. We'd take long walks or drive to the country. Now he spends all his time at the store without me."

"Nancy, don't jump to the wrong conclusion," Edith calmly reminded her. "Bob is probably not having an affair with another woman, but rather

30

a love affair with building a successful business."

Edith took her daughter-in-law's hand. "I've noticed the store seems to consume him. It's painful now, but I'm sure with time this too will pass away. Many men go through this as they begin to achieve a certain amount of success in their careers."

"I hope so," Nancy said with a faint smile. "I knew if I talked to you, you'd understand what was happening."

Their conversation was interrupted by the shrill ring of the telephone. Edith hurried to answer it with a "Merry Christmas," as she put the phone to her ear.

It was Jean. "Merry Christmas to you. Are you having a nice holiday?"

After exchanging family news with both Jean and Jim, Edith passed the phone on to Nancy, then Bob, Jay, and Dawn. Each had a chance to share their Christmas greetings. Geographical distance could not dampen their family love.

When the mantel clock struck nine times that night, Bob called an end to the visit. "Time to head home, kids. Gather up your toys. Mom, can I see you in the kitchen for a minute?"

Bob motioned for her to sit while he paced around the room. "Mom, why don't you reconsider going to Sun City this winter? There is nothing for you to do here in Rocky Bluff until spring. I can take over full control of the store, and you won't have a thing to worry about. Maybe you could look up the Millers and begin playing golf again."

Edith took a long, deep breath to calm herself before responding. "You're mistaken, Bob. There's plenty for me to do here in Rocky Bluff. Now that the holidays are over, I plan to find a part-time job, or I may get involved in volunteer work."

As she surveyed her son's determined eyes and set jaw, she tried to control her anger. "Again I want to remind you that Harkness Hardware is a family business, not a sole proprietorship."

"I'm sure you'll see it my way when the holiday excitement is over," Bob mumbled as he left the kitchen and turned his attention to the children. He helped them gather their packages and put on their coats. He left with only a cool thank you to his mother.

Edith stood in the window and watched them leave with tears in her eyes. She could face retirement, but the conflict with her son was another matter.

The next morning Edith stayed in bed later than usual after a fitful night's sleep. At nine-fifteen she wrapped her fleece robe around her and went to the front door to collect the morning paper from between the storm door and inside door. Unfolding the *Rocky Bluff Herald* she scanned the headlines and lead story.

LOCAL YOUTH DEAD OF OVERDOSE

Susan Youngman, seventeen-year-old daughter of Frank and Elizabeth Youngman, was found dead in her bedroom late Christmas night. Police found an empty bottle of unidentified pills beside her. An autopsy is being performed.

Edith remembered the blond-haired student in her last home economics class. She would have given her an A for the semester if she had a better fit on her final sewing project. Her eyes filled with tears as she stepped back into the warmth of her living room and closed the door and continued reading.

The victim had placed a call to the Rocky Bluff Crisis Center at 9:15 P.M. Because of the holiday season the volunteer force was insufficient to handle the overload of calls and Susan was put on hold. When the volunteer returned to Susan's call, there was no answer. The call was traced to the Youngman residence and police were summoned.

Funeral services will be held at 1:00 P.M. on December 30 at the First Presbyterian Church of Rocky Bluff. Interment will follow at the Pine Hills Memorial Cemetery.

I've got to go to those services, Edith determined as she sank into the rocking chair beside the window. Reaching for a tissue on the end table beside her, she sobbed softly as her mind drifted back to the two years she had Susan as a student.

Susan had always been a shy girl without many friends. Was there anything I could have done to help prevent this tragedy? Edith reached for another tissue. Her eyes wandered to the freshly fallen snow outside the window.

Could I have helped raise her self-esteem so that she would not have drifted to this level of hopelessness? Should I have referred her to the counselors when I noticed her avoiding the other girls? After spending a few minutes lost in grief, Edith reached for the telephone.

After hearing her daughter-in-law's voice on the other end of the line, she said, "Nancy, did you see this morning's paper?"

"You mean about Susan Youngman? Was she one of your students?"

"Yes, she was such a sweet girl. Do you think you could attend the funeral with me Friday?"

"Of course, Mom. We'll get someone to cover for me at the store. Besides, Susan's parents are regular customers. The least I can do is lend some support during this tragic time."

That Friday the First Presbyterian Church was packed with mourners. One section was exclusively high school students. Afterward as the crowd gathered at the Pine Hills Cemetery, Edith found herself surrounded by teenagers. Not only were her former students anxious to learn about her activities since she'd retired, but they craved her motherly support during their time of grief. Many of them had never lost a loved one. To them death only came to the elderly, not someone their own age, someone who had taken her own life.

The following Monday Edith spotted an advertisement in the classified section of the morning paper.

Wanted: Crisis Center Volunteers
No Experience Necessary
Training Classes Begin January 10th
To Preregister Call 789-3333.

That's exactly what I want to do, she thought excitedly. *I can take these classes and then work at the crisis center. Maybe I can make a difference for all the other Susan Youngmans who are out there crying for someone to listen to them.*

Edith grabbed the phone and dialed the advertised number. After the second ring a man answered. "Hello, crisis center. May I help you?"

"I saw your ad in the paper about training sessions for volunteers. I'm interested in more of the details."

"Good, I'm glad you called," a gentle male voice replied. "There's a twelve-week training session. During that time we determine who is suitable for the task. We're in desperate need of more volunteers. Could you give me your name and tell me a little about yourself and why you would like to help at the crisis center?"

"My name is Edith Harkness. I retired from teaching at Rocky Bluff High School last year and I'd like to devote a few hours a week to community service. I had Susan Youngman in my class and I'm willing to do whatever I can to help prevent another such tragedy."

"Mrs. Harkness, thank you for calling. I'm Roy Dutton, the director of the crisis center. I'll be leading the sessions and bringing in several specialists as guest lecturers. I'm looking forward to meeting you in person. Can you come to the first training session Monday, January tenth, at seven P.M.

in the hospitality room of the civic center?"

"Yes, I'll be glad to learn more about it. I'm looking forward to being there."

After they'd hung up, Edith paused to enjoy the warm glow that enveloped her. Now she would finally be contributing something to the community that she loved.

The next few days seemed to drag by as Edith sought ways to fill her time. Monday evening the streetlights glistened on the freshly fallen snow as Edith drove cautiously down Main Street to the civic center. A twinge of doubt haunted her. *At my age why do I think I'll be able to help young people going through problems so different from what I faced as a teenager? Although I've experienced my share of heartaches, I've led a fairly protected life compared to the temptations they face today.*

Edith parked her Ford Escort next to the side door of the civic center and wrapped her scarf around her face to protect against the harsh Montana wind. She hurried inside and located the meeting room at the end of the hallway. Seated at three tables were ten young women and five men. She was the only woman over thirty.

A distinguished looking gray-haired gentleman whom Edith vaguely recognized from church rose to greet her. "Welcome. You must be Edith Harkness. I'm Roy Dutton. I'm glad the cold weather didn't keep you away. Would you like to hang up your coat and join us?"

As Edith took a seat at the end of the far table, the director walked to the front of the room. "I'd like to welcome all of you to our first in a series of twelve training sessions for crisis center volunteers. Would each of you introduce yourself and tell us why you are interested in crisis intervention?"

After the introductions Roy began his presentation by distributing handouts describing the schedule of classes, the topics to be covered, and the guest speakers for the various class sessions. Edith quickly forgot her apprehension as she became engrossed in the techniques used in helping people in crisis. In no time at all Roy Dutton announced that it was nine o'clock and the session had ended.

As Edith was buttoning her coat, Roy approached her. "I'd like to say again how glad I am that you decided to join our group. We have been in dire need of mature people. The twenty year olds may be able to talk the language of those in crisis, but it has been my experience that troubled people have more confidence in older volunteers. Maturity has a way of providing stability and hope in what appears to be an impossible situation."

"I would like to think I have learned a few things during all my years of living, but the problems young people face today are so different from those I faced growing up."

"Yes and no," the director responded kindly. "Yes, young people are faced with problems of drugs, sex, and violence that were not as prevalent a few years ago. However, people still have the same basic needs of love, acceptance, and a feeling that their life has a meaning or purpose. Our biggest job is to strip away all the circumstantial smoke screens and get to the core of the problem. How about joining me across the street at Bea's for a cup of coffee? We can continue our discussion there."

Leaving her car in the parking lot of the civic center, Edith walked across the street with Roy. His calm and direct manner put her completely at ease.

After ordering coffee and pie, the conversation shifted from the crisis center to their families. Roy was aware of Harkness Hardware but had not made the family connection between Bob Harkness and Edith. After expressing concern about Edith's difficult transition into retirement, he began to share his own background.

"I guess I've lived a humble life compared to owning a hardware store and teaching school. I was a social worker all my life. I have one son, Pete, who absorbed most of my spare time. His was a difficult birth. The doctor was able to save his life, but he was left with some brain damage from lack of oxygen. Then when he was three years old, his mother developed cancer. We lost her a year later."

"I'm sorry to hear that. What a tremendous challenge to raise a handicapped child alone!"

"It was hard at times, but I just did what had to be done, the same as anyone would under similar circumstances. There's a terrific special education program here in Rocky Bluff. I don't know what I'd have done without it."

Edith admired his deep blue eyes and practical approach to life as he continued telling her about his son. "Where is Pete now?" she queried. "Still living at home?"

"No, while he was still in school they discovered that he had an unusual mechanical ability and were able to find a job for him as a handyman on a ranch near the Canadian border. He's coming home this weekend. I'd love to have you meet him."

"I'd like that very much."

"How about Friday night? After I meet his bus we have a normal ritual of going to McDonald's."

"Sounds like fun," Edith said genuinely.

"Good, I'll pick you up at five-thirty so you can come to the bus station with me." Roy reached for the check the waitress had left on the table.

"I hope you don't mind fast food?"

"Of course not. I frequently end up at those places with my grandchildren."

That Friday evening Roy and Edith waited in the Rocky Bluff bus terminal for the familiar Mountain Trailways bus to arrive. At exactly five-forty-five, headlights shone through the windows as the sixty-passenger bus pulled to a stop. Pete was the first one to step from the bus.

"Hello, Dad," he shouted as he hurried toward his father. "Can we go to McDonald's now? I'm hungry."

"Welcome home, Pete. As soon as we get your bags we can be off, but first I'd like you to meet a friend of mine, Edith Harkness."

Pete stared at the attractive, dark-haired woman standing next to his father. A look of bewilderment crossed his face. "Hello," he mumbled. "Me and my dad are going to McDonald's now."

"Hello, Pete. I'm glad to meet you," Edith said. "I've heard so many good things about you."

Roy tried to diffuse the awkward situation. "Pete, I've invited Edith to join us for hamburgers."

Pete remained silent as Roy took his baggage check and went to claim Pete's worn brown suitcase. Roy then led the way across the snow-packed parking lot to his aging Oldsmobile. He opened the back door of the car and Pete grudgingly slid onto the seat as Roy opened the front door for Edith.

Edith and Roy engaged in small talk as Pete sat glumly in the back. Upon arriving at McDonald's, Pete rushed to the counter.

"I'll have two Big Macs, a large order of fries, and a large chocolate milkshake," he told the counter employee as she quietly pushed the order buttons in front of her. After Roy and Edith had placed their order, Roy paid the bill and picked up the tray and followed Pete to a back booth.

"Why'd she have to come?" Pete demanded as he reached for his hamburger. "It's always been just you and me. That's the way it's supposed to be."

Edith shot an uncomfortable glance at Roy.

"Pete, it's always nice to make new friends. Edith is my friend and she wants to be your friend, too."

"No, she doesn't," Pete responded sharply. "She only wants to be *your* friend. I watched the way you acted in the car. You didn't even care if I was there or not."

Edith sat quietly as Roy tried to explain their budding friendship to Pete. Roy had been the center of Pete's life for so long that Pete was unable to accept the fact that his father could have a relationship with anyone else. To Pete, Edith was simply a rival for his father's affection. Friendship appeared out of the question, for now.

Chapter 5

All of you know it's been a long, cold winter in central Montana," Roy Dutton said at the beginning of the fifth training session. "Cabin fever has settled over Rocky Bluff and calls to the crisis center have doubled."

Of the original fifteen volunteers only five had continued the training program: Two were young housewives, one a bus driver, one a high school history teacher, and Edith.

"Because of the increased demand for more counselors, I would like all of you to complete the training as soon as possible. How many of you could come four nights a week for the next two weeks?" Roy looked from student to student.

The participants exchanged questioning glances. Finally Edith broke the silence. "I'm free for the next two weeks."

One by one the others echoed their agreement.

Roy smiled with appreciation. "Fine, then, we'll go ahead and meet since most of you are able to be here. If something comes up and you can't come, maybe you could get the notes from someone else. Better yet, I can tape each session."

The next two weeks flew by as Edith spent every Monday through Thursday night in class. Edith's family, however, was less than ecstatic about her involvement. Nancy and Jean were pleased she'd finally found fulfillment. Jay and Dawn continued to spend part of each Saturday with their grandmother and weren't even aware of her other interest. Bob felt the crisis center was complete foolishness, but he was glad that his mother's attention had shifted from store affairs.

At every training session Roy presented mock situations of different types of crisis calls. The trainees answered as if each call were a true-to-life one and they had to produce immediate verbal responses. Afterward everyone criticized the simulated crises. This became the most vital part of their training. Besides the guest lecturers from the welfare office and police department, a psychologist from the mental health clinic and a medical doctor offered helpful advice, but they in reality could only supplement the crisis intervention practice. The crisis center was only as effective as its volunteers' responses.

Finally the last night arrived and each trainee was handed a certificate of achievement. As Edith examined hers, she felt a satisfaction that rivaled that of receiving her college diploma many years before. Her most recent educational experience, however, had imparted an immeasurable benefit: She had learned more about helping others help themselves than during her four years in undergraduate school.

Following the last class session Roy and Edith shared their customary cup of coffee at Bea's. "Edith, I don't have enough people to fill the schedule at the center this weekend. Would you mind helping Friday and Saturday nights until midnight? We're the busiest over the weekends and occasionally I have two lines going at the same time. I'll be there to help, but after a few calls I'm sure you'll feel confident enough to handle them on your own."

"Sounds good to me. I should try while it's fresh in my mind."

"Good. I'll pick you up at seven-forty-five Friday. If you'd like, bring something to help pass the time. Some nights the phone rings constantly and other times I can sit for hours and nothing happens, except that I get a lot of reading done."

Friday night Roy arrived as planned and shook the snow from his boots before stepping inside. "Mabel will be there until we arrive," he informed Edith. "Most of the calls come after nine. The desperate ones seem to phone after the movie is over and people return to their empty homes."

On the way to the crisis center Roy explained the personal situations of those who had been calling regularly. "None of the regular calls during the last few months were life-threatening situations, just lonely people. But you never know, there are several delicate relationships that could erupt anytime."

As Roy parked his car in front of the center, Edith turned to him. "Thanks for the advice. I can use all the help I can get."

The pair hurried inside to escape the bitter cold and hung their coats on a rack behind the door. Across the room were two newly constructed desk cubicles with phones, paper and pencils, and a list of phone numbers of service agencies. Roy carefully reviewed which buttons to push for each line and which one to use to keep the call on hold and how to notify the telephone company to trace a call.

After Edith felt confident with the use of the phone, they made themselves comfortable on the fading green sofa that had been donated by one of the city council members. They were soon involved in a lively conversation that jumped from world affairs to their families. Just as Roy had said, the phone did not ring for almost two hours. While Edith talked, she crocheted several inches on her afghan and nearly forgot her reason for being there.

At nine-fifty-seven the shrill ringing of the telephone brought them both to attention.

"You're on," Roy whispered as Edith reached for the phone.

"Hello, crisis center. How may I help you?"

"I don't know if anyone can help." The man's voice was slurred and he spoke slowly and deliberately.

"Would you like me to try?" Edith asked, giving Roy a desperate glance.

"Well. . .it's kind of personal. My wife just took our baby daughter and left me. I don't know where they went. I called her mother's house, but she wasn't there."

Edith gave Roy another panicky look before she answered. "Do you have any idea why she left?"

"Well. . .it's sort of a long story," he mumbled. "I was coming out of Tony's Place as the movie was getting out. I stood there watching the people when I saw Sarah come out with another guy."

His voice broke while Edith waited patiently for him to regain his composure. "I followed them to the parking lot behind the theater. When I confronted them, this creep took a swing and leveled me."

"Were you hurt?" Edith's voice displayed her concern.

"No. . .I laid there for a moment, but I was okay. When I finally got home, Sarah was just walking out the door with a suitcase in one hand and our baby in the other. Over her shoulder she shouted, 'Don't call me, I'll call you.'"

"What did you do then?"

"I was going to run after her, but there was a black sedan with the same fellow in it waiting across the street. He shook his fist at me as she jumped into the car and they sped around the corner. They could be clear to Billings by now."

"That must've really hurt when she left without an explanation." Edith took a deep breath. "I am concerned about you. Have you been able to think about what you should do next?"

"I'm furious with the guy who took my wife. I would blow him away if I had half a chance. I don't understand how Sarah could do this to me. I love her so much. There isn't anything I wouldn't do for her. We have the sweetest six-month-old baby who's the spittin' image of her mother. My entire life centers around them. Without them there's no reason for me to go on living."

Cold chills went through Edith as she listened to his anger. She was reminded of Larry Reynolds. "Do you have any friends?"

"Well, there's a couple. . .but they're happily married. They'd never understand how Sarah could run off with another man. They think the world of her and probably would think I did something to drive her away. Besides, I wouldn't want to bother them with my troubles." His sad voice faltered as he shared his broken heart.

"Friends are for the bad times as well as the good," Edith tried to assure him. "I'm your friend and I'm concerned about your problems. My name is Edith. You don't have to give me your name, but what can I call you over the phone?"

"Jake. . .Jake Croder."

Edith listened to Jake pour out a lifetime of hurts and heartaches. After forty minutes she was able to convince him to make an appointment with one of the counselors at the local mental health center the next morning. She promised to call him the next day to see how he was doing. Fortunately another call did not come in during that time, so Roy was able to give his undivided attention to monitoring Jake's call.

"Good work," Roy praised as she hung up the phone with a sigh of relief. "I couldn't have done a better job myself."

"Thanks," Edith mumbled, laying her head on the desk to relax. "That was harder work than I expected. I certainly hope he keeps his word and sees one of the counselors tomorrow. If his wife doesn't come back, it will be a long time before he recovers."

Saturday night was even busier for Edith. Most of the callers needed someone to listen to their problems and could then find a solution themselves. In spite of the numerous calls there were long periods of time when neither line was busy and Roy and Edith engaged in personal conversation.

When the next shift of volunteers came at midnight, the older couple put on their coats and walked toward Roy's car parked in the back lot. "Can I pick you up for church in the morning? Pete is home again this weekend and will be with me. I could stop about ten-fifteen and we could make it a threesome."

"I'd love to." After a long pause she giggled. "We'll be the talk of the town by Monday morning."

Hurrying up her front steps, Edith turned on the light in the living room and hung her coat in the front closet. She stretched out in her recliner to relax before going to bed. A warm feeling enveloped her as she thought about her friendship with Roy. The warmth quickly faded as she considered Pete's hostility toward her.

I wonder how Pete will react toward me tomorrow at church when he wouldn't even speak to me at McDonald's the other night. I'll have to try my hardest to win him over. I wonder if Roy is actually aware of the depth of Pete's hostility.

When Roy stopped the car in front of Edith's home the next morning, Pete mechanically got into the back seat without saying a word. He continued to sulk as the two in the front seat carried on a lively conversation. The happier they appeared, the more miserable Pete became.

"Pete, how was work on the farm?" Edith asked, trying to pull him into the conversation.

"Okay," he mumbled.

"Did you have a good bus ride?" she probed.

"Nope."

Edith turned her attention back to Roy as he pulled into the church parking lot. Roy opened the car door for Edith as Pete bounded out of the back seat. In the church they found vacant seats in the third pew from the back and waited in silence for the service to begin. Edith felt as if all eyes were on Roy and her. She chuckled to herself as she imagined what they might be thinking.

Pete's scowl continued during the entire service; any gestures of kindness to share a hymnal were quickly rebuffed. When the service was over, Pete hurried to the door, while Roy and Edith tried to keep up with him and still greet those around them.

"Good morning, Mrs. Harkness." Pastor Rhodes smiled as he vigorously shook her hand. "How are you today?"

"Very well, thank you," she answered graciously as the minister turned to greet Roy.

"I see your son is home," Pastor Rhodes said as he shook Roy's hand. "It must be a special treat to have him with you."

"Dad hasn't any time for me," Pete interrupted rudely. "He's been too busy with Edith."

Pastor Rhodes gulped, his face flushed. "Your dad loves you just as much as he always has. I'm sure you will enjoy getting to know Mrs. Harkness. She's an excellent teacher and has a special love for young people."

"She doesn't love me," Pete blurted out as he shoved his way through the crowd into the parking lot.

"Please excuse his outburst," Roy apologized. "He usually loves everyone, but he's had a hard time accepting Edith's friendship."

"I understand. Think nothing of it. Maybe I'll be able to talk with Pete sometime this week."

"That would be thoughtful of you, but the Davidsons are picking him up this afternoon and taking him back to the ranch," Roy explained as the minister turned his attention to greeting the next person in line.

Following a quick lunch and without saying another word to his father, Pete hurried into his bedroom and began repacking his clothes. Normally he would have waited for his father's help, but today was different. As soon as the familiar gold Jeep Wagoneer stopped in front of the Dutton home, Pete bounded for the car without even a good-bye.

The next afternoon as Roy sat in his easy chair reading the current issue of *U.S. News and World Report,* the doorbell rang. He opened the door to his minister. "Pastor Rhodes, what a pleasant surprise. Do come in. Let me take your coat."

"When Pete left church yesterday I was extremely concerned about him." The minister made himself comfortable on the living room sofa.

"Pastor Rhodes, I've never seen him this upset before. I thought he would take kindly to Edith, but he's acting like a spoiled child."

"Mentally and emotionally Pete will always be a child. I hope you don't dampen your friendship with Edith because of it. You can't let Pete think he has control over you or he'll take advantage of the situation."

"But what can I do? I've tried everything I can think of and it only gets worse," Roy admitted, hoping for even a thread of insight into his dilemma.

"Maybe a few days away from home with your undivided attention would help. Would it be possible to take Pete on an extended fishing trip later in the spring? He used to enjoy your trips to Colorado."

"That's an excellent idea. Maybe then he'll realize that I'll always love him despite my friendship with Edith."

"Does Pete remember his mother at all?" Pastor Rhodes inquired as he thought back through the years of his relationship with the father and son.

"Not really. He's seen a lot of pictures of her though." He paused a moment and stared blankly out the window at the thawing snow. "Come to think of it, he's never had a good relationship with any woman. When he was in school he usually had male teachers, so perhaps he doesn't know how to interact with a mother substitute."

"That could be possible."

"He's accepted Martha Davidson, but their relationship is a more distant employer-employee arrangement. Martha's temperament displays her German background: hard-working, reserved, rarely displaying her true feelings." Roy tried to analyze his son's behavior. "I guess I'll just have to keep working on the situation and see what happens. It couldn't possibly get any worse than it already is."

"Let me know if there's anything I can do," Pastor Rhodes offered as he stood up to leave. "If you'd like, I'd be glad to meet with Pete when he comes home next time."

"Thanks for your concern," Roy said, walking him to the door. "I'll definitely be in touch."

Returning to his favorite chair, Roy sat bewildered. *What should I do about Pete? He's the last person on earth I'd want to hurt, but he refuses to accept Edith. . . . Maybe that fishing trip would be a good idea. Perhaps while we're alone in the Colorado wilderness I can make him understand my need for female companionship. . . . Maybe it wasn't wise for me to have devoted so much time to Pete when he was growing up while ignoring my own needs. I should have known that sooner or later I would become interested in another woman.*

The next Sunday afternoon Edith enjoyed the day with her family. Bob was absorbed with the figures on his laptop computer. Nancy worked on a pile of mending while she visited with her mother-in-law. As soon as possible the children monopolized Edith's time with table games. After an hour and a half Edith's desire flagged while the children were still going strong.

As the children finished gathering up the game pieces, Nancy joined her mother-in-law at the card table in the center of the living room. "Mom, can I get you a cup of coffee?"

"After a game like that I think I deserve one along with some adult companionship," Edith answered lightheartedly.

As Nancy prepared the coffee, Edith joined her son on the sofa. "Bob, you've been so quiet this afternoon. Is something on your mind?"

Bob shifted positions and cleared his throat. "Actually, Mom, I've been wanting to talk to you for some time, but I didn't know how or when."

"Just go ahead and say it and maybe together we can put it in the proper words."

Nancy returned with the coffee for her mother-in-law and a refill for her husband and herself. "Is this a private conversation or can anybody join?"

"Don't be silly," Bob answered, ignoring her dry humor. "This is a family affair. Maybe you could help explain this to Mother."

"Explain what?"

"Well, w—what exactly is your relationship with Roy Dutton?" Bob stammered, avoiding his mother's annoyed gaze.

"We are becoming very close friends. I help him at least twice a week at the crisis center, but you know all that. Why do you ask?"

"Can't you see what he's trying to do?" Bob demanded in a condescending tone.

"He's trying to help those in the community who are going through a difficult period in their lives. What's wrong with that?" Edith didn't try to hide the irritation in her voice.

"Is Roy showing a romantic interest in you?" Bob boldly continued.

Edith felt her cheeks redden. "We're becoming fond of each other and we're discovering that we share many of the same interests and hobbies. So again I ask, what's wrong with that?"

"He's taking advantage of your situation, Mom. Can't you see? You've just retired and don't know what direction you should take and a gray-haired knight in shining armor comes along and tries to sweep you off your feet."

Edith's eyes danced with anger. "Bob, that isn't exactly the way it happened. We began by having coffee together after classes, a normal situation, wouldn't you say? Then a friendship developed."

"Let's approach it from a different angle. What kind of work did Roy do before he retired?"

"I've told you that he was a social worker."

"And what kind of income do retired social workers have?"

"I really haven't given it much thought. I assume he receives social security and a stipend from the Montana Public Employees Retirement Fund. He doesn't seem to have any overwhelming financial need, nor is he living extravagantly."

"But Mother, can't you see what he's interested in? It's a classic soap opera. I can't stand by and let a Prince Charming who is barely making an existence sweet talk you out of all your savings. The money my father made belongs in the family, not to a fast-talking, gray-haired panther."

"Bob, that is the most absurd thing I have ever heard! Where does it say that every man over sixty-five who takes a woman to coffee is interested only in her money? We have the same need for human companionship as those under thirty."

As the tension mounted in the Harkness living room, Nancy again found herself in the position of family mediator. "I'm sure Bob doesn't mean to sound so cruel," she said as she shot a warning look at Bob. "If he knew Roy the way you do, I know he'd feel differently about the situation. Let's change the subject to something more pleasant. We invited you over to have an enjoyable afternoon, not to condemn your friendship."

"Thanks, Nancy. Where is the skirt you want me to hem? If you'll slip it on, I'll measure and pin it up for you."

For the next couple of hours Edith and Nancy worked in the bedroom that doubled as a sewing room. No mention of Bob's outburst was made, but his words had left a scar that would be hard to heal. Edith's thoughts, however, raged just beneath her calm exterior. If only her son would try to understand life from her point of view.

Chapter 6

"Hello, Mom," Jean said as Edith answered the phone late one Friday night in April. "I hope I didn't wake you. How's the weather in Montana?"

"Hi, dear. I'd just dozed off. It's good to hear your voice," Edith responded, waking from a light sleep. "To answer your important question, I hope spring has finally come. The snow is gone except on the mountain peaks and I have a couple tulips trying to force their way through the ground."

"Good. I hope you don't have any late spring blizzards this year. They are the real killers. At least the weather isn't nearly as severe here in Chamberland."

"Jean, what's up? You didn't call me at ten-thirty to talk about the weather."

"I called at ten-thirty because the rates are cheaper and to give you some good news."

"Don't keep me in suspense."

"You're going to have another grandchild."

Edith was now wide awake. "I'm so happy for you, Jean. When's the baby due?"

"The doctor says the middle of October. I hope that I'll be able to keep working through August. Jim's so excited about the baby that he has already become overly protective of me. I keep trying to convince him that pregnancy is a natural, normal condition, but he's carrying on as if our baby will be the first one born in history."

"Keep me posted on how you are getting along. Tell me if there is anything I can do to help."

"You don't have to worry about anything, Mother. I haven't been a nurse for six years for nothing. Sorry I woke you. I'd better let you go so you can get some sleep. Good night, Mom."

"Good night, dear. Take care of yourself and that new grandbaby."

As Edith drifted off to sleep that night, a sense of peace filled her. She was proud of her family and their accomplishments; she felt blessed to have Roy with whom she could share the joys and frustrations of life.

She'd have to tell him the exciting news first thing in the morning.

Pete's emotions were in constant confusion. When he returned to the ranch after his two-week visit in Rocky Bluff, he kept busy with farm chores. In the evenings he hid himself in his room and put model engines together. He didn't speak about his father for several days. One afternoon when he returned to the farmhouse after helping with the calves, Martha met him at the door.

"Pete, your dad called this afternoon."

"I never want to talk to him again," Pete said, pouting and stomping his foot in disgust. "He loves Edith, not me."

"But Pete, he called specifically to talk to you, but you were out haying the new calves and I couldn't find you in time. Why don't you call him back?"

"I won't do it."

"Your dad mentioned something about taking you on a fishing trip to Colorado. Why would you turn down a trip like that? I always thought you liked to fish."

Pete looked at Martha Davidson in disbelief. Gradually the tension left his face. "Well. . .maybe I'll call him. Can I have time off work to go on a trip?"

Martha breathed a sigh of relief. "Certainly. Now why don't you give your father a call and see what he has planned?"

Martha handed a reluctant Pete the telephone and slowly he dialed his father's number.

"Hello, Dutton residence."

"Hi, Dad. Martha said I should call you."

"I'm glad you did, Pete. How have you been?"

"I'm fine. Martha said you're going fishing in Colorado."

"Yes, and I was wondering if you would like to come with me."

Pete paused, torn between going on the fishing trip and avoiding Edith. "I'll go only if it's just you and me."

"I assure you it'll just be the two of us. I've already made the reservations at the Blue Lodge on Lake Branby for the twenty-first to the twenty-seventh of April. We should have a lot of fun. They say that April is the best time to catch rainbow trout and walleye."

"Okay. I'll go with you."

"Have all your things ready on the twenty-first and we'll leave bright and early. Mrs. Davidson invited me to spend the night with you at the ranch so we can get an early start. It's a long day's drive for us."

"I'll be ready. Thanks, Dad." With the promise of a week alone with his dad, Pete was back to his normal, talkative self. *Maybe I'll be able to convince Dad to forget all about his lady friend,* he thought eagerly.

Roy hung up the phone with a feeling of triumph. *Pastor Rhodes must have been right. A fishing trip alone with Pete is a great idea.* He poured a glass of milk and cut himself a large piece of chocolate cake. After enjoying his snack he called Edith to share the progress he was making with Pete. At last he had found someone who understood some of the problems of raising a handicapped child.

Three weeks later Roy and Pete left Montana as scheduled. After crossing the Colorado border on Interstate 25, the car began to lose power. Each hill became harder and harder to climb.

"Dad," Pete began with a worried look on his face, "would you turn off the radio? I want to listen to the engine. I think I know what's wrong."

Roy immediately turned off the radio and they both listened intently as the car slowly reached the crest of another hill. "What do you think it is, Son?" Long ago Roy had learned that although his son was classified as mentally retarded, he was a near genius when it came to mechanical things.

"I think the timing is off. Would you stop so I can check it?"

Ten miles farther down the road, Roy pulled the loaded car into a shaded rest area. Pete jumped out and opened the hood. His eyes lit up. "Dad, do you have a screwdriver? The timing is off. All it needs is a little adjusting."

Roy reached into the glove compartment and handed the tool to his son.

Moments later the engine was purring like a kitten. "There," Pete said with obvious pride. "The car should run all right now."

The two men climbed back into the car and within minutes they were cruising up a steep incline at sixty-five miles an hour without a problem. They made the rest of the trip without incident and at seven that evening Pete caught sight of Lake Branby. "Dad, look at the lake! It's beautiful. I can hardly wait to get out on the water."

The pair quickly unloaded the car and began preparing hot dogs and beans on the cabin hotplate. The lumpy beds supplied relief for their tired bodies. At dawn Roy and Pete were on the lake. The wind was biting and cold as it blew off the water, but they were both bundled in warm clothing and enjoyed the invigorating air. Little time passed before Roy pulled in a three-pound rainbow trout, and a half hour later Pete caught a walleye.

As the morning warmed, Pete shed one of his jackets. "Dad, do you love Edith?" he asked unexpectedly.

Roy paused. He had been wondering how he could bring up the subject, but this wasn't the way he'd anticipated. "Yes, I'm very fond of her."

"Are you going to marry her?"

"We don't have any definite plans," Roy replied hesitantly.

"Men always marry their girlfriends. I've seen it all on TV."

"Why are you worrying about me getting married?"

"Because then you won't have any time for me. You'll only have time for your wife."

Again Roy tried to explain that there would always be enough love to go around. Pete didn't respond but continued to stare blankly at the horizon.

For the remainder of the week their relationship was strained. Pete responded only to direct questions. His mood was cold and he displayed no emotion. Pete's mind was made up. If his father got married, he would lose him forever.

Roy was more concerned how he could communicate with Pete. Even a long-distance phone call to Edith gave him no new ideas.

The last afternoon on the lake Roy tried again to help his son understand the situation. "Pete, you've been the center of my life for the last twenty-eight years and I love you dearly," he began cautiously. "But ever since your mother died, there has been an empty spot in my life, that is, until I met Edith. But Edith will never change our relationship."

"I don't want to talk about Edith. You love her more than you love me. I want to go back to the ranch."

"The Davidsons will be coming to Rocky Bluff three days after we get back. That way you'll have time to see your old friends before going back to work and we can have a little more time together."

The long fishing vacation had ended on a sour note. Neither father nor son had accomplished his secret objective. The drive back to Montana was uneventful. Pete slept most of the way or stared blankly at the scenery. His normal zest for life seemed to have vanished. Roy's confusion about how to handle his son's jealousy increased with each passing mile. I'm able to help others deal with their problems, but I'm not able to deal with my own, he scolded himself as he followed his son into their home late that night.

Roy skipped church the next morning and unpacked the car. Pete continued to pout and avoid his father. He only left the TV to go to the kitchen or to the bathroom. Any offer of warmth by his father was rebuffed.

Monday morning Pete became even more bored and decided to take a walk around his hometown to enjoy the fresh spring air. As he stopped to look into each of the store windows, one particular store caught his attention: Harkness Hardware. Pete opened the double doors and quietly strolled down a side aisle. He began to idly examine the car repair tools. Within a few minutes a handsome, dark-haired man approached. "May I help you?"

"No, I'm just browsing," Pete mumbled.

"Say, aren't you Roy Dutton's son?"

"Yes. My name is Pete. What's yours?" He looked up from the display of sockets.

"I'm Bob Harkness. I imagine you know my mother, Edith."

Pete's body tensed. "I wish your mother would stay away from my dad. I don't like her."

"Pete, you must really be upset about their relationship. Let's go across the street to the drugstore and have a cup of coffee and talk about it. My wife Nancy can watch the store while I'm gone."

Pete felt important in the company of such an influential businessperson. He and his father had often had coffee accompanied by someone whom Pete felt was important, but never had anyone like that invited him for coffee. Pete obediently followed Bob into the drugstore. The two men found a back booth and ordered.

As the waitress returned with two steaming cups, Bob looked intently at Pete. "Why are you so upset about our parents' relationship?"

"My dad doesn't need a wife," Pete protested adamantly. "He only needs a son."

"Do you suppose he's just looking for a woman to do his housekeeping for him?" Bob asked, hoping to take full advantage of Pete's simple, naive mind.

"Why else do men get married?" Pete asked innocently. After a short time he gave a hearty laugh and answered his own question. "Unless they find someone with a lot of money. I once saw a movie on TV about how this younger man married an old lady only for her money. Does your mother have a lot of money?"

Bob's muscles tightened as he tried to maintain a relaxed smile on his face. "I'm afraid your dad is looking at the wrong woman if he is only looking for money. Is it getting hard for him to live on his pension?"

"I don't know," Pete responded blankly. "He complains a lot about not having much money. Maybe it's because he's spending all his money on your mother. Why don't you stop them?"

"I wish I could, but I can't find a way to do it. They're both acting like a couple of silly teenagers instead of mature senior citizens. What would they do if one of them became seriously ill?"

"If my dad got sick, I could take care of him myself," Pete boasted as he took his last sip of coffee.

A familiar voice interrupted their conversation. "Is this a private party or can anybody join?"

"Oh, hi, Mom," Bob responded, startled at Edith's sudden appearance. "Please sit down and join us. I was just getting better acquainted with Roy's son."

"Hello, Pete. How was your fishing trip?"

"Fine," he mumbled without looking from his empty coffee cup.

"Did you catch your limit?" Edith continued, hoping to somehow break the ice.

"Of course. I'm a good fisherman."

"When are you going back to the ranch?" Edith persisted, trying every possible way to draw him into a conversation.

"Wednesday. Then you can have my dad all to yourself."

"Pete, your father loves you very much. He talks about you constantly while you're gone."

"I better go now." Without further explanation, Pete rose and hurried from the drugstore.

"I don't know how Roy and I are going to be able to convince Pete that we both love him and want to have him around," Edith sighed to her son.

"Maybe it would be better if you didn't try so hard. It's not fair that you come between a father and son during this stage of their lives." Bob glanced at his wristwatch. "If you'll excuse me, I'd better get back to the store and help Nancy. I've been gone quite awhile now and we have a lot of new stock to check in."

The next day Bob dialed the Dutton home. "Hi, Pete. This is Bob. I'm sorry that you're leaving tomorrow to go back to the ranch. The next time you're home, would you come to the store and see me? Maybe if we work together we can convince our parents how foolish they are."

"I've tried to break them up and it hasn't worked," Pete answered excitedly. Finally he had met someone who understood his problem. "Dad should be spending more time with me."

"You're right, Pete," Bob continued, trying to incite Pete into action. "They don't belong together. He needs to be spending that time with you." Bob paused for emphasis. "After all, you're his only son."

Chapter 7

D o you have plans for Friday night?" Roy asked after Edith answered her telephone on the last Tuesday in April.

She smiled to herself. "Not really, just the usual 'Friday Night at the Movies' on TV or a good book. Do you have something better in mind?"

"You decide. There's a three-act play at the civic center presented by a traveling team of college students. People say they are pretty good. Would you care to join me?"

She chuckled. "What time does it start?"

"It begins at eight, so I'll pick you up about seven-thirty. I'm looking forward to seeing you then," Roy added as he bid her good-bye.

As Roy drove through the brightly lit streets of Rocky Bluff on Friday night, Edith turned to him, her face flushed and palms sweaty. "I almost called and broke our date this evening," she murmured. "I've been feeling very strange most of the day. I've been having strange chest pains today, so I assume I am coming down with some kind of viral infection. I figured that I'd feel the same whether I sat home in my easy chair or if I went to the play, so I decided to go ahead and enjoy the play."

"Are you sure you'll be okay?" Roy questioned gently, his blue eyes settling on Edith's tension-filled face. "The rest might be better for you."

"No, I'll be fine, really," Edith assured him as Roy pulled to a stop in the far corner of the civic center parking lot.

When they arrived in the lobby, they were surprised to find that the main floor of the auditorium was full and only a few seats were left in the balcony. Amid the constant stirring of people, Roy and Edith found two vacant seats close to the aisle near the back of the balcony. After they greeted friends from the senior citizens center in front of them and a couple of Edith's former students nearby, they settled into a few moments of idle chit-chat before the curtain went up.

As the play progressed Edith broke into a cold sweat. Her last conscious thoughts were of Roy. *I shouldn't have come, but I don't want to spoil Roy's evening and have him take me home. He has been looking forward to seeing this play all week.*

As the curtain fell after the second act, the pain in Edith's chest became unbearable, then she experienced the same horrible sensation traveling down her left arm. With a heavy gasp for air, she slumped sideways toward Roy.

"Someone call an ambulance!" he shouted as he stretched Edith out in the aisle. Quickly he checked for a pulse in the carotid artery. Nothing. Tilting her head backward, he cleared Edith's airways and began CPR. Fifteen chest compressions, then two breaths into her mouth, fifteen more chest compressions and two long breaths. After what seemed an eternity, Roy heard the sound of an ambulance in the street below. Moments later three emergency medical technicians rushed in with a stretcher.

The ambulance crew quickly assessed the situation and continued CPR as they placed Edith carefully on the stretcher and wheeled her to the waiting ambulance. Roy hurried to his car and followed them at full speed. His only thought was to get Edith to the hospital immediately.

As Roy entered the emergency room, three minutes behind the ambulance, he was faced with a smiling ambulance crew. "We made it," the short, dark-haired attendant shouted as soon as he saw Roy. "She started breathing on her own as we pulled into the hospital parking lot. Thanks to your quick action at the civic center, I think we have a good chance of winning this one."

Roy hurried to the admissions desk. "May I see Edith Harkness, please? She just arrived by ambulance."

"I'm sorry, but the doctors are with her now. Are you a member of the family?" The gray-haired nurse behind the desk took out a sheet to record Edith's background data.

"I'm a good friend," Roy replied nervously. "But I'll call them right away. Her son lives here in Rocky Bluff and her daughter is in Idaho."

"I'd appreciate if you'd do that for us. I'll wait for her son to arrive to get her background."

Roy hurried to the nearby phone booth, checked the number, and dialed the Robert Harkness residence. After several rings, Jay answered the phone.

"Hello, Jay. Is your daddy home?"

"Just a moment and I'll call him."

A deep voice greeted him after a few moments of silence.

"Hello, Bob. This is Roy Dutton. Your mother and I went to the community play tonight, where she became seriously ill. They brought her to the hospital in the ambulance. Would you come right away?"

There was an icy pause at the other end of the line. "I'll be right there. Thanks for calling."

Within ten minutes Bob and Nancy rushed into the emergency room waiting area. "How is she?" Bob demanded as soon as he saw Roy.

"The doctor is waiting to talk to you. Do you mind if I tag along?"

"No, of course not. You might be able to help us fill in the pieces."

Bob stepped up to the admissions clerk. "Could I see Edith Harkness's doctor? I'm her son, Bob."

"Just a moment, please. I'll have to page him."

"Dr. Brewer. . .paging Dr. Brewer. . .please come to the emergency room admissions desk."

Within moments a sandy-haired doctor in a white coat with a stethoscope around his neck appeared. He approached the worried trio. "Are you relatives of Mrs. Harkness?"

"Yes, I'm her son, Bob Harkness, and this is my wife, Nancy, and a friend of my mother's, Roy Dutton."

"It's nice meeting you. Let's sit over here." He motioned to a sofa and loveseat in a corner. They sat on the edge of their seats as the doctor continued. "Your mother is beginning to stabilize, but it will be several days before we know how much damage has been done. I've had her moved into the intensive care unit, where we can monitor her heart. We may decide to transport her to the Great Falls Deaconess Hospital, where they specialize in cardiac care."

"Is there anything we can do for her?" Nancy asked tearfully.

"Just pray. The medical profession will give her the best care possible, but only God can heal. You might want to call the rest of the family and warn them that she is in critical condition."

"We were planning to call her daughter in Idaho as soon as we'd talked with you and had more details," Roy explained. "I'm sure she'll want to come and be with her."

"I'll be on call all night if your mother needs me," Dr. Brewer assured them. "If you want to go to the ICU unit in the south wing you can see your mother for just a few minutes. She's not fully conscious, but she's beginning to respond to outside stimuli. There's a five-minute visiting limitation per hour. Feel free to call me if you have any questions." With that the physician disappeared down the long corridor to the doctors' lounge while the others sat in stunned silence.

"Let's go see Mother. I'll call Jean later," Bob directed as they rose from their seats at the same time and made their way to the south wing.

After finding the nurse on duty, Bob discovered Edith was in room 317. They all peered in through the glass window. "Your mother is resting well, but she's in critical condition. Only one person is allowed in the room at a time," the nurse directed.

Nancy slipped in first. After a few brief moments of watching Edith struggle with each breath, she left the room with tears in her eyes. Roy and Bob took a few moments with her without saying a word. Each was lost in his own thoughts.

As Bob joined the others in the hallway, he cleared his throat in an attempt to collect his composure. "I'll give Jean a call if you want to go home and get some rest. There is nothing we can do here. Mom seems to be receiving the best of care."

While Bob made his way to the phone booth next to the hospital lobby, Roy waved a sad farewell and stepped outside. A warm breeze struck his face. Normally he embraced the coming of spring, but tonight his body felt numb. He knew that he was becoming extremely fond of Edith, but he didn't realize how much she meant to him until he saw her lying pale and nearly lifeless in the intensive care unit. The memories of the happy times they had together and the joys they had shared flashed before him.

When he arrived home, Roy fixed himself a cup of hot cocoa and tried to relax. His mind kept drifting back to the hospital. He finally decided to go to bed, but the hours passed slowly as he tossed and turned.

By nine the next morning Roy had returned to the south wing of the hospital. As he approached the nursing station he found Nancy, Bob, and Dr. Brewer in the visitors' lounge. Roy hesitated in the doorway until Bob acknowledged him with a weary smile. "Roy, would you join us? We have some important decisions to make."

Roy took a seat on the couch next to the doctor. "How's Edith this morning?"

"She rested well all night and is beginning to regain consciousness, but she's in a great deal of pain," Dr. Brewer explained. "Bob and I feel it would be wise to transfer her to the Great Falls Deaconness Hospital as soon as possible. The Mercy Flight Ambulance has already been summoned."

"The problem is," Bob began hesitantly, "it will take me most of the day to arrange for help at the store so I can go to Great Falls. I talked with Jean last night and Jim is taking her into Coeur D'Alene this afternoon so that she can catch the evening flight to Great Falls. We need to have someone there to meet her flight at eleven-thirty. Would you be willing to drive to Great Falls and be with Mother and then meet Jean's flight?"

This was one of the most difficult situations Bob had ever faced. He had been trying his best to discourage Roy's friendship with his mother, but now he felt forced into seeking his help. *Maybe if he sees her at her worst it will convince him to end their relationship,* he thought. *Perhaps when he sees all her medical costs he'll really lose interest.*

"Certainly," Roy responded, completely ignorant of Bob's feelings toward him. "I'll go home and pack a few things and leave right away. What time will the air ambulance get into Great Falls?"

"It should be arriving here in about fifteen minutes," Dr. Brewer explained. "It will take less than three minutes to load the patient and then another forty-five minutes to fly back to Deaconess. If you leave right away, you might be a little over an hour behind her arrival. I'll let them know that you are coming."

"They're planning to do a heart catheterization soon after she arrives and from there they will decide if open-heart surgery is necessary," Bob continued, trying to mask his agitation. "I'll be there first thing tomorrow morning if they do surgery, but it's impossible for me to walk away from the store without prior arrangements."

"There's no problem," Roy assured him. "That's one of the advantages of retirement. I'm free to help anyone at a moment's notice. May I see Edith before I leave?"

"Certainly," the doctor agreed as he rose to check on another patient. "Just don't stay long. She's extremely weak."

Roy slipped down the hall and through the door to Edith's room. When he sat next to the bed, Edith opened her dark brown eyes and turned her head toward him. A faint smile spread across her lips.

"Hello, Edith," he greeted her softly as he took her hand in his. "How are you feeling?"

"Not too well," she whispered. "I feel like I've been run over by a steam roller."

"The air ambulance will be here in a few minutes to take you to Great Falls Deaconess. I'm going to drive to Great Falls to be with you and to meet Jean's flight tonight."

"Thanks for everything." Edith's eyes closed as she loosened her grasp on his hand.

"Don't worry about a thing. You have the best medical care available. I'll see you in a couple hours in Great Falls." With that he leaned over and gave her a quick kiss on the forehead, then quietly left the room. A trip to Great Falls was the least he could do for the one who was beginning to mean so much to him.

Two hours later Roy approached the admissions desk in the main lobby of Deaconess Hospital. "What is Edith Harkness's room number? She arrived about an hour ago by air ambulance from Rocky Bluff."

"Just a moment, please," the receptionist responded as she typed the name into the computer on her desk. "She's in acute cardiac care unit number three on the third floor. Please check at the nursing station on that floor."

Roy thanked the woman and hurried to catch the waiting elevator. Approaching the cardiac care nursing station, he was overwhelmed with the number of monitors with lines pulsing up and down. The nurse on duty did not look up from the screens as he approached. He waited in silence a few moments before a much younger nurse appeared from a small drug chamber nearby. She locked the door behind herself and placed the key in her pocket.

"May I help you?"

"Yes, I'm here to see Edith Harkness who arrived from Rocky Bluff."

"You must be Roy Dutton," she responded with a smile. "We've been expecting you. The flight attendants told us that you would be coming as a representative of the family. Edith is in ACCU number three, but they just took her down to have a heart cath. It'll be another hour to an hour and a half before she'll be back in her room. You may wait in her room, the visitors' lounge, or in the cafeteria on the main floor."

Roy felt disappointed that he couldn't see Edith right away. "I didn't have any breakfast before I left this morning so I think I'll catch a quick bite to eat in the cafeteria."

Roy found a table in the hospital dining hall beside a window. He relaxed with a bowl of ham and bean soup and a chef's salad. With each bite he felt his strength renewed. His body ached from lack of sleep and tension. After forty-five minutes of watching the hospital employees and the visitors come and go, he returned to the third floor to wait for word about Edith.

Stepping off the elevator, Roy greeted the staff at the nurses' station and tried to make himself comfortable in the lounge. He scanned the magazines on the table and picked up a few current issues, but the minutes dragged by. Finally a gurney appeared, pushed by two muscular orderlies dressed in green. Roy rose to meet them.

"The doctor will be here shortly to talk with you," the taller one explained as Roy neared the gurney. "We'll have Mrs. Harkness settled in her bed in a few minutes."

Roy paced nervously up and down the hallway until a balding doctor stopped him at the end of the hall. "Mr. Dutton?" he questioned, offering his hand in greeting. "I'm Dr. Pierce."

"It's nice to meet you," Roy responded. "I'm a good friend of Edith Harkness. How is she?"

"It's a miracle that she's still alive. She's quite a fighter." The doctor motioned for Roy to join him in the visitors' lounge. "Has any of her family arrived yet?"

"They won't be in until this evening. Her daughter is coming from Idaho tonight and her son is coming from Rocky Bluff in the morning. Is Edith going to be all right?"

"Mrs. Harkness suffered a serious cardiac arrest. The main artery into the heart is 95 percent blocked; another artery is 90 percent blocked and another 82 percent blocked. I've scheduled her for open-heart surgery first thing in the morning. I'll have her family finish signing the necessary papers as soon as they arrive. Edith has already signed the release to do surgery, but she is much too weak to question further."

"What are her chances of resuming a normal lifestyle?" Roy questioned with a worried sigh.

"I can't give you any percentages. She appears to be strong and in good health otherwise. We have an excellent staff of heart surgeons, so she has much in her favor. Many of our patients are back to their normal routines within three months, but each case is different."

The doctor paused, trying not to generate false optimism. "Edith's situation is extremely serious, however. I'll keep you posted on her condition and will talk more with you and the family after the surgery tomorrow."

After the doctor disappeared down the hallway, Roy sat in the visitors' lounge in stunned silence for nearly a half-hour. Although he knew there was a strong possibility of surgery when he came to Great Falls, the harsh reality of the situation sent cold chills down his spine. Finally he slipped quietly into Edith's room. While he stood beside her sleeping form an assurance of peace settled over him. In spite of the formidable circumstances, God still had everything under control.

Regaining his emotional equilibrium, Roy left the hospital to find accommodations. Less than a block away he spotted a modest motel with a flashing neon sign, Sunrise Inn. He parked the car in front and stepped into a clean, efficient office. "May I help you?" the manager greeted.

"I'd like to reserve three rooms for at least two nights. I need a single for Jean Thompson, a double for Bob Harkness, and I'll need a single for myself. My name is Roy Dutton."

"That will be no problem, Mr. Dutton." The manager smiled as she checked the register.

"We have a friend and family member who is going to have surgery in the morning," Roy explained, reaching into his pocket for his wallet.

"We serve many of the patients' families. You can let me know in the morning how long you'll be staying." The office manager hurriedly took down the necessary information and filled out the credit card forms. "Here are the keys to your rooms. I hope you enjoy your stay."

Roy kept the key to room 116 and dropped the other two into the pocket of his suit coat. After he unlocked the door and hung his suit coat on the back of a chair, he removed his tie and shoes and stretched out on the bed. A few hours of rest seemed extremely inviting to his weary body.

Later that evening Roy anxiously drove the quiet streets of the city to the Great Falls International Airport. He had seen several pictures of Jean, but he had never met her in person. Only a handful of maintenance people and baggage personnel were there to greet the arriving passengers. Finally the loudspeaker blared, "Horizon Flight Number 315 is now arriving at Gate Number 2."

Roy jumped to his feet and waited as the passengers began to file by the check stand. After a few moments a tall, dark-haired young woman began walking toward him.

"Are you Roy Dutton?" she asked confidently.

"Yes, and you must be Jean. You look just like your photos."

"It's nice to meet you, Roy. I've heard so many good things about you." As she extended her right hand, Roy noted how much her mannerisms were like her mother's. "How is Mother? I've been extremely worried about her."

"They did a heart cath today, and she's scheduled to have a triple bypass first thing in the morning," Roy explained as he picked up her suitcase from the luggage check stand. "The doctor says she's in extremely good health for someone her age, and I'm told the finest heart surgeons are on staff. The doctor would like to have you check in at the business office and the nurses' station as soon as you arrive at the hospital. There are still some forms that need to be signed."

"There's always so much paperwork at hospitals," she sighed. "I think I spend more time at work filling out forms than caring for the patients. Anyway, I appreciate your coming to be with Mother and to pick me up. Did you think to make a reservation at a motel for me?"

"Yes, at the Sunrise Inn, nothing fancy but comfortable and only a block from the hospital. Bob will be here first thing in the morning and his room is waiting whenever he arrives."

Later, alone in his motel room, Roy read his Bible, but his mind could only concentrate on his dearest friend lying weak and vulnerable in a strange hospital room. *At least God understands the needs and desires of my heart,* he thought as he closed his Bible. He turned off the bedside lamp and resigned himself to another night of fitful sleep.

Chapter 8

Roy was up at dawn and went directly to the hospital. He stopped at the nurses' station to inquire about Edith's condition.

"Mrs. Harkness has already been given her pre-op medications and she's a little groggy. I can tell you that she rested well through the night and did not have any further problems," the head nurse assured him. "The surgical procedure generally takes about five hours and we try to keep the family informed as to the progress of the surgery. You may stop in her room and see her, but don't stay long. There's a family room down the hall if you care to wait."

"Thank you for your kindness. Her daughter and son should be along shortly."

As Roy turned, Bob and Nancy appeared. "How's Mom?" Bob demanded abruptly.

"They said she had a good night's rest and they will be taking her to surgery in a few minutes. Jean should be here any time now. She had to stop at the business office."

"I'm sure everything will be all right," the younger man replied stiffly. "Thank you for coming ahead to be with Mother. If you want to go back to Rocky Bluff, I think we can handle it for a few days. I know Jean has taken a temporary leave of absence from work."

"That's all right. I didn't come this far to leave your mother now. I'll stay until she's better."

"Whatever you like, but I'd hate to have our family problems interfere with your personal life."

Just then Jean entered the waiting room. The few hours of sleep seemed to have refreshed her. "How's Mother this morning?"

Bob stood in detached silence while Roy answered. "Your mother is almost ready to go to surgery," he explained softly. "They have given her a shot so she's a little groggy, but I'm sure she'll want to see you."

The family walked toward Edith's room. Roy politely pushed the door open for Jean. She was professionally trained to deal with critically ill patients, but she was not emotionally equipped to deal with her mother lying in a sterile hospital room. She choked back her tears as she approached

59

the bed. Edith roused and turned her head toward her daughter. A faint smile spread across her face. "Jean, what a surprise," she whispered. "When did you get here?"

"I flew in late last night. Roy met me at the airport." Jean took her mother's hand in hers. "I plan to stay until you're able to take care of yourself again. While I'm gone, Jim is prepared to hold down the fort as long as necessary. You get some rest now and remember, we are all here with you."

Bob and Nancy stuck their heads into the room. "I know there is a limit of two visitors per patient, but can we have a quick prayer with Mother before she goes to surgery?" Nancy asked.

"Please do," Edith murmured as Roy walked around the bed and took her other hand.

The four together said a simple prayer for healing, comfort, and strength. As they were whispering their Amens, two orderlies appeared in the doorway. "Are you ready, Mrs. Harkness?" one of them asked as Jean stepped aside to allow the gurney to be wheeled next to the bed.

"As ready as I'll ever be," Edith responded weakly.

"Our prayers are with you, Mom," Jean said as the family turned to leave the room.

As soon as the gurney was pushed onto the elevator, Bob turned to Nancy. "Let's go downtown for breakfast. Hospitals are too depressing for me and besides, the surgery takes five hours and we can be back by noon. Anyway, there are some supplies I want to check on with the wholesaler."

Anger flashed through Nancy's dark brown eyes. She took a quivering breath. "There's a cafeteria right here in the hospital. Surely business can wait until your mother's surgery is over."

"There's nothing we can do here. I need to get outside and get some fresh air. Let's at least go downtown for breakfast and come back as soon as we've eaten."

Nancy turned to her sister-in-law with an embarrassed look. "Would you excuse us for a bit? We'll meet you here later. I'm anxious to hear all about the plans for my future niece."

"Or nephew," Jean corrected as Bob and Nancy disappeared down the hospital corridor. Shocked by her brother's lack of concern, Jean stood in silence with tears building in her eyes. Suddenly she began to sob. Roy wrapped his long arms around her in a fatherly manner as she buried her face in his sweater. The time when she felt that she should be the strongest she found herself crumbling like a little girl. The thought of the woman who had loved and nurtured her all her life lying on a surgeon's table had rendered her temporarily helpless.

After a few minutes, the tears stopped and Jean felt emotionally drained. Roy gave her a warm smile. "Let's go down to the cafeteria and have some breakfast. A cup of coffee and some toast will do us both good."

A friendship grew between Roy and Jean as they sat across the table from each other. Although they had met only the night before, they were bound together by a common concern.

Roy spread grape jelly on his toast and looked up at the young woman so like her mother. "You must be extremely close to Edith," he shrewdly observed.

"Much more than most mothers and daughters," Jean replied, relieved to have an opportunity to talk about her mother with someone who was also concerned. "We were among the few who made the transition from a parent-child relationship to an adult friendship. I can truthfully say that except for my husband, my mother is my best friend."

"She's a remarkable woman. You should hear her compassion and wisdom when she talks to crisis line callers. The depth of her character is astounding."

"It's too bad that Bob hasn't developed that relationship with Mother. After she retired he treated her as if she were a total invalid, of no value except to serve as a source of a sizeable inheritance."

Jean sighed with disgust. "I may be judging him wrong, but I get the feeling that his basic philosophy is life ends at sixty, so get all you can while you're young."

"That's a pretty miserable perception. You know, most people haven't discovered that the best part of life can be the retirement years."

"I'm beginning to understand what you mean. Sometimes I think that by the time we finally learn how to live the way God intended, our lives are almost over."

"Well, the nicest thing about being old is that you don't have to worry about getting old anymore," Roy chuckled as he pushed his plate aside and leaned back in his chair.

The two continued a lively conversation about world events and personal problems, staying in the cafeteria long after their meal was over. Occasionally Roy's eyes strayed to the scene outside the nearby window. A parklike courtyard was in the center of the hospital complex. "Let's go outside for a walk and get some fresh air and then go upstairs and see if there is any word from the operating room."

Jean stood up, pushed her chair under the table, and followed him out the cafeteria door. Slowly the two strolled around the tree-lined sidewalk that encircled the hospital. The spring morning reinforced their hope and faith that Edith would be restored to complete health. The God who created such a beautiful world could rebuild a damaged heart. But would He?

Around ten o'clock Jean and Roy returned to the third-floor waiting room, although they knew it might be another hour before they received word on the surgery. Much to their surprise they were greeted by Nancy and Bob.

"Where have you been?" Bob demanded as soon as he spotted his sister. "I thought you of all people—a nurse!—would be staying here in case someone came with a report on Mother."

Jean's temper flared as she tried to ignore his outburst. "We've been for a walk around the hospital."

Nancy shuffled nervously and reached out and took her sister-in-law's arm. "Jean, come tell me all about your plans for the baby. I'm so excited for you."

As the women attempted to engage in talk of babies and homes, the men each picked up a magazine and thumbed through the pages, neither acknowledging the presence of the other.

"It's nearly eleven o'clock. We should be hearing about Mother's progress soon," Jean observed half to herself and half to the others. "I'm sure everything is going okay. The doctors doing the surgery are highly respected by the medical people in Chamberland, but that still doesn't remove my fears."

Bob began to pace the floor. He paused before the open window for several minutes, admiring the sights of the city below and the majestic Highwood Mountains that silhouetted the horizon. Although no one spoke, the tension mounted in the small waiting room.

At eleven-thirty a nurse appeared in the doorway. "Are you the family of Edith Harkness?"

"Yes, I'm her daughter, Jean. How is she?"

"The surgery is taking a little longer than expected, but everything is under control. She should be out of surgery in another hour or so," the nurse assured them.

"It shouldn't be taking this long for a triple bypass," Jean responded, the creases in her forehead deepening. "Are there complications?"

The nurse cleared her throat. "This is a very technical surgery, so any minor problem can cause a major delay. I'll let you know as soon as I receive more news. Can I get anyone a cup of coffee?"

"Please," Roy responded to her questioning gaze. "Could I have a teaspoon of sugar in mine?"

"I'll take mine black," Nancy requested as both Bob and Jean nodded in agreement.

Nancy and Jean kept up a steady stream of small talk to keep their minds from dwelling on "what ifs." Each passing minute seemed like an hour. Even the aroma of fresh coffee couldn't calm their frayed nerves.

At one o'clock the same nurse reappeared in the doorway. "I know this has been a long wait for you. The surgery is progressing, but the last word from the operating room was that they will not be finished for another hour. There were a few minor setbacks along the way. I'll let you know as soon as I receive more news."

"What's going on down there?" Bob demanded rudely. "Did they make some sort of blunder and are now trying to cover it up?"

The nurse's eyes flashed. "Your mother has the finest doctors available. They will explain the procedure after the surgery is over."

After the nurse gave her second report, they were all afraid to leave the room for even a drink of water until they received further word on Edith's condition. Shortly after two o'clock Dr. Pierce entered the waiting room still dressed in his green surgical suit. All eyes focused on him.

Jean was the first to speak. "How is she?" was all that would come from her trembling lips.

"Your mother is out of surgery and is resting comfortably. As you may have suspected, we did have some complications," Dr. Pierce began.

Jean took a deep breath. "What were they?"

"Twice the blood pressure dropped severely, the result of internal bleeding. Consequently, we had to reopen the chest cavity and redo the suture. Everything appears normal at this time."

Jean sighed with relief. "How long will it be before we will be able to see her?"

"They will leave her in the recovery room for several more hours before they bring her back to the cardiac intensive care unit. However, she probably won't be too aware of things until at least tomorrow."

The doctor described the exact details of the surgery, complete with pictures of the damaged arteries. Jean felt a lump build in her throat. This was not a clinical textbook case but her own mother.

As soon as Dr. Pierce finished the medical description, Jean turned to him with tears in her eyes. "What's the prognosis? The little I know about heart surgery is that the longer one is in surgery, the less chance there is for a total recovery."

"That's not a hard-and-fast rule," the doctor stated matter-of-factly. "Each situation is different. We will not know for several days how fast your mother's system will recuperate from the intense shock of the surgery. She may have suffered a slight stroke while she was on the operating table. All we can do is wait and see."

"Thank you for all your efforts," Roy said with a relieved smile. "I don't know what we'd do without doctors like you."

"Let me know if there are any problems or questions concerning your mother," Dr. Pierce told them as he rose to leave.

"Whew! I'm glad that's over and Mother is holding her own," Bob said after a few minutes' silence as they all absorbed the doctor's news. "Now I can get back to work at the store by tomorrow if Jean's going to stay here. It's a busy time of year with the lawn and garden supplies just starting to sell."

All faces registered shock at Bob's blasé attitude. "As I said earlier," Jean replied tartly, "I plan to stay until Mother is home and able to care for herself."

Bob turned to Roy. "I assume you'll be going home tonight as well."

"No, Bob. I have enough trained volunteers to run the crisis phone for two or three weeks without a problem."

"Whatever you think, but I'm sure Jean can handle everything here. After all, she's a nurse by profession." Bob gave the last words an almost sarcastic emphasis.

"I'm certain Mother will enjoy his company while she's recovering," Nancy inserted, trying to break another tension-filled situation initiated by her husband. Without scarcely taking a breath, Nancy turned her attention to her sister-in-law. "Please cancel our reservations at the motel. I guess we won't be using them after all. If you need any help, just give me a call and I'll come right back."

"Thanks, I appreciate your offer. Roy and I will keep you posted on her progress."

Nancy gave her sister-in-law a quick hug as Bob hurried toward the door, expecting his wife to follow instinctively. Jean and Roy watched as the pair disappeared down the hall and entered the waiting elevator. As they sat together in silence, Roy observed from Jean's body language her barely suppressed anger at Bob's seemingly callous behavior.

"Jean, I don't mean to pry, but does Bob have a reason to resent my friendship with your mother?" Roy asked as he surveyed the attractive young woman who sat across from him.

"Truthfully, Bob has become nothing more than a greedy, self-centered slob. Although he's my only brother, I'm beginning to see him in a totally different light. Money is fast becoming his god."

"Those are pretty harsh words, but I've also observed a preoccupation with money. Maybe that's his problem. He probably thinks I'm only interested in your mother's money."

"Anything is possible. He's really becoming touchy about the store's future. Maybe when this is all over we can have a good talk with Bob. Everyone is becoming extremely sensitive to his attitude, but we all try to sweep it under the carpet and pretend that nothing is wrong."

"I'm sure it's not beyond hope," Roy assured her. "In spite of his outward expression of disinterest in his mother, I sense a real love and protectiveness underneath. The good side of Bob will eventually win out."

A smile spread across Jean's face as the tension lines relaxed. "I certainly hope you're right."

"Let's go to the acute cardiac unit and see your mother. I'll feel better just seeing her again even if she's sleeping." Roy gestured for Jean to follow him.

Edith lay motionless surrounded by tubes and monitors. Her gray-flecked hair framed her pale but serene face. They studied the scene for several moments in silence. Finally Jean spoke. "She's in good hands. Maybe we should go now."

Roy retired to the motel for some needed rest, which he admitted he had done without since Edith became ill. Jean decided to stay at the hospital, her only companions a few books and a troubled heart.

The days passed slowly for Jean and Roy as they kept a constant vigil at Edith's bedside. Within three days the doctors felt she was strong enough to move into a semiprivate room on the cardiac care floor. Due to the complications of the surgery, Edith did not regain her strength as fast as the medical team would have liked, but her positive attitude and a sustaining faith kept her constantly moving forward. Every day Nancy called Jean at the motel to inquire about her mother-in-law. Bob, however, was always busy at the store.

"Mother, some flowers just arrived," Jean said brightly as she set a beautiful arrangement of yellow and pink carnations on her nightstand.

"Who are they from?" Edith murmured, a smile spreading across her face.

"The card says, 'From your son, Bob,' " Jean replied as she noted a sadness in her mother's eyes.

"Isn't there even a note attached? I've been here over a week."

"I'm sorry, Mom. Just the flowers arrived. I'm sure Bob must be very busy this time of year."

Nothing more was said about the lack of support from Bob, but there seemed an emptiness in the family. Hopefully, things would be different when Edith returned to Rocky Bluff.

After two weeks of taking turns sitting at Edith's bedside, Roy and Jean began talking more and more about Edith's homecoming. As they talked, Edith's spirits lifted, but a sense of helplessness kept invading her speech. "I guess I don't have a heart like a twenty year old anymore. A year ago Dr. Brewer told me that I did, but now I'm beginning to wonder if I'll ever be able to take care of myself."

"Don't worry about a thing, Mom. I'm planning to stay with you until you can," Jean assured her as she took her hand.

"You don't want to be apart from your husband too long," Edith protested weakly. "That's not good for any marriage. The doctor said that I won't be able to climb the stairs to the bedroom for some time."

"Roy and I have been talking about that," Jean stated calmly. "We could convert the den into a bedroom."

"You know, I've been thinking the same thing." Edith adjusted her bed to an upright position with the automatic controls. "The furniture shouldn't be too difficult to move, but I'd want to keep the bookcase and my sewing machine in the den."

"I'll tell you what," Roy began, rubbing his chin thoughtfully. "Why don't I go back to Rocky Bluff tomorrow and rearrange the furniture? I can get a couple of kids from the school to help me. You won't have to worry about a thing. If you don't like where I hang the pictures and place the knickknacks, I can move them again when you get home."

Edith's eyes filled with tears. "That would be kind of you. Maybe Bob would help, if he's not too busy at the store. May is a such a busy time with the last-minute shopping for gardening supplies."

"Oh, I don't mind doing this at all. I'll get your bedroom ready, and then as soon as the doctor says you can come home, I'll drive back and get you and Jean. You're fortunate to have such a fine nurse for a daughter, or should I say such a fine daughter for a nurse? I imagine Dr. Pierce will let you come home earlier than normal just because of Jean."

True to his word, Roy spent the next few days rearranging Edith's house, occasionally with Nancy's help. When he received word that the doctor was going to dismiss Edith the following day, he called Nancy to relay the news.

"I'll be over this evening," she promised. "I want to make the bed and be sure that all the linens are handy. Maybe I'll pick up some groceries on my way. Jean's going to have enough to do caring for Mother without having to worry about the shopping for a few days."

That night Nancy and the children joined Roy at Edith's house. Jay and Dawn painted a "Welcome Home, Grandma" banner and hung it in the front window. They could scarcely contain their excitement at the prospect of seeing their grandmother again.

Roy left early the next morning for Great Falls. The miles of newly sprouting wheat fields flew by as the warmth of the bright spring morning enveloped him. His prayers had been answered: Edith was returning home.

When Roy arrived at the hospital, Jean had already helped her mother dress and she was sitting in the chair beside the bed. She had also fixed her mother's hair and helped her with her makeup. The sight of Edith looking so well uplifted Roy's spirits and convinced him she would completely recover.

Three hours later as they stopped in front of Edith's house, Roy and Edith began to giggle. Jay and Dawn's banner completely covered the full length of Edith's picture window.

"One thing I'm blessed with is a loving family and good friends. I don't know what I'd have done without each of you," Edith said as tears of gratitude filled her eyes.

Roy opened the car door and offered Edith his arm. Slowly they made their way up the sidewalk. "I've been in the hospital so long my legs feel like rubber," Edith complained as Roy wrapped his arm around her to help support more of her weight.

"Just a few more steps and we'll have it made," he assured her as he unlocked the front door. Roy helped Edith into the newly converted bedroom, while Jean followed closely behind with her mother's suitcase. "Well, what do you think?" Roy asked, pleased as a young boy bringing home his first A.

Speechless, Edith turned to give him a big thank-you kiss. Wiping a tear from her eyes, she managed, "Even the pictures are hung exactly where I would have put them myself."

"Then I think I'll run on home and leave you in the competent hands of Nurse Jean. You need to get to bed and get some rest."

"Thanks again for all you've done," Edith replied as Roy leaned over to kiss her good-bye. "I am a little weary."

When school was out that afternoon, Jay and Dawn hurried to their grandmother's house. "Hi, Aunt Jean. Can we see Grandma?" they begged as soon as she opened the door.

Jean gave her niece and nephew a quick hug. "She'll be glad to see you, but be real quiet, she's awfully tired."

Jay and Dawn tiptoed into their grandmother's bedroom. Edith heard them and rolled over. "Come here, both of you, so I can give you a hug." Edith sat up and gave each of her grandchildren a weak embrace. "I really missed you when I was in the hospital."

"I'm glad you're home," Jay said as he squeezed his grandmother. "Did you like our banner?"

"I loved it," Edith assured them. "It was the best welcome home I ever had." The children beamed with pride as Jean entered the bedroom.

"I hate to break up the party, but I think we'd better let Grandma get her rest. I have some cookies and milk in the kitchen," Jean said as she motioned for the children to follow her.

" 'Bye, Grandma," Jay and Dawn echoed in unison as they followed their aunt to the kitchen.

Edith leaned back with contentment. It was good to be home. She was determined to do her exercises and follow her doctors' orders explicitly so that she could regain her strength. She'd already set her goal to be well by the Fourth of July. Sharing the church's annual picnic with her family had always been—and would continue to be—the highlight of her summer.

Chapter 9

After Roy returned from Great Falls, he was anxious to see his son, hopeful that time would have healed their strained relationship. Through the weeks of concern for Edith, the tension with his son had been pushed into the background.

The last weekend of every month the Davidsons took Pete to a nearby town, where he caught the noon bus for Rocky Bluff. The following Tuesday they would meet him at the depot and take him back to the ranch.

Friday afternoon Roy nervously waited for the five o'clock bus. When the double-decker finally pulled to a stop, Pete was, as usual, the first to get off. "Hi, Dad," he greeted, giving his father a quick embrace.

"Pete, it's good to have you home. Let me get your luggage for you." Roy breathed a sigh of relief that his son seemed to be his normal, bubbly self.

"Can we stop at McDonald's before we go home? I'm starving."

"Good idea." Driving down the main street of Rocky Bluff, Roy turned to his son. "How's the ranch work coming along this month?"

"The planting's done. A lot of the equipment broke down, so I've been busy in the shop most of the time."

"You can fix almost anything, can't you?" Roy parked the car in the only slot left in the parking lot.

"Once I had trouble getting a transmission back in their half-ton truck. I never worked on that kind before. It was really hard, but I finally got it in and running."

They ate in silence in a corner booth until Pete finished his first Big Mac. "Dad, why did you go to Great Falls when Edith was sick?"

"I wanted to be with her and try to make her as happy as possible."

"The doctors and nurses are there to take care of people. Why did you need to be there?"

"It's pretty lonesome to be in a hospital in a city where you don't know anyone."

"Didn't her family go to see her?"

"Her daughter Jean and I took turns staying in the room with her. I think we were a big comfort to her. Would you like to go visit Edith this weekend while you're home?"

"No way! I don't want anything to do with her. You shouldn't, either."

"Pete, don't you think there's enough love in my heart for two people? I've found that the more love I give away, the more I have to give."

Totally unconvinced, Pete's cheerfulness turned to gloom and he finished his second hamburger in silence. Pete's thoughts turned to the one person who seemed to understand his dilemma. *Maybe Bob has thought of some way to keep them apart. . . . He doesn't want them to see each other, either.*

Pete spent the remaining hours of the day in front of the TV. At ten o'clock he switched off the set and headed for his bedroom without saying good night to his father.

Roy watched his son with anguish as he disappeared down the hall. He picked up a sports magazine from the coffee table and scanned the pages without focusing on the words.

The following morning Roy was up early to fix a breakfast of bacon, eggs, toast, juice, and milk. Pete ate his double portion in silence and then got up from the table and headed for the door.

"Where are you going, Pete?"

"For a little walk," he mumbled, not turning around. Roy watched the door close behind him. He and his son had been the closest of friends only a few months before. Now they acted like strangers.

Outside the well-kept bungalow, Pete took a deep breath. He needed help. He had to stop his father's friendship with Edith before they got married.

Pete increased his pace as he neared the business section of Rocky Bluff. Rounding the corner on Main Street, he entered Harkness Hardware and found the manager sitting at his desk in the back of the store. "Hi, Bob," he began weakly, afraid that Bob might have forgotten the talk they had a few weeks before.

When Bob looked up from his desk, his face broke into a broad smile. "Well, hello, Pete. Welcome home. What brings you out so early in the morning?"

"I wanted to talk to you."

"Good. I've been wanting to visit with you as well. Let's go across the street and have some coffee."

Bob put his hand on Pete's shoulder as they stepped outside. "There's no problem that the two of us can't figure out together," he said grinning.

"I hope so," Pete replied with his customary slow drawl. He felt better already. Bob seemed to be able to handle any situation that arose, even an enormous problem like the one he faced.

"What's on your mind today, Pete?" Bob asked as the waitress brought two steaming cups of coffee.

"My dad is still seeing your mother. It's worse than ever. You said you'd help me keep them apart, but he went to Great Falls when she was in the hospital. Maybe they'll get married and forget me."

"My mother is so sick that marriage would be the last thing on her mind."

In spite of his own reassuring words, Bob had his doubts. *What if Roy thinks she won't last much longer and tries to marry her to get his hands on my father's estate?* Lost in his thoughts, Bob had temporarily forgotten the young man sitting across the table.

Pete waited impatiently as Bob stared blankly out the drugstore window. Finally he demanded, "What are you thinking about, Bob? Do you have any ideas on how to keep them apart?"

"I just had an idea, but I don't know if it will work. Would you be able to talk your father into taking an extended vacation with you? Maybe going to Europe or someplace like that?"

"Go to Europe?" Pete asked excitedly. "That's way across the ocean. That would cost too much money."

"Maybe I could come up with some money for the plane tickets, but it'd have to be a secret between the two of us." Bob watched the look of eagerness on Pete's face. "I have an old army buddy who now heads a travel agency in Germany. When we were in Vietnam, I helped carry him out from behind enemy lines when he was wounded. He owes me a favor."

Pete looked puzzled. "But how can he help?"

"Maybe he'll be able to arrange free room and board and book you on some of the local tours."

"Do you really mean you'd help my dad and me go to Europe? Colorado is the farthest I've ever been. I've never even been on an airplane."

"Sure," Bob replied confidently. "Then you could have your father all to yourself. Why don't you tell your dad to come to the store about two-thirty this afternoon and talk to me about the trip? You can tell him I want to repay him for staying with Mother while she was in the hospital."

A few minutes later Pete burst through the living room door of the Dutton residence. "Did you have a good walk?" Roy asked as he looked up from the desk where he was balancing his checkbook. It was obvious that his son's mood had improved considerably.

"This wasn't a normal walk," Pete exclaimed, flopping onto the sofa and stretching his long legs under the coffee table in front of him. "We might get to go to Europe for free. They had a show on TV the other night about Europe and I really want to go."

"What does a free trip to Europe have to do with your walk?" Roy queried with amusement. Pete would often become excited and then be unable to separate his desires from reality. Years of experience had taught Roy not to challenge Pete's dreams directly.

Pete was puzzled over his father's lack of excitement about a trip to Europe. "I'm serious, Dad. Bob Harkness said that he'd take care of everything for us."

"Is the hardware store having a drawing for some lucky couple to win a trip to Europe? I've never been lucky at anything like that."

"Oh, no, nothing like that. Bob says that he owes you a favor for staying with his mother while she was in the hospital. He wants you to come to the store this afternoon and talk to him."

One word tumbled on top of the other as his simple mind tried to keep the real reason for the trip separate from the story Bob wanted him to tell his father. "Please, Dad, let's go to the store this afternoon and talk about it."

"There must be something else involved. I'll go talk to Bob and get this straightened out. People don't offer free trips to Europe to just anybody. But before I go to the store, I'd like to run over and see how Edith's feeling today. Do you want to come with me?"

"No, Dad!" Pete objected as his face reddened with anger. "This is the only time I have to be with you. I want you to play checkers with me. We haven't done that in a long time."

"Maybe I could play one quick game before I go. Do you want to get the checkerboard?"

But after a quick game, Pete was still not satisfied. "How about two out of three?"

Usually Roy let Pete win a game now and then, but this time he made sure he won so that the games would be short. As much as he loved his son, he did not want Pete to keep him from seeing Edith, especially now.

After losing a second game, Pete suggested a third one, but Roy was already putting the checkers in the box. Realizing that he would be unable to keep his father from seeing Edith, Pete decided to join him. He didn't want Edith to have him completely to herself for the afternoon.

Jean answered the door dressed in faded blue jeans and a plaid maternity top. "Roy, how good to see you again. Mother will be delighted."

"Jean, I'd like you to meet my son, Pete. He came home to be with me for the weekend."

"How do you do, Pete? I've heard many good things about you. Won't you come in and sit down? Mother will be out in just a minute."

Pete slouched in the rocking chair by the window and began thumbing through a sporting goods catalog beside him, completely ignoring the others in the room.

"Jean, before your mother gets here, do you know anything about Bob offering Pete and me a free trip to Europe? Pete came home this morning with the report that Bob had a friend in Germany who was willing to provide room and board for us for several weeks. Bob said he wanted to pay me back for staying at the hospital with your mother by providing us with the plane tickets."

Jean looked at Roy in amazement. *Surely Pete must have misunderstood,* she thought. "Bob has never been generous with money. I don't understand why he would start now."

"Does he really have a friend in Germany who'd be willing to do all of that for a total stranger?"

"Well, he did save a guy's life in Vietnam and has taken advantage of him ever since. This man went to Germany right after he finished his tour of duty and now he runs a large hotel and travel service. Beyond that I don't know much about him."

Just then Edith appeared in the doorway. "Roy, Pete, I'm glad you both came. Has Jean offered you a cup of coffee yet?"

"I'm sorry. We got busy talking and I forgot," Jean apologized. "Can I get you both a cup?"

"Certainly," Roy replied as he joined Edith on the sofa.

"How about you, Pete?" Jean asked.

"None for me," he answered, not looking up from the automotive section of the catalog. He was confused by Jean's response to her brother's generous offer. *How could she say that? Bob was such a nice guy. He's the only one who understands me. He knows that Dad and Edith don't belong together.*

Edith, Jean, and Roy talked about the upcoming vote to raise the mill levy in order to build a new wing on the high school. Pete sat in the rocking chair and sulked. Contempt for the former schoolteacher grew with each passing minute. Finally Pete couldn't stand it any longer. "Dad, let's go down to the hardware store and see Bob. I told him we'd be in around two-thirty."

"In a few minutes, Son," Roy responded kindly. "We still have plenty of time."

Pete slouched deeper into the chair, his chin resting on his chest. He kept his eyes fixed on the grandfather clock in the corner. At exactly two-twenty-five Pete spoke again. "Please, Dad. I don't want to keep Bob waiting."

"All right, Son," Roy answered reluctantly, joining him at the door.

"I'll see you later, Edith. Thanks for the coffee." Roy looked back at his dear friend dressed in a bright red lounging robe. The vivid color formed an attractive contrast against her hair. A smile spread across his face as their eyes met. "Take care of yourself."

"Don't be too disappointed if I turn down the offer to go to Europe," Roy told his son as he started the engine of the car. "It's not that I don't want to go, but I don't want to be away from Edith very long until the doctor has given her a clean bill of health. I also don't want to feel indebted to a stranger in Germany, much less to Bob. I hope you understand that."

The meeting between Roy and Bob was brief. Bob's explanation of the trip as payment for staying with Edith sounded suspicious to Roy. He did not want to be paid for helping someone whom he had grown to love.

"I appreciate your offer, Bob, but I can't accept it. I cannot take any more time away from the crisis center, and besides, I don't want to leave your mother until the doctor says she can resume normal activities," Roy explained as Pete sat beside him scowling. He thanked Bob again for his offer and left the store with Pete shuffling dejectedly behind him.

Frustrated that his initial plan did not work, Bob soon developed another. A few days later he stopped to visit his mother after work. "Mom, now that your health is failing, have you ever considered selling this big house?" he began as he paced nervously in front of the window. "Rocky Bluff has several openings at their senior citizens housing project. It'd be much wiser to plan for your financial future instead of waiting until you're desperate and are forced to take the only options left available."

"I don't want to give up this house," Edith protested adamantly. "I've lived in this house since I was married. Why should I leave it now after I finally got it paid for and fixed the way I like it?"

"It's too big for you to care for. Jean will have to go back to Idaho soon and you won't be able to keep it up. We could arrange a trust fund to take care of your future medical bills and also a fund for your grandchildren's education. Financial planning is the name of the game these days. I could oversee the entire plan myself so you wouldn't have to worry about a thing."

"The answer is no, and I do not want to hear anything more about it."

Jean was aghast at her brother's suggestion. Concerned that her mother was getting too excited, Jean immediately changed the subject to her expectant state. Nothing pleased Edith more than the thought of another grandchild. She was proud of the two she already had and prospects that a third one was on the way brought only joy.

Thwarted in his scheme, Bob soon found an excuse to leave. As he walked down the steps, Jean turned to her mother. "This is a terrible thing to say about my own brother, but how did he ever get a saintly wife like Nancy?"

"You're right, Jean. It's not nice to say," Edith scolded gently. "Maybe someday the good Lord will be able to help Bob straighten out his priorities. Bob has many good qualities. . .and he is my son. . .but I'm afraid he's too involved in trying to make as much money as possible in the least amount of time."

Yet what worried Edith most was that Bob was fast becoming his own worst enemy.

Chapter 10

As Edith rested in her recliner at the picture window, her thoughts were centered on her garden plot in the backyard, especially the lush and aromatic lilac bushes. Ever since her marriage to George Harkness, her summer days had been occupied with gardening. This summer, however, her garden would have to fend for itself. She was not willing to ask her pregnant daughter or her daughter-in-law to help her.

Jean suddenly interrupted her mother's train of thought. "It's beautiful outside. How about taking your walk a little earlier today?"

"Even if I can't work in my garden at least I can still enjoy the out of doors," Edith replied as Jean helped her with her sweater.

Slowly Edith and Jean descended the steps and made their way down the main sidewalk. They paused when they reached the end of the block. "Do you think there is any way I can go to church tomorrow?" Edith asked. "I've really missed it. Sunday just isn't Sunday without being in church."

"We'll try it," Jean promised as they turned and headed back to the house. "I can park the car in the handicap parking space and you can use the wheelchair ramp so you won't have to climb those steep front stairs. We'll slip out during the last hymn so you won't get caught in the crowd."

"When they remodeled the church five years ago, I didn't realize how important the changes for the handicapped would be until I needed to use them myself," Edith admitted, remembering all the discussions that went on about the ramp at that time. "If there's one thing I've learned through all of this, it's to be more sensitive to others."

The next morning Jean and Edith arrived at church twenty minutes early. Edith felt alert and invigorated by her first outing since her hospitalization. The warm Montana sun reflected off the golden steeple cross while a robin chirped happily from its crossbar.

"I wish I had my camera right now," Edith observed. "Seeing that robin reminds me that God still has everything under control."

During the last hymn Jean and Edith slipped out the side door. Once home Edith promptly changed into a lounging robe and stretched out on her bed with a smile of contentment on her face.

Later that afternoon Edith and Roy had time alone while Jean visited

Bonnie, a former high school classmate. The couple sat in relaxed silence for a few moments. Finally Roy cleared his throat. "Edith, have you ever considered remarrying?"

Edith looked up with surprise. "I guess I've never given it much thought. After George died, I devoted all my efforts and time to my students. Why do you ask?"

"I thought I was content living the life of a single man until I met you. As the months have passed, I'm more and more convinced that I'd like to share the rest of my life with you."

As their eyes met, Edith had to admit the feeling was mutual although she had never verbalized it. Yet it wasn't practical. "Roy, how can you say that, with my health lingering in the balance as it is? You don't want to spend the rest of your days caring for an invalid."

"But Edith, yours is not a permanent condition," Roy protested mildly. "Each day you're able to walk farther than you did the day before. It won't be long before you'll be walking around the block. In a few weeks you should be as good as new."

"I wish that were true." She paused and cleared her throat. "At my last check-up the doctor said there had been some permanent damage to my heart and I should avoid all strenuous activities. I'll have to ignore the fact that I have an upstairs and a basement in my house."

Roy took her hand lovingly. "We all have certain physical limitations. In a few weeks you'll be self-sufficient again and life won't seem nearly as dismal. I love you for what you are, not for what your body can or can't do."

"Roy, if only we'd met ten years ago things might be different," Edith sighed, tears glistening in her eyes.

"No self-pity allowed," Roy scolded kindly. "Have you already forgotten what Pastor Rhodes said in his sermon? We're to live one day at a time and we're to live it to the fullest."

"You're right," Edith confessed, forcing a smile. "I'm being rather silly, but marriage is a big step. Let's think about it awhile longer and see how fast I get my strength back."

When the next Sunday arrived, Edith was up early dressing for church. She had always considered her faith in Jesus Christ important, but now after her surgery, she realized that she could not survive without the Lord's sustaining hand.

Following the morning worship service, she greeted Pastor Rhodes at the door. "You can't imagine how good it is to be back in church. It seems to make my entire week go better."

"I'm glad you're able to get out again. I saw you here last week, but you slipped out before I had a chance to talk to you. If you're not busy Tuesday afternoon, I'll come by and visit for a few minutes."

"I'll have the coffee pot waiting." Edith moved out the side door as Pastor Rhodes turned his attention to the next person in line.

Tuesday as Jean was finishing the noon dishes, the phone rang. She reached around the corner of the cupboard and picked up the receiver. "Hello, Harkness residence."

"Hello, is Jean Thompson available please?" a woman asked in a pleasant, businesslike manner. "Long distance calling."

"Speaking," Jean answered, puzzled at who would be calling during the middle of the day.

"Jean, this is Sue Watkins at Chamberland Hospital. I don't want to alarm you, but your husband Jim was just brought to the emergency room following an accident at the sawmill."

Jean gasped. "Is he all right?"

"He's resting comfortably now, but he has three broken ribs and a broken sternum and will need to be hospitalized for several days," Sue went on to explain.

Jean grabbed the counter for support. Her face turned ashen as she listened, her mind in a spin. "Tell Jim that I'll be there as soon as possible. I'll call before I leave. Thanks for letting me know."

Jean nearly dropped the receiver as her mother entered the kitchen.

"What happened, dear? You look awful."

"Jim was injured at the sawmill. He'll be in the hospital for a few days. I wish I could go right away, but the bus doesn't leave until morning."

Edith stood in stunned silence. Her heart raced. "How bad was he hurt?"

"They said he had three broken ribs and a broken sternum." Jean's voice quivered.

"I'll call Roy and see if he can drive you home. Rush upstairs and get your things packed. I'll take care of the rest."

"But Mother, I hate to leave you," Jean protested, torn between her loyalty to the two people who were the dearest to her. "I wish I could be in both places at the same time."

"Don't worry about me. Your husband needs you now. I'll be able to work something out. The Lord has never left me stranded."

Jean rushed upstairs as Edith hurriedly dialed Roy's familiar number. She briefly explained Jean's situation and he immediately put her mind to rest. "Edith, give me about a half-hour to pack a few things and gas up the car and I'll be right over to get Jean. If we leave Rocky Bluff by one-thirty, she can be at the hospital in Chamberland by midnight."

"Roy, I don't know what we would do without you. You're always available to help whenever we have a crisis."

"Don't you think it's the least I could do for my future family?" he asked lightly, hoping to help her relax. "Your time is my time."

"Aren't you rushing me a little?" Edith teased, thankful for his note of levity to help break the tension she was feeling. "Remember, I haven't given you an answer yet."

"Just tell Jean I'll be there in a half hour. We'll have everything under control and you won't have to worry about a thing." Roy's confident tone belied his growing concern that this minor crisis might be enough to upset Edith and cause another heart attack. The doctor had warned her to avoid as much stress as possible.

Edith eased herself into her reclining chair, her heart pounding wildly. She achieved a temporary calm by taking deep breaths, but it was interrupted by the buzz of the doorbell. Edith sighed and then slowly rose to answer it.

"Pastor Rhodes," Edith motioned for him to come in. "I forgot about your coming this afternoon amid all the confusion of the last few minutes. Please sit down and I'll get you a cup of coffee."

"I've had my limit of coffee for the day, but thanks for the offer." Pastor Rhodes gently guided her back to her reclining chair. "Edith, your face looks flushed. Maybe you'd better sit and rest. What can I do to help?"

"Jean just received word that Jim has been injured at the sawmill and she's upstairs packing now. Roy is driving her back to Idaho. He'll be here in a few minutes," Edith explained wearily, leaning her head back on the chair.

Pastor Rhodes sat down on the sofa. "With your daughter gone you'll need someone to help you with the housework."

"You're right. I'm able to take care of my personal needs now, but I'm still not strong enough to do much cooking and cleaning, or the shopping."

"I'll try to find someone for you."

Jean had overheard snippets of their conversation as she entered the living room. "Pastor Rhodes, I can't thank you enough! What a load off my mind that would be, now that I'm on my way back to Chamberland," Jean said approvingly. She looked at her mother's weary face and shared a knowing look with the sensitive clergyman.

Chapter 11

Each afternoon Roy joined Edith for her daily walks, encouraging her to go a few yards farther than she did the day before and sharing items of interest from his own life. "Edith, I was finally accepted into the Thursday morning golf mixed foursome at the country club," he told her one day. "Sounds silly to say, but I've waited a long while for such an honor."

"That's quite an exclusive circle of folks. Who did they pair you up with?"

"A woman named Sally Pegram. I've never met her, but they say she's one of the leading women golfers in the city."

"I remember Sally," Edith recalled thoughtfully. "George and I played a few rounds with her once, and she beat us soundly."

"Well, I'll need a good partner to make up for my lack of ability."

Roy reported to the clubhouse at nine-forty-five the next morning. When he checked the schedule he found that he and Sally along with Sam and Beth Porter were the third foursome to tee off. Across the room he caught a glimpse of his old friend Sam and hurried to join him and his wife. "Well, hello, Sam, Beth. It's been a long time since we've played in the same foursome. I don't think we've been together since last year's Labor Day tournament."

"Roy Dutton! What a pleasant surprise," Sam exclaimed as he extended his right hand. "Aren't you the lucky one to have Sally Pegram as a partner? I don't think there's much chance of beating that partnership."

"She'll have to play doubly well to make up for me."

Sam lowered his voice to just above a whisper. "Not only did you luck out with one of the city's best golfers, but you also got one of the nicest looking single women around."

"I've never met her, but I have seen her picture in the sports pages," Roy explained. The teasing tone in Sam's voice was a little unsettling.

"The only problem with Sally is that she's desperate for a husband. I get the feeling that she's afraid of growing old alone. She might find one if she weren't so assertive around men, married or single."

"Sally couldn't be as bad as all that," Roy said, laughing. "At least I've found the woman I want to grow old with, but I'm having trouble convincing her of that fact."

"It's only a matter of time and persuasion before Edith comes around to your way of thinking," Beth observed good-naturedly.

Sally Pegram knew how to make an entrance. Wearing a bright blue knit top and light blue walking shorts that complemented her eyes and tanned body, she discreetly acknowledged the approving looks. "Hi, everybody," she greeted breezily. "I hope I didn't keep you waiting, but the traffic was terrible. There was an accident at the corner of Central and Sixth Street and only one lane of traffic for blocks."

Sally's gaze lingered leisurely on Roy and made him uncomfortable. Suddenly she turned back to Sam. "Aren't you even going to introduce me to my partner?"

"Oh, I'm sorry," he replied, sensing Roy's embarrassment. "Sally Pegram, I'd like you to meet Roy Dutton. Roy is the director of the crisis center."

"How do you do, Roy?" She smiled, reaching out to shake his hand. "I did hear there was a handsome widower working there. It must be awfully exciting trying to help all those troubled young people."

Unconsciously Roy stepped backward to give himself more space as he extended his hand. "Sometimes it seems overwhelming to think that a person's life might depend on what I say." He took a deep breath and sighed. "I suppose it would be even worse if I didn't try to help at all."

To divert attention from himself, Roy checked the green on the first hole. It was clear. "Looks like the others are far enough ahead that we can get started. Is Beth going to show us how to do it?"

They strolled companionably toward the first tee. For most of the game the foursome was evenly matched except for Sally, who always seemed to take at least one less stroke per hole. The talk remained strictly on golf until they reached the twelfth green. Casually Sally turned to Roy as the Porters walked on ahead. "I would have thought you'd have remarried years ago. It must have been very difficult living alone."

"It was at times, but I think I managed quite well. I raised a son by myself and am very proud of that boy. There are too many things happening in Rocky Bluff to become bored."

When they reached the thirteenth fairway, Roy was the first to tee off. After his slice to the left, Sally placed her tee in the ground and took her best driver from her golf bag. As she swung, Roy admired her athletic but feminine form and tremendous power. After several weeks of nursing Edith back to health, Roy felt invigorated sharing female companionship with someone who was physically active.

They placed third in their flight that day and made plans for the tournament the following Thursday. As Roy drove home, he again found himself wondering if Edith would ever have the strength to join him on the golf course. The physical exercise had revitalized his spirits and helped relieve the pent-up tension of the last few weeks.

That afternoon Roy busied himself at the crisis center. He had completed the installation of the sheetrock the day before and wanted to prepare the room for painting. The work was slow and tiring, but the mental picture of a comfortable, functional counseling area spurred him on. His mind drifted back to the hours he had spent with Edith in this room, helping to give her the confidence to counsel over the phone. *She always seemes to say the right words in almost any situation,* he mused.

Around seven o'clock Roy stopped in front of Edith's home and hurried up the front steps. As she opened the door with a friendly greeting, he gave her a quick kiss on the lips before he spoke. "It's a beautiful evening and I need a beautiful woman to share it with. Would you join me for a ride in the mountains? The fresh air will do you good."

"I've been a little down today, maybe a change of scenery will be good for me," Edith replied as she reached into the front closet for a sweater. "I'm anxious to hear about your golf game. I often considered taking up the game again after retirement." A note of resignation lingered in her voice. "I guess those days are gone forever."

The weeks of illness were beginning to pull Edith into a mild state of depression. Her strong determination, coupled with her faith of a lifetime, would not let her succumb to the discouragement for more than a few hours at a time.

As the pair turned off the main highway onto a narrow mountain road, Edith broke a long silence. "Is Sally Pegram as good as the sports writers claim?"

Roy smiled as the image of that feminine yet powerful form flashed before him. "Yes, she's good all right, but I think that the paper has overplayed her abilities. She's still human like the rest of us. What amazes me is how a woman that small can drive the ball with so much power. She can outdistance me by several yards."

"Never underestimate the power of a woman," Edith teased as they jostled over the twisting road. "Will you be playing with the same foursome next week or with different partners?"

"They have the foursomes set for the entire season, so I'll be playing with Sally for at least six more weeks. Except for the fact that our skills were a total mismatch, we had a delightful time being paired with the

Porters. They have a great sense of humor and keep the game lively."

Roy's eyes drifted across the horizon. The setting sun formed a picturesque landscape of bright pinks and oranges against the tree-lined mountaintops.

Roy cleared his voice and glanced at Edith from the corner of his eye. "Now that you're feeling better, do you think you'll be able to spend a few evenings a week at the crisis center? It would help break up your long evenings."

Tears glistened in Edith's eyes. "I'd like that very much, but I haven't felt strong enough to drive my own car yet. I'd hate to have to depend on others for transportation."

"There's always another way to accomplish the same goal," Roy persisted gently. "Would you be willing to have an extension phone installed in your house? I hate to have all of your newly acquired training go to waste."

"You do have a tremendous power of persuasion. After all that you have done for me, a few hours on the crisis phone is the least I can do."

"Good! I'll contact the phone company and see how soon they can install it. You can disconnect it any time you wish."

The following afternoon Roy joined Edith on the sofa. He wrapped his right arm around her and he pulled her next to him. "Honey, I asked you a question several weeks ago and I intend to keep on asking it. Are you ready to set a wedding date? Your health is improving daily, maybe not as fast as you'd like, but you are improving."

"Roy, I want to say yes in the worst way, but I don't think it would be fair to you. I'm not even able to do all my own housework yet, much less be an asset to a husband." She appeared cool in an ice-blue blouse that camouflaged her pounding heart.

"I've been keeping house for nearly twenty years, so I'm used to all kinds of domestic chores," Roy assured her. "It would be a pleasure to serve someone who likes to eat my cooking."

They sat in silence for several moments before Roy continued. "The greatest asset to me would be someone with whom I could share my love and life."

Roy's steel-blue eyes and silver-gray hair made it difficult for Edith to remember her objections. Yet not being able to fulfill the normal duties of a housewife discouraged her. "All the same, Roy, I appreciate your offer, but I don't want to be a burden on anyone. You have done so much for me already and I haven't been able to reciprocate. Ask me again when I'm able to maintain my own home."

Roy pulled her even closer. "I've told you before, Edith, that I want to marry you because of who you are, not what you can do. Take a few more days to consider."

Tears gathered in her eyes. "Maybe I just need time to get used to the idea. If you only knew how badly I want to say yes," Edith whispered softly as she laid her head upon his shoulder.

The next few days Roy busied himself with carpentry work at the crisis center and Edith began sewing a formal dress for Beverly Short to help pass the time. As the garment began to take shape, her self-confidence was gradually restored: She was finally able to be of service to someone else. Beverly had refused payment for her help in painting the house, so this was one way Edith could show her appreciation.

When the formal was completed three days before the reception for Bev's granddaughter, Edith invited her over for a fitting. As Bev slipped into the dress and returned to the living room to model it, Edith felt satisfied. She had successfully completed her first sewing project since her surgery.

"With work like this you can never say you're handicapped again," Bev teased as she stepped onto the stool so Edith could measure the hem. "You could become a professional seamstress."

"Flattery will get you everywhere," Edith laughed lightheartedly. "As long as I can do it sitting down, I'm okay. It's the physical exertion that does me in."

Normally Bob did not visit his mother unless he was bringing the children over, but for the next several days he stopped nearly every night. After the third evening Edith noticed that he disappeared into the other rooms with a tape measure and a sheet of paper. When he reappeared Edith confronted him. "Bob, I appreciate your stopping by each evening to visit. I've seen more of you this past week than I have for the last six months, but I have a feeling that something else is going on."

"Well, to be honest, there has been," he mumbled, stretching out on the sofa and putting his feet on the ottoman. "I've been visiting with Walton Realty Company and have given them the size and description of this house. They value it at $115,000 on the current market."

"Why have you been wasting your time with all that? I have no intentions of selling."

"I was just looking out for your well-being and future. Since you're not able to take care of yourself anymore, it might be wiser to sell the house and move into a nursing home. Your insurance plus Medicare should be enough to keep you comfortably in the finest home in the state for the rest of your days."

Edith glared at her son, anger and frustration written on her face.

Ignoring his mother's obvious rage, Bob continued. "If the house is sold and you invest the money wisely, there will be a steady income that would serve as a family legacy."

"I'm not ready to part with this house," Edith retorted sharply. "Your father wanted to keep this house in the family as long as possible. There are too many memories here."

"Then Nancy and I could sell our house and move into this one. We could always use the extra space. We could put our house on the market. Would you like to come with me tomorrow and talk with Richard Walton about the possibilities?"

Edith's eyes blazed with indignation. "How dare you become involved in my personal finances! I will do nothing of the sort. I'll sell this house when I feel good and ready and not a day before."

"Mother, don't get upset. I was only trying to help. Why don't you think about it for several days and then we can talk about it?"

"There is nothing to talk about, Bob," Edith retorted. "I will handle my own personal business affairs."

His face flushed with anger, he walked stiffly to the front door. "I'll be seeing you later. I have a lot of work to finish at the store tonight. Do try to relax and not let your blood pressure get too high. You know how dangerous that is for you."

With that Bob disappeared down the front steps as Edith remained in her lounge chair shaking her head. *If only Bob would understand my situation and help me instead of making life so complicated. I know I've tried to talk to him about his attitude toward money, but then so have his wife and sister and we've all failed. Only God can change him now.*

As Edith was leisurely finishing her evening meal that night, the ringing of her personal phone jerked her to attention. She reached for the receiver. "Hello, Mom. How are you?"

"Jean, it's good to hear your voice. I'm doing okay, but I'm still a little slow on my feet. How are you doing?"

"I'm doing great and Jim is almost healed from the mill accident. We thought we'd drive to Rocky Bluff for the Fourth of July weekend. Are you planning to go to the annual church picnic?"

"I sure would like to, but I don't think I'll be strong enough. Beverly Short offered to take me, but her family will be here and I don't want to take her away from them."

"Then we'll take you," Jean offered enthusiastically. "Would you call Bob and Nancy and make sure they'll be at the picnic? We'll make it a big family outing."

"Bob has been talking about working that day, but if he knows both you and Jim will be there, maybe he'll be able to make some time to join us. I'll talk to them and let you know. Thanks for the offer."

The two chatted for a few more minutes before saying good night. Edith doubted if Bob would go to the picnic after their heated exchange of this evening, but she would at least invite him. *The best way to get him to come is to first ask Nancy,* she thought. *Somehow she's generally able to remind him of his family responsibilities. I know the children will want to come if they know their aunt Jean and uncle Jim will be there.*

❧

The day of the picnic the Harkness clan brought a lawn chaise for Edith and gathered around a picnic table at the fringe of the group. Everyone was anxious to talk with Jim and hear more about his accident and the plans for their new baby. After an hour of small talk and heaping portions of summer salads and grilled fare, Edith began to get drowsy. Her eyes closed.

"Jean, look at her," Bob said as he motioned to his mother. "She's getting too old to come to functions like this."

"Bob, she's just taking a little cat nap," his sister responded with disgust. "What's so unusual about that?"

"Well, nothing, except she is no longer able to take care of herself. She has to have someone come in every day and help her. That house is much too big for her to manage and yet she refuses to consider selling it."

"Why should she?" Jim spoke up sharply. "It's been her home for over thirty-five years. I think she's still able to make her own decisions."

"Mother is not being realistic about her future. She should be in a nursing home where there is someone around all the time to help look after her," Bob persisted.

"People who are much more handicapped than Mother still enjoy independent living, why shouldn't she? Why are you so anxious to get rid of her?"

"I'm not trying to get rid of her," Bob insisted angrily. "I just think she deserves a rest."

"I want Grandma to keep her house," Jay injected. "I like that house. Dawn and I have a lot of fun there."

"I agree with you," Jean and Nancy spoke in unison.

"Well, it looks like you're outvoted," Nancy said in her typical moderator voice. "Everyone agrees that your mother should keep her house and do as much or as little as she is able to do. We will either do the rest or find someone who can."

Bob's eyes flashed, but he said nothing. Dawn suddenly saw the line-up for the three-legged race and grabbed Jay's hand to run and join the others. Bob continued to sulk during the remainder of the picnic while the others went on to lighter subjects. Everyone overlooked the cloud that seemed to hang over the Harkness family.

Chapter 12

One Saturday night as Edith was knitting a scarf and mittens for Jean, the crisis phone rang. "Crisis center, may I help you?"

"Nobody can help me," a young woman cried mournfully. "This entire mess is hopeless."

"Would you like to tell me about it?"

Through muffled sobs the answer came. "I. . .can't. . .stand. . .being. . . a mother." She struggled to continue. "Little Jeffy just keeps crying no matter what I do, so I finally hit him and threw him in his crib. I didn't hurt him, but I didn't mean to be so rough with him."

"I understand how you feel," Edith responded sympathetically. "Sometimes when my children were little, I felt the same way and had to struggle with myself to maintain control."

"But how did you do it?" the young woman questioned in a tight, controlled whisper.

"We find the inner strength to cope if we know where to turn." Edith paused to give the frustrated mother a chance to think, all the while wondering if she had come from a Christian home. "Has your baby had a medical check-up to determine the reason for his crying? Babies often have ear infections or sore throats and the mother can't tell whether or not they are in pain."

"I don't have any money to take him to a doctor. Even if I did, I'd be afraid to do it. The doctor'll only say that I'm a terrible mother. Then the authorities might take my baby away from me. If I didn't have little Jeffy, I wouldn't have anything to live for."

Edith cleared her throat and took a deep breath. "There are special medical and social programs to help people in your situation. I'm sure we can find a solution. You don't have to tell me your name, but what can I call you during our conversation?"

"I don't mind telling you. It's Beth Slater," she whispered.

"I'm glad to talk to you, Beth. My name is Edith. It's often difficult to know how to handle a new baby when the pressures of life bear down upon you. Do you have anyone you feel comfortable talking with? Your husband or mother or a good friend?"

"I'm not married. When my boyfriend found out I was pregnant, he left town. My mother wanted me to get an abortion so that none of her friends would know I was pregnant. I just couldn't kill my own baby, so I left home and moved to Rocky Bluff. I receive some government money, but that isn't nearly enough to support me and Jeffy."

Edith thought back to the years when her own children were babies. In modern parlance, she had had the support system of a husband, two grandparents, and scores of relatives and friends to teach her about motherhood. "Learning to be a good mother doesn't always happen automatically. Have you taken any classes or read any books on child care?"

"Well, no," Beth admitted hesitantly. "I'm nursing the baby and changing his diapers. That's about all I really know how to do. Babies are supposed to have shots, but I don't know when or what kind. I think I should start him on baby food pretty soon, but I don't know when or how much."

"I'm glad you called the center; it took a lot of courage. Would you let me make an appointment with a pediatrician for you? He or she will be able tell you about shots and exactly how and what to feed Jeffy. There is nothing to be afraid of. Doctors want to help mothers and their babies, not separate them."

"Will you promise me that you won't let them take my baby away from me?"

"I promise you that as long as a child is loved and well cared for, no one will separate him from his mother. I can tell by how you talk that you love Jeffy and want the very best for him."

"I do," Beth replied with a little more confidence in her voice. "I'd do anything for him, but I don't know what to do."

"I'll call you tomorrow after I've made an appointment for you. I'll also have someone give you a ride to the doctor and home again. In the meantime, the welfare department has many services available to help new mothers. Why don't you contact the social worker who oversees your ADC claim?"

"I don't tell her anything that she doesn't ask me," Beth replied bitterly. "I'm afraid she'll put Jeffy in a foster home. She thinks a sixteen year old shouldn't have a baby. I know she does."

"Beth, social workers are trained to help people who cannot help themselves. I'm sure she has worked with many other girls with similar problems. Would you trust me to talk to her for you?"

"Well, err, I suppose. I guess I'll have to trust someone. I sure am making a mess of things myself."

Later that day Edith contacted the doctor and the welfare department. An appointment was made for the following Tuesday afternoon, and the social worker promised to make an immediate home visit to Beth and explain the training programs and educational opportunities available to young mothers.

That evening Edith dialed the girl's number. "Hello, Beth," she said to the young voice that answered the phone. "This is Edith from the crisis center. How are things going for you now?"

"Hi, Edith. Things are a lot better now. When Jeffy woke from his nap, he was so much fun to play with. Then my social worker came to see me. She was extremely understanding. She told me about childcare classes at the community center and home study programs that will help me get my high school diploma. She left a lot of material for me to read. She said she'd come back again next week to see what I've decided to do. Thanks for calling her for me."

"I'm so glad things are going better for you," Edith replied. "I've called the pediatrician and made an appointment for Jeffy Tuesday afternoon at two-thirty. I also arranged for one of the women from the church to provide a ride for you. Her name is Grace Blair. She'll be by at two-ten to pick you up."

"I don't know how I can ever thank you, Edith," Beth said shyly.

"Just take good care of little Jeffy and give him an extra hug from me." A bond of concern began to grow between the two although they had never met.

"You know, Roy," Edith began as the two sat alone in her living room later that night. "Situations like the one with Beth make me feel the most worthwhile. All that child needs is for someone to care about her and teach her how to cope with the routine problems of life. There are many services available to people in crisis if they only knew what to expect from each agency."

"That's so true," Roy said, nodding in agreement. "Young people often consider government agencies as enemies instead of concerned, trained people who could help them. The crisis center serves as a liaison between a hurting person and the source of help."

⌇

For the next few days the thought of Beth and her problems were pushed to the back of Edith's mind as she coped with the antics of her grandchildren. The following Friday evening Edith again answered the crisis phone. Instantly she recognized Beth Slater's high-pitched voice.

"Well, hello, Beth. This is Edith. How are things going for you tonight?"

"I guess I'm okay," Beth confessed meekly, "but I still get lonely always being by myself. I wish that group for young mothers met more often."

"Why don't you bring Jeffy and visit me tomorrow afternoon? I'm not able to get out as much as I'd like, but I'd enjoy getting to know you better. I used to teach home ec at the high school, and I miss being around young people."

"Well, if you're sure I wouldn't be a bother. . .but I don't have a car."

"Where do you live? Maybe it's close enough to walk."

"Three eighteen South Windham. I have a two-room basement apartment."

"That's only three blocks from me. Why don't you bundle up Jeffy and come around two o'clock? We'll make a bed on the floor for him to take his afternoon nap and then we can have a cup of hot chocolate and a nice long visit while he sleeps."

"Thanks so much. I haven't been invited to anyone's house since I've been in Rocky Bluff."

The next afternoon Beth balanced her baby on her knee as she sat at the kitchen table while Edith made hot chocolate. As the older woman put a tablespoon of the cocoa mix into each cup and added boiling water, a look of pleasure crossed her face. "Except for my grandchildren, I haven't had anyone join me for hot chocolate for a long time."

"It's so kind of you to invite me. Since it's been cold, I haven't been able to get out much. Fortunately there is a corner grocery store a couple blocks from my apartment. I wish I had a car and knew how to drive."

Beth's eyes suddenly became distant. "I quit school the semester before I would have taken driver's ed."

"That's something you can take through the adult education center at the vo-tech high school. Maybe when Jeffy gets a little older you can find a part-time job and begin saving for a car of your own."

"I'd like that," Beth replied as she took a sip of her hot chocolate. After a long pause she looked across the table at Edith. "How do you make baby food? I have to figure out how to save money."

"The softer fruits and vegetables can be put in a kitchen blender and puréed at top speed. Carrots are more difficult and you may have to add a little water. If you don't have a blender, you can use a potato masher or fork. With a little practice you will discover the proper consistency."

"I don't have a blender. All I have are a couple of plates, some cups, a saucepan, and a skillet."

"You know, I think I have an extra blender. In fact, I have two of several kitchen appliances and utensils. Would you like to have them?"

"But I can't afford to pay you," Beth protested weakly.

"They are a gift to you from me. I'll sort through them later this week and maybe you could come back Saturday and I'll have my grandson help you carry them home."

Saturday morning Edith packed a large box for Beth. Shortly after lunch Jay and Dawn stopped to see their grandmother. After serving the children cookies and milk, Edith turned to her grandson. "Jay, in a little while a young woman with a small baby is going to stop for this box of pots and pans and dishes. We want to visit for awhile, but when it's time for her to go home, would you carry the box for her? She can't carry the baby and the box at the same time."

"It's not very far, is it?" Jay asked reluctantly as he stuffed his last cookie into his mouth.

"Only three blocks."

Just then the doorbell rang and Edith hurried across the room. When she opened the door she found Beth standing there with another teenager. "Edith, this is Anita. I hope you don't mind that I invited her to come along."

"Oh, no, I always enjoy company. Come in and make yourselves at home." Reaching for the bundle in Beth's arms, Edith gently uncovered the sleeping child. "Let me lay Jeffy in the corner and we'll sit around the kitchen table so we won't disturb him."

"Edith, I met Anita a few days ago when she moved into the apartment upstairs. She came here from New York to get married. But after she got here, her boyfriend changed his mind and went to Texas to work in the oil fields. She doesn't have enough money to get back home, so she's trying to find a job here. She's awfully homesick and I thought maybe you could help her."

"I can always offer a listening ear," Edith replied as she turned to Anita. The teenager's long blond hair fell loosely around her shoulders. The tension in her facial muscles made her appear years older. "Let's begin by having something hot to drink. The two of you must be frozen."

After Anita explained more about her situation, Edith's face lit up. "I can't promise you anything right now, but there may be a way for you to get a bus ticket home. The Salvation Army has a special fund to help people like you. Let me call Captain Barrett at the local mission."

The afternoon flew by as the three women shared their lives, completely ignoring Jay and Dawn at work on a jigsaw puzzle in the back bedroom.

After a couple of hours Jeffy awoke and Beth and Anita decided it was time to go. "Beth, don't forget your box of kitchen supplies," Edith reminded her as she began putting on her coat and wrapping Jeffy in his blankets. "I'll have Jay carry them home for you."

"That won't be necessary," Anita replied quickly. "I can carry them for her." Anita stooped down and picked up the box with ease.

"Thanks so much for all you've done for me," Beth said, giving Edith a quick hug.

"You're entirely welcome. I'm glad someone can use these things." Edith turned her attention to Beth's friend. "Anita, thanks for coming. Feel free to call or stop over any time you need someone to talk with. How can I contact you after I talk with the Salvation Army?"

"You can get hold of me at Beth's," the young woman replied as a warm smile spread across her face. "You remind me so much of my own mother. I don't know when I'll ever get to see her again. She has to work to support my seven brothers and sisters."

As the two young women walked down the sidewalk, Edith stood in the window and watched. *What a lot of potential those two young people have,* she thought. *I hope that I can help them over the hard spots.*

That evening Bob again stopped at his mother's home. "Mother, you look tired tonight," he said as he went to the refrigerator to get a soft drink.

"I'm fine," Edith replied as she straightened her recliner into the upright position. "Beth was over this afternoon and she brought a friend with her."

"You're spending an awful lot of time with those girls," Bob admonished as he sat on the couch. "Mom, you're getting too old to still be working with teenagers. I thought you'd given that up when you quit teaching school."

"I enjoy doing it, Bob. Why do you think I would ever be too old to help people?"

"That's n—not exactly what I meant," he stammered. "But look at you. You're exhausted. You should be having people take care of you instead of you still trying to take care of them."

Edith's jaw became fixed as she glared at her son. "I'll never be too old to help people. As long as my weak heart keeps pumping, I'll do whatever I can to help others." She paused as she sent up a quick prayer for inspiration. "You know, Bob, God has blessed me with a good life and I want to share it with those less fortunate as long as I can. Now is the harvest time of my life, and I'm reaping the rewards by helping others. You're still in the planting season, Bob, and I pray someday you'll understand what this means."

Chapter 13

"Hi, Bob, I'm back in Rocky Bluff," Pete Dutton exclaimed as he stuck his head into the backroom of Harkness Hardware where Bob was unpacking a crate of rakes.

"Hello, Pete. Pull up a chair and sit down," Bob invited as he took the last rake from the box and tossed the box into the storage bin behind him. "Can I get you a soft drink?"

"Sure," Pete replied. He surveyed the cluttered storage room while Bob reached into the cooler, handed him a Pepsi, and pulled up a chair next to him.

"How's ranch life?"

"Busy," Pete responded, trying to sound as businesslike as possible. "The machinery kept breaking down, but I was able to fix almost everything."

"I'm proud of you, Pete. You're a genius when it comes to machines." Bob reached over to pat him on the shoulder. "I'm glad you stopped by because I was almost ready to give you a call. What are your plans for the next few days?"

"I'm trying to find a way to keep Dad away from that woman."

"You must mean my mother," Bob replied sympathetically. "I've been trying for eight months to keep them apart. Nothing I've tried so far has worked."

"Dad's been playing golf with another woman. Maybe he'll forget Edith. I don't care if he has a golfing friend, but he doesn't need a wife."

Bob smiled to himself as he continued to manipulate information from Pete. "I wish that were true. I hear Sally is out to find a husband and she's not fussy about who it is. Some men are saying your dad is playing hard to get. All he can talk about is my mother."

"But if Dad could have a healthy golf star, why would he want a sick wife? He told me that he's asked Edith to marry him."

Bob's face turned red with rage. Could his own mother be considering remarriage without consulting him? He sat in silence for several minutes before he spoke. "Pete, don't worry about a thing. I just had an idea!"

"Good. What is it?" Pete's eyes widened with anticipation.

"Would you like to ride to Great Falls with me Monday morning?"

Pete was overwhelmed at the thought of an invitation from someone as important as Bob Harkness. "Sure, it sounds like fun. What are you going to do?"

"I plan to check the nursing homes there. I want to find the best one possible for Mother. After all the years of helping others, she deserves the best of care," Bob explained, wryly remembering his recent conversation with his mother.

A puzzled look spread across Pete's face. "But how can you get her to go if she doesn't want to?"

"I'll talk to her doctor. I'm sure he'll convince her that she needs constant care to protect her damaged heart." Bob's eyes shifted aimlessly around the storeroom before they rested on Pete. "Pete, I need you to tell the doctor the worries your dad has about my mom's health. I don't want it to appear like it was all my idea."

Pete became so excited he jumped up and down. "If Edith is in Great Falls, she and Dad can't get married! What time are we going to leave?"

"I'll pick you up at eight if you promise not to tell your dad why we're going. Just tell him that I have some supplies that I need to get and that I asked you to come along to help me load the car. I'll see you bright and early Monday morning." The conversation ended, Bob stood and began tearing open another shipping crate, completely ignoring the happy young man who slipped out the back door.

Pete nearly skipped down the street toward home. At long last Edith would be out of his father's life for good. She would be in a nursing home where she belonged and his father would only have one person to love.

That evening Roy and Pete picked up Edith and took her to the city-wide Little League championship game at the park. As they joined Bob, Nancy, and Dawn in the grandstands, Pete was back to his friendly self. He had no reason to hate Edith; Bob had everything under control.

"I sure hope Jay's team wins," Pete exclaimed as he watched the boys on the field warm up. "Which team does he play on?"

"Jay's the pitcher for the Blue Jays," Dawn announced proudly. "I think they named the team after him because he was so good and he likes the color blue. That's him warming up there by first base."

Edith and Roy exchanged amused glances but did not amend Dawn's explanation.

As the game progressed, Jay lived up to his sister's praise and struck out one batter after another. At his turns at bat he hit a double, a single, and drew a walk. Toward the end of the sixth inning, Bob leaned over the others and caught Pete's attention. "Want to come to the refreshment stand with me, Pete?"

Pete nodded vigorously and jumped to his feet.

"Can I come with you, Daddy?" Dawn begged as she took hold of his hand. "I want to get some popcorn."

"I suppose so," Bob agreed reluctantly. "You can get your popcorn and go right back."

The men led the way to the concession while Dawn tagged along a few paces behind. Not realizing that she was listening, Bob put his hand on Pete's shoulder. "Are you ready to go with me Monday? I'm going to need you to convince your dad how necessary the doctor said it was for Mother to have constant care."

"That won't be hard," Pete stated proudly. "My dad always listens to what I have to say."

"Good. I don't want to waste any time. Mother will be so much better off in a nursing home in Great Falls where she can receive the best health care available."

"We are only doing what is best for her," Pete said, trying to convince himself that what they were doing was in Edith's best interest.

"Remember, I don't want anyone to know our plans until we have the arrangements made. If your dad or my mother finds out, our entire plan will be ruined," Bob explained, again ignoring Dawn behind them.

"I promise not to tell a single person," Pete agreed. A depth of serious determination penetrated his voice. "At least she'll be a long ways away from my father."

Confused and upset, Dawn's eyes suddenly filled with tears. *Why don't they want Grandma in Rocky Bluff? Why are they taking her to a nursing home in Great Falls? I don't want her to leave us. I missed her so much when she was in the hospital.* She turned and started to run back to the bleachers. She must not leave her grandma, not now at least.

As Bob turned to Dawn to take her order, he caught sight of her bright red playsuit running toward the spectators. Bob shrugged his shoulders and dug in his back pocket for his wallet to pay for the snacks.

Pushing her way through the crowds, Dawn slipped in beside her grandmother and wrapped her small arms around her.

"What's wrong, honey?" Edith asked as the little girl tried to hold back her sobs.

"Nothing," she lied, burying her face in her grandmother's chest. "I just want to be with you and watch Jay play ball."

Within a few minutes Bob and Pete returned with their popcorn and drinks. Bob turned to his daughter, now leaning against his mother. "I brought you a bag of popcorn and a drink. I figured when you saw ours you'd want some, too."

"Thanks, Dad," she mumbled as she shoved a handful of popcorn into her mouth and offered some to her grandmother.

When the game had ended with a victory for the Blue Jays, 5 to 3, Jay beamed with excitement as he and his team walked across the field to receive their trophy. The Harkness and Dutton families were on their feet with the others to cheer them. Dawn pushed her fears to the back of her mind as she joined the celebration. Victory meant ice cream sundaes for everyone!

Monday morning Bob was busy at the store and didn't arrive at the Dutton home until nine. Pete hurried to the curb as soon as the familiar sedan appeared around the corner. After exchanging quick pleasantries, the pair was on their way to Great Falls.

"Your mother sure looked old at the ball game. She's way too old to live alone and way too old to marry my father!"

"I'm certain the doctor will agree with us. Besides, the nursing home will have so many social activities, it won't be long and she'll forget about your father. She's always liked to be around people," Bob assured him with pride in his ingenious scheme.

As soon as he was at the city limits, Bob pressed down on the accelerator. Pete's face became ashen and he clutched the dashboard so tightly his knuckles turned white. "Aren't you going over sixty-five?"

"No cops patrol here this time of day," Bob rationalized as he pressed the gas pedal still closer to the floor. "Besides, I have to make up an hour since we were late getting started. Why don't you lie back and take a nap? It'll make the miles go faster."

In spite of his fear of speed, Pete had complete confidence in the respected, dark-haired man beside him. Within minutes he laid his head against the door frame and was fast asleep. Glancing sideways and seeing Pete's lack of attention to the speedometer, Bob accelerated even more and pulled into the other lane to pass a cattle truck.

In the oncoming lane a semi-trailer truck was only one hundred yards away. Choosing between a ten-foot ditch and the truck, Bob swerved toward the ditch. He wasn't fast enough. The front end of the semi slammed into the right side of the car where Pete was sleeping. There was an instant of breaking glass and grinding metal, and then deathly silence. No one moved within the battered car.

Sirens disturbed the morning calm of Rocky Bluff as the ambulance raced toward Community Hospital. Roy Dutton, busy sanding the door frame at the crisis center, recalled Pete's new attitude toward Edith and him at Jay's baseball tournament. Suddenly the crisis phone rang.

No one ever calls the crisis center until evening, Roy thought strangely as he reached for the receiver.

"Roy Dutton?" a businesslike voice asked on the other end of the line.

"Yes," Roy replied, wondering who would know he was working here so early in the morning.

"This is Dr. Brewer at the emergency room of Community Hospital. Your son has been in a serious car accident and was brought to the hospital. Would you meet me at the emergency room right away?"

While waiting for Roy's arrival, Dr. Brewer caught sight of Pastor Rhodes, who was making his routine Monday morning hospital visits.

"Pastor Rhodes, I'm glad you're here," Dr. Brewer began as he motioned for him to follow him into an empty visitors' lounge. "Is Roy Dutton a member of your congregation?"

"Yes. Is there a problem?"

"I was hoping that you might be able to help me. His son was just brought in as a DOA from an accident twenty-five miles out of town. The driver, Bob Harkness, was injured and admitted to the west wing. I called Roy and asked him to come to the hospital. Would you stay and help him during this difficult period?"

"Certainly. Has anyone contacted Edith Harkness yet? If her son was injured I'm afraid the shock might be too hard on her weak heart."

"She's been called and told about her son, but she's not aware of Pete Dutton's death. Her housekeeper is bringing her to the hospital. I'll call the nurses' station and have them watch for her. They can tell her to meet us in the emergency room as soon as she arrives. I'd rather she learn the sad news from us than from someone else."

At that moment the automatic door to the emergency room slid open and Roy Dutton walked in. Spotting Dr. Brewer with Pastor Rhodes, a lump built in Roy's throat.

Dr. Brewer motioned for him to sit down. "Roy, I have some bad news," he began as he joined Roy on the sofa. "Bob Harkness and your son were in a car accident earlier this morning. Bob suffered three broken ribs and lacerations, but he should be fine in a few days." The doctor took a deep breath. "Your son was killed instantly."

Roy sat in stunned silence. Pastor Rhodes rested his hand on Roy's shoulder as Roy leaned forward and buried his head in his hands and sobbed. Leaving Pastor Rhodes alone with Roy, Dr. Brewer went to meet Edith, who was walking down the long corridor to the emergency room. Her face was flushed from exertion and worry.

"Mrs. Harkness, have you seen Bob yet?" Dr. Brewer asked softly.

"I was just in his room, but he was resting so I didn't stay. There was a message at the nurses' station for me to come to the emergency room. No one will tell me how Pete is."

"I'm sorry, but Pete Dutton did not survive the accident. He was killed instantly." Edith's face flushed even more and her heart pounded. "Mrs. Harkness, please come and sit down," Dr. Brewer encouraged, putting his right arm around her to help support her weight. As he led her to the waiting room, she spotted Pastor Rhodes and Roy with his face buried in his hands.

Edith hurried to Roy's side and touched his arm. Instinctively he pulled her next to him and the two clung to each other in a silence that was punctuated only by an occasional sob. After several minutes Dr. Brewer took both their hands in his. "If there is anything I can do to help, please feel free to call me."

Roy took a deep breath and stood up. "I suppose I better make the funeral arrangements and begin notifying family." Pastor Rhodes offered to join him as he helped Edith to her feet.

Two hours after arriving at Community Hospital, Bob regained consciousness. As his eyes began to focus, he saw Nancy sitting in the chair next to the bed. Tears were flowing down her cheeks. His chest was heavy with pain and there were bandages on his left arm and face.

Instinctively Nancy became aware of his stirring and went to his side. She took his head in her hands and pressed her lips against his.

"What happened?" Bob whispered with great effort.

"You collided with a semi. You have three broken ribs and other cuts, thirty-five stitches in your arm and twenty in your face, but the doctor says you should be as good as new."

"I feel miserable," Bob moaned. "How's Pete?"

If only Pastor Rhodes were here to help her break the news, she reflected with a sigh. She continued to clutch his hand in hers. "This is very hard to say," she choked, "but Pete is dead. He was killed instantly."

Bob took a deep breath, realizing his mental anguish far outweighed the pain of his body. The final moments before the impact flashed before him with clarity. He began to cry uncontrollably.

Within minutes a nurse rushed in with a hypodermic needle filled with a clear liquid. "He needs to rest. I know he's in a great deal of pain. This should help him for awhile."

Bob's sobs subsided in a few moments as he drifted into a drug-induced sleep and Nancy returned to her vigil in the chair beside his bed.

Three hours later Bob again became aware of his pain and the sterile hospital room around him. "Nancy," he whispered, as his wife tiptoed to his bedside. "Did you say that Pete Dutton was dead?"

Nancy shuddered, afraid the truth would cause the same reaction. "Yes, Bob, I'm sorry."

"I killed him!" Bob's whisper had become a drugged shout.

"Honey, you didn't kill him," Nancy said softly, cradling his head in her hands. "It was an accident."

"No, I killed him the same as if I had taken a gun and shot him," Bob persisted. "Pete warned me that I was going too fast before he went to sleep, but I was too anxious to get to Great Falls. I shouldn't have passed the cattle truck. I killed Pete Dutton!" His hysterical cries were underscored as he pounded his fist into the mattress.

As Bob's sobs and shouts again echoed up and down the west wing, the head nurse immediately called the doctor for clearance and returned to administer another shot. Within minutes Bob was asleep again.

Nancy collapsed from emotional exhaustion into the chair beside the bed. Her husband, who had always been able to control his entire world, had been completely broken within a few short hours.

When Bob awoke again, a heavy gloom hung over him and he refused to discuss the accident. When visitors came, he remained cold and aloof. His previous fragile emotional state had given way to listless, mechanical behavior.

Wednesday morning he was dismissed from the hospital. As Nancy drove the car into the driveway, Jay and Dawn came running to receive their customary hugs and jostling. Bob merely pushed them aside, complaining that his chest hurt too much to hug anyone.

As the day passed, one hour of mental torment seemed to blend into the next. *Bob Harkness is a killer,* he kept repeating to himself. *I killed Pete Dutton.* His thoughts were confirmed when the sheriff's deputy came to his home and charged him with speeding and imprudent driving.

Thursday afternoon nearly a hundred friends and relatives gathered at the graveside after the funeral service. Bob stood as far from the others as he could. Choosing words from Paul's letters to the Corinthians and Thessalonians, Pastor Rhodes spoke in a commanding voice that echoed across the hillside:

"Eye hath not seen, nor ear heard, neither have entered into the heart of men, the things which God hath prepared for them that love him.

"For our light affliction, which is but for a moment, worketh for us a far more exceeding and eternal weight of glory.

"For if we believe that Jesus died and rose again, even so them also that are fallen asleep in Jesus will God bring with him."

"Pete, even if I did kill you, you are with God today," Bob whispered as if he were standing beside him instead of lying in the coffin about to be lowered into the ground.

Suddenly Bob felt a firm hand on his shoulder and he was brought back to reality. "How's it going, Bob?" Pastor Rhodes asked as the mourners began to file back to their cars.

"I don't know," he confessed sadly. "I used to have my entire world under control and now it has disintegrated into a million useless pieces. I don't know where to turn, what to do. How can I face the people of Rocky Bluff after what I have done? How can I face my own family? How can I face God?"

Wisely Pastor Rhodes momentarily ignored his questions and suggested an alternative. "Come. Let's talk in my study." Bob rode back to the church without saying a word. After the two men were seated in the minister's study, Pastor Rhodes said, "I know you lost a friend, but is there something more that is troubling you?"

Bob stared at the floor and his eyes settled on an ant as it scurried across the room. His first instinct would have been to step on it, but not today. Finally he blurted out, "I killed Pete Dutton."

The minister tried to hide his shock. "Wasn't it an accident, Bob? Did you intentionally hit that truck?"

"No, I didn't plan for it to happen, but I was driving too fast and I didn't watch what I was doing. I shouldn't even have been going to Great Falls in the first place."

"Roy told me that Pete said you were going after supplies. Was there another reason for your trip?"

Bob stammered. "I–I–I was going to find a good nursing home for Mother and then talk with the doctor and work up a legal form for her admittance. I only had selfish motives that were not in the best interest of my mother."

Pastor Rhodes watched the private battle raging inside Bob. Finally words began to tumble from Bob's mouth as if a dam had broken. "My reasons for the trip weren't at all Christian, and I took advantage of Pete's simple trust in me. I'm the one who puts on a big Christian businessman's facade, but that's all it is. Attending church is always good for business in a small city like Rocky Bluff. I've made my best contacts there. While you were speaking at the graveside, I realized I really didn't know what Christianity was about. All I have been thinking about lately was how to get total control of the family business. My entire life has been centered on making money, despite the cost to anyone else."

"Bob, it's never too late to turn your life around and get into a right relationship with God. In spite of everything, your family still loves you, and, most importantly, God still loves you." Pastor Rhodes took his large black study Bible from his desk and handed it to Bob. "Would you read First John, chapter one, verse nine for me?"

Bob thumbed through the New Testament hoping to stumble across the tiny book. He might be a whiz in the business world, but he was a biblical illiterate. After several minutes of searching, he began to read aloud:

"If we confess our sins, he is faithful and just to forgive us our sins, and to cleanse us from all unrighteousness."

A light bulb seemed to go on within Bob's mind. The fragmented pieces of his Christian upbringing were beginning to fall into place: He could be forgiven. As long as there is life, there is hope for changes and new beginnings. "Maybe someday God will forgive me for what I have done," he muttered.

"God forgives sins whenever we confess them, but we also have to forgive ourselves," Pastor Rhodes challenged kindly. "I realize it has been a difficult day for you. Why don't you think about God's forgiveness and the meaning of the Christian faith for a few days? I'll give you a list of Scriptures to study. We can meet again next week after you've had time to rest and seriously consider them."

"Thank you," Bob replied as he rose to leave. "Money almost became my god. It has nearly destroyed my life and the lives of those I've loved the most. There has to be a better way to live and I'm determined to find it."

Over the next few days Bob spent many hours resting in bed. When he was not sleeping he was studying his Bible and thinking. *Why have I been so inconsiderate and uncaring toward Mother? She taught me the right way to live and I refused to listen. Because of that I indirectly caused Pete's death. There will never be a time that Mother will be too old to know what is right and wrong. Her body may be slowing down, but her loving spirit will always be young and alive.*

Bob paused. A special peace surrounded him. *If Jesus could forgive the thief on the cross, surely He can forgive me.* Bob questioned himself and his motives for some time. In the end, there was no booming voice or flashing lights, but in that afternoon stillness the same Savior who had been a constant companion and friend of his mother became a reality to Bob Harkness. A serenity filled his troubled mind as he thought of ways he could show his mother his gratefulness for all she had done for him.

First, however, he had to face Roy Dutton.

Chapter 14

The morning after Pete's funeral, Roy awoke with a dull headache. As he lay in bed trying without success to go back to sleep, he came to a stark conclusion. The world of grief and sudden loss was his to face alone. After an hour of staring blankly at the ceiling, he stumbled out of bed. He paused at the closed door to Pete's room and then hesitantly opened it. Waves of happy memories washed over him. *Why did that senseless accident have to happen?* he asked himself. *Pete led a life of simple innocence, why did it have to end this way?*

After a spartan breakfast of cold cereal and black coffee, Roy dressed in an old plaid shirt and faded blue jeans and headed for the crisis center. "Good morning, Roy," Dan Blair, one of the volunteers, greeted as Roy strolled into the center with an emotionless expression on his face. "I'm sorry to hear about the loss of your son. I thought you might like some help with the painting."

"Thanks, Dan," Roy responded, sinking into the padded chair by the door. "I don't know what I'd have done without you taking over the switchboards and organizing the volunteers for me. With so many things on my mind this week, I'm afraid I abandoned the crisis center."

"That's understandable. I enjoy helping. Our union went on strike last week and I don't know when we'll be called back to work. Most of the other bus drivers are spending their time walking the picket line, but I'm not the militant type. I'd rather be working at something. I suppose I might feel differently about the strike if I had a wife and children to support."

"I'll be able to put you to good use here if you have the extra time," Roy replied as he picked up a paint roller and began spreading light blue paint on the west wall. "I can finish the manual labor, but I'm not ready to deal with other people's problems. Dan, would you mind taking over for me until you're called back to work?"

"Not in the least. Just let me know what needs to be done and I'll see that it gets done."

The two men finished painting the room in less than two hours. Few words were spoken between them, but Dan's presence was a comfort to Roy. Before leaving, Roy took out a sheet of paper and briefly outlined the procedures of the crisis center and the personnel involved. As he handed it to Dan, he breathed a sigh of relief. The work of the center could go on without him.

On the way home Roy decided to stop at Bea's for a bite to eat. As he gazed idly through the side window, Sally Pegram approached his booth and silently slid into the seat across from him.

"I'm sorry to hear about your son," she began as she took his hand in hers. "If there's anything I can do, please let me know."

Roy's eyes met hers, but the feeling of despondency remained. "There's not much anyone can do right now. I guess I just need time to help fill the void."

"How about a game of golf in the morning? We were such good partners during the mixed foursome tournament, I'd hate to let our talents go to waste."

"Sally, I'm having trouble getting interested in anything at this point."

"You need to force yourself to do something. The fresh air and crisp September wind will be good for you. Playing golf always lifts my spirits and gets my mind off my troubles."

"It might be worth a try. I can't keep my mind on anything else, but I warn you that I'm pretty lousy company right now."

"I'll take my chances," Sally said lightly as she stood to leave. "I'll meet you at the clubhouse at ten."

Roy watched her as she strolled gracefully out of the restaurant. *Maybe she's right. A change of pace might be good for me. I do need some good old-fashioned relaxation.*

❧

The next morning as they approached the green of the seventh hole, Sally had endured enough of Roy's sullen silence. "I know it hurts deeply that Pete died, but don't take it so hard," she said nonchalantly. "Maybe it was for the best anyway. After all, he was mentally retarded, and who would have taken care of him if you died first?"

Sally's words cut through Roy like a surgeon's scalpel. *Surely she doesn't realize what she is saying,* he tried to rationalize. *Maybe she's one who stumbles over words in a tight situation.* After a long pause Roy answered, "The Davidsons would have always provided a home and job for him. Even if he were retarded, he could have been an excellent mechanic for any rancher or farmer." His speech was slow and deliberate and his face reddened with anger.

"I didn't mean to upset you," Sally replied in a sugary sweet voice as she took her putter out of her golf bag. "But this way Pete will never be a drain on society. He's happier where he is now."

105

"Pete had more love and compassion than most of the leaders in our community. He was an asset to society, not a detriment," Roy snapped. "I can't imagine anyone thinking otherwise." With that he approached the eighth tee-off area. He firmly pushed his tee into the ground, placed the ball on it, and with one powerful swing sent the ball farther than he ever had in his life.

"I'm sorry," Sally said quietly, while pouting as Roy placed his driver back into his bag. "I thought maybe I could help you see things more realistically."

The pair finished the ninth hole in silence and Roy hurried to his car, scarcely saying good-bye. Sally tagged behind him with a puzzled look on her face. "Do you think we could get together for another game before the weather turns cold?"

"I think I've had enough golf for the season," Roy answered dryly as he opened his trunk and laid his clubs next to his spare tire.

Instead of heading home, Roy turned down a side street and went straight to the Harkness home. The thought that somehow Edith's son may have been responsible for Pete's death had created an uneasy tension between them. He tried to shove those thoughts into the background and visualize the laughing, caring person who had been his prize student in the volunteers' class.

Edith answered the door dressed in a crisp lavender pantsuit. The worry lines that had appeared during her surgery had reappeared on her flawless skin. "I'm glad to see you," she greeted as she motioned for him to have a seat on the sofa. "I've been concerned about you. I've scarcely talked to you since we left the mortuary Monday afternoon. I called your house several times, but you weren't home."

As Roy sat on the living room sofa, a warmth began to replace his numbness. He marveled at Edith's compassion and depth of character that far outweighed what he had experienced with Sally. He basked in the silence of her presence before he spoke. "I finished painting the walls at the crisis center yesterday and then I went golfing this morning with Sally."

"The exercise should have been good for you," Edith replied, taking his hand in hers.

Roy gave a sarcastic laugh. "The exercise was great, but the company was devastating."

"What happened? It's not like you to talk that way about anybody."

"I've never known anyone to have such a low regard for human life, almost a Nazi-like mentality, and believe me, I cringe at that description. She would have been perfectly content in a society intent on destroying all misfits to produce a perfect race."

Edith paused, searching for the appropriate words. "I don't know exactly what she said and I'm probably better off not knowing. This is the time when our faith is put to the greatest test. You must forgive even when you heart is broken."

"I wish I could honestly say I can, but all I can say at this moment is that I'm willing for God to help me forgive. I'm not able to do that with my own strength."

"Our willingness is all He expects. If we trust God, the details will take care of themselves."

For the next hour the two shared their thoughts more deeply than they had before. All of their hurts and heartaches were exposed as their mutual love and trust blossomed. Finally Edith looked at the clock and gasped. "Roy, it's nearly one-thirty and I'll bet you haven't had any lunch."

"You're right. I was so angry I forgot all about food."

"The housekeeper fixed a large pot of chili last night before she left. How about having some with me? It's not any fun eating alone."

Roy heartily agreed and followed her to the kitchen. He began getting the bowls and silverware from the cupboard as Edith took the pot of chili from the refrigerator. They worked in peaceful silence until lunch was at last on the table, and then Roy asked the blessing. As Edith filled the bowls, she began a humorous digression of Jay and Dawn's start of another school year that buoyed Roy's downcast spirits.

"Edith, why don't you go lie down and rest? I'll finish the dishes," Roy volunteered as the last bite of chili disappeared from her bowl. "I'll see you at church tomorrow."

"I've learned never to turn down an offer for help. I am getting a little tired." She gave Roy a kiss on the lips and disappeared into her bedroom as he began clearing the table. The bond between them had not been weakened because of Pete's accident, Roy realized, but any mention of the tragedy had been tactfully avoided.

The next morning Bob and Nancy and the children gave Edith a ride to church. While Bob seemed happier and more relaxed than he had in years, his behavior seemed strange to Edith after such a traumatic week. The children chattered about their new year in school. The joy in the car was in sharp contrast to the pain and heartache that Edith kept hidden within herself.

As the organist played the prelude, Roy quietly slid into the pew next to Edith. They both whispered soft hellos and then withdrew into their own thoughts. As Edith studied his sturdy, handsome face, she realized she had not noticed the night before how he had aged in the last week. The laughter lines that she cherished had deepened into crevices of worry.

As the congregation sang "What a Friend We Have in Jesus, All Our Sins and Griefs to Bear," Edith again glanced at Roy and noticed a tear sliding down his cheek. *If only Roy would let Jesus carry his grief instead of trying to carry it alone,* she prayed with tears welling up in her own eyes.

As the congregation gathered in small groups on the sidewalk outside the church following the worship service, Nancy turned to Roy as he descended the front steps. "Mom is coming home with us for Sunday dinner. Why don't you join us? We'd love to have you."

Roy hesitated and gazed into the distance. "Thanks for the offer, Nancy, but could I take a rain check? I think I'd prefer to be by myself for awhile. Last Sunday Pete was sitting beside me in the pew and today he's gone."

"Well, if you change your mind, please feel free to come over later," Nancy encouraged, giving his arm a gentle squeeze.

Roy was embarrassed to offer such a lie when the truth was vivid in his mind. He could not bear to face the man who was responsible for his son's death. Although everyone said it was an accident, he still needed someone to blame. After all, the accident report had stated that excessive speed was involved.

After dinner, instead of going directly to his bedroom to rest, Bob stretched out on the living room sofa. Mentally Edith kept rehearsing what she would say to Nancy and hoped that Bob would soon retire to his bed. However, none of her rehearsed words seemed suitable to the situation, and her son did not budge from the couch.

As the women joined Bob in the living room, he sat up and a flood of words poured from his mouth like a bursting dam. "Mom, I don't know how to say this, but I'm really sorry for the way I have treated you lately. I was more concerned about making money than your personal welfare."

Edith stared at him in disbelief. After a long silence she replied softly, "What brought all that on?"

"It's a long story. But as I was standing over Pete's grave, I realized what an innocent trust he had in me, and, more importantly, what a simple faith he had in God. I felt pretty ashamed of myself. After the funeral I had a long talk with Pastor Rhodes and he gave me some Scripture to study. I came home and did a lot of soul searching. You know, Mom, I sat beside you in church every Sunday for many years and I don't think I ever listened to a word that was said until I had made such a mess out of my life that I didn't know how to get out of it. Only when I was at the end of my rope did I turn to God for help. I can honestly say that from now on I'm going to follow Christ, whatever the cost, even if it means I have to give up the business."

Edith could not contain her excitement. She had been waiting for years to hear those words. "I'm so happy for you," she said as she gave him a hug. "My deepest prayer has been that my entire family would surrender their lives to Christ before I die."

"There's one other thing I need to say," Bob continued as he lowered his gaze, afraid to make eye contact with his mother. "I think you ought to keep the house as long as you can. I can help you with the regular maintenance and Nancy said she'd help with the inside work. To be honest, I only wanted you to sell so that I could protect my personal inheritance. That's how ugly I had become. Please forgive me. I'll try to make it up to you any way I can."

Tears filled Edith's eyes at Bob's honest confession. The integrity he had been taught by his father was finally beginning to show. "I knew all along that was what you were trying to do and that's why I refused to sell. Let's put all the hard feelings behind us. I came over today to talk to Nancy about helping me with the housework until I can find a buyer. *I* have decided to sell the house."

"But Mother, are you sure you want to sell?" Bob questioned softly. "Don't let anyone influence you one way or the other. We know how much your home has meant to you throughout the years. Remember all the good times you've enjoyed in that house. You shouldn't make such an important decision on the spur of the moment."

Edith's eyes roamed idly out the picture window. The leaves on the willow trees were turning a golden brown. Another season was beginning. "I have to be realistic about my physical limitations and accept the fact that my house is too big for one person. I probably could find a small, one-bedroom apartment that would fit my needs much better."

"If you're certain that's what you want, I'll be willing to help you," Bob offered cautiously. He paused for a few moments, deep in thought. "I'd feel better if you set up your assets to go to your favorite charity. That way I can prove to you that I'm interested in you and not the family inheritance."

Edith studied her son. The change in him between Thursday and Sunday was unbelievable. Yet underneath his brazen exterior she had always sensed the gentle, compassionate spirit that had now surfaced. "Bob, I do want your help. Now maybe I can begin to put some trust in your judgment and financial advice. I'm proud of you. It takes a pretty big man to admit his shortcomings. I feel that a new era in our relationship is before us."

Chapter 15

The following Monday Roy drove Edith to Great Falls for a follow-up visit with her cardiologist. The news was worse than expected. Edith's heart had suffered permanent damage and she would have to limit her activities.

Upon returning home, Edith had just unlocked the back door and invited Roy inside when the phone rang. "Hello, Grandma." Dawn's words were punctuated by muffled sobs. "You did come home after all. Can I come and see you?"

"Well, certainly, honey, if it's all right with your mother. But why are you crying?"

"I just want to see you," Dawn managed through her gasping cries. There was a momentary silence while the weeping child raced to find her mother. "Mommy said I could come so long as I am home by bedtime. I'll ride my new bicycle and be there in a few minutes."

Edith hung up the phone and turned to Roy. "That was strange. I've never heard Dawn this upset before. She acted like she didn't think I was ever coming home again. I wonder where she got that idea?"

"Children have a way of misinterpreting things. I'm sure that it's nothing serious."

When Edith opened the front door to greet her granddaughter, Dawn wrapped her arms around her waist, buried her head on her chest, and continued to sob. Edith led the child to the sofa and cuddled her while Roy watched with compassion. "Why did you think that I was never going to come home again?"

"Because you went to Great Falls. I thought Roy was going to put you in a nursing home there and I'd never get to see you again."

"Whatever gave you that idea? I merely went to see the doctor."

"At Jay's last baseball game I heard Daddy and Pete talking about going to Great Falls to find a nursing home for you. They were on their way to Great Falls when the accident happened."

Roy's face turned red with anger as he attempted to control himself in Dawn's presence. He remained rigid on the living room sofa while Edith led her granddaughter to the kitchen.

Edith fixed Dawn a cup of hot chocolate and handed her the cookie jar. "Dawn, the doctor said I'm still strong enough to live by myself. I just won't be able to do all the things I used to do. If I ever do need to go to a nursing home, I'll go to the one here in Rocky Bluff. That way you will be able to come and see me every day."

After finishing her snack, Dawn returned to her normal bubbly self. "Grandma, I'm glad you're going to be in Rocky Bluff forever. I'm going home now to tell Jay." With that Dawn raced out the front door, barely managing a quick good-bye to Roy on her way.

Edith turned to Roy. "I'm sorry you had to hear the reason for Bob's trip this way. I didn't learn about it until the other day and I didn't know how to tell you. I didn't want to hurt you anymore. You've already been through so much. I was going to wait until the timing was right to tell you."

"I think the time is right, right now." Edith had never heard Roy's voice so harsh and demanding. "After all, it was my son who was killed in the accident. Why would he be a part of putting you in a nursing home?"

"Pete was jealous of our relationship. We both knew that. I'm sorry to say that it was my own son's idea for him to come along. Bob took full advantage of Pete's innocent trust."

"How can you forgive him for such a thing and pretend like nothing ever happened?" Roy demanded, pounding his fist into the arm of the chair. "While being part of this fiasco to get rid of you, he killed my son."

"Roy, I had to forgive Bob because Christ forgave me for all the selfish things that I've done. What is helping me the most is to know that God is bringing good from a tragic situation."

"What good could possibly come from Pete's death?" Roy demanded.

Edith took a deep breath as she tried to choose her words carefully. "The day of Pete's funeral Bob realized what he had done and became truly remorseful. He has had a complete change of heart and is now beginning to be less concerned about money and his own self-interests and more concerned about other people. You won't believe how different he is now."

"I'll believe it when I see it. The jails are full of people who suddenly 'get religion' after they've gotten themselves into trouble," Roy shouted. "You expect me to take it lightly that Bob could kill my son and then make it right by a simple confession of faith and begging forgiveness? I'll have to see the change before I'll believe anything."

"Spend more time with him, Roy. Then you'll see what I mean. Don't just take my word for it. Bob didn't intend for Pete to die. He wants to beg your forgiveness and to make amends for what has happened, but he doesn't know how. He is carrying around a tremendous sense of guilt."

"I don't know if I can face that man again as long as I live." He paused and took a deep breath. He was torn between the woman he loved and the hatred he felt toward her son, the man who had killed, albeit accidentally, his only son.

The room seemed to fill with tension as the clock ticked loudly from the mantel. "Maybe I'd better go home now and cool off. I'll call you in the morning. Good night, Edith." With that Roy turned and stomped out the back door, slamming it behind him.

Edith took a deep breath and then checked the phone directory and dialed the Rhodes residence. In a few moments a deep voice answered. "Pastor Rhodes. May I help you?"

"Hello, Pastor, this is Edith Harkness. I hate to disturb you at home, but I have a problem that I don't know how to handle, and I thought you might be able to help."

"I'll be glad to do anything I can. What's happening?"

"Roy just found out that Bob and Pete were on their way to Great Falls to arrange to put me in a nursing home when the accident happened. I've never seen him so angry. He feels that Bob manipulated Pete and then accidentally killed him. I tried to explain that Bob has since repented and turned his life around, but I felt like I was talking to a brick wall. I'm frightened for him. Is there anything you can do?"

"Don't let Roy's anger upset you. It's a very natural emotion for him at this time. Anger is one stage of the grieving process. I'll go and visit with him right away. Don't worry, I won't let on that you sent me."

Edith breathed a sigh of relief. "Thank you for your concern. I don't know how we'd get along without you during this difficult time."

"That's what I'm here for."

As Edith prepared for bed that night, she felt she carried the weight of the world on her now drooping shoulders. The doctor's diagnosis, Dawn's knowledge of the accident, and Roy's outburst of anger all contributed to her mental and physical exhaustion. As she straightened the heirloom quilt on her four-poster bed, the ringing phone made her lose her balance momentarily.

"Hello, Grandma. Congratulations!" Her son-in-law's cheerful voice greeted her.

"Well, hello, Jim. Do you have some good news for me? I need some for the day."

"I sure do. Jean had a baby girl at nine o'clock tonight. Gloria Lynn weighs eight pounds and three ounces and is the most beautiful child I've ever seen. Jean will be out of the hospital in a couple days. Will you be able to come and stay with us like we planned?"

"I'd love to, but I'm afraid I wouldn't be much help around the house. The doctor has placed so many limitations on me."

"That's all right, Mom. I'll get the housework done, but Jean insists that it's traditional for the maternal grandmother to come and give a new mother pointers on child care. How soon will you be able to leave?"

"I suppose I could take the bus that arrives in Chamberland at eight-twenty the day after tomorrow if you'll meet me. I have several things I need to do tomorrow."

"Great! I'll meet the Friday night bus from Rocky Bluff. Just don't spoil my daughter too much. That's my job."

As Edith lay in bed that night, the intensity of her life engulfed her. Never before had she felt so many conflicting emotions at the same time: the love of her family, the joy of a new grandchild, the pain of death, and the helplessness of being unable to comfort the man she loved. The doctor had been right. During her latter years she had learned what things in life were important and what things would pass away.

The next morning Edith wanted to call Roy and tell him the exciting news, but she was afraid he might be sleeping late. The night before he had promised to call, but the phone had been silent all morning. Early that afternoon the doorbell rang. She expected to see Roy but found her minister standing there instead. "Hello, Pastor Rhodes, do come in."

"Good afternoon. How are things going today? Were you able to get a good night's rest?"

Edith sighed as she remembered her sleepless night. "Not really. I'm extremely concerned about Roy, plus I received word that Jean had a baby girl last night."

"Congratulations. Are you planning to go to Idaho to be with them?"

"I hope to leave on tomorrow morning's bus, but I don't really want to leave Roy. You know how despondent he's been since the accident."

"I understand why you feel that way, but I would suggest that you go ahead and be with your family. I had a long talk with Roy last night. Right now he is having trouble dealing with his own feelings about the accident, but he doesn't want that to destroy your relationship. That is why he asked that I come by and talk with you."

"But what did he say?" Edith's eyes froze. The thought of losing Roy's friendship was overwhelming.

"He's afraid to see you for a few days for fear he would say something that he would later regret. I'm certain everything will work out in the end," Pastor Rhodes assured her. "Roy needs time to grieve over his dead son."

Edith's mind drifted back nearly twelve years to when she had suffered a similar loss. "I've been there myself. When George died I stayed in the house for almost three weeks before I even ventured to the store. Then I had so many conflicting feelings that I needed time by myself to sort them through. I know people had trouble understanding my need for solitude. Roy must be experiencing the same thing, but I'm concerned about him being alone."

"I assure you I'll be visiting Roy as often as possible while you're away. We must put him in the Lord's hands during this difficult time. In the end there is little either you or I can do; only God can heal a broken heart."

The first Sunday after Edith left for Chamberland, Roy stretched out in front of his TV and watched a football game. His peace was abruptly disturbed by a loud knock on the front door. Suddenly he found himself face-to-face with Bob Harkness.

His attitude toward Bob was beginning to soften, but he was not yet certain that they could carry on a worthwhile conversation. Almost mechanically, he invited him in and turned off the TV.

"I hope I'm not disturbing you," Bob began as he entered the living room with reluctance. "I have wanted to talk to you for some time, but I didn't have the courage."

"Please sit down and I'll get you a soft drink. Do you like yours in a can or with ice?"

"I'm not fancy. Straight from the can is fine."

In a few moments Roy returned with a drink for Bob. "Have you been following the Vikings this season?"

"I catch a game now and then. I hear they're having a pretty good season."

"That they are."

The two men sat in uncomfortable silence for a few minutes. Finally Bob cleared his throat and spoke. "This is the hardest thing I have had to do in my life. Six months ago I would never have dreamed that I would be begging someone's forgiveness. I thought I had my entire life under control. Roy, I regret that I have hurt so many people and I know I am responsible for Pete's death."

"Regrets will never bring Pete back to life," Roy replied without emotion. His body became rigid and his icy gaze froze Bob to his chair.

"How well I know. I've agonized over this ever since the accident. Although I was raised in the church with fine Christian parents, I completely missed the love and forgiveness that Christ offers."

There was a long, tense silence before Bob continued. "When I was faced with the fact that it was my own selfishness that indirectly led to Pete's death, all I could do was plead for mercy. I wish there was some way I could make up for what happened, but all I can do is beg for your forgiveness."

Roy's scowling expression caused Bob to hesitate and take a deep breath. "Also, I can't find words to tell you how much I appreciate your love and concern for my mother, especially during her long illness."

Fragments of the Lord's Prayer flashed through Roy's mind. "Forgive us our trespasses as we forgive those who trespass against us." *Can I live what I speak? Bob seems sincere. Can I turn him away when he is literally begging for my forgiveness?*

The struggles within Roy mounted. He must completely forgive Bob or become hard and bitter for the remainder of his life. After an unbearable silence Roy looked the young man straight in the eyes and whispered, "Yes, I do forgive you. I accept the change that God has made in your life."

Suddenly tears of relief filled the older man's eyes and his shoulders shook with his sobs. Washed away with these tears were his hostilities, frustration, and anger toward the man whom he'd considered responsible for his son's death.

As Bob watched him tears also filled his eyes. Words were not necessary to express the healing that was transpiring between the two men. Life could now go on without the shadow of the accident casting a pall over their relationship and Roy's relationship with Edith.

After that Sunday Roy was able at last to face the empty room in his house. At the same time he began to miss the companionship and good times he had shared with Edith. When he called her in Chamberland the next evening, he learned that she would be coming home the following Wednesday. She sounded so excited about the new grandbaby and promised scores of pictures to substantiate her claim of a beautiful child.

Wednesday afternoon Roy busied himself with preparations for Edith's return. He made a pineapple upside-down cake, a tossed salad, and a large pot of spaghetti sauce. That evening Bob, Nancy, and the children joined him at the bus station. Everyone was anxious to hear about the new baby and to welcome Edith back to Rocky Bluff.

After the evening meal, the Harkness family remained around the dining room table while Roy stacked the dishes in the dishwasher and then returned to his place. They reveled in a new openness and freshness in their family love. Finally Roy, unable to contain himself, rose to his feet in a mock formal manner.

"Ladies and gentlemen, we have gathered here at this joyful occasion to make public the engagement and approaching marriage of Roy Dutton and Edith Harkness. Everyone in favor, please say aye."

The children immediately shouted their approval while all heads turned toward Edith. Tears filled her eyes. "After hearing the doctor's discussion of my physical limitations, are you sure you want to go through with this?"

"The doctor didn't say you were mentally limited, did he?" Roy teased as the children giggled.

"Well, of course not."

"Then this is what I want to do. We are taking a family vote. Edith Harkness, how do you vote?"

Words failed her as she stood and embraced her dearest friend. As their lips touched momentarily, Nancy and Bob clapped and shouted their ayes and laughter filled the room.

The next morning Roy awoke to a city blanketed with snow. As he peered out his frosted window, he saw a parallel between the winter scene and his life. As the stark bareness of the oak trees was now covered with a snowy comforter, so the nakedness of his anguished soul was now clothed with a new love. Edith had agreed to be his bride, and they had the full support of her family.

After breakfast Roy bundled himself up for the winter weather and walked to the crisis center, invigorated by the crisp morning air. As he entered the back room of the center, Dan Blair had just finished sweeping the tile floor and rearranging the throw rugs.

"Good morning, Dan."

"Roy, it's good to have you back! The calls have nearly doubled with the approach of the colder weather. I was beginning to think that we might need two volunteers on duty again to help prevent what happened last year with Susan Youngman."

"We'll call a meeting of all the volunteers and work out a schedule for the holiday season sometime next week."

"That sounds like a good idea." Dan hesitated before continuing. "My union settled their strike late last night and they are calling all bus drivers back to work Monday. Can someone else carry on?"

"Don't worry about a thing. I know it's been difficult for you and the others who have been on strike for six weeks. I appreciate all the work you've done."

The men visited for another hour concerning the events of the past few weeks. Roy felt he was again in contact with the needs of the community. It was good to be back at the center after so many weeks of only feeling his personal pain. After Dan left, he stayed at his desk for another hour to catch up on the mounds of paperwork.

The next afternoon Roy parked his car in Edith's driveway. Instead of going to the door, he found a shovel in the garage and began clearing a path down the front sidewalk. Halfway down the walk Roy took a rest and spotted Edith standing in the picture window smiling. He waved at her and returned to scooping snow as she returned the gesture. *How can she consider herself an invalid when she has so much to offer?* he thought suddenly.

When he finished the walk, Roy leaned the shovel beside the garage door and slipped into the back porch to take off his boots and shake the snow from his coat and hat. Edith greeted him with a smile. "You didn't have to do that. I could have Jay shovel the sidewalk when he gets home from school."

"It was my pleasure." Roy stepped into her warm kitchen and took off his coat. "The least you could do for a freezing old man would be to offer him a hot cup of coffee," he teased, pulling up a chair at the table.

As they sipped their coffee in silence, Roy searched for exactly the right words. "Edith, I don't want to wait any longer. We've been through so much together. Let's get married as soon as possible." He took a deep breath. "How about December thirty-first?"

At first Edith hesitated as if she had not heard what he said. Marriage to Roy seemed the natural and right thing to do. She entwined her fingers through his as her face glowed with love.

"That's fine with me, but why did you pick New Year's Eve of all times?"

"We'll only have our family and close friends at the wedding, but the entire world will be celebrating with us. How's that for logic? We can start out the new year afresh with a new life together. I wonder if Pastor Rhodes will be able to perform the ceremony that night?"

"That all sounds so easy, but we have two separate homes to combine," Edith protested weakly. "I know I have been hesitant to part with this house, but why don't we just let Bob go ahead and sell it?"

"That's fine with me," Roy agreed as he took her face in his hands. "Edith, my dear, my place is plenty big enough for the both of us."

Chapter 16

The day after Thanksgiving the phone rang in the Harkness home as Edith was finishing the lunch dishes.

"Hello, Edith, this is Grady Walker at the school. It's been a long time since I've seen you. How have you been?"

"I'm moving slower, but I seem to be keeping busy. How are things at school?"

"We've all been involved in the new building project. If you've been by the north side of the building lately, you've probably seen that the new wing is nearly completed."

"It doesn't seem like any time at all since they had the ground-breaking ceremony."

"Why I called, Edith, is to see if you would come to the school sometime this week. There are a few things I'd like to discuss with you."

"I don't see a problem. How would tomorrow afternoon be?"

"That would be great. How about two-thirty?"

With the time agreed upon, Edith hung up the phone mystified as to why Grady would want her to come to the school. Grady knew that she was no longer able to substitute teach and she had had very little contact with the school since she retired.

The next afternoon a flood of memories overwhelmed Edith as she walked into Rocky Bluff High School. The walls had been repainted and the floors shined. The faces of the students were different, but it felt like she was coming home. Viola greeted her warmly and ushered her into the principal's office. Grady was sitting at the table with Dick Ritter, chairperson of the school board.

The principal greeted her and extended his hand. "I think you know Dick Ritter."

"Oh, yes," Edith assured him as she shook hands with a long-time acquaintance. "It's good to see you again."

After a few minutes of small talk shared over coffee, Grady finally came to the point of the meeting. "I suppose you're wondering why I had you come today. Your contributions to Rocky Bluff High School have not gone unnoticed. In fact, I most likely would not be here today if it weren't for your quick actions."

"I only did what had to be done at the time," Edith insisted. "I think if I'd had time to think, I would never have been brave enough to take the gun away from Larry."

"You not only saved my life, but for ten years you provided the best education and role model Rocky Bluff students could have. In recognition of your contribution to Rocky Bluff High, the school board has unanimously voted to name the new addition the Edith Harkness Wing, with your permission of course."

Edith sat speechless. Never had she thought she would receive such an honor after such a quiet, ordinary life. "But I don't deserve such an honor," she objected weakly.

"The school board believes you do. No one has consistently made as many contributions to Rocky Bluff High School as you. If you agree, I'll make the decision public next week."

"Oh, Grady, I feel so humble at this moment. Of course, you may name the new wing after me, but I still say I don't deserve this honor."

In the days that followed, Edith was overwhelmed, but she could not spend time thinking about it. She was in a flurry of wedding and moving plans. Everything seemed to be happening at once.

On December thirty-first Pastor Rhodes stood before a small gathering in the intimate church chapel. As he read the timeless words pronouncing Roy and Edith husband and wife in the name of the Father, and of the Son, and of the Holy Ghost, he beamed approvingly at the couple standing before him. He had shared many joys and heartaches with them over the years as their pastor. Tonight was a milestone in their lives, and he was honored to be a part of it.

"Pastor Rhodes, you and your wife are planning to join us at the reception at Nancy and Bob's home this evening, aren't you?" Roy asked after the ceremony. "The women have been working for several weeks to provide us with a gala affair."

"I wouldn't miss it for the world. I'll be over in a few minutes after I turn down the heat and lock the building."

"Don't wait too long," Nancy teased. "You don't want to miss the cake cutting."

Among the guests who had traveled great distances to celebrate the New Year's Eve wedding were Jean and Jim with Gloria Lynn from Idaho, Roy's brother and his family from Miles City, Montana, and Edith's sister from California. When Gloria Lynn let out a big cry, Jean hurriedly bundled her in the afghan that Edith had crocheted as a Christmas gift.

"It sounds like it's feeding time," the new mother sighed contentedly. "If you all don't mind, Jim and I will leave for Bob's now so I can perform my duties."

"The housekeeper is at the house now to finish setting up and welcome guests, so just make yourself at home," Bob said as he walked them to their car. "We'll be along shortly."

Within a half hour more than fifty guests were gathered in the Harkness home. Jay and Dawn were beside themselves with excitement. "Grandma, I bet I'm the only one in my room at school who got to go to their grandmother's wedding!" Dawn giggled. "I hope I can have a picture to prove to everyone that I did."

"As many pictures as your uncle Jim has been taking, I'm sure there'll be enough for the entire town," Edith replied as she winked at her overeager photographer.

Eyeing her mother-in-law across the room, Nancy motioned her to join the group assembling around the beautifully decorated serving table. "Mom, do you and Roy want to cut the cake so we can begin serving?"

Edith took Roy's hand as she led him behind the table. Her fingers covered his as she helped guide the knife through the thick icing, cutting two small pieces.

"We have to do this properly," Jim teased. "The most important picture at the wedding is the one with the bride and groom feeding each other a piece of wedding cake." After adjusting the lens, he snapped the shutter as Roy and Edith simultaneously shoved a piece of cake into each other's mouth. Everyone cheered with delight. Edith reached for a napkin to wipe her face and fingers as Roy chuckled at the frosting on her nose.

As midnight approached, the wedding guests prepared to toast the bridal couple with the fruit punch Jean had prepared that afternoon. "To a long, happy life together," Pastor Rhodes began.

"Best wishes to the newlyweds," Bob said as he lifted his glass. His eyes misted over as he looked deep into his mother's eyes. "Mom, I want you to know you'll never be too old to enjoy life. I wish you both happiness, good health. . .and the presence of mind to throw me out the door if I should ever interfere! I love you both."

Laughter erupted in the dining room and then one by one each of the guests proposed a toast to the radiant Mr. and Mrs. Roy Dutton.

Contagious Love

*This book is dedicated to my mother, Frances Hartman,
and to my late father, Walter Hartman,
my two children, and my four stepchildren.
I trust that our love is contagious to our grandchildren
Ryan Orr, Vanessa Sanchez, and Michael Mishler.*

Chapter 1

Hello, crisis center. May I help you?"

"I hope so," a frightened voice whispered. "I can't talk long. My husband is going to be back in a few minutes. He's been beating me. My eye is swelling so badly that I can hardly see."

Edith Dutton took a deep breath and whispered a quick prayer for wisdom. This was her first call at the crisis center after returning from her honeymoon, and in spite of her sixty-seven years, the potential for serious consequences sent chills down her spine. "What do you think will happen when he gets back?"

"He left to buy more beer, so it'll probably only get worse. I'm really scared. He told me that if I didn't have this house spotless by the time he got back, he'd beat me bloody. I've really tried, but I've been sick lately. I'm always nauseated and can hardly keep any food down."

"We'll have to get you out of there right away. Do you have any friends or relatives where you'd be safe?"

"No. My mother died when I was twelve, and my dad and stepmother live in Iowa, but they wouldn't be able to help. I've been so busy with the baby that I haven't had time to make friends of my own."

"There are several local agencies that can help. In fact, we have a spouse abuse shelter here in Rocky Bluff. Hurry and pack a few things for you and your baby, and I'll have the director of the shelter come and get you right away. Of course, the police will have to be notified."

"Do they have to be?" Terror vibrated through her words. "He'll really be mad then. I know they'll put him in jail because he's already on probation."

"Right now your safety and the safety of your baby is what's important. What's your name and where are you?"

"My name is Libby. . .Libby Reynolds. My baby's name is Vanessa. I'm at 2519 Frontage Road. Please hurry. I'm expecting him back any time and I haven't gotten everything done he told me to do."

"I'll call the police and they'll be there in just a few minutes," Edith assured her. "Now what's the name of your husband and what kind of car is he driving?"

Libby hesitated. *What will he do to me if I tell? If only I'd been a better wife maybe this wouldn't have happened.* The silence became penetrating. Finally she whispered. "He's driving a red Ford Maverick. His name is Larry Reynolds."

Edith's face whitened, her hands turned clammy. Her mind flashed back nearly three years. She again felt the terror of staring into the muzzle of a .38 Police Special in the hands of Larry Reynolds with her principal, Grady Walker, lying wounded at her feet. She had not seen Larry since that time, and she had desperately tried to block those memories out of her mind.

Edith took a deep breath. *I have to keep my composure. This girl's life is in danger.*

"Libby, my name is Edith Dutton," she said, trying to keep her voice calm. "My husband and I will be there with the director of the spouse abuse center in fifteen minutes. Be waiting for us at the door."

Edith hurriedly hung up the phone, thankful that she had an extension of the crisis center line in her own home. "Roy," she shouted as she rushed to the coat closet beside the front door. "Get your coat. There's a young woman in serious danger."

Roy laid his newspaper on the end table and helped Edith with her coat before reaching for his own. As the director of the crisis center, he was used to handling problems over the phone, but never had he seen his best counselor so intent to personally intervene in a case. "What's happened?" he queried, fearing for the health of his beloved bride.

"We've got to get Larry Reynolds's wife to the spouse abuse shelter. He's been beating on her and then left to get more beer. She's scared to death and so am I. We can call Teresa from the car phone and tell her we'll stop by her house on our way to get Libby."

"I was afraid that boy would end up a menace to society," Roy said as they raced to the car. "A lot of people have tried to help him, but he refused to listen to anyone. I bet he's going to be spending time in the state penitentiary in Deer Lodge before his life is over. I like to give people the benefit of the doubt, but with Larry I question if there is much hope for him."

Roy opened the left door of their Chrysler LeBaron for Edith and then hurried around the car and slid behind the wheel. "I'm sure glad we have such a flexible spouse abuse director as Teresa. She's done so much for this community."

Edith picked up the car phone, dialed, and waited. *What if she's not home?* She worried with each passing ring. Suddenly the ringing stopped.

"Hello."

Edith breathed a sigh of relief. "Teresa, thank goodness you're home. Roy and I are on our way over to get you. Larry Reynolds's wife just called the crisis center and he's been beating her. After my dreadful experience with him, I'm afraid for her life. I told her we'd take her and the baby directly to the spouse abuse shelter."

"I'll get my coat and be watching for you," Teresa assured her. "Sonya, one of our best volunteers, is staying at the shelter tonight, so she'll have an extra bed and crib waiting for her. Have you called the police yet?"

"That's my next call."

Roy looked over at his trembling wife. The streetlights magnified the tension in her face. Those same wrinkles that he had watched gradually fade after Edith's near-fatal heart attack were now spreading across her face. The same young man who had caused enough fear in the calm home economics teacher of Rocky Bluff High School to raise her blood pressure to dangerous heights was again threatening Edith's serenity and the life of his own wife and child.

Edith quickly dialed 9-1-1.

"Emergency services. May I help you?" a confident voice said.

"Hello, this is Edith Dutton. I'd like to report a case of domestic violence with the wife's life in imminent danger. My husband and I, along with Teresa Lennon from the spouse abuse center, are on our way to get her, but he's been drinking and we could run into problems. Could we have a police officer meet us there right away?"

"Don't worry, they'll be right there. Where are you going?"

"We're on our way to 2519 Frontage Road to get Libby Reynolds," Edith explained as she tried to keep her voice under control. "Her husband, Larry Reynolds, just left to get more beer and threatened to beat her more when he got home."

"You said his name was Larry Reynolds." The dispatcher's tone indicated he was familiar with the name.

"Yes," Edith gasped.

"Do you know what kind of a car he might be driving? Maybe they will be able to stop him before he gets home."

"Libby said he was driving a red Ford Maverick. She didn't say what year."

"That information is extremely helpful. I'll have the police on their way. Now be careful," the dispatcher warned. "If Larry is any place in the vicinity when you get there, don't approach the house until the police arrive."

Edith's hand trembled as she hung up the car phone. She was torn by her desire to help Libby and her fear of having to face Larry Reynolds again. She visualized that same .38 police special pointed at a young, frightened woman and knew what she had to do.

Just then Roy turned their Chrysler from Main onto Sixth Street. He immediately discerned a trim figure hurrying toward the curb. He steered to the edge of the street and stopped. Teresa wasted no time in opening the door and sliding into the back seat.

"Hi. Thanks for taking such a personal interest in this case. It could be real touchy. Were you able to get hold of the police?"

"Oh yes," Edith replied. "I called them as soon as I hung up from talking with you. The dispatcher said she would send a squad car there immediately. It looks like Larry will be spending a lot more time behind bars."

"I would think so," Roy responded dryly. "The last time he pled temporary insanity and only spent six months in a mental hospital. He obviously didn't learn anything from that. I've heard he's been involved in all kinds of fights at the bars after he's had a few drinks under his belt. I hope we don't have to deal with that."

"No," Edith assured him. "The dispatcher advised us that if Larry is around, we are not to go near the house until the police arrive. They will handle the situation."

As Roy turned onto Frontage Road, a red Maverick sped around them and nearly hit a parked car. The trio gasped.

"Better hurry," Edith directed. "I want to be waiting in the car in case Libby runs from the house with nowhere to go."

As Roy increased the pressure on the accelerator, he spotted blue and red flashing lights three blocks behind them and gaining on them quickly. They all breathed a sigh of relief as Roy pulled to the right and the patrol car sped around them.

"Thank you, Lord," Edith whispered as they followed the authorities to the Reynolds residence.

"Boy, am I glad to see them," Teresa gasped. "I've been in tough predicaments before with domestic abuse, but never this bad."

Sergeant Philip Mooney and Officer Scott Packwood stopped in front of 2519 Frontage Road and stepped from their patrol car. Having recognized the Dutton car as they had sped past them, they waited on the curb for the fast-approaching Chrysler.

In the glimmer of the streetlight, Edith recognized one of the officers. *I'm sure glad Phil's on duty now,* she mused. *He did such a good job handling Larry three years ago.*

Roy pulled up behind the police car and the threesome hurried toward the waiting officers.

"I'm glad you're here," Sergeant Mooney greeted. "Depending on how much Larry's been drinking, we could have a real problem on our hands. I don't want to put his wife or child in danger. He's on parole, so he's not supposed to own a firearm, but we don't want to take any chances. At this point he could use anything as a weapon, even his fists. I'm hoping there's some way we can talk the wife and baby out of the house before we have to confront Larry."

"Since I was the one Libby spoke to, maybe if I went to the door alone as a friend I could get Libby and the baby outside without upsetting Larry any more than necessary."

"Edith, I can't ask you to do that," Sergeant Mooney protested weakly. "We're the ones who are paid to take the risks, not you."

"Phil, I faced Larry once with a loaded gun and God gave me the strength. If He could protect me three years ago, He can do it tonight."

"I'll admit that method might be least likely to cause Larry to fly into a rage. Are you sure you're up to it?"

Roy was filled with trepidation as he surveyed his wife's strained face. His love and admiration for her escalated with each passing moment. He wondered how he had ever survived the long, lonely years of widowhood without her. And now the thought of her voluntarily putting her life on the line for someone she had never met was nearly overwhelming.

Edith looked at Roy for assurance. Their eyes met, but no words escaped their lips for several seconds. Finally, Roy nodded his head up and down.

"I have the best protection in the world," Edith replied bravely. "And with everyone here for backup, I'll try my best."

"Don't forget, we'll be hiding in the bushes with revolvers drawn if you have any problems," Sergeant Mooney responded as he and Officer Packwood moved toward the shadows of the bushes surrounding the house.

Roy squeezed Edith's hand. She took a deep breath and walked slowly toward the front door. She could hear shouting within, but could not make out the words. Hesitantly she reached for the doorbell.

"Who's there?" a gruff voice shouted.

"I'm a friend of Libby's. I wanted to come by and say hello. I haven't seen her for several weeks."

"She's busy now and doesn't have time to see anyone."

"I'll only be a minute. Please tell her she has a friend."

Edith could hear muffled sobs behind the closed doors. "No. . .wait a minute," a female voice cried. "Please don't go away. I need your help. You sound like the woman I talked with on the phone tonight."

"What do you mean? Were you wasting your time talking on the phone tonight? You were supposed to be cleaning this pig sty while I was gone," the male voice growled.

"I. . .I'm sorry. I was just lonely. Please let me talk to her for just one minute. I promise I'll not call anyone again."

"You don't need to see anyone. Do I have to blacken your other eye to get you to understand that?"

Suddenly Baby Vanessa began to cry. The entire household was a mass of crying and shouting. Time was suspended as the male curses behind the thin walls increased. Slowly the door opened. A young emaciated woman with swollen eyes and bruises appeared in the doorway holding a scream-ing baby. Edith grabbed her arm and dragged her down the three steps with a husky male figure close behind.

"Get back here you worthless, no-good piece of. . . !" Larry shouted. His voice trailed off as a glimmer of recognition spread across his face. He grabbed the poker from beside the fireplace as he followed his wife through the open door. "What are you doing with my wife? You messed up my life once before while I was in high school. I won't let you do that again."

With revolvers drawn, Sergeant Mooney and Office Packwood came between the two women and their assailant. "Larry Reynolds, you're under arrest for violating probation and assault and battery."

While the arresting officials were reading Larry his Miranda rights, Teresa led Libby and the crying baby to the Dutton vehicle. Although she had cared for many troubled families throughout the years, she always felt ill-prepared for the pain that they shared. She wrapped a blanket around the sobbing woman and put her arms around her. Not a word was spoken as the sobs subsided and Libby relaxed with her head on Teresa's shoulder. All energy and emotion seemed to be drained from the frightened woman.

"Our first stop will be the emergency room," Teresa explained gently. "We need to have your injuries checked."

"I'll be okay," Libby sobbed. "Besides, I can't go to the hospital. I don't have any insurance."

"Don't let insurance stand in the way of your health," Teresa replied. "I'll be able to help you get financial assistance for medical care."

"But what'll I do after they've patched me up? If I come back here, he'll only beat me again."

"The police will have him busy in jail for a long time tonight. After Larry is gone, we'll come back and get your things. Has the baby been hurt in any way?"

"Oh, no. She's just scared." Libby's voice trembled. "She's the apple of her daddy's eye. He said if I ever left him, he'd get custody of Vanessa 'cause he could prove I was an unfit mother."

The young woman watched as the officers handcuffed her husband and placed him in the back of the patrol car. "The only reason why I've stayed with him was because of Vanessa. I take really good care of her. Do you think he'd be able to take her away from me?"

"Of course not. He's just using that to scare you. You won't have to worry about him bothering you again," Teresa assured her. "I think the officers have plans for him for a long time."

"But I don't want to be the one who caused him to go to jail. After all, it wasn't all his fault. I should have had the house cleaned up when he got home today, but I've been so sick lately."

"No one deserves to be treated the way you've been. Your immediate need is medical care, a good hot meal, and a warm bed. We'll begin working on the rest of your life tomorrow."

"It's strange," Libby sighed. "I know I can't keep living with Larry like this. However, sometimes I still feel a spark of love, in spite of everything he's done."

"Libby, love is complex and multifaceted. Tomorrow will be soon enough to begin evaluating your feelings toward Larry. Right now it's time to get you to the emergency room."

While the police officers were leading Larry to the police car and Teresa was comforting Libby in the back seat of the car, Edith and Roy clung to each other under the reflection of the streetlight. Edith laid her head upon Roy's chest. Her breathing was rapid and her heart raced. "Edith, you're one brave lady. I've never seen anyone as self-sacrificing as you. But are you going to be okay?"

"A cup of hot tea and a good night's sleep will go a long way." Edith's words sounded strong, but the quiver in her voice betrayed her weak heart.

"While Libby is being examined in the emergency room, I think we better have your blood pressure checked."

"I hate to admit that I'm not as strong as I used to be, but I guess you're right. I don't want to go through heart surgery again. I have too much to live for now." Her eyes twinkled as she lightly brushed her lips across his. "I have the best husband in the world," she whispered as the pair walked to their car hand in hand.

Chapter 2

"Mom, I just heard the news and I came over as soon as I could," Bob Harkness said as he walked into his mother's kitchen. "It's all over town."

"Word travels fast in a little town," Edith smiled. "I was just getting ready to call you at the store when I saw your car in the drive. Now that you're here, would you like a cup of coffee?"

"I'd love it," Bob replied as he reached for a mug in the cupboard over the coffeepot. "With your increasing reputation for bravery, you're quickly becoming the community folk hero."

Edith chuckled as she admired her son's muscular shoulders. Years of work at the family hardware store had developed his physical strength. Edith thought back to the days when he first returned to Rocky Bluff to manage Harkness Hardware Store after her first husband, George, died. She had worked as the bookkeeper while her husband ordered the merchandise and waited on customers. Feeling inept at managing the entire business without him, she asked Bob to manage it for her while she returned to teaching.

Bob pulled up a chair at the kitchen table. "Mom, you're one brave lady. You always put the needs of others ahead of your own. I hope that experience last night didn't put too much strain on your heart."

"I feel perfectly fine today. Knowing that Libby is being cared for at the shelter and Larry is in jail gives me a great deal of peace."

"I don't think Larry will be in jail long." Bob hesitated as he surveyed the dark circles under his mother's eyes. "The rumor on the street is that bail will probably be set at five thousand dollars. I saw his parents go into the bank first thing this morning, so my guess is that they'll take out another mortgage on the ranch in order to post his bond."

Edith stared out the kitchen window at the barren elm tree in the backyard. She well understood the pain Larry's family must be feeling. "I'm sure his parents must be heartbroken. I know they were crushed after the trouble Larry got into three years ago."

"From my observation, they appeared to be so ashamed that they quit going to church and community events for several months. It wasn't until

130

their pastor and church people rallied behind them that we began seeing them in Rocky Bluff again," Bob replied. "I don't think they realized how much the community hurt for them. The town knew it was Larry's decision to pull the gun on the principal, not theirs, but until people began articulating their feelings to them, they had no way of knowing."

"In a way I understand what they must be going through. Although it's the child's decisions, a parent is programmed from the time they hear the first cry to feel they are responsible. I guess I've never quite gotten over feeling responsible for you and Jean, in spite of the fact that you both now have your own families."

"Mom, I wish you wouldn't try to carry my burdens. I'm the only one responsible for the times when I mess up. I'm just glad that we have a forgiving Lord and you have a forgiving husband."

"I have to agree with both those statements," Edith replied as she reached across the table and patted her son's hand. "Plus I have to add that I'm also thankful for a repentant son who was willing to own up to his mistakes. Without that I would never have had this beautiful marriage to enjoy during my later years."

Edith's mind drifted back to the time of Bob's opposition to her relationship with Roy. He'd been more interested in preserving his portion of the family inheritance than concerned for his mother's well-being or happiness. The tragic part was that Bob had involved Roy's mentally handicapped son, Pete, in his scheme to keep them from marrying. That scheme culminated in a fatal car accident that left Pete dead and Bob in the hospital.

"Bob, what you've done with your life since the accident is nearly miraculous, especially the work you've done to help the local boys club. The parents of those kids appreciate it very much."

"I want to help the kids enter adulthood with the right values, decision-making abilities, and proficiency in handling stress. I know I had the right values taught to me, but I never saw how important they were until I destroyed another person's life."

Edith sighed. "Larry Reynolds had the right values taught to him, but sad to say he never learned them. I hope something can be done to help him before he destroys his life and the lives of those around him."

"If there's any way I can help him, I sure would like to try." Bob refilled his coffee cup before he continued. "I need another challenge to keep my mind off my difficulties at the store. Things are really getting tough."

"Are you having problems getting your shipments on time? I know that was one of your father's biggest concerns."

"I wish it were that simple. This recession is taking its toll on our sales.

With farm prices so low, farmers and ranchers can't afford new equipment. All of them seem to be fixing what they have and trying to make do to get through another season."

Worry spread across Edith's face. "How bad is it?"

"I have three large payments to major vendors next week and I'm not sure how I'm going to pay even one of them. I'll probably have to go talk to our friendly banker and take out a loan. I hate to take on more indebtedness with the economy this shaky, but I don't see any other way to handle it."

"Maybe if you talk to the vendors, they'll accept partial payment for a month or two."

"I tried that. They said I have to pay in full or they will be forced to cut off all sales to me until the entire bill is paid. They are key suppliers; I can't be without their products."

"I guess you don't have any other choice than to see Rick at First National. He always treated us fairly during the recession of the late seventies."

Bob rose from the kitchen table, rinsed out his cup, and set it in the sink. "I better get back to the store. I told Nancy I wouldn't be gone long. She's been such an encouragement for me. I don't know how I'd ever have gotten along without her."

Edith spent the remainder of the morning reading the *Rocky Bluff Herald*. The silence of the empty house was relaxing as she stretched out in her favorite chair, and it wasn't long before she dozed off with the paper across her chest. Promptly at twelve o'clock she was awakened when the back door banged.

"Is that you, Roy?"

Roy wiped his feet on the doormat, crossed the kitchen and living room with several long strides, and planted a kiss on his drowsy wife's forehead. "How's my lovely bride? I hope you've had a chance to rest from your exciting evening last night."

"Hi, dear. I guess you caught me napping," Edith sleepily replied. "I'm doing great. Bob came over a little while this morning. It seems the whole town is talking about Larry's arrest."

"I'm sure they are. By the way, while I was working at the crisis center this morning Teresa called. She was concerned how you were doing and didn't want to bother you in case you were resting."

"I'm glad everyone's concerned, but people worry too much about me," Edith assured him. "I'm fine. There's not much the Lord and I can't handle together. Did she say how Libby was doing?"

"Except for being covered with bruises, she'll be okay. However, Teresa would like you to call her sometime this afternoon." Roy paused a moment and then chuckled. "I think she needs some of your motherly advice."

"She's a good social worker. I'm sure I can't tell her anything that she doesn't already know."

"I take it last night's experience really unnerved her. She asked me to let her know the next time we have a training program for volunteers at the crisis center. She believes that training would be invaluable for her."

"It would be good for anybody," Edith reminded him, as she remembered how valuable her training had been. "Textbook learning can only do so much. It might help if Teresa spent a few weekend evenings answering the crisis line. You get a totally different image of life in Rocky Bluff than from what you observe on Main Street during the daytime."

"That's true. Few people realize the heartache that goes on behind closed doors." Roy glanced toward the kitchen clock. "Edith, I bet you haven't had anything to eat yet. Why don't you let me fix you a tuna salad sandwich?"

"That sounds good. While you're doing that, I'll warm up a can of tomato soup."

After lunch Edith dialed and waited.

"Hello."

"Hello, Teresa. This is Edith. How are you doing today?"

"I'm fine, but more importantly, how are you? You had quite a fright last night."

Edith smiled. "My blood pressure is back to normal and I had a good rest this morning. How's Libby doing?"

"Outside of being black-and-blue, she's going to be okay physically. However, I'm really concerned about her emotional stability. She bears many of the classic symptoms of spousal abuse. Her self-esteem is at rock bottom and she seems to think she deserved it."

"That's too bad," Edith responded as she imagined the pain Libby must be experiencing. "However, even though it looks pretty bleak now, nothing is too difficult for God to heal."

"That's what impressed her the most about you. . . . Your faith in God is unshakable." Teresa hesitated. "That's the area I feel the most limited to talk about and Libby kept asking questions. I was wondering if you'd have some free time when I could bring her over so you could answer some of her questions."

"I promised my grandchildren they could come over and play Monopoly this afternoon. Jay and Dawn are hard to turn down. Could we make it tomorrow afternoon?"

Teresa giggled. "I didn't think kids played Monopoly anymore."

"They do at my house. I'm not into video games, yet."

"Edith, I'm taking Libby some disposable diapers this afternoon. I'll see if tomorrow will be okay with her."

"I'm looking forward to meeting with her. If there's anything more I can do to help, please let me know."

"You've done more than your share. However, I get the feeling Libby is going to be turning to you more and more. She was very impressed with the love you and Roy have for each other and can't understand why she and Larry can't have the same."

Promptly at two o'clock the next afternoon, Teresa's Chevy Capri stopped in front of the Dutton residence. Edith watched out of her front window as Libby unfastened Vanessa from the car seat and joined Teresa on the sidewalk. Her heart sank as she observed the dejected slump in the young woman's walk. *Poor self-esteem is written all over her,* Edith mused.

"Welcome. Do come in out of the cold," Edith greeted as she flung open the door before Teresa had a chance to reach for the doorbell.

The two women stepped into the entryway. "Edith, it's good to see you again," Teresa said as she automatically wiped her shoes on the doormat. "I'd love to stay, but I have a few errands to run. I'll be back in about an hour. You two have a nice visit."

"I'm sure we will," Edith responded as she opened the hall closet and took out a coat hanger for Libby. "I'll have the coffeepot on when you get back."

Teresa shut the door quietly behind her as Edith turned her attention to the baby in her mother's arms. "Libby, may I hold Vanessa while you take your coat off?"

Libby handed the baby to the older woman, hung her coat in the open closet, and glanced around the room. "You have a lovely home. It has so much warmth and charm. I don't think I'll ever have a decent home of my own. I can't even keep a husband."

Edith gulped. Right away she was searching for the right words. "Libby, what happened last night was not your fault. Larry has never been able to handle stress. He's like the person who's angry with his boss and feels he can't do anything about it so he takes it out on his innocent dog when he gets home."

"Yeah, I know what you mean," Libby sighed. "Every once in awhile I see Larry kicking our dog, Ralph. The poor thing just looks up at him with his big brown eyes that say, 'What did I do to you?' "

"I'm afraid Larry treats you the same way he treats Ralph. Beating on you is merely a way for him to relieve stress."

"But I so wanted our marriage to work." Libby bit her lip. "I did everything I could think of to make him happy, but it still wasn't enough."

"I'm sure you did," Edith sympathized. Sensing the conversation was about to become intense, Edith motioned toward the door at the side of the room. "Let's go to the kitchen; I seem to have my best conversations around my kitchen table."

"Vanessa is acting sleepy. Do you have a place I can lay her down?"

Edith smiled as she remembered other young mothers, such as Beth Slater, who found their way to her kitchen table while their babies slept on a blanket folded up in the corner of the living room. She reached into her closet and took out a faded quilt. "Vanessa should be comfortable in this corner and we can watch her from the kitchen," she said as she spread the quilt on the floor.

While the baby slept peacefully, the two women sipped on their coffee. "Libby, it's very natural that you have mixed feelings toward Larry. You have good reason to be angry for how much he hurt you both physically and emotionally. I'm sure the emotional pain is far worse than the physical abuse you took."

Libby took a Kleenex from her purse. "It was awful. He would claim he loved me one minute and be shouting at me and insulting me the next. He was always angry about something."

"Honey, the most important thing you'll need to do in your relationship with Larry is try to understand what is actually your problem and what is his," Edith comforted with her typical maternal instinct.

"It just seems like one massive problem to me, not part his and part mine."

Edith surveyed the tear-filled eyes of her young guest. "It will probably seem that way for awhile, but little by little you'll look at a particular situation and say, 'That's Larry's problem and I can't do anything about it.' Other times you'll be able to say, 'That's my problem and I can do something about it.'"

Libby thought a moment, sighed, and then smiled. "I guess you're right. I really can't help it when he forgets where he left his tools when he's fixing the car. But somehow I've been led to believe that it's my responsibility to always have everything available for him whenever he wants them."

"You're learning fast," Edith assured her as she poured another cup of coffee. "You're off to a good start and there are many great things ahead for you."

The hour passed quickly as Libby unloaded her fears and doubts to the retired home economics teacher. It wasn't long before Teresa was ringing the doorbell. At the first buzz, Vanessa awoke with a whimper as Edith went to answer the door.

"Teresa, do come in. We still have a little coffee left in the pot," Edith greeted as she motioned for the social worker to enter.

"Thanks. I'm sure you two had a good visit. I'm sorry it took longer than I expected. The traffic was terrible and the lines were long. The usual routine."

"No problem. We did have a good visit. I know it's difficult for Libby at the shelter without transportation, but do you think someone could bring her to see me every two or three days? We have so much we want to talk about."

"That shouldn't be a problem. We have a good crew of volunteers, especially Sonya and Patricia. Most of them have been right where Libby is today. They know what it's like to be abused and are anxious to help others in the same situations."

Teresa followed Edith into the kitchen. "I will take you up on your offer for a cup of coffee," she said as she pulled out a chair and sat down. "There is something we need to discuss with Libby."

The young mother picked up her baby from her makeshift bed in the corner and followed the others to the kitchen. A frightened, bewildered look spread across her face. *This must be serious. I must be in a lot of trouble now,* she thought.

Sensing her concern, Teresa reached over and patted her shoulder. "Relax. Everything's working out for the best. You just have a decision to make."

Libby gave a weak smile as she returned to the chair she had just left. "I don't know if I'm up to making a rational decision now or not."

"We're here to help you," Edith assured her as she refilled Libby's cup.

Teresa took a deep breath while she studied the frightened girl's face. "I saw Sergeant Mooney this afternoon. He'd just been out to the shelter to talk with you, but of course you were gone. Anyway, he needs to know by tonight whether you want to press assault and battery charges against Larry."

Libby's face whitened. "If I press charges, he'll try to take Vanessa away from me."

Teresa gulped. "Even though he'll probably be out on bail in a few days, there's no chance that he could get custody at this point since he has violated parole," she assured Libby. "Vanessa is still nursing and must have her mother."

Silence enveloped the room as Libby remained deep in thought. "I think I still love him; I don't want him to go to jail."

"You would not be the one who sends him to jail, that's a decision for the judge," Edith assured her. "Larry knew drinking alcoholic beverages was against his parole. That was his decision and not yours."

"But what good would it accomplish if I did press charges?"

"The decision is entirely yours," Teresa assured her. "The important thing is that you will never again be abused. No woman deserves that kind of treatment."

Libby again paused before she spoke. "Larry doesn't know how to control his temper. I wonder if there is some way he could learn how to do that without having to go to jail."

"The mental health clinic does provide training in stress management. We might suggest that Larry be required to attend," the social worker explained. "But again, it's the judge's decision."

"I'm really scared to live with him. . .but I don't want to press charges . . .I don't want to go back home, but I don't have anywhere else to go."

"You and Vanessa can stay at the shelter for up to a month. During that time we'll see that you find a place to stay. We'll help you get government assistance and obtain training or employment."

Libby gasped as a smile spread across her face. "You mean you'd do all that for me? I don't deserve it."

"Of course you do," Edith quickly replied. "The only requirement is that after others have helped you, it will be your turn to pass it on."

"That's right," Teresa agreed. "All the volunteers of the spouse abuse center once came to us as victims. Many of the crisis center volunteers once struggled with difficult problems themselves. It's their way of passing help on to others."

"If they can do it, so can I." Libby snuggled her baby to her chest. "However, I don't think I could live with myself if I pressed charges against Vanessa's father. As long as he never hurts me again, I think I'll be able to forgive him."

Chapter 3

"Good afternoon. May I help you?" Bob asked as he approached a middle-aged couple standing in the middle of a section of snow blowers.

"Hello, Mr. Harkness. I'm just pricing snow blowers. Mine gave out during the last blizzard and I can't decide whether to have it fixed or buy a new one."

Bob gulped as he recognized Donald and Frances Reynolds. *I wanted to find a way to help Larry and here I am face-to-face with his parents. I hope I'll be able to encourage them instead of hurting them any more than they already are.*

"Mr. Reynolds, now is a good time to buy. We have a midwinter sale on all winter equipment."

Donald silently walked through the row of snow blowers and examined the price tags. "This one's not bad. Could I buy it on time? Things are kind of tight at the ranch right now."

Bob's mind raced. *I'm not making any money at all with this sale and selling anything on credit only makes it worse, but I've got to turn over this inventory in order to get at least a little cash flow.*

"How about seventy-five a month until it's paid off at 9 percent?"

Donald rubbed his chin and then looked at Frances. She nodded in the affirmative.

"Mr. Harkness, I do appreciate you doing this for us. Things are pretty tough right now," Frances said weakly.

"Do call me Bob," the storeowner insisted. "I sympathize with what your family is going through. If there is anything I can do to help, please let me know."

"Your family has already done so much to help. I know Larry doesn't see it this way, but your mother has stepped in twice and kept him from getting in even more trouble. If she hadn't protected Libby last night, who knows what Larry would have done to her."

"I'll admit my mother is one brave lady, but we both believe that Larry has a lot of potential. Hopefully, he can work out his problems before he destroys himself."

"I'm glad that someone else believes in him," Frances smiled. "Most people act like we're crazy to take another mortgage on the ranch to bail him out of jail. Even Rick at First National thought long and hard before he signed the papers, but we just can't give up on him despite what he's done. After all, he is still our son."

"With God's help anyone can change no matter what they've done," Bob assured her. "I wish there were some way I could befriend Larry. I'm sure he feels the entire world is against him now."

"He's felt that way since his senior year in high school," Donald replied. "After his scholarship to Montana A&M was canceled because of smoking pot after the state basketball tournament, his entire world seemed to fall apart."

"We're going to be picking him up from the jail later this afternoon. We'll tell him about your offer. I'm sure he'll appreciate it."

That afternoon Frances and Donald Reynolds walked into the Little Big Horn County courthouse in Rocky Bluff and went directly to the Clerk of Court's office with a five-thousand-dollar check in their hands. The paperwork for Larry's bail was processed quickly, and within a few minutes the Reynoldses were face-to-face with their son.

Larry's face was tense and pale as he approached his parents. "Hello, Mom. . .Dad. Thanks for posting bond. That jail is definitely not a nice place to be. I didn't sleep all night. There were all kinds of weird things going on. I don't deserve to be in a place like that."

"Those were pretty serious charges brought against you," Donald reminded him gently. "Sergeant Mooney doesn't take lightly to parole violation. I guess you're fortunate that Libby didn't press assault and battery charges against you."

"Son, why don't you come back to the ranch and stay with us until your case comes to trial? The fresh, clean air will do you good." Frances choked back her tears.

Larry remained silent as the threesome walked slowly to the family Bronco. They felt eyes from every store around the town square peering out at them. Larry slid into the backseat as his father started the engine of the four-wheel drive. "Going home with you sounds like a good idea. I can't stand this stinking town any longer. Let's go by my house and I'll get some of my clothes and Ralph. I'm sure Ryan would like to help care for him."

Donald smiled as he watched his older son's face in the rearview mirror. "Your little brother will be glad to do that. He's always thought Ralph was the most intelligent dog in the world and he's wanted to spend enough time with him to teach him to do tricks."

"Before I forget to tell you," Frances began hesitantly, "we stopped in Harkness Hardware Store earlier today to get a new snow blower. Bob Harkness said to tell you if there's anything he can do to help, you let him know."

"Humfff," Larry scowled as he slammed his fist against the seat. "I wouldn't accept help from him if he was the last person on earth. Because of his mother, I've spent time in jail twice. That entire family is my enemy, not someone I'd want to be friends with."

The Reynoldses finished their drive to the younger man's home in silence. Words could not express the confused emotions they were each feeling. Larry hurriedly packed his clothes, tools, stereo, and TV. As he was loading the Bronco, he noticed the two dog dishes on the back stoop. *Good grief, Ralph hasn't had anything to eat or drink for twenty-four hours.*

"Ralph!!! Here Ralph!!!" Larry picked up the half-empty bag of dog food from the back porch and carried it to his father's car. "Where could that dumb dog be?" He glanced toward the garage and there was his mixed-variety mutt slithering toward him with his tail between his legs.

"Hello there, old buddy. I bet you're kind of thirsty." Larry patted his mangy dog and put some water in his dish from the outside water spigot.

"Dad, do you and Mom want to go on ahead of me? I'll follow you in my car. I want to give Ralph a chance to eat something first."

An hour later Larry pulled his Maverick into the familiar homestead. Ryan ran outside to greet him. Larry had never noticed before how much his little brother had grown to look like him since he'd gotten into junior high. "Hi," Ryan shouted. "Do you have Ralph with you?"

"I sure do," Larry answered as he alighted from his car with Ralph close on his heels. "I sure do. In fact, I have a deal I want to make with you. If you'll promise to take good care of him, I'll let you have him. I'm going to be too busy trying to get my family back."

"Hey, thanks! That's great!" Ryan exclaimed. Then he stopped and looked at his older brother with puzzlement. "What do you mean you want to get your family back? I thought they threw you in the slammer for beating your wife."

"Just for your information, little brother, I still love her and the baby, and I'm going to get them back, regardless of what I have to do."

"Boy, that's a strange way to show love."

"There's a lot of things you'll never understand. There's two things I'm going to do. . . ." Larry paused as if he were talking more to himself than to his brother. "I'm going to get my family back and I'm going to get even with the Harkness family."

Ryan's face whitened as he saw his brother in a totally different light. "But you can't do that. Jay's my best friend."

Late the next week Bob stopped at his mother's house on his way home from work. Roy, Edith, and Bob exchanged pleasantries and made themselves comfortable in the living room before Bob came to the point of his visit.

"Well. . .the worst has happened," Bob faltered before continuing. "Rick turned down my loan. He said it wasn't anything personal, but because of the recession and low farm prices, I'm no longer a good credit risk."

Edith looked stunned. "This is the first time in history Harkness Hardware has been disapproved for credit. . .but then, it is the first time in history that the farm economy has been this bad."

"The farmers are really hurting. The only major piece of equipment I've sold all month was a snow blower to Donald Reynolds. But I had to sell it on credit, so it didn't help my cash flow at all. On top of my three main vendors screaming at me for money, I have a large insurance premium due next month. I just don't know what I'm going to do. I have to maintain fire insurance or my entire mortgage becomes due."

Wrinkles began to deepen on Edith's face. "The only thing I can think of is to pray," Edith replied. "There has to be a way out of this, but I'm afraid I don't have an easy answer to your dilemma."

The trio stared out the window in silence for several minutes before Roy tried to move the conversation to a more pleasant subject. "How's Jay adjusting to junior high this year? I can't believe he's grown as much as he has in the last few months."

The topic of his two children, Jay and Dawn, was usually enough to bring a smile to Bob's face and provoke several minutes of bragging of their latest accomplishments, but all he could say was, "That's the sad part. That store is the only means I have to support those kids, and it won't be much longer before they'll be looking at going to college. Nancy may have to get a job outside of keeping the store books just to support the family. It really hurts my pride to even consider that."

To help reduce the gloom that settled over the Duttons' living room, Bob succumbed to Roy's lead and began talking about the children. Anything to keep from thinking about the "what ifs" of life.

Every other day either Sonya or Patricia would bring Libby to Edith's home and then leave for an hour and a half before returning to take her back to the shelter. Libby and Edith's conversations covered everything from Libby's early life, parenthood, her relationship with Larry, faith in God, and the love and forgiveness offered through Jesus Christ. No subject was off limits for discussion.

"I've been at the shelter for nearly three weeks now, and I feel I'm over the hump and can begin looking for an apartment," Libby confided to Edith as she balanced Vanessa on her knee. "Teresa has helped me apply for welfare, and we are looking into different programs so that I can support myself and Vanessa."

"I'm glad to hear you're so optimistic," Edith replied. "Since you began to realize how much Christ loves you, your self-esteem has skyrocketed. I'm sure you'll go far in life."

"I still kind of wish it could be with Larry, but I'm never going to let myself be abused again."

Edith poured Libby and herself another cup of coffee. "You're being very wise. Before you can have a successful marriage, both parties have to be emotionally and spiritually healed. One person cannot do it by themselves." Just then the doorbell rang. Edith hurried across the living room and opened the door. Sonya was beaming from ear to ear.

"Come in, Sonya. You look like you're bursting with good news."

"I am," the young woman replied as she stepped into the entryway. "Libby is still here, isn't she?"

"Oh yes, we were just starting our second cup of coffee. Would you care to join us?"

"I'd love to."

Sonya handed her coat to Edith, who quickly hung it in the hall closet. The young woman followed Edith into her kitchen, where Libby was sitting with a puzzled look on her face.

"Sonya, you're back early."

"Yes, and I have some great news," Sonya replied as she made herself comfortable at the end of the table. "I just ran into a friend of mine, Pam Claiborne, and she is getting married next week and will be moving out of her apartment. She has a real cute place over on Ash Street. It's kind of small, but it would be just perfect for you and Vanessa."

Libby's eyes lit up, then she hesitated. "It sounds terrific, but I can't afford even the first month's rent, much less a deposit."

"This apartment complex is approved for Section Eight, which means the amount of rent you pay is based on your income. I'm sure we can work something out. Pam can show you the place today if you'd like."

"Libby," Edith inserted, "our church has a fund to help those who have special needs. While you and Sonya go look at the place, I'll give Pastor Rhodes a call and see if he can help. You can repay the fund when you get back on your feet."

"That's a great idea," Sonya said. "Edith, would you mind if I use your phone to give Pam a call? I want to tell her we'll be right over."

Sonya's conversation with Pam was short. The two young women slipped into their coats and Libby hurriedly put Vanessa in her snowsuit and grabbed her diaper bag. This could be a major turning point in her life.

The following Saturday the young adult's group from the church gathered to help Libby move into her new apartment. When Libby returned to her former home on Frontage Road, she was relieved to discover that Larry had not taken the furniture. Mixed feelings flooded her. *Is this a new beginning in my life or just the end of a marriage? I have no choice but to go through with this. I know I can't afford the rent on this house any longer and it's obvious that Larry just walked away and abandoned it.*

At the end of the day tears filled Libby's eyes as she surveyed her new living room cluttered with boxes. "How can I thank you for helping me this way?" she told the small band of new friends.

Patricia smiled. "We've all been in situations where we needed another's help. This group has helped me move at least twice. We meet every Wednesday night for study and old-fashioned fun. I hope you'll be able to join us. We even provide baby-sitters for those who need them."

"I. . .I don't know what to say," Libby stammered. "Nobody has ever helped me before. You've all been so good to me. I'd love to come."

"Good. I'll pick you up around seven o'clock Wednesday," Patricia replied.

The next two weeks went quickly for Libby as she unpacked boxes, hung pictures, and settled into her new apartment. Her visits with Edith became less frequent.

Late Friday night, the phone rang at the Dutton residence. "Hello," Edith greeted as she pushed her gray-flecked, black hair away from her ear.

"Hello, Edith. This is Libby. I'm sorry to call so late, but I didn't know what else to do. I'm really scared."

"What's the matter, Libby?"

"Larry must have found out where I live because he's been in front of the apartment in his red Maverick all afternoon. When I walked to the grocery store, he followed me. He waited outside and followed me home."

Wrinkles appeared in Edith's forehead. "Did he say anything to you?"

"All he said was, 'I'm going to get Vanessa.' I won't let anyone take my baby away from me."

"Libby, Montana has just passed some very strong antistalking laws. Is Larry still in front of your house?"

Libby pulled the drapes back a few inches. "Yes, he's still there. I wonder if he'll ever leave."

"I'll give Sergeant Mooney a call and see if he can come and have him move on. Also, tomorrow you may need to have a restraining order drawn up to keep Larry from bothering you and Vanessa," Edith replied.

"How do I do that? I can't afford an attorney."

"We can give Legal Services a call tomorrow. They take cases for those who can't afford regular legal fees. Maybe Sonya or Patricia could give you a ride. I'll talk to you tomorrow about that. Right now we better hang up so I can call Sergeant Mooney. Call me in a few minutes if Larry is still there. In the meantime, make sure all your windows and doors are locked."

Chapter 4

A Rocky Bluff police car cruised quietly down Ash Street toward the Forest Grove Apartments. Sure enough, a red Ford Maverick with a man slouched behind the wheel was parked in front of the complex. Sergeant Mooney stopped his car behind the Ford and cautiously approached the driver.

"Larry, would you mind getting out of your car and talking with me?" Sergeant Mooney asked.

The young man moaned, shrugged his shoulders, and grudgingly stepped from his car.

"I haven't done anything. I was just sitting here taking a rest. There's no law against that."

"That depends," the police officer replied as he surveyed both the car and the suspect. "What are you doing here?"

"I told you, I was just taking a nap."

"Aw, come on, Larry. You know Libby is living in the Forest Grove Apartments. Were you wanting to see her?"

"It would be nice to see my wife and baby again. No one has the right to split up our family."

"It's been reported to us that you have been following Libby wherever she goes."

"That's not true!" Larry shouted as he slammed his fist into the side of his car. "I've kept my distance from her. I've just been interested in what she's been doing."

Sergeant Mooney took a deep breath. "I must advise you that the state of Montana has very strict antistalking laws. Therefore, you'll have to stay away from this part of Ash Street and make no attempt to see Libby. Otherwise, I'll have to file charges against you."

"That's not fair. I have a right to see them."

"Libby has been advised to see an attorney and obtain a restraining order to keep you away from her and Vanessa."

"And who advised her to do that?" Larry demanded. "I suppose it was that Dutton woman again. She's always meddling in my affairs."

"Whom Libby talks with is no concern of yours. You need to worry about keeping your nose clean while you're on probation. The judge doesn't look kindly on anyone who makes trouble during probation. Now get in your car and go on home. I don't want to receive another report of you being near these apartments."

Larry opened the door, slipped behind the wheel, and intentionally made his tires throw gravel as he sped away. Philip Mooney shook his head with disgust. *Will Larry ever accept responsibility for his behavior and quit blaming others for his problems?*

As Larry cruised the streets of Rocky Bluff, his anger escalated. *I've got to put a stop to that old lady's continual interference with my life. If she's going to interfere with my family, I'll just interfere with hers.*

As he turned onto Main Street, his eyes fell upon a sign in front of a local prominent business. He steered his car into an empty parking space in front of Harkness Hardware Store. Ignoring the expired parking meter, he stormed toward the door, forcing other pedestrians to move out of his way.

"Is Bob Harkness here?" Larry demanded of the attractive woman behind the counter.

Nancy Harkness gulped as she recognized the disturbed young man. "He's working in the storeroom if you'd like to go on back."

Not waiting for her to finish her sentence, Larry charged toward the back of the store. Bob was mixing paint in the side room when Larry burst through the swinging doors. Larry paused for a moment, not knowing what to say. He wandered aimlessly around and began picking up antique bottles and jars, which were on display in the corner. Confusion and rage enveloped him. This seemingly kind family was ruining his life.

Finally, Bob heard the tinkle of glass when Larry replaced a jar onto the shelf. "Well, hello, Larry. It's good to see you. What brings you here today? I was hoping we could get together sometime."

"Yeah, sure," Larry grunted. "My mother told me you wanted to help me. Well, if you want to help me, keep your mother from interfering in my personal life. What my family and I do is none of her business."

"Larry, we are all concerned for you, Libby, and the baby. We just want to have what's best for all of you. Mother has a very soft heart for young people who are hurting."

"Oh garbage. She's just a meddlesome old busybody. I want you to tell her to quit talking to Libby. She's filling her mind full of ridiculous ideas and trying to keep us apart. If she doesn't stop interfering in my life, I'll have to do something drastic."

Bob's face turned ashen as he recalled the painful physical and emotional scars Larry's attack on the high school principal had left on his

146

mother. "Larry, just don't do anything to get yourself in more trouble. You're very upset now. I don't know what has happened, but why don't you sit down and tell me all about it."

"Forget it," he sneered. "Just tell your mother to quit talking with Libby, or else. . . ." With that Larry turned and stomped toward the front and out the door.

Nancy rushed toward her husband. "Do you think he'll try to make good on his threat? I've never seen so much built-up anger in my life."

"Nah," Bob tried to assure her. "He's just blowing off steam. He's all talk. He'll cool off in a little while."

"I sure hope you're right. I don't take threats like that lightly. Are you going to tell your mother that he was here?"

"No, I don't want to worry her and I sure wouldn't want to discourage her from helping Libby. She's doing such a fantastic job with her. I'm sure everything will be okay."

❧

Unaware of Larry's threatening encounter with Bob the day before, Libby joined Edith in her kitchen for coffee and encouragement.

"Have you given any more thought about getting a restraining order to keep Larry away from you?" Edith queried. "I'm sure Stuart Leonard at Legal Services could draw up the paperwork for you. He's a fine young attorney."

"I've been thinking about it a lot since I talked to you yesterday. Soon after I hung up I saw Sergeant Mooney drive up. He was talking to Larry for awhile. Larry really appeared angry and was slamming his fist against the side of his car. He then got in his car and sped away. He hasn't been back since."

Edith surveyed Libby's face with concern. She understood how difficult it was for Libby to take a stand against Larry even when her personal safety was in jeopardy. "I wonder how long he'll stay away? A day? A week?"

"As stern as Sergeant Mooney looked, I bet he scared him off, but I don't want to take any chances. I'll make an appointment with Legal Services tomorrow."

"That's a good idea," Edith reminded her. "If circumstances change, you can always have a restraining order lifted."

Libby sighed. "At least I'm not doing something that can't be undone." She stared out the window at the buds that were beginning to appear on the bare elm tree. The encased buds seemed to give her a ray of hope. Soon new leaves would be springing forth. *I feel like those buds. I want to break out of my shell and make something beautiful of myself like the elm leaves do.*

"Edith, the other day you talked to me about going back to school and getting some training. At the time I didn't think I was smart enough to, but I think I'd like to give it a try. How do I go about it? I'm not sure what I even want to do."

"What are some things you're interested in?" Edith asked as she poured the young woman another cup of coffee.

"Well. . .this may sound kind of strange, but since Larry has been in so much trouble with the law, I've been fascinated with the law shows on TV. I even stay up late at night to watch the old Perry Mason reruns. But I know I'd never be able to be a lawyer."

"Have you ever considered becoming a paralegal? Lawyers can't function without them."

"That might have possibilities, but I don't know how I'd ever be able to pay for it."

"They have all kinds of grants and scholarships available for those who attend Rocky Bluff Community College. Teresa keeps abreast on all the different programs available. Why don't we give her a call and ask her to come over?"

"Sure," Libby said with a smile. "Can I use your phone? I have her number memorized by now."

Libby took the phone and dialed the familiar number. There was a long pause as Libby waited impatiently for a response.

"Hello."

"Hello, Teresa. This is Libby. How are you today?"

"I'm doing great and you?"

"Things have really changed since I got my own apartment. Why I called is I'm here at Edith's now and we were wondering if you were free and could come over for a few minutes."

"I'd love to. Just give me a few minutes to freshen up. I'll be there in a half-hour."

Edith and Libby chatted and played with Vanessa as they waited for Teresa. When Teresa arrived, the three women made small talk over cookies and coffee before coming to the point of the meeting.

"Teresa, Edith said you're familiar with different assistance programs that I might qualify for so that I could attend college."

"Familiarity of assistance programs is part of my responsibilities as head of the spouse abuse center. Career training is an important aspect in helping abused women get on their feet again. Is there a particular field you're interested in?"

"I'm wondering if I'm smart enough to become a paralegal."

"Of course you're smart enough. When you get back in the studying mode, your self-confidence will come back. The main concern is supporting yourself and Vanessa. Social Services has several programs that can help with living expenses and child care. Also, the county bar association provides several grants every year for those interested in paralegal studies. I don't think they've all been claimed for this past school year."

Libby beamed as her thoughts turned inward. *There may be hope for me yet. I might be able to make it on my own without Larry.* "How soon do you think I could start?"

"Right now," Teresa assured her. "Registration for spring quarter is next week. You could begin by taking a lighter load to get back in the swing of things. Then with a couple courses in the summer, by fall you'll be able to lead the pack."

Tears filled Libby's eyes. "Do you really think so?"

"Of course I do," Teresa responded, giving Libby a hug as Edith looked on with pleasure.

<hr/>

For the next few days Edith was busy with projects in the church and entertaining her grandchildren after school. However, after four days without hearing from Libby, she began to wonder if Libby had given up on her plans to attend college and was afraid to tell her. Her concerns were removed when her phone rang late Friday afternoon.

"Hello, Edith. This is Libby. I've been meaning to call you for the last few days, but I've been extremely busy."

"I'm glad to hear from you. How are things going?"

"Great. I have all the paperwork filled out for college. I was able to get financial assistance and I register for classes next week. My only problem is I can't find anyone to take care of Vanessa while I go to class. All the daycares are full and no one wants a child for only a few hours a week. You know lots of people in town. Do you know anyone who might be interested?"

Edith thought for a moment. "This may be a long shot and you might not like this idea at all, but I have a young friend who is a teenage mother. She's doing an excellent job with her baby and is trying to get on her feet the same as you are. Would you be interested in meeting her?"

"Sure. If she's nice maybe we can help each other. I qualify for subsidized childcare, so I'll be able to pay the going rate in the community. How can I get in touch with her?"

"Her name is Beth Slater. I met her via the crisis center. I'll give her a call and maybe she could come over Monday afternoon and the two of you could meet."

"That sounds good to me. Call me when you find out if she can come and I'll see if Sonya wouldn't mind driving me over on her way to aerobics class."

Monday afternoon Beth Slater knocked on the door of the Dutton residence. Edith eagerly flung the door open and greeted her with a warm hug as she motioned for her to enter.

"Beth, it's good to see you again. It's been too long since we've gotten together. I hardly recognize little Jeffy."

Beth smiled as she stood her toddler on his feet and removed the coat from his chubby shoulders. "I don't think you've seen him since he began walking. He's become a regular terror on two legs."

"He looks perfectly healthy and happy. I'm so proud of the care you've taken of him."

"The parenting classes you suggested were extremely helpful. Plus, I'm going to get my high school diploma in May. By taking those special classes I was able to catch up with my classmates. I'll graduate a week after my eighteenth birthday. I'm so glad you were on the crisis line the first night I called. I never would have gotten my life together without you."

Edith hung Beth's coat in the hall closet and motioned to follow her to the kitchen. "I have another friend coming over in a few minutes whom I'd like you to meet. She has many of the same challenges you have. Right now she's getting ready to attend the community college."

"Sounds great to me. I've been so busy taking care of Jeffy that I haven't had any time for a social life."

"She is looking for someone to take care of her seven-month-old baby while she attends class. All the daycares are either full or won't take children for only a few hours a week."

Beth raised her eyebrows. "Would it be a paying job?"

"Of course," Edith assured her. "She'll be getting government assistance to help with child care while she goes to classes. She can pay the going rate for day care. Are you interested?"

The young mother beamed. "Sure. This would be my first paying job. I like the idea of being able to pay some of my own expenses. I've had to be on ADC for so long."

"Good. Libby should be here any time. She has a beautiful baby girl named Vanessa. She'll win your heart immediately."

Just then the doorbell rang. Edith moved to the front door as quickly as she could. "Libby, please come in. Beth is anxious to meet you and little Vanessa."

Libby hung her coat in the hall closet as she had so many times before and followed Edith to the kitchen.

"Libby, this is Beth Slater and Jeffy. Beth, I'd like you to meet Libby Reynolds and Vanessa," Edith said as she motioned for Libby to have a chair.

"Hi, Libby. You have an adorable baby."

"Thanks," Libby grinned and turned to inspect Beth's baby. "Jeffy is a real sweetheart with those big brown eyes."

"You wouldn't be any relation to Larry Reynolds, would you?" Beth asked innocently.

Libby flashed a look of embarrassed panic at Edith before she answered. "Yes, he's my husband. . .we're separated right now."

"Oh, I'm sorry. I didn't mean to pry," Beth replied meekly. "I had a friend who said that when she was in junior high, Larry was always her hero. He was talented in all sports, good looking, and had a neat sense of humor. She had him up on such a high pedestal that she was devastated when he shot the principal."

"Larry's had many inner struggles. He's such a neat guy and I think I still love him, but I don't dare live with him until he works out his problems. I'm afraid he'll hurt me or Vanessa."

"I hope things work out for you. I know raising a baby by yourself and trying to study is pretty hard."

"Right now I'm trying to find someone to watch Vanessa three mornings a week while I go to class. I'm at the point of no child care, no class."

"I take classes for my high school diploma in the evening and I'd love to take care of Vanessa for you."

The girls began exchanging details of their lives and situations, and before the afternoon was over, both were on their way to becoming close friends. Edith sat back and smiled at the mutual support and encouragement they were able to give each other. Mature encouragement was vital in both their circumstances, but the encouragement of a peer in the same circumstances helped to fill a void in both their lives.

Chapter 5

The crocuses were in full bloom beside the front steps of Edith Dutton's home as Sonya Turner rang the front doorbell. She nervously tightened her scarf against the crisp spring winds.

"Hello, Sonya. Please come in," the former home economics teacher greeted as she thrust open the storm door. "We haven't had a chance to visit since Libby moved into her own apartment."

"Hi, Edith. I'm glad you could see me on such short notice. Your reputation of being the problem-solver of Rocky Bluff is getting around."

Edith chuckled as she hung Sonya's coat in the hall closet. "I'm sure there are others who would describe me differently. Larry Reynolds describes me as a meddlesome old lady."

"I bet someday he'll learn to respect you the way the rest of us do," Sonya assured her.

"Why don't you join me in the kitchen for a cup of coffee? I have a feeling you came over for more than just a casual visit."

Sonya obediently followed her into the bright, airy kitchen. "Yes," she hesitated, "I do need some personal advice. You're pretty good at reading people."

"Comes with experience," Edith chuckled. "Now why don't you tell me about it?" Edith poured the coffee and sat the pot between them.

"Remember Pam Claiborne, who was living in the apartment that Libby moved into?"

"I've never met her, but I've heard a lot of good things about her. Didn't she marry Ed Summer, the new music teacher?"

"Oh, yes. And she's been floating on cloud nine ever since. You'd think she was the only woman who has ever been in love," Sonya giggled.

Edith wrinkled her forehead. "So where is the problem?"

"Pam has just begun selling Beautiful You Cosmetics and she's trying to arrange as many makeup parties as possible. I'd really like to help her, but my apartment is too small. Since I'm working all day, I don't know many people to invite."

"Now that is one of the easiest problems I've been asked to solve. I have plenty of space here and I know quite a few young women about your age. Why don't we turn this into a real get-acquainted event?"

"Pam says a makeup party works best if there are between eight and ten guests. I can only think of Libby and Patricia to invite. Can you think of any others?"

"Do you know Beth Slater? She's taking care of Libby's baby while Libby attends classes. And Libby told me about her new friend, Liz, who lives across the hall from her. Maybe she would like to invite her." Edith paused for a moment as she stared out the window. "What about Patricia's sister, Jenny?"

Sonya beamed. "We're now up to seven. There's a lady at work that I know. Her name is Joan. Maybe she would like to come and bring her friend, Kristen, with her."

"Well, that's our guest list," Edith responded. "Now when do you want to have the party?"

"I'll have to clear it with Pam, of course, but how about a week from Wednesday?"

"Sounds good to me. I'll make one of my specialties for dessert."

"I can't let you do that," Sonya protested. "I'll bring the refreshments. It's enough that you provide the place for us to meet."

The two women chatted about Sonya's job and mutual acquaintances for another half-hour and then Sonya hurried to the spouse abuse center, where she was scheduled to work for the evening. Edith watched through her picture window as she drove away. *It's so uplifting to have the younger women find their way to my kitchen table. When I retired I was certain I would live in isolation with only friends from the senior citizen's center.*

The days passed swiftly before the scheduled makeup party. The Saturday before the party Edith hired Hilda to clean the house for her. It was going to be fun to have a houseful of young women along with their babies gathered in her home. With a houseful of women coming, however, Roy decided Wednesday night would be a good time to catch up on his paperwork at the crisis center.

Promptly at seven o'clock on the night of the party, Sonya and Pam arrived at the Dutton residence loaded with boxes and a small suitcase.

"Do you mind if we use your kitchen table?" Pam queried. "It's easier to spread the different products out on the table and it's closer to water."

"Certainly. I guess I'm a little rusty on the requirements of makeup parties." Edith motioned for the pair to follow her to her much-used kitchen table.

While Pam arranged her assortment of products in the center of the table, Sonya set up extra folding chairs and organized the refreshments. By seven-thirty all the details were prepared for the guests.

Within fifteen minutes eight young women were gathered around Edith's kitchen table. Sonya served lemon bars, mixed nuts, and tropical punch while Pam explained the advantages of Beautiful You Cosmetics. When she completed her presentation, Pam asked for questions.

Libby looked pensive for a few moments and then finally got up enough courage to speak. "All of your pictures and examples only show gorgeous girls. What about those of us who don't have any natural beauty? I can't see spending my money on something like this."

"Libby, you have a lot of natural beauty," Pam assured her. "But you've been so busy being a mother and student that you haven't had the time to develop it. We're all going to have complete facials. We'll experiment with the different techniques and shades of makeup and compare the difference."

"I don't think anything could make a difference on my ugly face, but I'm willing to give it a try," Libby chuckled.

Pam spent the next few minutes going from guest to guest, helping them completely remove their old makeup and selecting the most attractive shade for them to try. Little by little Libby's skepticism was replaced by genuine enthusiasm. She learned how to select the right color for different types of lighting. She learned how to blend the blush high on her cheekbones and how to merge three different shades of eye shadow.

"Wow, you look terrific," Jenny observed. "You could get any man you'd want looking like that."

Libby gulped. Her eyes turned distant. "I only want Larry, but I don't think we'll ever be able to get our marriage together again."

"Time will tell," Edith responded. "The important thing is that you feel good about yourself. Go look in the full-length mirror in my bedroom and see the difference in yourself. Hold your head up and be proud of who you are."

Five minutes later Libby returned to the kitchen with her eyes aglow. "I couldn't believe that was really me in the mirror. The only problem is, my new face makes my clothes look shabby."

The entire group broke into gales of laughter. "I have just the solution for you," Pam said as soon as the laughter subsided. "I've also begun selling a line of women's clothes, Fashions by Rachel. They sent me a lot of samples so that I could begin to spread the word around Montana about their outstanding clothes. If you're not busy in the morning, I'll bring some over to your apartment and see how many fit you. You can be the walking advertisement for Fashions by Rachel at Rocky Bluff Community College."

Libby's face flushed. "I've never been a model before, but it might be fun trying."

The party broke up within an hour with everyone convinced that they were much more attractive than before. Libby could scarcely contain her excitement about the change in her appearance and eagerly awaited Pam's visit.

❧

Early the next morning Pam pulled into her old parking stall at the Forest Grove Apartments. She unloaded the clothing traveler and headed for Libby's apartment. Libby greeted her with even more enthusiasm than she had the night before. Before the morning was over, Libby had learned how to select the right colors and lines for her particular figure. She learned what types of slacks and skirts helped slim her hips and thighs. Best of all, she had an entirely new wardrobe of clothes for only guaranteeing to help Pam introduce Fashions by Rachel around the state.

That afternoon, dressed in her favorite slacks outfit, Libby put Vanessa in a new sweater that Edith had given her and headed for the neighborhood supermarket. As she was pushing the stroller across the parking lot, a familiar Maverick pulled up beside her.

"Wow, you're looking great," Larry sneered. "Where did you get those clothes? A new boyfriend buy them?"

Libby's face turned ashen. She looked over her shoulder, but another car was behind her and there was nowhere for her to run. "Larry, you're not supposed to bother me. Did you forget about your restraining order?"

"I didn't look you up. This is merely a chance meeting. Now tell me where you got your new look. Is it some other guy?"

"I'm too busy now to be interested in men." Libby did nothing to hide her disgust. "If you really must know, I was over at Edith Dutton's last night and. . ."

Before she could finish her sentence, Larry snapped, "I might have known that old biddy was interfering in our lives again. I bet she's trying to get you to look nice so you can find another man. Just you wait. I'll get even with her yet." With that he stomped on the accelerator, left a strip of rubber on the asphalt, and sped out of the parking lot. Libby took a deep breath, tried to force a smile on her face, and headed for the front entrance of the store. *I'm glad Larry liked my new look. I only wish he'd waited long enough to hear the real story. When will he ever get over his insane jealousy?*

❧

At 3:22 A.M. the next morning fire sirens pierced the stillness of Rocky Bluff. A red glow lit the business district as flames leaped out the windows of Harkness Hardware Store. Officer Scott Packwood blocked off the street while the firemen hooked up their hoses to the fire hydrant in front of the store. Heavy black smoke poured from the back of the building as the fire consumed the paint inventory. Sharp, piercing explosions followed as the fire ignited the locked case of ammunition. In spite of the hour, a crowd began to gather across the street on the courthouse lawn.

Having secured the area, Officer Packwood called the police dispatch. "Steve, phone Bob Harkness and tell him there is a fire at his store and to come immediately."

"I'll get right on it," Steve responded crisply as he reached for the local phone book.

Within minutes Bob and Nancy were dressed and on their way to the store. Expecting to find a localized fire that was under control, they were horrified at the flames and billows of black smoke that were consuming their building. Bob parked his car on the far side of the courthouse square next to a red Maverick. He took his wife's hand and raced across the lawn toward the burning building. He quickly spotted Officer Packwood.

"Scott, what's happened? How'd it start?" Bob gasped. "It looks like we've lost everything."

"I don't think anything could have survived that intense heat. Fire Chief Hatfield is suspicious of arson, but they won't be able to begin their investigation until it cools down. Do you have any idea what might have started the fire?"

"No, everything looked normal when we left at seven-thirty. I can't imagine that we have any firebugs in Rocky Bluff."

"Rumor has it that finances were getting kind of tight for you right now," Scott said as his eyes pierced through the darkness toward Bob.

Just then Nancy began to sob hysterically. Bob wrapped his long arms around her and pulled her next to him, completely ignoring the policeman's comment. They stood and trembled together as the roof crashed into the building.

"Pretty bad fire, huh?" said a deep voice from behind the couple.

Bob turned and found himself face-to-face with Larry Reynolds. "The worst I've ever seen in my lifetime," he stammered.

"Might put you out of business, huh?"

"Probably so."

"Have you told your mother that her pride and joy has burned to the ground? I bet she'll really be upset," Larry snarled with contempt. "Could I have the honor of telling her?"

Bob glared at the young man. He was in no humor to deal with a smart-mouthed punk.

As dawn broke over Rocky Bluff, Harkness Hardware lay in ruins. Bob and Nancy waited until the firetruck left and then drove directly to the Dutton residence.

"Bob, Nancy, do come in," Roy greeted as he opened the door wearing his robe and slippers. "Your mother and I were just sitting down to breakfast. Would you like to join us?"

"Thanks for the offer," Nancy replied. "But I'm afraid food would stick in my throat right now."

"Bob, Nancy, is that you?" a female voice shouted from the kitchen. "Would you like some scrambled eggs?"

"No food for me, Mom. We are bearers of bad news," Bob stammered.

Edith surveyed their tear-stained faces as the couple entered the kitchen. "Sit down and tell me what has happened. You look like you've lost your last friend."

"It's even worse than that," Bob replied as he poured himself a cup of coffee. "We lost the entire store."

"I knew you were having financial problems, but it all couldn't have gone up in a puff of smoke overnight. You'll have time to reorganize and liquidate some of your assets."

"Mom, that's exactly what happened. It all went up in a puff of smoke. There was a fire about three-thirty last night and the store is a pile of rubble."

Edith sat in stunned silence as her weakened heart pounded within her chest. "I can hardly believe it. After all the years of hard work George and I put into that store, I can't imagine it a pile of rubble. Give Roy and me a few minutes to dress and take us downtown."

Edith and Roy quickly forgot their breakfast and rushed to the bedroom to dress while Nancy and Bob paced nervously around the living room.

As the foursome headed toward the business section of Rocky Bluff, Bob explained the details of the previous night as best he could. "Mom, the strangest part was the number of people that had gathered that time of night to watch the fire. Even Larry Reynolds was there."

"That kid sure gets around," Edith sighed. "Bob, have you contacted your insurance agent yet? I'm sure there'll be a major investigation."

Bob scowled. "I never thought about an investigation. I'll have to wait until ten o'clock until his office opens to call." He hesitated, then took a deep breath. "It's hard enough losing everything. I don't think I can fill out a pile of papers. All our records would have been lost in the fire. I don't even know how I can validate my exact inventory."

Bob parked the car in front of the courthouse across from what remained of Harkness Hardware Store. Roy helped Edith from the car and pulled her close to him as she surveyed the rubble. Tears built in her eyes.

"Edith, are you all right?" Roy queried gently. "I don't want this to be too much of a strain on you."

Edith forced a smile. "Of course this is hard, but I know that with Bob and Nancy's skills and the good Lord's help, they'll be back in business in a few months. This isn't the end of Harkness Hardware Store; it's a new beginning."

"Mom, I wish I had your faith. You see good during even the worst circumstances." Bob took his wife's hand. "But if everyone will stand behind us with prayer, Nancy and I will do our best to carry on."

Chapter 6

Bob, I realize this is a tough time for you and that most of your business records were destroyed in the fire, but we're going to have to reconstruct your assets and liabilities as best we can," Warren Engelwood said as he opened his laptop computer and placed it on Bob and Nancy Harkness's dining room table.

"I'll do my best," the shattered storeowner replied as he poured his insurance agent a cup of coffee. "Nancy might be better at remembering the details than I am. She worked with the figures at the end of each day."

"My mind is blank," Nancy stammered. "It quit functioning the night of the fire."

Warren looked at her sympathetically and then turned his attention back to his computer."First, how much inventory did you lose in each category?" Warren asked as he selected the appropriate data field on his laptop.

Bob sighed, looked over at his wife, and shrugged his shoulders.

"I honestly can't remember. We had a backup tape locked in a metal cabinet in the office, but it wasn't fireproof, so I don't know if it survived or not."

"Why don't we go down to the store and see if we can find it?" Warren said as he closed his computer. "If it isn't damaged too badly, I can send it to our central office. They are equipped to restore damaged computer tapes and disks."

"We can take my pickup," Bob volunteered as he reached for the keys on a hook beside the back door.

Nancy slumped deeper into her chair. "If you don't mind, I think I'll wait until later to see the rubble. Besides, I promised the kids I'd take them down this afternoon."

⟡

Solemnly, Bob and Warren climbed over the yellow barricade tape on the side of the building where the office was once located. They moved a burnt beam from the rafters that had lodged against the charred remains of the desk and the metal cabinet.

"Be careful, Bob," Warren reminded his client. "This could be dangerous. We don't know if the floor or walls are weakened enough to collapse.

All we want is to get into the file cabinet, then let the demolition crew take over."

"Except for being covered with soot, the file cabinet doesn't look in too bad a shape," Bob replied as he forced the key into the lock and turned. "I'm glad I've kept a duplicate key on the same ring as the house and car keys."

Both men held their breath as he shook the key until he felt the lock release. There on the second shelf, seemingly untouched by water or heat, was the backup tape.

"Great," Warren beamed. "It looks like it's still pretty much intact. To save our time, I'll take this back with me. I can do most of my report from the office. Meanwhile, I'll arrange for the crew to come and level the building. They won't be able to begin until the fire inspectors have finished their investigations, but that should be completed within a few days."

The two men climbed into Bob's pickup and headed back to the Harkness home. "Thanks for the ride," Warren said as Bob parked his vehicle in the drive next to the family car. "I'll be getting back to Great Falls and try to get as much done on this today as I can. Good luck."

❧

"Hello, Jean," Edith Dutton greeted as her daughter in Idaho answered her ringing phone. "How are you and Gloria doing?"

"We're doing great. Gloria's a little fussy from teething, but nothing beyond the normal."

"I have some bad news for you," Edith continued. "There was a fire at the store last night."

Jean remained silent for several moments, trying to grasp what her mother had said. The store had always stood as an indestructible monument for her. "Did Bob lose much?" she finally queried.

"The store was a total loss. He's meeting with his insurance agent now. I sure hope the insurance will cover enough so that he can rebuild."

"Do they know what caused it yet?"

"The fire inspector is still working on it, but they're suspicious of arson."

"Arson in Rocky Bluff?" Jean shook her head in disbelief. "That doesn't seem possible."

"I know," Edith sighed. "But a lot of strange things have happened here. It's not the sleepy village you grew up in."

"In my time no one would have imagined that a school principal would be shot by a student," Jean said with disgust.

"Not to change the subject, but it sure is nice to have a nurse for a daughter," Edith said, trying to ease the tension.

Jean giggled. "I see it's time for free medical advice coming up."

Edith's voice became serious once again. "You guessed it," she replied as she took a deep breath. "I'm getting concerned about Roy."

"What seems to be his problem?"

"He's tired all the time. It's all he can do to walk from his recliner to the kitchen table."

"Fatigue can accompany a multitude of maladies. Is there anything else?"

"Well, it's all kind of elusive," Edith explained. "He just sits in his chair all day and drinks water. I've never seen anyone consume that much water, even when they were working in the hot sun. On top of that, Roy has become extremely moody, and that isn't like him at all."

"Without taking a blood test I can't be sure, but the symptoms sound a lot like diabetes. He needs to see a doctor right away to have it checked out."

Edith sighed. "That won't be easy. He's having trouble admitting that anything is wrong. He thinks it's just a sign of advancing age."

"Mom, do your best to convince him that there's a big difference between being old and being sick," Jean begged. "It's imperative that he gets to a doctor right away."

Later that afternoon when Edith confronted Roy with the possibility of diabetes, his reaction was much different from what she expected.

He sat frozen and expressionless for a few moments and then his eyes lit up. "Edith, I should have thought of diabetes before," he said as he took her hand in his. "Maybe I should give Dr. Brewer a call. My mother suffered from it before she died of a heart attack. I'll always remember the final heart attack, but what led up to it faded from my memory. But I do remember her taking shots at least twice a day."

"If you'd like, I'll go ahead and make an appointment for you. You just stay here and rest." Edith leaned over and gave him a hug. Roy had been so good about taking care of her during the long months in which she recuperated from her heart problems, she would do as much as she possibly could in her weakened condition to take care of him.

Two days later, Nancy drove her in-laws to the Professional Medical Clinic. She entertained herself by flipping the pages of *Redbook* and *Better Homes and Gardens*. Thirty minutes later the solemn couple emerged arm in arm from the examining room.

"Nancy, they did some lab work and my blood sugar level was nearly 400," Roy began, trying to force a smile. "Dr. Brewer wants to put me in the hospital for a few days to monitor my blood sugar and do further tests to make sure none of my organs have been affected. Would you mind stopping by the house first so I can pick up my robe and slippers?"

"No problem at all," Nancy replied. "Is there anything you need from the store on the way? A new toothbrush or anything?"

"I'm just too tired to get out of the car. But if you wouldn't mind, would you run into the grocery store and get me a soft-bristled brush?" Roy chuckled weakly. "Toothbrushes they provide in hospitals are like emery boards."

"I'd be glad to." Nancy motioned to a bench just inside the front door. "Why don't you two wait here and I'll go get the car. I had to park at the far end of the lot."

Roy and Edith sank onto the bench and waited for their ride. Neither one wanted to admit the anxiety they were feeling. Edith didn't dare tell Roy that she felt her heart pounding within her chest.

Bob generally relied on his mother to keep him informed about the news of his sister, but now, more than ever, he needed his sister's encouragement in this latest family crisis.

"Hello, stranger," he greeted as he recognized his sister's gentle voice. "How have you been? I'm sorry I haven't checked in with you lately."

"Bob, it's good to hear from you. I understand you're going through some pretty tough times. . .losing the store and everything."

Bob sighed. "That's the understatement of the year. And to make matters worse, they admitted Roy to the local hospital this afternoon."

"What's wrong? I hope it's nothing serious."

"His blood sugar was nearly 400. The doctor wants him in the hospital to regulate his insulin and to do further tests to make sure none of his organs are damaged."

"With blood sugar that high it could be serious. How's Mom holding up?"

"You know Mom. She's the strength for everyone. However, when I left the hospital, her face was terribly flushed and she looked awfully tired. I tried to get her to go home and rest, but she didn't want to leave until Roy was asleep."

"I think I'd better come," Jean replied without hesitation. "Jim has a few days of personal leave. Now that Gloria's older, it won't be difficult to travel with her. We'll leave first thing in the morning."

"I sure would appreciate that," Bob responded. "I'd imagine when Roy gets out of the hospital, Mom is going to need some help. I wish you didn't live so far away. You're such an encouragement for everyone."

By seven o'clock the next morning, Jean and Jim Thompson locked the front door of their home in Chamberland, Idaho, and fastened their daughter in her car seat. The miles flew by as they cruised the familiar interstate highway and then turned onto a two-lane highway outside of Missoula. They had driven this route many times before, and each time it was different. The freshness of the mountain springtime was all around them.

Twelve hours later the young family pulled into the parking lot of the Rocky Bluff Community Hospital. They checked at the front desk for the room number of Roy Dutton and then hurried down the west wing toward room 116.

As they quietly peeked into the room, they saw Roy peacefully sleeping in the bed by the window, while Edith was busy knitting in the green chair in the corner.

"Hello, Mother," Jean whispered as she hurried across the room to give her mother a kiss.

Edith looked up with a tired smile. "Hello, Jean. I'm so glad you could come. Bob said you'd be in sometime this evening."

Edith turned to Jim, who was holding the baby. "Hi, Jim. How's Gloria? She has grown so much since I last saw her."

"Gloria's doing great," Jim replied as he admired his smiling daughter. "However, I think she's entering her terrible twos early," he chuckled. "When I put her down, she can really move."

Jean glanced at her sleeping stepfather. "How's Roy?"

"He's resting comfortably, but it's been quite a struggle. If you wouldn't mind driving me home, I'll fill you in on the details later."

The day after Jean arrived, Roy was dismissed from the hospital. However, before dismissal, Edith and Roy received a mini training session on how to check Roy's blood sugar at home and how to inject his daily insulin shots. Jean had their home spotless upon their arrival. She had spent that morning in the grocery store in an attempt to restock their refrigerator with foods that were suitable for a diabetic diet. She also knew that same diabetic diet would be healthy for her mother as well.

Jean was not only concerned about her mother and stepdad, but her brother as well. She tried to console him that as soon as the insurance company finished their audit, he could begin to rebuild.

Early the next Monday morning the doorbell rang at the Harkness home. Jay hurried to answer it.

"Hello, is your daddy home?" Warren Engelwood asked as Jay recognized him as the man who came the day after the fire.

"Yeh, just a minute." Jay stepped back and shouted. "Hey, Dad, someone's here to see you."

Bob hurried from the back bedroom, where he had been going through hardware catalogs, dreaming of the day he could rebuild.

"Warren, do come in. Can I get you a cup of coffee?"

"I think I'll wait on that." The insurance agent's face was glum. "I'd like you to meet Craig Goosemont. Craig, this is Bob Harkness."

Bob reached out his hand. "It's nice to meet you, Craig. Won't you sit down?"

The three men sat stiffly on the living room sofa and chair. Warren cleared his throat. "Bob, I have some bad news for you. We were able to reconstruct your backup computer tape. The data showed that your business was in serious financial trouble when the fire occurred. Under those circumstances, combined with the fire chief's conclusion that arson was the probable cause of the fire, we have no alternative but to turn our audit over to the county attorney. No insurance claim will be paid until the county attorney's investigation has cleared you of any involvement with the fire. I'm sorry it had to turn out this way."

Bob's face turned ashen. He could not speak for several minutes. His body trembled. "That is absurd. Yes, we were having financial problems, but we were eventually going to get out of it. I'd never think of starting a fire to collect insurance money."

"I'm sorry," Warren repeated. "We have to report our findings to the county attorney. My advice to you is to hire the best attorney in town."

The two men excused themselves and walked briskly from the house. Bob watched from the window as they got into Warren's car and drove away.

"Dad, why did they accuse you of starting the fire? You'd never do anything like that. You're the best dad and the best Christian in town." Jay sobbed as he clutched his father around the waist.

"I don't understand this, Son," Bob assured him. "But God has brought us through good times and bad. He won't let us down now when we need Him the most."

Suddenly, Nancy appeared at her husband's side and placed her arm around his broad shoulders. "I don't know how things could get any worse," she muttered through tear-filled eyes. "This is a time when the Harkness clan pools their strength and comes up with a solution. I'm glad Jim and Jean are here now. I think we better have a family meeting before we do anything else."

"I don't want to burden them with my problems when they have enough of their own, but they'll be upset if we don't let them know right away. I'd hate to have them learn from someone else that I'm suspected of arson."

Roy was sitting in his recliner watching TV and Edith was resting on the sofa when Bob, Nancy, and the children entered through the back door. Jean was there to greet them.

"Would you like something to eat to start your day out right?" Jean asked lightly.

Bob and Nancy stood in solemn silence.

"Oh, dear. Did I say something wrong?"

"You sure did, Sis," Bob said as he gave her a hug. "Things have gone from terrible to unbelievable. Is Mom busy?"

"She's resting on the sofa. What's this all about?"

"Let's go to the living room and we'll tell everyone our sordid tale of woe."

After retelling the conversation with Warren and Craig, Bob was surprised with how calmly everybody took the news that he was about to be accused of arson.

"Bob, things are going to work out. They don't have any substantial evidence against you. Having a business in financial trouble is not a crime. It happens every day." Edith's voice was calm and steady. "However, I have two suggestions for you. First, go talk with Pastor Rhodes and seek his support and prayers, and then go see Michael Miller. He's the best criminal attorney in town and a good Christian man. I'm sure he'll be able to get things ironed out for you."

Roy rose from his chair and put his hand on Bob's shoulder. "Bob, you stood up and confessed when you were wrong regarding the car accident and Pete's death, and God forgave you and saw you through those difficult times. You came out of that a much stronger person. Now when you are falsely accused, God will continue to protect you and make you a better person. We're all standing behind you."

Bob relaxed, and the tension lines began to fade from his face. His mother's and Roy's words were a salve to his troubled spirits. With a family like this standing behind him, he could survive anything.

Chapter 7

Gentlemen, I just had an interesting talk with Warren Engelwood and Craig Goosemont, the agents of Bob Harkness's insurance company," Carol Hartson began as Philip Mooney and Scott Packwood made themselves comfortable in the modest office of the county attorney.

"They gave me a copy of an audit they did of Bob's store. It seems that the office safe protected the store's computer backup tape from the fire. The picture the audit shows is not very pretty. Bob was in serious financial trouble. So serious in fact, that as I see it, he only had three options to save his business. He could hit up the bank for another loan, he could go belly up through bankruptcy, or he could torch the place for the insurance. Check with the bank to see if he applied for a loan and if they turned him down. He did not file for bankruptcy and, as we know, the store burned. I want you to go back over your entire investigation step by step. The arson inspector for the insurance company believes that Bob Harkness started the fire himself to hide his financial problems."

Phil and Scott looked at each other in shocked disbelief. "That doesn't seem possible," Phil protested. "I've known Bob since he was a kid. He's not an arsonist."

Carol's lips remained tight as her forehead wrinkled. "Phil, I've known Bob all of my life, too, but we can't allow our emotions to prevent us from enforcing the law. Go back to the crime scene. There has to be something we have overlooked. Also, this is an election year. We can't let the biggest crime Rocky Bluff has had in years go unsolved."

"We'll do our best," Scott assured her as he and Phil left the room shaking their heads. "We've been through every aspect of this case at least twenty times, but we'll give it another shot."

Phil and Scott strolled briskly across the courthouse lawn toward the burnt-out store. "This is what we get when we have a new county attorney who's out to make a name for herself," Phil sighed. "Ever since she took office she's been no end of grief for the police department. She treats us like we're all totally incompetent."

"It's rumored around town that Stuart Leonard is planning on running against her in the next election. My guess is that if he runs, he'll get it," Scott replied. "He's very well liked because of his work with Legal Services and the representation he provides for the poor."

"He's got my vote," Phil declared. "He's got a good head on his shoulders. He wouldn't be expecting us to waste our time digging through this rubble for the umpteenth time."

"Okay. Let's play her game one more time," Scott declared as the pair walked gingerly through the burnt-out building. "We'll pretend this is our first investigation after the fire."

Phil shrugged his shoulders. "It's obvious the fire started here in the paint room. The fire was much hotter here and even some of the metal shelving melted and the walls are much more charred."

"Paint's pretty flammable. It wouldn't have taken much to ignite it." Scott took several deep breaths as he moved around the building. "There's no odor of gasoline in here."

"Even if there had been gasoline in here, by now its scent would be pretty well gone," Phil replied as he poked the rubble in the back corner. Taking a pencil from his shirt pocket, he leaned over and inserted the pencil into a circular piece of glass.

"What do you have there, Phil?" Scott asked, hurrying toward his friend for closer inspection.

"Looks like the neck of an old glass gallon jug."

"I've never seen one of those before," Scott replied.

"Come on," Phil snickered. "Don't try to tell me that this was before your time. Ma and Pa stores used to sell orange juice in jugs like these. Then along came supermarkets and plastic containers."

Phil placed the piece of glass into a cellophane envelope and handed it to Scott. "Take this over to the lab and see if they can lift any prints from it."

"You're thinking maybe that jug was used as a Molotov cocktail to fire this place?"

Sergeant Mooney shook his head with dismay. "Could be. . .it's possible. We don't have anything else to go on. Get this over to the lab right away. Meantime, I'm off to the bank; then I'll bring in Bob Harkness for questioning."

❧

Edith tried hard not to let the latest family crisis upset her. She knew she would have to find something more to occupy her time and thoughts. The crisis line had been fairly inactive during the pleasant summer months. Libby Reynolds was busy taking classes at Rocky Bluff Community

College while Beth Slater watched little Vanessa and her own baby, Jeffy. The warmth and fellowship of the makeup party remained with her. Little by little plans began to materialize in her mind. Wednesday afternoon she gave her pastor a call at his church study.

"Pastor Rhodes," she began after sharing a few moments of small talk. "If you have some free time this week would you mind stopping by for a cup of coffee? I have an idea for a church project I'd like to talk to you about."

"Sounds good to me. How does tomorrow at two o'clock sound to you?"

"Great, the coffeepot will be ready."

Edith hung up the phone and scratched a few notes to herself. She wanted to have her plan well thought out before she presented it to anyone else. An undertaking like this had never before been attempted in Rocky Bluff.

⊗

"Roy, how have you been?" Pastor Rhodes queried as he shook the older man's hand.

Roy beamed. He was always glad for a visit from his pastor. He had been with him through good times and bad. "I'm doing a lot better," Roy assured him. "I've really been trying to take care of myself. I take my insulin faithfully, and Jean prepared a pretty rigid diet for me to follow before she went back to Idaho."

"I'm glad to hear that." Pastor Rhodes gave a playful glance toward Edith. "I'm certain your wife is keeping you in line."

"You better believe it. All sweets are barred from the house and a lock has been placed on the refrigerator door."

After Edith served coffee and placed a vegetable tray in front of them on the coffee table, Pastor Rhodes looked over at Edith. "What kind of project do you have in mind for the church? I'm always interested in ways to expand our ministry."

"I know you've been aware of my activities with some of the young mothers in the community." Edith's eyes sparkled with enthusiasm. "I'd like to help start a group for young mothers who have little training and little support from family members. I envision a multigenerational group that would help fill the parenting gap. We could call it MEM—Mothers Encouraging Moms."

Pastor Rhodes remained silent a few moments as he stared out the picture window. *That's a fantastic idea. Why hadn't I thought of that years ago?*

He then turned his attention back to Edith. "I like that. Tell me more while I take some notes. I don't want to miss a thing."

"I thought each session could feature a topic presentation, perhaps a local authority. There could also be a craft time, musical entertainment, devotions, and 'ice-breaking' games," Edith explained.

"It sounds like you've really thought this through. How do you propose we start?"

"I was thinking that we could form an executive committee. Maybe Beth and Libby would like to help us." Edith paused and cleared her throat before continuing. "Perhaps a couple of ladies from the ladies aid could also serve on the executive committee. They could have a wealth of ideas of things to try."

"Edith, since you seem to have a pretty good handle on this, why don't we set up a meeting date, call the group together, and officially lay the groundwork? The church calendar is pretty open this summer, so you could pick any time you'd like."

"How about a week from Wednesday?" Edith queried. "That would give me time to get a few women together to brainstorm. I'll host the get-together. Could you be able to join us then, Pastor?"

"I wouldn't miss it for the world. I'll try to compile a list of local human resources you might consider for speakers."

After Pastor Rhodes left the Dutton home, Edith immediately set about calling potential executive committee members. She knew she had to keep her mind busy so she would not think about the loss of the store and her son's uncertain future.

❦

"Rick, I appreciate you taking the time to visit with me," Sergeant Mooney said as he entered the plush office of the president of First National Bank in Rocky Bluff. "I'll try to keep this as brief as possible."

"This sounds serious," the middle-aged banker replied as he motioned for his guest to be seated. "What can I do to help?"

"I understand the Harkness Hardware Store had an account in your bank."

"They've been customers of ours since George Harkness originally opened the store."

"Could you tell me a little about its financial condition before the fire?"

"Of course I don't know about his other liabilities, but I do know that a few weeks before the fire, Bob Harkness filed an application for a loan with us so he could pay some of his vendors. I guess they were pressing him pretty hard."

"Did you give him the loan?"

"That was one of the hardest things I've had to do as a banker," Rick confided. "I hate denying a loan to a longtime friend, but the recession has hit the local farmers so hard that they're not buying anything from anyone right now. They're just making do with what they have. Our loan committee felt a loan to Bob at this time was too great a risk for us to take."

"Do you have any ideas how he was going to meet his financial obligations?" Philip asked. The possibility of a solid Rocky Bluff citizen being an arsonist sent chills through his body.

Rick shook his head sadly. "I haven't a clue. But with the figures he put on his loan application, he was going to have to do something fairly soon."

Phil thanked the banker for his help and shuffled through the lobby into the brightness of the summer afternoon. *I wish I wasn't the one responsible for this investigation. I'm just too close to the family to be objective. I've participated in a multitude of church and community activities with the Harkness family. Bob just couldn't have started the fire.*

He trudged back to the police station and slumped into his chair. He took the manila folder from his "Active" file and shuffled through a few pages. Finding what he was looking for, he copied a telephone number to a piece of scratch paper and dialed the phone.

"Mr. Warren Engelwood, please. This is Sergeant Mooney of the Rocky Bluff Police Department calling."

"Just a moment, I'll buzz him," a pleasant voice replied.

Within a few seconds a male voice came on the line. "This is Warren Engelwood. May I help you?"

"Yes. This is Phil Mooney and I'm investigating the Harkness Hardware Store fire. I understand that the store was insured by your company."

"That's right," Warren replied. "We hired a special arson investigator and the circumstances do not look at all good for the owner of the store. In fact, we had a long conversation with your local county attorney. She's quite a go-getter."

Phil shook his head with dismay. "That she is. What's the company's opinion of the case?"

"First of all, Bob had a strong motive to collect fire insurance. According to his records that we were able to salvage from his computer backup tape, he was on the verge of bankruptcy." Warren was unable to hide his disgust for small town law enforcement. "Being the owner of the store, he obviously had all kinds of opportunity to start the fire, plus he had the means to do it."

"That's all circumstantial," Philip reminded him. "Do you have anything concrete?"

"I gave everything we have to your county attorney. How she uses it is up to her."

Unable to get any satisfaction from the insurance agent, Phil ended the conversation and took his pocket tape recorder from his desk and added a new cassette. The only thing left to do was interview Bob Harkness.

Sergeant Mooney again picked up the telephone and dialed the familiar number of Bob Harkness's home.

Bob answered the telephone on the first ring. "Hello, Phil. What a pleasant surprise. What can I do for you today?"

"I'm sorry, but this is not a personal call. I'm going to have to ask you to come down to the station. We need to question you further about the fire. I'll spare you and your family the embarrassment of coming to your house to pick you up."

"I'll be glad to do anything I can to help, but I think I've told you everything I can about the fire. I just wish I knew how it started."

"Please come down right away. I'll be in my office."

"Thanks for the courtesy, Phil. I'm on my way."

When Bob arrived at the police station, Phil directed him to a small conference room in the back and started his tape recorder. "Bob, I understand you were having some financial problems at the store shortly before the fire."

"I'll have to admit I was," Bob mumbled. "I was considering bankruptcy, but I knew that would kill Mother. She and Dad had worked so hard to build up the business."

"So what were you planning to do?"

"I had hoped to get a loan from the bank, but they turned me down."

"Was the store well insured?"

"That is the only good thing about this entire situation. Mom and Dad took out an excellent policy when they first opened and I've kept it up through the years." Suddenly he stopped and stared at the police officer. Disbelief enveloped him. "Phil, you don't honestly think I started the fire in order to collect the insurance?"

"The circumstances don't look very good for you right now."

Bob glared at the officer. "You've got to be kidding. We've known each other for years. You know I could never do anything like that."

"Our personal relationship has nothing to do with this. We have to look at the facts, and right now the facts don't look very good for you. Bob, whenever police anywhere investigate a crime, they seek the answers to three questions. Who had the motive to commit the crime, who had the opportunity to commit the crime, and what means were used to commit the crime. You definitely had a motive to torch your store and plenty of opportunity.

As of right now, we don't know how it was done—the means. But you fit the answers to two of those three questions."

Bob clutched his fist under the table as he tried to maintain control. "This is absolutely preposterous. I don't want to answer any more questions until I have a lawyer present."

"That's a very wise decision," Phil assured him. "You're free to go now, but we'll be in touch. Until this is solved, you are not to leave town."

Bob Harkness left the conference room not knowing whether to cry or to fly into a rage. He felt as if his world had just crumbled around him. Everything he had ever stood for had been called into question.

On the way down the hall, Bob passed Scott Packwood. "How's it going, Bob?" Scott asked and was surprised when Bob didn't respond.

With a shrug of his shoulders, Scott entered Phil's office, where Phil sat dejectedly.

"Phil, good news!" Scott almost shouted. "You were right. We hit pay dirt. There were prints on that bottleneck. You'll never guess whose."

"All right, I'll bite—whose?"

"Larry Reynolds."

Chapter 8

Bob stepped into the brilliant Montana sun. *What right do the birds have to sing and the sun to shine?* he pouted as he walked toward his car. *This entire thing is absurd. Mother will be heartsick to think they're seriously considering pressing arson charges against me. I have to find a gentle way to break the news to her.*

Bob blindly drove across town and parked his Ford Taurus in his driveway. He burst through the back door, slamming it behind him.

"Bob, what happened?" Nancy asked as she turned off the vacuum cleaner.

"The police actually think I started the fire for the insurance money. Their entire case is based on the store's financial problems."

"That can't be." Nancy was adamant as she put her arms around her husband. "We've known most of those policemen all our lives. They're our friends. How can they possibly think that?"

"That's what I said, but Phil told me that our personal relationship has nothing to do with this. They have to look at the facts."

"But what facts?" Nancy protested. "They don't have any."

"It's all circumstantial." Bob headed for the refrigerator and took out a pitcher of tea. "Otherwise, they would have arrested me on the spot. They even told me not to leave town until this is over. Would you like to have a glass of iced tea with me?"

"I need something to help me cool off," Nancy replied as she pushed her dark hair back from her face and slumped into a chair at the kitchen table.

Bob handed a glass to his wife and then took a big sip from his own. "I'm the one that has to cool off. I don't think I've ever been this angry in my life. I know right always triumphs in the end, but it sure looks bleak now. I'm going to have to break the news to Mom and Roy, and that's not going to be easy."

"We've gotten so used to being concerned about her health, but now we also have to be concerned about his. They say stress is one of the most dangerous agitators of diabetes."

"Mother always taught me about inner strength and peace with God. I often wondered how she did it," Bob admitted. "Now I'm the one who's going to have to ignore my feelings and fall back on what she taught."

Bob took several deep breaths followed by another swallow of iced tea. "I think I can handle talking about this without being angry. Let's go over and see them before they hear it from someone else."

Roy and Edith Dutton were resting in their recliners in the living room when Bob and Nancy arrived. Bob tapped on the door, opened it, and exclaimed, "Don't get up. We'll let ourselves in."

Edith released her footrest and sat upright. "Do come in. It's good to see you both. I was wondering how you were doing."

Bob gulped. He had to choose his words carefully. "We're doing fine. We just wanted to stop over and check on you." Bob studied his stepfather relaxing in his chair. "How have you been doing today, Roy?"

"To be honest, this isn't one of my better days," he confided. "I feel extremely nervous and irritable. Sometimes, I wonder how Edith puts up with me."

Edith smiled as she reached out and took his hand. "I'm beginning to understand the symptoms. I generally know when it's really the disease complaining or you."

"Bob, I hope you realize what a jewel of a mother you have. She's always putting everyone else's needs before her own."

"It took me many years to see it, but she's definitely head and shoulders above the rest of us." Bob paused and studied his mother's graying hair and smooth complexion. Her peaceful serenity glowed through her wrinkled face. "I did have a minor setback today. Philip Mooney called and asked me to come down to the police station. It seems they are seriously investigating me for arson."

Roy looked puzzled. "But why? They couldn't possibly have any evidence against you."

"I know," Bob sighed, "but because of my financial problems, they assumed I had a motive and, of course, I would have had all kinds of opportunity. All they're looking for is how I supposedly started the fire. I'm going to have to see my attorney tomorrow to find a way out of this."

"Any good lawyer will be able to clear your name," Edith assured him. "I don't think you'll have anything to worry about. It's all part of the process until they find the cause of the fire."

Bob nodded in agreement. "But it sure makes it difficult being accused of something as absurd as that. God has seen me through some other pretty tough times. I'm sure He'll see me through this as well."

❦

Philip Mooney stared at his partner. Embarrassment and shame enveloped him. "Scott, I've just done the most absolutely stupid thing in my entire career. I caved in to the influence of our novice county attorney and believed that Bob was guilty of starting that fire. I came as close to arresting him as I possibly could without actually doing it. I feel like such a fool."

Finally, Phil cleared his throat and gazed at his partner with intensity. "Now tell me more about the prints on that bottleneck."

"There are prints on the glass and they definitely belong to Larry Reynolds."

"How did the lab make the identification so quickly?"

"They decided to compare them against our local bad boys' prints on file before sending them to the FBI. Larry's were the sixth set they compared and they got a match."

"Funny," mused Phil. "I had never even thought of Larry for this one, but remember all the talk he's been doing about getting even with the Harkness family? That kid really hates those people. Blames them for all of his troubles, yet if Edith hadn't stopped him when she did, he would have killed Grady Walker and be doing life today instead of probation."

"Yeah," agreed Scott. "He's one weird dude. Shall we bring him in?"

"Yes, go over to the city magistrate's office and get a warrant for his arrest, then meet me back here. I've got some paperwork to do. We'll head out to his parents' ranch as soon as I finish it."

"That's one reason I'm glad I'm only a patrolman—no paperwork," Scott teased as he left Phil's office.

❧

That afternoon Nancy and Bob rented a video and went to the Dutton home just to try to get their minds off their problems. When the movie was over, Edith gazed at the tension-filled face of her son. She longed to help take the burden away. "It's a beautiful day. Why don't you and Nancy go play a round of golf and get your minds off all this? Take Nancy out to the steakhouse afterwards. Stay out as long as you like. Roy and I will stay with the kids."

"We can't impose on you like that," Nancy protested weakly.

"It's no imposition. We can rest just as well at your house as at our own," Roy grinned. "When it's mealtime we'll just call Pizza Palace for home delivery."

Bob studied his mother's tired face. "Mom, I appreciate this. You're a real jewel. I'll bring the car around to the front so you won't have to walk so far."

❧

As Phil and Scott drove to the Reynolds's ranch, each felt a deep sense of

175

relief. Finally, the case would be closed and they would have Carol Hartson off their backs. As the patrol car entered the lane to the ranch, they spotted Ryan playing in the yard with his dog.

"Pretty fancy tricks you have your dog doing," Scott shouted as he got out of his car.

"I've taught Ralph a lot of new stuff," Ryan responded proudly. "I don't think Larry taught him a thing when he had him."

"Speaking of your brother, is he home now?" Phil asked.

"Yeah. He's in watching TV. He's been a real couch potato since he moved back home. What do you want him for?"

Phil gulped. It was obvious that Ryan thought the world of his brother, in spite of his mocked sarcasm. "We just want to talk to him for a few minutes."

Ryan turned his attention back to Ralph while the officers stepped onto the wooden porch of the old ranch house. Mrs. Reynolds answered the door dressed in a flannel shirt and blue jeans. The lines on her face tightened.

"May I help you?"

"We would like to talk with Larry. Is he home?"

"Yes. He's in the living room. Won't you come in?"

Larry rose from the sofa as the two officers entered the room. "What do you want?"

"We have a warrant for your arrest, Larry. The charge is arson for starting the Harkness Hardware Store fire."

"I don't know anything about it. All I know is that they got what they had coming."

Frances Reynolds scowled at her son. "Be quiet, Larry. You're in enough trouble as it is."

"I was just a bystander," Larry sneered. "It sure was fun watching that building burn."

Scott didn't say a word as he took Larry by the arm and led him to the patrol car. The three men rode back to town in silence. They led the young suspect back to the same conference room Phil had used a few hours earlier with Bob Harkness. They closed the door behind them.

Philip cleared his throat. "Larry Reynolds, you're under arrest for the arson fire of the Harkness Hardware Store. You have the right to remain silent. You have the right to have an attorney present during all questioning. If you cannot afford an attorney, one will be appointed for you. Anything you say can and will be used against you in a court of law. Do you understand these rights?"

"Of course. I've heard 'em all before," Larry snarled. "I didn't start that fire, so I don't need a lawyer."

Phil and Scott had perfected their interrogation techniques after years of working together. They had the "good cop-bad cop" routine down to a science. Phil, the more experienced of the two, was always the "bad cop."

They had also devised a technique of their own they called "knock 'em-sock 'em." They would seat the suspect in a chair positioned in the middle of the room. Phil would stand to the suspect's right while Scott stood to his left. First Phil, then Scott would bombard the suspect with questions, scarcely giving him time to answer. They would keep this up for hours until the suspect either told them what they wanted to know or until they were convinced the suspect was innocent.

Phil decided to employ "knock 'em-sock 'em" in their interrogation of Larry. Scott positioned the chair and directed Larry to sit. Larry, ever contemptuous of authority, moved the chair a few inches before sitting.

"Okay," he stated in his most arrogant and cynical voice. "I'm ready whenever you are."

Phil scowled at the suspect. "Why did you set fire to the Harkness Store?"

"I didn't."

Then it was Scott's turn. "We know you did."

"No, you don't," Larry countered.

Phil stared at him sternly for several moments before he spoke. "You tossed a glass jug filled with gasoline through the store's rear window and then followed that up with a lighted match."

Larry sighed with disgust. "I did no such thing."

Gradually Larry became less cocky as his self-confidence was continually challenged. Phil would ask him a question, he would turn his head toward Phil to answer, and then Scott would throw a question at him. When he turned toward Scott to answer, Phil would query him. It was all extremely unnerving and Larry hoped it would end and soon.

"Why do you hate the Harkness family?" Phil snarled.

"Everybody knows how much trouble they've. . ." Larry suddenly realized what he was saying was self-incriminating and he let his voice trail off.

Scott could not let this opportunity pass. "You admit you hate them then?"

Larry looked at the floor. "Yes. . .er. . .no, I don't. . ."

"You've told everybody in Rocky Bluff who'd listen how much you hate them," Phil reminded him.

"That was just talk." Larry was blubbering now, on the verge of crying.

"We can put fifty witnesses on the stand who will testify you swore to them you would get even with the Harkness family," Scott retorted, unmoved by Larry's whimpering tone.

"I. . .I was just running off at the mouth."

"Tell us how you torched the place, Larry. It'll go easier for you," Phil explained sternly.

Larry's voice began to break. "You got nothing on. . ."

"Oh, yes we have," Scott assured him. "You got away with the attempted murder of Grady Walker because your smart lawyer pleaded your youth and temporary insanity, but this time we have the goods on you."

Larry began to panic. "No, you haven't!" he screamed.

Phil's eyes seemed to pierce the suspect's soul. "You're an adult now, Larry, and you told too many people that you would get even with the Harkness family to plead temporary insanity this time."

Larry started sobbing. "I didn't do it."

Scott looked at his partner. "Shall I show him, Phil?"

"Go ahead. It will cut down on his excuses."

Scott held up the cellophane envelope containing the bottleneck. "Remember this, Larry? It's the neck of the glass jug you filled with gasoline and then threw through the rear window of the store."

Larry was now utterly confused. "I didn't do it. I never saw that thing before."

"If you never saw it before, then how come your fingerprints are all over it?" Phil challenged.

Larry was totally dumbfounded and couldn't speak. He tried to choke back his sobs.

"We found it in the paint room where the fire started," Scott stated firmly.

Larry's face whitened. His hands and shoulders began to tremble. *These guys are for real. I could go to the state pen in Deer Lodge for something I didn't do. I was able to plead temporary insanity as a minor when I shot Mr. Walker, but nobody will defend me now.*

Vanessa's innocent face flashed before him. *I can't let my little girl grow up knowing her daddy's in jail. Libby's done such a good job taking care of her, while I was never there to help. Now there's a court order keeping me from seeing them. And it was all caused by my own stupidity.*

Larry pictured Libby's sweet face and long blond hair on their wedding day. He pictured her the day he saw her in the supermarket parking lot with her new hairdo, makeup, and clothes. *How can I possibly throw away such a thing of beauty? And to think I would actually beat up on her for the dumbest reasons.*

178

Finally, Larry, shaken and more afraid than he had ever been in his life, was able to respond. "I don't doubt that you found my prints in that room. I was there with Bob Harkness less than two weeks ago. Ask Bob, he'll tell you so himself."

Phil shook his head in disbelief. He had heard so many excuses throughout his law enforcement career that this was just another one to add to his list. "Larry, you're entitled to one telephone call before I take you to your cell. You can make it now. I suggest that you call an attorney."

"I want to talk with Bob Harkness. He has always offered to help me, but I've been the one who's been obnoxious toward him."

"Come on," Philip retorted. "You don't think Bob Harkness is going to get you out of this mess. Remember, you've been telling everyone around town that you were going to get even with him and his mother. Now you've been arrested for taking away their years of hard work. I know they're good people, but they are not going to come to your defense. You'll now finally have to pay for the consequences of your own behavior."

"I know it would take an act of God for anyone to come to my rescue in such circumstances. But I have nowhere else to turn. Please let me try," Larry pleaded as tears streamed down his cheeks. Every fiber in his being cried for help and there was only this faint ray of hope. *If God and the Harkness family will help me now, I'll make a whole new shift in my life. I'll get a steady job, I'll quit drinking, I'll be the best husband and father out there.*

Larry looked nervously around the bare room. The two police officers stared at him. A dismal cell waited for him just a few yards away. *Dear God, I've been such a fool. Please help me. Show me what to do. Please forgive me and help others forgive me, too, especially Libby.*

Scott stood up and went to the next room. He returned in a few moments with a telephone and Bob Harkness's phone number written on a scrap of paper.

Larry hurriedly dialed the number.

"Hello," a mature voice greeted.

"Hello, is Bob Harkness there?"

"I'm sorry. He and his wife are out for the remainder of the day. This is Bob's mother. May I take a message?"

Chapter 9

"Hello, Mrs. Dutton, this is Larry Reynolds. I need to talk with Bob right away," Larry stammered into the phone.

"I'm sorry, but Bob won't be home until late tonight. Is there something I can help you with?"

Larry hesitated. *Is this offer coming from the same person I wanted revenge against?* he wondered. "You mean after all I've done, you'd be willing to help me?" he said with disbelief.

"Of course I'll help you, Larry," Edith replied. "I'd like to see you have a productive life. Yes, you've made your share of mistakes, but you have a lot of potential. Your parents have given you a good foundation, and you have a lovely wife and child. I remember the days when you were on the honor roll and were a class leader as well as a star athlete."

Tears welled in Larry's eyes. "The good times seem like another lifetime ago."

"But your life isn't over," Edith explained. "It is never too late to turn yourself around."

"I'm beginning to doubt that," the young man whispered. "If things don't change in a hurry, I'm looking at spending the next ten years of my life sitting in the state pen in Deer Lodge."

"Why is that? You're out on probation. There's a restraining order keeping you from bothering Libby, but that isn't enough to send you to Deer Lodge."

"Those are the least of my worries," Larry explained. "I've been arrested for starting the fire at the hardware store. I'm in jail until I can prove I didn't do it."

Edith visualized the panicking young man on the other end of the line. "Larry, Bob won't be back until late tonight, but I'll have him come to the jail first thing in the morning to see what he can do to straighten out this mess."

"Thanks, Mrs. Dutton," Larry sighed. "You won't be sorry you helped me this time. I'm really sorry for telling everyone that I was going to get even with you for messing up my life. If you hadn't intervened, I might have killed Mr. Walker and anyone else who was in my way. If you hadn't intervened, I might have seriously injured Libby and Vanessa. I promise you'll never regret this. Someday you'll be able to be proud of me again."

Edith hung up the phone, returned to the living room, and sunk into her recliner. *Whatever happened to the simple, happy days of Rocky Bluff? Life is becoming too complex and stressful for our young people. I wanted my grandchildren to enjoy the same peaceful community and state that I did, but I fear those days are gone forever.*

By nine o'clock the next morning, Bob walked into the police station. Sergeant Philip Mooney was working the front desk. He looked up and smiled. "Good morning, Bob. What brings you out so early in the morning?"

"Mother got a strange phone call from Larry Reynolds late yesterday. What's going on?"

"We've arrested him for arson. We now have evidence that he started the fire at the hardware store," Philip explained.

Bob could scarcely conceal his annoyance. "But early yesterday you were almost ready to charge me with starting the fire. What's changed?"

"When we went back to the store, we found the neck of an old glass jug with Larry's fingerprints all over it. It's the perfect shape for a Molotov cocktail."

"Can I see the piece or is it confidential?" Bob queried.

"I don't see a problem with you looking at it," Philip replied. "Just a moment and I'll get it from the safe."

As the police officer laid the clear cellophane envelope on the counter, Bob burst out laughing. "That's the top of an old orange juice jug that my dad used to cool his drinking water. Dad kept it full of water in an old icebox. I haven't used it in years and it was on a shelf with a bunch of old jars and bottles in the paint room."

"But how would Larry's fingerprints have gotten on it if it was in the back of the store?"

"About a week before the fire, Larry stopped at the store to talk to me. He was pretty steamed about my mother's influence in getting a restraining order to keep him from bothering Libby. He marched right to the back room where I was mixing paint. I did notice him handling the bottles. I imagine he'd never seen any like those before."

"Well, I guess you just shot down the only substantial evidence we have against him. I'll have to have the charges dropped against him. Would you like to come back with me while I tell him?"

"Sure." Bob followed the police officer down the long corridor to Larry's cell. The clang of the doors behind him sent shivers through his body. *So that is the most feared sound to any prisoner. That ought to be enough to scare anyone straight.*

"Larry," Sergeant Mooney began as he unlocked the cell. "You have a visitor. You were right. Your faith in God and the Harkness family has paid off. Bob told me you were in the paint room visiting with him about a week before the fire. I understand you were pretty interested in his antique bottle collection."

"Yeah, I'd never seen anything like them before. I got so interested in them that I almost forgot what I'd come to see Bob about," Larry replied. "I think I picked up nearly every bottle on the shelf before he turned around."

"Since Bob came and collaborated your story, I'll let you go home now. Just don't leave town until this is settled," Sergeant Mooney said as he motioned for him to leave.

Larry did not waste any time leaving the cell. As he walked down the narrow corridor, he turned to Bob. "Thanks. I really appreciate this. I don't know how I can ever repay you."

Bob put his hand on Larry's shoulder. "Why don't you come home with me for a little coffee and conversation, and then I'll drive you back to the ranch?"

"I'd like that. I'm really serious about getting my act together. I can hardly believe that after all I've done, you and your mother are willing to help me."

For the next two hours Larry and Bob visited around the kitchen table. The topics ranged from everything from stress management, anger control, and problems with the law to the fire and their individual families. As time passed, Larry kept eyeing the phone on the wall. "Would you mind if I used your phone? I'd like to give Libby a call."

"You know you have a restraining order not to contact her in any way," Bob reminded him. "How about I call her, explain the circumstances, and then ask her if she'd like to talk to you?"

"Sounds good. At least that way she wouldn't get scared and hang up before I had a chance to explain what I have to say."

Bob reached for the phone. "Do you know her number?"

"I've had it memorized since the day she got her apartment. It's easy to remember."

Bob dialed the number and waited. One ring. . .two rings. . .three rings.

"Hello."

"Hello, Libby, this is Bob Harkness. How have you been doing lately?"

"I'm doing great. I'm really busy with school and taking care of Vanessa."

"Why I'm calling concerns Larry. I suppose you've heard they arrested him for starting the fire at the hardware store."

"I heard that before class today," Libby replied. "I know he doesn't have a great track record, but I can't believe he actually did it."

"You're right, he didn't do it," Bob assured her. "His fingerprints were found on the neck of a glass jug in the paint room. I went to the police station this morning and explained that Larry had been there just a week before the fire and he was handling the jars then. They released him and their investigation is continuing. He's with me now."

Libby broke into a broad smile. It felt as if a weight were lifted from her shoulders. "I just knew it couldn't be true. In spite of everything, I've always believed in his innate goodness."

"Libby, we know there is a restraining order that keeps him from calling you, but he's sitting right here and would like to talk with you."

"Please put him on. I want to hear directly from him what is going on."

Bob handed the phone to Larry. "Hi, Libby. Thanks for talking to me. I've done a lot of stupid things in my life. Most of the time I never got caught. This time I could've got sent to Deer Lodge for something I didn't do. If it hadn't been for the Harkness family coming to my aid, I'm sure they would've convicted me."

Libby's heart began to soften as she listened to that familiar voice. "When I heard that you'd been arrested, I just couldn't believe you did it."

"I'm really serious about getting my act together this time," Larry tried to assure her. "I know you've heard that from me a lot. Every time I hit you I promised you that I'd never do it again, but I always did. I'm truly sorry for the hurt I've caused you. Someday I hope you'll be able to forgive me."

"Larry, I forgave you a long time ago. But there's more involved here than simple forgiveness. I have to be certain that you have changed. I can't risk you hurting me or Vanessa the next time you become angry."

"I understand what you are saying, but would you be willing to start over fresh? Not from the night they took you to the battered spouses home but from the night we first met."

"Are you saying you want to start dating all over again?"

"Exactly," Larry replied with confidence. "We'll take it slow and easy and not repeat the same mistakes. Maybe we can begin by starting to go to church together."

Libby's eyes filled with tears. "I think I'd like that. But I don't want to feel any pressure. There are a lot of hurts that need to be healed."

183

"Thanks, Libby. Of course, first we have to get the restraining order lifted. Then after that we can start dating again."

"I'll see what I can do," Libby promised with tears running down her cheeks. "It was good talking to you. Good-bye. We'll be in touch."

Larry breathed a sigh of relief as he hung up the phone. He turned his attention back to Bob. "Thanks for letting me use your phone. Would you mind giving me a ride back to the ranch now? I have a lot of fences to mend with my family."

That afternoon Philip Mooney and Scott Packwood were summoned to a meeting with Carol Hartson, the county attorney.

"Well, guys," Carol began. "Let's review where we are so far." She took out a manila folder and began to refer to some handwritten notes. "We know Bob Harkness was in dire financial straits and pulling every string he could to stay in business. He applied for a bank loan but was turned down. His creditors were pressuring him to pay up. That's sure motive aplenty to fire the place for the insurance. As the owner, Bob had access to the store any time. So much for opportunity. But thus far, we haven't been able to ascertain the means. How the fire was started. Bob is smart enough to fire his place without leaving any clues. But I've known Bob Harkness all of my life and I can't believe he would do anything like that."

She paused for a few moments, chewing on the end of her pencil. "Then we have Larry Reynolds. He hates the Harkness family and holds them personally responsible for all of his troubles. He has vowed revenge to everyone who will listen. That's motive. And let's not forget his fingerprints were found in the paint room, Bob's explanation notwithstanding. That points to opportunity. I've also known Larry Reynolds all of my life, and I wouldn't put anything past him. But I don't believe Larry is smart enough to start a fire without leaving some telltale signs behind."

Carol surveyed the two police officers slumped in their chairs before her. She could not let this case go unsolved. After all, this was an election year. The local newspaper was calling her constantly for an explanation. "Well, gentlemen, does this mean we are stumped?"

The two uniformed officers looked at one another and then at Carol. Both nodded their heads in the affirmative.

"Is it time to call in the experts?"

Again Phil and Scott nodded their agreement.

Carol pressed the push to talk button on her intercom: "Lily, get me Bruce Devlin at the state crime lab in Missoula, please."

Carol held the phone loosely to her ear and turned her attention back to the officers. "Kind of hard on the old ego to have to admit we can't solve this one without help, isn't it?"

Phil shrugged his shoulders in disgust. "This is the first time in my career as a police officer that I've been unable to complete an investigation."

Lily's voice came over the intercom. "Miss Hartson, Mr. Devlin is on line one."

"Thank you, Lily." Carol put the phone tightly against her ear and pressed the flashing light on the phone base before her. "Hello, Bruce. How is the luck of the Irish these days?"

"Carol, you don't need luck if you're Irish. Just being Irish is enough. What can I do for you?"

"We have a situation here that cries of arson. Two viable suspects, each with strong motives and ample opportunity. But we can't put our finger on the how. May I borrow Marty Sanchez for a day or two?"

"Well, Marty's in Kalispell right now on another case, but I can probably shake him free by Friday. But you'll have to pay his transportation. I'm over budget now."

"Friday will be fine. Go ahead and send him down round-trip air and my office will reimburse yours."

"Right, I'll get back to you on flight numbers and times. Have a good day, Carol."

"You, too, Bruce, and thanks."

Carol hung up the phone and turned back to the officers. "As soon as Bruce gives me Marty's arrival time, I'll let you know. Thanks for coming in."

Once the two officers were out of Carol Hartson's office, Scott turned to Phil. "Who is Marty Sanchez?"

"Just the best arson investigator in the western United States and Canada. Quite possibly the best of all in both countries," Phil replied. "He started out working for an insurance company, but as his fame grew, so did the demand for his services. He's been in the business over twenty-five years. The past ten with the state crime lab."

"Do you think he can put his finger on our case?" Scott queried. "We've been over it from every possible angle."

"I'd stake my reputation on it. Marty Sanchez is one of the most respected arson investigators in the country. He's probably investigated more torchings than anyone in the field. Whenever cops in the West have a burn they can't make out, they call on Marty. Beats me, though, how a greenhorn like Carol heard about him."

"I'll bet she called some old-timer somewhere and asked his advice," Scott retorted. "I bet it really hurt her pride to have to ask someone for help."

Phil laughed. "You're probably right, Scott. Few people outside of law enforcement ever heard of Marty."

"In other words," summarized Scott, "if Marty Sanchez says its arson. . ."

"It's arson." Phil finished Scott's sentence for him and then added, "Let's get back to headquarters. I wouldn't want the chief to hear about Marty Sanchez coming in from anybody but us. Word travels in Rocky Bluff faster than our feet can get us across the street."

"Boy, that's for sure," agreed Scott. "Rumors are generally a lot more interesting than the facts."

Chapter 10

Libby paced around her living room. This was almost too good to be true. *I have always said I believed in miracles and that people can change. But could it happen to Larry? He has claimed he was going to change so many times before, how can I know that this time is different?*

She picked up Vanessa and cuddled her against her breast. *Wouldn't it be better if Vanessa were raised in a two-parent family instead of only having one? Why do the innocent have to suffer from the stupid actions of adults?*

Realizing that she needed another adult to talk with, she picked up the phone and called a familiar number.

Edith Dutton answered on the fourth ring of her phone. "Hello?"

"Hello, Edith. This is Libby. How are you doing today?"

"I'm doing great. How are you and Vanessa?"

"We're fine. In fact, I think that we're on the verge of a real breakthrough, but I'm just not sure," Libby explained, scarcely able to contain her excitement.

"Larry and I just had the first seemingly honest conversation in our lives."

"But I thought there was a restraining order prohibiting him from contacting you." Edith could no longer contain her puzzlement. The last she had heard from anyone was when Larry called the night before from the jail asking for Bob.

"Bob was able to have him released. Bob called me from his home and asked if I wanted to talk to Larry. Of course, I had to say yes. My curiosity was getting the better of me. When Larry started talking, I couldn't believe what I was hearing. He always apologized every time he beat me, but it never really sounded sincere. This time he sounded like he really meant it. He wants to start our relationship all over again. In essence, he wants us to start dating again. I'm excited and scared at the same time."

"I imagine you would be having a lot of mixed feelings. This afternoon the executive committee of MEM is meeting here at my house. Why don't you plan to stay for dinner afterwards and we can have a long talk about this?"

Libby smiled. "Thanks for the offer. I really need to talk to someone."

"I'm always here to listen," Edith replied. "That's the least I can do."

"You know the new MEM group has meant so much to me. Just meeting with others who have also gone through the same frustrations of raising children has really been an encouragement to me," Libby explained. "I'd like to do more to help others who've gone through some of the same problems I've had."

"I'm sure you'd be good at that," Edith replied. "You've learned a lot about yourself, the meaning of love, and marriage these last few months. In fact, I was talking with Teresa the other day and she was commenting that they were needing more volunteers at the spouse abuse center. Why don't you give her a call?"

"Do you really think I'm ready?"

"With God's help you can do anything," Edith assured her. "Teresa will provide you with the training each step of the way."

The two women chatted a few minutes about the latest antics of Vanessa and then hung up. They both felt they were on the edge of something great, but they had to be sure.

❧

At nine-fifteen Friday morning, Philip Mooney and Scott Packwood waited impatiently for the Treasure State Airline flight from Missoula. Julio Raphael Martinez-Sanchez was the last to deplane from the twin-propeller eighteen-seater, affectionately called a "flying cigar." Although his wife called him "Julie," no one else would dare. A third generation Montanan, he was proud to be an American, but yet equally as proud of his Mexican ancestry. Marty was dressed in a plaid western shirt and blue jeans. When traveling out of state, he always wore a three-piece business suit, but when he was home in Montana, he dressed for comfort.

Scott watched the graying expert approach as he clutched a manila file folder tightly in his hands. He thought about what Phil had told him about Marty. *If anyone could figure out how the fire started, it would be Marty Sanchez. Marty had twenty-five years' experience as an arson investigator and was well respected by all the police forces in the western United States and Canada. When Marty says its arson, it's arson.*

"Welcome to Rocky Bluff," Philip said as he extended his hand to the investigator. "How was your flight?"

Marty burst into uproarious laughter. "Remember I came in a 'flying cigar,'" he responded with glee. "It was similar to the roller coaster rides I enjoyed as a kid."

"They do have that reputation," Scott agreed. "Yet, we're thankful Treasure State flies into the small towns. Otherwise, we wouldn't have any air service at all and we'd have to drive one hundred fifty miles to Great Falls to catch a flight."

"Only those who really want to get here will fly those things," Marty chuckled. "That way Montana is preserved for only the adventuresome at heart."

"By staying semi-isolated, we protect Montana as the last best-kept secret of the country," Philip said as the three men headed toward the waiting patrol car.

"By the way," Scott interjected as he handed the manila folder to Marty, "we brought the file on the Harkness fire along with us. I thought maybe you'd like to review it on the way to the site. It definitely has me stumped."

"Thanks, I appreciate that," the arson expert replied as he opened the back door of the patrol car.

The three men rode in silence as Marty perused the material. Every word was filed in his long-term memory bank for future reference. Upon arriving in the business district, Philip parked the car in front of the courthouse and the trio walked across the street to the burnt-out remains of Harkness Hardware. Not waiting for an explanation, Marty started right to work.

After a few minutes of watching Marty work in absolute silence, Scott whispered to Phil. "He doesn't talk much, does he?"

"No, but he doesn't miss much, either," Phil whispered back.

Marty repeatedly returned to the paint room. Phil, Scott, and the local fire investigators had all concluded the fire had started there. But how?

With a pencil firmly gripped at the eraser between the thumb and forefinger of his right hand, Marty stirred through the rubble. Pausing at an electrical outlet in the northeast corner of the paint room, using his pencil, Marty pulled up the remains of the electrical wiring for a closer look. He took out a small pocketknife and scraped the wiring free of debris.

Phil and Scott watched in amazement while Marty concentrated on the outlet itself. He examined it thoroughly. Using the blade of his pocketknife, he scraped through debris to the metal of the two screws in the outlet. Finally he stood and took a long look at the only window in the room now devoid of panes. He then looked at the only door leading from the paint room to the main part of the store.

The two police officers remained silent while the arson investigator wandered around the room, poking here and there with his pencil. Evidently, he found what he was looking for as he held up the remains of a tin can, smelled it, tossed it aside, and then picked up several more just like it.

Tossing the last can aside, Marty left the paint room and went to the rear of the building. He stopped at the window and peered through it into the paint room. He then directed his attention to the ground as if looking for something. Finding what he was looking for, he poked it with his pencil.

Phil could no longer contain his curiosity and silently went over to see what Marty was so interested in. To his surprise it was pieces of glass. *Why would he be so interested in the glass?* Phil wondered. *There is broken glass all over the place.*

Marty then walked back to the rear of the building and stood by the window. He removed a carpenter's tape measure from his pants pocket and handed one end to Phil.

"Phil, hold this for me."

The police officer dutifully obeyed. Marty measured the distance from the window to the glass. He placed the tape measure back in his pocket and returned to the paint room. He then went directly to the electrical outlet in the northeast corner and again picked up the burned and frayed electrical wiring.

Phil and Scott could scarcely contain their suspense when Marty finally spoke. "This is a paint room—here the store owner mixed the paint the customer wanted. His paint is stored here along with his paint thinner. Paint thinner is a highly flammable liquid and it also gives off noxious fumes. The ventilation in this room consists of only one window and only one door. That should be enough if both of them were kept open, but according to the fire chief's report, they were both kept closed. The door was kept closed to prevent the paint odors from entering the main part of the store and the window was always closed for security purposes."

Holding up the electrical wiring for Phil and Scott to see, Marty continued. "See this electrical wiring? It's copper." He then held up the electrical outlet. "See these two screws in the outlet? The copper wires are wrapped around these screws that are then tightened to hold the wires in place. These screws are aluminum. Copper and aluminum are incompatible in electrical fixtures. When electrical current is passed through them, they vibrate. But copper and aluminum vibrate at different speeds. This vibration causes friction. Friction generates heat. The heat then became so intense, it caused this union of copper and aluminum to spark."

Marty cleared his throat and wiped the sweat from his brow with his red checkered handkerchief before he continued. "In this enclosed room with all of its paint thinner fumes, the sparks ignited the fumes and we had a tremendous explosion, so tremendous that pieces of glass from this window were blown twenty-seven feet from the rear of the building. With the window gone, oxygen was sucked into the room and everything went up in flames."

Phil and Scott look at each other in amazement. He had it all figured out in thirty minutes, while they had been working for weeks on this case. Finally Phil spoke, "You mean it's not arson?"

"No way. Given the ingredients of paint, paint thinner fumes, no ventilation, incompatible electrical wiring, you have a catastrophe just waiting to happen," Marty replied with confidence. "Say, can one of you drive me back to the airport? I'd like to catch the next 'flying cigar' back to Missoula. My grandson's playing in his first Little League game tonight and I promised him I wouldn't miss an inning. Tell your county attorney I'll mail her my written report in a few days."

That afternoon, Scott and Philip returned to Carol Hartson's office. Carol surveyed their confident stride and smiles as they entered the room. "You look like you have some answers," she observed. "So whom do I prosecute? Bob or Larry?"

"Neither one," Philip replied with a scowl. "It was not arson. The fire was caused by old, incompatible wiring in a room filled with highly flammable fumes."

"To me it's a relief that we don't have to prosecute a community leader or a scared kid," Scott interjected, unable to hide his disdain for the county attorney's eagerness to have a high-profile case. "Would you like to contact the *Herald* or should we?"

Carol slumped in her chair. "I'll call them. They called me this morning while I was in court and I was supposed to return their call. I was waiting for your report before I phoned, so I better get on it. It'll probably make the lead story for the Sunday edition," she sighed.

The two officers left her office shaking their heads in dismay. "I'm even more convinced than ever to see Stuart Leonard in that position. Let's go talk to him tonight about getting his campaign organized. We'll volunteer our wives as campaign managers."

Scott look at Phil with amusement. "You mean you can get by with volunteering your wife without first asking her?"

"Of course not," he snickered, "but it's fun thinking about it. Now let's go finish our paperwork. This case is closed."

As soon as the two officers returned to their headquarters, Phil briefed his chief on the case and received his permission to notify the two former suspects that they were off the hook. Scott called Larry at his parents' ranch and relayed the good news to a very relieved young man.

Phil called Bob Harkness, who was equally relieved that the ordeal was over. Phil explained to Bob that the county attorney would notify the *Rocky Bluff Herald,* but that he wanted Bob to hear it from the police before he read about it in the paper.

Bob was absolutely dumbfounded that such a devastating fire could have been caused by something so simple as incompatible electrical wiring. He resolved then and there that his new store would have state-of-the-art electrical fixtures and plenty of ventilation.

Three days later the phone rang in the Robert Harkness home. Nancy sighed as she headed toward the phone. "I wonder who that could be. The phone seems to be ringing off the hook these last few days."

"Hello, Mrs. Harkness?" a cheerful voice greeted.

"Yes it is," she replied politely. "May I help you?"

"Is Bob home? This is Warren Engelwood in Great Falls."

Nancy took a deep breath. The last few times he had called had only brought disappointment and accusations. "He's in the basement. Just a moment and I'll get him."

Nancy walked to the top of the stairs. "Bob," she shouted. "Warren Engelwood is on the phone. Something must be wrong. He almost sounds cheery this time."

Bob hurried up the steps three at a time. "Hello," he panted into the phone.

"Hello, Bob, this is Warren. I finally have some good news for you. I just received the arson investigator's report from the crime lab in Missoula. We are ready to settle your insurance claim for the full amount. We'll have the check in the mail first thing Monday morning so you can go ahead and level the building and begin reconstruction. Good luck with your new store!"

Bob's face began to glow. He could hardly keep from shouting, but he controlled himself and calmly replied, "Thank you. Thank you very much. I really appreciate you getting this settled so soon."

Bob hung up the phone, picked up his wife, and whirled her around the kitchen. "Bob, what is it?" she gasped as the air was nearly pressed out of her lungs by Bob's excitement.

"They just received the arson investigator's report and we're going to be reimbursed for the total value of the store. We can begin rebuilding immediately."

"Praise the Lord!" Nancy shouted and then in a calmer note added, "It's been tough, but I never doubted that God would see us through this."

Chapter 11

Mother, great news!" Bob shouted as he stuck his head through the Duttons' back door.

Edith straightened her reclining chair. "Bob, come on in. Is the rest of your family with you?"

"Of course," he replied as Jay and Dawn hurried past their father to give their grandmother a hug.

Nancy could scarcely contain her excitement. "We stopped to get you and Roy and treat you to dinner at the steak house."

"I'm always ready for a juicy steak," Roy grinned. "What's the occasion?"

Bob stretched out on the sofa, extended his long legs, and placed both hands behind his head. "I just got a call from Warren Engelwood. They just received the report from the crime lab and they're going to mail me a check for full replacement value. We're back in business again."

Edith beamed. Instinctively, she walked across the room and gave her son a hug. "I'm so happy for you. I knew everything would work out in the end."

"I'm sure glad I listened to you and Dad and kept full coverage on the store. You don't know how much I was tempted to cut back on coverage when the premiums were due and the cash flow limited," Bob admitted.

"I learned a long time ago to expect the unexpected," Edith replied as she sat next to her son. "I've lived through floods, droughts, hail, and even shootings. I didn't see any reason why we'd eventually face fires as well. I just didn't expect one of this magnitude."

"Edith, why don't you hurry and freshen up?" Roy chided. "I can almost taste my steak already."

Minutes later the family was gathered around a large, circular table in the center of the dining room at Beefy's Steak House. Dawn's eyes bounced around the room, awed with her acceptance in an adult environment. Jay was able to mask his excitement. After all, he was almost thirteen and needed to appear cool and very mature.

"Pick the best on the menu," Bob encouraged lightheartedly. "Tonight we celebrate. Monday we start work and won't have time for anything more than hamburgers."

"So how do you plan to attack the rebuilding of Harkness Hardware?" Roy asked as he closed his menu with decisiveness.

"Labor costs are what's going to kill me," Bob replied. "So I want to do most of the work myself. I think my old pickup is going to make lots of trips to the landfill."

"You won't be able to do all the cleanup yourself," Edith insisted. "It takes at least two strong backs to move the heavy stuff."

Roy leaned back in his chair and took a sip of his water. "I've been thinking about that. Good help is hard to find, especially here in Rocky Bluff. Everyone who wants a job already has one."

"This may be a long shot," Edith replied hesitantly, "but what about Larry Reynolds? He's applied for several jobs around town, but everyone's afraid to hire him because of his police record."

"Hmmm. I never thought about that." Bob paused a moment and stroked his chin. "I can't afford to pay him much, but maybe if I offer the spare room in the basement, he'll be a little more interested. Working long hours like we'll be doing for awhile, I can't expect him to make that long trip from the ranch every day."

Just then the waitress appeared to take their orders. Building plans were postponed until Monday. Tonight was a time to enjoy each other and good food.

Dawn was anxious to tell about the events of the first week of school, while Jay was excited about having made the middle school's flag football team.

"I'm glad they changed to flag football this year," Nancy said as she took another bite of her chocolate mousse dessert. "There were getting to be too many injuries during the middle school's tackle football games. Last year alone there were a dozen boys on the injured list. I was to the point of not letting Jay play football this season if it was going to be that rough."

"The decision to switch from tackle to flag football in the middle school was a long time in the making. Traditions die hard in Rocky Bluff," Edith recalled. "Even when I was still teaching there were all kinds of studies showing the permanent damage done to growing bodies when they were forced to produce before they were developed enough to do so. I'm glad the kids can now learn the fundamentals of football without risking major injury."

Roy turned to the young man sitting beside him. "Jay, I want to be at your first game. When is it?"

"Right after school next Friday. I was hoping that you and Grandma could come. You never missed any of my Little League games."

"We wouldn't miss it for the world."

The celebration evening ended much too soon. Everyone knew it would be constant hard work until the store was back in operation, but the Harkness/Dutton family was a family that thrived on challenges.

One night while Libby was studying for her class on bankruptcy forms, her mind kept drifting back to Larry's phone call. She closed her book and stared out the window into the blackness. It was now time to take action. She picked up the phone and dialed the Donald Reynolds home. Ryan answered the phone and promptly shouted, "Larry, it's for you. Sounds like Libby."

"Hello," Libby said as her estranged husband answered the phone.

"Hello, Libby, how have you and Vanessa been doing?" Larry asked.

"I'm fine," the young mother replied. "However, Vanessa is having another bout with an ear infection. The doctor says that if it persists, she'll have to have tubes put in her ears."

"I didn't know she was having trouble with her ears." Larry's voice portrayed his genuine guilt. "I'm not much of a father when I don't know when my own child is sick, am I?"

"There was no way you could have known. After all, there is still a restraining order in place that keeps you from contacting us."

"Libby, would you consider having that order lifted? I'd really like to spend time with you and Vanessa, but I don't want to do anything to jeopardize my probation. I had an awfully close call of going to jail for a long time, and I don't want to have even a minor offense held against me. Would you like to have the restraining order lifted?"

Libby took a deep breath. This was a time she had been hoping and praying for, but was she ready? Could she trust being with Larry again? Yet, the softness and concern in his voice softened her doubts. "I'd like that. It is more difficult than I expected being a single parent of a baby. There are so many decisions to make as to her care that I'd like to share."

"Then if it's okay with you, I'll go down to Legal Services tomorrow. Maybe Stuart Leonard will be able to convince the judge to have the restraining order lifted. I heard he is thinking about running for county attorney, but perhaps he'll have time for another case."

"If it would help, I'd be willing to testify that I'm no longer afraid of you and that Vanessa needs to get to know her daddy."

A lump built in Larry's throat. "Thanks, Libby, I can't tell you how much this means to me. It's one thing to say you forgive me, but it's something else for you to believe in me enough to put aside your own fears and doubts and act like I'd never hurt you."

"Larry, I've always seen the gentle side of you and have known your potential, but it was your temper that always seemed to get the better of you."

"I know," the young man mumbled, "but from now on I'm going to think first before I shoot off my big mouth and make stupid mistakes. The consequences just aren't worth it."

"Larry, as soon as the restraining order is lifted, I'd love to see you again. You won't believe how much Vanessa has grown," Libby said. Suddenly a cry came from Libby's bedroom. "Sorry, I have to run. It sounds like she's waking up from her nap. Motherhood beckons."

" 'Bye, Lib. I'll be in touch."

Saturday morning Larry paced restlessly around his parents' ranch home. He would go from one minor project to another. TV had long since lost its appeal to him, especially Saturday morning TV. He ignored the distant ringing phone and his younger brother's muffled response. Suddenly there was a loud and clear shout, "Larry, telephone!"

Larry hurried to the phone. "Hello?"

"Hello, Larry, this is Bob Harkness."

After a few moments of small talk, Bob got to the point of his call. "Larry, I just received word that the insurance company is going to provide complete replacement value for the store, so I'm ready to rebuild. However, I'm going to need another set of strong muscles to help clean up that mess. Would you be interested?"

Larry stood motionless. He had never been offered a job before. Until now he had to try to support himself and family by doing handyman jobs on demand. No one trusted him with anything more than a lawn mower or snow blower and an occasional hammer or paintbrush. "Yeah, sure, Bob. When would you like me to start?"

"Eight o'clock Monday morning sound okay to you?"

"I'll be there."

"Larry, I want to warn you up front that I won't be able to pay anyone more than minimum wage until the store is in operation again. We'll be working from sunup to sunset for as long as we can. Time is getting short, and we need to get as much done as possible before the snow flies."

"I understand. I'm just anxious to get back to work. Life has seemed so pointless since I moved back to the ranch."

"I can imagine," Bob agreed. "I've been getting plenty bored myself waiting for the insurance company to come to a decision." He paused a few moments before continuing. "Larry, I have a spare bedroom in the basement. If it would be more convenient for you, you can use it until you get your feet on the ground again."

Larry could hardly contain himself. "I'd love to. In the evenings I'd like to begin spending time with Libby and Vanessa, and it would be great if I didn't have the long drive to the ranch every night."

"But what about your restraining order?" Bob queried. "I don't want you to do anything to put your probation in jeopardy."

"Oh, I'm getting that taken care of," Larry assured him. "Stuart Leonard is petitioning the court to lift the order. He's pretty sure it will go through because Libby said she'd testify that she is no longer afraid of me and that it would be in Vanessa's best interest that I take a more active parenting role."

"That's great," Bob replied. "If you need another character witness, I'll be willing to testify to the change you have made and that you now have steady employment."

"Thanks for the offer. I need all the help I can get." Larry gazed out the kitchen window. The leaves on the trees in the yard and the field beyond reflected brilliant orange, yellow, and red. Never before had the colors seemed so vivid. "If it's all right with you, what if I bring my toothbrush in about eight o'clock Sunday night? Then I'd be ready for a bright and early start Monday morning."

"Sounds good. We'll leave the light on in the basement for you."

The first week of work sped by for Bob and Larry. The cleanup was tiresome and dirty. After numerous trips to the landfill at the end of each day, they both hurried home and showered, ate a huge dinner that Nancy had prepared, and dropped into bed. Mutual understanding and respect came with each backbreaking hour.

At two o'clock Friday afternoon, Bob looked at his watch. "How time flies when you're having fun," he chuckled. "I almost forgot that Jay's flag football game is at three-thirty. I promised him I'd be there and bring Mom and Roy. Doesn't your brother Ryan play on that same team?"

"That's all he could talk about since school started."

"How about coming with us? We can always squeeze another person into the car."

"Do you think people will accept me back? I haven't set foot in that school since I was unceremoniously led out by the police after I shot Mr. Walker."

"You've paid for that. No one holds that against you anymore," Bob assured him. "Your presence will be a testimony to the entire community that you've changed."

"Well, I've always wanted to see Ryan play. I'm sure Mom and Dad will be there, too."

∽

Two hours later, Bob, Nancy, and Dawn Harkness, Roy and Edith Dutton, and Larry Reynolds huddled together on the wooden bleachers of Rocky Bluff Middle School's football field. Gaiety was in the air as the crisp fall air whisked about them.

"Larry, isn't that your mom and dad coming in now?" Edith asked as she pointed to a middle-aged couple at the far right of the bleachers.

"It sure is," Larry replied as he waved to his parents.

"Why don't I go down and ask them to join us?" Bob said as he stood and began climbing across the bleachers.

The Reynoldses beamed at the invitation of socializing with another family of their son's teammate, but even more, the chance to watch their older son enjoy the friendship of those he'd considered his enemies just a few weeks before was overwhelming. Maybe there was hope for him yet.

Ryan and Jay both carried the ball several yards while their families stood to cheer them onward. During the second quarter, everyone was on their feet with excitement when Ryan made a forty-yard touchdown.

During the halftime, Larry and his father decided to go to the refreshment stand. After they received their hot dogs and soft drinks, they turned to go back to the bleachers. As they rounded the corner, they were face-to-face with Grady Walker. Larry froze in his tracks. This was a moment that he had dreaded ever since he shot Grady, but he knew that someday he would have to face it. *What to say? What to do?*

"Hello, Mr. Walker," he said cautiously. "I'm glad to see you again."

"Hello, Larry. How have you been doing lately?"

"I've been doing great these last few weeks." Larry paused and cleared his throat. "Mr. Walker, there is something I've been wanting to say to you for a long time. I'm truly sorry for all the pain and suffering I've caused you. I know there's nothing I can do to make it up to you. I just want to beg your forgiveness, although I know I don't deserve it."

Mr. Walker shook Larry's right hand vigorously while he clasped Larry's shoulder with his left. "Thank you, Larry. I forgave you many years ago. However, there is one way you can make things up to me. Have a full, rich, productive life."

"Thank you so much," Larry stammered. "I won't disappoint you this time."

199

It was a large and happy throng that exited the Little Big Horn County courthouse in Rocky Bluff, Montana, that Tuesday morning. Larry and Libby Reynolds led the procession followed by Roy and Edith Dutton, Bob and Nancy Harkness, Grady Walker, Donald and Frances Reynolds, along with Sergeant Philip Mooney and Officer Scott Packwood of the Rocky Bluff Police Department in full dress blues, minus sidearms. Along with them, lest we forget the man who orchestrated it all, was Legal Services attorney Stuart Leonard.

Thanks to Stuart's excellent presentation and expert examination of the witnesses who volunteered to testify on Larry's behalf, Judge Milton Eubanks lifted the restraining order he had imposed on Larry to prevent him from seeing or otherwise annoying Libby and Vanessa. They were now legally free to start their lives over again.

Stuart called Libby first and she told the judge that in the past few weeks Larry had changed and was again the man she knew and loved. Edith Dutton related that she had always known that Larry was innately good and needed love and patience more than he needed punishment.

Grady Walker followed Edith. He had a two-and-three-quarter-inch scar that ran along his left temple and over which no hair would grow. The scar was put there by the bullet fired by Larry Reynolds. Grady testified that the Larry Reynolds who had begged him for forgiveness at the flag football game was the same Larry Reynolds he had known as an outstanding student and athlete at Rocky Bluff High. That was typical of Grady. He would carry the scar and the memory of that shooting to his grave, but in his heart he had only forgiveness.

Bob Harkness pleaded with the judge to show Larry the same compassion Roy Dutton had shown him after his son's death in an auto accident for which he, Bob, was responsible.

Phil and Scott were not there as friends of Larry Reynolds. They were there because they were proud members of one of the most outstanding law enforcement communities in the nation. Montana's peace officers had a code of ethics they had forged over a hundred years of bringing rustlers, claim jumpers, horse thieves, bank robbers, murderers, and highwaymen to justice. They would fight just as hard to free an innocent man as they would to convict a guilty one. Larry's response to their "rock 'em-sock 'em" interrogation was what they had come to expect from an innocent man. They would testify on Larry's behalf, not because they were friends of his, which they were not, but because they had seen a change in him they believed to be sincere; and as Montana peace officers, their code would permit them to do no less.

There were hugs, handshakes, tears, and backslapping all around. The tears mostly came from Larry, who thanked his God for blessing him with friends and neighbors like these.

Chapter 12

Kim Packwood and Jessica Mooney had never taken an active role in the political process, but this year they were shaken out of their complacency. Law enforcement had become a second love for them, and they felt it imperative to elect an experienced lawyer to the position of county attorney. To their way of thinking, Stuart Leonard had the most integrity and was the most intelligent, compassionate lawyer in the county. One crisp, fall afternoon, they drove to the Rocky Bluff Legal Services office.

"Hello, ladies, may I help you?" The receptionist behind the desk greeted the pair as they stepped into an unadorned office.

"Hi, Pat," Kim responded. "It's good to see you again. Is Stu busy? We have a proposition we'd like to discuss with him."

"Just a moment and I'll buzz him," Pat replied as she lifted the receiver and pushed the red intercom button.

"Yes," a deep voice answered.

"Kim Packwood and Jessica Mooney are here to see you."

"Send them right in."

Before the pair could reach the office door, Stu emerged to greet them. "Do come in," he said as he held the door open for them. "Make yourselves comfortable. Can I get you a cup of coffee?"

"Thank you, I'd appreciate that," Jessica replied.

Kim nodded in agreement. "Thanks. I'll have one as well."

After exchanging a few moments of social pleasantries, Jessica got right to the point. "Stuart, the entire community appreciates the work you're doing at Legal Services. You've been a friend to the poor for many years. You're an excellent lawyer and you're well respected in the community."

Stuart's face flushed. "Well, thank you. I appreciate your confidence. However, I have a feeling I'm being flattered for a reason."

Kim chuckled. "I guess you can see right through us. We do have ulterior motives."

Jessica studied his dark, inset eyes. "Stu, we were wondering if you would run for county attorney," she continued. "You know how many problems we've had with the present county attorney. Carol just doesn't have the

202

experience to handle the pressure. Maybe in five or ten years she'll be ready, but not now."

Stu stroked his chin. "Hmm," was all he said as he sat silently gazing at the bright orange elm tree outside his office window.

The two women sat uncomfortably waiting for him to answer. *Are we being too presumptuous in trying to get someone to run for political office? After all, we have no experience in politics ourselves.*

"The thought has crossed my mind. In fact, my wife and I were just discussing the possibility the other night," Stuart finally admitted. "However, I'd hate to give up my work at Legal Services. Here I feel like I'm making a major contribution to the unfortunate people in our county, but there are times when I do feel restless and ready for a change."

"You would make an even greater contribution in the county attorney's office," Kim replied. "If you choose to run, Jessica and I are willing to work for your campaign."

Stuart chuckled. "How can I turn down an offer like that? Two co-managers right at my doorstep."

"We could also recruit some students of the paralegal department at the community college to help with your campaign," Jessica explained. "For many, this will be the first election that they will be able to vote in and a good time for them to get involved."

"Okay," Stu replied. "With support like this, I guess I can't say no. I'll go over to the county clerk's office tomorrow and file the necessary paperwork as candidate for county attorney. I'll be in touch with you in a few days so we can hold a planning meeting by next Saturday. Maybe you could even have a few recruits from the college attend."

The two women grinned, thanked him profusely, and shook his hand as they left his office. Excitement was in the air.

*

At the next meeting of MEM, Edith gave a half hour presentation on long-range goal setting. Then they broke into small groups to discuss their individual goals. Beth and Libby ended up in the same group.

"I'm having trouble making long-range goals," Libby admitted. "It seems all I can focus on is how I can survive my next exam."

The others in the group snickered sympathetically. "We've all been in that position," Bea Short said. "You at least have a midrange goal to finish your paralegal course. Otherwise, you wouldn't be working so hard."

Libby smiled. "I guess you're right. I'm really looking forward to getting my diploma in December. Last year at this time I never would have dreamed that I could even get into college."

"Libby, I don't think I've ever told you this before," Beth Slater began. "But you've been a real inspiration to me. I've watched you go to college and make good grades while still taking care of Vanessa. I'm beginning to wonder if I could do the same myself."

Edith Dutton, who had been rotating from group to group, joined their group in time to hear the longing in Beth's voice. "Of course you can go back to college, Beth. Nothing is impossible with God's help."

"Yeah, Beth, if I can do it, you can do it," Libby chimed in. "Fall quarter is over in December and winter quarter begins the first of January. Why don't you start then?"

Beth hesitated as all eyes were focused on her. "Maybe I will," she said thoughtfully. "When I was a little girl I always imagined myself as a secretary, but I'm having to go to night school to get my high school diploma."

"Several people in my class did the same thing," Libby assured her. "They went back to school and got their high school diploma, then they were accepted into the community college. I'll go with you to the student services center tomorrow and they can help you get registered."

Beth beamed as everyone in the small group, both the young moms and the older women, encouraged her to go for it. A deep sense of satisfaction enveloped Edith. Her primary goal of the group was being met—mutual encouragement across generational lines.

❧

"Before we start class today, I have a few announcements to make," Libby's instructor in her bankruptcy forms class began after the students had made their way noisily into the room. "One of the advantages of attending the community college is that you are close to the political process. Regardless of what your particular political persuasion may be, I urge each of you to get involved in the local elections coming up this fall. One such opportunity is the organizational meeting of the "Stuart Leonard for County Attorney" committee this coming Saturday morning. It will be at ten o'clock in the meeting room of the Downtowner Hotel."

Libby's ears perked up. *I've got to go to that,* she told herself. *Stuart was so good to Larry and me when he took Larry's case to have the restraining order lifted. Maybe I should call Larry and tell him about Stuart running for county attorney.*

Libby's attention focused back on the instructor in front of the room. "And now, class, please take out today's assignment and pass it forward."

❧

At nine-thirty that night, Libby phoned the Bob Harkness residence.

"Hello, Nancy," she greeted as a friendly voice answered the phone. "This is Libby Reynolds. I hope I'm not calling too late."

"No, of course not," Nancy assured her. "I was just finishing loading the dishwasher. With the men working until the last ray of sunlight is gone, we have been having some pretty late dinners."

"Does Larry happen to be handy?" Libby asked.

"He just went to the basement. Just a moment and I'll call him."

As soon as Larry heard that Libby was on the phone, he came bounding up the stairs and rushed to the phone. "Hi, Libby, how are you?"

"I'm fine," she assured him. "I'm sorry I called so late, but I knew you worked until dark."

"I'm glad you called. I've been missing you a lot lately."

"Why I called is I just learned today that Stuart Leonard is running for county attorney. They're having an organization meeting Saturday for his campaign committee. I'm planning on attending and I thought you might be interested also."

"He'd make a great county attorney," Larry replied. "If it wasn't for him, I wouldn't be able to see you and Vanessa on my days off. Bob was going to let me have both Saturday and Sunday off this weekend, so maybe I will go to that. How about if I picked you up around nine-thirty Saturday morning?"

"Larry, we've never been in public together since we separated. This could really get the town talking," Libby chuckled.

"It's about time they said something good about me for a change," Larry replied. "I need to change my reputation. It's no fun being known as 'the town bad boy.' "

❦

That Saturday Larry and Libby Reynolds walked self-consciously into the meeting room of the Downtowner just as Jessica Mooney took the podium. "I'd like to welcome everyone to the meeting today," she began. "Although some of us may have never met, I'm sure we will be close friends by the time the election is over. We are bound together by one common belief and goal: Stuart Leonard is the best qualified person for the Little Big Horn county attorney post."

With those words the entire group burst into loud applause and cheers. Stuart rose and raised his right hand for silence. "Thank you all for your support. I promise that if I am elected, I will not let you down."

"I have listed some things that need to be done between now and election day," Jessica explained after Stuart returned to his seat. "I'll pass a sheet of paper around with the tasks and a tentative timetable. Please sign your name and telephone number beside the task and the times you could work."

When the sheet got around to Larry, he studied it carefully and then shook his head. "Since I work six days a week from dawn to dusk, there's no way I can help," he whispered to his estranged wife.

"I'm sure they'll understand, just as long as Stuart has your vote."

Larry's face turned glum. "I haven't registered to vote yet and there are only a couple days left to get that done. I've never voted before in my life. I never thought one vote would count for anything before."

"You'd better run, not walk, to the clerk's office first thing Monday morning and get that done," Libby whispered. "It's a good thing the court-house is right across the street from where you're working."

Libby turned her attention back to the sheet now in front of her. WORD PROCESSING NEEDED EVERY AFTERNOON FROM 4:00–5:00. *That's something I can do,* she thought. *I've spent enough time in the campus computer center typing papers. In fact, I'm getting pretty good at it.*

Libby quickly signed her name and number and passed the sheet to the middle-aged lady sitting beside her.

When the meeting was over, Larry invited Libby to the hotel cafe for a sandwich. After Larry had placed his order for a French dip and Libby ordered a club sandwich, they turned their attention back to each other.

"You know, Libby, this was the first time I've ever felt really accepted in the adult world. Even though I'm a complete novice, at least I feel like I am working for a worthwhile goal instead of just hanging out somewhere."

"I'm looking forward to doing the typing on Jessica's computer. They say her system is as sophisticated as those used in most law offices. This could be good experience for me."

Larry studied his wife. She was a totally different woman from the scared girl who had to call the police to protect her from his cruelty. She was now sporting a new hairdo and had learned to use makeup wisely. By working with Pam Summer, she had modeled or sold enough clothes that she now had an entire wardrobe of Fashions by Rachel. However, these superficial changes were far less important than the inner strides his wife had made. *In a few weeks Libby will have completed her paralegal course and will be working in some law firm. I hope I can make that much of a change in my life.*

"A penny for your thoughts," Libby said as Larry's silence became almost deafening.

"I was just thinking about how lovely you are and how much I like the changes in you," he admitted as he reached across the table and took her hand. "I hope someday I can earn your love and respect."

"You have made a good beginning," Libby assured him. "But we both need time to grow up before we can put our family back together again."

"How well I know," Larry replied. "Like we said before, we have to start dating all over again. However, that's been kind of hard with the long hours I've been working." He paused a moment before continuing. "How about a date tomorrow morning?"

"But it's Sunday," Libby protested. "Ever since we separated, I've been going to Edith's church. It somehow gives me enough strength to get through another week."

Larry smiled and a twinkle sparked each eye. "I know tomorrow's Sunday. That's why I asked. Would you accompany me to church tomorrow?"

Libby and Larry arrived at church early the next morning and took seats in the back reserved for parents with small children. "I used to think the roof of the church would fall in if I went in," Larry whispered.

"See, it didn't," Libby giggled back.

"I'm glad we have Vanessa with us. That gives us an excuse to sit in the far back. Otherwise, I'd feel like everyone was looking at us instead of the minister," Larry confided.

"I've always been shy and wanted to stay in the background, but Edith, Teresa, and all the others have made me feel so welcomed here," Libby whispered as the organist began the prelude.

Pastor Rhodes based his sermon that Sunday on 2 Corinthians 5: 17–20 (KJV): "New Life and Reconciliation."

"Therefore if any man be in Christ, he is a new creature: old things are passed away; behold, all things are become new. And all things are of God, who hath reconciled us to himself by Jesus Christ, and hath given to us the ministry of reconciliation; To wit, that God was in Christ, reconciling the world unto himself, not imputing their trespasses unto them; and hath committed unto us the word of reconciliation. Now then we are ambassadors for Christ, as though God did beseech you by us: we pray you in Christ's stead, be ye reconciled to God."

How appropriate, thought Libby. *This just has to be God's seal of approval on the change in Larry and my reconciliation with him.*

Larry sat glued to his seat throughout the sermon. *Why, Pastor Rhodes seems to be speaking directly to me. Thank You, Lord,* he prayed silently, *for giving me a new life and reconciling me to my wife and daughter.*

Leaving the church, they stopped to chat with Roy and Edith Dutton and were soon joined by Bob and Nancy Harkness accompanied by Jay and Dawn.

"We are having dinner at my place," Nancy said as soon as there was a pause in the conversation. "Why don't you three join us?"

"Oh, I don't know," Larry hesitated. "We wouldn't want to impose."

"Nonsense," retorted Bob. "You're not imposing, you're invited."

"Well, okay, if you think it will be all right," Libby replied meekly.

Larry turned to Bob. "We'll follow you."

With that each one shook hands with Pastor Rhodes at the door and headed for their vehicles. For the first time a church service had been a place of peace for Larry and not a place of boredom.

❧

When the Sunday dinner was over and the dishwasher loaded, the six grown-ups adjourned to the living room. Jay and Dawn disappeared outside to play, while Vanessa slept soundly in her daddy's arms.

Edith looked over at the shy blond across the room. "Libby, I hope things have been going well for you."

"Oh, yes. Much better than I expected," Libby replied with satisfaction. "My only frustrations at the moment are my kitchen appliances; they keep breaking down. I guess I should expect that since I got most of them from the thrift store on Second Avenue."

Edith shook her head with understanding. "I know that can be plenty annoying."

"My toaster is on the blink and so is my electric coffeemaker." Libby paused and then sighed. "I can live with that, but yesterday my blender stopped as well. I need the blender to puree Vanessa's baby food. I guess I'll have to buy a new one, but that could be difficult on my budget."

"Well, why didn't you say something?" interjected Larry. "I'll buy you new ones the first thing tomorrow."

"No, Larry, don't do that," protested Edith. "I have a better idea. Why don't I throw a shower for you, Libby? This will give me an opportunity to be active again and I'll put a list of things you need on the invitation."

"There's a big disadvantage in eloping like you did two years ago," Nancy chuckled. "You miss out on bridal showers and you have to start housekeeping totally from scratch."

"Are you sure you want to go to that much trouble, Edith?" Libby asked.

"It's no trouble at all," Edith replied.

"I have a better idea," Nancy inserted. "Hold the shower here and I'll take care of the eats."

"Then it's settled," Edith stated as the others nodded their heads in agreement. "I'll try to arrange it for the middle of next week."

Chapter 13

Jay and Dawn were sitting on the living room floor watching TV cartoons when their mother returned from the supermarket. "Come on, kids," she pleaded. "Get with it. You promised to help me decorate the place. The guests will be arriving in less than three hours."

Jay reluctantly turned off the television, and he and Dawn stood on the sofa to hang the banner they had made for Libby's shower. The banner read: WE LOVE YOU, LIBBY AND VANESSA. Jay then left the remaining chores to Dawn and dashed out to play, mumbling, "This is girl stuff."

From the kitchen, Nancy heard the doorbell ring and Dawn shouting, "I'll get it!" And then, "Hi, Grandma. Come in and see the banner Jay and I made."

"Dawn, you remember Teresa Lennon, don't you?" Edith said as she motioned toward her companion. "She was kind enough to give me a ride over here."

"Oh, sure," Dawn replied. "I see her at church all the time."

Edith then turned her attention back to the banner. "It's very nice, Dawn. You and Jay did an excellent job. I'm sure Libby will love it."

"I'm in the kitchen, Edith!" shouted Nancy, who was unable to stop spreading the icing on the cake for fear it would harden too soon.

"I'll be right there to give you a hand," Edith replied. "I brought some extra help along with me."

Nancy greeted Teresa as she entered the kitchen. "I just had to give you a hand," Teresa said. "Libby is one of the major success stories of the spouse abuse center and I want her to know how much we all appreciate her courage."

"What needs to be done?" Edith asked as she looked around the kitchen.

"How about you two making the relish tray? The carrots, celery, pickles, and olives are in the refrigerator."

Promptly at seven o'clock the doorbell began to ring almost incessantly. The room was soon filled to overflowing. Pam Summer came, as did Beth Slater, Jessica Mooney, Kim Packwood, and Mary Barker, wife of Libby's landlord. Patricia Reagan and Sonya Turner, volunteers at the spouse abuse center, were bursting with excitement.

The table in the corner designated for gifts was stacked with packages of every size, shape, and color. Libby opened each gift with gratitude. Never before had she received so much love and attention at one time. Surprising enough, none of her gifts were duplicates. She was suspicious that Edith was behind that strange coincidence, but she did not dare ask.

After all the gifts were opened and the papers thrown away, Teresa turned her attention to Beth, who was sitting beside her. "Beth, how are things going with you now that you've started the community college?"

"Classes are going great and I'm happier than I have ever been in my life," she replied. She paused before she continued. "However, I am also beginning to get worried. I just received a letter from a girlfriend in my hometown last week. She said that Mickey Kilmer had been kicked out of the Marine Corps and was back in town looking for me and Jeffy."

"He's Jeffy's father, isn't he?"

"Yes. But I don't want Mickey back in my life again. He's bad news. I'm afraid that one day he's going to show up here and try to take Jeffy from me."

"Just remember, Beth, you have a lot of friends in Rocky Bluff who will go to bat for you."

"Thanks, Teresa. I'll remember that."

"Nancy, I'd like to thank you and Edith for the beautiful shower and all of my friends here tonight for the wonderful gifts. You've all been just swell. I'll never forget what you've done for me, for Vanessa, for Larry. You've helped turn our lives around. Thank you and may God bless you."

As the guests were leaving, Jessica Mooney yelled, "Don't forget to vote tomorrow. Who do you want for county attorney?"

"Stuart Leonard!" came the response loud and clear.

❧

Election day dawned sunny and crisp in Rocky Bluff. The anticipated blizzard did not materialize. Stuart Leonard's campaign staff was out in full force. Libby Reynolds was busy on the telephone arranging rides to the polls, while Kim Packwood and Jessica Mooney drove voters to and from their polling sites.

During a midmorning break, a thought flashed through Libby's mind. *What about Edith and Roy Dutton? Roy has limited his driving since he was diagnosed with diabetes, and Edith has rarely been behind the wheel since her heart attack. Maybe I should give them a call.*

Libby dialed the Dutton residence and waited for the familiar answer. "Hello?"

211

"Hello, Edith. This is Libby. Thanks again for that beautiful shower last night. I can't tell you how much I appreciate your efforts." Libby paused a moment before continuing. "I was wondering if you and Roy need a ride to the polls today. We have some critical local races being contested this time."

"Nancy and Bob were going to come by tonight right before the polls close to give us a ride. They're all tied up with the construction of the new store. However, I'd like to get it done earlier because we're both going to be pretty tired by eight o'clock."

"Kim and Jessica are providing rides to the polling places today. I can have one of them stop by and pick you up. What time would be convenient?"

"Any time is great," Edith replied, "but right after lunch would probably be the best. Then Roy would have time for his afternoon nap when he gets home. It's so kind of them to be doing this today."

"We're enjoying it," Libby replied. "I hadn't realized how much of a problem lack of transportation was for senior citizens. I've had to do without a car since Larry and I separated, but there's always a lot of younger people with cars going to the same places I am or else I'm able to walk. But some of the people I've called are practically stranded every day."

Edith sighed with understanding. "It's difficult losing your independence once you've been active all your life. Roy and I are fortunate that we have family close by who are willing to take us anywhere we want to go, but many people have no family nearby."

Libby and Edith chatted for a few more minutes and then Libby excused herself to continue calling people from a list provided by the senior citizens' center.

By four-thirty that afternoon the list had been exhausted. The three women, along with Vanessa went to Jessica's home to begin preparing for the victory celebration at eight o'clock. Stuart Leonard and his family and all those who helped on the election committee were going to sit glued to the local radio station and listen to the election results.

The women quickly prepared a finger food buffet and began decorating the home. Jay and Dawn Harkness came early to help blow up and hang balloons and crepe paper streamers. They were elated to be included in the gala event, especially on a school night.

The first guests began to arrive promptly at eight o'clock. All speculated on the outcome of the election based on their own personal exit polls. After the living room was crowded with people, Stuart and his wife arrived with their two children. Everyone was eager to talk with him, but he motioned for silence so they could hear the radio. The local radio talk show host was carrying on an annoying monologue to fill the time while the ballots were being counted. At nine-thirty a telephone call interrupted the noisy chatter of the celebration.

Everyone held their breath while Phil rushed to the phone. "Hello?"

"Hello," a businesslike voice responded. "Is Stuart Leonard there?"

"Just a moment please." Phil handed the phone to Stu, who had quietly slipped to his side as soon as he heard the phone ring.

"Hello, this is Stuart Leonard."

"Hello Stu, Alex Snyder here at the election center. All precincts but one have reported in and I'm happy to inform you that you have been elected to the position of county attorney of Little Big Horn County by a two to one margin. Congratulations!"

Stuart gave the victory sign to the hushed group and everyone broke into cheers. Larry Reynolds had brought two bags of confetti for the occasion, much to the delight of the Harkness and Leonard children. "Speech! Speech!" echoed throughout the crowd.

Stuart raised his hand for silence. "I want to thank each of you for all your hard work. I couldn't have done it without you. I am really looking forward to serving as your county attorney and will do my utmost to enforce the laws of the great state of Montana. I would also like to announce my selection for staff. There is already a secretary in the office who will remain, but I am allowed to hire one paralegal. I have selected someone who through hard work and determination has proven that nothing is too difficult to conquer. She has put in many tireless hours working for my campaign."

Everyone looked from one person to another. Who among them had paralegal training? Few thought about the shy blond standing in the corner holding her baby. Their eyes returned to Stuart with anticipation.

"My selection is Libby Reynolds," he announced. "She will be graduating from the paralegal department at Rocky Bluff Community College December fourteenth with a straight A average. It is an honor to have her on my staff."

Libby stood in shocked silence. Never in her wildest dreams had she imagined herself as a paralegal for the Little Big Horn county attorney. Less than a year ago she felt that she deserved nothing more from life than to have her husband beat her, yet tonight she was entering on a promising new career.

Tears filled her eyes. "Thank you, thank you," she whispered as she moved closer to Stuart, who held out his hand for her to join him in the center of the room. "I'll try my best to live up to the confidence you're placing in me."

The entire group cheered, but the loudest cheers of all came from her handsome husband, who had been standing beside her. Instead of living a life breaking the law, he had become an enthusiastic supporter of those enforcing it.

The following Friday night as Roy and Edith were relaxing in front of the television set, Edith glanced over at Roy. Instead of his customary relaxed position, Roy's eyes were spacey and distance. He was perspiring and jittery. "Are you all right, Roy?" She asked.

Roy did not react, but continued as if he were not present in his body. "Roy, are you okay?" Edith said as she hurried to his side.

"Yeah, I guess. Pete was just here to see me."

Edith's face turned ashen. His son Pete had died more than two years before. She picked up Roy's wrist and felt his pulse pounding. She hurried to the phone and dialed for help.

"Emergency services," an efficient voice responded. "How may I help you?"

"This is Edith Dutton. I need an ambulance right away. I think my husband is going into diabetic shock."

The dispatcher took Edith's address and advised her to remain calm and that an ambulance was on its way. Within minutes she could hear the sirens approaching and saw the reflections of the red lights. She flung the front door open as the paramedics appeared with a gurney. They immediately took a sample of blood from Roy's finger and placed a drop on a stick that they stuck into a small gray box.

"How low is it?" Edith asked as she leaned closer to read the meter.

The medic reached into his bag and took out a gel-covered capsule. "Thirty-five. We have to get glucose into him immediately." He then broke the capsule open and forced the liquid down Roy's throat.

In a few minutes Roy began to respond. "Roy, let's get you onto the stretcher. We're going to take you to the hospital for a few tests. Your blood sugar's way out of balance."

Edith took her coat from the front closet and followed the gurney to the waiting ambulance. She watched as they loaded her husband in the back, and then one of the paramedics helped her climb into the front. On the way to the hospital, they radioed Dr. Brewer that they were in transit with one of his patients.

Events moved swiftly upon arrival at the emergency room. Roy was immediately surrounded by Dr. Brewer and two nurses. While he was being treated, Edith found a pay phone in the corner of the lobby and phoned her son.

"Hello, Bob," she said, unable to hide her urgency. "Could you come to the emergency room right away? Roy had another bad spell. I think he's going to be okay, but it was pretty touch and go for awhile."

"I'll be right there, Mom," Bob responded as he motioned to Nancy to come with him.

By the time Bob and Nancy got to the hospital, Roy had been taken to a semiprivate room and was resting comfortably. "Hello, Mom," Bob whispered as he tiptoed into the room. "How is he?"

"There's no need to whisper," Roy retorted. "I'm doing fine. Everyone just overreacted. They're going to keep me here overnight and then I can go home in the morning."

Bob went over to his bed and took his hand. "I'm glad to hear that," he said. "If it's all right with you, can I take Mother home so she can get some rest?"

"Please do," Roy chuckled. "She looks more tired than I do. Just remember to have someone here to get me first thing in the morning."

"Don't worry. I'll be here," Bob promised. "Now get some rest and we'll see you in the morning."

That weekend Roy and Edith remained home and rested. Nancy stopped by and prepared Sunday dinner for them. The next Tuesday morning the phone rang. Edith was greeted by a cheerful voice. "Hello, Mrs. Dutton. This is Barbara Hall, the head of United Charities. Is Roy available?"

"Just a moment, please."

Roy slowly raised his reclining chair and walked to the kitchen phone. "Hello."

"Hello, Roy. This is Barbara Hall. I'm pleased to inform you that at the United Charities committee meeting last night we voted to increase the allocations to the crisis center. We decided to hire a full-time coordinator. Would you be willing to accept the position?"

Roy paused. Suddenly he realized that his desires were in direct conflict with reality. "Of course, I'd like nothing better than to accept," he replied dejectedly. "But now that I have diabetes, I am unable to do so. It wouldn't be fair to the community if I took the position. But may I recommend someone else?"

"We're open for any suggestions," Barbara replied. "We hope to find someone who's experienced in the area of crisis intervention."

"I know just the man for the job," Roy stated. "He managed the crisis center by himself for several months a couple years ago when my son was killed. He drives a Western States bus between here and Spokane,

Washington. If it's a livable wage, I'm sure he'll be interested."

"Sounds perfect. What's his name?"

"His name is Dan Blair. Just a moment and I'll give you his number." Roy thumbed through the list of frequently called numbers in front of him. "Here it is."

"Thank you for your help and for all your years of service," Barbara replied. "Your recommendation is good enough for us. Dan Blair is our man."

Eight o'clock on December fourteenth, friends and family members of Rocky Bluff Community College students gathered in the fieldhouse for the fall commencement ceremony. Edith was there with Bob and Nancy, while Roy stayed home to rest. Teresa was there grinning from ear to ear. Libby was one of the major success stories of the spouse abuse center. *It's times like these that make it all worthwhile*, she told herself.

Beside Teresa sat Beth Slater holding her two-and-a-half-year-old son. *If Libby can do it, so can I*, she thought. *I can make it through the secretarial course.*

Proudest of all was Larry Reynolds, who sat with his parents and his younger brother. Suddenly the school band began to play "Pomp and Circumstance," and the audience rose to their feet while the graduates slowly filed in. There was Libby, sixth from the end. Her face was serious and intent like her fellow graduates, but she winked at Larry as she passed his row.

How could I possibly have abused such a lovely, intelligent woman? Larry scolded himself. *I can hardly wait for Bob to get the store open so he can pay me a living wage. Then Libby and I and Vanessa can live together as a family again. I'm so delighted with the change in her. Only God could have produced such a miracle.*

Chapter 14

"Jim, be careful," Jean gasped as the car began fishtailing down the highway.

Jim Thompson took his foot from the gas pedal and began to steer in the direction of the skid. Fortunately no cars were approaching in the other lane. The Thompson car slid back and forth across the road for another fifty yards before Jim had it under control again.

"I certainly didn't expect roads like this," Jim exclaimed as he wiped the sweat from his brow. "The weather was perfect when we left Chamberland."

Jean breathed a sigh of relief. "I'm sure glad we have Gloria fastened in her car seat. I don't think she realized anything happened. I know it's early, but let's stop in Lincoln for the night. It's not worth the risk to go any farther. Roger's Pass could be a real bear."

"We promised Bob we'd be in late tonight so we'd have all day tomorrow to help him set up the displays, but they'll have to go it alone," Jim said as he turned off at the Sleepy Eye Motel. "He still has three days before his grand reopening, so we can work like crazy to help once we get there."

Bob and Nancy Harkness along with Larry Reynolds had spent twelve hours per day at the store since the first of the year. First there were the walls to paint and then the display cases needed to be put together. Nancy's big day came when the new computer system arrived. Not only was she going to have new hardware to work with, but she had entirely new software.

As she poured over the manuals and did the trial exercises, Larry was drawn more and more to what was happening on the monitor. "Nancy, I know you're too busy right now, but sometime I'd sure like to learn more about computers."

"I'd be a poor teacher," Nancy chuckled. "I'm having trouble enough trying to get this supposedly easy program functioning before we open the doors for business." Nancy thought for a moment. "I think Paul's Computer Store gives introductory classes every so often. Why don't you take your coffee break and walk down the block and ask them?"

"I think I'll do that," Larry replied as he reached for his coat. "Computers were just getting started when I was in high school, but at the time I thought it would be too much work to learn. Now they look absolutely fascinating."

Twenty minutes later Larry opened the front door and stomped the snow from his shoes on the mat. His cheeks were pink from the biting wind. "Paul has a good thing going at his store. There is a small classroom in the back and introductory classes will be meeting for the next four Wednesday nights. The only problem is I don't have fifty dollars. My car insurance is due this month."

Bob looked up from the box of screwdrivers that he was trying to arrange on the shelf. "Larry, you've more than kept up your end of the bargain. You've been putting in some pretty long hours working at minimum wage. I told you I'd put you on regular salary as soon as we opened the store. Obviously, that's just days away. But as a bonus I'd like to pay your tuition for that class. I'll go down and talk to Paul a little later and get things set up for you."

"Thanks, Bob. You don't know how much I appreciate this."

Bob slapped Larry on the shoulder and snickered. "Since you'll be making a living wage, I bet you'll be getting anxious to get a place of your own and out of our cramped basement."

"You were reading my mind," Larry replied. "I was thinking about a place of my own not because your basement room is small, but because I'm planning to ask Libby to rejoin me. I want us to live together again as a family. Just watching you and Nancy with the kids makes me homesick for my own family."

Libby walked up the steps of the courthouse. Her high heels echoed down the hallway as they hit the marble floor. She paused in front of the Little Big Horn county attorney's office and took out a key. Opening the door, the enormity of her job enveloped her. The desk before her was her desk, complete with a picture of little Vanessa in the corner. The computer was there for her sole usage. *If there ever was a miracle, it's plain and simple here: me doing research for a county attorney. I could never have done it on my own.*

"Hi, Libby," a friendly voice called from the next room. "I've been waiting for you. When you get settled, come into my office. I have a search I want you to do on the online legal database."

"I'll be right there," Libby replied as she hung her coat in the closet and put her purse in the drawer beside her desk.

"What can I help you with?" Libby asked as she stepped into Stuart

Leonard's modest office. "Another heavy case?"

"It sure is," Stu replied. "I'll need all the help I can get. I'm glad you have the latest training available in telecommunications. I missed all of that when I was in law school. Would you dial up the legal database and find everything you can on this subject?"

He handed her a scrap of paper with several terms scribbled on them. She smiled at the nearly illegible handwriting that she was beginning to learn to decipher. "I'll get right on it," she promised as she hurried back to her office and flipped the switch to her computer.

Nancy and Bob Harkness had just ordered a quick sandwich at the Corner Grill when Stuart Leonard walked in. "Hi, Stuart," Bob said as the county attorney passed their table. "Care to join us for lunch?"

"Sure," Stu replied as he pulled up a chair. "Beats eating alone."

Stu motioned to the waitress. She immediately returned to the table with a menu in hand. He quickly glanced over the menu and said, "I'll have a ham sandwich on rye bread, please, with a cup of split pea soup."

"Thank you, sir." She smiled as she took the menu from his hand.

Stu turned his attention back to the Harknesses with a twinkle in his eye. "I've noticed my employee is showing a lot of interest in your employee."

"They've been having lunch together nearly every noon," Nancy replied with satisfaction. "And even better than that, they've been in church together every Sunday since Thanksgiving. I think things are beginning to come together for them."

"Larry mentioned to me the other day that he was looking for a two-bedroom house or apartment. It wouldn't surprise me at all to see a complete reunion within a month or two. They're both making a decent wage now."

"When I went before the judge to request Larry's restraining order be lifted, I did so with a great deal of misgiving," Stu admitted. "However, Larry is proving that he is worthy of our trust. After seeing so many young people throw their lives away, it's good to finally see a success story. Hopefully, other troubled teens will notice from their examples that there's always hope that life can get better, regardless of how bad things appear at the time."

The next day the phone rang in the Little Big Horn county attorney's office. The secretary promptly answered and then turned to Libby, who was busy inputting data into the computer. "It's for you."

"Hello, this is Libby Reynolds."

"Hi, Lib, I'm sorry to bother you at work," Beth Slater replied. "I have some good news and I just couldn't wait to tell you."

Libby swirled in her chair, "That's okay. I need a momentary break. What's going on?"

"I got my first test back at the college and I actually got an A. I've never had an A before, except for maybe third grade gym class," Beth exclaimed excitedly. "I know it's old hat to everyone else, but I always thought I was too stupid to learn much."

"Beth, I knew you could do it. If I could do it, so can you. Have you told Edith Dutton yet?"

"I want to see the look on her face when I tell her." Beth hesitated. "In fact, I think I'll take my paper over and show it to her. As soon as Jeffy wakes up from his nap, I'll put him in the sled and walk over there. None of this would have been possible without her. And to think it all started with a desperate call to the crisis center."

⁂

Jim and Jean waited until late morning before they left the Sleepy Eye Motel. They wanted to give plenty of time for the road crews to clear the pass. The remainder of their trip was uneventful.

"I hope your mom's not in bed when we get there," Jim said as he and Jean reached the outskirts of Rocky Bluff.

"I can see her now," Jean replied as her eyes held a distant gaze. "She's lying on the sofa in her robe watching TV and listening for every car that comes down the street. She could never sleep until she knew her family was home safe and sound. Particularly if we were traveling during the winter."

Just as Jean had expected, the faint flicker of the TV was seen through the drawn blinds of the Dutton residence. Jean hurriedly unstrapped the sleeping Gloria from her car seat while Jim hurried to the trunk to get the luggage. The biting winter air stimulated their weary bodies. The front door flung open just as Jean reached the top step.

"Jean, honey, it's so good to see you," Edith exclaimed as she gave her daughter a hug. "How was your trip?"

"Tiring." Jean laid the baby on the floor while she took off her coat. Her first instinct was to hand the baby to her mother, but she thought better of it. Gloria was getting to be a chunk and Edith's arm strength had been greatly weakened since her heart attack.

"How's my baby?" Edith queried as she admired her dark-haired granddaughter lying on the floor.

"She's doing great. She got a little tired of her car seat for awhile this morning, but she soon went back to sleep. All considered, she traveled extremely well."

Jean quickly unbundled the baby and sat with her mother on the sofa while Jim brought the luggage in from the car and carried them to the guestroom. "How's Roy been doing?" she inquired.

"He's sleeping now," Edith explained as she fought back a yawn. "Basically he has his good days and he has his bad days. However, I'm afraid that the bad days are becoming more and more frequent."

"I'll do what I can to help while I'm here," Jean assured her and then quickly changed the subject. "How's Bob coming with the store?"

"It's been a long haul, but he's just about finished. I think he only has a couple more shelves to price and fill and he'll be ready to roll."

"He'd like to have Roy and me along with you and Jim there serving cake and coffee during the three-day reopening. He's put a lot of money into advertising the event, so if the weather cooperates, we should have a good turnout."

"I hear he's hired Larry Reynolds full time now. How's that been working out?"

"Unbelievably well," Edith assured her daughter. "Larry has gotten so involved that he's even taking computer classes to help with the business part of the store. Bob has been an outstanding influence on him."

Jean giggled. "My former self-centered, money-hungry brother is now the community role model. Miracles do happen."

The sun shone warmly as Bob Harkness unlocked the front door of the *new* Harkness Hardware Store on the day of the grand reopening. Jean dropped Gloria at an old high school friend's home for the day and then drove Jim, Edith, and Roy to the store. Edith and Roy made themselves comfortable at the refreshment table by the door while Jean and Nancy finished putting the finishing touches on the serving table. Everything was arranged perfectly. The day they'd worked toward for so long could begin.

Bob glanced out the window as he arranged the supplies under the front counter. The delivery van from Specialty Florist pulled to a stop. The driver jumped from the cab and opened the side door and took out a huge bouquet of flowers and entered the store.

"Where would you like these?" he asked Bob.

Bob hurriedly surveyed the front of the store. "How about on this stand?" he replied. "Who are they from?"

"This one is from Rick at the bank," the deliveryman replied as he set the bouquet on the stand. "But I have others."

He turned and hurried from his van with another bouquet with *Good Luck* written on its ribbon. "This one is from Warren Engelwood in Great Falls."

He went to the van again and returned with another. "This one is from Paul's Computer Store."

He hastened to his van and returned with still another. "Good luck, from Mr. and Mrs. Stuart Leonard."

Before he was finished, twelve different bouquets lined the walls of the hardware store. Even the president of the chamber of commerce sent a congratulatory bouquet.

Nancy put her arm around Bob's waist and laid her head against his chest. Tears filled her eyes. "I never dreamed we'd have this much support. A few months ago it seemed like the entire community was against us, and now they're all behind us." She shrugged her shoulders and laughed. "That's life in little town Montana."

Edith looked at Roy, who was obviously enjoying stuffing himself with refreshments. "Roy, remember your caloric intake and absolutely no sweets. I want to walk around and look over the new inventory. Will you be okay for awhile?"

"Edith," Roy scolded, "you worry too much about me. Please go. I'll be fine."

As Edith walked around the new store, she marveled at the different tools and equipment farmers and ranchers used today. She saw very few farm implements that were familiar when she and George ran the store. *I hope all of these new devices help take some of the backbreaking drudgery out of farm work,* she mused.

She glanced around the store and spied Roy talking to Dan Blair and hurried to greet him. The last time she saw Dan was at her and Roy's wedding reception.

"Dan, so nice to see you again. How have you been?"

Dan extended his hand. "Edith, it's great to see you again. I was just telling Roy that Barbara Hall of United Charities has offered me the position of full-time director of the crisis center."

"And he accepted," Roy chimed in.

"Yes, thanks to Roy's outstanding recommendation, Barbara offered the job to me. It doesn't pay as much as the bus company, but at least I'll be home every night."

Just then a crisp breeze of winter air hit their faces as the front door opened. All turned to greet Beth Slater as she walked by carrying little Jeffy.

"Oh, Beth do come and meet Dan Blair, the new director of the crisis center," Edith said. "Dan, this is Beth Slater and her son Jeffy."

"Pleased to meet you, Beth," Dan said graciously as he reached out to shake her hand.

"And I, you," she replied with a smile. "I'm an alumnus of the crisis center," she chuckled. "I don't know what I would have done without Edith's and Roy's assistance. I'm glad that Roy's passing the directorship to such capable hands."

Dan grinned as his face flushed. "Thank you for those kind words. I'm certainly going to try to live up to Roy's faith in me."

"Well, Beth," Edith broke in. "Little Jeffy is his usual well-behaved self. It must be fun having him learning how to talk. It doesn't seem like any time at all since he was just a tiny one in your arms." Edith then turned her attention to the young man beside her. "Dan, Beth just enrolled in the secretarial school at the community college."

"That's tremendous. I'm sure you'll do well." Dan could not take his eyes off Beth's sparkling blue eyes. "There's always room for one more secretary in Rocky Bluff. Perhaps after you finish the course you can help me type the crisis center's weekly reports. My typing ability is pretty limited."

"I'd be happy to," Beth said and smiled. "Well, if you folks will excuse me, I'd like to take a moment to congratulate Bob and Nancy. They've worked so hard on this place. Then I better take Jeffy home and put him to bed. It's way past his afternoon nap time."

"Stop by the house and see us sometime," Edith invited. "Our doors are always open."

"I'll do that," Beth assured her. "It's good to see you again." The young woman turned her attention to Edith's husband. "Roy, I do hope you get better. I'll remember you in my prayers." Beth then paused as she turned to her new acquaintance. "Dan, nice meeting you, and if I ever master the art of typing, I promise to help with those weekly reports."

As the front door closed behind Beth, Edith turned to Roy. "There goes one sweet lady."

"That she is," he agreed as his thoughts flew back through the last few months. "She's come so far from the scared little girl I met two years ago."

"She seems like a very nice person. I'm surprised I've never seen her before. Who's her husband?" Dan asked.

"She's not married," Edith replied. "She was very much in love with her fiancé, but when she became pregnant, he beat her and left town. That was more than two years ago and she hasn't seen or heard from him since, not that it makes any difference. As far as she's concerned, it's all over between them, and Beth is better off without him."

"She's too lovely for anyone to abandon," Dan sighed.

Chapter 15

Libby, now that the store is open again, Bob gave me a substantial raise. It's time for me to find a place of my own," Larry said as the young couple relaxed in Libby's small apartment the week following the reopening.

Tears welled in Libby's eyes as she took his hand. "I'm so proud of you, Larry. Everything's turning out better than I could ever have imagined."

"Libby, would you be willing to come back and live with me? I could look for a house or apartment big enough for the three of us and possibly someday the four of us."

Libby hesitated. She had been dreaming about this day for months, but now that it had happened, she was speechless. She had gotten used to an independent lifestyle. Would she be able to readjust to married life once again? Then she looked into Larry's deep, intense eyes. *How can I possibly hesitate? Here is the same boy I fell in love with more than two years ago who has matured into one of the kindest men in Rocky Bluff. My cup runneth over.*

"Yes. . .of course," she stammered.

Larry took her into his arms. "You'll never regret this. I promise. I'll be the best husband and father in the county."

"You'll have to be," Libby giggled. "After all, you're married to the paralegal for the county attorney."

"I've been watching the paper for rental units and there just aren't many available," Larry admitted dejectedly. "I don't know how soon I'll be able to find a place for all of us."

"Rumor has it that a two-bedroom apartment is going to be available here in the Forest Grove Apartments the middle of February. But I'm not sure which one it is."

Larry brightened. "I'll check with your manager in the morning and see if we can rent that one. What apartment is he in? Not having to rent a truck would sure make moving day a lot easier."

"He's in number seventeen. . .the end unit. His name is Ron and his wife's name is Mary. They have a real cute place." Libby hesitated before she spoke again. "Larry, there's something else I'd really like to do before we become a family again." Libby leaned against his chest with his arm wrapped around her. "I'd like to renew our wedding vows. This time we can make our promise before God and really mean it."

"That's a great idea." Larry's voice was firm with conviction. "I'll add one more thing on my list to do. I'll contact Pastor Rhodes and see if he would conduct a simple ceremony in the church sanctuary." Larry stroked her cheek softly as he gazed into her blue eyes. "Libby, you'll never regret this."

The pair continued their discussion far into the night, forgetting that they both had to be up early for work. At midnight, Libby began to yawn and they bid each other good night. Neither one slept well that night. This time it was joy and excitement that kept them awake, not frustration.

The next morning Libby sleepily dragged herself out of bed, got herself and Vanessa dressed, and hurried Vanessa to the day care center. Soon she would have someone to wake up with and help her with her early morning chores. No longer would she have to sit alone over her morning cup of coffee.

During her morning break she dialed a familiar number.

"Hello?"

"Hello, Edith. This is Libby. How are you and Roy? I haven't seen you since the store's reopening."

"We're doing fine," Edith assured her. "But we're not doing as much as we'd like."

"I have some great news," Libby continued excitedly. "Larry and I are going to get back together just as soon as we can find a place to live."

Edith's eyes sparkled as she remembered the broken young woman and baby she had taken to the spouse abuse center more than a year before. "I'm so happy for you both. You're an encouragement to other young people to tough it out through the hard times."

"Larry's going to talk to Pastor Rhodes about using the sanctuary of the church to renew our wedding vows."

"Libby, that's perfect. Would you let Nancy and me plan a reception afterwards in your honor?"

The young woman hesitated. She had never had a regular wedding and reception before. She and Larry had eloped to Coeur D'Alene, Idaho, two years before, been married in the "Lovers' Chapel," and had spent the night in the Pink Flamingo Getaway. "Oh, Edith. I don't deserve anything that nice," she muttered. "People have been so good to us."

"We'd love to do it," Edith assured her. "This time I want to make sure you have a memorable fresh beginning. Start thinking about some of your friends that you would like to have attend."

Libby then glanced at the clock over her head. "Oh, dear. I better get back to work. I'm in the middle of some pretty heavy research for Stu."

That afternoon, Larry called Pastor Rhodes at the church study and asked him if he would conduct a renewal of wedding vows ceremony for Libby and him.

"I'd be delighted to," Pastor Rhodes assured him. "However, since you did not have a traditional wedding before, I would like to meet with both you and Libby for a couple of counseling sessions. I'd like to cover some of the basic marriage principles that I discuss with all engaged couples."

"That seems reasonable," Larry replied. "We want to make sure everything goes right this time. Not too many people get a second chance like we have."

"How about you and Libby coming to my study Saturday at two o'clock? We could make specific plans as to date and time then," Pastor Rhodes suggested as he thought back through the changes, both the good and the bad, he had seen in Larry from the time he first met him ten years ago until today.

That evening after work when Larry stopped at the Forest Grove Apartments, he found the manager, Ron, extremely accommodating.

"Yes, Larry, apartment twenty will be available February fifteenth. The tenants are moving out the first and we need a couple weeks to clean and paint the walls. The carpeting is getting plenty worn, so we thought this would be the best time to replace it. Are you interested in renting it?"

"I sure am," Larry assured him. "Do I need to put down a deposit to hold it?"

"Normally there would be a three hundred dollar cleaning deposit, but since Libby already lives in the complex, it won't be necessary. Just pay us two weeks' rent for the remainder of February when you move in."

"I'm sorry I can't show you the apartment until the current tenant moves out, but I can show you this one. They're exactly the same except the rooms are reversed."

Ron led Larry through his immaculate two-bedroom apartment. "Your wife has excellent decorating tastes," Larry observed.

"That she does," Ron agreed as he grinned at his wife, who was at the dining room table helping her son with his homework. "She could make a storeroom into a work of art."

Larry could hardly wait to get to Libby's apartment to share the news of the day. She was busy getting Vanessa ready for bed when Larry knocked on her door. She hurried to the door and flung it open. "Come in, Larry. I'm glad you're here in time to say goodnight to Vanessa before she goes to bed."

Larry took off his coat, laid it over the arm of the sofa, and picked up his daughter. She was looking more like her mother with each passing day. Vanessa giggled as Larry began making faces at her as he held her gently in his arms.

"Don't get her too excited," Libby cautioned. "I want to get her to sleep tonight."

"Let me read a quick story to her before we put her to bed. Does she have a favorite?"

"She seems to like the one about the kittens," Libby replied as she reached for a cardboard book on the shelf. "She likes to hear me try to imitate the kittens while she looks at the pictures."

Vanessa was soon asleep in her daddy's arms. Larry quietly laid the book back on the shelf and tiptoed into the bedroom. He laid her sleeping form in the crib and paused. He held his breath as she stirred and then rolled to her side and was fast asleep.

Libby watched from the bedroom doorway. *It is so important for little girls to have father figures to identify with. I'm so thankful Vanessa will now be able to grow up with her daddy to help guide and comfort her.*

Larry took Libby's hand and gently led her back to the living room sofa. "This has been one perfect day," he whispered.

Libby's eyes glistened. "Why? What has happened?"

"First I called Pastor Rhodes and he said he would be honored to help us renew our wedding vows. He would like us to come by the study next Saturday at two o'clock to set up the details and to have some basic marriage counseling."

"It's all so exciting," Libby replied. "When I called to tell Edith the good news, she said she and Nancy wanted to have a reception for us. It's going to be like a regular church wedding, which we didn't have the first time."

"That's not all," Larry interrupted. "I talked with your manager on my way over to see you. He said we could move into apartment number twenty on February fifteenth. He said we wouldn't be able to see that apartment until the current tenant moves out, but he showed me his apartment, which is just like it except the rooms are reversed. You were right. Those two-bedroom apartments are really nice."

Libby sat in silence for a moment before reacting. "Do you know what would be romantic?"

"Just being with you is romantic," Larry said as he pulled her closer to himself.

"You know what I mean," she snickered. "Wouldn't it be romantic to renew our wedding vows on Valentine's Day? The following day we could move into our new apartment."

"Sounds good to me. Let's suggest that to Pastor Rhodes Saturday," Larry replied. "Say, what all does Edith have in mind for the reception?"

"I don't know for sure, but she wants us to make a list of friends we want to include. I haven't started the list yet, but I do know I want Beth Slater to be at the very top of that list. She's been there whenever I've needed a friend."

Larry took out a sheet of paper and began listing people with whom they'd like to share their happy day. Before they were through, they were shocked that there were more than fifty friends and relatives listed. "Are you sure Edith is expecting a list this long?" Larry queried as he finished counting the names.

"She said the sky's the limit," Libby replied, wanting to share the happy day with the entire world. "She said she wanted to invite a few friends of their own as well. Especially those who work at the crisis center. Roy wants them to see one of their victory cases. She says they go a long time without seeing positive results, so our renewal of vows could be a real encouragement to them."

Larry shrugged his shoulders with delight. "The more the merrier."

On February fourteenth, Nancy and Beth spent all day decorating the fellowship hall of the church with hearts and cupids among the red and white streamers. Edith worked awhile in the morning and then brought Dawn by after school to put on the finishing touches. The Goody Bakery had designed a three-tier wedding cake, which graced the center of the serving table. Everything was perfect.

Promptly at seven o'clock the wedding march began. Libby, dressed in a pale pink and white dress, started down the aisle on the arm of Roy Dutton. If ever there were a model father to help a young woman take the crucial steps toward a successful marriage, it was he.

Larry's face broke into a broad grin as he saw his wife begin the long descent down the aisle to the altar. The beautiful bride on the arm of a distinguished father-figure was an image from a storybook.

The actual renewal of vows took only a few moments. Tears filled Libby's eyes. *The last time I said these words, I didn't know what I was getting into, but it seemed like it would be fun. Tonight I know what I am getting into, and I know we have to have God's help to make a marriage work.*

Larry and Libby moved easily through the crowd, accepting congratulations and expressions of good luck. They came face-to-face with Viola Tomkins, Grady Walker's secretary, whom Larry had scared that horrible day so long ago.

Neither spoke at first. Then Larry cleared his throat. "Forgive me, Viola. I'm truly sorry for what happened and that you had to witness such a terrible deed. I wasn't thinking straight."

With that Viola gave Larry a quick hug. "Oh, Larry," Viola exclaimed. "The important thing is that you're thinking straight now. The past is past."

"Thank you," he murmured as he turned to the woman at his side. "I'd like you to meet my wife, Libby."

Libby extended her hand. "I'm glad to meet you, Viola. Thank you for coming."

"I had to. The whole town is so happy for you and Larry. From the bottom of my heart, I wish you both the best."

"Excuse me," Larry interrupted. "I see the Mooneys and the Packwoods over there and I want to thank them for standing behind me at the court hearing."

Larry took his wife's hand and led her across the room. "Phil, Scott," Larry began. "Words can't express how much I appreciate what you two have done for me. You're the greatest."

"Not to worry, Larry. Now that we no longer have to contend with you, we can concentrate on the real criminals among us," Phil quipped to the amusement of all.

"Jessica, you remember the famous Larry Reynolds. Larry, my wife, Jessica."

"I'm delighted to see you again, Mrs. Mooney. We met at Stu Leonard's election headquarters. But Phil should have introduced me as infamous."

"You have rehabilitated yourself, Larry, and Rocky Bluff has dropped the "i" and "n" but kept the famous."

"That's true," chimed in Kim Packwood. "I hope you and Libby have a long and happy marriage."

"That goes double for me, too, Larry," Scott Packwood said as he shook Larry's hand.

"Your wedding dress is just gorgeous. Did you make it yourself?" asked Grady Walker's wife, Phyllis.

"Oh, no," Libby replied. "I could never do anything this nice. I had lots of help. Beth Slater chose the material and Pam Summer designed it. Edith introduced me to her former next-door neighbor, Beverly Short, who made it for me. Mrs. Short is an amazing woman. She's over seventy, but she does wonders with her fingers."

"I agree with you," Grady said. "We've known Bev Short all our lives. She made our daughter's wedding dress a few years ago. Libby, Phyllis, and I wish you and Larry all the best."

"Thank you, Grady. Coming from you that means so much to us."

Larry continued to move around the room greeting well-wishers, when he spied Amy Wallace, the Rocky Bluff High School nurse. Larry permitted himself to reminisce. *Beautiful Amy. She hasn't changed a bit. She's just as lovely now as she was when I was in high school. I had such a schoolboy crush on her back then. But so did half the male student body.*

"Oh, Larry." It was Edith Dutton. "Please come here. I want you to meet someone." Larry moved to Edith's side. "Larry, this is Grace Blair and her son, Dan."

"It's a pleasure to meet you both," Larry said as he and Dan shook hands.

Edith continued. "Dan is the new director of the crisis center."

"Oh, yeah. I remember reading about that. Congratulations. That center is doing a great job. My wife can attest to that."

"Nice of you to say so. Mother and I hope that you and Libby will be very happy."

"With friends like these," Larry waved his arm around the room, "how could we not?"

A hush came over the room as Roy Dutton loudly tapped a spoon against a decanter.

"Folks, could I have your attention, please? Will everyone fill their cup with some of the delicious punch my daughter-in-law Nancy made. I want to propose a toast to the bride and groom."

There was a mad dash to the punch bowl and some good-natured shoving that caused no little amount of punch to be spilled on the carpet. Pastor Rhodes grinned as he remembered it was Bob and Nancy's turn to clean the church that week. Finally the room settled down and all the guests faced Roy, who now had Larry and Libby by his side.

"To the bride and groom!" Roy shouted as he raised his cup. "May the good Lord richly bless and keep them both."

Shouts of "Hear-hear," "all right," "you bet," and "God bless you," filled the room. And then "Speech, speech" was followed by a thunderous applause.

"I don't know what to say. You've all been so wonderful," Larry began.

"I just thank God that I live in Rocky Bluff with all of you wonderful people. I feel like I have been handed a second chance at life and I promise you I will devote the rest of my life to making my wife and baby happy. Thank you all."

Libby was too overcome with emotion to speak and could only wave to the cheering and understanding crowd. As Larry and Libby stood facing their guests, a familiar figure made his way to the front. He stood before Larry with his left arm behind his back as though concealing something.

"Coach Watson!" Larry shouted with undisguised glee. Todd Watson was coach of the Rocky Bluff High School basketball team. Not since that horrible day in Larry's life when Todd Watson entered the principal's office and led Larry away after Edith had disarmed him had Larry seen his old mentor.

Grady Walker also came to the front of the room and stood beside Todd.

"Larry, Grady and I have something for you. You would have received this on your graduation night if you'd been there. We've been saving it for the right moment and we can't think of a moment more right than this one." With that, Todd brought his left arm from behind his back and handed Larry a beautiful trophy. "There's an inscription on it. Won't you read it for us?" Grady asked.

Larry took the trophy with trembling hands and began to read: "To Larry Reynolds," he read aloud. "Rocky Bluff High School's Most Valuable Player Award. Montana State Class A Basketball Championship Game, Billings, Montana, March fifteenth. . ." Larry couldn't finish. It was all too much for him. So many good things had happened to him in such a short period of time. He buried his head in his hands and cried like a baby.

Libby threw her arms around him as his mother and father rushed to his side. The crowd once again applauded. There were few dry eyes among them.

When Larry regained his composure, Bob Harkness asked the Reynolds family to pose for a family photo to memorialize the happy occasion. Larry, Libby, and Donald and Frances Reynolds stood side by side as Bob focused and snapped the picture.

"Wait a minute, Bob. I want Ryan in this, too," said Larry. "Ryan," he yelled. "Where are you?"

There was no answer.

"I think Ryan's among the missing along with Jay and Dawn," Bob observed with a chuckle.

The three were on a self-appointed mission in front of the church, where Larry had parked his car. They were preparing Larry's car for the honeymoon getaway. Dawn stepped back to admire her handiwork. With a bar of white soap, she had drawn a heart on the passenger's side door with an arrow running through it. Inside the heart she had added "Larry and Libby."

Ryan had been busy collecting soda pop cans for days and stringing them together. He tied the noisemakers to the rear bumper, laughing all the while. "Boy, that's going to make a lot of noise," he giggled with self-satisfaction.

"It sure will," agreed Jay as he busied himself soaping "JUST MARRIED AGAIN" across the rear window.

"I wish my dog, Ralph, could be here. I'd hide him in the backseat. That would shake them up."

Finishing their happy chore, the children hid in the shrubbery by the church building to watch the fun when the bride and groom emerged.

Meanwhile, after the toast and the presentation, the crowd began to mill around again in the fellowship hall. Dan Blair spotted Beth Slater across the room. Little by little he inched his way in her direction, trying not to be too obvious. Finally, he was beside her.

"Hello, Beth," he began politely. "I'm Dan Blair. We met at the reopening of Harkness Hardware Store."

"Hi, Dan," she replied cheerfully. "I remember you. You're now the full-time director of the crisis center."

"You do have a good memory," he chided.

"How could I possibly forget anyone who works for the crisis center? That was how I met Edith and got my life straightened around."

"She and Roy have been an inspiration to many people," Dan reminded her. "Look how much they've done for Larry and Libby."

"That couple proves that with God's help, nothing can stand in the way of true love." Beth's eyes became distant. "But in my case it's doubtful if love is possible since I already have a child."

"Beth, you were the one who caught the bridal bouquet." Dan grinned as he observed the flowers in her hand. "Isn't that proof enough that love can be possible with or without a child? Give it time. A year ago Libby would never have thought she would be where she is today."

❧

"What are they doing in there?" asked Dawn from her hiding place in the shrubbery.

"I don't know," Ryan whispered. "Why don't you go and see?"

"Okay, I'll be right back," Dawn mumbled as she dashed up the steps

233

of the church. She entered the church and turned to go to the fellowship hall when she heard a loud commotion as the reception party began to leave. Flying out of the church and back to her hiding place, she yelled, "Here they come!"

The guests broke into squeals of laughter as they saw Larry's car. "Ryan!" Larry yelled in mock despair. "Just wait until I get back."

From the safety of their hiding places, the three children shook with laughter.

At last it was time to go, and Larry and Libby waved to the crowd as they sped off trailing five feet of soda pop cans noisily behind them.

Edith turned to Roy. "The Lord works in mysterious ways His wonders to perform."

"Amen to that," said Dan Blair as he squeezed Beth Slater's hand.

Inspired
Love

This book is dedicated to the memory of two great Montana women,
Monida Vaughn and Muriel David.
Their "kitchen table" ministries served as a model for
the character Edith Dutton.

Chapter 1

The comanager of Sleepy Eye Motel in Rocky Bluff, Montana, forced a smile as the young, slender stranger approached the desk. "May I help you?"

The weary traveler glanced nervously around the lobby. "I'd like to rent a room with a kitchenette," he snarled.

Anita Reed shuddered. "We only have three kitchenette units and they're generally full, but someone just checked out this morning, so number thirteen is available." She reached for the room key behind her and the registration form under the counter.

The young man reached for a pen and began filling out the form. A scowl crossed his face. "I hope it's on the back side of the building. I don't like being disturbed."

"Yes, it's right off the alley. It'll provide you with a lot of privacy. How long do you plan to stay?"

He nervously took a round can from his hip pocket. He opened the container and placed a small wad of tobacco in the side of his mouth. "I'll be in Rocky Bluff until I decide to move on."

"Our policy is that the kitchenette units must be rented for a minimum of three days," Anita stated firmly. "After that it can go on a day-by-day basis with the checkout time at eleven o'clock."

The stranger took his wallet from his tattered GI fatigues and handed her a hundred-dollar bill. "Take the first three days out of this."

Anita counted back the change and then reached for the partially completed registration form. She glanced suspiciously over its contents. "I'm sorry, sir, but you didn't fill out your model of car and license plate number."

He grabbed the paperback and reached for the pen on the counter. "Boy, you hick-town people sure are snoopy. It's none of your business what kind of car I drive."

"It's one of our regulations. It also helps us provide better protection for our guests." Anita breathed a sigh of relief as her husband entered the side door of the lobby.

The disgruntled traveler scribbled a response on the form and handed it back to Anita without muttering another word.

Anita handed him the key to room thirteen. "Have a good day. If there's anything we can do to make your stay more pleasant, please let us know." Her kind words did not betray her inner fear and concern.

Grabbing the key, the young man stomped from the room, oblivious of Dick Reed's presence.

Dick shook his head with disgust. "Boy, he's a mean-acting dude to be driving such a late model Porsche. Most Californians leave their fancy cars behind and only bring their all-season vehicles when they come to Montana on vacation. Generally, they want to see the beauty of the backwoods, not try to impress the natives."

Anita glanced out the window. "I wonder what he's up to here in Rocky Bluff," she responded. "We're too far off the normal tourist route between Yellowstone and Glacier Parks for casual visits."

"I think we'd better keep an eye on him. If he does anything suspicious, we ought to let Phil Mooney know down at the police station. I heard that Little Big Horn County is seeing a great increase in drug traffic. There's a lot of flat land here for traffickers to land small, private planes."

Anita looked quizzical for a moment. "I have heard a lot more low-flying planes lately, but I just assumed they were crop dusting."

"That's what they want us to think, except it's long past the spraying season. I just hope that our new guest isn't one of them. But drug money could explain the fancy car."

⊗

Beth Slater arranged a pile of toys on the kitchen floor and then joined Edith Dutton at the table for a leisurely cup of coffee. "I hope Jeffy won't be in your way if he plays with his trucks in the corner."

"That's perfect," Edith assured the young mother. "It's been such a pleasure to watch Jeffy grow. It doesn't seem like any time at all since you brought him over for the first time. He was all wrapped in blankets and spent most of his time sleeping in the corner."

A faraway gaze settled on Beth's face. "I don't think I could have gotten through those early days without you. I often wonder what would have happened if you hadn't been working the crisis line the first time I called it."

"I'm sure the good Lord would have brought someone else into your life at that time." Edith paused as memories of the last four years flooded her. "I'm just glad I was the one who got to know you and little Jeffy. It's been so encouraging to watch a scared sixteen year old learn to care for her baby, then get her high school diploma and go on to take secretarial courses at the community college."

"At the time I never thought it would be possible, but here I am getting ready to go on a job search myself." Beth took a long, pensive sip of coffee before continuing. "When Libby Reynolds graduated and got her first job as a paralegal, it all looked so easy. Now when it's my turn to go out into the workaday world it seems so difficult. I don't even know how to begin."

Edith handed Jeffy another chocolate chip cookie. Before she retired as the home economics teacher of Rocky Bluff High School, her recipe for chocolate chip cookies had become famous throughout the state of Montana. Her cookie jar was rarely empty.

Jeffy dropped his Matchbox truck and reached for the cookie. "Thank you, Mrs. Dutton."

"You're welcome, sweetie," she replied. Edith turned her attention back to the proud mother. "I'm glad to see that you're teaching manners early to Jeffy. It makes it so much easier when they get in school."

Beth's baby was growing into a normal, happy child. "Jeffy seems to have been born with a sweet spirit," Beth beamed. "I'm so glad you directed me to the necessary social services when I needed them. But now it's time I get off welfare altogether," she declared. "Edith, do you have any tips on how to begin job hunting?"

"Have you tried to put a résumé together yet?"

"How can I prepare a decent résumé when I've never had any job experience? And no one is going to give me a job without experience."

"You've taken care of Libby Reynolds's baby regularly," Edith reminded her. "That would count toward demonstrating dependability and responsibility."

"Hmm. I never thought of that."

"If you listed the skills you've learned in your various classes, you'd have a lengthy list. Why don't you sit down tonight after Jeffy's asleep and jot down the highlights of each class?" Edith suggested. "We can go over it in a few days and compile a list of your qualifications and draft your résumé so all you'll have to do is go to the computer center and type it."

Beth glowed as a weight of concern was lifted from her shoulders. "I sure appreciate your help," she replied. "Will you be busy Wednesday afternoon to go over the details?"

"I'll be here," Edith assured her. "How does two o'clock sound?"

Edith went on to remind Beth to read the job ads in the *Rocky Bluff Herald* newspaper every day and to stop at the Montana State Job Service at least once a week.

Beth nodded her head in agreement with each suggestion Edith made. "And, most importantly," the older woman continued, "do as much volunteer work as you possibly can. You never know what might turn into a full-time position."

"Libby's volunteer work on Stuart Leonard's election committee for county attorney sure won her a jewel of a position," Beth giggled. "I don't know where to begin looking for a volunteer position. I faint at the sight of blood, so I wouldn't be any good at the hospital."

"I volunteered at the crisis center when I first retired," Edith reminded her with a twinkle in her eye. "In fact, I found more than just a few hours of fulfillment. That's how I met Roy. We were married several months later."

Beth sighed as her shoulders slumped. "I wish something like that would happen to me, but I don't think there's much of a demand in Rocky Bluff for single mothers as wives."

"Don't give up hope so soon. You never know what the future will hold," Edith consoled as she patted Beth's hand. "Just go on with your plans and Mr. Right will sneak into your life in the most unexpected way."

Beth straightened her shoulders as Edith's wisdom reached deep into her spirit. "You're right," she smiled. "The most important thing right now is finding a job so I can support myself and Jeffy and get off welfare."

Beth paused and took another sip of coffee before continuing. "Several months ago the director of the crisis center asked me if I would have time to help with the clerical work there. I was too busy with classes then, but from now until I find a full-time job I could probably help at least once a week."

"That's perfect," Edith replied enthusiastically. "Why don't you give Dan Blair a call when you get home? We could then include your volunteer work on your resumé."

Just then Jeffy crashed two trucks with disgust. Beth motioned for him to stop and then began helping him pick up his toys and placing them in his bag. "Edith, you've been a great help, but I think I better get Jeffy home for his afternoon nap. It looks like his frustration level is getting too high."

Edith fetched Beth's and Jeffy's coats from the front closet, then helped the four year old get his arms into the sleeves. "I'm looking forward to our visit Wednesday," she said as she opened the door for her guests.

Beth smiled. "Thanks. I need all the help I can get. I'll take your advice and give Dan Blair a call as soon as Jeffy is down for his nap."

Edith watched the young mother and child from her living room window until they rounded the corner. *So many troubled young people have found their way to my kitchen table for encouragement since I retired,* she mused. *My heart attack may have slowed my body, but as long as my welcome mat is out, I don't have to feel trapped within these walls.*

Returning to the sofa, Edith reached for a pillow, slipped off her shoes, and stretched out for a quick nap. As soon as she had dozed off, she was awakened by the shrill ring of her telephone. *I wonder who that could be?* she thought as she rubbed her eyes and hurried to the phone.

"Hello, Mother," Jean Thompson greeted when Edith picked up the receiver. "How are you and Roy doing today?"

"I'm doing well, just my usual slow self," she responded with a chuckle. "However, we're having trouble getting Roy's diabetes stabilized. One minute he's fine, the next minute his blood sugar may drop to a dangerous level. Last night it zoomed up to four hundred again."

"Has he been staying on his diet?" Jean queried. "I know how much Roy likes his sweets."

"Surprisingly enough he's followed his diet religiously, so I don't understand the fluctuation," Edith stated. "It sure is nice having a nurse for a daughter to share my concerns with."

"At least my advice is free," Jean laughed. "However, maybe you should notify your doctor and not wait for his regular appointment."

"I suppose you're right," Edith sighed and then searched for a way to ease the tension building within her. "Now enough about us. How are you and Jim and little Gloria?"

"We're doing great. I enrolled Gloria in nursery school three days a week while I work, and she loves it. She brings home all kinds of artwork for our refrigerator."

Edith grinned. "I hope you'll share some of it with me," she said. "When Jay and Dawn were little, Bob and Nancy made sure I was supplied with all kinds of 'Grandma's art.' "

"Mom, do I still have to keep competing with my big brother?" Jean teased. "My kid's artwork is as good as his kids'."

"Don't be ridiculous. I'm just saying I like to see the work of all my grandchildren, not just those who live close by," Edith scolded gently and then took a deep breath before continuing. "Not to change the subject, but how's Jim doing? I hope the problems at the sawmill are being resolved."

"I wish they were," Jean replied, not able to hide the pain in her voice. "The environmentalists won," she stated sadly. "The spotted owl controversy was enough to close the area woods from logging, which is forcing all the sawmills around Chamberlain, Idaho, out of business. It's really a sad time for our town. I don't know if it will ever be able to recover."

"Does Jim know what he's going to do yet?"

"Since he's working in the office, he'll be one of the last ones to leave. He has to make sure all the financial accounts are balanced before they lock the doors. Then I don't know where we'll go. There's already talk of having to close the local hospital because of declining support. That means I'll be out of a job as well."

"If you do decide to leave Chamberlain, it sure would be nice if you'd move a little closer to Rocky Bluff. It's awfully hard to have family so far away."

"We'll have to see what happens. I'll call you in a few days and let you know what's developing," Jean replied. "Mother, promise me you'll call the doctor about Roy," she added as she ended the conversation and returned her phone to its cradle.

Edith had just made herself comfortable in her recliner when Roy came out of the master bedroom to join her. "You sure have had a busy afternoon," he said, brushing his lips against her cheek. "Who was that on the phone?"

"Jean just called to let us know the mill where Jim works will be closing and they'll probably be looking for jobs somewhere else."

"I sure wish they'd move back here. I'm getting kind of attached to Gloria," Roy commented as his eyes sparkled. "She's getting to be a real charmer."

"That's exactly what I told her." Edith paused as her eyes caught a glimpse through the window of Bob's Ford Taurus pulling into the drive. "I wonder what Bob's doing here in the middle of the day?"

"I guess we'll soon find out," Roy replied as he opened the front door for his stepson. "Bob, glad you could stop by. What brings you out at this time of day?"

"Coffee break time," the dark-haired businessman countered as he made himself comfortable on the sofa. "Besides, I need some words of wisdom from Mother and you."

Edith raised her eyebrows as she remembered the days when Bob wanted sole control of the family business that his father started more than thirty-five years before. *Bob has changed so much since the car accident that killed Roy's son, Pete,* she thought. *That guilt nearly destroyed Bob before he came to terms with his responsibility.*

"Mom," Bob began as he surveyed his aging mother. The wrinkles around her eyes and forehead seemed deeper each time he saw her. "Since the grand reopening of the store after the fire, I'm finding myself in an extremely unique situation. With the settlement of the insurance company and the extra business that has been generated, I'm going to have to invest in a hurry or pay a tremendous tax bill. Do you have any ideas?"

"For someone who was contemplating bankruptcy just a little over a year ago, this is a major miracle," Edith chuckled. "Just off the top of my head, my only suggestion would be to open a satellite store. Your father always wanted to do that, but the cash flow was never there at the right time."

Bob scratched his head and stared out the window for several minutes. "That's a good idea," he said thoughtfully. "But where would I build it? Great Falls and Billings are crowded with hardware stores."

"Bob, why don't you try one of the smaller towns around here?" Roy suggested. "All of them cater to the farmers and ranchers, but no one is willing to invest in their towns. The businesspeople want the major cities, and the retirees and new transplants all want the mountains. No one seems interested in the foothills and the prairies, so that's a ripe market for investment."

Bob grinned from ear to ear. "That's a fantastic idea. I could do a little investigative work as to the local economy and the support a new store might expect to receive from the locals. Do you have any suggestions for location?"

Edith mentally scanned the geography of central and eastern Montana. Suddenly her eyes brightened. "How about Running Butte? It's only a little over an hour's drive from here. It's a well-kept little town with a lot of community pride, even after they closed the school and bussed the children into Geraldine. The reservation towns are often neglected by the outside world."

"Hmm, not a bad idea," Bob replied as he stroked his chin. "Maybe Nancy and I will drive out there this weekend and look around. Would you and Roy like to come with us?"

Roy and Edith exchanged glances. "Sounds good to me. I'm always looking for a chance to take the prettiest woman in town out to the countryside," Roy chuckled.

"Oh, by the way, Bob," Edith inserted. "Your sister called this afternoon. It seems that the environmentalists temporarily won the battle in the Northwest and shut the woods up for logging. They're going to be closing Jim's mill. The entire town of Chamberlain is pretty upset about their loss. Right now Jim and Jean don't know what they're going to do. However, with Jim's accounting skills, I'm sure he'll be able to find another job, but I'm sure it will mean they'll have to relocate."

"I wonder how they would like to live in Running Butte," Bob snickered as he slipped on his coat and headed for the front door.

Chapter 2

P retty flashy car for someone hanging around Rocky Bluff," Lieutenant Philip Mooney commented. He and Sergeant Scott Packwood were passing the Pizza Palace on the way back to the police station after investigating a minor traffic accident.

"I've seen that Porsche parked at the Sleepy Eye Motel the last couple of nights when I've had graveyard patrol," Scott replied. He peered through his side window hoping the driver would return to his car. "I hope they're just here on vacation and not someone trying to bring in drugs. We've had a lot of suspicious activity lately that we just can't put our finger on."

"Let's keep an eye open for the driver, but we have to remember that just because most young people in Rocky Bluff drive a pickup truck, it's not a crime to drive a Porsche," Phil chuckled.

The pair rode in silence for the next couple of blocks as they surveyed the community, which they were proud to protect. "Phil, isn't that Beth Slater coming out of the Job Service building?"

"Sure is," Phil replied. "I wonder if she's trying to get a job. She sure has been working hard to improve herself. She went to night school to finish her high school education and then took a secretarial course at the college. I don't mind paying taxes to help people like her get back on their feet."

"I know Edith Dutton has taken her under her wing and provided her a solid role model," Phil observed. "It's amazing the impact a few quiet people can have on this community. Edith has proven to the rest of us that age and physical limitations don't keep a person from influencing troubled youth."

Unaware of being watched, Beth turned the corner and headed for the Dutton residence. The crisp fall breeze whipped through her hair as it rustled the leaves around her feet. Jeffy was staying with a friend while she began her first official day of job hunting. The Job Service clerk had told her about a vacancy at the high school. Beth could hardly contain her enthusiasm. Could this be the lead she needed? Only an expert in the field would know, and she could hardly wait to see her.

Roy Dutton had just returned to the living room from finishing lunch when he noticed Beth hurrying up their front walk. "Edith, Beth is here a little early this afternoon. Judging by the way she's walking, she's pretty excited about something."

"I hope she has good news about a job," Edith responded as she went to open the door for her young friend. "She's been working hard enough to get one."

Before Beth had a chance to ring the bell, the front door of the Dutton home flew open. "Beth, do come in," Edith invited. "I'm all ready to help you with your résumé."

"I'm sorry I'm early," Beth explained as she took off her jacket. "I got a lead at the Job Service and I can hardly wait to talk to you about it."

Edith smiled and motioned for her to follow her to the kitchen. "Let's have a cup of coffee while you tell me about it."

"Getting this job would be an answer to my prayers," Beth confided as she made herself comfortable at the kitchen table.

"So where is it?" Edith teased. "Don't keep me in suspense."

"It's at the high school. They are looking for a clerk-secretary in the library to begin the first of November. The Job Service counselor said the woman who has this position now is moving to Denver."

Edith thought a moment while she poured two cups of coffee. "That would be Jenny Jones's job. I did hear that her husband's trucking firm was doing some reorganization and he was being transferred. She did an excellent job keeping the library organized when I taught at the high school."

"Hmm." A puzzled look spread across Beth's face. "Jenny Jones? Didn't I meet her a long time ago at a cosmetic party you hosted?"

"I forgot about that," Edith admitted. "She was here that night. She's a sister of Patricia Reagan, who used to do volunteer work at the spouse abuse center."

"Well, tell me more about the job," Beth urged. "It's sounding better all the time. I especially like the idea of having summers and holidays to spend with Jeffy."

Edith passed a plate of cookies to her guest. "Rebecca Sutherland is the librarian. You'll enjoy working with her," the former home economics teacher stated. "She has about twenty-five years of library experience with twenty of those here in Rocky Bluff. It wouldn't surprise me if she retires before too long."

"Well, do you think I've had the right kind of training for the job? I don't want to apply for a job I couldn't handle."

"With all the computer classes you've had, you'll be a 'shoo-in,' " Edith encouraged. "I heard that the school just received a grant to automate the library and that means there will probably be a lot of data entry. They say it's a pretty complex procedure to enter the entire card catalog into the computer."

"Then in my résumé I better emphasize my computer skills," Beth replied as she took a pad and pen from her oversized purse. "I'll need to come up with some profound objective for desiring this job. I obviously can't say I just want to earn money," she chuckled.

Edith beamed. "It looks like you came prepared."

"I've been giving this a lot of thought," Beth admitted. "In fact, I went to the public library this morning and photocopied some samples of different formats of résumés." She reached into her purse and took out six pieces of paper folded in half. "I think I like the top one the best, but the second one isn't bad."

In an hour both Edith and Beth were satisfied with the rough draft they had tailored specifically for the Rocky Bluff High School library position. "Since Jeffy's at the sitter's, I'll have time to run over to the computer lab and type this now. I can file my application at the school the first thing in the morning."

Beth rose and began putting on her coat. "Edith, thanks for all your help. If I get this job, it will only be because of your help."

"If you get this job, it will be because of your own hard work," Edith reminded her. "If you need a good recommendation, be sure and use my name."

❧

Saturday afternoon an oversized moving truck stopped in front of the home of Bob and Nancy Harkness. Twelve-year-old Dawn rushed out the front door. "Hi, Uncle Jim. I've been waiting all day for you," she exclaimed as she gave Jim Thompson a big hug. "When are Aunt Jean and little Gloria going to get here?"

"They had to stop for gas so they should be along shortly. Is that big, mean dad of yours home?" he chided.

"Dad said to have you call just as soon as you got in and he'll come right home. I think there may be some change of plans," Dawn explained.

Just then Jean and Gloria drove up in the family minivan. Jim and Dawn hurried to the curb. "Hi, Aunt Jean. How's Gloria?"

"We'll find out in a moment," Jean laughed as she gave her niece a squeeze. "She's been sleeping ever since we left Missoula. It's time to wake her or she'll never go to bed tonight."

When Jean opened the car door next to the sleeping child, the cold blast of fall air brought her to sudden alertness. "We're here," Jean whispered as she lifted her daughter from her car seat.

Within minutes after Jim called him, Bob joined his sister and brother-in-law in his spacious living room. "I'm glad you were able to pack up and move so quickly," Bob said as he poured a cup of coffee for each of his guests. "I didn't expect this deal to go through so fast."

"That's one of the few benefits of renting and not owning a home," Jim replied with a touch of sarcasm in his voice. "However, we're now going to be home owners. . .sort of."

"I'll have to admit it was kind of nerve-wracking to select a double-wide mobile home sight unseen complete with floor plan and colors," Jean said. "The colors were rather limited, but I think we'll be happy with what we bought. We did want an extra bedroom in case we have an addition to the family before long."

"Are you trying to tell me something?" Bob teased.

Jean shook her head. "Not yet, but don't be surprised."

"So when's the mobile home coming?" Jim asked as he took another sip of his coffee. "We don't want to impose on you too long."

"The workers brought it in yesterday and they're assembling it today. It sure simplified things to be able to find a lot that already had a septic tank and electricity," Bob explained. "Why don't we take your van to Running Butte tomorrow afternoon and see how it's coming along? If they're done, I'll take off work Monday and help you unload your truck."

"Sounds good," Jean replied. "Maybe we could take Mom and Roy along. I'm sure they need an outing."

"They do keep busy, but I sense they feel trapped since neither one is able to drive anymore."

"How have they been doing lately?" Jean queried. "When I've talked to them on the phone, they've sounded a little discouraged."

Bob shook his head. "Mom's been busy helping anyone in town who seeks her out. However, Roy seems to be slowing down an awful lot."

Jean wrinkled her forehead. "She told me several weeks ago that they were having trouble keeping his blood sugar under control. If we go out of town, we'll have to be sure to take his insulin in an insulated kit and have some extra sweets in case he has a problem. I'm sure the fresh air and ride in the country will do him a lot of good."

"I think we'd better let them know that we're in here," Jim chuckled. "It doesn't take long for word to spread that a moving van is in town. They would be awfully hurt if they knew we were here and didn't go to see them."

Bob hurriedly gathered up the coffee cups and placed them in the sink. "Mind if we take your van so we don't have to move the car seat?"

"I was just getting ready to offer."

Just as Jim was turning onto Main Street, a shining black Porsche sped around them. "Where did he come from? It sure looks like the locals are getting mighty prosperous in the last few months."

"Sorry, that one has California plates," Bob observed with a note of cynicism. "We're not getting many California escapees in this part of the state, but the Gallatin and Flathead Valleys are having real growth problems. Their infrastructure can't adapt to such rapid change all at once and our state coffers are too broke to help them out. I don't know how it's going to turn out. I'm just glad I live in Rocky Bluff."

"That's an interesting phenomenon," Jean noted. "Montana used to be the place for only the most hardy, and few people paid any attention to us. Now it's become the ideal escape from big city problems."

Both Roy and Edith were dozing in their recliners when their family entered through the back door. "Mom, we're here!" Jean shouted.

"Come on in, everyone," Edith replied as she adjusted her chair to the upright position. "We were wondering what time you would be getting in. We'd like to treat everyone to dinner at Beefy's Steak House tonight."

"That will be a treat," Jean replied as she leaned over to kiss her mother. "Are you sure they are prepared for a three year old?"

"I've seen more poorly behaved children than her eating there," Edith laughed. "Besides, my grandchildren are always good. Right, Dawn?"

"Right, Grandma," she giggled as she held her cousin's hand tightly.

Roy finally aroused to alertness. "Hello, everyone. Glad to have you back in God's Country for good," he chuckled. "How are the plans coming for the store at Running Butte?"

"We're on a roll," Bob assured him. "One reason why I wanted Jim and Jean here long before the store actually opened was to become familiar with the community. Since Running Butte is next to a reservation we need to know how best to stock the shelves to meet their needs. The land over there isn't nearly as productive as it is around Rocky Bluff."

"I'm looking forward to working with the Native Americans," Jean added. "I heard a rumor that a new medical clinic is coming to Running Butte and I'd like to get in on the ground floor of that project."

"That sounds exciting," Dawn exclaimed. "Maybe someday I can come up and help you."

"I'd like that," Jean assured her. "Your schooling has to come first, but maybe you could come for the summer and help with Gloria."

Monday morning while Beth was doing the breakfast dishes, she was interrupted by the shrill ring of her telephone.

"Hello."

"Hello, may I speak with Beth Slater, please."

"This is she."

"This is Viola Tomkins, the secretary at Rocky Bluff High School. The administration has reviewed your application and the principal has asked me to set up an interview time for you. Would you be available at three o'clock Wednesday to meet with Mr. Walker and the librarian?"

Beth could hardly believe her ears. She had worked and prayed for this moment and now she was nearly speechless. "Yes. . .sure. . .I'll be there Wednesday. Thank you for calling."

Beth hung up the phone and picked up her startled child and danced around the kitchen.

"Mommy, what happened?" Jeffy asked, barely able to talk beneath her bear hug.

"I have an interview for a job," Beth explained as she set him back on the floor. "That means we'll have enough money to buy a car and get some of the things we've never had before."

"Can we get a fancy black car like the one we saw going down the street yesterday?" he begged.

Beth giggled. "We won't be able to afford anything that fancy, but maybe I can find a Matchbox car like the one you saw. It was so far away I couldn't see the exact model, but maybe we could match it up pretty close."

Beth picked up the phone and dialed a familiar number. "Hello, Edith," she greeted when she recognized the voice on the other end.

"Well, hi, Beth. How's it going?"

"I just got a call from the high school and they want me to come for an interview on Wednesday. Isn't that exciting?"

"I'm so happy for you," Edith replied as she sat down in the chair next to the phone. "Grady Walker called me as a reference late yesterday and he was extremely impressed with your training at the community college. I take that as a very positive sign."

Suddenly Beth's voice softened. "I won't know what to say. I've never had a job interview before."

"Just be your usual sweet self and answer their questions. Mr. Walker is a friendly kind of person. There's nothing to be afraid of."

"The librarian will also be at the interview," Beth explained.

Edith chuckled. "Don't worry about Rebecca. She's the kind of person who can put the most fidgety neurotic at ease."

"If that's the case, I'll feel right at home immediately."

Wednesday afternoon, dressed in her best Fashions by Rachel dress, Beth dropped Jeffy off at a friend's house and walked the six blocks to the high school. The thought of having a car of her own made the distance seem even longer. Promptly at three o'clock she was ushered into the administration office.

"Hello, Beth," Viola greeted. "Would you like to have a seat? Mr. Walker got detained with a parent, but he'll be free in just a few minutes. Can I get you a cup of coffee while you wait?"

"Thank you. I'd like that," she replied as she made herself comfortable on the padded chair. *So this is where all the excitement happened,* Beth mused. Knowing Larry and Libby Reynolds now, it didn't seem possible that he could have shot Mr. Walker. *It's amazing how life has gone on as if nothing happened. I wonder if Mr. Walker still flinches every time he sees an unruly student walk through his door? It takes a mighty big person to forgive someone the way he forgave Larry.*

Beth's thoughts were interrupted by a tall, middle-aged man. "Hello, Beth. I'm Grady Walker. I'm sorry to keep you waiting, but I had a minor crisis occur right before you got here. Won't you come in, please?"

Beth obediently followed him into his office. She surveyed his cluttered office and the family pictures on his desk. *He must be extremely proud of his family,* she thought.

A well-dressed woman in her late fifties rose as she entered the room. "Beth, I'd like you to meet Rebecca Sutherland, our librarian. Rebecca, this is Beth Slater."

Rebecca extended her right hand. "It's nice to meet you."

The trio sat at a round table in the center of Mr. Walker's office. Beth found herself immediately at ease as she explained her background and experience with clerical work and computers. Finally, after an hour of discussing Beth's qualifications and explaining the job responsibilities, Mr. Walker said, "Beth, I'm sure you're anxious to see the library. We're mighty proud of it since we moved it into the new Edith Harkness wing. Rebecca will give you a grand tour. We'll make our decision this evening and will be in touch with you in the morning. Thank you for your time."

When Beth entered the spacious, well-lit library, she immediately understood why they were so proud of it. Everything was clean and organized with the latest audiovisual equipment lining the walls.

"As Mr. Walker told you, we're planning on automating next year, so for the next few months we're going to be placing bar codes on all the books," Rebecca said.

"That's going to be a massive job," Beth noted, as she tried to estimate the number of books on the shelf.

"That it will be, but I'm sure we can finish before the school year is over," the librarian assured her.

Beth felt as if she were floating on clouds as she walked to her friend's house to pick up Jeffy. She had only been at Rocky Bluff High School for a little over an hour and yet she felt she was already a part of that institution. *Imagine me, Beth Slater, four years ago a high school dropout, possibly being offered a job in a high school,* she thought as she crossed the street.

Suddenly her thoughts were brought back to her immediate environment as a black Porsche sped past her, nearly bumping her off the curb. "Crazy driver," she mumbled. "Why don't you watch where you're going? Don't you know pedestrians have the right-of-way?"

The hours passed slowly that night as Beth tossed and turned in her bed. *Did I get the job or didn't I?* she wondered. *I felt like the interview went well and they liked me, but I don't know who else applied for the job. There are thousands of people out there who are a lot more qualified than I am.*

The next morning Beth busied herself baking cookies as she waited for the phone to ring. At nine-fifteen it rang. Beth hurriedly wiped her hands and reached for the receiver.

"Hello."

"Hello, is this Michael's Computer Store?"

Beth's heart sank. "I'm sorry, you have the wrong number."

Beth went back to her cookies. Each minute seemed like an hour. Exactly at ten o'clock the phone rang again.

"Hello."

"Hello, is this Beth Slater?" a man's voice greeted her.

"Yes, it is."

"This is Grady Walker. I would like to offer you the job of clerk-secretary of the Rocky Bluff High School library. Are you still interested in the position?"

Still interested? Beth could hardly contain her excitement. "I'd be delighted to accept. Thank you for your offer."

"Good," the principal replied. "Could you be at work November first at eight o'clock? Report directly to my secretary. She'll have some paperwork you'll need to fill out. I'm looking forward to your joining our school family."

Chapter 3

The workmen on the new store sure started early this morning," Jean Thompson observed as she prepared breakfast in her new double-wide mobile home. "They're a dedicated bunch."

Jim smiled as he peered out the kitchen window. "That's one of the advantages of hiring local help. The unemployment rate is so high on the reservation, I have a waiting list for workers. It probably won't be long before other businesses will recognize the eager supply of labor and relocate to Running Butte as well."

"The plans for the new medical clinic are nearly finished and I imagine they'll be ready to build about the time the store is complete," Jean said as she placed three bowls of oatmeal on the table. "I think they're planning to do about the same thing Bob did. . .bring in a preconstructed metal building and then hire local help to complete the interior. The weather is so unpredictable here, the less outdoor work the better."

Jim spread homemade strawberry jam on his toast. "These metal buildings can get pretty hot in the summer, but with air-conditioning it shouldn't be a problem."

"Hopefully we'll be open before spring planting begins," Jean replied. "I was in the grocery store yesterday and overheard some locals talking. They're looking forward to not having to drive one hour each way just to buy a handful of nails."

"That's what I like to hear. It's going to take a lot of community support to make this work," Jim paused. "At first I was concerned they might not be as supportive of non-Native Americans, but I guess I can put that fear to rest."

Jean leaned over and picked up a piece of toast that Gloria had tossed on the floor and then turned her attention back to her husband. "I talked to Bob last night and he's going to bring the entire family up this weekend to inspect the progress. Hopefully, Mom and Roy will be able to come with them. I'm planning on a big dinner for my official house warming."

"Sounds good to me," Jim said as he glanced at the clock. "I better get out there and get to work," he chuckled as he stood and pushed in his chair. "I don't want to be labeled as 'one of those lazy outsiders'."

As soon as Grady Walker called, Beth Slater could scarcely contain her excitement about obtaining her first job. She immediately picked up the phone and dialed a familiar number.

"Hello, Edith," she exclaimed as soon as she recognized the voice on the other end of the line. "I have great news, but I don't want to share it over the phone."

"I can hardly wait to hear it," Edith responded. "Why don't you bring Jeffy and come on over? Can you have lunch with us?"

"Thanks," Beth replied, as she eyed her son playing on the floor. "We'd like that. Jeffy always likes to go to his granny Edith's house."

Beth hurried into her bedroom to freshen up and then put clean clothes on Jeffy. She packed a toy bag for him, grabbed their coats, and headed for the Dutton residence. This news was too good to wait.

Edith was watching for them as Beth and Jeffy came up the front steps. She flung the door open before Beth had a chance to ring the doorbell. "Hello, Beth. . . Jeffy. Do come in out of the cold."

"That fall wind is kind of nippy. I hope we don't have a storm moving in," Beth replied as she removed her coat.

"Mommy got a job and we're going to get a car," Jeffy blurted as soon as he walked in the door.

Edith beamed and looked at Beth for confirmation.

Beth nodded. "Grady Walker called this morning and asked me if I wanted the clerk-secretary job in the library."

Edith hugged her young friend. "When do you start?"

"The first of November. I have so much to get done before then."

"I'm sure you'll be able to do all that has to be done," Edith encouraged. "Let's go to the kitchen and make some plans. I guess the obvious question is, who'll take care of Jeffy while you work?"

"I know several women who take children into their homes, but at Jeffy's age, I'd rather have him somewhere he'll get preparation for school," Beth explained. "I know I'm biased, but he appears to be extra bright for his age."

"That's not prejudice," Edith chuckled. "That's a statement of fact."

"I've heard some of the mothers in my classes at the community college talk about Kinder University Day Care. I thought I'd go by there tomorrow and talk to the director. It's just three blocks from the high school, so I could walk over and see Jeffy on my lunch break."

"Sonya Turner and Patricia Reagan are codirectors of the day-care center. They have a pretty good thing going for them," Edith replied, as she poured them each a cup of coffee. "They used to be volunteers at the spouse

253

abuse center. While they were there, they saw that the biggest need of this community was adequate day care. I've only heard good things about them."

"The only thing that bothers me about going to work is that I was just beginning to do the clerical work at the crisis center for Dan Blair. I'll hate to let him down. He's swamped with paperwork."

"Since you'll be off work at three-thirty every day, maybe you could spend a little time after work at the crisis center. Why don't you go down and talk with Dan and see what can be worked out?" Edith suggested. "When I was doing volunteer phone work there, I found everyone extremely accommodating to the various work schedules of the volunteers."

Beth paused for a moment before she spoke. "That's a good idea. Tomorrow after I go to Kinder University I'll stop and see Dan. The crisis center was responsible for me getting my life turned around, so I'd really like to give back as much as I possibly can."

The next day Beth Slater lifted the latch to the front gate of Kinder University. The yard was full of brightly painted play equipment. One teacher was supervising eight children as they scampered around the yard, each bundled in a heavy coat and hood. Jeffy's eyes brightened. "Can I go play with them?"

Beth beamed. Her son seemed to love the day care on first sight. "Maybe later," she replied. "First we need to talk to someone."

The young woman by the swings quickly approached Beth and Jeffy. "Hi, may I help you?"

"Yes. I'd like to talk to the director about possibly enrolling Jeffy in the center."

"Great. We still have room for several more children," the teacher replied. "Either Patricia or Sonya can help you. If you ring the front doorbell, one of them will be right with you."

Beth rang the bell and within moments a young woman dressed in stylish slacks and a sweater came into the doorway. "Hello," she greeted. "May I help you? My name is Sonya Turner."

"Hi, I'm Beth Slater. I think we met several months ago at a cosmetic party at Edith Dutton's," Beth said as she extended her hand. "I just got a new job and I wanted to check into enrolling Jeffy in day care."

"That's right. I remember you now," Sonya smiled. "You were considering taking classes at the community college at the time but were afraid you wouldn't be able to make it. Do come in."

"Well, I did take those classes and it wasn't nearly as bad as I thought it would be," Beth responded, immediately feeling at ease. "In fact, because of them I was able to get my first job."

"Great," Sonya smiled as she led the way to her office. "Maybe Jeffy would like to play with the others while we talk."

That was all the invitation the four year old needed before he was right in the middle of the other children. The rocking horse with a rope mane held the greatest appeal.

Sonya and Beth visited as if they were long lost friends. Sonya explained their procedures and day-to-day routine, and Beth shared some of Jeffy's interests and favorite foods. Within minutes Beth was certain this was the right environment for her son. He would not only be well cared for here, but he would also receive the mental stimulation he needed.

"Jeffy," Beth called. "Time to go."

"Do I have to?" the young boy pleaded. "I'm having too much fun."

"You can come back next week and stay all day while I go to work. Won't that be fun?"

"Yeah," he replied as he obediently followed his mother out the door, giving the playroom one last glance.

Beth's next stop was the Rocky Bluff Crisis Center. It was an eight-block walk from the day care, but fortunately the anticipated storm had not moved in and the walk was invigorating. She shyly pushed open the door and found Dan surrounded by a pile of papers when she walked into the workroom.

Hearing the door open, Dan looked up. "Boy, do I need you!" he chuckled.

"It's always nice to be needed," she replied lightly.

"Take off your coat and stay awhile," Dan invited as he rose from his chair. "Can I get you and Jeffy something to drink? A cup of coffee or a soft drink?"

"Thanks, Dan. Don't go to any extra trouble. We can share a Coke."

Dan went to the half-size refrigerator and took out a can of pop while Beth and Jeffy made themselves comfortable on the sofa. "Why I stopped by, Dan," Beth began hesitantly, "is to tell you that I just got a full-time job. I'm going to be a clerk-secretary at the high school library."

"Fantastic. When do you begin?"

"Next Monday."

Dan gave a sheepish grin. "Why am I so happy? That means I'm going to lose you as my steady assistant just when you were figuring out my messy system."

"The crisis center did so much for me that I want to be able to help as much as possible," Beth explained. "I was thinking maybe I could stop over for an hour a couple times a week after work and help you out. You sure look overwhelmed now."

"Beth, you're a lifesaver. I'll be eternally grateful," he chuckled.

"Mommy's going to get a car," Jeffy volunteered.

"Good for you," Dan replied as he eyed the mother, amused at the little boy's enthusiasm. "What kind do you want to get?"

"I want to get one like that black fancy one I saw yesterday," Jeffy replied, thinking Dan was talking to him. "But Mom said she'd get me a Matchbox car just like it."

Dan roared. "That black Porsche does get around. I think you'll want something a little more conservative."

"And a lot less expensive," Beth echoed.

"I heard that Teresa Lennon was trying to sell her Chevy Capri. Maybe you'd be interested in that," Dan suggested.

"Right now I don't know how I'd pay for it."

"A dollar down and a dollar a month. Maybe if you'd talk to Rick at the bank, he'd be able to set up a loan for you now that you have a job."

Beth took a deep breath. "I don't even know how to begin the process. I've never owned a car before and I just got my driver's license a few weeks ago at the college, but I've never had time to do much driving in the drivers' education car."

"I'll give you a hand," Dan promised as he reached for the phone. "Let's call Teresa and see what she wants for her car. Then you can go to the bank with the exact car and price in mind. They'd be more willing to talk to you then."

Dan dialed Teresa Lennon and had an animated conversation with her as he negotiated a price for her eight-year-old car. When he hung up the phone, he turned back to Beth. "I think I got the best possible price for this car and she says it's in excellent mechanical condition. Are you still interested?"

"If the payments aren't too high," Beth replied.

Dan reached for his coat. "Then let's go down to the bank and see what they say. I'm parked out back."

Beth's mind spun as Dan and Rick discussed high book values, low book values, and current interest rates. Finally, they settled on a monthly payment schedule. "Does this seem like something you can handle on the salary you'll be making?" the banker asked.

Beth gulped. "Yes, I think so. . . . I just don't understand how all of this will work. I don't even have my first paycheck yet."

"The school has a direct deposit arrangement with this bank. We can do an automatic loan withdrawal from your account the day after your check is deposited so you'll never have to worry about missing a payment," Rick explained as he handed the papers to Beth to sign.

"Sounds too good to be true," she replied as she scanned the forms in front of her. "I'm glad Dan was able to help me get the car. I could never have done it by myself."

Monday morning Beth drove Jeffy to Kinder University and then parked her car in the faculty parking lot and hurried inside. Viola was already in the office waiting for her. It took over an hour to fill out the necessary paperwork and to explain the benefit package that came with the job. *I didn't realize that Jeffy and I would be covered under a real medical insurance policy,* Beth thought. *I'll no longer have to depend on Medicaid.*

After finishing the paperwork, Beth began her duties in the library. Rebecca Sutherland explained the policies, procedures, and basic routines of the library. By lunchtime Beth was checking out books to the students and helping them with simple questions. *I never dreamed I could ever be helping students in school,* she mused. *I'd always thought school was too difficult for me and I couldn't wait to get away from it.*

At three o'clock that afternoon Viola Tomkins was standing in the window of the high school office watching the students board the school buses parked along the curb. All the buses had their stop signs extended and red flashing lights on. Suddenly a black Porsche sped past the buses, just missing a couple students who were trying to cross the street.

Viola reached for the phone and dialed the emergency number. "Hello, I'd like to report a black Porsche that was speeding past school buses while they were loading students."

Phil Mooney groaned when Viola's report came in. "That guy in the Porsche really gets around," he said to the dispatcher. "I'm glad I took down his license number earlier. Here," he said to the dispatcher, "fax this to the California Bureau of Motor Vehicles and request information they have on this license number."

Within minutes the return fax was in. The black Porsche was registered to:

Lance Corporal Mickey Kilmer
Marine Barracks
U.S. Naval Station
San Diego, California

"Hmm. Time to do some more investigative work," Phil said as he read the incoming fax. "What is one of their marines doing here in Rocky Bluff?"

Phil went back to his desk and prepared a request for information about Lance Corporal Mickey Kilmer from the commanding officer of the marine barracks, U.S. Naval Station, San Diego, California. Soon that fax was also on its way.

"While I'm waiting for a reply, I think I'll cruise the streets and see if I can find our offending black Porsche. Montana state law is very strict about not passing a school bus from either direction while it's loading and unloading passengers," Phil said as he placed his hat on his head and slipped out the door.

Lieutenant Mooney drove past the Sleepy Eye Motel. No black Porsche. He drove past the high school. No black Porsche. No Porsche was found parked in front of any of the fast food restaurants in town. *I guess I struck out this time,* he mused. *I might as well go back to the station and wait for the reply to my fax.*

Phil Mooney was stopped at the door as he entered the station. "The answer to your fax just came in," the dispatcher said as she handed him a sheet of paper.

Phil hurried to his desk and slid into his chair before reading the much-awaited fax.

FAX TO: Chief of Police, Rocky Bluff, MT
FROM: Commanding Officer, Marine Barracks, U.S. Naval Station, San Diego, CA
REF: Your Request for Info on Kilmer, Mickey (NMI), LCpl. USMC SSAN: 247386225
Name: Kilmer, Michael (NMI)
Description: Age: 23   HT: 5'10"   WT: 165 lbs.
Build: Slender   Hair: Brown   Eyes: Hazel
Complexion: Tan. No identifying marks or scars
Home of Record: Rte. #2, Box 37,
          Elders Point, Montana

Subject EM tried and convicted by Special Court Martial, this station, for violation of Article 112a UCMJ—Wrongful use, Possession, etc., of Controlled Substances, To Wit: two grams of cocaine.

Subject was sentenced to be reduced to lowest enlisted grade

with a forfeiture of all pay and allowances due or to become due
and to be dismissed from the United States Marine Corps per
Bad Conduct Discharge.

Subject waived appeal and was dropped from the Rolls of
USMC 93 days ago.

Major Barton Sends

Chapter 4

Roy, Dan Blair's on the phone," Edith called, rousing her husband from a nap in his recliner.

"At least the phone is finally for me," he chided good-naturedly. "I was beginning to think it was strictly a private line."

"Hello, Dan," Roy greeted as he took the phone from his wife. "How are you doing?"

"I'm okay. More importantly, how have you been doing?"

"To be honest with you, this stupid diabetes has really slowed my body down, but, like I tell Edith, my mind is functioning A-OK but no one will believe me."

Dan chuckled. "I'll believe you, even if no one else will. In fact, that's why I'm calling. I need some advice about the crisis center. Who better to ask than the former director?"

"Why don't you come over and I'll have Edith fix us a cup of coffee," Roy invited. "It's her turn this week to do kitchen duty," he joked.

Edith glared at him across the room and shook her head. She had long since learned that some of his humor was not worth responding to.

A half hour later Roy was offering his guest a cup of coffee. "Dan, I hope you like the coffee. I made it myself. It seems right after I talked to you, Edith had something urgent to tend to which kept her tied up for quite awhile. I knew I'd promised you a cup, so I went ahead and made it myself."

"The timing was perfect," Edith snickered. "I just can't let him get too dependent on me."

Dan took a sip of his coffee. "I'm glad to see you two haven't lost your sense of humor."

"It's the only thing that's keeping me going," Roy retorted. "Now what great words of wisdom would you like to hear from me?"

"I've noticed an increasing number of noncrisis calls," Dan began. "People seem to be lonely and simply need a sympathetic ear."

"That's a good sign that you've touched a nerve in the community, but it also ties up the phone lines for the true emergencies," Roy replied thoughtfully. "I guess that leaves you with two options."

260

"What's that?"

"Either you cut all the noncrisis calls short and risk offending the caller, or you can expand your services by putting in more phone lines and recruiting more volunteers," the former director advised.

"But it'll take more than is allotted in my budget to expand, and I don't want to harm the compassionate reputation we've built in the community. I feel like I'm in a catch-22 situation."

"Not necessarily. Why don't you try writing a proposal to the director of United Charities, Barbara Hall, outlining your needs and how you plan to meet those needs? Occasionally they're able to tap other sources and provide emergency assistance for those over budget. However, it'll take a lot of clerical work to write the proposal."

Dan thought a moment. "I know just the person who can help. The problem is she's a mighty busy lady."

"Those are generally the ones who do the best job," Roy reminded him.

Promptly at three-forty-five that afternoon, Beth Slater breezed into the Rocky Bluff Crisis Center. "Sorry, I'm late. Some students had blocked the faculty parking lot when I went to leave."

Dan glanced at the clock overhead. "I was expecting you at three forty-two, what took you so long?" he teased.

Beth giggled as she hung her coat on the wire-framed coat stand. "What's up for today? I can work exactly fifty-eight minutes before I have to pick up Jeffy."

Dan suddenly became serious. "This project could take more than fifty-eight minutes. I'm considering writing a proposal to United Charities for increased funding so we can add more phone lines and volunteers to handle the noncrisis calls."

"That's a great idea," Beth exclaimed as she opened the refrigerator for a soft drink. "There were many times I wanted to call the crisis center when I was lonely and just needed someone to talk to. I was fortunate that Edith Dutton had given me her home phone number so I didn't tie up the crisis lines for the ones who really needed it."

"But that means a lot of typing," Dan warned her.

"I'm up to it," Beth assured him. "I could talk to the computer lab teacher and maybe he'd let me take one of the older computers home for the weekend to work on this project."

"Beth, you're an absolute dear. I'm sure you'll have a lot of extra stars in your crown when you get to glory for taking on this project," the director of the center teased.

Beth helped Dan outline what he wanted to say in the proposal and then hurried to Kinder University.

"Hi, Mommy!" Jeffy shouted as his mother entered the playroom. "Do you want to see the pictures I drew today?"

Jeffy took his mother's hand and proudly led her to the table in the corner. "The fancy black car kept driving past our school while I was outside for recess, so I decided to draw some pictures of it. They're pretty good, aren't they?"

Cold chills traveled down Beth's spine. *What is Jeffy's fascination with that car?* she thought. *That car seems to be every place and yet it's never close enough to see the driver.*

A fresh blanket of snow covered Rocky Bluff when Beth left for work the next morning. The biting cold dampened her spirits and the fear of her first drive on snow-packed streets enveloped her. A sense of apprehension tried to smother her, but she took a deep breath. *I'm a working woman now. I'm only experiencing what every other Montana woman is facing this morning. With God's help I can handle it.*

Beth eased the car slowly toward Kinder University. Jeffy was eager to play with his new friends. However, this was the first time it was hard for Beth to say good-bye. *I'm merely suffering from separation anxiety.* She tried to console herself.

The grayness of the skies echoed Beth's spirit. She tried to keep a smile pasted on her face while she checked out books to students and shelved those they returned. As she was walking down the hall from lunch, Grady Walker approached her with a grim look on his face. "Beth, would you come into my office please?"

Panic raced through her as she followed her principal down the hall like a disobedient student. *Have I done something wrong? Aren't they happy with my work here? I just bought my car, so I can't afford to be fired now.*

Mr. Walker motioned for her to enter his office and then he closed the door behind him. Terror gripped her as she saw Lieutenant Mooney and Sergeant Packwood standing there.

"Beth, won't you sit down," Mr. Walker said, as he pointed to the same table and chairs she sat in during her interview two weeks before.

"Beth, I have some bad news for you," Phil Mooney began. "Jeffy has disappeared from Kinder University Day Care."

The young mother sat in stunned silence. She wanted to scream, but her mouth froze shut. Finally, she was able to whisper. "You must be mistaken. Jeffy loved it there. He would never run away."

"We don't think he ran away," Sergeant Packwood tried to explain.

Beth began sobbing hysterically. "Then what happened to my baby?"

"At this time all we know is what the directors and teachers have told us. The teacher was outside with eight children when one of them fell on the ice and received what she thought might have been a concussion. After taking care of the injured child, she returned to the others, but Jeffy was missing. There were small footprints in the snow up to the fence, large men's boot prints on the other side of the fence, and tire marks near the sidewalk. The police are now trying to identify the kind of car by the type of tires."

Beth continued sobbing while the three men sat there in tense silence. Nothing would be able to take away her pain until her child was in her arms. Her baby was gone.

Finally, Mr. Walker put his hand on Beth's shoulder. "Beth, is there somewhere you'd like to go? I'll drive you there myself. Your car will be all right in the faculty parking lot overnight."

"I want to see Edith Dutton," Beth mumbled between sobs.

Mr. Walker had his secretary go to the library and get Beth's coat and purse. He then told Viola to call Edith Dutton and tell her they were on their way and they would explain the circumstances when they got there.

"If we have any developments, we'll be in touch with you either at Mrs. Dutton's or at your home," Lieutenant Mooney explained softly. "Do try to get some rest. You'll need all the strength you can muster."

Numb with shock, Beth scarcely felt the cold, biting wind that blew across the faculty parking lot. Grady gently directed her to the principal's parking stall. She sobbed softly as he drove on the snow-packed streets to the Dutton residence.

Mr. Walker escorted Beth to the door and rang the bell. "Do come in out of the cold," Edith invited, as she observed the distraught young woman before her. "What has happened?"

"Jeffy disappeared from Kinder University," Grady Walker explained. "It looks like a kidnapping."

Edith's face blanched as she wrapped her arms around Beth to comfort her. "How can that be? They take such good care of the children there."

"One of the new teachers took the older children outside for a few minutes to play in the snow," Grady explained. "One of them slipped on the ice and hurt his head. While her attention was directed to him, Jeffy vanished."

"Do they have any idea who did it?" Roy asked as he straightened himself up in his recliner.

"Lieutenant Mooney said the leads are pretty slim now, but they're doing all they can." The principal turned his attention back to the stunned mother. "I need to get back to school now, but if there's anything I can do, don't hesitate to ask. We'll give you a few days personal leave until Jeffy is found."

"Thank you for all you've done," Beth muttered as she slowly regained her composure.

"Beth, let me hang up your coat," Edith said gently. "Why don't you stretch out on the sofa and rest while I make some herb tea. That always seems to have a soothing effect for me."

As Edith walked to the kitchen, the phone rang.

"Hello."

"Hello, Edith," a worried voice greeted. "This is Sonya Turner. Does Beth Slater happen to be at your house? I called the school and whoever answered the phone said she left with Mr. Walker."

"Yes, she is. Would you like to speak to her?"

"If it's okay with you, I'd rather see her in person," Sonya replied.

"I'm sure that would mean a lot to her. Do stop over," Edith invited. "I'm just putting on a pot of herb tea now."

Within minutes, Edith, Beth, and Sonya sat glumly in the Duttons' living room sipping herb tea while Roy reclined restlessly in his chair, unable to comfort the grieving women.

"Beth, you don't know how sorry I am about this," Sonya said with tears in her eyes. "If only we hadn't let the children go out and play in the snow today, this wouldn't have happened."

"I didn't think anything like this would happen in Rocky Bluff," Beth muttered. "Occasionally we hear of something happening in Billings, but never here. And why Jeffy? He's such a sweet, loving child."

Sonya bit her lip. "I just don't understand," she confided. "I know the police are doing all they can. They worked quite awhile in front of the day care. Scott Packwood said they're going to make plaster models of the foot and tire imprints in the snow and send them to the crime lab in Missoula. Hopefully, that'll give them a lead."

"I just don't see how anyone could do such a thing to an innocent child," Beth muttered as she tried to hold back her tears. "Don't they have any human decency?"

"I hope they catch the guy, lock him up, and throw away the key," Roy said, unable to hide his anger.

The women each nodded in agreement.

"I wish I could stay longer," Sonya said as she stood to leave. "But I need to get back to the center so others can take their break. If you hear any word on Jeffy, would you let me know? We'll all be praying for him."

"Thanks," Beth mumbled as Sonya slipped quietly out the front door.

Beth stretched out on the sofa and pulled the afghan over her. Nothing could remove the cold chill that encased her except the warm embrace of her son. She wanted to slip into unconsciousness, but sleep avoided her as memories of Jeffy laughing and playing danced before her.

A cloud of gloom hung over the Duttons' home. An hour later the silence was broken by the ringing of the doorbell. "I hope that's the police with some word on Jeffy," Roy exclaimed as he went to answer the door.

Roy was unable to hide his disappointment. "It's Dan," he announced, motioning for him to come in.

"Don't sound so unhappy with my arrival," Dan said, trying to ease the tension.

"I'm sorry," Roy apologized. "We were just hoping it was the police with some word about Jeffy."

The director of the crisis center forced a faint smile. "That's okay. I just came by to see how Beth was doing." He walked across the room and took her hand.

"I'm doing terrible," she said as she sat up so he could join her on the sofa. "I just want my baby back."

"The police are doing all they can." Dan squeezed her hand tighter. "I'm sure Jeffy has an entire legion of guardian angels taking care of him right now."

"I hope you're right," Beth replied. She sat in silence for a moment before she spoke. Then turning to her friend, she said, "Dan, would you mind giving me a ride home? My car is still in the school parking lot. I want to be home in case the police call with any word on Jeffy."

"Sure," Dan replied as he rose from the sofa. "Let me get your coat. I'll take you home and then walk over to the school and get your car for you. While I'm doing that, would you mind ordering out for pizza?"

"Food is the last thing on my mind," Beth replied as she slipped into her coat. "But I guess it's getting about that time."

"Time is getting away from us," Edith reminded her. "You need to keep up your strength for when Jeffy comes home."

"When I get home I should call my parents in Glasgow," Beth sighed. "They disowned me when I got pregnant with Jeffy, but I suppose it'll be on all the evening news broadcasts tonight, so they probably should hear it first from me."

"I know calling your folks will be difficult, but I'll be by your side to give you moral support," Dan encouraged as they walked to his car parked in the drive.

"I'm sure they'll tell me, 'I knew you couldn't handle that baby by yourself. You should have had an abortion like we wanted you to,'" Beth sighed as she choked back the tears. "Can you imagine having aborted little Jeffy? He's the most precious child there ever could be."

When Beth opened the door to her apartment, she burst into hysterical sobs once again as Dan held her gently in his arms. Jeffy's favorite stuffed toy was on the chair. His artwork covered the refrigerator and his inflatable chair was still in front of the TV, where he left it that morning. Just as her tears began to subside and her body relaxed, the doorbell rang.

"I hope that's the police with word about Jeffy," she said as Dan answered the door.

"Hello, Pastor Rhodes," Dan greeted.

"Is Beth home? I just heard what happened to Jeffy and I wanted to stop and see how she was doing," Pastor Rhodes said as he stomped the snow from his shoes and entered the cozy apartment.

"Things are plenty tough," Beth admitted as the pastor took the chair next to the sofa.

"I imagine they are," he acknowledged. "We just have to trust that Jeffy's in God's hands right now and He is protecting him from all harm. The church prayer chain is praying for him right now and will continue to do so until he's returned."

"Thanks for your support," Beth replied as she glanced at the clock overhead. "It's time for the five-thirty news. I want to see if they have any news about Jeffy."

Dan took the remote and clicked on channel five just as the theme song of the news broadcast began. Sure enough the lead story was: CHILD SNATCHED FROM LOCAL DAY CARE. Beth's eyes filled with tears as she listened to the newscaster rehash the events of the day. They ended with a picture of Jeffy that was taken the first day at Kinder University. The public was asked that if they had any knowledge as to the whereabouts of the child to please call the Rocky Bluff Police Department.

After the evening news, Pastor Rhodes led the worried mother in a prayer of protection for her child and comfort and strength for herself.

Beth felt more at peace as she closed the door behind her pastor. "I don't know what I'd do without the love and support everyone has shown me," she said to Dan as she squeezed his hand. She then took a deep breath. "Now I have to call my parents. I hope they didn't see the news, but I think they can get this channel on cable in Glasgow now."

Beth checked her address book and dialed the long-forgotten number.

"Hello, Mother," she greeted as a familiar voice answered the phone. "This is Beth."

"Honey, how are you? We've been so worried about you, not knowing where you've been for so many years," Mrs. Slater said as she choked back her tears.

"Mom, something terrible has happened," Beth sobbed.

"We know. We just saw your baby's picture on the evening news. He's a beautiful child. Your dad and I are going to leave first thing in the morning to come to Rocky Bluff and help with the search for him. We love you, darling."

"Mom, you haven't said that since I was a little girl," Beth sobbed.

"I'm sorry," Mrs. Slater admitted. "But those times are over. We want to be a family again with our beautiful grandson. Will you please forgive us for not standing behind you when you needed us the most?"

"Of course," Beth assured them with tears streaming down her cheeks. "I need you more than ever right now."

Chapter 5

Where are you taking me?" Jeffy cried as the black Porsche sped away from Kinder University.

"I thought you'd like to ride in my new car," the stranger replied. "Only extra special people get to ride in this car. Do you like it?"

The child leaned back in the seat and relaxed. "Yeah, it's neat. I have a Matchbox car just like it."

Jeffy sat in awe as the Porsche reached the outskirts of Rocky Bluff. His dream of being in a fancy car had come true.

"Do you want to see how fast the car can go, just like in the races?" the driver asked.

"Yeah, that'd be fun," Jeffy shouted excitedly. "I've never been to the races, but I've seen them on TV."

The black Porsche raced west toward Great Falls. Occasionally, it slid on the icy snow-packed pavement, but the driver immediately regained control and regained speed.

"Jeffy, do you know who I am?"

"No, but you have a neat car," the child innocently replied.

"I'm your daddy."

"I don't have a daddy," Jeffy stated in a matter-of-fact tone. "It's just me and my mommy."

"She didn't tell you about me because I was in the marines."

"You mean you were a real GI Joe?"

Mickey Kilmer laughed. "Something like that. Now that I'm out, you and I can do a lot of fun things together."

"But what about Mommy?"

"She has a new job. Wouldn't you rather ride in my car than go to day care every day?"

Jeffy thought for a moment. "I guess so. But I like Kinder University. It's fun."

The warmth from the car heater made Jeffy sleepy, and he laid his head against the back of the seat and went to sleep. The highway became more snow-packed and slippery with each passing mile. Mickey was forced to decrease his speed just to stay on the road. The miles passed slowly for him.

Ten miles out of Great Falls, Mickey awakened the sleeping child. "Jeffy, we're going to stop here. I need to get some snow tires. The roads are just too slick to drive on. If anyone asks you, tell them we're on our way to see your grandma."

"But I don't have a grandma," Jeffy protested. "Except for my granny Edith."

"You'll be meeting all kinds of new people," Mickey explained, trying to calm the child's fears so he would not alert a passerby. "Until today you didn't know you had a daddy and now we're the best of friends. Right?"

"Yeah, I guess so," he replied doubtfully.

Mickey turned his car into the first tire shop he came to on Tenth Avenue South—Don's Tire and Rubber. "Wait here a minute while I see if they have what I need," he directed the child.

Mickey got out of the car and hurried into the sales shop. "Do you have any snow tires to fit my Porsche?" he demanded of a nearby salesman.

"Pretty fancy car to be driving on these kind of roads," the salesman commented as he looked out the plate glass window. "I'll have to check the computer to see if we have any that are compatible. It's not very common in Montana."

Mickey nervously watched the traffic while the salesman punched the keys of the computer. He stood motionless as a Great Falls police car stopped at the corner light.

The salesman looked up from the computer screen. "Looks like you're in luck," he assured Mickey. "We still have two left, but we have such a backlog because of this storm, we won't have time to get to them until tomorrow."

"But I have to get on the road as soon as possible," Mickey pleaded. "My mother is critically ill and my father asked me to come home right away. If I don't get home tonight, I may not get to say good-bye."

The salesman stroked his chin. "Hmm. If that's the case, maybe we'll be able to slip you in right now. It'll take us about an hour and a half if you want to go and get something to eat."

We Montanans are so naive we'd believe any hard luck story, Mickey snickered as he walked back to his car. "Come on, Son," he said loud enough for the salesman to hear. "Time to get something to eat before we go on to Grandma's house."

⌘

After hanging up from talking with her mother, Beth Slater paced nervously around her small apartment. "Beth, why don't you sit down and try to watch television with me? You're only wearing yourself out by pacing."

"I wonder if the police have any new leads?" Beth said as she peered into the night blackness. "Statistics say that the longer a child is missing, the less likely you are to get him back at all," she sighed.

"Why don't you call the police station and find out?" Dan suggested.

Beth dialed the nonemergency police number. "Hello, is Lieutenant Mooney there please?" she asked the receptionist. "This is Beth Slater."

"One moment please."

The silence on the line was nearly deafening before a deep voice answered. "Hello, Beth. This is Lieutenant Mooney. How are you doing?"

"I'm plenty worried. Have there been any developments?"

"We probably won't know anything until morning," Phil explained. "Scott caught the last Treasure State plane to Missoula this afternoon to hand carry the plaster molds of the footprints and the tire print to the crime lab. He's supposed to call me first thing in the morning with results. I don't think we'll know anything until then. But I'll let you know as soon as I hear anything."

"Thanks," she muttered as she hung up the phone.

"No more news," Beth sighed as she turned her attention back to Dan.

"Say, we forgot all about the pizza we were going to order. What kind do you like?" Dan asked, trying to ease her troubled mind.

"Jeffy and I usually have Canadian bacon," she replied.

"That sounds good. Now how about you calling the Pizza Palace and placing the order? If you'll give me the keys to your car, I'll walk over to the school and drive it back. If they guarantee thirty-minute delivery, I should be back long before the pizza gets here."

Beth reached for her purse and handed Dan her keys. He slipped out the door into the night blackness while she took out the phone directory and searched the yellow pages under P.

A string of friends and well-wishers either came to Beth's apartment or called that evening. Dan remained constantly by her side, helping her tell the story of Jeffy's disappearance over and over again. By ten o'clock the last of the guests left and Beth and Dan turned on the ten o'clock news. Again Jeffy was the lead story.

"Flashing his picture all across the state on TV, someone's sure to recognize him," Beth sighed as the same picture of him appeared on the screen.

"I'm sure we'll have some good news in the morning when Scott calls from the crime lab," Dan assured her as he patted her hand and stood to leave. "Now why don't you go to bed and try to get some rest? I'll call you first thing in the morning."

Eight o'clock the next morning Dan was knocking at Beth's door with a sack of groceries. "I thought I'd make you one of my specialties for breakfast," he said when she opened the door dressed in a crumpled sweat suit. "How does a Denver omelet sound?"

"I appreciate your efforts," Beth sighed as she motioned for him to enter. "I'm just not in the eating mood. I don't think I slept a bit all night."

"That's all the more reason to have a hearty breakfast."

Within thirty minutes Dan had a lavish breakfast on the table. Beth did her best to compliment him on his cooking, but every bite laid flat in her mouth. When they finished, Dan insisted on doing the dishes alone so she could get some of the rest she missed during the long night.

Beth's state of semiconsciousness was broken with the ring of the doorbell. Dan hurried to answer it.

"Phil, do come in. I hope you have some good news for us," he said as he swung the door open and then stepped aside.

"Let's just say I have some interesting news," the officer responded as he headed for an overstuffed chair beside the sofa where Beth was resting. "Scott just called from the crime lab in Missoula. They found that the car tracks were made by a Pirelli radial tire size 25540 Z R 17. This particular tire is manufactured by Pirelli Tire Company in Italy. It's standard equipment on all model 911 Porsches. The boot print was made by a size ten army issue style combat boot. The weight of the wearer is estimated between 155 and 175."

"Well, at least that's a beginning," Dan replied. "Not too many people in Rocky Bluff drive a Porsche."

"How about that black Porsche that's been cruising around town for the last week or so?" Beth asked. "Who does that belong to?"

"Interesting enough, we just ran a make on it the day before yesterday when the driver failed to stop for the school buses that were loading students," Lieutenant Mooney explained. "We traced it to a Mickey Kilmer who was kicked out of the marine corps with a bad conduct discharge about three months ago for possession of cocaine."

Beth gasped and turned ashen.

"Do you know him?" Dan and Phil asked in unison.

"He's Jeffy's father. I haven't seen him since I told him I was three, months pregnant."

Lieutenant Mooney tried not to display his shock. "We've placed an all-points bulletin out for his arrest," he explained matter-of-factly. "I'm sure we'll have your baby back in a few days. I better get back to the station in case we have any response to our APB."

After the police officer left, Beth turned to Dan. "Would you mind driving me to Edith's? I want to tell her about the latest developments, but I don't feel up to driving on these slick streets."

"I'd be delighted to," Dan said as he reached for his coat. "Get your coat."

As they turned the corner toward the Dutton residence, they could scarcely believe their eyes. Cars lined both sides of the street. "They all seem to be at the Duttons'. I hope they're both okay," Beth said, trying to mask her sense of panic.

"I haven't heard an ambulance siren this morning, so I assume that they are," Dan assured her.

When Beth entered the Duttons' living room, she found herself surrounded by hugs and well-wishers. "We're in the process of organizing a Bring Jeffy Home Committee," Edith explained as she helped Beth off with her coat. "We have a number of ideas that we're working on."

"What do you think of this as a missing child poster?" Teresa Lennon asked as she held up a neatly printed poster with Jeffy's enlarged photograph in the center.

Tears welled in her eyes as she surveyed the notice with Jeffy's picture, description, and the phone number of the Rocky Bluff police department. "It's perfect," she murmured. "I don't know what to say."

"If you like it, Teresa said she'd take it over to the print shop and have ten thousand copies made," Edith explained as she patted the frightened mother on the shoulder.

"But I don't make enough money to pay for it," Beth said meekly.

"We'll worry about the financing," Edith assured her. "We have already begun placing jugs in all the stores to help meet expenses."

"The president of the bank has set up a Jeffy Slater account and he donated the first one hundred dollars," Teresa exclaimed excitedly.

Beth shook her head in amazement. "I can't believe everyone is doing this for me."

"We're doing it for both you and Jeffy," Patricia Reagan replied as she hugged her friend. "We love you both."

Teresa Lennon, the director of the spouse abuse center, was obviously one of the leaders of the ad hoc committee. "We've also contacted several dairies that distribute milk in schools in the northwestern United States and Canada," she explained as she laid her poster aside. "They've agreed to print Jeffy's picture on the missing children's milk cartons. Someone's bound to recognize him."

"Canada?" Beth questioned. "Do you really think he could have gone up there?"

"Anything's possible," Teresa replied. "The border is only two hundred miles away. It's a mighty long border, with a lot of crossings between Montana and Canada."

"We're in the process of listing US and Canadian agencies to notify and provide them a copy of the poster," Edith went on to explain. "I'm sure we'll need more than ten thousand, but that's a good starting number."

"That's not all we're doing," Larry Reynolds added. "I've gotten fairly efficient with the computer since I started working at Harkness Hardware Store. I've placed Jeffy's picture in an on-line database of missing children that's available to all computer enthusiasts, social services, and law enforcement agencies. Perhaps someone will recognize him there."

"You've all been so kind," Beth said. "Even my parents are coming from Glasgow to help look for Jeffy."

A look of shock spread across Edith's face. "I thought they had disowned you when you got pregnant and didn't get an abortion."

"They did," Beth replied. "But I called them as soon as the news was on TV. When they saw Jeffy's picture on TV last night, they said they felt terrible about the way they acted toward me. They want to get to know their grandson that might not have been if I had listened to them and had an abortion."

"I wonder if they'll be able to travel from town to town, truck stop to truck stop hanging Jeffy's posters," Edith pondered. "Most of us aren't able to get away from our families and jobs for very long and Montana has a lot of territory to cover."

"I imagine Dad would like to do that," Beth responded thoughtfully. "He used to be an over-the-road trucker and knows all their hangouts. He's really missed the road since he retired. They should arrive late this afternoon and we can ask them then."

The ringing of the phone interrupted the enthusiastic plans being made. Edith hurried to the phone. "Hello."

"Hello, Edith. This is Phil Mooney. Does Beth Slater happen to be there? I checked her apartment and no one was there."

"Yes, she is," Edith chuckled. "Along with half the town of Rocky Bluff. Just a moment and I'll put her on."

The entire group went silent as Beth took the phone.

"Beth, I just got our first response to our all-points bulletin."

Beth's eyes lit up. "What was it?"

"The police department in Great Falls just called and said they did see a black Porsche about five P.M. yesterday getting snow tires at Don's Tire and Rubber on Tenth Avenue South," Lieutenant Mooney explained.

"Were they sure it was Mickey?"

"They're pretty confident," Phil assured her. "When they talked with the salesman at Don's Tire, they said that the driver fit Mickey Kilmer's description and he was traveling with a small boy. He gave them some story that he was on his way home to see his ailing mother."

"But Mickey's mother lives in Elders Point," Beth protested. "That's in the far southeastern part of the state. He's going the wrong direction."

"Don't worry. We're contacting all the border crossing stations to make sure he doesn't enter Canada. It'll be a lot harder to locate Jeffy if Mickey does cross the Canadian border." Phil could scarcely hide the frustration in his voice. "Let's hope he kept going west or turned south from there."

Beth hung up the phone and turned to the group. "That was Lieutenant Mooney from the police department. He came by my place earlier today and told me that the car tracks found where Jeffy was kidnapped belonged to that black Porsche that has been seen all over town. The Porsche belongs to Mickey Kilmer, who was kicked out of the Marine Corps three months ago." She hesitated as all eyes remained glued on her in astonishment. "Mickey is Jeffy's father." Beth took another deep breath. "Lieutenant Mooney said that the Great Falls police just called and that Mickey and Jeffy were spotted in Great Falls about five P.M. yesterday."

With that Beth collapsed to the floor. Dan was immediately kneeling beside. "Are you okay?" he whispered.

"I'm sorry," she murmured. "I'm so tired I guess I can't keep my body functioning."

"I'll take you home, where you can rest," Dan said, helping her to her feet. "The Bring Jeffy Home Committee is in good hands."

Dan took Beth home, where she immediately flopped on her sofa. He gently covered her with an afghan and sat down in the chair to read the morning newspaper. Of course, the disappearance of Jeffy Slater was headline news. Dan dozed off himself, but was soon awakened by the doorbell.

"Scott, you're back from Missoula already," Dan said as he opened the door.

"I took the next Treasure State flight home. We don't have any time to lose in finding Jeffy," he explained. "I just wanted to stop by and see how Beth was doing."

"She's holding up fairly well," Dan assured him. "But she's extremely tired. She didn't get much rest last night."

"I can imagine," Scott sympathized. "When she wakes up, would you tell her that a border guard outside Sweetgrass just called and said that a man driving a black Porsche with a young boy sleeping in the backseat crossed the border just before midnight last night? He said the driver appeared so distraught about getting home to his ailing mother that he did not detain him."

"Oh, no," Dan sighed. "Only a miracle will get him home now."

Chapter 6

Mr. Walker, thanks for letting me have a few days off work after Jeffy was kidnapped," Beth Slater said as she entered his office the week after her child had disappeared. "I just can't stay alone in that apartment waiting and watching, wondering if he'll ever come back. Even my parents returned to Glasgow until we get word on his whereabouts. At least I can try to earn a little to help pay for his search."

"I'm glad you're back," Grady Walker said as he rose from his chair. "I know Rebecca Sutherland really missed you."

"I'm sure she's way behind in her clerical work. I'll try to help her get caught up as fast as possible."

Beth had trouble smiling at the students as she checked out books and reshelved the returned ones. Many teachers and school personnel stopped to encourage her, but nothing would take away the pain of seeing the many posters with her giggling son's face. Still, school was better than sitting alone in her apartment waiting.

At three-thirty Beth dreaded going home. She drove aimlessly downtown and parked her car in front of the crisis center. Her shoulders drooped as she walked into the center.

"How was your first day back at work?" Dan asked as he surveyed her lined face.

"All I can say is that I survived another day without Jeffy," she muttered as she took her coat off and hung it on the coat rack. "I hope he'll be home for Thanksgiving."

"You're doing a great job hanging in there," Dan said. "Have you had any news today?"

"I'm afraid not. Everything's at a standstill. Do you have any clerical work you'd like to have done? I need to do something to keep my mind busy. When I think about Jeffy I nearly go crazy."

"I still haven't typed the proposal for additional funding for the crisis center. Would you like to work on that?" he asked as he took a manila folder from the cabinet beside his desk.

"Sure. Maybe something good will come out of it."

"Beth, do you know Jean Thompson, Edith's daughter?"

276

"Yes, I met her at the Harkness Hardware Store grand reopening after their big fire. Edith talks about her a lot. Jean's daughter is just a few months younger than Jeffy."

"Did you know that she and her husband moved to Running Butte to open another hardware store?" Dan queried as he joined Beth on the sofa.

Beth nodded her head in agreement. "I'd heard that. Edith was real excited about them coming back to Montana."

"Anyway, while her husband is busy getting the hardware store set up, Jean is head-over-heels trying to get a medical clinic started for the Native Americans. That tribe has been neglected by the government for a long time."

"Jean would be good at that," Beth smiled. "They say she did a fantastic job at the Chamberlain Hospital and they hated to lose her."

Dan propped his feet on the ottoman and grinned. "Jean called this morning and asked if I could come for lunch Saturday and bring Roy and Edith along. She wants to start a crisis center similar to what we have in Rocky Bluff only on a smaller scale."

"That sounds like a great idea," Beth responded. "You know what I think of the necessity of crisis lines. I don't know where I'd be if Rocky Bluff hadn't had one when I needed help."

"Jean said she needed all the help she could get from the experts in the field. Imagine me an expert at anything," Dan snickered.

A smile spread across Beth's tense face. "Anyone who can do what you do is an expert. Not everyone can look at other people's problems as compassionately and objectively as you do."

Dan reached for her hand. "Flattery will get you everywhere," he replied lightheartedly. "She also wondered if you could come along. She knows you're one of our strongest supporters."

"I can't plan anything until Jeffy is home," Beth replied. "Everything is hour by hour."

"If there's any news on Jeffy, I'm sure none of us will want to go. We'll just call and reschedule."

"It sounds good to me. I'll let Lieutenant Mooney know where I'll be so he can call me there if there are any new developments."

Beth remained at the crisis center and typed on the proposal until five o'clock and then hurried home to watch the evening news. The disappearance of Jeffy was no longer the lead story, but occasionally someone came up with a new theory and got a little media time. The evening news was the same as nearly every other day: Tribal warfare in Africa, corruption in Washington, and another Speedy Mart was held up in Billings.

The following day at work went better for Beth. The pain was still there, but her smile for the students came a little more naturally. At three-thirty she drove directly to her apartment complex and parked her car in the stall. She hurried to the boxes on the curb to get her mail. Usually she only got "Current Occupant" mail, but today she discovered a business envelope with no return address. The postmark was smudged, but it looked like it was mailed within the state.

This is different, she mused. *Usually the envelopes I get say "To the lucky winner: please send money to collect your prize."*

Beth unlocked her door and stepped inside. The letter was typed on cheap, plain paper using an old-fashioned typewriter whose ribbon had seen many miles.

To: Beth Slater

I saw your baby Jeffy's picture on television. He's an adorable child. He does not deserve to grow up with an unwed teenage mother living off welfare. Our tax money does not need to support the likes of you. Women with low morals should not be allowed to keep their babies. Your child is better off with his natural father, who would be willing to work and earn a salary and not live off welfare the way you do.

You should clean up your life, get a job, and don't spread any diseases.

Signed,
A Concerned Citizen

Beth stood in stunned silence and then burst into tears. She took her keys from her purse, locked the door behind her, and ran to her car. She could hardly see through her tear-filled eyes as she drove toward Edith Dutton's home. Parking her car in the drive, she raced toward the front door.

"Beth, what's happened?" Edith asked as the young woman fell into her arms sobbing.

Beth reached into her coat pocket and took out the crumpled envelope. "This came in the mail today. I don't even know how they got my address."

"The phone book is easy enough," Edith replied as the pair sat down together on Edith's living room sofa. A scowl spread across Edith's face as she read the offending letter.

Edith shook her head in disgust. "This person is full of hate. We needn't concern ourselves with this garbage. He, or she, doesn't even have the facts straight. You're an excellent mother," Edith assured her. "You know you don't have loose morals. You know you used the welfare system the right way—you used it to support your baby while you got an education so you could support both of you. You also know that it's the baby's father who has the questionable morals."

"Does everyone think this of me?" Beth sobbed.

"Of course not, honey," Edith comforted. "However, there are all kinds of kooks out there. That's why Jeffy is not with you right now."

"I really tried to be a good mother," Beth continued to sob. "I know it was wrong that I got pregnant in the first place, but that was such a long time ago. Will I be condemned all my life for that? Is that why God let Jeffy be taken away from me?"

"Beth, Jesus died on the cross for your sins along with everyone else's. God didn't let Jeffy be taken from you because of your sin. Jeffy was taken because Mickey is acting very irresponsibly."

"Pastor Rhodes explained that to me a long time ago," the distraught woman confided, "but sometimes I still feel guilty even though my affair with Mickey happened five years ago. I'm afraid people will always look down on me."

"The writer of this letter has not walked in your shoes. He or she doesn't understand what you've been through," Edith tried to explain. "He's the one that should be pitied. He must have an awfully miserable life to be filled with this much hate."

"I don't think I'll ever get this letter out of my mind," Beth whispered. "It hurts so deeply."

"Let's turn it over to Lieutenant Mooney to add to Jeffy's file. That way you'll never be tempted to go back and reread it. Who knows, maybe the sender had something to do with Mickey." Edith went to the phone and dialed the local police station. Beth did not need anything else to torture her troubled mind.

❧

Constable Gene Hanson parked his Royal Canadian Mounted Police cruiser in the West Elementary School visitor's spot. Law Enforcement Day in the Calgary Schools was one of his favorite assignments. He spent the entire day going from class to class teaching the children about safety and law protection. He had time to meet one-on-one with them during recess, and he especially enjoyed eating lunch in the noisy cafeteria.

At eleven forty-five the mountie found himself surrounded by twelve third-graders complaining about their hot dogs while they enjoyed every bite. "Do you know why these kids' pictures are on the milk cartons?" he asked the freckled-faced redhead across from him.

"Yeah, I think they got kidnapped or something," he responded matter-of-factly. "We're supposed to watch for them and then call the police if we see them."

"You learned your lesson well," Constable Hanson replied.

"Look at this little kid," the petite brunette next to him said. "His name is Jeffy Slater. He sure is cute. We drove through Rocky Bluff, Montana, last summer on vacation. I wonder if we saw the kidnapper and didn't know it."

"You can never tell a kidnapper by just looking at them," Constable Hanson explained. "Sometimes they'll even try to be your best friend."

"What are you going to do when you leave the school?" a pudgy boy queried.

"I'll probably go catch a speeder or a motorist who ran a stop sign," he responded lightheartedly. "All the vacationers have left, so business is pretty slow this time of year."

That afternoon, while Gene Hanson and his partner, Kenneth Hogan, were on routine patrol, they noticed a black Porsche speeding down Main Street as they approached the intersection. Gene immediately turned on his red lights and siren and gave pursuit.

"Can we get close enough to read the plates?" Constable Hogan asked.

"The traffic is so heavy I'm afraid we'll endanger someone if I go any faster," Gene replied as his knuckles gripped tighter around the steering wheel. "We're already going sixty-five kilometers in a thirty-five zone and he's pulling away from us. We better radio ahead for someone to block his path."

Ten blocks further down the street near the outskirts of town two more police cruisers joined the chase, and the three of them forced the black Porsche into a used car lot. Constable Hanson approached the car where the other mounties had the driver spread-eagled against the side of the Porsche. A frightened child whimpered in the front seat. Seeing that his colleagues had the situation well in hand, he turned his attention to the child.

"Hi, what's your name?" Constable Hanson asked.

"Jeffy."

Suddenly the face on the carton at lunch flashed before him. "Is your last name Slater?"

"Yeah," he mumbled in amazement. "How'd you know?"

"You're a pretty famous guy," Constable Hanson reminded him. "I bet you're even from Rocky Bluff, Montana."

"Wow, you're good."

Constable Hogan joined the arresting constables. "I just ran a computer check on that California license plate and there is an all-points bulletin on it from the state of Montana for kidnapping."

"I didn't do anything," Mickey snarled. "He's my own kid."

"We'll have to check into that," Constable Hogan replied firmly. "First we'll need to inspect your car." Kenneth opened up the front door of the Porsche and began looking around. Under the front seat was a small brown box. He opened it to find a fine white powder. He put it to his nose and then rubbed a few particles between his fingers.

"Looks like we have a couple of kilos of cocaine here, boys," he said as he handed the box to Constable Hanson. Kenneth Hogan continued in his search. Inside the glove compartment he found a small handgun. He checked the trunk, but it contained only a set of tools and a man's suitcase full of clothing.

"I've finished the search," Constable Hogan stated. "Let's take him in. You guys can have Mickey and we'll take the child. I'll call for a tow truck to bring the Porsche down to headquarters."

Jeffy sat in the backseat of the police car with his eyes wide and frightened. On the one hand he was excited about getting to ride in the police car, but on the other hand he was frightened seeing the man who claimed he was his daddy being arrested. "Where are we going?" he cried. "I want my mommy."

✦

Nine o'clock that night, Lieutenant Phil Mooney was finishing the daily paperwork at Rocky Bluff police station when the phone on his desk buzzed.

"Phil, a Constable Hanson from the Canadian Mounties would like to speak with you," the night dispatcher said as he picked up the phone.

Phil pushed the red flashing button on his phone. "Hello, this is Lieutenant Mooney."

"Lieutenant Mooney, in response to your APB we have arrested Mickey Kilmer. The child, Jeffy Slater, was with him. However, we found two kilos of cocaine and a handgun in his possession, so we will be having plans for him for a long while."

"How is the child?" Lieutenant Mooney asked.

"He's fine, but extremely frightened," Gene Hanson replied. "He keeps asking for his mother. We've put him in protective custody until we can get this sorted out. With the laws of two countries involved, both the mother and the father are going to need a couple good attorneys."

"I'll let the mother know right away that the child is safe."

"Would you have her get an attorney right away? We'll be calling first thing in the morning with arrangements from this end," Constable Hanson explained.

"We already have counsel for the case," Lieutenant Mooney replied. "Our Little Big Horn county attorney Stuart Leonard is already on top of the case and will do a fine job. Thanks for calling. We'll be in touch tomorrow."

All the employees in the police station burst into an excited cheer when they heard that Jeffy had been located.

"Come on, Scott, let's go tell Beth," Phil said as he motioned toward his partner.

Beth sat in front of the TV mindlessly watching the images flicker across the screen. She was scarcely aware when one show ended and another began. She was brought back to reality with the ringing of her doorbell. Cautiously, she opened the door and saw the two police officers standing there. Unlatching the chain, she invited them in.

"Did they find Jeffy?" she pleaded as she observed the broad smiles on both their faces.

Phil smiled. "He's in protective custody in Calgary, Alberta, Canada."

Beth gave a shout for joy and spontaneously hugged each of them. "Is he all right?"

Phil placed a hand on her shoulder. "They say he's fine, just a little frightened. He keeps asking for his mother."

"When can I go get him? I could leave first thing in the morning."

"Getting him back won't be that simple," Phil explained. "Since he was with his natural father and the laws of two different countries are involved, it's going to take some legal legwork. I'm sure Stuart Leonard will do a good job for you, and Jeffy will be home in a few days."

"Thank you. Thank you." Beth shouted as she shook both their hands and then began to dance around the room as they slipped out the door. "Jeffy's coming home. Jeffy's coming home. Thank You, Jesus. Jeffy's coming home."

After several minutes of privately rejoicing, Beth had to share this news with someone. The clock said it was too late to bother Edith. Both she and Roy retired early. She immediately called the crisis line. *This is a crisis,* she told herself. *Jeffy's coming home and I've got to shout it to the world.*

"Hello, crisis center. This is Dan, may I help you?"

"I've already been helped!" Beth shouted. "Jeffy's coming home."

Chapter 7

A half hour before school started, Beth Slater burst into the administration office. "They found Jeffy," she exclaimed excitedly.

"Where was he?" Viola Tomkins asked.

"Mickey had taken him to Calgary and then got himself arrested for possession of cocaine."

"Beth, what are you doing here then?" Grady Walker queried. "You should be on your way to Canada."

"I wish I were," she sighed. "But there's a lot of legal red tape between the two countries. Stuart Leonard is working on it now. Hopefully he'll be home by Thanksgiving."

Teachers and students alike went by the library giving Beth hugs and rejoicing with her. At nine o'clock Beth turned to her supervisor. "Rebecca, would you mind if I take a break and go to the teacher's lounge to use the phone?"

"No problem at all," the librarian assured her. "I can watch the floor while you're gone."

Beth dialed the familiar number and waited for an answer. "Hello, Edith. Guess what happened?"

"They found Jeffy," the older woman replied lightheartedly.

"How'd you know so early? It's scarcely nine o'clock," Beth protested, wanting to be the first one to break the news.

"I see you didn't read the morning paper," Edith chuckled. "It's the headline in the *Herald*."

"I never have time to read the paper until after work," Beth confessed. "There's no need for me to tell anyone else since the entire town knows now."

Edith nodded her head. "I'm sure the coffee shops are buzzing."

"I've got to call my parents. They had planned to return to Rocky Bluff just as soon as Jeffy was found. I've got to tell them not to come until I have an exact date for his return. I'm going to throw the biggest Thanksgiving bash ever for Jeffy and them."

&

Forty-five minutes before Stuart Leonard's secretary, Pat Crouse, and his paralegal, Libby Reynolds, were due at work, the telephone rang in the

Little Big Horn county attorney's office. *Who could be calling this time of the morning?* Stuart groaned as he reached for the phone. *I came in early so I wouldn't be disturbed.*

"County attorney's office. May I help you?"

"Stuart Leonard, please."

"Speaking."

"Mr. Leonard, my name is Greg McIntyre. I'm an attorney in Calgary, Alberta. I've been retained to represent Mickey Kilmer for violating Criminal Code Canada. He's been charged with importing two kilos of cocaine into Canada and illegal possession of a handgun."

"Sounds like Mickey's been a very busy man," Stu broke in. "We're preparing kidnapping charges against him down here for violating the Montana criminal code."

"Stu." It was Greg's turn to break in. "We both know you can't make it stick. And even if you could, the Crown will never agree to an extradition hearing on Mickey. Importing drugs into Canada is a major felony up here, not to mention illegal possession of a handgun. I sent my paralegal to Helena Tuesday and she obtained a copy of Jeffy's birth certificate from your Bureau of Vital Statistics. It shows Mickey as Jeffy's natural father. In the absence of a court order to the contrary, the natural father has just as much right to custody of the child as the natural mother."

Although Stuart resented the early phone call, he resented foreign interference in the Kilmer case even more. But he understood where Greg was coming from. He even knew what point Greg was going to make next.

"It's going to be next to impossible to make a case of kidnapping against the natural father," Greg chided. "Oh, you might be able to make out a case of custodial interference, but even that's debatable, because no court has ever awarded custody of Jeffy to anyone."

"What's your point, Greg?"

"Look, Stu, I'm a good attorney. I can modestly say I'm as good an attorney as you'll find in my country or in yours. But I can't beat this charge against Mickey. Six RCMP constables were present when Mickey was stopped per your APB and in their search of Mickey's Porsche they found the cocaine and the handgun. It's an open-and-shut case. Mickey's going to jail all right, but he's going to jail in Alberta, not Montana."

"I can live with that, but we want Jeffy back," Stu stated firmly.

"Here's my point," Greg continued. "We're asking you to drop all charges against Mickey in Montana. In exchange, he will surrender Jeffy without a fight. That way when he gets out of jail up here in three or four years, he won't still have the Montana charge hanging over him."

"I'll have to think on that for a while, Greg, and do a little research to see if I can find a precedent."

"I've already found one for you."

"Your court or mine?"

"Yours," Greg retorted. "Have you read *Wilson v. Barlow*? It's a recent Montana case."

"No, I haven't," Stu admitted.

"How about reading it and calling me back? Call collect if you wish."

"All right, give me a couple of hours, Greg, and I'll get back to you."

"Thanks for your time, Stu, have a nice day."

"You, too. 'Bye for now."

As soon as Stuart hung up the phone he went to his library and read *Wilson v. Barlow*. In that case, the court held that the statute provides that a person who has left the state does not commit the offense of custodial interference if he returns the individual taken to lawful custody prior to arrest. Greg had done his homework before he called. Stuart was impressed with this brash young Canadian.

Mickey had been arrested, but not by U.S. law officers, and he was arrested for possession of cocaine and an illegal handgun, not for kidnapping, not for custodial interference.

Stuart returned to his office and called Milton Eubanks, Chief Judge of the Little Big Horn County District Court. He explained the legal problems he had encountered with the Kilmer case and recommended that they accept Greg's offer.

Judge Eubanks readily agreed. It would not only save the taxpayers of Little Big Horn County thousands of dollars, but most importantly, the child would be returned to his mother's arms almost immediately.

Stuart dialed Greg's number and was greeted by a pleasant feminine voice with a decidedly French accent. Then Greg came on the line. "Stu, that was fast and you didn't even call collect. What's the verdict, old buddy?"

"We'll go along with you. You set up the time and place for us to pick up Jeffy. I recommend the border crossing station at Sweetgrass."

"No problem. The border crossing station at Sweetgrass it is. How about noon Monday?"

"I'll be there. Say, Greg, when you come, can you bring me some Fraser River salmon?"

"I will," chuckled Greg, "if you bring me about four buffalo steaks."

"Consider it a done deal. Oh, by the way, Greg, I don't know whether you're as fine a lawyer as I could find in your country, but you're certainly as fine a lawyer as I could find in mine."

"Thanks for the compliment, Stu." Greg tried to act serious for a moment. "Do you like hockey, Stu?"

"I sure do. I never miss a Bulls home game in Billings and I'll make a bet with you."

"What's your bet?"

"I'll bet you our Canucks can whip your Canucks."

On that frivolous note, the two attorneys hung up, looking forward to meeting face-to-face on Monday.

That Saturday Dan picked up Edith and Roy Dutton and then Beth Slater for their trip to Running Butte.

"Rebecca Sutherland and I would like to throw a welcome home party for Jeffy Tuesday afternoon in the library right after school," Edith said as they passed the Rocky Bluff city limits. "We wanted to use the gym, but they have basketball practice until seven o'clock."

"Everyone is being so good to me," Beth replied. "I don't know what to say."

"Just to have Jeffy back in Rocky Bluff will be enough," Edith replied. "What arrangements have been made for bringing him home?"

Beth smiled as she thought of being reunited with her giggling child. "Stuart Leonard, Dan, and I are going to drive to Great Falls tomorrow afternoon and get a motel room for the night. It's just too far to make it to Sweetgrass from here by noon."

"I'm along as the chaperon," Dan inserted as he winked at Beth sitting beside him.

"I need all the moral support I can get," Beth responded quickly. "I'm not used to dealing with law enforcement people, attorneys, and customs agents."

"We plan to go back to Great Falls Monday night and leave for home first thing Tuesday morning, so we should be back by two or three o'clock that afternoon," Dan explained.

"That's perfect. You could come directly to the library as soon as you get back in town. Sonya and Patricia said they would bring Jeffy's friends from Kinder University to the party."

"Jeffy will be pleased. He really likes the new friends he's made at the day-care center."

"Rebecca is already collecting gifts for him, so he'll have an early Christmas."

"It may be Christmas for him, but Thanksgiving for me," Beth responded. "My parents will be coming Tuesday, so they should be here in time for the party. It will be the first time they've held their grandson. I've never known them to be this excited before."

"I'm sure there'll be reporters from both the *Herald* and the television station at the celebration. Jeffy has become quite a celebrity throughout the state," Edith reminded her.

"What about all the notices that have gone up all around the country?" Roy queried in his usual practical manner.

"Teresa Lennon has been busy notifying business establishments to take down Jeffy's posters because the missing child has been found. Larry Reynolds immediately put a notification on the on-line database that Jeffy had been found," Edith answered.

"It looks like you've been a busy bunch," Dan chided. "Nothing can beat the community support of the citizens of Rocky Bluff."

Jean Thompson had the table set with several different salads and sandwiches when the foursome arrived at her new double-wide mobile home. A sweet aroma filled the air. "This looks like quite a feast," Roy exclaimed as she motioned for him to sit at the head of the table.

"It needs to be," she chuckled. "I'm getting free advice. Besides, it gave me a chance to try a recipe that I got from one of my new friends here in Running Butte."

"So what is it I smell?" Edith asked.

Jean's eyes sparkled. "Indian fry bread," she replied. "I'm sorry I'll have to ration the portion I give to Roy. It's definitely not designed for a diabetic. Gloria sure loves it."

After they finished lunch, Jean stacked the dishes in the dish-washer, then she and Jim led the way across the street to the new store. The exterior of the building was finished, complete with a sign, HARKNESS HARDWARE II. Jim put his key into the keyhole, flung the door open, and shouted, "Ta-daah."

The interior walls were framed, but no sheetrock had been hung yet. Sawhorses and lumber cluttered the floor. "If you would all step this way, I will show you the front counter, over which thousands of dollars of merchandise will pass each month." Jim grinned as he motioned to an empty space close to the door. "In this section will be the household goods and to your right will be yard supplies."

Jim led the gathering through the framework of a partitioned wall. "To your right are the men's and ladies' rest rooms and to your left is the paint room." He observed the investigative looks on Roy and Edith's face and continued, "Of course you will note that the paint room will be well ventilated. We want to be far above code and not even have any cause for suspicion of a fire here."

"Jim, you're doing a great job here," Edith observed. "How soon do you plan to open?"

"We'd like to be open in February," he replied. "It would mean a lot to the locals not to have to drive into Rocky Bluff for their spring supplies. However, we still have one hitch."

"What's that?" Roy asked.

"I don't have time to learn to run the computer system and Jean is busy getting the medical clinic set up," Jim sighed.

"Another reason, I have trouble understanding computers," Jean explained. "To me it's like, if it doesn't breathe, I can't comprehend it."

Edith hesitated. "This is a long shot, but what are the chances of Larry Reynolds coming to Running Butte to help with the computers? Nancy can handle the Rocky Bluff store."

"Do you think his wife would be willing to leave Stuart Leonard's office?" Beth questioned. "She worked pretty hard to get that paralegal degree. It would be difficult for her to put it behind her now."

"There would have to be a pretty big carrot offered to entice her to come to Running Butte, but anything is possible," Jim exclaimed thoughtfully.

"A very big one," Beth murmured.

"So what do you think of our project so far?" Jim asked as he surveyed the expressions on each of their faces.

"It's almost unbelievable," Edith responded. "George always wanted to build a satellite store, but the timing never seemed right. He would be very proud of what you and Bob have done."

"Now it's my turn," Jean said as she led the group out the front door of the building. "If you'll follow me just one block south, you will find yourselves in the waiting room of the Running Butte Medical Center."

Edith took Jim's arm as they slowly walked down the only paved street in Running Butte. "Sorry we can't offer you a sidewalk, but the founding fathers did not foresee any expansion in their community," Jean chuckled.

"You really have to use your imagination on this," Jim teased as he pointed to a vacant lot with string connecting numerous stacks.

"The federal government promised us a building by springtime, but I'm getting a little apprehensive," Jean sighed.

"But if it goes as fast as the store has once they get the frame here, it shouldn't be a problem," Jim tried to encourage. "The committee is really working hard to get this up and operational."

"Anyway, the front will be the lobby," Jean explained. "The medical wing will be on the left, complete with a major trauma facility. We hope to be able to fund our own ambulance."

"They think they could save several lives a year if they didn't have to wait for an ambulance to be dispatched from Rocky Bluff," Jim inserted.

Jean's eyes brightened. "The wing on the right will have rooms for miscellaneous services. This is where we'd like to have the crisis center lines installed."

"It would be so much handier to have it adjacent to the medical clinic than clear across town as it is in Rocky Bluff," Roy noted. "I hope you'll be able to fund it."

"It looks good right now, but we're also trying to get a social worker and a tribal attorney as well."

"That might be your carrot," Beth giggled.

Jean's eyes twinkled. "You mean for Libby?"

"Who knows?" Beth replied.

"The committee has been negotiating with a local man who is at the University of Montana Law School right now," Jim explained. "They're trying to convince him to come home and work as the tribal attorney. Their reservation legal system is in shambles right now, and the people are so confused they don't know what to do. They feel like they're neither fish nor fowl."

"We wish you luck," Edith said. "I know these people have been neglected far too long. In fact, Pastor Rhodes has even mentioned the possibility of starting a mission work out here. So many of the people have given up hope and turned to alcoholism."

"Only one or two stay in school until they graduate, so we're fortunate to have one of them finishing law school this spring," Jean said as she looked at her mother. "Mom, you're looking tired. Maybe you'd like to take a short nap before you head back to Rocky Bluff?"

"I guess I am getting a little weary," Edith confessed. "Why don't we head back to your house? I'll take a quick nap while the rest of you plan the new crisis center."

⟡

As the sun was setting, Dan stopped his car in front of Beth's apartment. "Thank you for such a lovely day," Beth said as Dan walked her to her door. "It helped make the time go faster until Jeffy is home."

Dan roared. "I hope I mean more to you than just a way to kill time."

"I'm sorry, Dan. I didn't mean it that way. You are a fun person to be around. It's just I don't know how to relax and have fun, especially since Jeffy's been gone."

"Jeffy will be back in your arms Monday and then maybe I can teach you how to trust God, relax, and have fun. I'd like to start tonight, but I'm scheduled to work at the crisis center in a half hour."

"I'm looking forward to seeing you tomorrow when we leave for Great Falls," Beth responded. "Just remember you're along only as a chaperon," she chuckled.

Chapter 8

"This is your wake-up call," Dan Blair chuckled as Beth answered the phone in room 113 of the Sunrise Inn in Great Falls. "Breakfast is in thirty minutes in the motel restaurant."

"I've been up since five o'clock," Beth replied. "I was too excited to sleep. Just think, in five hours I'll have Jeffy in my arms again."

"Since you're ready, why don't you meet Stu and I in the restaurant in five minutes? Then we can have an early start for Sweetgrass."

"I'll be there." Beth quickly stuffed her curling iron and makeup into her bag, grabbed her coat, and hurried to the restaurant.

"Good morning, Beth," Stuart Leonard greeted as he motioned for her to join them in the booth. "I understand you didn't sleep well last night."

Beth smiled as she slid in beside Dan. "All I could think about was Jeffy. I bet he was totally confused with the entire ordeal."

"All they told me was that he kept saying, 'I want my mommy,'" Stu told her for what seemed the tenth time.

"We called the highway patrol for the road report and they say there's snow on the highway farther north, so it'd be best if we get an early start," Dan explained as he reached for one of the menus the waitress handed the trio.

The drive to Sweetgrass from Great Falls was uneventful, and the hours seemed to drag by. Beth felt like a little child every time she asked, "How soon are we going to get there?"

They arrived at the customs office in Sweetgrass at eleven forty-five. The officials on duty had neither seen Attorney Greg McIntyre nor a small child. Beth paced nervously across the lobby, inspecting every car approaching the check station. No one who was traveling with a small child fit the attorney's general description.

"Would you like a cup of coffee while you wait?" the customs agent asked as he sensed her nervousness.

"Yes, that would be nice," she replied as she waited while he filled a Styrofoam cup for her. As she was taking her first sip, a brown Bronco stopped in the parking lot. A young man in a business suit got out along with a well-dressed middle-aged woman. The woman opened the door to

291

the backseat and unlatched a child's car seat. She took the child by the hand and walked around the back of the vehicle toward the lobby of the inspection station.

"Jeffy!" Beth shouted as she ran out the door and across the parking lot just as fast as she could.

The child broke away from his caregiver's hand. "Mommy!" he shouted as he ran toward her with his short legs moving just as fast as they could.

Beth picked up her son in the middle of the snow-packed parking lot and held him tight. It was hard to tell which one was crying the hardest. Dan and Stuart stood nearby with tears in their eyes.

"I take it you're Greg McIntyre," Stu said as he extended his right hand. "I'm Stuart Leonard and this is Dan Blair."

"It's nice meeting both of you," Greg replied as he shook hands with both men and then turned to the woman at his side. "This is Victoria Marshall. She's head of protective services in Calgary. She's been seeing that Jeffy has been getting the best of care."

"It's nice meeting you both," she said as she extended her hand in greeting. "There's no doubt at all who the mother is," she said as she nodded toward the young mother still embracing her child.

The five happy adults went into the lobby to sign the necessary legal papers. While Stuart and Greg shuffled papers, Beth gave Jeffy a new stuffed panda bear that she had purchased at the mall in Great Falls.

"That should about do it," Greg said as he closed his briefcase. "Now, did you bring the buffalo steaks that you promised?" he teased. "I heard they're out of season now."

"Just a moment. I'll have to go to my trunk and get the cooler," Stu replied smugly. "The local grocer keeps a supply in the freezer for the tourists."

Greg's face dropped. "I didn't think you were serious, so I didn't bring the Fraser River salmon."

"There's one thing you need to learn," Stu chided. "A Montana attorney always keeps his word."

On the way back to Great Falls, Beth and Jeffy sat in the backseat and played nursery rhyme games. Finally, Jeffy fell asleep with a contented smile on his face. Beth memorized every line on his body before she, too, dozed off. This was the day the entire town of Rocky Bluff had been praying for.

❧

"Mrs. Dutton, I hope you don't mind us stopping by unannounced," Suzanne Slater said as Edith opened her door. "Since Beth is on her way to bring Jeffy home, we just wanted to come and personally thank you for all you've done for our daughter and grandson."

"Do come in," Edith replied as she motioned for them to enter. "Have you met my husband, Roy Dutton?

"Roy, I'd like you to meet Beth's parents, Suzanne and Ed Slater. I met them briefly at a 'Bring Jeffy Home' Committee meeting."

The couple crossed the room to shake hands with Roy. "We heard so much about you from Beth."

"Please have a seat," Edith urged. "Would you like a cup of coffee?"

"That would be a nice warmer-upper," Ed replied. "It was a long, cold trip from Glasgow, but we wanted to be here when Jeffy and Beth got back."

Edith disappeared to the kitchen and was back within moments with four cups of coffee on a serving tray. "We're planning a welcome home party tomorrow at the school library where Beth works and we'd love to have you join us."

"Don't you think our presence would be awkward after we disowned our daughter for so long and did not even acknowledge that we had a grandson?" Suzanne queried.

"We were so angry and foolish when Beth told us she was pregnant," Ed confessed. "We tried to tell her that Mickey was a worthless drifter, but she was sure she could change him."

"When we forbade her from seeing him, she started sneaking around to meet him," Suzanne continued. "Her grades started dropping and she seemed totally out of control. I just didn't know what to do."

"I could imagine it was extremely difficult for you," Edith comforted. "Raising teenagers is never easy."

Ed's face lengthened as he stared out the window. "Beth never actually told us she was pregnant, but when her clothes started getting tight, we confronted her. It wasn't a very pretty scene."

"We tried to have her get an abortion so no one would know she'd ever been pregnant, but she wouldn't hear of it," Suzanne recalled. "For some strange reason that unborn child was important to her, and she refused to consider an abortion. She disappeared the next day. I cried for weeks, and then I turned numb inside. It was like a part of me had died until I saw Jeffy's picture on the TV news and knew that Beth was all right."

"We're so proud that she stood up to us about an abortion. All we thought about was that she was carrying a product of her sin, not a child as precious as Jeffy," Ed continued.

"Beth told us the last time we were here that Mickey had left Glasgow the day she told him she was pregnant, but had given her three hundred dollars to help pay for her medical bills. She used that money to get a bus ticket to Rocky Bluff." Suzanne took a tissue from her purse and dabbed her eyes. "All she could talk about was all the people here who helped her, especially you and Roy."

"Beth worked very hard to finish her education, obtain a secretarial degree, and get a job," Edith replied. "She's an inspiration to a lot of young girls who have made bad choices in their lives."

"We're just glad you were there through the tough times," Suzanne said. "You did what I should have done. You were a mother to her when she needed it the most. I don't know how I'll ever repay you."

Edith smiled. "You can repay us by starting a brand-new relationship with your daughter and grandson. Your attendance at the party tomorrow would mean so much to Beth. It would demonstrate to the community the power of forgiveness on both your parts."

Ed smiled. "Put in those terms, we'll be honored to be there. We brought our video camera and won't miss a precious moment of it."

The next afternoon Stu Leonard pulled into a truck stop on the edge of Rocky Bluff. "I'm sorry to stop so close to home, but I've been driving on empty for the last forty miles and I'm afraid to go a mile farther. The service station where I usually fill up on my way home from Great Falls was closed and I've been driving on fumes ever since."

"That's okay," Beth replied. "I need to change Jeffy into some new clothes before his party. I didn't want to dress him at the motel because I was sure he'd have them messed up before we got home."

"You're coming to Jeffy's party at the school library, aren't you, Stu?" Dan asked as Stu inserted the nozzle into the gas tank.

"I'd like to, but I have an appointment with Judge Eubanks at four o'clock. That's one I don't dare be late for."

A half hour later, Jeffy walked into the Rocky Bluff High School hand-in-hand with his mother. He felt very important getting to come into the "big kids" school. However, when Beth opened the door to the library and stepped inside, Jeffy clung tightly to her when a crowd of friends and strangers shouted, "Welcome home, Jeffy!" Cameras flashed all around him.

Suddenly Jeffy spotted a group of friends from Kinder University playing in the corner and was immediately in the middle of them, ignoring all the other guests.

"Jeffy, we have some presents we'd like to have you open," Edith said as she pointed to a table piled high with brightly wrapped gifts.

"You mean these are all for me, Granny Edith?" he grinned.

"They sure are. Maybe your mother could help you open them."

For the next twenty minutes Jeffy opened presents. There was a fire truck from Sonya Turner, a musical toy from Roy and Edith Dutton, and numerous stuffed animals and cars from other community members. Finally, Larry Reynolds brought a large gift from behind the counter.

"I wanted to save the best for last," Larry chuckled. "If Jeffy's going to make a hit in Rocky Bluff High School, there is one thing he's going have to learn young."

Beth's eyes twinkled. "And what's that?"

"Have him open the box and find out," Larry said as he set the box in front of the child.

Jeffy was soon tearing the paper and throwing it in all directions. Beth had to ask for a pair of scissors to help her son open the taped box. Suddenly she started giggling. Inside the box was a nerf ball along with a miniature basketball hoop.

"We have to start teaching them to play basketball young in Rocky Bluff," Larry chided. "We have to keep up our state championship record."

The entire group roared as they remembered Larry's ill-fated basketball days and the community pressures for a winning team.

Beth was extremely conscious of a video camera in the background. Yet, she had little time to respond to its operators. Finally, Jeffy looked up from his toys. "Jeffy, I'd like you to meet your grandma and grandpa," Beth said as she motioned for her parents to come to the front.

Jeffy looked stunned. "I didn't know I had anymore grandmas. I just thought I had Granny Edith."

"This is my mother and father, your grandma and grandpa," she explained as she embraced them both. Not wanting to be left out on any loving, without a moments hesitation Jeffy ran immediately into his grandma Slater's arms for a hug. Not a single eye in the room was dry. This was the miracle the Slaters had almost missed because of their lack of forgiveness.

❦

Jim Thompson and Bob Harkness poured over catalogs and inventory sheets far into the night while their wives spent a leisurely evening with Roy and Edith Dutton. A December snow was slowly inundating the entire state.

"I'm glad we brought a change of clothes so we can spend the night," Jim remarked as the two walked to Bob's hardware store. "I've already slid into the ditch once this season. We were fortunate that time, but I don't want to push my luck again."

"At least we won't be able to complain about not having a white Christmas this year," Bob noted.

"That is, unless a chinook wind comes in at the last minute," Jim reminded him. "A couple of Christmases ago, when we came for the holidays, there were fourteen inches of snow on the ground when we went to bed and it was all gone the next morning."

"Now back to the books," Bob sighed as the two gathered around the computer screen. "It looks like our best move would be to keep the inventory level at the Running Butte store at one-half of the level here for at least the first year."

"I guess if I needed something in a hurry I could send someone to Rocky Bluff to get it," Jim responded as he refilled his coffee cup. "I like the idea of having internal modems and faxes to link our two systems, but I'm still concerned about doing the book work and managing the store at the same time. Computers have never been my forte. I wish there was some way I could steal Larry Reynolds from you."

Bob thought for a moment. "That would be an ideal situation, but Libby is pretty entrenched in the county attorney's office."

"We've done some prework and we might have a paralegal job for her in Running Butte."

Bob surveyed his brother-in-law with amazement. "Come on," he chuckled. "The only thing Running Bluff has going for it is the soon-to-be-opened Harkness Hardware II."

"You sure underestimate the influence of your sister," Jim chided. "She's nearly single-handedly taken on the Bureau of Indian Affairs. Besides helping get the medical clinic open, she is trying to get an ambulance service, a home health care worker, a social worker, a crisis center, and a tribal attorney for the reservation people."

"I see I should make it to Running Butte more often just to keep up on things," Bob replied as he visualized his vivacious sister. "Now that Jay's old enough to drive, I've been sending him with the needed supplies."

"They broke ground for the medical clinic last week, and Jean made sure there was a wing for social services." Jim nearly exploded with pride. "Last week Jean drove to Missoula with the chief of the tribal council to try to convince Stephen Yellowtail to come back to the reservation after he graduates from law school in June."

"Were they successful?"

"I think so, but they have no final agreement yet," Jim explained. "He's pretty aggressive and is requesting suitable housing along with office space and clerical and paralegal help before he agrees to come. The last tribal council meeting voted to meet his demands."

"I know where they can get an excellent paralegal, don't you?" Bob winked.

"Why don't we present this proposition to Larry first thing in the morning and give him and Libby time to think about it?" Jim suggested. "The paralegal position would have to be advertised to the public and meet all government regulations, but with Libby's training and experience, she would be a shoo-in for the position."

Larry Reynolds stomped the snow off his cowboy boots as he entered the back door of Harkness Hardware Store the next morning. "Kind of cold out there." He shuddered as he rubbed his hands together and took off his parka.

"Hi, Larry!" Bob shouted out to him. "When you get your coat off, join Jim and me in the office. We have something we want to discuss with you."

"I hope it's good," Larry responded as he entered the office. "I need something to warm me up this morning."

Bob filled Larry's mug. "How would a cup of coffee do for a starter?"

Larry surveyed the pair with suspicion. They had something up their sleeve. "Yeah, sure," he replied.

"Larry, you look like you don't trust us," Jim teased. "Why, we're about to offer you the opportunity of your lifetime."

Larry raised his eyebrows. "Now that sounds like an offer I can't refuse."

"You've learned our computer system backwards and forwards since we put it in," Bob began, trying to chose his words carefully. "Since we're expanding, we really need your services in Running Butte. Would you and Libby consider a transfer there?"

"Where would I live? The few livable houses there are all owned by long-term residents," Larry protested.

"There's land on the edge of town where you could put a mobile home," Jim responded. "We could help you get a good deal on a brand-new one."

"I know Libby would hate to leave her job with Stuart Leonard," Bob inserted. "But there's a good possibility of a paralegal job with the tribal attorney's office that's opening soon."

"It might not be as difficult as you think to get her to quit her job," Larry replied with a smile.

Both men exchanged puzzled glances. The paralegal job for the Little Big Horn county attorney was a coveted position.

"Libby hasn't told anyone yet, but she just found out she's pregnant and she's concerned that taking care of two children and working in such a high-pressure job might be too much for her. I think she might be amenable to a low-profile job for awhile. We'll talk about it and I'll let you know in a few days."

"Sounds like a fair deal," Jim replied. "If Libby has any questions about the job with the tribal attorney, she might give Jean a call. It's exciting being on the ground floor of several projects at the same time."

Chapter 9

Beth, remember when Jeffy was missing you told me you didn't know how to relax and have fun?" Dan queried as they sat in her living room watching TV together after Jeffy had gone to bed.

Beth flushed. "Yes. I was really uptight then. I just didn't know what to do with myself without Jeffy. He'd become my entire life."

"Now that Jeffy's home and the holiday season is over, I think it's time you learn to have some fun in your life."

"Working full time and then coming home and taking care of Jeffy and the apartment, there's not much time for anything else."

"When you're busy helping everyone else, that's the time when you need a special time for yourself, otherwise you burn out and don't enjoy anything," Dan insisted.

"You're probably right." Beth sighed and then she giggled. "The high school kids can often get as demanding as my four-year-old son."

"Then let's see what we can do to help you learn to have fun," Dan said as he took her hand. "What do you like to do?"

"All I've ever done in my spare time is watch TV. I know that makes me sound like a boring couch potato, but since Jeffy was born, I haven't had the money or the time to do anything else."

"What did you like to do when you were still in school?"

"Not much," Beth confessed. "I was too shy to make many friends. I would occasionally go to a basketball game with one of my girlfriends, but when Mickey and I started dating, all we did was cruise around town. I didn't do anything with my girlfriends after that."

"Did you participate in any sports?"

"Nope. I was afraid everyone would laugh at me. I guess I was a pretty self-conscious kid."

"Most young teens miss out on a lot of positive experiences because of a low self-esteem, but now that you're older, you've learned that the only ones you need to satisfy are God and yourself," Dan reminded her. "You can forget about what other people think."

"I used to spend a lot of time worrying about what other people thought about me, but now I've noticed that people are so busy worrying about their own problems that they don't have time to think about me," Beth chuckled.

"Is there a certain sport you'd like to learn but are afraid to try?" Dan queried.

Beth thought a moment. "I always thought tennis looked like fun, but we don't have any indoor courts in Rocky Bluff. The regular tennis courts at the country club don't open until spring."

"In Montana our winter sports are pretty much limited to skiing and snowmobiling," Dan noted as he visualized Big Sky Ski Lodge outside of Bozeman, where he used to ski as a teenager.

"Even if I'm a native from the coldest part of the state, I still can't stand the cold," Beth snickered.

Dan shook his head in amusement. "If you don't like the cold, that eliminates almost everything." He paused for a moment before continuing. "What about bowling? The Westend Bowling Alley has quite a few leagues."

The thought of meeting different people and just relaxing intrigued Beth, but a practical cloud enveloped her. "No one would want someone as inexperienced as I am on their team."

"I'm pretty rusty myself, but maybe if we practice a lot this year, by fall we'd be ready for regular leagues." Dan chuckled. "If we weren't, no one would be the wiser and we wouldn't embarrass ourselves by pulling down the team scores."

"I thought you weren't interested in what other people thought of you," Beth teased.

Dan grinned sheepishly. "Just part of my male ego." He hesitated as he gazed into her deep blue eyes. "How about asking one of your high school students if they could come and baby-sit Jeffy Friday night while we go bowling?"

"I've never used a teenage sitter before," Beth cautioned. "They get kind of expensive."

"Don't worry about a thing," Dan assured her. "I'll pay her and give her a ride. Do you know anyone who might be interested in earning two or three dollars for sitting here watching your TV while Jeffy sleeps?"

Beth thought a moment and then her eyes brightened. "I have one student assistant who might be interested. I could ask her tomorrow."

"Great," Dan replied as he squeezed her hand. "Be sure and find out where she lives so I can pick her up."

❧

Friday night Beth and Dan had more laughs and enjoyed themselves more at the Westend Bowling Alley than Beth had ever thought possible. For the first time in her life she felt she was truly a woman with her own identity, not just Jeffy's mommy, or even worse, a single mother. She learned about strikes and spares, and most importantly, how to avoid gutter balls.

After a couple hours of bowling, Dan suggested, "Let's go to the Pizza Palace to top off the evening. I'm just not ready for this evening to end."

Beth smiled. "Sounds great," she replied. A mischievous twinkle came into her eyes. "See, I didn't have any trouble at all learning how to relax and have fun."

"Well, I don't know about that," Dan said as he helped her with her coat. "I think you'll need another lesson next Friday night. Having fun could be a pretty difficult skill to learn."

"That'd be marvelous," Beth responded. "If I can't get one of the high school girls to baby-sit, maybe Liz who lives across the hall wouldn't mind watching my TV instead of her own."

A few minutes after midnight when Beth closed the door behind Dan and the baby-sitter whom he was driving home, a warmth enveloped her. *I've never had this much fun before in my life*, she mused. *Dan was always with me for support during those awful days without Jeffy, but I thought I was just a charity case he was helping. Tonight was different. I've never felt this way before. We didn't talk about my problems, we just relaxed and had fun.*

The mood of the previous evening remained with Beth the next day and she was anxious to share it with one of her best friends. After lunch she bundled Jeffy in his new snowsuit and drove to Edith Dutton's home.

"You look cheerful and all aglow," Edith said as she greeted Beth with a quick hug.

"I didn't realize it showed that much," Beth giggled as she took off her coat. "I guess it's safe to say that I had more fun last night than I ever thought possible."

"So what happened? I'm dying to hear what has brought our sweet, serious Beth out of her shell."

"That's just what Dan called me. . .serious," Beth replied as the pair made themselves comfortable at the kitchen table and Jeffy opened up his toy bag on the floor nearby.

Edith nodded with understanding. "You've had to grow up in a hurry and have missed many activities that others your age have enjoyed."

"Dan's trying to bring that to a screeching halt."

Edith's eyes brightened. "I take it your relationship is becoming more than a benevolent concern of his," she teased.

"We did have a lot of fun together last night," Beth admitted, "and we're planning to go out again next Friday."

"Good for you. I'm glad you're beginning to realize that although you have the responsibility of a beautiful child, you can still have a life of your own."

Beth stared into space for a few moments before she spoke. "I've never felt this way about anyone before," she whispered. "Not even when I thought I was madly in love with Mickey."

"Mature love is different from teenage love," Edith reminded her. "It can see you through both the good times and the bad. It doesn't have the roller coaster effect that you see in today's high school students."

Beth again was slow to respond. "I never really thought of this as love. It's just I'm comfortable with Dan. We can laugh together, cry together, or just sit in silence and it doesn't make any difference."

"That's how you know when you've found Mr. Right," Edith replied. "When they feel as comfortable as an old shoe. Men of excitement and glamour may come and go, but life is not excitement and glamour. It's day-to-day events, highlighted with special milestones."

"But I can't fall in love," Beth sighed. "Not now. Not after what has happened."

Edith was puzzled as she surveyed the young woman across from her. "What terrible thing has happened that would keep you from being loved and loving in return?"

Tears filled Beth's eyes. "I had a child out of wedlock. After Jeffy's disappearance was covered nationwide, the entire world knew about my sin."

"But God forgave you a long time ago," Edith reminded Beth as she patted her hand. "And now even your parents have forgiven you. Why don't you forgive yourself?"

"Sometimes I think I have and then other times I still feel so guilty."

"Beth, it's time to let go of the past and go on with your life. You have a good education, a good job, and a beautiful child. Don't let the mistakes of your youth damage the rest of your life," Edith pleaded. "You're an entirely different person now."

"Sometimes when I'm alone and depressed, these things keep coming back to haunt me." Beth shrugged her shoulders. "It's like a thief trying to sneak in and steal my happiness."

How often Edith had faced similar situations herself, but through the years she had developed a strong mental discipline. "Don't let the black thoughts destroy you. Every time one crosses your mind, remind yourself that Jesus is stronger than your memories and He'll protect you from your own destructive thoughts."

Beth's eyes brightened as the tears disappeared. "I'll try to oust the annoying memories when they occur," she responded. "But it's going to take a lot of practice."

"You've conquered a lot of problems in your short life," Edith reminded her. "I'm sure you can get control of this one as well. Just don't let your memories stand in the way of developing a relationship with Dan or anyone else."

Beth beamed. The weight of her past felt like it was lifted from her shoulders. She could begin to admit the possibility that she might be falling in love. . .real love, for the first time in her life.

༚

Larry Reynolds waited until Saturday night after Vanessa was in bed before he brought up Jim Thompson's offer. "Libby," he began as he laid the newspaper beside him on the sofa. "Have you done any more thinking about what you'd like to do after the other baby comes?"

"I really don't know what to do," Libby sighed. "That's why I haven't told anyone I'm pregnant. That's the first thing they'll ask me. 'How much time are you going to take off work? Are you going to be able to work and care for two children?' "

"I'm going to leave that decision up to you," Larry responded gently. "I know it will be a lot of work to do both. It would be tight, but if we budget carefully, we might be able to get along on just my salary."

"I know," Libby sighed, "but I've worked so hard to get my paralegal education, and if I don't keep up-to-date, I'll have trouble getting back in the job market when the kids get older."

"I had an interesting offer that might make a difference." Larry hesitated. "I've been waiting until we had some time alone to discuss it."

"So, what's the other possibility?" Libby queried. "I feel pretty indecisive at this point."

"Bob called me into his office when Jim Thompson was in town last week and asked me if I wanted to work at the Running Butte store," Larry explained as he studied his wife's face for a reaction. "They think I've learned their computer system so well I'd be a lot of help there. Since I've worked so closely with Nancy here, they think they'd maintain a much more consistent bookkeeping system if I used the same procedures in that store."

"What did you tell them?"

"I told them I'd think about it and talk it over with you. They both realize how important your job is for you right now, but they didn't know you were pregnant."

"I bet as a proud father you broke the news," Libby chided.

"Well, I was forced to when they had a possibility of a paralegal job for you in Running Butte, but I told them not to tell their wives or Edith until

303

you could break the news."

Libby and Larry discussed the future baby along with the pros and cons of moving to Running Butte far into the night. When they crawled into bed that night, they had both agreed it was a good opportunity for the entire family.

The next afternoon while Larry and Vanessa were taking their Sunday afternoon nap, Libby drove to the Dutton residence.

"Libby, it's so good to see you," Edith greeted as she invited the young woman into her living room. "Since you've been working we haven't had much time to spend together."

"I know," Libby agreed meekly. "It's been much too long."

Edith and Roy and Libby visited about routine life in Rocky Bluff before Libby explained the real reason of her visit. "Larry and I have some good news that we've been keeping to ourselves for some time."

"Let me guess," Edith said with a gleam in her eyes. "You're expecting another little one."

"Did Larry tell you?" Libby scowled good-naturedly.

Edith giggled. "You have that motherly glow about you. You're just radiant."

"It can't be that obvious," Libby protested. "I'm sure someone told you."

"That will always be my secret," Edith replied. "When is the baby due?"

"The middle of June, hopefully on my birthday."

"Do you plan to take a leave of absence from work?" Roy queried. "I know Stuart Leonard would be lost without you."

"Larry and I are talking about it, but we haven't completely decided," Libby explained. "Did you know Bob and Jim offered Larry a job at Running Butte?"

"Yes, we discussed it while we were there several weeks ago, but we didn't know if it was possible or not," Edith replied. "Everyone knew how well you liked your job."

"I do like it, but with a second child to take care of, I don't think I'll be able to do it justice," Libby explained. "So moving to Running Butte isn't out of the question. What do you think?"

"Of course, it's something you and Larry will have to decide," Edith replied, "but perhaps a change of scenery would be good for you."

"I've often thought about that," Libby replied. "We have so many memories here. Not all of them are good. I keep wondering if people are still influenced by Larry's past whenever they see us."

"Larry has been a wonderful testimony to the community that people can change," Roy responded, "but some people refuse to let people change.

I think it helps make them feel bigger when in actuality it only shows how small they are."

"Not only what people think about us bothers us, but even more importantly, I still have memories that are triggered every time I drive past the house we used to have on Frontage Road. Every time I pass the high school I think about the worst day in Larry's life," Beth replied as she gazed aimlessly out the window.

"Then maybe moving is the best thing for you," Edith responded. "I've never believed that a person should run from their problems, but both of you have overcome a lot of obstacles. If you moved, you would leave Rocky Bluff victoriously."

Libby smiled. "That's what I've been thinking. I think I'd like a fresh beginning, and no time is better than when we have another child on the way."

Just then the Duttons' doorbell rang. When Roy opened the door, there stood Larry holding Vanessa. "Larry, do come in. We were just talking about you."

"I'm sure you were," he laughed. He gave his wife a quick kiss as Vanessa reached for her mother. "Vanessa and I woke up and decided we hadn't visited the Duttons in a long while.

"I suppose Libby has told you the good news." Larry grinned.

"Of course," Roy answered. "I just don't know how you kept it quiet for as long as you did."

"We just wanted to know what to do before we started broadcasting the news, but word has a way of getting around Rocky Bluff ahead of us."

"That's life in a little town," Edith replied.

"We'll have to get used to it," Larry replied. "If Libby is agreeable, it looks like we'll be living in an even smaller town."

"I was leaning that way before," Libby said as she took her husband's hand, "but after talking with Roy and Edith, I'm sure that's what I want to do."

"Not everyone gets a second chance in life the way we have," Larry replied. "This could be one of the best things that ever happened to us." Larry put his arm around Edith and gave her a warm hug. "It seems that my worst enemy has become my best friend."

Chapter 10

The sharp ring aroused Dan Blair. He reached sleepily for the phone. "Hello."

"Hello, Dan, this is Jean Thompson." She hesitated as she noted the slowness in his voice. "Did I awaken you?"

Dan rolled over and studied the red numbers on his alarm clock. Ten-thirty-five. "I should have been up a long time ago," he admitted. "I worked late at the center last night so I slept in a little. Thanks for calling. I was planning on getting some book work done before noon. What can I do for you?"

"Jim and I will be coming to Rocky Bluff this afternoon and I was wondering if we could get together and discuss the new crisis center for Running Butte."

"I'd love to. Where would you like to meet?"

"How about at my mother's at two o'clock? That way they can have some input as well."

Dan was now fully awake. "Sounds good. I'll see you at Edith's at two."

Jean hung up the phone and stood in her kitchen window, marveling at the construction on the new medical center going on just a couple blocks down the street. *A month ago it looked like it would be a couple years before they would begin work on the building and now the exterior is nearly completed. At this rate it's going to be open about the same time as the hardware store.*

That afternoon Jean, Edith, Roy, and Dan each enjoyed a cup of coffee and carrot cake in the Duttons' living room. Jean had a yellow tablet and pen beside her. "Dan, what is the first step I need to take in organizing a crisis center?"

Dan looked at her across the room. "Roy, I think you'd be a better one to answer her questions. What were some of the first things you did in starting the one here in Rocky Bluff?"

Roy set his coffee cup on the end table beside him. "First, and most important, you'll need volunteers. That's where good advertising comes in."

"When I first volunteered, it was in answer to an ad in the *Herald*," Edith recalled. "However, without a community newspaper, you'll have a bigger challenge on your hands."

"Whenever anything is going on in Running Butte, a sign is always posted in the local grocery store," Jean said and grinned. "Everyone in town gets to the store at least once a week. Also, Pastor Rhodes is very good about putting community announcements in the church bulletin."

"I'm glad our church established a mission to the Native Americans at Running Butte," Edith noted. "I know our congregation worked extremely hard renovating an old abandoned school into a church. It's quite a sacrifice for Pastor Rhodes to drive out there every Sunday afternoon, but he says he loves the people there."

"Those who attend his services really appreciate all that he's doing, and each week we gain a few more worshippers," Jean replied.

The foursome remained quiet as each entertained his or her own thoughts of the enormity of the challenges in Running Butte. Finally Roy broke the silence. "Jean, I hope you get this crisis center off the ground as soon as possible," he said. "I heard that the suicide rate among those on the reservation is almost three times the rate for all other races in our country. Do you have a place and time to meet in mind?"

"I arranged to use the church fellowship hall every Saturday afternoon at three o'clock," Jean explained. "I would like to have some of your specialists from Rocky Bluff come and talk to us. They could stay overnight with Jim and I and attend church with us the following day."

"That sounds like an excellent plan," Edith encouraged. "You've put a lot of thought into this project."

Jean then turned to Dan, who was lost in thought. "Dan, do you think you could prepare a training program for me and arrange for guest speakers when necessary?"

"I thought you'd never ask," he grinned. "I could bring the speakers with me when I come. Probably the same ones who share with our volunteers wouldn't mind taking a Saturday afternoon drive with me. Also, there's a certain young lady I know who has a great deal of personal interest in the success of crisis centers and who would like to accompany me."

The three exchanged knowing glances. "Looks like things are getting pretty serious between you and Beth," Roy chided.

Dan's face became somber. "I wish they were more serious than they are," he replied. "I think because she has been hurt so badly, she's afraid to love anyone for fear she will be hurt again."

Edith surveyed the handsome young man beside her. "Dan, you've been just the thing she needs," she assured him. "Little by little she'll relax and come around. Just give her a little more time."

"I know," Dan sighed. "Maybe I'm just more ready for a permanent relationship than she is. Perhaps the age difference is a problem."

"At your age, eight years doesn't seem like a lot," Edith replied. "Beth has had to accept more responsibilities than most twenty year olds. She needs time to learn to trust her own feelings. Life has changed so fast for her these last few months."

"We're all proud of her," Roy added. "She's going to make someone a mighty fine wife some day."

Dan grinned at the others and then the conversation went back to who should be invited to speak to the Running Butte volunteers. They were motivated by the memory of the crisis center's success with Beth. By the time her husband came to pick her up, Jean had five pages of notes.

Now that the planning of the Running Butte Crisis Center was in the competent hands of Dan Blair, Jean Thompson was able to turn her undivided attention to obtaining a tribal attorney for the members of the reservation. The next week she and Chief Joseph Black Hawk drove to the campus of the University of Montana in Missoula, where they met with Stephen Yellowtail.

"Steve, we've made the most generous offer we possibly can to convince you to come back to Running Butte as our tribal attorney," Chief Black Hawk began as the trio met in the lobby of the law school. "We must have a final commitment now, otherwise we will have to begin looking elsewhere. We have to act when the funding is available."

"Well, I have been offered a prestigious position with a law firm in Washington D.C., but I had the feeling they were only trying to meet some kind of quota. They didn't seem at all interested in my ability as a lawyer," the law student sighed. "Besides, I would never be happy in a big city."

"There's something about the wide open spaces and the call of the land that's inbred in us," Chief Black Hawk replied. "It's just part of being a Native American. Something we can all be proud of."

A look of determination spread across Steve's face. "I can't leave Montana while my own people suffer injustices and I have the skill and training to help them. I plan to move back to the reservation as soon as I graduate in June."

Chief Black Hawk could not conceal his delight. "Great," he exclaimed. "We'll try to have everything ready for your arrival. That's Jean's job."

"Steve, if you have any questions or problems in the transition, feel free to contact me," Jean said, knowing the reluctance of many Native Americans to ask for help.

Steve lowered his eyes. "Yes. . .sure."

"I brought along the floor plans of several mobile homes that we could have situated on a lot within three blocks of where your office will be," Jean explained as she took a manila file folder from her briefcase. "All of these come completely furnished—however, you may choose to substitute your own furniture if you'd like."

"My tastes are rather basic, so whatever interior design you choose will be fine with me," Steve replied as he thumbed through the pictures and brochures from the mobile home dealer in Rocky Bluff. "However, I do have one request. I would like a three-bedroom. I need an extra bedroom for when my family comes to visit and one for a home office. I'm a big one in getting up in the middle of the night to work."

Jean opened a colorful brochure and placed it before the young law student. "How does this one look?"

Steve studied the floor plan and description for a few minutes in silence before he spoke. "I like it," he replied seriously. "I've never lived in anything that nice before."

"Good," Jean smiled. "I'll have the dealer order it and he'll have it ready for you by the middle of June."

Chief Black Hawk leaned back in his chair. "Another hurdle you'll need to cross is passing both the tribal and the Montana state bar exams," he began. "We've arranged for the county attorney of Little Big Horn County to help you study for the state bar exam. Stuart Leonard has a brilliant mind and I'm sure he'll be a big help."

"Also, Stuart's paralegal will be moving to Running Butte before the new hardware store opens," Jean inserted. "Her name is Libby Reynolds and she comes highly recommended. Of course, you can hire your own staff, but she's more than qualified for the position."

Steve's eyes filled with tears. "I'm so glad someone is finally helping my people. It breaks my heart every time I go home and see the misery on the reservation."

"It's interesting," Chief Black Hawk explained. "Once a local church in Rocky Bluff became interested in our people and our problems, things began to happen. They were even able to shake up the government bureaucracy to get the promised government programs started."

"Do you have a doctor, yet?" Steve queried. "It would be a shame to have a fancy building and no doctor."

"Right now we have a physician's assistant lined up to come," Jean explained. "He's a member of the Blackfoot tribe in Browning. He'll be coming in June when he finishes his training. The hospital and doctors in Rocky Bluff have promised to work closely with our clinic."

Chief Black Hawk looked proudly at the woman beside him. "Jean was director of nursing at the Chamberlain, Idaho, hospital before moving to Running Butte, and she'll be in charge of the nurses and nurses' aides in the clinic. We're getting a lot more experience than we'd ever dreamed possible."

"I'm glad to hear that," Steve replied. "I just read some alarming statistics about reservation health care that made me want to leave law school and go to medical school. However, my queasiness at the sight of blood was the deciding factor to stay where I am."

"The statistics are frightening," Chief Black Hawk admitted. "Especially when those statistics are your own family and friends. Three times more American Indian babies die of sudden infant death syndrome than any others. The pregnancy rate among high school-aged Native American women in Montana is more than three times greater than the rate for all other women ages fifteen to nineteen. Diabetes and cirrhosis of the liver are also rampant on the reservation."

Steve shook his head sadly. "I can hardly wait to get back home to help my people. If there's someone coming to care for their medical needs, I'll do my best to meet their legal needs."

◈

That winter, basketball fever had again swept Rocky Bluff. This year not even Dan Blair could avoid the enthusiasm. Wednesday night he gave Beth a call. "Beth, I know we were planning to go bowling Friday night, but how would you like to go to the high school basketball game with me instead?"

"That sounds like fun," she promptly replied. "Since I've been working in the library I'm getting to know some of the players. I rarely went to the ball games when I was in high school, but now basketball has an entirely different appeal to me."

"Then you have a lot of making up to do," Dan chuckled. He hesitated before continuing. "Do you think Jeffy would like to come with us?"

"He'd love it. Larry Reynolds gave him a toy basketball set at his welcome home party and he plays with it all the time."

"The game is supposed to be a real barn burner," Dan continued. "They're playing Lewistown for the championship. The winner will advance to the class A tournament in Billings."

"I overheard the kids talking about the game in the library today. They're all excited about it. I hear the combination of Ryan Reynolds and Jay Harkness is unstoppable."

"We'll see if they're that good," Dan chuckled. "I'll pick you and Jeffy up about seven o'clock."

"I'll be looking forward to it. See you Friday night."

◈

Jeffy could scarcely contain himself at the thought of going to a real basketball game. When they arrived at the Rocky Bluff High School gym that

310

Friday night, he insisted on a bag of popcorn and a small cup of pop before he even entered the gym.

Dan selected seats midway up the bleachers near the halfway line of the court. The teams were still doing their warm-up drills as the threesome made themselves comfortable. Jeffy was mesmerized with the pep band as they played all of the upbeat favorites. He was soon clapping his hands in time with the music along with the cheerleaders. Suddenly everyone rose to their feet and sang the school song while the cheerleaders did their acrobatic stunts.

"Wow, those girls are good," Dan whispered. "Cheerleaders never did those kind of feats when I was in high school."

"They spend a lot of time in the weight room building up their strength so they can lift each other that way. The cheerleaders are even stronger than some of the guys, much to their frustration," Beth snickered.

Suddenly a hush fell across the crowd as they began to introduce the team members. "Number twenty-three, Ryan Reynolds," the speaker shouted. The Rocky Bluff supporters cheered. "Number fourteen, Jay Harkness." The crowd cheered even louder. The noise level increased as the other members of the team were introduced. Finally, the crowd was seated, the referee blew his whistle, and the game began.

The score remained close throughout the first three quarters. First Rocky Bluff would lead by two or three points and then Lewistown would lead. For a while it looked like the high school students were right. . .Ryan and Jay were unstoppable.

Jeffy could scarcely contain his excitement as he sat between Beth and Dan. Dan had almost as much fun watching Jeffy enjoy the game as he did watching the game himself. During a time-out, Jeffy looked up at Dan. "Gee, you're a lot of fun," he giggled. "You're almost like having a real daddy."

Beth and Dan exchanged nervous glances. "You're a lot of fun yourself," Dan said as he tousled the boy's hair. "I'd like to consider you as my son."

Jeffy suddenly became serious. "I had a daddy for three days once, but he was mean and went to jail. You're a lot nicer than he was."

Beth bit her lip to keep back her tears while Dan reached behind the child's back and gave her hand a comforting squeeze. "I hope the three of us will get to do a lot of things together," he replied just as the buzzer rang, announcing the end of the time-out.

As the minutes ticked away on the clock, the game became even more intense. Both teams resorted to a run-and-gun style of play. Suddenly, the referee blew his whistle and pointed to Jay as he held up one finger on his left hand and four fingers on his right. Jay walked meekly to the bench.

"What happened to Jay?" Jeffy queried.

"He had too many fouls and the rules say if you've touched another player too many times you're out of the game," Dan explained.

A Lewistown player advanced to the free throw line. He shot and made it. His next shot swished the net without even hitting the backboard. Lewistown was now three points ahead with only twenty seconds left in the game.

Rocky Bluff worked the ball down the floor, but Lewistown increased their defensive pressure. With eight seconds left Ryan Reynolds shot and made it. The score was now Rocky Bluff seventy-seven and Lewistown seventy-eight. Lewistown took the ball and slowed the game to nearly a standstill.

"Why don't they run and shoot like they've been doing?" Jeffy asked.

"They don't want to run the risk of Rocky Bluff getting possession of the ball and making another basket," Dan explained.

Suddenly the buzzer sounded. The game was over. A heavy gloom settled over the Rocky Bluff supporters as they began filing out of the gymnasium.

"It's too bad they lost," Beth said as they began putting on their coats. "This game meant so much to the entire school. They haven't had a championship team since Larry Reynolds led the team six years ago."

"The kids may think so, but life isn't over," Dan chuckled through his own disappointment. "Jay and Ryan are only juniors. They're sure to take the team to the class A state championship next year."

"Dan, I wish I had your spirit of optimism in spite of disappointment," Beth sighed as she looked into his steel blue eyes. "You're the best encourager I've ever known."

Dan wrapped his right arm around Beth while he took Jeffy's chubby hand in his left. "The two of you mean more to me than I can ever express in a crowded gym," he laughed.

Chapter 11

Jeffy finally fell asleep," Beth sighed as she sank into the cushions of her sofa. "The flu that's going around this winter is really wretched."

Dan put his arm around the tired young mother. "It's tough to see these little guys be so miserable and not be able to do much to help them."

"I'm glad you could come and stay with him while I was at work," Beth responded. "That's one of the disadvantages of being a working mother. . . what to do when the kids are sick and can't go to day care."

"Since I've been taking the night shift at the crisis center, this worked out perfect for both of us. I love that child as if he were my own."

Beth smiled as she stretched her feet upon the footstool and rested her head upon Dan's chest. "He thinks the world of you. That seems to be all he can talk about lately. . . When's Dan coming?"

Dan paused a moment and admired the young woman beside him. "I'd like to make our relationship more permanent. Dropping in every few days, going out to eat or going bowling or to a ball game seems pretty limiting. Beth, will you marry me so we could spend the rest of our lives together?"

Beth sat in stunned silence. Tears filled her eyes. "Dan, you deserve someone better than I. You deserve someone who's not tainted by a sinful past that keeps coming back to haunt her."

"Beth, don't be ridiculous. We've been through this many times before. You're not tainted. While you were a silly teenager you fell in love with a number one jerk. God has forgiven you for what has happened and has blessed you with a beautiful son. Please try to forgive yourself."

"I'm trying," Beth confessed, "but it's so difficult at times. I don't understand how you could love me like you do."

"I love you because you're a mature, compassionate young woman with whom I enjoy spending my time." Dan's voice became emphatic. "We've grown closer together through the good times and the bad. There seems to be nothing we haven't shared."

"Doesn't being eight years older than me bother you?" Beth queried.

"If you were fourteen and I was twenty-two it would make a big difference, but you are a mature woman now. After you get out of your teens, age becomes irrelevant. Please put aside your fears and say yes."

Beth again sat in silence. "I want to say yes," she stammered, "but I need more time to think about it. I made such a big mistake five years ago that I don't trust my own decisions."

Dan pulled Beth tighter against himself. "I'll give you all the time you need. I know this is the biggest decision you'll ever make in your life."

Suddenly Dan's eyes rested at the clock over the television. "Beth, I didn't realize it was getting so late. I'm supposed to be at the crisis center at nine o'clock. It could be a busy evening."

The couple embraced quickly and rose to their feet. "I'll call you tomorrow," Dan promised. "I'm afraid I'll have to spend most of Saturday at the center, but I'll be by first thing Sunday to take you and Jeffy to church, providing he's feeling better."

Beth smiled as Dan slipped out the door. "Thanks for all you've done. I don't know what I'd do without you."

As Beth laid restlessly in her bed that night, the words *I don't know what I'd do without him* kept running through her mind. She pictured herself alone with Jeffy in five years. She would do her best to raise him properly, but it would be hard to face life's challenges alone.

She then pictured Dan across the kitchen table every night discussing the day's happenings. She pictured him coaching Jeffy's little league team as she sat proudly in the stands. She imagined family camping trips into the nearby mountains. *Dear God,* she prayed. *I want a normal married life so badly. Do I really deserve it after what I've done?*

Suddenly a peace came over Beth. *Christ died so that I could have life and have it abundantly. Why shouldn't Jeffy and I be happy and have a normal family life? We both love Dan and he loves us. I want to talk this over with Edith before I give Dan a firm commitment. I don't want to hurt him in the slightest way.*

❧

"That show wasn't worth watching," Edith sighed. "I wish I'd spent the evening with a good book. I think I'll head off to bed now. Are you coming, Roy?"

Edith looked over at her husband. His eyes were glazed. Without saying a word, he stood and then crumpled to the floor. Edith was immediately at his side. "Roy, are you all right?" she pleaded as she reached for his pulse.

The elderly gentleman did not respond except for several involuntary muscle spasms. Edith ran to the phone and dialed 9-1-1.

"Rocky Bluff Emergency Response. May I help you?"

"Yes," Edith responded breathlessly. "I need an ambulance at the Roy

Dutton residence at 923 Maple Street right away. Roy has collapsed and won't respond to anything."

"We'll have an ambulance right there, Mrs. Dutton," the dispatcher assured her. "Please try to remain calm until they arrive and turn on an outside light so they can read the house numbers."

Edith returned to the living room and knelt by her husband. He still did not respond to her voice or touch. Outside she could hear the siren of the ambulance approaching. The flashing lights reflected through the picture window. She ran to the front door and flung it open just as a police car pulled up behind the ambulance. Four medics jumped from the ambulance. Two raced to the back and pulled a gurney onto the street while the other two medics joined Phil Mooney as they raced to the Dutton home.

"Am I glad to see you," Edith exclaimed as she nodded to her husband on the floor beside his chair.

"What happened?" the tallest medic asked as he took a stethoscope from his bag and knelt beside Roy.

"I don't know," Edith murmured. "We were just watching television and when he stood to go to bed, he collapsed."

"His heartbeat seems fairly strong and regular," the same medic observed. He then turned to his colleagues who had just appeared with the stretcher. "We need to get him to the hospital right away."

Phil Mooney put a comforting arm on Edith's shoulder. "Put your coat on and I'll take you to the hospital in the police car."

While the medics were loading Roy into the ambulance, Edith grabbed her coat and purse, flipped off the lights, and locked the door behind her. Phil took her arm as they hurried to the patrol car. Edith's face flushed with worry and excitement as her heart pounded in her chest.

"Phil, would you see that Bob and Jean are notified that they are taking Roy to the hospital?" Edith begged.

"Certainly," Phil responded as he reached for the car radio and called his dispatcher.

"I'm accompanying the ambulance to Rocky Bluff Community Hospital. Would you notify Bob Harkness and Mrs. James Thompson of Running Butte that Roy Dutton collapsed in his home and is on the way to the hospital?"

"Consider it done," the voice replied over the radio. "I hope Roy will be okay."

When the ambulance pulled into the emergency entrance with the patrol car right behind it, Edith could see Dr. Brewer's tall, lean form hurrying across the parking lot.

"What happened?" he asked as he accompanied the gurney through the automatic doors.

Edith again relayed the same story as before as they steered her husband toward examining room number three. "Why don't you wait here in the lobby while we examine Roy?" Dr. Brewer said as he pointed to the familiar emergency waiting room. "The receptionist will get a cup of coffee for you."

Lieutenant Mooney remained in the waiting room with Edith until Bob and Nancy hurried into the hospital twenty minutes later, and then he quietly slipped out the side door.

"How's Roy doing?" Bob asked.

"Not well," Edith sighed. Wrinkles increased on her forehead. "I think they've ruled out a heart attack. They are now trying to get the staff and equipment ready to do a CAT scan."

"Mom, how are you holding up?" Nancy queried as she noticed the flush in her cheeks.

Edith took a deep breath. "I haven't had time to think about myself. I've been so worried about Roy. He has suffered enough with his diabetes; he doesn't need anything else."

Edith, Bob, and Nancy watched nervously as the staff bustled in and out of the third emergency room.

"Have you talked with Jean, yet?" Edith murmured.

"They're on their way," Bob assured her. "They're going to drop Gloria off at our house so Dawn can baby-sit. I think it's going to be a long night."

As they sat quietly in the emergency waiting room, Edith's mind drifted back through the different crises that brought their family together in this very place. . .the death of her first husband, George. . .her own heart attack. . .the car accident that killed Roy's son and injured Bob. . . Roy's coming down with diabetes. . .and now this.

"We're very fortunate to have such a good hospital and professional staff," she commented as a nurse hurried by with more supplies. "Many smaller communities in Montana are not able to support a hospital or keep doctors, while we seem to have one of the best facilities in the area."

Nancy nodded in agreement. "I'll admit we do have one of the finest. Not very many towns have a doctor as concerned about his patients as Dr. Brewer. With his skills I'm sure he could make it big in any large city, yet he chose to treat families in a small town in Montana."

"Quality of life is something money can't buy," Bob replied. "I had to learn that the hard way."

As Bob stood to get another cup of coffee, he saw his sister and her husband coming down the corridor. He hurried to meet them. Giving his sister a quick hug, he pulled her aside where his mother could not see them.

"Hi, I'm glad you made it," he said with a forced smile. "They are doing a CAT scan right now on Roy. It doesn't look good. I'm also concerned about Mother. Her face is awfully flushed, but she won't consider being checked until she knows how Roy is. I hope your medical background can help console her. She's been through so much."

"I'll do my best," Jean replied as they turned the corner to the waiting room.

"Hello, Mom," Jean said as she leaned over and embraced her weary mother. "How's it going?"

"Not good, I'm afraid," Edith sighed. "We should be hearing the results of the CAT scan soon."

Edith repeated the events of the last few hours while Jean listened attentively. It was easier to explain medical symptoms to her daughter than anyone else.

"It sounds like a stroke to me," Jean said hesitantly. "It will be interesting to see what the scan shows."

Just then Dr. Brewer emerged from the emergency room and approached the family. His eyes immediately rested on Jean. "Hi, Jean, I'm glad you could get here so quickly. Roy is going to need all the support he can get."

"How is he?" Jean asked as she scrutinized the doctor's expressions.

"I'm afraid he had an aneurysm that burst," Dr. Brewer replied. "There is a good chance that surgery will improve his chances, but we can't guarantee anything."

Edith's flushed face turned ashen. "Are you sure he's going to make it?"

"Probably so," the doctor explained to her. "His heart is still strong, and that's in his favor. However, we don't know how much damage has been done to the brain."

Dr. Brewer paused to give time for the prognosis to settle over the worried family. He sat down in the chair next to Edith and took her hand. "If we do surgery, I'll need your permission."

"What's the prognosis without surgery?" Edith queried.

"Not good," Dr. Brewer replied. "There's a chance he might not even regain consciousness."

"Then what is the prognosis with surgery?" Edith continued to question.

"Surgery at his age and with diabetes is risky, but there's hope that he'll be able to have at least partial recovery."

Edith studied the faces of her grown children. They both nodded their heads affirmatively. "Then let's go ahead with the surgery and trust God to protect him."

"That's a wise decision," Dr. Brewer replied. "We'll schedule the surgery for ten o'clock in the morning. We're going to be moving him to intensive care now if you would like to see him for just a few minutes."

The doctor studied Edith's weary face and then continued. "I'd suggest you go home and get some rest. It's going to be a long day tomorrow." He rose and turned his attention back to the entire family. "I'll see you all tomorrow. Good night, now."

Jean was first to take control of the family crisis. "Mom, Jim and I will spend the night with you while Gloria can stay at Bob's. I'm sure she's asleep by now. It's fortunate that tomorrow is Saturday so Dawn will be home to watch her."

That night Edith tossed and turned in her bed from excess caffeine and worry. She tried lying crossways in the bed so she would not be as conscious of the emptiness, but nothing could lift her loneliness and concern. *Will I ever be able to share this bed with Roy again? He brought so much meaning and joy into my life.*

The next morning Edith bathed and dressed, then joined Jean and Jim in the kitchen, where Jean had prepared a hearty breakfast of hot cereal, fruit, and toast.

"You better eat well," Jean reminded her mother. "Who knows how long it will be before we'll be able to eat again."

"I'm really not hungry, but I better have something to keep my strength up," Edith replied. "Roy needs me more than ever now."

Just then the phone rang. The three exchanged nervous glances. "I hope it's not the hospital calling," Jean said as she reached for the phone.

"Hello, this is the Dutton residence. Jean Thompson speaking."

"Hi, Jean. This is Beth Slater. I'm surprised to hear you at your mother's home so early in the morning."

"We came in late last night," Jean explained. "Roy had a stroke last night and is scheduled for surgery at ten this morning."

There was a long silence on the other end of the phone line. "I'm sorry to hear that," Beth faltered. "If there's anything I can do, please let me know."

"Prayer is the main thing," Jean reminded her.

Beth's voice quivered. "If I can find someone to stay with Jeffy, do you think it would be okay if I came to the hospital and sat with Edith during the surgery?"

"I'm sure she'll appreciate that."

"Edith always stood by me during all my troubled times. The least I can do is to be there during her difficult times. She and Roy have taught me so much about love."

"We will be leaving for the hospital in fifteen minutes. If you'd like to join us, please do. We'd all enjoy seeing you again," Jean replied. "You've been such a vital part of their lives."

The two visited for a few moments about Roy's condition and then hung up the phone, agreeing to see each other within an hour.

Edith, Jean, and Jim arrived at the hospital just as the staff was preparing Roy for surgery. Tears filled Edith's eyes as she watched them shave his distinguished gray hair. "I love you, Roy," she whispered as she took his limp hand. "Hang in there. We'll all be praying for you." She leaned over and kissed his lips and then stepped back so the orderlies could lift him onto the cart and take him to the operating room. Everything was right on schedule as Dr. Brewer had promised the night before.

Within minutes Bob and Nancy joined the rest of the family in the family lounge. "I brought some knitting along to keep my hands busy," Nancy said after greeting her in-laws. "It helps the time go faster for me."

"That's a good idea," Edith replied, "but I'm so nervous now I don't think I could even sign my name."

Nancy reached into her knitting bag. "In that case, I stopped and bought some new magazines for you to look through. The ones in the hospital are always months old."

"Thanks, Nancy," Edith replied. "You always think of everything."

Minutes later Beth Slater walked into the family lounge. She immediately went to Edith and embraced her. "I'm so sorry about Roy. You both mean so much to me."

Edith's voice was weak and tired. "You've brought a great deal of joy into our lives as well."

"Your mature love and marriage is an example for everyone," Beth continued. "You weren't afraid to take a risk with a relationship even though you had to overcome many obstacles. You stood beside each other through both sickness and health."

Edith smiled. "Those words have much more depth than when they are recited at a young couple's wedding ceremony. They are the confidence that love provides, knowing your spouse will be there no matter what happens. The human body can withstand a lot of physical pain if the person knows they are loved unconditionally. That's what mature love is all about."

Beth smiled. "That's what I want in my life as well," she said as she took Edith's hand. "Because of the love I've seen between you and Roy, in spite of all the difficulties you've faced, I'm not afraid to say 'yes' to Dan's proposal. With God's help we, too, can promise 'in sickness and health'."

Chapter 12

The minutes ticked by slowly as the friends and family of Roy Dutton huddled together in the family lounge of the Rocky Bluff Community Hospital. Nancy busied herself with her knitting and found that she was having to undo as much as she was doing, but it helped pass the tense hours during the surgery. Beth Slater turned the pages of the magazines, but was unable to concentrate on reading. Only Edith appeared relatively composed.

Beth studied her older friend's face with bewilderment. "Edith, how can you appear so calm when the life of the man you love is on the line?"

Edith chuckled softly. "You should have seen me last night," she confessed. "I was a nervous wreck."

"She's not kidding," Jean teased. "I was afraid we were going to have to get a hospital room for her as well."

"I tossed and turned most of the night. Roy and I have been so happy together these last four years, I didn't want to lose him," Edith explained. "While I was sitting here this morning a peace settled over me, and instead of becoming angry about Roy's illness, I became thankful for the four years we have had together. I have completely put his life in God's hands."

"That takes a lot of courage," Beth replied. "I only wish my faith were as strong."

Edith patted the young woman's hand. "God doesn't provide the strength until you need it. This morning I accepted the fact that if he goes to be with the Lord now, it will be alright. He will no longer be in pain. He has been talking more and more lately about how beautiful heaven must be. I know that we'll have eternity to be together. However, I want to keep him with me for as long as possible. He's added so much joy to my life."

Everyone in the room exchanged looks of embarrassment. Here they were supposed to be comforting Edith and yet she was the one consoling them.

Just then Pastor Rhodes stepped into the room. He nodded to each of the family members and then turned to Edith. "How's it going?"

"The last word from the operating room is that the surgery is going well," Edith responded. "But we won't know for several days how much damage has been done. There's a good chance of paralysis."

"We know he's in God's hands," Pastor Rhodes reminded them. "The church prayer chain is praying for all of you right now. God has been faithful to your family through many crises and He's not going to let you down this time."

"Mother's the pillar of us all," Jean responded. "She's the first one to accept the fact that whatever happens will be God's will."

"Honey, don't make me out to be the saint I'm not," Edith chided. "You saw how I was last night."

All eyes shifted as Dr. Brewer appeared in the doorway. "The surgery went well. The aneurysm was tied off and the blood clot was removed. However, there seems to have been some leakage into the brain. We won't know for several days if there will be any paralysis, but judging by where the leakage occurred, I'm fairly certain the right side of his body will be affected somewhat."

"When can I see him?" Edith pleaded.

"He'll be in the recovery room for about an hour and then they'll move him to intensive care, where you can see him for only five minutes every hour," Dr. Brewer explained. "Why don't you get a bite to eat in the hospital cafeteria? The food there is pretty good."

"Thanks so much for all you've done," Edith said as she shook the doctor's hand. "I don't know where our family would be without your excellent care and concern. Rocky Bluff is fortunate to have you."

After Dr. Brewer bid them farewell and returned to the doctors' lounge, where he changed into street clothes, Pastor Rhodes smiled and turned to Edith. "We can thank God that the surgery went well and continue to pray for Roy's complete recovery."

"Thank you for coming, Pastor," Edith replied. "I appreciate your concern."

Beth likewise said good-bye as the Harkness family headed for the hospital dining room. Their mood lightened as they each selected their favorite sandwich and soup. Together they had survived another family crisis.

An hour later Edith slipped into Roy's intensive care unit and took his limp hand. His eyes slowly opened. "Hello, Roy," she whispered. "How are you doing?"

A faint smile spread across his face. The muscles around his face began to twitch. "He. . .he. . .he. . .lo," he stammered. "I. . .I. . .I'm. . .s. . . s. . .slee. . .py." Roy closed his eyes and faded into a deep slumber.

Edith leaned over and kissed him on the forehead and slipped out of the room to join her waiting family. "Jean, I know it's too early to tell for sure, but I'm afraid his speech is going to be impaired. He had a lot of trouble forming his words."

"That's fairly common after all that he's been through," Jean explained. "It could be that the anesthetics have not worn off."

"But this was different from slurred, drugged speech," Edith persisted. "He tried so hard to communicate with me, but he wasn't able to make the sounds."

One by one the other family members slipped into Roy's room, but he did not rouse. As Jean slipped out of the room, Edith looked wearily at her daughter. "Would you mind taking me home? Now that I know Roy is okay, I think I could sleep for a week."

"That's a good idea. We could all use a good nap."

Edith slept most of that afternoon. Jean fixed her mother's favorite dish for dinner. . .spaghetti and meatballs. As soon as she had finished eating, Edith went back to bed and slept the entire night. Every cell in her body seemed to be craving complete rest.

By eight o'clock the next morning, Edith was dressed and in the kitchen preparing breakfast for Jean and Jim. Jean stumbled into the kitchen in her bathrobe with her hair tousled. "Mother, you shouldn't have to fix breakfast for us," she protested. "Give me a few minutes and I'll have breakfast on the table."

"I need to make myself useful sometime," Edith teased. "Besides, I'm anxious to get to the hospital and see Roy. He should be alert today."

"Well, if you insist," Jean replied with a twinkle in her eye. "We'll be with you in just a few minutes. Jim is finishing showering now."

An hour later Edith, Jean, and Jim stopped at the nurses' station at intensive care.

"Hello, Edith," the nurse greeted. "How are you today?"

"I'm fine," she replied. "How is Roy doing?"

"He rested well," the nurse replied. "But he seems to have some paralysis on his right side and his speech is slurred. I'm sure Dr. Brewer will want to talk to you about physiotherapy as soon as Roy is strong enough. His body has suffered an awful shock and since he's a diabetic, it will take even longer for him to heal."

"I'm so thankful he's pulling through the operation," Edith sighed. "When he left the house in the ambulance, I wasn't sure of anything."

"I'll admit it was kind of touch and go for awhile," the supervising nurse explained. "But Roy has a tough constitution and a strong will to live. Others would have given up under much less difficulties."

Edith eyed the door to her husband's room. "May I see him now?"

"I'm sure he'll enjoy it. Just remember he's only allowed one visitor at a time for only five minutes."

As Edith opened the door, Roy's face broke into a broad grin. "H. . .h. . .h. . .i, E. . .E. . .d. . .d. . .ith," he stammered.

Edith took her husband's hand as she leaned over to kiss him. "How are you doing?" she whispered.

"F. . .f. . .f. . .i. . .i. . .ne. . . ."

"That's good," she whispered, trying to mask the lump in her throat. "We'll have you up and running in no time."

"C. . .c. . .c. . .a. . .n. . .n. . .t m. . .m. . .o. . .v. . .ve."

"There's all kinds of gadgets to help," Edith reminded him gently. "Dr. Brewer is probably planning a pretty extensive workout for you. Are you up to it?"

Roy grinned and nodded his head affirmatively.

"That's the spirit," Edith replied. "You'll have to show the world that one's never too old to keep fighting for the good life."

Roy squeezed Edith's hand as he smiled.

"Jean and Jim are anxious to see you," Edith explained. "They came down late Friday night, but Jim has to be in Running Butte by early morning. They're expecting a big shipment for the new store, but he'll be by later today to see you."

Roy nodded his head affirmatively.

"They're really protecting you now," Edith teased. "They'll only let one of us in at a time, so I better go now so everyone else can see you before they leave. I love you."

"I. . .l. . .l. . .o. . .v. . .ve. . .y. . .y. . .y. . .ou."

After watching how Roy struggled to form each letter, Jean had a running monologue explaining the progress of the Running Butte Crisis Center. She could sense his intense interest by the sparkle in his eyes. Roy was trapped in a body that was unable to communicate with his loved ones.

While Edith was waiting in the hallway in front of her husband's room, Dan Blair, Beth Slater, and Jeffy entered. "We had to come and see how Roy's doing before we go to church," Dan explained. "I was shocked to hear what happened. Roy seemed to be doing so well lately."

Edith shook her head. "One never knows when something like this is going to happen. He had one close call."

"If there is anything I can do to help, please feel free to ask," Dan stated. "Will you be needing transportation to the hospital or anything like that?"

Edith's eyes brightened. "Jean and Jim are going home this afternoon and, of course, Bob and Nancy work all day, so I'll be needing rides to the hospital until Roy's released."

"Consider it done," Dan replied. "Just tell me what time you'd like a ride and I'll be there."

"Would ten o'clock every day be too much of an inconvenience?" Edith replied. "I feel like a terrible burden since I haven't been able to drive myself after my heart attack."

"No problem at all," Dan assured her. "There are some advantages of working the night shift."

The days passed slowly for Edith. Promptly at ten o'clock each day Dan took her to the hospital and then returned to get her at three. Edith did her best to keep Roy's spirits high and chatted about the grandchildren, school, church activities, and the progress of the new hardware store.

Three weeks after Roy's stroke, Dr. Brewer invited Edith to join him in the family lounge. "Edith," he began cautiously. "This is very difficult for me to say, but the restoration of Roy's functions are not going as easy as I'd like. Through physical therapy he is beginning to get some range of motion in his right leg and arm, but he is far from being able to walk and feed himself. I think it's time we begin considering other options."

Edith's chin dropped. "What options are left? I would really like to bring him home, but I won't be able to care for him in the condition he's in now."

"Edith, Roy is going to need physiotherapy and specialized health services for a long time and strong backs that will be able to lift him from his bed to his chair. My advice is to place him in a long-term skilled nursing facility," Dr. Brewer replied gently.

Edith sat in stunned silence. "You mean he'll have to be in a nursing home?" she murmured.

"I'm afraid so," Dr. Brewer responded. "People often think placing a family member in a nursing home is a sign of self-centeredness and cruelty when in reality it can be the kindest thing you can do for your loved one."

"But I promised before God that we'd be together until 'death do us part,'" Edith protested with tears in her eyes.

Dr. Brewer took Edith's hand. "Just because Roy's in a nursing home does not mean you'll have to abandon him." He paused before continuing. "We have a fine facility right here in Rocky Bluff. You could visit him every day and even make arrangements to have your meals together in the dining room with the others."

Edith shuddered at the thought of nightly separation from her beloved husband. "The house is so lonely without him. It would not only be an adjustment for him but also for me."

"With the nursing home connected to the hospital, Roy will be able to continue his daily physical therapy treatments," Dr. Brewer explained. "If he ever becomes able to walk and take care of himself, I'll be the first one to recommend him returning to his own home."

Edith thought back through the years of the times she visited the nursing home with either a church group, a school group, or just to visit an elderly friend. "There is one advantage to a nursing home in a smaller community over one in the city," she noted.

"And what is that?" Dr. Brewer queried.

"There is a lot of community involvement in the activities of the home. The program coordinator generally has something different going on every afternoon."

Dr. Brewer nodded with agreement. "That's true. Often the patients have a lot more social activities than when they were alone in their own home."

"That's true for most people," Edith replied, "but Roy always seemed to have a string of friends stopping by the house for a cup of coffee. We've gone through three coffeemakers just in the short time we've been married."

"Then I'm sure Roy won't be lacking in company while he's in the community nursing home." Dr. Brewer gazed out the window at the freshly fallen snow. Helping family members accept the perhaps permanent limitations of a loved one was one of the hardest parts of his job as family doctor. "Edith, should I go ahead and make arrangements with the director to have Roy transferred as soon as the next bed is available?"

"Could I have a couple days to talk with my family?" Edith queried. "I don't want to make such a big decision without first consulting them."

"Of course," Dr. Brewer responded. "We probably won't need a decision until the end of the week. Would you call me by Friday and let me know what you've decided?"

"Sure," she responded. "I just want to make certain I'm doing the right thing for Roy."

That afternoon Edith rode home in silence, lost in her own thoughts. Dan Blair had long since learned that there comes a time when people need to be alone to sort through their own feelings and did not pressure her for details. As soon as she walked in her home, Edith hung up her coat and went directly to the phone.

"Hello, Jean," she said when her daughter's voice echoed through the receiver.

"Hello, Mom. How are you doing?"

"I'm fine. How are you and Gloria?"

"We're doing great. We're as busy as we can be with the new medical center being so close to completion. How's Roy?"

"That's what I'm calling about," Edith confessed. "Would you and Jim mind driving to Rocky Bluff tomorrow night? I want to get the entire family together and discuss his condition."

"No problem," Jean replied, sensing the concern in her mother's voice. "In fact, I'll come down early enough to make a big dinner for our family."

The next afternoon when Dan dropped Edith at home after her daily visit to the hospital, she found Jean busy in her kitchen. She gazed around the counters and smelled the ham cooking in the oven. "This is going to be better than a Christmas dinner the way you're going at this," she teased.

"Any day is a good day to make special," Jean replied as she finished tossing the salad. "Besides Jay and Dawn are going to come and I don't want them to think I've lost my touch."

"I'm glad they're going to be here," Edith replied. "Those two are extremely mature for their years."

The Harkness family chattered back and forth about the routine issues of daily life in Rocky Bluff, each knowing that something important was to be decided, but the dinner table was not the time nor the place to address it. After everyone had finished dinner and Jean and Dawn had loaded the dishwasher, the entire family gathered in Edith's living room. All eyes settled on her. Now was the time.

Edith cleared her throat as she surveyed her family. "I had a long talk with Dr. Brewer yesterday," she began. "He said that Roy's rehabilitation is not coming along as well as he'd like and that we need to consider other options."

Jean studied her mother's face. "Is he suggesting we put Roy in a nursing home?"

"Exactly. He felt Roy needs intense physical therapy and specialized care that we can't provide at home."

Tears filled Dawn's eyes. "But he can't go to the nursing home. He needs to be at home so we can visit him all the time," the thirteen year old protested. "Jean's a nurse. Couldn't she care for him the way she took care of you after your heart attack?"

Jean put her arm around her niece. "I wish it were that simple," she sighed, "but Roy's medical problems are much different from what your grandmother experienced. Roy is not able to walk, so two strong people will have to lift him every time he needs to get out of bed or go to the bathroom. I'm not strong enough to do that alone."

"Also, Dawn," Edith continued, "Roy has to have physical therapy every day so he can learn to reuse his right arm and leg. We wouldn't have any way to get him back and forth to the hospital from here."

"It just seems so mean to put him in the nursing home," Jay protested.

"I felt the same way until Dr. Brewer talked to me," Edith confided. "Now I feel like it's the kindest thing I can do under the circumstances. He told me I can have my meals in the dining room with Roy every day so it won't be like we're abandoning him. Even if he can't talk to communicate, we are still spiritually one."

"We can all visit him regularly," Bob stated. "He's done so much for us that it's time we give something back. I know it's hard when he can't talk the way he'd like, but he still talks with his eyes and with time he can get a few words out."

Finally, the wisdom of specialized care became a reality for Dawn. "The nursing home isn't that far out of my way home from school," she noted. "I can stop by nearly every evening and bring my friends with me."

"We want to let the entire world know how much we love our grandpa and make him the most visited resident in the home," Jay inserted.

"Then everyone is in agreement that I should let Dr. Brewer go ahead and make the transfer to the nursing home?" Edith queried.

Everyone nodded their heads affirmatively.

"Thanks," Edith smiled. "You've made this decision so much easier for me. It's comforting to know that when problems arise, we can always stand together as a family."

Chapter 13

B eth, did you notice how Roy looked at Edith today while she was reading to him? He may not be able to verbally communicate well, but his eyes spoke volumes," Dan said as the young couple relaxed in Beth's living room after Jeffy was in bed.

Beth's voice softened. "Their devotion is an inspiration of the faithfulness of love, even through the toughest times."

Dan put his arm around Beth. "The more I see the fruits of their marriage, the more I want to experience some of the same benefits with you," he implored. "Beth, when will I get an answer to my proposal?"

"Tonight," she whispered as she laid her head on his chest. "I feel just the way you do. After seeing Roy and Edith's love through the most difficult of times, I'm no longer afraid to love someone unconditionally."

The young couple embraced with ecstasy. Never had either one of them been happier. Love rushed into the empty hole in both their lives. "Honey, I'm so happy every time I'm with you," Dan murmured into her ear. "Let's set a wedding date as soon as possible."

Beth pulled back from their embrace. "There's so much going on now and it will take several months to make wedding plans," she protested good-naturedly. "I couldn't possibly be ready until after school is out in June."

"Then June it is," Dan declared. "On Saturday let's go down to Rothstein's Jewelry Store and pick out the biggest diamond we can afford."

Beth gasped. "A diamond? I never expected a real diamond. Aren't we being frivolous when there's so many bills to pay?"

"Diamonds are an investment, not a luxury. You deserve the very best. Our love is forever."

Beth hugged her fiancé with delight. "Dan, I love you so much. I never knew life could be so good."

"If you can find someone to watch Jeffy, I'll pick you up at one o'clock on Saturday."

"I don't think that'll be a problem," Beth replied. "Several girls at school nearly beg to baby-sit him."

"Great," Dan nearly shouted with exhilaration. "Saturday, after I take Edith to the nursing home, I'll come and take you downtown. Be sure and circle that day on the calendar in red."

Saturday afternoon found Dan and Beth perched on two bar stools in front of the diamond case of Rothstein's Jewelers. "Which one do you like the best?" Dan asked as they peered through the glass.

"I don't know what to say. They're all beautiful."

"Do you like a round or an emerald cut?" the jeweler asked as he took an example of each from the showcase.

"I like that one best," Beth replied as she pointed to a one-half karat solitaire.

"Try it on and see how it looks," Dan begged.

Beth slid the ring onto her third finger, left hand. "It's beautiful," she gasped. "I can't wear something like this all the time."

"Of course you can," Dan reminded her as he pointed to a bridal set in the back corner of the diamond case. "Why don't you try that one?"

The jeweler took out the bridal set Dan selected and helped Beth slide it onto her finger. The solitaire engagement ring was accented by the swirl of smaller diamonds of the wedding band encircling it.

Beth gasped, "I've never seen anything as exquisite as this."

Dan turned to the jeweler. "We'll take this one."

Beth handed the set back to the jeweler, who placed it in its box. "Will it be cash or charge?" he asked Dan.

"I'll write a check," Dan responded proudly. "I've been saving for this day for a long time."

"But we only agreed to marry this week," Beth teased suspiciously.

"I had you picked out a long time ago," Dan laughed. "I knew it would just be a matter of time before you came around."

"Fortunately, Beth's ring size is a perfect six, the same size in which most of the bridal sets are initially manufactured, so there won't be a need to size them. You can take them with you now if you'd like," the jeweler explained.

Dan wrote the check while the jeweler filled out the guarantee papers. The transaction was soon completed and the happy couple walked out the door holding hands. As soon as they were inside the car, Dan took the little box from his pocket.

"Beth, I can't wait to have you begin wearing this," he said as he held out the engagement ring. "I want to shout it to the world that you have agreed to be Mrs. Dan Blair."

Dan slid the ring onto her finger. Forgetting the passersby on the sidewalk, their lips met for a lasting moment. Soon they would be one family.

"I can't believe this is happening," Beth exclaimed.

"Let's go by the nursing home and show the ring to Roy and Edith," Dan replied eagerly. "Without them I don't think any of this would have been possible."

Beth squeezed his hand as Dan reached for the ignition. Rarely did she have trouble finding something to talk about, but the excitement of this moment left her speechless. Dan parked his car in front of the care center and they hurried inside. They found Edith in Roy's room reading the *Herald* to him.

Seeing the young couple, Roy broke into a broad grin. "H. . .h. . .he. . . l. . .l. . .lo, D. . .D. . .D. . .an."

"Hi, Roy. You're looking good today," Dan greeted as he shook his hand. "Hello, Edith. How's it going for the both of you?"

"Really good," Edith replied. "Roy is getting the best of care here. And, believe it or not, the food here is really good. I am so grateful that you're able to bring me over every day so I can have lunch with him."

"I enjoy doing it," Dan replied as he pulled up chairs for himself and Beth. He looked over at his fiancée and lifted her left hand. The diamond flashed in the sunlight that streaked through the window.

Edith took Beth's hand from Dan. "Beth, that's beautiful. Congratulations," she exclaimed. "I'm so happy for you."

Beth beamed. "I never thought anything like this could ever happen to me. I feel like a princess being swept away by my Prince Charming."

Roy reached for Beth's left hand. He smiled as he gazed at the diamond and then lifted her hand to his lips in a form of blessing. Being mute didn't prevent him from communicating his true feelings.

"Have you set the date yet?" Edith queried.

"I'm awfully busy until school is out," Beth replied, "but hopefully we can get married in June so we have the entire summer together before I have to go back to work."

"We haven't talked with Pastor Rhodes, yet," Dan inserted. "I hope our wedding won't interfere with his vacation."

"I doubt it," Edith replied. "He usually takes his family on vacation late in the summer."

Beth glanced at Roy. His chin had sunk against his chest and his eyes had closed. "Looks like it's afternoon nap time," she whispered.

Edith smiled. "Dan, would you mind taking me home now? I think Roy's had enough excitement for the day. Seeing the two of you so happy will give him pleasure for days to come."

The next day Dan, Beth, and little Jeffy lingered behind the congregation so they could speak with Pastor Rhodes a few moments privately.

"Dan. . .Beth, you both look extremely radiant today," Pastor Rhodes greeted.

"We have a reason to be," Dan chuckled. "Beth has agreed to marry me," he said as he lifted Beth's left hand.

"Congratulations," the pastor smiled. "That is a beautiful ring."

"We were wondering if there would be a weekend in June in which you could perform the ceremony for us?"

Pastor Rhodes took his black schedule book from his coat pocket. "It looks like the last three weekends are open, so you can have your pick of dates. I like to have at least four premarital counseling sessions with the engaged couple before the ceremony. Could we set up a time this week to get together and discuss the details?"

Dan looked at Beth. They were already beginning to think as one. "With our strange work schedules, Saturdays seem to be the best time for both of us," Dan told the pastor.

Pastor Rhodes flipped a couple pages in his schedule book. "How does two o'clock in my office sound?"

"We'll be there," Dan promised as he took Beth's hand in his right and Jeffy's in his left.

That is a mighty promising family in the making, Pastor Rhodes mused as the three walked happily down the front steps of the church.

It did not take long the next morning for word to spread through the faculty and students of Rocky Bluff High School that the library clerk had just become engaged and was sporting a new diamond. The teenage girls rushed to the library as soon as they had a break between classes. Beth could scarcely get her books shelved for the day.

"Miss Slater, let me see your ring."

"It's beautiful."

"Are you going to invite us to your wedding?"

"I wish my boyfriend would give me a diamond like that."

At lunchtime Beth was surrounded by well-wishing faculty members. Beth scarcely knew how to respond to their enthusiasm. The most enthusiastic of all was the librarian, Rebecca Sutherland.

"Beth," she exclaimed over cafeteria hamburger. "We're going to have to throw a big shower in celebration. It's not often we get to help start one of our own out on a voyage of marital bliss."

The entire faculty lounge burst into gales of laughter.

"Men's dirty socks stuck under the bed," one teacher chided.

"Caps left off the toothpaste," added another.

"Someone drinking directly out of a milk carton instead of using a glass," laughed another.

Beth blushed. "I don't know what to say. It's all so exciting. Even if I have to reach under the bed to find the dirty socks," she teased back.

"Consider the formation of the shower committee made, and invitations for a party sometime in May will be forthcoming," Rebecca said just as the bell rang, summoning them back to class.

The next Saturday afternoon Beth and Dan arrived at Pastor Rhodes's office promptly at two o'clock. After exchanging pleasantries, the first thing on the agenda was to select a wedding date. With little discussion, June twenty-first was written on the church calendar.

Pastor Rhodes then looked at the future bride across the room from him. "Beth, your entire countenance has changed since you became engaged."

"There's a good reason," Beth beamed. "I'm happier than I've ever been in my life. After all I've done in my life, I feel like I don't deserve all this, but yet good things keep happening to me."

Pastor Rhodes became serious. "Jesus not only died for what you've done in the past," he assured her. "He also came that you might have life and have it abundantly."

Beth grinned. "Well, having Dan's love is definitely making my life abundant."

"How's Jeffy accepting the idea of you getting married?" Pastor Rhodes asked. "After all, he's had your undivided attention all his life."

"Jeffy's excited that he's finally going to have a daddy," Beth responded. "He thinks the world of Dan."

"I've noticed that in church," Pastor Rhodes responded. "He spends a lot of time sitting on his lap or holding his hand."

"I'd like to adopt him if it's at all possible," Dan stated. "But I don't know where to begin since his natural father is in jail in Canada."

"Why don't you talk with Stuart Leonard about that?" the pastor suggested. "He'll probably be able to help you out. He's already familiar with the law enforcement agencies in Canada after he worked to get Jeffy released back to Montana last fall."

"Dan, I wish you would talk to Stu as soon as possible," Beth pleaded. "Jeffy's adoption would make us truly a traditional family. . .something I thought I would never have because of my stupidity with Mickey."

"I'll call him Monday and make an appointment," Dan assured her as he took her hand. "Jeffy is already so much like a son to me that I want to make it official at the same time I make you my wife."

Pastor Rhodes directed the remaining conversation toward the characteristics of a Christian marriage and some common pitfalls that might befall them. Both Dan and Beth were eager to begin their married life with a firm commitment that together they could conquer anything.

The following Wednesday afternoon Dan greeted Pat as he entered the Little Big Horn county attorney's office.

"Hello, Dan. It's good to see you," the secretary greeted. "Won't you be seated? Stu will be right with you."

Just then the distinguished county attorney appeared in the doorway. "Dan, how are you doing?" he said as he extended his right hand. "Won't you come into my office?"

Stu motioned for Dan to be seated in a chair to the right of his desk. "What can I do to help you today?" he queried.

Dan took a deep breath. "I suppose you know that Beth and I are getting married in June."

"In Rocky Bluff there are no secrets," the attorney chuckled.

"Well, I was wondering what my chances would be to adopt Jeffy?"

"It's within the realm of possibilities," Stu replied. "It mainly depends on whether or not the natural father would sign a waiver giving up his rights as a father."

"Since he's in jail in Canada, wouldn't that be pretty hard to do?"

Stu surveyed the earnest young man's intense expression. "Not necessarily. We do have several things in our advantage. First, we know exactly where he is; and second, we also know his attorney. I can draw up the papers and call Greg McIntyre in Calgary and see if he will go to the jail and ask Mickey to waive his paternal rights."

"After all the trouble he went to in kidnapping Jeffy and taking him to Canada, I doubt if he'd sign anything," Dan said dejectedly.

"I don't think Mickey's behavior was caused by any paternal instinct. He only wanted revenge on Beth and a cover for his criminal activities. If he thought he'd have to pay child support just as soon as he returned to the States, I think he might be glad to have someone else take over his responsibilities. Give me a few days to work on it."

"Thank you so much," Dan said as he rose to leave. "I'd like to make Jeffy my son at the same time as I make his mother my wife."

"I'll be in touch with you in a couple of days after I've talked with Greg McIntyre. I think we have a good shot at this one."

The next few weeks flew by for Beth and Dan as they made plans for their upcoming wedding and honeymoon. There were bridesmaids' dresses and a bridal dress to order. . .flowers. . .invitations. . .food. . .showers. Beth was astir with all the excitement, but she had the best advisor possible in planning a social occasion, the former home economics teacher, Edith Dutton.

"Mickey, you have company," the prison guard said as he unlocked the cell and motioned for him to walk down the corridor toward the visitors' room.

"Who is it?"

"I think it's your attorney."

Mickey smiled as he sat at the table and peered through the mesh separating the prisoner from the guest.

"Hi, Greg, did you come to get me out of here?"

"You don't have a chance for parole for several more months," the attorney stated flatly. "However, I do have a proposition for you to consider."

"What's that?"

"Beth Slater is planning to get married in June and her fiancé, Dan Blair, would like to adopt Jeffy. They need you to sign a waiver giving up your parental rights."

"I'm not going to do that," Mickey sneered. "He's my kid."

"That's right, Mickey, he is," Greg McIntyre replied. "However, since he's your child, you're responsible for child support payments under United States law. As soon as you cross the border, you'll be expected to pay child support."

"Ah. . .I suppose I could kick in fifty dollars a month if they force me to."

"Child support payments in the States can run five to six hundred dollars a month," Greg explained.

"You mean that as soon as I go home, I'll have to pay that much? Even if I did get a decent job, I wouldn't be able to support myself and give that much to Jeffy. Besides, Beth will only spend it on herself. She has a good job; she can support him."

"Legally, you're still responsible until Jeffy becomes eighteen."

Mickey sat in silence. "That's a heck of a lot of money. How am I going to get out of this?" he sighed. "If I'm not in a jail with four walls and bars, I'll be in financial jail for the rest of my life."

"You could sign the waiver giving up your parental rights and then Dan would be responsible for paying all his bills."

"If I sign this, as soon as I get out of jail I can go back to the States and get a job without having anything hanging over my head?"

"Yes, Jeffy will be entirely Dan's and Beth's responsibility."

Mickey's eyes began to moisten. "I've always wanted to go back to Montana as soon as I get out of here. I left the state when I joined the marines and I don't think I could be happy any other place. Where do I sign?"

Chapter 14

B eth, would you and Jeffy like to go to Running Butte with me a week from Saturday?" Dan asked as the pair sat watching TV in Beth's cozy apartment.

"Sure, what's the occasion?"

"Libby Reynolds called today. They've settled into their new double-wide mobile home there and she'd like to have a little housewarming dinner. She asked if we'd be able to bring Edith Dutton with us."

Beth smiled. "That sounds like a good idea. I wish I could have helped them move, but I had to work that day."

"They had plenty of help," Dan assured her. "Since Libby is pregnant, no one would let her lift even the smallest box."

"I am anxious to see their new place. When does the new store open?"

"That Saturday is the grand opening of Harkness II. That's why she'd like us to bring Edith. Larry and the rest of the Harkness clan are going to be busy at the store all day."

Beth's thoughts drifted back through the months that she had known Libby Reynolds. "So much has happened since Edith introduced me to Libby and I started taking care of her little Vanessa while she went to para-legal school."

"I don't think Rocky Bluff will ever forget the night the Harkness Hardware Store burned down, the arson investigation, and their grand reopening." Dan's face broke into a broad grin. "I know I'll never forget the grand reopening," he said as he put his arm around his fiancée. "That was the day we met."

"It's interesting how a serendipity happens when we're going about our daily routines." Beth sighed as she laid her head upon his chest. "Who would have thought the reopening of a local business would affect me for the rest of my life?"

"That fire had a life-changing effect on Larry and Libby as well," Dan replied. "Before that time Libby was a terrified, young, abused wife calling the crisis line. Within months they were renewing their wedding vows, and here they are now with a new home of their own and another baby on the way."

"Isn't it interesting that here in Rocky Bluff, when people's lives change for the better, somewhere in the background is the influence of Edith Dutton?"

The leaf in Libby's kitchen table extended to include Beth, Dan, Jeffy, and Edith into the Reynolds's family circle.

"I'm glad you could come to our grand opening," Larry said as he passed the mashed potatoes to Edith. "This store is like a miracle springing up in a decaying hamlet. The reservation people are so appreciative of anyone investing in their world."

"I'm looking forward to seeing the store," Edith noted as she looked out the front window and saw cars lining the road for two blocks.

"The store's just packed," Larry continued. "Bob and Nancy, along with Jim and Jean, are really busy. I promised I wouldn't be gone long so they can each take a few minutes to catch a bite to eat."

Edith turned to Libby. "When do they expect to get the new clinic open?"

"They're looking at the middle of June for the construction to be completed. Both the physician's assistant and the new attorney will be moving into Running Butte about that time," Libby explained. "Their grand opening is scheduled for the second week of July."

"How exciting," Beth declared, trying to grasp the enormity of the project. "But isn't that about the time your baby is due?"

A look of pleasure settled across Libby's face. "The exact due date is the fifteenth of June, so it ought to be a busy month for us."

"It's going to be a great month for us as well," Dan chuckled. "I'll be gaining a wife and a son at the same time."

"I sure hope I'm not in the hospital and will be able to come to your wedding," Libby replied. "I hated having to decline being your bridesmaid, but it's not a very good time for me."

"Actually, it's because you won't know what size to make your bridesmaid's dress," Larry chuckled as he patted his wife's tummy.

Libby blushed and then took Vanessa from her high chair before she began clearing the table. "Let me help," Beth said as she began to stack the plates to carry them to the sink.

Within half an hour the small gathering in the Reynolds's kitchen had moved to the new hardware store. Edith's eyes filled with tears as she approached her son. "Bob, you've done an excellent job. Your father would be proud of you. It was always his dream to expand the store to another community, but he never had a chance. That heart attack just came too early for him."

"Mom, we couldn't have done it without you," Bob replied as he hugged his mother. "You've stood behind us through thick and thin."

"There were a lot of times we all felt like we were on pretty thin ice," Edith chuckled. "But fortunately the ice never broke."

"Hi, Grandma. Isn't this store neat?" Dawn exclaimed as she hurried down the aisle leading her cousin Gloria. "I've been helping pour punch and serve cookies. Would you like to have some?"

"I'd love to," Edith replied as she followed her granddaughter to the serving table where Dan, Beth, and Jeffy had already joined Nancy and Jean.

Jean leaned over and kissed her mother. "Hi, Mom. I'm so glad you could come."

Edith grinned. "I wouldn't miss this for the world. How's it going?"

"Really great," Jean replied, "but I don't know what we would have done without Larry. As soon as they moved here, he unboxed the computer system and had everything up and running in no time."

"He's come a long way since he played basketball at Rocky Bluff High School," Edith replied.

Suddenly Jean spotted a friend down a side aisle. "Mother, there's someone I'd like you to meet. Wait a minute and I'll go get him."

Within moments Jean returned followed by a heavyset, middle-aged man wearing two braids that extended past his shoulders. "Mother, I'd like you to meet Chief Joseph Black Hawk. Chief Black Hawk, this is my mother, Edith Dutton."

"It's nice to meet you, Mrs. Dutton. I've heard so many good things about you. Your daughter and son-in-law have been a great asset to our community the few months they've been here. We're all looking forward to not having to spend two and a half hours on the road just to get a simple nut or bolt."

"I'm sure it's been a real trial for you, especially in the winter," Edith replied. "Also, having your own medical and legal centers here should help Running Butte develop a sense of self-reliance and encourage the young people to strive for higher goals."

"Jean has worked hand-in-hand with us trying to bring these social services to the local people. She's considered one of our kindred spirits. You should be mighty proud of her."

Edith beamed. "That I am. Her forte has always been to help others, regardless of the personal sacrifice to herself," she replied. "It was very nice meeting you and I hope we'll have a chance to get together again at the grand opening of the new medical clinic."

Rebecca Sutherland was just finishing typing a purchase order when Beth arrived at work Monday morning.

"Good morning, Beth," she greeted. "How was your weekend?"

"Great," Beth replied. "Dan and I took Edith Dutton to the grand opening of Harkness II in Running Butte Saturday. They really did a good job getting that store set up."

"They are a multitalented family," Rebecca noted. "I enjoyed working with Edith when she was the home economics teacher here. She had so much concern for each individual student whether she had them in class or not."

"Since she's retired, Edith seems to have spread that same concern throughout the community," Beth replied as she sat down at the desk opposite Rebecca's.

"Beth, I have some exciting news to tell you," the older woman began. "I've put in twenty-five years in school libraries and I figure it's time for me to make a change."

Beth's heart sank. She'd enjoyed working with Rebecca these last few months. "You're not thinking of retiring are you?"

"Not exactly," Rebecca replied. "But I've received a contract from a private high school in Guam to come for two years and organize their library."

"Guam? Where's that?"

"It's a little island in the Pacific that's one of our U.S. territories. We have both a naval station and an air base there. I heard they needed a lot of help with their educational system, so I thought it might be a good place to put my experience to work."

"Sounds exciting, but do they speak English there?" Beth queried as pictures of coconut palms and brown-skinned natives flashed before her.

"Oh, yes," Rebecca grinned. "Everyone speaks English, but most of the natives are bilingual and also speak their local Chamorro language. It's going to be quite a challenge."

The thought of a close friend in a distant land overwhelmed Beth. "When do you plan to leave?"

"Probably the first part of August," Rebecca explained. "I'd like to take a couple weeks to tour the Hawaiian Islands on my way over."

Beth's eyes gleamed. "Lucky you."

"I've been saving for a long time for such a vacation," Rebecca responded with a distant gaze in her eyes. "Beth, there's one thing I'd like you and Dan to think about. Maybe it would be advantageous for the both of us."

"What's that?"

"I need to have someone live in my house while I'm gone and take care of general maintenance, plus water my plants, and feed and love my Pekingese, Shushu. I could move the furniture you don't want to use to the basement. I want someone who I know and trust to live there while I'm away. I wouldn't charge you any rent."

Beth's eyes widened as she visualized Rebecca's large brick home on the edge of town. "You have such a beautiful home. It's hard to imagine myself living in something that nice. It would be quite a responsibility. I'll talk to Dan and get back to you in a few days. Thanks for the offer."

Beth could hardly wait to see Dan that evening. When he arrived at seven o'clock, she breathlessly told the story of Rebecca's offer. She concluded her monologue with, "But I've never lived in anything like that before. I've always been in awe of people who live in beautiful homes."

Dan smiled. "Behind the fancy homes they're just ordinary people like you and me," he assured her. "There's nothing at all snobbish about Rebecca, is there?"

"No. She's one of the most down-to-earth people I know," Beth agreed. "God just seems to have blessed her with that home and now she's willing to let us live there free for two years."

"This could be a real godsend for us," Dan noted. "For two years we can save the money we'd normally spend for rent and use it toward a down payment on a house of our own."

Beth's eyes became distant. "This is like a fairy tale. Just a few months ago I was struggling on welfare and now I'm making plans to become a homeowner," she murmured.

"Then you agree we should take her up on her offer?" Dan queried.

"I'm a little concerned having Jeffy in such a beautiful home. What if he spills something on her plush beige carpet or breaks one of her lamps?"

Dan took her hand to calm her fears. "That could happen to anyone. If it happens, we just have the carpet cleaned or replace the lamp. You should be very proud of Jeffy. He's such a well-behaved child."

Beth nodded in agreement. "Okay, then let's go for it. I'll tell her tomorrow that we'll be happy to do it. Then when the time for her to leave gets closer, we can get together and discuss the details."

The next day Edith invited Dan into her home for coffee after he brought her home from visiting Roy in the nursing home. Edith poured two cups of coffee and took a half dozen home-baked cookies from the cookie jar before she joined Dan at the kitchen table.

"Roy didn't look as well today," Dan noted as he took his first sip of steaming coffee.

"His color wasn't good at all and his expression seemed blank and distant," Edith sighed as the wrinkles deepened in her forehead. "The head nurse said he had a very restless sleep. They're suspicious that he is having minor strokes, but no one can be sure."

"I admire your persistence in visiting him every day in spite of the weather."

"Roy's body may be wearing out, but as long as he has breath, his gentle spirit will always shine through," Edith replied. "Have you noticed that despite how miserable he may feel, he rarely complains?"

"You both have been a real inspiration to Beth and me. We hope we can demonstrate our love for each other the way you and Roy have."

"I'm sure you will," Edith assured him. "You both know what it's like to suffer misfortune and to keep your eyes on the Lord through the tough times as well as the good times."

Edith's interest in talking about herself and her own problems was short-lived. "How are the wedding plans coming?"

Dan beamed. "Beth has all the wedding details under control. The gals at the school are throwing a shower for her next week, so she's really busy. She's leaving the big things to me, like planning a honeymoon and where we're going to live."

"And where will that be?" Edith queried. "Both your apartments are too small for three people."

"We'll have to stay at Beth's until the first part of August. After that Rebecca asked us to house-sit her home while she's in Guam for two years," Dan explained.

Edith poured Dan another cup of coffee and passed the plate of cookies to him. "That sounds like a good deal for the both of you. I'm really excited about Rebecca's contract on Guam. With her experience she'll be able to build an outstanding library for them."

"It's an opportunity of a lifetime for her," Dan agreed. "I hope someday Beth and I will be able to travel abroad."

Edith smiled. "It's hard to know what bend in the road our lives will take," she replied. "Life-changing events happen when we least expect them."

Later that afternoon when Dan returned to his apartment, the phone rang. "Hello."

"Hello, Dan. This is Stuart Leonard."

"Oh, hi, Stu. Any word yet?"

"That's why I'm calling," the county attorney replied. "I just got word from Greg McIntyre in Calgary. He said that Mickey Kilmer signed the papers surrendering his paternal rights, so you're free to adopt Jeffy."

Dan's eyes filled with tears. "I don't know how to thank you. Now what do I do next?"

"Now it's time to hire an attorney," Stu explained. "I'd like to help, but as county attorney I can't engage in private practice."

"Yes, I know. There are a couple of attorneys in town I could call. Thanks so much for your help," Dan said as he hung up the phone.

The next day after driving Edith to the nursing home, Dan went to the newest lawyer in town, Dave Wood. Dave greeted him at the door and immediately ushered Dan into his humble office. The diploma on the wall reflected graduation from the University of Montana Law School just one year before. Dan explained his desire to adopt Jeffy and the circumstances in which the father had surrendered his parental rights.

"This should be a fairly simple procedure," Dave explained thoughtfully. "I'll simply petition the court for you to adopt Jeffy. You'll probably have a hearing before Judge Milton Eubanks. If everything goes well, the court will grant the petition right away." Dave was unable to disguise his eagerness. "I'll get right on it and will let you know in a few days when the hearing will be."

"Thanks so much for your help," Dan said as he rose to leave. "I'd like to make Jeffy my son at the same time I make his mother my wife."

"I'll have to check the court calendar, but with your wedding date so close, I can't guarantee anything."

The two men shook hands and Dan left the small office at the edge of town. He nearly floated down the steps. It would only be a matter of weeks before his dreams would come true.

❧

A week later, after an extremely busy night at the crisis center, Dan collapsed on his bed at four o'clock in the morning. Scarcely a muscle twitched until the phone rang promptly at eight-thirty. Drowsily he reached for the receiver.

"Hello."

"Hello. Dan Blair, please."

"This is he. May I help you?"

"Dan, this is Dave Wood. I have some good news for you."

With those words Dan was immediately awake. "What is it?"

"I was able to get your day in court scheduled for June twenty-third at two o'clock."

"Thank you. Thank you so much," he stammered.

Dan hung up the phone and looked at the calendar. The big day was

Saturday, June twenty-first. Beth's parents had agreed to come from Glasgow for the wedding and then stay with Jeffy while they took a ten-day honeymoon to Lake Coeur D'Alene, Idaho. *Surely, Beth won't mind postponing our departure for a couple of days so Jeffy could legally become my son,* he mused as he rolled over and fell back into a deep, peaceful sleep.

Chapter 15

Beth kicked off her shoes, sank into the sofa, and placed her feet on the ottoman. "Thank goodness Jeffy is asleep. It was a busy day at work and I'm beat."

"I wish there was something I could do to help," Dan replied as he put his arm around her shoulder.

"It's just something only Rebecca and I can trudge through," Beth sighed. "The end of the year inventory is bad enough, but with Rebecca retiring, she's trying to teach me as much as possible and leave the library as well organized as possible for the new librarian."

"Have they hired anyone yet to replace her?"

"They've advertised locally and in all the statewide agencies and they've been amazed at the response. Since there have been so many budget cuts it seems like the libraries are the first place they cut and there's a lot of well-qualified school librarians out there," Beth explained. "Jobwise, I don't think this is a good time to be a school librarian. Rebecca did say they wanted to have someone hired before the last day of school."

"Even with school ending you're still going to be busy planning for the wedding, but at least that's something I can help you with," Dan replied.

"Just getting all the invitations addressed has become a real chore. I didn't realize we had so many friends and family until I began making a list," Beth smiled. "I hope everyone can come. I have a couple aunts that I haven't seen since I left Glasgow."

"Teresa Lennon has offered to take care of all the details for the reception, plus plan the decorations and flowers of the church. Why don't you take her up on the offer?" Dan suggested. "You have enough to do just getting yourself and Jeffy ready for the wedding."

"I hate to impose on her. Teresa has been so good to me."

"Teresa loves to plan social events," Dan coaxed. "It's her form of recreation. She'll be disappointed if she can't help."

"I suppose you're right," Beth responded. "I'll give her a call after work tomorrow and see if there's some time we can get together and plan the details. It sure would take a load off my mind if I didn't have the reception to worry about."

"After this is all over you're going to be ready for ten days of relaxation at Lake Coeur D'Alene. I already have our reservations made at the Pink Flamingo. We can sleep until noon, then rent a boat and cruise around the lake and admire the wildlife and the beautiful sunsets."

"That sounds heavenly, but it's going to be the first time I've been away from Jeffy since his kidnapping. I don't know how he's going to take it."

"Your mom and dad will be here and he'll be just fine," Dan reassured her. "You're the one who'll suffer separation anxiety."

"I suppose you're right," Beth laughed. "I know he is really looking forward to having a daddy."

"I wish we could go before the judge the day before the wedding instead of postponing the honeymoon for a couple of days, but it'll be well worth it. When we leave for Coeur D'Alene he'll officially be my son. I've already checked into picking him up on my health insurance. There's no problem at all adding him.

"When we get back I'll just move my clothes over here and I'll put my extra things in a storage shed for a couple months until we move into Rebecca's house. My studio apartment isn't even big enough for one person, much less a family."

"I still can't get over the thought of living in a home as nice as Rebecca's and not having to pay a cent for the privilege."

"Don't forget you'll have to walk her dog and water her plants," Dan chided. "Nothing in life is ever free."

The pair continued their marriage discussion for another hour when Beth began to yawn and her eyes drooped. "Honey, I'd better let you get some sleep," Dan said. "I'll call you later tomorrow evening after you've talked with Teresa and see how things are going."

They embraced tenderly and Beth walked him to the door. "See you tomorrow," she murmured. "I love you."

"I love you, too," he responded as he slipped out the front door.

✑

Beth and Jeffy had scarcely gotten in the door the next afternoon when the phone rang.

"Hello," Beth greeted as she laid her purse on the table.

"Hello, Beth, this is Teresa. How are you doing?"

"Keeping busy," she replied. "I was just getting ready to call you. How are you doing?"

"I'm doing well," Teresa replied. "I wanted to follow up on my offer. Is there anything I can do to help you with your wedding plans? I know it's hard work to follow through on all the multitude of details."

"Why don't you come over tonight or tomorrow evening and we could talk about the details? I'm feeling extremely overwhelmed right now."

"How about if I come over tonight at seven?" Teresa queried.

"Sounds good," Beth replied. "I'll be looking forward to it."

Beth had a pot of coffee and a plate of cookies waiting when Teresa arrived that evening. They discussed each aspect of the reception and decorations. Finally, Teresa became very serious. "Beth, what are you planning for a wedding dress?"

"I know the time is getting close, but I haven't decided," Beth admitted. "Even if I had the cash, I'd hate to put a lot of money in something I'll only wear once. Since it wouldn't be socially proper if I wore a pure white one, I don't know what to do."

"I'll admit there isn't much of a selection here in Rocky Bluff," Teresa replied. "But I was talking with Rebecca last night, and we thought that if you hadn't picked out a dress yet, we'd like to get one for you as our special wedding gift."

Beth was speechless and then began to stammer. "I. . .I couldn't let you do that for me. You've already done so much."

"It's something we'd really like to do," Teresa persisted. "Rebecca said that she doesn't know what she would have done without your help this past year. Don't deny us the chance of helping a good friend."

"How can I turn down that kind of offer?" Beth chuckled.

"You can't," Teresa replied firmly. "Now, what do you have planned for Saturday?"

"Just the usual. . .laundry, cleaning, and shopping."

"How about getting up early and the three of us going shopping in Great Falls? There's a real nice bridal shop there. I'm sure we could find a dress that would be just perfect for you. Time's a-wasting."

"Sounds like fun," Beth agreed. "I'll see if Dan will be able to stay with Jeffy all day. If he's with Dan, I don't think he'll even miss me."

◈

Edith Dutton had just finished eating lunch when the phone rang. "Hello."

"Hello, Edith. This is Larry Reynolds. How have you and Roy been doing?"

"I'm doing fine, but Roy seems to be failing more every day. I'll be seeing him this afternoon and hopefully he'll be better. Dan should be coming any time to take me to the nursing home."

"Good, maybe we'll see you there," Larry responded cheerfully.

"Are you at the nursing home now?"

"Not exactly. I'm next door at the hospital. Libby just had another baby girl at ten o'clock this morning."

Edith beamed. "Congratulations. How are they doing?"

"They're both great. She's the cutest little thing and already has a full head of hair. Vanessa was nearly bald until she was a year and a half. She weighed in at seven pounds, eight ounces."

"What did you name her?" Edith could scarcely contain her excitement.

"Charity Rae," Larry responded proudly. "We named her that because she's a symbol of our newfound love."

"That's beautiful. I'm so happy for you."

"Can you stop and see us while you're at the nursing home?" Larry queried.

"I wouldn't miss it for anything. What room is Libby in?"

"Room 115. They've already taken Charity to the nursery."

"Good. I'll see you within an hour," Edith promised and hung up the phone just as the doorbell rang.

Edith hurried to the door. "Dan, do come in," she greeted. "I have some good news."

Dan's eyes widened with anticipation. It had been many weeks since he'd seen Edith this excited. "What's up?" he asked.

"Larry Reynolds just called. Libby had a baby girl this morning around ten. She weighed seven pounds, eight ounces and they named her Charity Rae," Edith explained breathlessly. "Larry said they named her that because she was a symbol of their new love."

"Knowing what all they've been through as a family, that is the most fitting name possible for their baby," Dan observed. "I'd like to stop and see them when we go to the nursing home."

"Larry said they're in room 115. Would you mind waiting a minute until I find my Polaroid camera?"

Dan and Edith reminisced about the changes in Larry and Libby's life on the way to the hospital. A new baby was the climax of years of struggling to find their way in life. As they entered the hospital room, Larry was sitting in a chair beside the bed holding Libby's hand. Both their faces were radiant.

As soon as Larry was aware of someone else in the room, he rose to greet them. "Edith, Dan, I'm so glad you could come."

"I wouldn't miss this for anything," Edith assured him and then turned her attention to Libby. "How are you doing?"

"I'm doing great," she beamed. "Have you been down the hall yet to see Charity?"

"Not yet. I wanted to see how you were doing first."

"I'll go with you," Libby responded as she started to get up from the hospital bed.

Larry took her arm firmly. "Wait just a minute and I'll get a wheelchair for you," he insisted. "You've worked hard enough for one day."

The new father proudly wheeled his wife down the hall of the Rocky Bluff Community Hospital with Edith and Dan close behind. They stopped in front of the nursery windows. Three babies were sleeping peacefully in their bassinets in front of the window.

"Charity is the one on the left," Larry stated. "Isn't she beautiful?"

"She sure is," Dan agreed as his eyes became distant. *Maybe in a year or two Beth and I will be standing in this same spot looking at our baby,* he mused.

"I can't tell which one of you she looks like the most," Edith commented as she studied the infant.

"I hope neither one of us," Larry chuckled. "We want her to be an even mix of both our good points and none of the bad."

Libby smiled up at Dan. "I'm glad Charity came this week. I didn't want to miss your wedding. Now we'll be able to take her and show her off."

"It wouldn't be complete without you and Larry," Dan chuckled. "However, I don't want your two adorable little girls upstaging my beautiful bride."

"Nothing could upstage Beth," Libby stated. "She's become simply radiant since she fell in love. You make a beautiful couple."

"They sure do," Edith agreed as she patted Dan's arm. "It's been a real pleasure to share these special moments with all of you." Edith paused and glanced back at the baby sleeping peacefully in the nursery. "If Roy's having a good day I'm sure he'd like to see Charity. Why don't I go down and see how he's doing?"

"We'd like to come with you. Larry's doing such a good job driving this chair," Libby chuckled. "I'm not used to having this kind of treatment."

When the foursome entered Roy's room, he was sitting in his recliner watching TV. His eyes sparkled as soon as he saw that he had company, and he immediately hit the mute button on the remote.

Edith leaned over and kissed him. "Hi, Roy. How are you doing today?"

"G. . .g. . .g. . .ood."

"Libby and Larry just had a new baby," Edith explained with a smile.

Larry wheeled Libby's chair close enough so she could take Roy's hand. "She's a beautiful little girl whom we named Charity. Would you like to go see her?"

Roy smiled and nodded his head affirmatively.

Edith slipped out of the room and headed for the nurses' station. Within moments she returned with two nurses' aides and a wheelchair.

"I understand you want to go for a little outing," the taller one said to Roy. "If you'll help us, we'll lift you into your wheelchair. It looks like you'll have a lot of help getting down to the nursery."

The nurses' aides gently lifted Roy and sat him in his wheelchair and adjusted the footrests.

"Enjoy yourself," they called as they disappeared down the hall to care for other residences.

"Roy receives such loving care here," Edith said. "I hate being separated from him, but I could never give him this kind of care at home. He still has a lot of friends stop to see him, and every afternoon the activities director brings in different entertainment so he never gets bored."

The small band walked slowly down the hallway to the nursery. Larry pushed Libby's wheelchair while Dan pushed Roy's. Roy's eyes danced and a grin spread across his face as he looked through the window of the nursery.

"Save that look," Edith said as she took out her Polaroid camera.

With one click the photo session was on. Every possible grouping was made as the camera was passed from person to person. They waited for each picture to develop before deciding what grouping to take next. Finally a nurse came out of the nursery.

"Libby, would you like to have the baby in the pictures as well?"

"We'd love to," Libby smiled. "I'd especially like to have one with Roy holding Charity. It would be one she could cherish for life."

The baby was brought out and gently laid in Roy's arms. Even his lack of speech could not prevent him from communicating the pleasure he felt at that moment. The camera clicked freely and only stopped long enough to add new film. Pictures were then taken of Roy and Edith with the baby. When it developed, Larry replied, "This one I want to have framed. Without the loving guidance of both of you, I don't think there ever would be a Charity to bless our lives."

After the picture taking session, Roy's eyes began to droop and his shoulders slumped. "Are you getting tired?" Edith asked.

Roy nodded. The small party of baby admirers bade each other good-bye. Larry wheeled Libby back to her room while Dan wheeled Roy down the long corridor to the nursing home with Edith at their side. Within minutes the same nurses' aides had Roy comfortably in his bed. Dan and Edith slipped quietly out of the room, down the long hall, and out the front door. In spite of Roy's failing body, his spirit was still strong.

Promptly at two o'clock on the twenty-first of June the organist at Rocky Bluff Community Church began to play. Pastor Rhodes, Dan Blair, and two groomsmen entered from the side door and took their places in front of the congregation. One at a time two bridesmaids dressed in lavender strolled slowly down the aisle. Then Vanessa Reynolds came slowly down the aisle dropping petals as she came. She blew a kiss to her new sister as she passed her parents, who were sitting on the aisle near the front of the church. Beside her was Jeffy Slater, dressed in a miniature tuxedo, carrying a pillow with a ring pinned to it. Jeffy beamed as soon as he saw Dan standing in the front. "How am I doing?" he whispered.

Everyone in the front snickered as they heard Dan whisper, "You're doing great, Son."

The organ tempo increased as Mrs. Slater stood, with the entire congregation following her lead. In the doorway stood Beth dressed in a beautiful off-white gown on the arm of her father. Her face grew radiant as she saw her fiancé and her son waiting for her at the end of the aisle.

Beth scanned the room. The church was full. Nearly everyone she had invited was there. Her favorite aunts were sitting in the pew beside her mother. Edith Dutton was also included in the honored pew. Teresa had done a great job, and the flowers, candles, and bows on the pews were perfect. Beth's eyes filled with tears. *God has been so good to me,* she mused. *Five years ago I was a scared unwed teenage mother with nowhere to go and no friends to turn to and now look at this.*

The next few minutes were a blur to Beth as her father escorted her up the aisle, the vocalist sang, and the pastor gave appropriate marital instructions. Her dream world was interrupted as she was staring into Dan's loving eyes and heard him say, "I, Dan, take thee, Beth, to be my wedded wife and Jeffy to be my precious son, to have and to hold from this day forward, for better for worse, for richer for poorer, in sickness and in health, to love and to cherish, till death us do part, according to God's holy ordinance; and thereto I pledge thee my faith."

Dan kissed his bride and picked up Jeffy and gave him a hug. "I love you, Son," he whispered.

There was scarcely a dry eye in the church as Dan took Jeffy's hand in his and Beth took Dan's arm and they marched victoriously down the aisle into a new life as one family.

As the couple reached the door, Pastor Rhodes lifted his arms in benediction. "What God has joined together, let no man put asunder."

Distant Love

*This book is dedicated to the gallant people of Guam
who during World War II endured three years
of a brutal Japanese military occupation but never once lost
their faith in God and the United States of America.*

Chapter 1

"Help me, someone, please help me!"

Rebecca Sutherland bolted upright in bed. *Am I dreaming or is someone actually calling for help?* The pounding on the front door continued along with the intermittent ringing of the doorbell.

"Fire. . . Fire. . . My house is on fire. My wife and children are inside. Please help me."

Rebecca grabbed her robe from the foot of the bed as she ran to the front door. She flung open the door. There stood Dick Reed barefoot, dressed only in a pair of boxer shorts. A red glow radiated from the house next door.

"Rebecca, call the fire department! Anita and the kids are still inside."

Rebecca rushed to the phone and dialed 9-1-1.

"Emergency Services. May I help you?"

"There's a fire at the Dick Reed residence, 2515 Rimrock Road. The wife and four children are still inside," Rebecca panted.

"The fire trucks and ambulance will be right there," the dispatcher assured her. "Try to remain calm until they arrive."

Rebecca ran outside. Dick was just coming around the side of the house with four-year-old Donna in one arm and two-year-old Jackie in the other. Pat Crouse came running across the street with her robe wrapped loosely around her. Sirens could be heard in the distance. Flames were now leaping from the windows of the Reed home.

Pat took the two children from their father's arms, while Rebecca tried to comfort her next-door neighbor. "I've got to go back!" Dick shouted as he turned back toward the house. "Anita, Chris, and the baby are still in there."

Rebecca held his shoulder. "The fire's spread throughout the house," she stated firmly. "The fire trucks are on their way. They'll get them out for you."

The fire truck screeched to a stop in front of the Reed home and eight firemen began running hoses to the nearby fire hydrant. The fire chief's car stopped behind the truck and the ambulance parked behind him. The neighborhood was a flurry of activity. Additional volunteer firemen appeared in pickup trucks from all directions.

The cool mountain breeze enveloped Fire Chief Andrew Hatfield as he quickly approached the small band huddled by the curb. "Dick, who's left in the house?"

"My wife, Anita, six-year-old Chris, and the baby."

"What rooms did you last see them in?"

Dick bit his lip. "Anita was asleep in the master bedroom and the baby was in a bassinet in the corner of the room. Chris was asleep in the room across the hall."

"We'll get them out," Chief Hatfield assured him and then turned his attention to Rebecca. "Mrs. Sutherland, would you take Dick and the children to your house and warm them up? Could we use your place as a command post for a few hours?"

"Certainly," Rebecca replied. "I'll put on a large coffeepot for anyone who needs to get out of this wind."

"Dick, we'll let you know just as soon as we locate the rest of your family," Chief Hatfield assured him. "We have the ambulance standing by and have notified Med-Evac from Great Falls. They'll have their helicopters land in the school parking lot, where they can be transferred to the burn center, if necessary. All you can do now is go with Rebecca and wait and pray."

Rebecca put her arm around Dick and directed him toward her front door. The tranquility of the living room conflicted with the terror and confusion outside. Pat sat the two stunned toddlers on the sofa and reached for the afghan to wrap around Jackie's trembling body. Rebecca grabbed another blanket from the hall closet for Donna.

"Dick," Rebecca said as she hugged Donna against her chest. "I'm sorry this house is devoid of men's clothes, but I do have a sloppy pair of sweats that might be big enough to fit you."

"Anything'll be fine," Dick mumbled as he slumped into the recliner. "I wish they'd hurry and tell me something. They should've found them by now."

Rebecca handed Donna to Pat as she hurried to the bedroom. "Is Mommy going to be okay?" the child sobbed.

"The firemen are working as fast as they can," Pat assured her as she cuddled the two children. "Why don't you and Jackie stretch out on the sofa and try to get some sleep? We'll let you know how they are as soon as we know."

Donna pulled her two-year-old sister close to her as she put her head on a pillow and straightened her legs. She sobbed softly as she watched Jackie close her eyes.

Rebecca returned to the living room carrying a pair of faded gray sweats and handed them to her neighbor. The warmth of the clothing felt good to Dick as he pulled them over his shivering body and slumped into the recliner.

"I better get the coffeepot started," Rebecca stated as she hurried to the kitchen. "Dick, can I make you a cup of instant while the pot's brewing?"

"I'm fine," Dick muttered as he stared nervously out the window at the activity next door.

Pat went to the window. "It looks like they're getting the fire under control. I'm sure we'll be hearing something soon."

"I hope so," Dick muttered. "This night seems like an eternity."

Pat had just returned to the sofa where the children were sleeping when the doorbell rang. She hurried to the door and flung it open. There stood Police Captain Philip Mooney holding a small bundle. "Any news?" she begged.

"The firemen kicked in the door to the back porch and found the kitten. I thought the children would like to cuddle it as they wait," the officer explained as Donna let go of her sleeping sister and hurried to retrieve her pet.

"How's my mommy?" Donna begged as she cuddled her kitten.

Captain Mooney knelt before the child. "We haven't found them yet, but it shouldn't be long now. Will you take care of the kitten while we keep looking?"

Donna nodded and then took the kitten back to the sofa, where her sister was beginning to stir. "Look, Jackie. They found Muffie."

Just then Rebecca appeared from the kitchen and nodded to the officer. "How's it going?"

"We haven't found them yet," Phil Mooney replied. "This is the worst tragedy I've seen in my life. The night Harkness Hardware Store burned was bad enough, but at least lives weren't involved there."

Dick appeared detached from the tragedy going on around him when Captain Mooney approached the recliner by the window. "I'm sorry for what is happening. I wish we could do more. Chief Hatfield will be by shortly to talk with you."

"I appreciate your concern," Dick replied with a glaze in his eyes. "I know you're doing all you can."

No sooner had Captain Mooney left than the fire chief arrived at Rebecca's door. He greeted everyone and then pulled a chair close to Dick.

"I'm sorry, Dick. We did the best we could, but the flames were too hot by the time we arrived. We found your wife by the children's window, the matting on the baby's bassinet melted, and the baby fell through to the floor. We found the older child's body in the hallway. He must have been trying to escape by himself. Our first observations are that Anita broke the window and got the first two children out but was overcome with smoke when she turned to get the other two. Where were you when the fire broke out?"

A long silence enveloped the room. Dick's eyes became even more glazed than before. "I. . .I. . .I was in the living room watching TV," he mumbled. "I must have fallen asleep on the sofa because when I awoke, the house was full of smoke and flames were coming from the hallway. I didn't know what to do, so I came to get Rebecca."

Chief Hatfield cleared his throat. "The bodies are being taken to the hospital for autopsy. You'll need to select a mortuary to handle the final arrangements," he said. "I'll have more questions in the morning after we've begun to investigate the cause of the fire. In the meantime, if there's anything we can do, please feel free to call." Chief Hatfield shook Dick's hand and started for the doorway. He paused as he noticed Rebecca standing in the kitchen doorway dressed in a royal blue robe, her hair tousled around her face.

"Rebecca, may I speak to you privately in the kitchen?" the fire chief asked.

"Certainly," she responded as she led the graying career fireman into the kitchen and pointed to a chair by the window. "Would you care for a cup of coffee?"

"I'd appreciate one. It's been a long night and I'm afraid it's going to get even longer," Chief Hatfield sighed as he slumped into a chair. "There's a lot of suspicious loose ends about this fire."

"How's that?" Rebecca queried as she poured two mugs of coffee.

"Don't you think it's pretty unusual that Dick would come to your home before he tried to get his family out of the fire?"

Rebecca sat in a chair across from the fire chief. She was still shaking, she noticed, but she made herself choke back the sorrow and horror she felt about Anita and the two children who had not escaped the fire. She took a sip of coffee. "That bothered me from the beginning, but he said the fire was so intense in the hallway and he was frightened and couldn't think straight. I took that explanation at face value."

"I guess I have a suspicious mind," Chief Hatfield confessed, "but my years in investigative work have taught me to question everything. Tonight after things settle down, would you jot down every observation and impression you had from the moment you first heard pounding on your front door? I'll be by tomorrow and take a complete statement. The arson investigation will begin just as soon as it is light."

"You don't think Dick actually started the fire, do you?"

"I'm not making any accusations at this point," Chief Hatfield stated. "I'm merely trying to make a thorough investigation as to the cause of the fire. Thanks for all the help you've been. I'd better get out there and see how the cleanup is progressing. I'll see you tomorrow."

Her haze of grief parted for a moment, and a puzzled expression covered Rebecca's face as she followed the fire chief to the door. She closed the door behind him and turned to the dazed father sitting in the corner.

"Dick, I suppose you'll be wanting to make some phone calls."

"I guess I'd better give Anita's family a call, but my address book burned in the fire," Dick mumbled as he followed Rebecca to the kitchen phone. "They live in Spokane."

"What's her father's name? I'll call directory assistance for you."

"Kenneth Taylor. Her mother's name is Laura. Kenneth has a bad heart, so I hope the shock won't be too hard on him."

Rebecca dialed directory assistance for the Spokane area and wrote the number on scratch paper. She dialed the number and waited. When the phone began to ring on the other end, she handed the receiver to Dick and left the room. This was a time when he would need privacy the most.

The former librarian of Rocky Bluff High School returned to the living room and sat in the chair next to her neighbor. "I'm glad to see the children finally went to sleep," she whispered. "When Dick gets off the phone, I'll see if he wants to get some rest in the guest room. We're going to have a long few days."

"It's a good thing tomorrow's Saturday and I'm off work," Pat replied. "I'll begin getting community assistance organized. I assume Dick will want to stay at his motel with the children until he's able to find another place."

"Perhaps," Rebecca replied. "But for the next few days they're more than welcome to stay here. He's going to need a lot of help caring for the children while making the final arrangements for Anita and the other two children. He must be numb with grief."

Pat wiped the tears from her eyes. "It's such a tragedy. They were the model family. They built the Sleepy-Eye Motel from a depressing flophouse to the nicest motel in town. They both were so devoted to their children."

"That's what bothers me," Rebecca replied. "Why didn't he try to get his family out before he came here to report the fire?"

Pat's eyes widened and then she shrugged her shoulders. "I guess one never knows how they might react under pressure," she sighed.

"Pat, why don't you go on home and get some rest," Rebecca said as she patted her friend on the arm. "I'm going to be depending a lot on you during the next few days."

"Are you sure there's nothing else I can help you with before I leave?"

"No. I think I've poured the last cup of coffee for the evening and I'm sure Dick will want to get some rest as soon as he finishes calling relatives."

Dick insisted on the two children sleeping with him, so Rebecca carried Jackie while Dick carried Donna into the guest room. He thanked her for her hospitality and closed the door. Rebecca returned to her bedroom and collapsed onto her pillow. She tossed and turned the remainder of the night without ever completely returning to sleep. When the sun began to shine through the closed blinds, Rebecca arose. She showered and then began brewing a fresh pot of coffee and fixing herself a couple pieces of toast.

As she was spreading the strawberry jam on her toast, the doorbell rang. She laid the knife on the corner of the plate and hurried to the front door. "Chief Hatfield, do come in."

"I'm sorry I'm so early, but the investigation team rolled into action at dawn. They're next door right now securing the premises."

"No problem," Rebecca assured him. "Can I pour you a cup of coffee and fix you a bite to eat?"

"I'd appreciate that," he grinned as he eyed her plate. "Do you have a couple more pieces of bread to slap in the toaster?"

"Chief Hatfield, it'd be a pleasure," she responded, trying to mask the fatigue and strain of the night before.

"To you it's Andy," he chuckled and then became serious. "Are your guests still sleeping?"

"I haven't heard any stirring coming from that room since I've been up," Rebecca replied as she hurriedly set another place at the table and poured a cup of coffee.

Andy shook his head with approval. "Good, because I think we have a real tiger by the tail. This investigation is becoming more and more suspicious and I'm going to be depending on your observations a great deal to provide us with possible leads."

"I'll help all I can," Rebecca promised, "but I'm afraid I haven't noticed anything out of the ordinary. Dick talked with his wife's parents for quite awhile last night. Anita's parents and her sister and husband are flying in this afternoon from Spokane. They'll be staying with Pat Crouse for a few days while the Taylors will probably stay with Edith Dutton."

Andy wrinkled his brow. "Why don't they all stay at the motel?"

Rebecca shrugged her shoulders. "Dick said it would be too hard for them to stay in the motel that he and Anita worked so hard to build."

Andy's expression softened as he eyed the middle-aged librarian across the table. "The strain of this is going to be hard for the next few days. Are you sure you want to be headquarters for all the commotion?"

"I think I'm up to it," Rebecca assured him. "Besides, the first of August I'm leaving for a two-week vacation in Hawaii before I go on to Guam and my new job. I'll just leave Rocky Bluff with a blaze of excitement."

"That it will be," Andy replied. "I brought my tape recorder along to begin taking your statement as to the events of last night. If Dick gets up, we'll have to stop and continue another time. However, your first impressions are crucial to the investigation."

For the next hour and a half Andy questioned Rebecca concerning every detail of the events of the night before. She answered the best she could, but the stress of the ordeal was beginning to take its toll. Her voice faltered. Andy's concern for her mental stress became apparent as he sat in silence while Rebecca stared out the kitchen window.

I haven't had any personal contact with Andy since he moved to Rocky Bluff five years ago, and yet there is something familiar about him, Rebecca mused. *I wonder who he reminds me of?*

Rebecca's thoughts drifted back through the years. She had grown up in a little town in Iowa and had gotten her teaching degree from the University of Northern Iowa. Two weeks after graduation she married Eric Sutherland and moved to Mason City, Iowa, where he was the social studies teacher and she was the school librarian. Everything was going well for them and they were making plans to start a family in a couple of years. However, the Vietnam War was at its peak and Eric's number was drawn in the lottery for military service. Within months Eric was a first lieutenant in the United States Army and leading a platoon in the Tet Offensive.

After she was notified of his death, she stayed in Mason City for a couple more years, but could not shake loose his memory. Rebecca sold their small home in Mason City and accepted a position as the high school librarian in Rocky Bluff, Montana. Using part of his insurance money, Rebecca bought one of the nicer homes there. Since she was certain she would never be able to fall in love again, her home, school, and church became a replacement for intimate relationships. No one would ever be able to match the pedestal her war hero had been placed upon.

Rebecca visualized Eric's warm compassionate eyes and suddenly saw that same compassion in Andy's eyes. *I wonder if Eric would look like that today?* she pondered. *Would he have distinguished gray hair or would his hair have thinned and left him bald?*

"Rebecca, I know you're getting tired," Chief Hatfield said as her faraway gaze remained. "Why don't I come back later today after you've had time to rest."

"I'm sorry," she replied. "I'm having trouble keeping my mind on task. Maybe I'll be able to remember more after I've rested. I certainly hope you can complete the investigation soon."

Suddenly Jackie's cry could be heard from the guest room and then Dick's low voice trying to comfort her. "I'd better be going. At this point the less Dick knows, the better off the investigation will be."

Rebecca escorted the fire chief to the door and then returned to her private thoughts. *The terror of last night is bad enough, but why do the memories of thirty years ago come back and haunt me now?*

Chapter 2

There's Grandma and Grandpa!" four-year-old Donna shouted as the distraught couple emerged from the Treasure State Airlines landing gate. She released her daddy's hand and ran to her grandfather, who picked her up and hugged her tight.

Tears built in his eyes. "How are you doing, sweetheart?"

"I miss my mommy," she sobbed. "Our house burnt down last night and she went to heaven."

"I know," Ken Taylor choked. "We came to say good-bye to her along with Chris and the baby."

Laura Taylor hesitantly approached her son-in-law. "Dick, how are you holding up?"

"Not well, but the people of Rocky Bluff are being extremely supportive." Dick forced a weak smile. "I'm staying next door with Rebecca Sutherland, the high school librarian. I can't bear the thought of going to the motel where Anita worked so hard."

"We feel the same way," Ken replied. "We don't think we'll be able to go near the motel or the burned-out house."

"One of the elderly women of the church has offered to let you stay with her. Her husband's in the nursing home and she complains that her home is too large for just her," Dick replied. "She's an absolute jewel. Her name's Edith Dutton."

"That's one advantage of a small town," Laura sighed. "Spokane has lost the neighbor-helping-neighbor environment. We scarcely know those who live in the same apartment complex."

"Everyone's been so good to us. Several women have already begun gathering clothing and household goods for us." Dick paused and the distressed family began to move slowly toward the baggage claim. "I have an appointment with the funeral director and the pastor later this afternoon to make funeral arrangements. Would you like to join me?"

Laura gulped. "I'd appreciate that. It's the least I can do for our beloved Anita."

"I'll take you to Edith's so you can settle in and then come back and get you at three o'clock."

The Taylors clung to their grandchildren as their son-in-law drove the familiar streets of Rocky Bluff. Within twenty minutes Dick, his daughters, and his in-laws were ringing Edith Dutton's doorbell.

"Welcome," Edith greeted. "Do come in."

"Edith, I'd like you to meet Anita's parents, Kenneth and Laura Taylor. Ken and Laura, this is Edith Dutton. She's been an inspiration and comfort to the entire town."

Laura reached out and took Edith's hand. "We appreciate you opening your home to us. With Anita's love and hard work in the motel business, it's too painful for us to stay in such a cold environment."

"I understand only too well," Edith replied as she squeezed the grieving mother's hand. "You're welcome to stay here for as long as you need."

"Thank you. We appreciate your thoughtfulness," Laura said as she wiped a tear from her eye. "The town seems to be doing everything possible to help."

"It was such a shock to us all," Edith replied. "I only wish there was more we could do."

Up to that moment Dick had been standing restlessly in the entryway. "If you would excuse me for a little while, I'd like to take the girls back to Rebecca's and rest. I don't think I got any sleep at all last night."

"Daddy, can I stay with Grandma?" Donna begged as she wrapped her arms around her grandmother.

Dick looked at his mother-in-law, who nodded her head with approval. "If you'd like. I'll be back in an hour so we can go to the funeral home."

As soon as Dick left with two-year-old Jackie, Donna crawled into her grandmother's lap and sobbed. Laura held her tightly as she shared her grief.

Tears gathered in Edith's eyes as she watched the two.

Gradually Donna's sobs subsided. "Mommy and Daddy had a big fight last night. They yelled a lot. Mommy said she wanted to take us and come and live with you."

Everyone's face blanched as they exchanged questioning glances. *Surely nothing suspicious happened,* Edith mused, *but there are so many details that don't add up.*

Laura masked her suspicions as she tried to comfort her granddaughter. "Maybe after the funeral you and Jackie can come stay with us. Your mother's old room has been empty ever since she grew up."

"We don't have anyplace to live here," Donna replied somberly. "Will Daddy come, too?"

Laura exchanged glances with her husband. "Probably not for awhile. He still has the motel to take care of."

To break the tension, Edith showed Laura to the guest room and invited her to unpack. Stretching out on the bed did little to relax the grieving couple.

As promised, Dick returned within an hour. "That short nap certainly helped me," he stated as he surveyed his weary in-laws. "Are you ready to go?"

The Taylors bade Edith good-bye and followed Dick to his waiting car with Donna clinging tightly to her grandmother's hand. A sense of terror enveloped them. Would they be able to view their only daughter's body lying in a casket with two of her children in tiny caskets beside her?

Rebecca had several things she wanted to get done, but her body wanted to sleep. It took several chimes from the doorbell before she was fully awake. She rubbed her hands over her hair and hurried to the front door.

"Chief Hatfield, do come in."

"I hope I didn't come at an inappropriate time. I knew that Dick was going to be at the funeral home late this afternoon, and I wanted to talk to you when he wasn't here."

"He's planning to spend the evening with his in-laws and probably won't be back until bedtime. Chief Hatfield, please have a seat. Can I get you a cup of coffee?"

"I'd love a cup, but please call me Andy."

Rebecca rushed to the kitchen and poured two cups of coffee and arranged a half dozen homemade cookies on a dessert plate. Within five minutes she joined the fire chief at the other end of the sofa.

Andy took a long sip of his coffee and a bite of cookie before he spoke. "Rebecca, how would you evaluate Dick and Anita's marriage?"

Rebecca hesitated. She gazed out the window toward the charred house next door. "On the surface they appeared like a model, hardworking family, but occasionally I sensed some unrest underneath."

"How's that?"

"Well. . .on cool evenings when I'd turn off the air conditioner and open the windows, I often heard angry shouts, but I passed them off as normal family squabbles."

"Did you hear anything specific?" Andy cleared his throat. "Threats or the like?"

"Not really. The exact words were not distinct. However, once I did hear her shout, 'Why do you hate me so?' "

Andy's eyes widened. "Did you hear a response?"

"I didn't pay much attention," Rebecca replied, "but I do remember hearing him say that she was an albatross around his neck and that he could go a long way in life without her."

"Do you have any idea why he came to your door without first trying to get his family out?" Andy queried.

Rebecca shook her head. "I've asked myself that repeatedly and can't come up with a good explanation. Dick said he was sleeping on the sofa and when he awoke the heat was too intense to get down the hallway to the children's bedroom."

"That's what he told us last night, but somehow the excuse just doesn't ring true. Although now I only have a gut-level feeling."

"It sounds awfully suspicious to me, too, but I can't put my finger on anything specific. Maybe I've watched too many TV mysteries."

The couple went over what seemed like every conceivable detail of the night before, but were unable to come to any conclusion. The sun was setting before Andy finished his interview with Rebecca.

Andy looked at her tired eyes. "I appreciate all the help you've been. The least I can do is treat you to dinner at Beefy's Steak House. I'm sure the last thing you want to do is prepare a meal for yourself."

"I was planning on heating up a TV dinner, but the steak house sounds a lot tastier. However, I'll have to warn you that I'm too tired to be reasonable company."

"That's okay," Andy grinned. "I won't be the life of the party myself."

As the evening progressed, the table conversation between Andy and Rebecca was limited, but a nonverbal bond developed. Each had the maturity to relax and accept the other's fatigue without further social demands. After the final bite of dessert and the last sip of coffee were enjoyed, Andy drove Rebecca home and walked her to her door.

"Our evening dialogue may not have been the most exciting," Rebecca concluded with a smile, "but I feel a lot was said in our silence."

Andy gave her hand a squeeze. "I feel much the same way. After this case is settled, maybe we can get together under more desirable circumstances."

Rebecca's smile became even broader. "I'd like that, but right now a good night's sleep is my highest priority."

Donna and Jackie Reed fell into an exhausted sleep on the makeshift beds that Edith Dutton had prepared for them in the corner of her living room. Ken Taylor turned to his son-in-law.

"Dick, Laura and I have been talking. It's going to be several weeks before you'll be able to get settled again, so we'd like to take the girls back to Spokane with us after the funeral."

Laura held her breath, expecting a near-violent objection from Dick. Instead a mysterious sense of relief came over him. "Yes. I suppose you're right. It'll take me awhile to find another place to live. The motel is no place to keep two small children for very long."

"Tomorrow we can go shopping and get a minimum wardrobe for them and buy the rest when we get back to Spokane," Laura suggested.

"A couple of the ladies have been collecting clothing, toys, and household goods for the Reeds," Edith explained, hoping to alleviate some of the tension that hung over the room. "Tomorrow maybe you'd like to stop at Pat Crouse's and see what fits them. I was talking with Teresa Lennon while you were out, and she said the community response has been overwhelming. Pat's basement is nearly full of donations."

"I don't like being considered a charity case," Dick retorted. "I do have a profitable business, I want you to know."

Edith gulped and took a deep breath. "Everyone's aware of that. They just want to help. They thought the world of Anita and the kids, and they wanted to help make the transition through this difficult time as easy as possible."

Dick focused his eyes through the window onto the neighbor's roof. "I suppose you're right. I don't have anything to dress the girls in. Could you meet me at Pat's around ten-thirty tomorrow?"

"No problem," Ken responded briskly.

Dick eyed his sleeping children on the floor. "I need to go and get some rest, but they're sleeping so soundly. I hate to awaken them." Dick yawned. "Laura, would you mind watching them tonight and bringing them to me at Rebecca's in the morning?"

"I'd be glad to," the children's grandmother replied. "They look like such sleeping angels now. Yet they've been through so much."

As Dick slipped out of Edith Dutton's front door into the darkening skies, Ken's face reddened. "There's something wrong here. That boy's acting awfully strange after just losing his wife and two children."

Edith shook her head. "I don't know what to think," she sighed. "I know people react differently during crisis situations. But in all the years I've known the Reeds, I've never seen Dick so detached from what's going on around him."

❦

Storm clouds hung heavy over Rocky Bluff as the town's people crowded into the church to say farewell to Anita Reed and little Christopher and Ricky. Before the service the family gathered in the basement. Relatives from several states who had not seen each other in years greeted each other with unashamed tears.

Upstairs Rebecca Sutherland slid into the pew next to Edith Dutton. "Hello," she whispered. "How are you doing?"

"It's such a difficult time," Edith whispered back. "I'm so glad I could be hostess to the Taylors. They're such delightful people and are so grief stricken."

"After meeting them I can understand where Anita got her strength of character," Rebecca responded. "It's too bad that her life had to be cut short before she could reach her full potential."

Fire Chief Hatfield slipped quietly into the seat next to Rebecca just as Pastor Rhodes stepped to the pulpit. The two exchanged nods of greeting and then turned their attention to the front of the church.

"May the peace of God be with you," Pastor Rhodes began as the soft organ music trailed into the background. His words of comfort and encouragement taken from the Bible helped lift the troubled spirit that enveloped the congregation that Friday morning. The vocal music continued to remind the mourners of God's promise of a better life after death.

After the service, first the family and then the rest of the mourners filed out of the church and proceeded to Pine Hill Memorial Cemetery. "Would you two ladies like a ride to the cemetery?" Andy asked as he turned his attention back to Rebecca and Edith.

"Thanks for the offer," Rebecca replied. "We'd appreciate it."

Edith nodded her approval. "I hate to impose, but I can no longer drive myself."

"That's why we're a community," Andy replied as he put his arm on her shoulder. "You've done your part by providing housing for Anita's parents."

A faint smile crossed Edith's face. "I think they were more of an encouragement to me than I was to them."

Andy showed the women to his car and then waited his turn to join the procession. At the cemetery he offered his arm to Edith as they walked to the gravesite over the loose gravel path. Rebecca, who was a little more surefooted, followed closely behind.

After everyone had gathered, Pastor Rhodes gave the final benediction for the lives of three young people that ended prematurely. Donna Reed clung tightly to her grandmother's hand, while Dick held two-year-old Jackie. "Grandma, do we have to leave Mommy here in the cold ground alone?" Donna cried. "I want to stay with her."

Laura Taylor knelt before her granddaughter and took her in her arms. "Honey, only your mother's body is in that box. She's in heaven with Jesus now. Someday we'll all go to be with her and the entire family will be together again."

Just then the sun began to move from behind the clouds in the southern sky. The rays that descended appeared as rays of hope to the mourners as they departed the cemetery.

After Andy drove the two women back to the church to get Rebecca's car, the two longtime friends decided on having lunch at Bea's Restaurant. While waiting for the waitress to bring their sandwiches, Rebecca turned to Edith.

"How did you ever handle retiring so easily? I'm having all kinds of problems accepting the fact that I won't be returning to Rocky Bluff High School next year, although I'm looking forward to my two-year adventure in Guam."

Edith chuckled. "You're looking at me as a model of accepting retirement? I left the high school mentally kicking and screaming all the way."

"It didn't appear that way to the rest of us," Rebecca replied. "You always seemed so gracious and composed."

"It wasn't until I had a heart attack that I fully accepted the fact that my life would never be the same again." Edith smiled as she placed her napkin on her lap. "Now I'm enjoying my independence from the seven to four routine more than teaching. The only thing I miss is not having Roy home with me. It's difficult only being able to spend a few hours a day with him at the nursing home."

"I feel like a new high school graduate," Rebecca said. "Everything I'm familiar with is behind me and a strange unknown beckons."

Edith chuckled. "That's a poetic way to put it."

Rebecca stared out the window and the passing traffic. "To be honest," she finally admitted, "I'm afraid of growing old alone. Up until now I've immersed myself in Rocky Bluff High School, but now that period is over. You at least found Roy to share your life with after you retired. I'm too set in my ways to share my life with anyone."

"After George died I accepted the fact that I would never remarry. I certainly didn't go out and look for love; it just happened as an added blessing in my life," Edith explained with a peaceful smile. "One never knows the twists and turns her life may take. I'm just glad we have a God who guides and comforts us through all the hills and valleys. These last few days have been a pretty deep valley, but the happiness from our shared love gives us strength to continue on."

The waitress set two plates of French dip sandwiches before the women. They nodded their appreciation and returned to their private conversation.

"I'll have to rely on the shared love with the people of Rocky Bluff while I'm alone in Guam," Rebecca admitted. "I have such mixed emotions about going. I'm both excited and fearful."

"It sounds like a wonderful adventure," Edith replied. "If Roy and I were ten years younger, we'd probably join you. My motto has always been to live each moment to the maximum."

Chapter 3

Chief Hatfield leaned back in his chair and stretched his legs. "Rebecca, I hope you've recuperated from your week of helping the Reeds."

"I'm beginning to get caught up on my sleep," she sighed. "But every time I go outside and look at the charred house, all I can think about is Anita and the children."

Andy smiled at the middle-aged woman across the table. "I know that must be difficult. Maybe it's a good thing you'll be leaving soon for Guam. A different environment will help erase the nightmare of that night."

"I hope so," Rebecca agreed. "All the arrangements are made. I have a real nice couple moving into this house next week. I suppose you know Dan and Beth Blair."

"Oh, yes. He's the director of the crisis center. I've heard a lot of good things about his work. He took over the directorship right where Roy Dutton left off. It was interesting that he married one of his callers."

"They had an interesting beginning," Rebecca replied. "I've been impressed with what Beth has done with her life. She came to Rocky Bluff as an unwed teenage mother and was able to finish high school and a secretarial course at the college. When she got a job at the school she was a tremendous help to me in the library."

"She went through a lot when her son was kidnapped. I never thought she'd see him again, but her prayers paid off."

"Even when he was gone, she was disciplined enough to focus her attention on her job. Everyone admired her for that."

"Dan and Beth would be the kind of people I would like caring for my home if I were to be gone for an extended period of time." Andy paused for a few moments before continuing. "The reason why I stopped over is to find out if you've noticed Dick Reed around the house."

Rebecca looked puzzled. "I haven't seen him since the day after the funeral. Dick and Anita's parents took the girls to Pat's basement to go through the clothes and toys donated to them. Dick said he was going to stay at the motel."

"I know," Andy replied. "I stopped by the motel a couple days ago to ask him more questions and the manager said he left town and he didn't know where he was."

"That's strange. Does anyone know where he went?"

The fire chief wrinkled his forehead. "Not as far as I can discover. I called Anita's parents in Spokane and they were surprised that he was gone."

"Have they found the cause of the fire yet?"

"Not yet. But it looks like it started in the hallway near a space heater. That's why I wanted to talk to him."

"You aren't suspecting foul play are you?"

"At this point we're not ruling anything out. I need to know the condition and history of the space heater."

"I'm curious how all of this is going to develop. I hope that I'll be able to keep in touch with people in Rocky Bluff and not miss out on any of the news."

"I'll try to keep you updated," Andy assured her. "After all, if this does go to court, you'll be one of the star witnesses."

"I won't be of much help half a world away, but I'll make a written statement of what I know."

"That's all that's necessary," Andy assured her. He glanced at his watch. "It's getting late. I promised the crew I'd be back at the fire hall by four and it's nearly five till. I hope I'll have a chance to see you before you leave."

Blood rushed to Rebecca's face. "I'd like that. I'm leaving on the seven o'clock flight to Billings and then on to Seattle."

"How about a farewell dinner for two at the steak house Saturday night?"

"Sounds good to me," Rebecca's replied with a smile. "This time I hope I'm a little more alert than the last time we were there."

Andy grinned as he stood to leave. "Even in our most exhausted state we had a good time together, so Saturday has got to be exciting."

The days passed quickly as Rebecca sorted and packed her personal belongings. What to take and what to store was a constant dilemma. During her busy moments she looked forward to a relaxing evening with Andy at the steak house. She wanted to savor every moment she had with her friends in Rocky Bluff, knowing that it probably would be two years before she would see them again.

"Rebecca, I really envy you getting to spend a couple weeks in Hawaii," Andy said as he finished his baked Alaska that Saturday evening. "My favorite aunt lives there, and when I was a boy we'd go visit her every couple years."

"What fond memories," Rebecca smiled. "What was she doing on the islands? Did she have an outside job?"

"My uncle was stationed at Scofield Barracks during World War II. After the war was over, he got a civilian job at the naval shipyard and she opened a dress shop in downtown Honolulu," Andy explained. "He died fifteen years ago. Aunt Lucille sold her store five years later and has spent the last few years basking in the sun."

Rebecca's eyes sparkled with interest. "When was the last time you got to see her?"

"I went over for Uncle Gene's funeral and I haven't been back since. They never had children of their own, so they kind of adopted me, especially after my folks died while I was in college. Do you think you might have time to call her while you're there? I'm sure she'd love to hear from someone from Rocky Bluff. I've told her so much about Montana and this town."

"I'd love to," Rebecca replied with a smile. "Just write down her phone number and I'll do my best. Since I'm not traveling with anyone, it will be good to talk with someone I have something in common with."

Andy took a notepad from his pocket along with his address book. He hurriedly copied the ten digits on a scrap of paper and handed it to Rebecca. She folded it and placed it in the outer flap of her purse. In the process she glanced at her watch. "It's been a delightful evening," she said, "but I'm afraid all good things have to come to an end. I still have a lot more packing to get done before I can go to bed tonight."

Sadness enveloped Rebecca as Andy drove her home. She had spent many years in Rocky Bluff without any serious interest in male companionship, but on the eve of her departure, Andy had ignited a warmth in her that she thought had long since been extinguished.

That Sunday afternoon, Rebecca stopped at the Dutton residence. "Edith, I wanted to be sure and see Roy before I left town. Would you like to ride to the care center with me?"

"Thanks for the offer," Edith replied. "Usually Dan Blair gives me a ride, but he had to work."

As Rebecca turned onto Main Street, she smiled at her friend beside her. "I appreciate you letting me store my car in your garage while I'm gone. I was at a loss as to what to do with it since it's too new to sell."

"I'm glad I could help," Edith assured her. "The garage has been empty ever since Roy had his stroke and we gave his car to our grandson Jay."

"I've seen it parked in the student parking lot," Rebecca said. "Jay's a responsible young man and is taking good care of it. That car seems to be his pride and joy."

Rebecca was not prepared for the change in Roy's condition since she had last seen him a couple months before. He had lost over thirty pounds and his hair hung limp and lifeless. He forced a smile as the two women entered his room.

Rebecca approached his recliner and took his hand. "Hello, Roy," she greeted. "How are you today?"

"F. . .f. . .fine," he whispered.

"I'm glad to hear that," Rebecca replied with a forced smile. "I'm leaving for Guam Monday and wanted to come and say good-bye. I'm going to miss you."

Roy tried to speak, but Rebecca could not understand his words. She looked at Edith.

"He's trying to say, 'Please write,'" Edith explained.

"I'll try to write often," Rebecca assured him as she held his hand. "I'm going to take a two-week vacation in Hawaii on my way over, so I'll send you some picture postcards from there."

Rebecca took a chair in the corner while Edith shared the family news with her husband, read a few articles of interest from the *Rocky Bluff Herald* and a couple of chapters from his Bible.

A few minutes later, while they walked down the corridor toward the nurses' station, Rebecca made sure she didn't look Edith's way. Tears filled her eyes. *Will this be the last time I'll get to see Roy?* she mused as a wave of melancholy enveloped her.

Just as planned, at seven o'clock that evening, the Blairs rang Rebecca's doorbell. "Welcome to your new home," Rebecca greeted. "Do come in and I'll show you around."

Dan, Beth, and four-year-old Jeffy followed Rebecca into her spacious living room.

"It's beautiful," Beth gasped. "You have excellent tastes in decorating."

"Thanks," Rebecca smiled. "I hope you'll be as happy in this house as I've been."

"I'm sure we will be," Beth replied. "I feel honored that you asked us to care for it while you're gone."

Rebecca patted Beth on the shoulder. "After working with you for the last few months, there's no one else I'd rather have live here."

"I promise I'll take good care of your dog," Jeffy said as he knelt to pet the Pekingese at his feet. "I've never had a dog of my own. This'll be fun."

"Her name is Shushu. Come and I'll show you where her food is kept,"

Rebecca said as she motioned for them to follow her to the back porch.

While Jeffy played with Shushu, Rebecca showed Dan and Beth where the fuse box was, the water and gas shutoff valves, along with the lawn mower and other outdoor tools. Beth felt overwhelmed with the responsibility of such a large home to care for, but Dan took it in stride and rose to the challenge.

After discussing every possible problem that might arise, Rebecca handed a set of house keys to Dan. "I wish I were able to give you a forwarding address and telephone number, but I won't know until I get there. I'll call you long distance as soon as I have that information. Good luck."

Beth hugged her former supervisor and bade her farewell. She had depended on Rebecca a great deal during Jeffy's kidnapping the previous fall and it was hard to say good-bye. Yet, the excitement of her new life with Dan could not be dampened.

The warm tropical breeze rushed through Rebecca's hair as she stepped from the Honolulu Airport. The van to the Royal Hawaiian Hotel waited at curbside. A flood of memories enveloped her as she directed the redcap where to unload her luggage and then handed him a tip. This was a part of her life that she rarely shared with her friends from Rocky Bluff.

As the van weaved in and out of the traffic, everything seemed so different, and yet Rebecca felt so connected to the island. It had been more than twenty-five years since she was last there, but now it seemed like only yesterday. She remembered standing at Eric's gravesite at the Pacific War Memorial Cemetery in the Punchbowl. He had been cited for bravery after being killed trying to save his platoon during the Tet Offensive of the Vietnam War. *I wonder what our lives together would have been if he would have returned? Would we still be teaching somewhere in Iowa? Would we have had a family?* Rebecca wondered.

Rebecca's attention was shaken back to reality as the van swerved to avoid hitting a group of pedestrians illegally crossing the street. *I have to enjoy today,* she scolded herself, *instead of dwelling on what might have been. I want to enjoy the island like all the other vacationers and not play the grieving widow of bygone days.*

Just as she promised herself, Rebecca spent the next three days playing tourist. She lounged on the beach, she walked the Ala Moana Mall, she visited the *USS Arizona* Memorial, yet amid all the glitter and excitement of Hawaii, a nagging emptiness hung over her. She tried writing postcards to her friends in Rocky Bluff—Edith Dutton, Beth Blair, Andy Hatfield, Pat Crouse, Teresa Lennon. Yet even the memory of her favorite people could not remove loneliness.

The walls of the Rocky Bluff High School library had always served as her refuge and a cushion against pain. This fall someone new would be in her place and Beth Blair would be that person's loyal assistant. *Am I strong enough to face another culture alone for two years?* Rebecca worried. *I've always prided myself on my independence and self-reliance, so why should I be so fearful about being alone?*

Rebecca's attention returned to the tropical surroundings. *This is silly,* she scolded herself as she watched the native dancers perform at the luau on the beach. *Tomorrow I'm going to take the city bus to the Punchbowl. I know he's no longer there, but maybe by being at his grave this restlessness will disappear and I'll be able to face the future unencumbered by memories.*

Just as she had planned, the next day Rebecca hiked a mile uphill from the last bus stop to the cemetery. The view over the city was awe inspiring. Yet, something was missing. The beauty and dignity of this honored cemetery had been transformed into a park atmosphere. Tour buses containing visitors from seemingly every country in the world converged on what she considered sacred ground. *These are our country's honored dead,* she thought. *The foreigners have no concept what this place means to us. Before I leave Hawaii, I must register my protest of turning a national memorial into a tourist attraction.*

Rebecca walked directly to her husband's gravesite. Every blade of grass was well manicured. She knelt beside the marker expecting a flood of ancient grief to overwhelm her; instead a calm peace settled over her. Eric had been in the loving hands of God for more than a quarter of a century, yet she had not released his memory and could not develop a deep friendship with any other man.

As the freshly mowed grass tickled her knees, she felt as if she heard him say, "Rebecca, I loved you dearly during the brief years we had together. Don't hide your life surrounded by books; learn to love again. Life is too short to waste a single moment."

Joy swelled up from within as she rose to her feet. That inner emptiness that had long imprisoned her faded. During the downhill walk to the bus stop, she felt as if she were gliding on a cloud.

The next morning at breakfast the date on the morning newspaper nearly jumped off the page. *My vacation is nearly over and I haven't called Andy's aunt like I promised him.*

After finishing her breakfast of tropical fruit, Rebecca hurried back to her room. She thumbed through her purse until she found the wrinkled paper containing Lucille Hatfield's telephone number.

Rebecca dialed the number and waited. "Hello. Lucille Hatfield residence," a familiar male voice answered.

Rebecca hesitated. "Andy, is that you?"

"Rebecca, I was hoping you'd call. I wanted to call you, but I had no idea where you were staying."

"What are you doing in Honolulu?"

"Two days after you left, I received a call that Aunt Lucille had passed away. Since I'm the next of kin, I caught the next flight out of Rocky Bluff so I could be here to make the final arrangements."

Rebecca sank onto her hotel bed. "I'm sorry to hear that. I know she'd been extra special to you throughout the years."

"That she was," Andy confessed. "It was very hard for me to leave the cemetery yesterday. I'm trying to get all the loose ends tied together today so I can leave first thing in the morning. It's vacation time and I can't leave. The fire department is shorthanded."

"Lucille was fortunate to have a nephew as considerate as you," Rebecca reminded him as she pictured his concerned eyes and broad shoulders.

"This is my last night on the island and I'd love to spend it with you," Andy replied. "Where would you suggest?"

"They're serving dinner on the hotel patio here at the Royal Hawaiian this evening. They're bringing in native dancers and we could dine by the beach and watch the sun go down."

"That sounds perfect," Andy replied as his sense of mourning for his favorite aunt lifted. "I have some errands to run and then I'll meet you at six-thirty."

The musicians strummed their ukuleles while Andy and Rebecca sipped their fruit drinks on the patio of the Royal Hawaiian. The palm trees rustled gently in the background. Tonight was the first time in more than twenty-five years that Rebecca had felt the concerned friendship of a man. They laughed and talked and shared many of their hopes and dreams of the future. There was never a mention of the tragedy that had occurred next door to her that brought them together. The sparkle in her eyes was like that of a woman of eighteen facing the world of love for the first time. Was it possible for a relationship to develop when they were eighteen thousand miles apart and would not see each other for two years?

Chapter 4

"Hafa adai," the clerk at the rent-a-car booth in the Won Pat International Airport greeted. "May I help you?"

"I'd like to rent an economy car for a week," Rebecca said as she parked her luggage cart in front of the counter.

"We have a two-door Mazda available," the bronze-skinned woman responded briskly as she reached in the file beside her. "If you're interested, please fill out the following forms."

Rebecca surveyed the questionnaire and shook her head with frustration. "What do I put down for an address? I just got off the plane and haven't had time to go apartment hunting."

"Just write in the name of the hotel where you'll be staying. On Guam, we know the car won't be going far," the clerk chuckled.

"I haven't checked into a hotel yet," Rebecca sighed. "Do you have any suggestions?"

"I suggest the Pacific Star, it's one of the nicest on Guam. Would you like a map of the island?"

"I'd appreciate that," Rebecca replied as she continued filling in the blanks. "I'll treat myself to a nice room tonight and go apartment hunting tomorrow."

The clerk entered the data into the computer and handed her a set of keys. "You'll find your car parked in space A-17."

"Thanks for your help," Rebecca replied as she adjusted the luggage on her cart. The rusted wheels balked as she headed toward the automatic door. She looked for redcap assistance, but none was available. People from all nationalities filled the lobby. Everyone seemed oblivious of her presence. *I have to learn to be totally self-sufficient,* Rebecca reminded herself. *I've been spoiled by having spent most of my adult life in Rocky Bluff. If I were struggling with this load there, I'd have a host of people helping me.*

The heavy tropical air smothered Rebecca as she stepped from the airport in Tamuning, Guam. Perspiration began running down her forehead. She was used to the temperatures occasionally reaching the high nineties in Montana during July and August, but those couldn't compare with the oppressive eighty-eight humid degrees of island life. She piled her luggage in the trunk of the rental car, returned the cart to the terminal, and started the engine of her rented Mazda. *Ahh, air-conditioning at last.*

Rebecca was scarcely able to absorb the extreme contrasts in her surroundings. She expected Guam to be just like Hawaii, only smaller, but the differences shocked her. While driving the few miles to the Pacific Star, she marveled at the international cosmopolitanism side by side with tin shacks. Chickens ran loose through the yards. Small children played barefoot while older ones gathered under the palm trees with soft drinks in their hands. Life seemed as if it were right out of *National Geographic.* She surveyed the young people she passed with wonderment. *Could they be some of my future students?* she mused. *Will I be able to relate to them and help them learn to use a library? Did I do the right thing to come so far by myself?*

Rebecca stopped her rented Mazda at a corner gas station and studied her newly acquired map. After surveying her surroundings and the traffic patterns, she started the car. At the next corner she turned west toward Tumon Bay. She gasped as she saw the marble-colored hotel rising above the bright blue shoreline. This was more beautiful than anything she had seen in Hawaii. *The rental agency clerk was right,* she mentally gasped. *This one night of luxury will be well worth the investment.*

Within minutes Rebecca had checked into the Pacific Star and was helped to her room on the fourth floor. After tipping the bellboy, she turned to the window and pulled open the drapes. The sky was ablaze with reds and oranges as it settled upon the watery horizon. Instead of being overwhelmed by the beauty so different from the majestic mountains of Montana, tears filled Rebecca's eyes. *I've never felt this alone since I got word of Eric's death more than twenty-five years ago. Instead of the ocean welcoming me, it feels like a chasm separating me from my loved ones in Rocky Bluff, Montana.*

Rebecca opened the drawer of the dresser and took out the hotel stationery. She flopped across the bed. *I haven't written a letter for years. Picking up the telephone is too easy, but I need to share the mixed emotions welling within me.*

Dear Edith,

After a five-hour nonstop flight from Hawaii, I finally arrived in Guam. It's so different from what I expected. I thought it would be a miniature Hawaii, but it's like I am in a foreign country instead of a U.S. territory.

Last night I was dining under a palm tree on the patio of the

Royal Hawaiian Hotel on Waikiki Beach with Andy Hatfield. I was shocked when I called his aunt and Andy answered the phone himself. His beloved aunt had passed away suddenly. I was glad I could be there during that difficult time for him. I never thought I'd ever again have a deep relationship with another man, but since the Reeds' fire, I'm catching myself thinking more and more about Andy. The few hours we've had together have meant so much to me.

As I look across the Philippine Sea from my hotel room, memories of home envelop me. I remember the glow that grew within you as your relationship with Roy deepened. At your retirement party from the high school, I knew you'd continue to have a productive life, but little did I imagine that love could happen to someone over sixty. Now that I'm nearing that age myself, I'm wondering if the same thing could happen to me. However, I won't be back to Rocky Bluff for nearly two years, so there's no way love can grow across the distant sea.

I suppose I'd better close now and get some sleep. Jet lag is beginning to set in. It will probably be several days before my internal clock adjusts to crossing the international dateline. The next few days are going to be extremely busy. I have to stop by Guam Christian Academy and let them know I'm on the island. I hope I can find an apartment right away. (I can't afford to stay in this luxury for long.) I'll also need to buy a car right away. Renting one can certainly add up in a hurry.

I'll let you know my permanent address just as soon as I find an apartment. Say hello to Beth and Dan for me, and give a special greeting to Andy.

May God continue to bless you and Roy,
Rebecca

The day after Chief Hatfield returned from Hawaii, Captain Philip Mooney walked into his office at the fire station. "Andy, it's good to have you back. How was your trip?"

"I wish I could say it was a delightful vacation of lying on the beach at Waikiki, but it was extremely difficult saying my final farewell to Aunt Lucille. The only enjoyable thing about the entire week was that I met up with Rebecca Sutherland. Just having a sympathetic ear of someone from Rocky Bluff meant so much to me. I just hope and pray things go well for her on Guam. From some of the stories I've heard about Guam, I'm concerned about her being over there by herself."

"I'm sure she'll be all right," Phil tried to assure him. "We both saw how good she was in crisis management the night of the Reeds' fire."

"She was brilliant and rose to the occasion," Andy agreed. Suddenly his eyes became serious. "Have there been any new developments in the case while I was gone?"

A scowl spread across Phil's face. "We haven't been able to figure out the exact cause of the fire. We're sure it started around a space heater in the hallway in front of the master bedroom, but it appeared to be a new heater, so it doesn't make sense." Phil shook his head with despair. "Dick Reed has left town and no one seems to know where he went. . .not even his in-laws. Add to that, he took out a million-dollar life insurance policy on his wife just three months ago. They're holding payment until we complete our investigation."

Andy stroked his chin. "Sounds pretty suspicious. Do you think it's time we call in Marty Sanchez again? He did wonders in finding the cause of the Harkness Hardware Store fire a few years ago."

Phil stroked his chin. "Speaking of Harkness Hardware, I wonder if the Reeds bought the space heater there. It looks fairly new. I think I'll stop by there later this afternoon and see if Bob has any records on it."

"Sounds like a good possibility," Andy replied. "We don't have many clues to go on. Maybe Marty will unearth the truth."

"We need all the help we can get. I'll give the state crime lab a call in the morning," Phil replied. "Hopefully they can get their top arson investigator here before the end of the week."

"If there's proof of arson, we don't want to let Dick get too far away from us." Andy hesitated. "Three months ago Dick Reed seemed like such a respectable family man, and now all sorts of weird things are surfacing."

☙

"Dan, I certainly appreciate you giving me a ride to the nursing home each afternoon. I don't know how Roy or I can ever repay you," Edith said as they approached the Rocky Bluff Care Center.

"You and Roy have meant so much to Beth and me that even if we lived until we were a hundred, we could never repay you for what you've done for us." Dan's mind drifted back through the years. "Roy was the one responsible for getting me involved in the crisis center, and you were always there for Beth when she first came to town as a frightened single mother. Even little Jeffy thinks you're the greatest."

Edith smiled. "We've certainly been through a lot together, haven't we?"

Dan reached across the seat and patted Edith's hand. "You've been there for us during both the good times and the bad. You've literally become our surrogate parents."

The pair rode in silence for several blocks before Edith spoke again. "I just got a letter from Rebecca. She says hello to you and Beth. She sounds awfully lonesome."

"Beth and I would like to write to her, but we don't have an address yet," Dan acknowledged. "I suppose we could write to her in care of the school where she's going to work. She's planning to check in there just as soon as she gets to Guam. I'm sure she'd like to know how Shushu is doing."

Dan stopped the car in the handicapped parking spot in front of the nursing home so Edith would not have to strain herself with a long walk. "I'll see you in a couple hours," he said as his older friend opened the passenger door. "I have a few errands to run for the crisis center this afternoon."

As Edith stopped at the nurses' station to check on Roy's condition, Liz Chapman, the activities director approached. "Edith, how good to see you."

Edith beamed as she took the young woman's hand. "Hello, Liz. You're looking extremely vibrant today. Things must be going well for you."

"I've never found a job as rewarding as this one. I only wish I had more time to arrange for local talent to perform at our afternoon get-togethers."

"Rocky Bluff has a lot of untapped talent," Edith replied. "I'm amazed every time I attend a school or community activity."

Liz nodded as she remembered the high school music concert the previous week."Would you be willing to run interference for me? I'd like to schedule performances every Monday, Wednesday, and Friday, and in-house games on Tuesday and field trips on Thursday."

"I'd be honored. In fact, I know of several groups who would be happy to play here."

"Thanks a heap. It'll mean so much to the residents," Liz replied.

"Roy looks forward to your talent days and is always asking when the next one is going to be. Making contacts is the least I can do to help. I'll get on the phone just as soon as I get home," Edith promised.

Edith said good-bye to Liz and then slipped into Roy's room. Seeing his bride of less than five years, Roy sat up in his recliner and beamed. "H. . h. . .hi. . .h. . .h. . .hon. . .n. . .ney."

Edith leaned over and kissed him on the lips. "Hello. How are you doing?"

Roy nodded affirmatively as Edith pulled a chair close to his. "I brought the mail along to read. I got a letter from Rebecca Sutherland in Guam. Would you like to have me read it to you?"

Roy again nodded his head. His eyes portrayed intense interest as

Edith read the letter. "N. . .n. . .nice," he muttered as she finished reading and folded the letter.

Edith then read the main articles in the *Herald* to him. Before she was finished with the sports page, Roy was asleep. Edith took her knitting from her bag and began working on a new lap robe for him. She treasured every moment she had with her husband, even those when he was sleeping.

It didn't seem long before Dan was there to give her a ride home. "Hi," he greeted as he stepped into the room. "I was looking forward to visiting with Roy a few minutes before we left, but I see he's sleeping."

"No problem," Edith replied. "The nurses have encouraged me to awaken him when he has company. They feel he can sleep anytime and the mental stimulation of a familiar face will help keep his mind in touch with the outside world."

Edith gently shook her husband's shoulder. "Roy, you have company."

Roy sleepily opened his eyes. A broad grin spread across his face. "D. . .D. . .Dan," he stuttered.

Dan shook his older friend's hand and then began sharing some of the events of the crisis center. Roy listened with great interest. He started the Rocky Bluff Crisis Center soon after he retired from his social services career. Turning the center over to Dan was one of the hardest things he had ever done. Roy's eyes sparkled with each new event, and he nodded with approval with each change. Although Roy's speech was limited, his eyes still communicated his inner vitality and strength.

❧

Ten days after arriving in Guam, Rebecca walked into the principal's office at Guam Christian Academy. The room was not air-conditioned, but the louvres were open and a tropical breeze greeted her.

"Mr. Diaz, I'd like to thank you for helping me get settled here in Guam. I found a nice one-bedroom furnished apartment in Dededo. It's a little farther than I'd like to drive, but this was the best I looked at."

"I'm glad I could help," David Diaz said as he motioned for her to sit down in the chair beside his desk. "How is the Toyota working out for you?"

Rebecca smiled. "Great. I understand it belonged to the social studies teacher."

"It's kind of a custom here," Mr. Diaz smiled. "When people return to the mainland, they need their car until they step onto the plane and they don't have time to find a buyer. When the new teachers arrive late in the summer, the first thing they need is a car. We like to take the cars from the departing teachers and make them available to the incoming ones."

"It's a great system. It saved me a lot of problems."

"There are enough difficulties just getting here and settled. We like to make it as easy as possible. When we hire teachers from the mainland, we look for those with good problem-solving abilities," Mr. Diaz explained. "You came highly recommended. Too many statesiders think coming to Guam will be like moving to another state. When they find they can't cope with the cultural differences, they're on the plane home before their first Christmas here."

"That's too bad," Rebecca replied, "but I can see how that can happen." Her mind drifted back to the petite blond she had met the day before. "A young teacher just moved into the apartment across the hall. She returned from shopping yesterday nearly in tears. Someone had referred to her as a 'haole.' She hadn't heard the term before, but it was said with such disdain that she knew she was being put down."

Mr. Diaz nodded his head knowingly, his bronze face reflecting a depth of understanding. "I'm sorry to say, that is a common occurrence here. The word 'haole' is Hawaiian, not Chammoro. It means 'boss.' During plantation days in Hawaii, the bigger plantations imported laborers from Japan, Korea, China, and the Philippines and overseers from the U.S. mainland, Scotland, and Portugal. The overseers were called 'haole.' Since the bosses were all white, the word was soon corrupted and came to mean white. Unfortunately, today it has taken on a derogatory connotation, and some of our people who should know better have adopted it as their own. The present interracial climate here is becoming more and more volatile. Is this your first experience as a minority?"

"I'll admit I've been pretty sheltered from racial slurs in Rocky Bluff. But being a minority here will give me a better understanding of what our Native Americans go through in Montana," Rebecca said. She hesitated as she grasped the enormity of the challenge of helping a people who might resent those of her homeland. "I'll do my best to provide the best school library possible and try to avoid any political or racial confrontations," Rebecca assured her new principal, trying hard to hide her trepidations.

"We're extremely fortunate to have you on our staff," Mr. Diaz replied. He then paused and pulled open his left-hand drawer. "By the way, several letters for you have already arrived. You must be a pretty popular person back in Montana."

Rebecca blushed as he handed her a stack of letters. "I'm sorry for the inconvenience. I had to give the school as my address until I found an apartment."

"No problem. Most of our new teachers do the same thing. In fact, we're still getting letters for teachers who left the island several years ago."

Principal Diaz handed Rebecca several brochures about the culture and life on Guam. "These might help you understand the local customs and people."

Rebecca thanked him and walked into the bright Guam sunshine. On the way to her car, she thumbed through the pile of envelopes in her hand. *Hmmm. . .a letter from Beth Blair, one from Edith, one from Pat Crouse, another from Teresa Lennon.* Rebecca's eyes froze, her heart raced. The return address on the next envelope read: "Andrew Hatfield, 708 Maple St., Rocky Bluff, Montana." *Does Andy care enough about me to carry on a relationship from such a distance? Or. . .maybe there's been new developments in the investigation of the Reeds' fire.*

Chapter 5

Rebecca hurriedly unlocked the car door and rolled down the windows. She could not wait to drive across the island to her apartment before reading her mail. Her hand trembled and her palms became sweaty in the tropical heat as she tore open the letter from Andy.

Dear Rebecca,

It was extremely fortunate that we were able to spend time together in Hawaii. I felt the loss of Aunt Lucille more intensely than ever I thought I would. Having you there did more than fill the void of Aunt Lucille; for the first time I felt what the Bible must mean when it says, "It's not good for man to be alone." All my life I've devoted myself to my career, but now I'm discovering another dimension to my life that I never thought existed. . .a need to share the joys and disappointments of everyday life with someone. Rebecca, when I was feeling low in Hawaii, you were the one who helped lift me from despair. I'm looking forward to the day you return to Rocky Bluff for good.

Incidentally, to bring you up to date on the happenings of Rocky Bluff, Dick Reed has left town and no one knows where he is. The fire is still under investigation and it's looking more and more suspicious with each passing day. Philip Mooney is going to call the crime lab in Missoula to send out their best arson investigator. Marty Sanchez did a tremendous job at getting to the source of the fire at Harkness Hardware Store a few years ago, so hopefully he'll be able to solve this one as well. I'll keep you posted as to the developments.

Do be careful while you're overseas. Guam is not nearly as safe as Rocky Bluff.

God's blessings,
Andy

The tropical breeze could not melt the oppressive heat within Rebecca's Toyota. She started the engine, rolled up the windows, and turned on the air conditioner. The cool air refreshed her perspiring body.

She turned onto the highway and headed toward Dededo. The other letters could wait. Her mind was in a spin. In less than a week school would be starting and she had so much to learn. Life on Guam was so different from life in Rocky Bluff. The easy-going, relaxed atmosphere was foreign to the work ethic displayed in a cold climate. The emphasis on education had always been vital to rural Montana, while education on Guam was just beginning to experience its awakening. *Maybe I should enroll in the class "Education and Culture on Guam" that's being offered at the University of Guam this fall,* Rebecca mused as she parked her car in front of her apartment building. She took the letters from the dash of her car and hurried inside. *I'm sure glad friends in Rocky Bluff haven't forgotten me,* she sighed. *I feel like a fish out of water walking on the beaches under the palm trees watching people relaxing in the sun.*

Rebecca took a soft drink from the refrigerator and sank into the cushion of her wicker sofa. She tore open Edith's letter, hoping to find words of encouragement. She was not disappointed. Her eyes moistened as she read Edith's prompting to rely more on Christ during her lonesome moments than she ever had in her life.

"Situations that you normally would have discussed with a friend here in Rocky Bluff," Edith wrote, "you'll now have to talk to the Lord instead. Your friends may have given you some misguided advice throughout the years, but God will never lead you astray."

Rebecca paused. *Edith is right as usual. I have become too dependent on my friends instead of leaning totally on God. That's why I'm feeling so alone.*

❦

"Grandma, what would you think if I joined the air force after I graduate instead of going to college?" Jay Harkness asked as he sat across the kitchen table from his beloved grandmother.

Edith surveyed her handsome, athletic grandson. The resemblance to his father, Bob, at that age was remarkable. "Each person has to decide what's best for them," she replied. "What to do after high school is one of the biggest decisions you'll ever have to make."

"So I'm finding out," Jay replied. "I know you and Dad have assumed I'd go to the University of Montana and get a degree in business so I could come back and run the hardware store."

Edith looked stunned. "I'm sorry if I ever gave you that impression. More than anything I want you to be happy. Your grandfather and I enjoyed our life together running the store, but that doesn't mean everyone else would."

"Dad has always been wrapped up in the store and never seemed to have time to spend with us when we were little," Jay lamented. "Only once did we take an extended family vacation. That was when we went to California to see Great Aunt Phyllis when Uncle John died."

"That's true," Edith agreed. "As a store owner, long vacations are often out, but you took many short vacations to Yellowstone Park, Glacier Park, and Flathead Lake. People drive clear across the country to see what we have right at our back door."

Jay blushed. "I don't want to seem ungrateful, but I guess I'm suffering from wanderlust. I want to travel and see the world. I figure the best way to do that is to join the military. I can still work on a college degree while I'm in the service."

"You don't have to convince me of that," Edith replied. "Both Roy and your grandfather served in the second world war. They had pretty horrible stories to tell, but they both said the same thing. . . It gave them a better appreciation of different cultures and the value of human life."

"Dad doesn't see any future in military service. He seems to think the military is only for those who wouldn't be able to make it in college."

Edith paused. Her mind raced back through the years of political and social change she had seen in her lifetime. "Regardless of the isolation we sometimes feel in Montana, world events do shape individual attitudes and perceptions," she explained. "Your dad grew up in the Vietnam era. He served time in the army, but fortunately the war was over before he had to go overseas. Several of his friends from basic training were killed in the war, and he never could find a reason for their death. Since then he's totally blocked out the necessity for a national defense system."

Jay nodded. "That explains his refusal. Every time we go to Great Falls, I've always wanted to stop and visit Malmstrom Air Force Base, but he's always had a reason not to. It's like a curtain is drawn around him."

Seriousness entered Edith's soft voice. "Jay, you'll have to make your decision with your own life goals and objectives in mind. Your father loves you, he may object at first, but in the end he'll be the strongest ally you'll ever have."

"Dad has never let me down yet," Jay replied. "Right now I just want to get outside of Rocky Bluff and see the world." The young man shrugged his shoulders. "Maybe someday I'll want to move back to Rocky Bluff, but not for a long while. I envy Mrs. Sutherland getting to go to Guam to work for a couple years. I can just picture her lying under a palm tree drinking guava juice."

"Life in a distant land isn't always as glamorous as it may seem," Edith chuckled. "There's also the inconvenience of not having all the amenities of home. There's the loneliness of not being accepted into another culture. Judging from Rebecca's letters, that seems to be her biggest concern at this time. It takes an extremely mature personality to do what she has done, and I'm certain that Guam Christian Academy will profit greatly from her expertise."

The conversation shifted to the start of football season. Ever since Edith was the high school home economics teacher, she had always enjoyed following Rocky Bluff High School athletic games. Now that her grandson played both on the football and basketball teams, she enjoyed them even more. Before each game Jay always looked into the stands to locate his family.

A note of sadness enveloped Jay. This year Roy would not be at his grandmother's side. A series of strokes had made it impossible for him to leave the nursing home. "Grandma, would you like to ride to Great Falls with me Saturday? I'd like to visit the base there before I talk to the recruiter. I want to make sure this is the right decision without any outside pressure or fantastic offers."

"I'd love to," Edith replied. "I'll treat you to the best restaurant in town while we're there."

⚜

Captain Philip Mooney reached for the phone in the Rocky Bluff police station and dialed the number of the state crime lab in Missoula.

"State crime lab. How may I direct your call?"

"Director Bruce Devlin, please."

Phil listened as he heard several clicks on the line. Then a friendly voice said, "Director's office. May I help you?"

"This is Captain Mooney of the Rocky Bluff Police Department. Is Bruce Devlin available?"

"He's on another line. Would you care to hold?"

"Sure," Phil said as soft music began playing in the background. He reached for some paperwork on his desk to occupy his time while he waited.

Within minutes a voice came over the phone. "Hello, Phil. How are things in Rocky Bluff? Are you staying above the crime wave?"

"Speeding tickets are my specialty," Phil chuckled as he recognized the voice of the head of the crime lab. "However, this time I'm stymied by a possible arson case."

"Did you have another hardware store burn down?"

"Worse than that," Phil replied. "This time it was a house fire. The mother and two children died in the blaze. It's a strange situation, and now the husband has left town and we don't know where he is."

Bruce Devlin's voice became somber. "Sounds pretty serious. With the husband having left town, a lot of the evidence probably left with him. I'll send Marty Sanchez over first thing in the morning."

"Our fire chief, Andrew Hatfield, will be glad to see him," Phil replied. "He's becoming extremely frustrated with the situation. He has strong suspicions but little evidence."

"That's Marty's specialty," Bruce replied. "Please have someone meet the ten-thirty Treasure State flight from Missoula tomorrow morning."

At ten o'clock the next morning, Chief Hatfield and Captain Mooney drove to the airport outside of Rocky Bluff to meet Julio Raphael Martinez Sanchez. The eighteen-passenger Treasure State commuter had become an invaluable link between Rocky Bluff and the rest of the world.

The pair peered toward the western sky until the small plane appeared. It rolled to a stop and the side door opened, releasing the steps. Marty was the first off the plane, dressed in his customary Montana traveling garb of blue jeans, western shirt, and cowboy boots.

"Welcome back to Rocky Bluff," Captain Mooney greeted as he extended his hand. "I believe you met Fire Chief Hatfield during your last visit."

Marty nodded in greeting and shook both men's hands. "It's good to see you again. I only wish we could meet under better circumstances."

"After the investigation is over, why don't you stick around and I'll treat you to dinner at Beefy's Steak House?" Phil offered.

"Sounds good to me," Marty replied. "But first things first. Let's go over the evidence you have so far."

"Right now everything's locked in my office awaiting your arrival," Andy explained. "Our prime piece of evidence is a space heater. We believe it started the fire. The thing that has me stumped is that it's a brand-new heater. We checked with Bob Harkness at the hardware store. He went through all his back records and found that Dick Reed purchased the heater just a week before the fire. A new heater shouldn't have overheated."

On the way to the fire station, Andy rehashed the events of the night of the fire. "The temperature dipped to a new record low for the month of June that night," he explained. "Around two in the morning, Dick Reed awakened the next-door neighbor and asked her to call the fire department. We found it extremely strange that he didn't try to get his family out first, but he maintains he was confused and frightened by the intensity of the flames. Also, he had taken out a million-dollar life insurance policy on his wife just three months prior to the fire."

"I'd like to talk with that neighbor," Marty stated. "Maybe in the confusion Dick might have said something that would help the investigation."

Andy's eyes became distant. "I'm sorry, but that won't be possible. Rebecca Sutherland is now on Guam. I did interview her extensively before she left, and you're welcome to use those notes and tapes."

Marty sighed. "That will help."

"I have her address and telephone number," Andy replied. "We could always give her a call. International calls have become nearly as easy as local ones."

"I'll make my investigation and then if there's any missing pieces, I'll try to contact Mrs. Sutherland," Marty said. "A telephone call may not be necessary."

The three men hurried into the fire chief's office. The charred heater was on a table in the corner. Without saying a word, Marty picked up the heater and studied it from every possible angle. "Hmm. . .interesting," he muttered as the two Rocky Bluff residents waited in silence. They had learned during his last investigation not to ask questions until Marty had completed his analysis.

Finally Marty looked up. "Andy, do you have a Phillips head screwdriver handy?"

"It's in the back cupboard. Just a minute and I'll get the key to it," Andy replied as he reached into his desk drawer. He took the key and jiggled the lock until it opened and quickly located the desired tool.

Marty took the screwdriver and removed the screws holding the casing to the rest of the heater. "Hmm. . . These are turning too easily. Has anyone taken this apart during the investigation?"

Andy's faced reddened. "I never thought to take it apart," he confessed.

"Most people don't," Marty replied as he removed the case. "It appears this heater has been tampered with."

Marty continued working in silence. "Hmm. . .interesting," he mumbled. Finally he turned to his companions and pointed to the heater in his hand. "Do you notice anything missing?"

"No, I can't say that I do," Phil replied.

"The thermostat has been removed. When the heater was plugged in without a thermostat, the coils just got hotter and hotter until they ignited the closest flammable item. Had there been a thermostat in the heater, chances are there would have been no fire. The thermostat would have automatically turned off the heater when the temperature of the coils reached seventy-seven degrees. It also looks like the heater was lying on its side." Marty pointed to the inner coils. "Notice how one side of the coils are darker than the other? That is not a normal burn mark."

"Yes, I see it now," Andy said as he peered through his bifocals. "I should have thought of that myself."

"Has anything been moved in the house?" Marty asked. "I know it's been two months since the fire."

"I went in there once with Dick to see if there was anything that could be salvaged, but it's been sealed ever since," Phil answered.

"Good. Let's go see the fire site," Marty responded as he moved toward the door before the others had a chance to respond.

Phil drove the police car down the familiar route to Rimrock Road. The charred house continued to send chills down his spine as memories of that tragic night two months before flashed through his mind. He waved at Dan Blair, who was mowing the lawn next door as they stepped from the car. The contrast of the normal tasks of life and the horror next door momentarily paralyzed him.

Phil unlocked the door and Marty led the way into the house. He went straight to the hallway where the heater had been located. "Hmm. . . interesting," Marty repeated. He got down on his hands and knees and felt the burnt carpeting. He picked up the charred remains of a child's receiving blanket. "Where was this located when you removed the heater?" he asked.

"It was underneath the heater," Andy replied. "With four small children in the house, I assumed one of them had dropped it too close to the heater."

"A child would drop a blanket on top of a heater, not under it." Marty's eyes sparkled. "So. . .o. . .o," he stated as his voice trailed out. "The person who started the fire removed the thermostat from the heater, laid it on its side on top of a highly flammable blanket. The blanket ignited the carpet, which is very cheap and gives off noxious fumes when it burns. It's a miracle that the mother was able to get two of the children out of the house before the fumes overcame her."

"That's all I need to know," Phil stated, his eyes ablaze. "I'll prepare a report immediately for our county attorney so that he can get the ball rolling for an arrest warrant. We can charge Dick Reed with three counts of homicide. We'll put that sleazeball away for good."

Chapter 6

Three hundred students and faculty gathered in the Guam Christian Academy gymnasium for the opening assembly of the new school year. Rebecca watched as the students filed in, giggling and laughing, glad to be back together after summer break. *There's little difference between these kids and those in Rocky Bluff except their skin is darker and their hair is shiny black,* Rebecca observed. *It looks like only ten percent of the student body are Anglos, or Haoles as they call us.*

"Hello," a voice from beside her greeted. "I take it you're the new librarian. I'm Mitzi Quinata, head of the English department."

Rebecca turned and smiled. "Hi. I'm Rebecca Sutherland. It's nice meeting you."

"It's good having you at GCA. I've been pushing for two years to get a full-time librarian," Mitzi replied. "Without a good library it's nearly impossible to teach English properly. You have your work cut out for you."

Rebecca laughed. "To be honest, I was a little overwhelmed when the principal first showed me the library. Boxes of books are stacked everywhere. A computer in the corner is still in boxes and the software is beside it. Within a short time I have to turn those boxes into an organized library."

"From what I've heard of your credentials, I'm sure you'll do a great job," Mitzi replied. "If there's anything I can do to help, please let me know. When you're ready to shelve books, I'll have my students help you. It'll be a good learning experience for them. Most of them have never heard of the Dewey decimal system."

"Thanks for the offer," Rebecca replied as the principal moved to the podium.

"Welcome to a new and exciting year at GCA," the principal began. "Let us all rise and sing the national anthem and the Guam Hymn."

A lump gathered in Rebecca's throat as the familiar strains of the national anthem began. Home seemed so far away, yet she was bound to this room full of strangers by the stars and stripes on the far wall. As soon as the excitement of the "Star Spangled Banner" ended, a soft hush filled the room. The students and teachers displayed a deeper respect as they sang the Guam Hymn in their own Chamorro language.

This feels like a strange contradiction, Rebecca mused. *A moment ago I felt a part of these people. Now I feel like a visitor in a foreign country.*

The crowd remained standing while the principal led them in prayer for wisdom and guidance. He asked for a special blessing for all the students, faculty, and support staff. After the final amen, everyone was seated as the principal surveyed his student body with pride.

"Hafa adai. Greetings to each one of you. We've made a lot of changes since last year. As you may have noticed, there's a new paint job throughout the school. The new wing housing the library and audiovisual center has been completed and we've hired a full-time librarian." He paused as he surveyed the section where the faculty was sitting. Spotting Rebecca, he motioned for her to stand. "Please make our new librarian, Rebecca Sutherland, feel welcome."

Loud cheers and applause filled the gymnasium. Rebecca smiled and waved to the student body.

"Mrs. Sutherland, would you like to come to the microphone and say a few words?" Mr. Diaz said as the gym became quieter.

Rebecca walked to the front. "I'd like to thank you all for your warm welcome. I'm looking forward to getting to know each of you individually and having a great year together. May God bless you all."

The crowd again burst into cheers as Rebecca returned to her seat. "They're an enthusiastic bunch," she whispered to Mitzi as she joined her colleague.

"That's a Guamanian welcome," the English teacher whispered back. "The Chamorros are an extremely warm and friendly people."

After the assembly Rebecca returned to her library full of boxes. *Where do I begin?* she mused as she scrutinized the room. *I suppose I should assemble the computer first and load the software. Then I can catalog the books as I take them out of the boxes.*

The rest of the day flew by, and when it was time to go home, Mitzi stuck her head into the library. "No one's allowed to work late on the first day of school," she teased as she scanned the room. "It looks like you got a lot done today."

"I feel like it," Rebecca sighed. "I'm exhausted, but at least I'll be able to begin cataloging books tomorrow."

Rebecca locked the library door, and the pair walked to the parking lot together, exchanging first day of school stories. It was comforting to Rebecca for a local teacher to take her under her wing and explain the similarities and differences of the two cultures. Mitzi had been educated at Portland State University and was well aware of the subtle adjustments in moving from the mainland to Guam.

As Rebecca parked her car at her apartment in Dededo, Ella Mae Jackson pulled in beside her.

"Hello," she greeted. "How was your first day of school?"

The trim blond locked her car and joined her new friend on the curb.

"Much different from what I expected," she confessed in a soft Southern drawl. "Guam's nothing like Abbeville, South Carolina."

Rebecca snickered. "It's a lot different from Rocky Bluff, Montana, too. Why don't you come to my apartment so we can compare tales of woe?"

"Thanks," Ella Mae smiled, trying to hide her frustrations of the day. "I've been busy with students all day and have scarcely had a chance to talk with any adult."

Rebecca unlocked her apartment door and motioned for Ella Mae to make herself comfortable on the wicker sofa while she went to the refrigerator for soft drinks.

"You're lucky," Ella Mae began as her hostess handed her a glass of cool refreshment. "You've had a lot of experience as a librarian and teacher before you came to Guam. This is my first year teaching and I have to get used to both teaching and a different culture."

Rebecca surveyed her young friend's wrinkled forehead.

"What school were you finally assigned to?"

"George Washington High School. They say it's one of the roughest ones on the island."

"Did you get a chance to meet any of the other faculty today?" Rebecca queried.

A faint smile began to spread across Ella Mae's face. "The head of the ROTC program stopped by my room during his lunch break to welcome me," she replied softly. "His name is Major Lee. I watched him work with the kids on the track, trying to teach them to march. I thought he was terribly harsh and strict with them, but when he stopped to visit, he was extremely kind and compassionate."

"That's what makes a good army officer," Rebecca replied with a smile, not wanting to mention her firsthand experience with an officer who was now buried in the Punchbowl near Honolulu.

"In talking with him just those few minutes it seems like Major Lee has a tremendous background in history. He'll make a good resource person if I have students smarter than I am."

"We need all the friends we can make."

"We haolies have got to stick together for moral support," Rebecca laughed. "It'll make our adjustment to Guam a lot easier."

393

The pair continued the conversation for over an hour. Finally, Ella Mae looked at her watch. "Oh dear. It's getting late and I've got a lot of lesson plans to make before tomorrow. Tomorrow you're invited to my apartment for soft drinks after work."

Edith Dutton waited eagerly at the nurses' station of the Rocky Bluff Care Center for the activities director. Within moments Liz Chapman was inviting her into the office. "Edith, it's good to see you again. I've heard by the grapevine that you've been doing a lot of contacting for us."

"People have been extremely accommodating and I have a tentative schedule of performers for every Monday, Wednesday, and Friday from now until Christmas," Edith explained as she took a folded piece of paper from her purse and handed it to Liz.

Liz smiled as she scanned the list. "I see you have a lot of local talent here."

"Oh, yes," Edith smiled. "I contacted the music teacher, Ed Summer, and he was extremely interested. He thought it would build his students' self-confidence to perform before an appreciative audience."

"You're amazing," the activities director replied. "You're one of the few people who is truly intergenerational and sees the importance of each stage of life. I hope your enthusiasm is contagious."

"It will be," Edith replied. "Everyone must grow older, and after experiencing the entire life cycle, one can't help but gain the intergenerational perspective."

"I understand you organized the Mothers Encouraging Moms group at your church," Liz said. "That's one of the best examples of one generation helping another that I've ever heard of."

Edith smiled. "The response has been good. Both the mothers and grandmothers have become extremely committed to helping each other. Now we want to expand to include the great-grandmothers," she explained. "Many of them are here in the care center."

"That's perfect. The residents enjoy the visits of younger people, and those who are able like to get out and mingle with the rest of the community." Liz could scarcely contain her excitement.

"Teresa Lennon has been working on that part of our outreach," Edith explained. "I'll have her get in touch with you and see what can be worked out."

"Edith, I can't tell you how much I appreciate all you're doing for the care center," Liz declared as she gave her older friend a hug.

"The feelings are mutual," Edith replied. "I can't thank you enough for all you've done for Roy. I was so afraid he'd feel neglected when I had to place him here, but with all the loving care he gets, he's adjusted extremely well."

Edith then left the office and went to Roy's room. Her visits had become routine. She first greeted him, read a couple chapters from the Bible, read the important sections of the newspaper and letters, and caught him up on the happenings of the family and community. By that time Roy would fall asleep and Edith would work on her knitting until Dan Blair came to give her a ride home. She was happy if Roy made even the slightest attempt to communicate.

After the cause of the Reeds' fire was determined and a warrant was issued for Dick's arrest, life returned to normal for Chief Hatfield. He spent at least ten hours a day at the fire station. He went to his weekly Lions' Club meeting and church on Sundays. However, the after-events of the fire had opened a part of his life that he never knew existed. He had shared the early frustrating hours of investigating that fire with an understanding woman. When his beloved aunt had died, that same woman was there to help him through the grieving process. Now that the crisis was over, he longed to share the routine of life with her, but she was fifteen thousand miles away.

This weekend I think I'll surprise Rebecca and call her. I'm going to need to do some exact calculations to get my time right. Andy pondered for a few minutes and made some scratches on his notepad. *They are one day ahead of us minus eight hours for daylight time. If I call around nine o'clock Saturday night, it would be one P.M. Sunday afternoon on Guam.* Andy could hardly wait for Saturday night to come. This was going to be one of the most unpredictable things he had done in his life.

The next Sunday afternoon, Rebecca returned from church, changed into her favorite pair of shorts, and fixed herself a hamburger with all the trimmings. She took her plate onto the balcony of her apartment and watched the children in the playground across the street. The tropical breeze blew through her hair. Suddenly the relaxing scene was interrupted by the shrill ring of the phone. She hurriedly pushed back the screen door and ran to the phone.

"Hello."

"Hello, Rebecca. How are you?"

Rebecca paused. *The voice is familiar, but it couldn't be,* she thought. *Maybe if I keep talking I can figure out who it is.*

"I'm doing fine. How are you doing?"

"Rebecca, you still don't know who this is, do you?"

"You sound so much like a friend in Montana, but I really can't tell."

Andy laughed. "This is your friend in Montana, Andy Hatfield. It's been several weeks since I've heard from you and wondered how things were going."

"Oh! Andy, thank you for calling. I'm so homesick I could cry. To answer your question, it was a hard adjustment at first," Rebecca admitted, "but except for being lonesome, I'm beginning to get settled in."

"I'm glad to hear things are going better. Have you made any new friends?"

"The head of the English department has kind of taken me under her wing. She's a native Chamorro who was educated in Portland, so she has a pretty good understanding of both cultures. Her daughter who's a senior has been working in the library as a student aide, so I'm getting personally involved with the entire family."

Andy smiled. "That was one of the reasons you wanted to go to Guam."

"It's a broadening experience for me, that's for sure," Rebecca replied. "A young teacher from South Carolina lives across the hall. This is her first teaching assignment and it's quite a struggle for her. She's in the toughest high school on the island and she lacks the experience and self-confidence to meet the demands."

"I imagine you're taking her under your wing the way Edith Dutton has helped most of the struggling young people in Rocky Bluff," Andy said.

"I'm trying," Rebecca admitted, "but I'd never be able to match Edith's achievements. She has so much wisdom and understanding."

"Although she always appears poised and in control, she's had many heartaches in her life," Andy reminded her. "I'm sure that's how she developed her compassion for others."

"Not to change the subject, but what do you hear from the high school? I really miss Grady Walker and all the other people there."

"Everything seems to be going well. The football team has won most of its games," Andy explained. "Ryan Reynolds suffered a sprained ankle and had to sit out a few games, but he's back in action as good as ever. I don't think the football team is good enough to make it to the state tournaments this year, but everyone is counting on the basketball team going all the way to the top."

"There are high school football and basketball teams here, but the main sport is soccer. I'm getting to be a real fan of our local team, especially the girls."

"Have you heard the outcome of the Reed fire?" Andy asked.

"No, I often wondered what happened to Dick Reed," Rebecca replied. "The first few weeks I was here, I received a lot of letters from Rocky Bluff, but they're getting few and far between now."

"We couldn't find the exact cause of the fire, so we called the state crime lab to help us. Marty Sanchez was here the next day. His brilliance never ceases to amaze me," Andy explained.

"So don't keep me in suspense," Rebecca chided. "What caused the fire?"

"It didn't take long for Marty to determine that the thermostat on the space heater in the hallway had been removed. Also, the heater had been lying on its side on top of a child's receiving blanket. To add to that, Dick had taken out a million-dollar insurance policy on Anita just three months prior to the fire. Needless to say, there's a warrant out for Dick's arrest, but no one knows where he is."

"Hasn't he even tried to contact his two remaining children?" Rebecca queried.

"Anita's parents haven't heard from him since they took the children back to Spokane with them," Andy explained. "It's all pretty strange."

"It's hard for me to believe that Dick Reed would be capable of murder," Rebecca replied. "He seemed to be such a strong family man."

"That's what we thought until we started checking his background," Andy replied. "It seems that he was married before and his first wife died mysteriously in a boating accident. Nothing was ever proven, but he had just taken out a large life insurance policy on her right before the boating accident also."

Rebecca looked worried. "Do the police have any clues at all?"

"He simply turned the running of the motel over to the handyman and disappeared. He's now on the FBI's most wanted list, but he seems to have vanished into thin air. The longer he's gone, the less likely it'll be that we'll find him."

Andy took a deep breath before continuing. "Rebecca, I don't want this conversation to end on a downer," he said. "I wanted to let you know that amidst that tragedy there was a good thing that came out of it."

"What's that?"

"I discovered that I enjoy being with you," Andy replied. "I just regret that it took so long for me to realize that I occasionally need female companionship. When I finally did, you were half a world away."

Rebecca's heart raced. "I feel much the same way," she replied. "Two years seems like a long time to be gone."

"I know," Andy sighed. "Maybe there'll be a way we can get together next summer. Right now it doesn't seem realistic, but stranger things have happened."

"You don't know how much I'd like that, but I signed a two-year contract and I can't let GCA down. The library is just beginning to take shape." Rebecca chuckled. "Maybe you could use some of those weeks of vacation time you've accumulated through the years."

"Don't laugh. Maybe I will."

Chapter 7

"Mom, I hope you'll be able to be at the store for our fortieth anniversary sale," Bob Harkness said as he relaxed in his mother's living room. "We're planning to have a big media blitz the week before, with ads in the paper and on TV and radio. We'll be serving the customary coffee, punch, and cookies, and I was wondering if you'd be there to greet people."

"I'd love to," Edith smiled. "It doesn't seem like its been forty years since your father first opened for business."

"It's seen a lot of changes through the years," Bob replied. "I guess the biggest tribute to Dad is when we opened the satellite store in Running Butte and Jean and Jim returned to Montana to run it."

"I thought when they moved to Idaho I'd only get to see them once or twice a year, and I would be just a voice on the telephone to my grandchildren. It is so nice to have them less than a hundred miles away."

Bob stretched out his legs and placed them on the footstool. "They're planning on being here for the big sale," he explained. "Larry Reynolds is more than capable of handling things without them. In fact, it won't be long before we might want to consider opening a third store and have him manage that one."

Edith beamed. "That'd be exciting. Not only from the business point of view, but from Larry's position. We've sure been through a lot with him through the years. He's grown from a rebellious sports star and abusive husband to a solid family man and business manager."

"Yes, and most of those changes have come about because of your influence."

"I haven't done anything out of the ordinary. I just happened to be in the right place at the right time." Edith took a deep breath as her mind raced back through the years. "I didn't choose to be the first one into the school office after he shot the principal. A few years later it was just a coincidence that it was my night to answer the crisis line when his wife called begging for help."

"Mom, stop being so modest. Anyone else would have panicked, but you had the calming words to defuse a hostile situation. You not only took care of the crisis, you followed up and became their friend and mentor, always expecting the best out of them."

"Through the years of teaching I've discovered that if you have high expectations for people, they will generally rise to the challenge. If you don't expect them to amount to anything, they won't," Edith explained.

"With that philosophy I can see why they named the new wing of the high school after you." Bob became silent as he stared out the picture window for several minutes.

"Mom, I'm afraid I'm not nearly as good a parent as you and Dad were," he muttered.

Edith studied her son's face, trying to understand the depth of his concern. "You have two beautiful teenage children," she protested.

"That I do, but they both have a mind of their own."

"You wouldn't want it any other way, would you?" Edith countered.

"Well, I was hoping that Jay would enroll in the business college at the University of Montana, but all he can talk about is joining the air force as soon as he graduates."

"What's wrong with that?"

"Dad worked hard to start this store and I was hoping we could pass it on to the next generation of Harknesses."

"The thing your dad would have liked the most is for his grandchildren to follow their own dreams and set their own course in life."

"I know, but I've always felt that joining the military out of high school was only for those who didn't have the ability to go on to college."

Edith smiled. "You've been too absorbed in that store to see what's going on with the career choices of young people lately," she chided. "Many use the military as a way to an education, not a way to escape it. Let Jay make his own decisions and he'll be okay."

"You're probably right," Bob sighed, "but it seems so unnatural to have a daughter who's more interested in the hardware business than a son. It's amazing to watch Dawn tinker with the broken lawn mowers that come in. At fourteen I think she knows how to use every tool in the store."

"Maybe she's your answer to keeping the store in the family," Edith replied. "Who says a woman can't successfully run a business? I was afraid to try when your father died, but times are different now. Businesswomen are finally obtaining their due respect."

Bob smiled as he again gazed out the front window. His mother always seemed to have the right words to keep the struggles of day-to-day life in perspective.

✑

"Ella Mae, it looks like school must be going better for you," Rebecca said as she met her neighbor on the steps to their apartment building.

"Oh, yeah," Ella Mae grinned. "I only had two discipline referrals today. Why don't you stop over at my apartment and I'll update you on the exciting happenings of GW High School."

The change in Ella Mae's mood was enough to peak Rebecca's curiosity as she followed the young teacher into her one-bedroom apartment. "Okay, what gives?" Rebecca teased. "Discipline referrals don't bring that kind of grin."

"Seriously," Ella Mae tried to protest. "My classroom control is getting better, but I don't think it's because of my great teaching ability."

"What else could it be?"

"Major Lee spotted my frustrations right away. He also noticed that the ring leaders were in his ROTC program and that was all it took."

Rebecca looked puzzled. "What difference would that make?"

"A lot," Ella Mae laughed. "Instead of writing a referral to the office, where they could sit in the detention room and sleep for an hour or two, I send them to Major Lee. No one likes that. He has them running laps and doing push-ups. My discipline problems are down seventy-five percent and the principal thinks I'm a great teacher to have the students under such good control."

Rebecca broke into gales of laughter. "It may not be the conventional way of doing things, but nothings works better than success."

"Major Lee has been stopping by my classroom after school nearly every day. It gives me something to look forward to after a hot, frustrating day," Ella Mae confided.

Rebecca's eyes danced. "O. . .o. . .oh. . .sounds serious."

"Nothing like that," the young teacher protested. "We're both lonesome and need someone to talk to. He's from Elberton, Georgia, which is only thirty-five miles from where I grew up in South Carolina. We 'rebels' have to stick together. There's few of us left."

"I bet you still sing 'Dixie' every day," Rebecca teased.

"Naah. . . They outlawed that a long time ago."

Rebecca's voice became serious. "Has Major Lee been on Guam long?"

"This is his second year of a two-year contract," Ella Mae replied. "He's already counting the days until he can go home. His brother wants him to come back to Georgia so they can go into the publishing business together. Now he wishes he would have returned as soon as he retired from active duty, but he'd never served in the Pacific before and found the possibility of coming to Guam intriguing."

"He sounds interesting," Rebecca said. "I'd like to meet him sometime."

"I'm sure you'd like him. We were planning on attending the Christmas parade. Why don't you come with us?"

"I wouldn't want to intrude on your date," Rebecca protested.

"It's not a date. A group of stateside teachers from GW were planning on going together and making it a day."

Rebecca looked at her friend with interest. "In that case, where and when is it?"

"It's the Friday after Thanksgiving. The entire island turns out and they block off Marine Drive for part of the day. They say the floats made from palm fronds are beautiful. I'd really like you to join us. It should be a lot of fun," Ella Mae insisted.

"Thanks," Rebecca smiled. "I wouldn't miss it for the world."

"Major Lee is making arrangements for us to go to Tarrague Beach at Anderson Air Force Base after the parade. He says that's one of the perks he gets for having stayed in the army for twenty years."

"Mitzi was telling me about that beach," Rebecca replied. "They say it's the most beautiful one on the island, but the locals don't have access to it since it's on a military reservation."

Ella Mae shrugged her shoulders. "I don't know anything about that. I'm just anxious to see the beach. Our gym teacher is planning on bringing a volleyball and net and we're all chipping in on the food."

"Let me know what I can bring," Rebecca replied as she rose to leave. As she returned to her own apartment, Rebecca became pensive. *I've spent most of my time here thinking about how lonely I am and how much I miss Rocky Bluff. I haven't ventured farther than the school, church, and grocery store. If I'm going to take fullest advantage of my time on Guam, I've got to experience more of the culture and see more of the sights.*

The next morning when Rebecca signed in at the school office, there was a poster on the bulletin board.

EVERYONE'S INVITED TO THE ALL-SCHOOL FIESTA
THANKSGIVING DAY FROM NOON—?.
PLEASE SEE MITZI QUINATA FOR
MENU SUGGESTIONS.

Rebecca's interest was peaked. She had heard of Mexican fiestas, but never a Guamanian fiesta. She hurried to the library and began setting up for the day. It wasn't long before the door opened.

"Hi, Rebecca. Are you coming to the Thanksgiving Day Fiesta?" Mitzi asked.

"Perhaps," Rebecca said as she laid a stack of books on the table. "I'm anxious to learn more about it."

"We want to make our stateside teachers and students feel welcome. I know it must be hard to be away from your families during the holiday season, so we're throwing the fiesta in your honor. You don't have to bring a thing. We want to share some of our Guamanian dishes with you."

"What's different here than on the mainland?" Rebecca queried.

"By eating in the school cafeteria, you've already experienced our red rice," Mitzi explained. "We have our own version of Southern spareribs. You won't want to miss out on our chicken *kelaguen,* which combines coconut, chicken, onion, peppers, salt, and lemon juice. However, there's one dish I want to warn you about and that's *finadene.* It's a very, very hot sauce using deceivingly small Guamanian peppers. The kids like to coax the newcomers into taking a mouthful of it and then sit back and watch the reactions."

Rebecca laughed. "Thanks for the warning. I'll be suspicious of any sauce the kids are too anxious for me to try."

As Rebecca went about her daily tasks, her sense of isolation was replaced by the sense of adventure that she once felt when she first began considering coming to Guam. Instead of being alone for the holidays, she had many new friends to share the festivities with.

⚘

"Fetch it, Shushu," Jeffy Blair shouted as he threw the rubber ball across the front lawn for the Pekingese to retrieve. Shushu scampered across the lawn, picked up the ball, and dropped it at Jeffy's feet. Jeffy took the ball and threw it again. At first the game was fun for the five-year-old, but it didn't take long for its repetitiveness to become boring. Seeing his dad raking leaves on the other side of the drive, Jeffy could not resist the three-foot pile. He took a running jump into the very center. Leaves flew everywhere.

"Jeffy, I've been working all afternoon trying to get these raked before the first snowfall," Dan scolded lightheartedly. "I don't want them scattered all over the lawn again."

Dan's words were lost in the crisp autumn air as Jeffy took another flying leap into the pile. As Jeffy lay giggling in the leaves, a screech of tires echoed from the street, accompanied by a loud yelp. A car door slammed as Dan and Jeffy ran toward the curb, where Shushu lay shaking on the side of the street. His back leg twisted into contortions. Chief Hatfield knelt beside the stricken dog and shook his head.

"It doesn't look good," he said to Dan.

Dan nodded in agreement as he put his arm around his son.

"It's my fault, Daddy," Jeffy sobbed. "I was supposed to watch Shushu and keep her out of the street. If anything happens to her, Rebecca will really be mad at me."

"Let's take her to the vet and see if Doc Howe can fix her up," Chief Hatfield said. "I really feel bad about this."

Dan hurried to the back porch and found an old blanket. Gently he wrapped the dog in the quilt and climbed into the backseat of the fire chief's car, followed closely by his crying son. Chief Hatfield took a short-cut across town to the animal clinic. Fortunately, when they arrived, Doc Howe was just returning from the Reynolds' ranch, where he'd been vaccinating cows.

"What happened here?" Doc Howe asked as he surveyed the bundle in Dan's arms and the sobbing child beside him.

"I'm afraid I wasn't watching close enough and the dog ran into the street in front of me," Chief Hatfield explained. "I hope you'll be able to fix her up. She belongs to Rebecca Sutherland and Jeffy was taking care of her while she's on Guam."

"We'll have to take some X-rays and see what's broken," Doc Howe said as he motioned for Dan to bring the dog to the examining room. "The way she's shivering, I'm afraid she's going into shock."

As Shushu laid on the table, each breath became further and further apart until there was no movement at all.

"I'm afraid she's gone," Doc Howe said softly. "Would you like me to take care of her?"

"I'd appreciate it if you would," Chief Hatfield replied. "Would you be able to have her buried at the pet cemetery on Boot Hill? I'm sure that's what Rebecca would want."

"No problem at all," the veterinarian assured them. "I'll have a wooden marker made with her name and date of death."

"What am I going to tell Rebecca when she comes home?" Jeffy sobbed. "I promised her I'd take good care of her dog."

Andy put his arm around the boy. "Don't worry about a thing. I'll call her this weekend and tell her it was all my fault. I should have been watching closer as I pulled away from the Reeds' home."

"I should be responsible for the long-distance call," Dan protested.

"No problem," Chief Hatfield replied. "I wanted an excuse to call her anyway. I just didn't want it to be one with bad news."

That Saturday evening Andy dialed Rebecca's number on Guam. He waited as he heard a number of clicks on the line and then ringing.

"Hello," a soft voice answered.

"Hello, Rebecca. How are you?"

"Andy, this time I know your voice."

"It's amazing that our connection is as clear as if we were just across town," Andy responded.

"They say that when they laid the fiber-optic cable to Guam a few years ago, it made a big difference in the telephone reception," Rebecca explained. "Before the cable, the signal had to be beamed to a satellite and back down, so it was subject to a lot of weather interference. Now it just zips along on the cable."

"You're definitely on the information superhighway now," Andy chuckled.

"So much the better for keeping up on the Rocky Bluff news," Rebecca replied as floods of memories engulfed her. "What's going on there?"

Andy took a deep breath. "I have some bad news for you. There was an accident in front of your house and I'm afraid I'm the one who's responsible."

"What happened?"

"I went to the Reeds' house to secure it before winter set in," the fire chief explained. "When I was leaving, I saw Jeffy playing with Shushu in your yard. All of a sudden the dog darted in front of my car and I didn't have time to stop. We took her to the vet's, but it was too late. I had her buried at the pet cemetery on Boot Hill. I'm really sorry."

There was a long pause before Rebecca replied, "Those things happen. Did Jeffy see the whole thing?"

"I'm afraid he did and he blamed himself for not watching the dog closer, but there was nothing he could have done. I think he cried for hours."

"I feel so bad for him," Rebecca sighed. "He has such a tender spirit and hurts so easily. I'll call him and let him know that I don't hold him responsible. I appreciate you calling and letting me know."

"I wanted an excuse to call you anyway, but I'm sorry it had to be bad news. I'm anxious to know how things are going in Guam."

Rebecca began telling about her experiences at her first Guamanian fiesta, the Christmas parade, and her trip to Tarrague Beach. "The strangest part of the holidays here is seeing Santa and his sleigh on top of a palm tree," she giggled. "Everyone seems to take it as normal, while I nearly laugh out loud every time I see one."

While the conversation continued in a jovial vein, the bond of commonality and depth of understanding grew with each passing moment. When they finally hung up the phone, Rebecca smiled to herself. *Mother* used to tell me that 'Absence makes the heart grow fonder' was just a cliché and it never happens that way, but this time I think Mother was wrong. The longer I'm away from Rocky Bluff, the fonder I'm becoming of Andy.

Chapter 8

Dawn, do you think you'd be able to sing here at the care center sometime this month?" Edith queried as her fourteen-year-old granddaughter pulled up a chair beside her step-grandfather.

"I'd be glad to," Dawn replied, "but I'll have to have clearance from the principal."

Edith smiled as the face of her former employer flashed before her. "I'll give Grady Walker a call. He's been extremely cooperative in excusing the students to perform here."

Dawn turned her attention back to her grandfather. "Would you like me to sing for you and your friends?"

Roy smiled and squeezed Dawn's hand. He tried to talk, but his words were inaudible.

Dawn turned her attention back to her grandmother. "I never get nervous when I perform here," she confided. "These people make me feel so welcome and appreciate everything I do, despite how bad I might sound."

"I've been extremely pleased with the community's response to my request for local talent," Edith said. "Even the fire chief has consented to come and play his accordion."

Dawn giggled. "You mean Andy Hatfield has musical ability? He always appeared as an athletic junkie to me."

"I've never heard him myself, but those who have say he has quite a repertoire of the golden oldies," Edith explained. "Those are the kind the residents seem to enjoy the most."

Dawn stayed for fifteen more minutes and shared the activities that were going on at the high school.

"Grandma, if you'd excuse me, I'd like to visit some of the others. There are a couple of ladies on the next wing I've gotten kind of attached to."

Edith beamed as she watched her granddaughter leave the room. *It's refreshing to see interest in other generations spreading throughout Rocky Bluff. I hate to see each age group become isolated.*

❧

"Rebecca, what are you planning to do over Christmas vacation?" Ella Mae asked as the two relaxed on the patio of Rebecca's apartment.

"I thought it might be a good time to take in some local flavor," Rebecca replied. "For a beginning I wanted to go boonie stomping through the jungle and visit Talafofo Falls."

"Sounds like fun." Ella Mae watched the children in the playground below before continuing. "Major Lee is planning on flying back to Georgia to help his brother. They'd like to be able to open their doors for business as soon as he gets back in June. He's going to take some Christmas presents back to my family in South Carolina."

"Why don't we plan to do something special together while we have the free time?" Rebecca queried.

"Major Lee said I shouldn't return to the mainland without first visiting Saipan. He says there are a lot of World War Two relics there and an old jail where it's rumored that Amelia Earhart and her navigator were held by the Japanese before they died."

"Hmmm. I never thought about island hopping," Rebecca replied. "The other Mariannas Islands are only a hundred miles from here. They say the planes that dropped the atomic bombs on Hiroshima and Nagasaki took off from the airstrip on Tinian. That ought to be interesting to see."

Ella Mae was bursting with excitement. "I'll stop at the visitors' bureau for travel guides. Major Lee can point out the best places to see and where to stay. This could be the most exciting Christmas vacation we'll ever have."

After school the next day, Ella Mae knocked at Rebecca's door with a handful of travel brochures in her hand.

"Rebecca, look at these," she exclaimed as soon as her friend opened the door. "We've got to take our cameras and stay on Saipan as long as we can. It's dotted with beaches and breathtaking precipices. There's Bird Island and the Grotto, which is a sunken pool connecting the ocean by twin underwater passages. I can hardly wait."

"Slow down. Slow down," Rebecca chided. "Let me see what you have."

Ella Mae and Rebecca spread the literature across the kitchen table. Their eyes danced as they surveyed the pictures of secluded sandy white beaches and windsurfers frolicking on the waves. "This is the place for me," Ella Mae announced. "In fact, I've found the perfect hotel to stay at."

"Where's that?"

"Right here at the Pacific Regency," Ella Mae replied as she uncovered a brochure hidden on the bottom of the stack. "Look, it includes twelve acres of lush gardens and international gourmet dining. There's tennis and windsurfing. What else could we want?"

"Fantastic," Rebecca exclaimed. "Let's call the travel agency and make the reservations. "How about flying over the day before Christmas and coming home the second of January?"

Rebecca took the phone and dialed the number on the back of one of the folders. Within minutes they both had given their credit card numbers, and the hotel and flight reservations were confirmed. They began to plan what they would pack. This was going to be their most exciting Christmas vacation ever.

Two weeks later Rebecca and Ella Mae deplaned at the Saipan Airport. Instead of a rolling passenger gate meeting the plane, they deplaned into the tropical sun on the landing strip and walked into the nearby terminal. They waited in line to show the immigration inspector the necessary paperwork. Although Saipan is a commonwealth of the United States and passports are not needed, both women were glad they had brought theirs along to expedite their entrance into the terminal. They hurried to the car rental agency near the entrance.

"Hafa adai," Rebecca greeted.

"Hello," the local agent responded. "May I help you?"

"We'd like to rent an economy car until the second of January," Rebecca replied.

"We have just the one you need," the agent replied as he pointed to a small Japanese car parked outside his window.

"That'll be perfect," Ella Mae said as Rebecca began filling out the paperwork.

The two women finished packing their luggage into the small trunk and slid onto the front seat of the car. Rebecca started the engine and they both breathed a sigh of relief as the air conditioner began blowing cool air.

"Ahh. This is the life," Ella Mae uttered as Rebecca steered the car onto the main street.

Both were amazed at the lack of hustle and bustle compared to Guam. Somehow Saipan had been able to retain the quietude of a getaway island.

"Let's check in at the Pacific Regency and then go exploring," Rebecca said. "Would you look at the map and tell me where to turn?"

Upon arrival at the hotel parking lot, Rebecca and Ella Mae took their luggage from the trunk of the car and walked toward the front door. As soon as the door opened in front of her, Rebecca gasped and froze. She immediately jumped backward away from the doorway.

"What's wrong?" Ella Mae asked. "You look like you've seen a ghost."

"I have," Rebecca stammered. "The man working the front desk used to be my next-door neighbor. He's accused of setting his house on fire where his wife and two children died. He's wanted in Rocky Bluff on three counts of homicide."

Ella Mae trembled with excitement. "What are you going to do?"

Rebecca's heart raced. "I've got to get to a phone where I can call the mainland."

"I think I saw an international telephone center on our way in," Ella Mae replied.

The women hurried across the parking lot, threw their luggage back in the trunk, and jumped into the car. Rebecca retraced her path toward the airport until she saw the phone center sign. They parked the car by the curb and rushed inside. The room was lined with oversized booths.

"Can I make a call to Montana from here?" Rebecca asked the woman behind the desk.

"That's what we're here for," the clerk smiled. "I'll punch in your code for booth twenty-three. It'll record the cost of your call and you can pay as you leave."

Rebecca reached in her purse, which contained her address book with Andy's phone number. She closed the door to the booth and punched the necessary thirteen digits. It seemed forever before a familiar voice was on the other end of the line.

"Hello, Andy," Rebecca gasped without waiting for a response. "I just saw Dick Reed."

"You what?" Andy shouted into the phone.

"A friend and I came to Saipan for the holidays. We were about to check in to the Pacific Regency Hotel when I saw Dick behind the desk," Rebecca explained.

"Did he see you?" Andy asked excitedly.

"I don't think so. I stepped back outside the door just as soon as I saw him. What should I do next?"

"The Commonwealth of the Northern Marinas Islands is a part of the United States and the FBI should have an office there. Go to their office and report what you have just seen to the special agent in charge. Dick Reed is on the FBI's most wanted list. I'm sure the special agent there will recognize his name. If the FBI agent needs more information have him contact Stuart Leonard, our county attorney. Just don't let Dick Reed know you're on the island."

"Thanks a lot," Rebecca sighed. "I hope they can catch him and put him away for a long time. I'll try to call you after I've been to the FBI."

The conversation was kept brief and to the point. Rebecca hung up the phone and returned to the counter. "That will be eighteen dollars and thirty-five cents," the clerk said as she checked the monitor and punched the amount into the cash register.

Rebecca handed her a twenty-dollar bill and waited while she counted back the change.

"Is there an FBI office on Saipan?"

"Yes, they're in the same office as the U.S. Attorney in the Horiguchi Building in Garripan," the clerk replied with a quizzical look.

"How do I get there?" Rebecca queried. "I have a map here if you wouldn't mind tracing the route."

The clerk took the map and made a dotted line to the Horiguchi Building. "This should help," she replied as she handed the map back. "It's not hard to find since it's the tallest building on the island."

"Thanks for your help," Rebecca replied as she and Ella Mae hurried out the door.

Upon arriving at the government building, Rebecca and Ella Mae consulted the building directory and took the escalator to the third floor. After passing through security, they were admitted to the U.S. Attorney's Office. Rebecca asked to see the special agent in charge of the FBI office. She was immediately ushered into a small, plain office.

"My name is Eric Grimes. How may I help you?"

Rebecca introduced herself and explained about Dick Reed and the fire. She then went on to tell how she had just seen him at the front desk of the Pacific Regency Hotel and had called the fire chief of Rocky Bluff, Montana, who had suggested she come to see him.

The agent took frantic notes as she was speaking. When he had finished, he typed Dick Reed's name into the computer. Instantly his picture, description, and criminal charges appeared on the screen.

"Here's our man," Agent Grimes exclaimed, slamming his fist on the desk.

"It's quite common for fugitives to come to the U.S. islands in the Pacific. They are as far away from the mainland as they can possibly be and they can enter without a passport, but I'm going to need an official request from the local police authorities before I can pick him up."

"Our fire chief said you should contact our local county attorney, Stuart Leonard, in Rocky Bluff, Montana," she replied. "But it's now late at night in Montana."

"Would Dick Reed recognize you if he saw you again?" Agent Grimes asked.

"Certainly," Rebecca replied. "We were next-door neighbors for many years."

"Do you think he saw you at the hotel?"

"I think I stepped back fast enough."

"Good. I recommend you spend the night at another hotel," Eric suggested.

"But we already have reservations at the Pacific Regency," Rebecca protested.

"That's no problem. Let me make some phone calls."

Rebecca and Ella Mae sat quietly while the special agent made two brief calls. After hanging up the phone, he turned back to them.

"You're all registered at the Hikishi Hotel just a couple blocks from the Regency. I'll let you know just as soon as we have him in custody and then you can go wherever you like."

"Thanks for your help," Rebecca replied as she rose to leave. "I don't want to have someone who's responsible for the death of his wife and children living in luxury on a tropical island."

When Rebecca and Ella Mae finally checked into their hotel room, Ella Mae collapsed across the bed.

"I said we were going to have the most exciting Christmas ever, but I didn't expect all of this."

"You and me both," Rebecca agreed as she looked at her watch and thought a moment. "It's so late back home I don't dare call Andy now. Let's go get something to eat and I'll call him in the morning and wish him a Merry Christmas."

After a delicious Christmas Eve dinner, the pair sat on the lanai of the hotel and watched the sun set over the Pacific. The meaning of Christmas for all people took on an even greater significance for Rebecca after interacting with a multitude of cultures within the last five months.

The first thing Christmas morning, Rebecca calculated the time difference and dialed the familiar Rocky Bluff telephone number.

"Merry Christmas," Andy greeted.

"Merry Christmas to you," Rebecca echoed. "I hope I called at a good time."

"For you any time is a good time. I was hoping you'd call last night after you'd been to the FBI."

"It would have been too late," Rebecca explained, "and I didn't want to disturb you."

"Don't worry about the time. I never have a problem getting back to sleep. So how's it going?"

"Special Agent Eric Grimes did verify that Dick Reed is his man, but he's waiting to get verification from Stuart Leonard before he picks him up.

Christmas is a hard time to carry on business," Rebecca replied. "He made reservations for Ella Mae and me at the Hikishi Hotel and told us to stay away from the Pacific Regency until they have Dick Reed in custody."

The wrinkles on Andy's forehead faded. "I've already talked with Stu and he's so excited about locating Dick he could scarcely contain himself. Call me again as soon as you know more. I'll never be able to thank you enough for what you've done."

Rebecca laughed. "All I've done is come to Saipan for Christmas break to relax in the sun."

"You've demonstrated all kinds of wisdom ever since the frantic ringing of your doorbell the night of the fire," Andy replied. "Although you're miles away, I feel so close to you."

Rebecca's eyes misted as she shot an embarrassed glance toward Ella Mae, who was reading another travel guide. "Andy, I feel the same way. I can hardly wait to see you again. There isn't a day that goes by that I don't think about you and Rocky Bluff. I can't believe it'll be over a year before I can go home again."

"Maybe it will be sooner than you think," Andy replied. "If things continue going the way they are, Stuart Leonard will probably need to have you come back to testify at the trial. We'll just have to see what happens."

Rebecca looked pensive. "If it goes to court, I hope it's during summer vacation. I was planning on taking a few courses at the University of Guam this summer, but I could take what I was going to spend on tuition and fly home."

"Who knows. Maybe the court will think your testimony is so vital they'll fly you home to testify," Andy pondered. "Please let me know as soon as you hear from Eric Grimes. I don't care what time it is, night or day. You have my work number, so don't hesitate to call me there if I'm not at home."

"Will do," Rebecca promised.

Again the conversation ended on a jovial note of the description of relaxing on the beaches of a tropical paradise. It wasn't as much the words that were shared as it was the unspoken feelings that flowed over the phone lines that added excitement to Rebecca's spirit.

"Love is connected to a telephone wire," she snickered to herself.

Ella Mae watched her older friend as she hung up the phone and stared out the hotel window to the ocean below.

"You seem like you're a thousand miles away," she chided.

"More like seventeen thousand," Rebecca replied as she turned her attention back to her friend. "I'm letting myself do what I said I wouldn't. . .

reminiscing about home. What are we going to do tomorrow?"

"There's an announcement in the lobby for snorkeling lessons. It said they'd provide all the gear. Want to give it a try?" Ella Mae coaxed.

"Me snorkel?" Rebecca chided. "There are some things people over fifty just shouldn't do!"

"Perhaps," Ella Mae teased, "but snorkeling isn't one of them. In fact, you're probably in better physical condition than I am."

Rebecca grinned. "Then it's a deal. Tomorrow I'll go make reservations for the two of us. If we do this, I want lots of pictures. No one in Rocky Bluff will believe I had the courage to go snorkeling. In fact, most probably don't even know what it is."

The next two days Rebecca and Ella Mae took advantage of every possible tourist activity available. Rebecca thought she had never had as much fun as she was having, however a nagging worry kept hanging over her. *When will Eric Grimes call about Dick Reed? I don't dare go near the Pacific Regency until this is all over.*

Finally, Friday afternoon, when they had just returned from the beach to change before dinner, the phone rang.

"Hello," a deep male voice greeted. "May I speak with Rebecca Sutherland?"

"Speaking."

"This is Special Agent Eric Grimes. I just wanted you to know that I talked with the county attorney in Rocky Bluff, Montana, and he verified that he was the one who issued the warrant for the arrest of Dick Reed. We now have Mr. Reed in custody and he'll appear before the U.S. District Court in Saipan in two weeks for extradition to Montana. After that, marshals of the U.S. Justice Department will escort him back to Rocky Bluff. You may now travel anyplace on the island without fear of being spotted by Mr. Reed. I want to thank you for your cooperation. Citizens like you make this job so much easier. If there's anything I can do to make your stay on Saipan more pleasant, please let me know."

Rebecca hung up the phone and collapsed on the bed sobbing.

Ella Mae put her hand on Rebecca's shoulder to comfort her. "What's wrong? Can I do anything to help?"

"No," Rebecca smiled through her tears. "I'm just relieved. It's finally over. Dick Reed is behind bars. Justice can now be served."

Chapter 9

E dith, would you like to have dinner with us Sunday?" Dan asked as he drove his older friend home from one of her daily visits to the care center. "We've been so busy during the holiday season that Beth and I haven't had much time to socialize."

"I'd love to," Edith replied. "Besides, I haven't seen Jeffy for several weeks."

Dan smiled mysteriously. "He's been asking about you lately. He has some exciting news for you."

"And you won't tell me what it is, will you?" Edith teased.

"I wouldn't ruin his surprise for anything."

The next Sunday the pew next to Edith was vacant when the Blair family entered the church. Jeffy was the first to spot his adopted grandmother and hurried for the seat beside her. His parents followed close behind.

"Hi, Grandma Edith. Can I sit with you?"

"Sure, Honey," Edith responded as she patted the spot next to her. "This seat has your name on it."

"I have a secret," Jeffy whispered, "but I can't tell you until dinner."

"Can you give me a clue?" Edith smiled.

"Just one clue. It has to do with Mommy."

"Is she fixing your favorite food for dinner?"

Jeffy shook his head as the organist began to play the prelude and a quiet hush spread throughout the church.

Edith surveyed the couple. A little more than six months before they had said their wedding vows before this same altar. Dan not only promised to take Beth as his wife, but Jeffy as his son. The adoption was finalized within days after Dan and Beth's marriage. *I've never seen Beth this radiant,* Edith thought as the congregation stood to sing the opening hymn. *Married life must be good for her.*

That afternoon as Edith and the Blairs finished their dessert around the dining room table in Rebecca Sutherland's home, Edith turned to Jeffy. "When are you going to tell me your secret?"

Jeffy looked questioningly at his mother, who nodded her approval.

"I'm going to have a new brother," Jeffy announced. "His name's going to be Danny."

Edith reached out and patted Beth's hand. "I'm so happy for all of you. When is he due?"

"The end of June," Beth replied. "Having Dan's child would be the best anniversary present I could possibly have."

"I get to help take care of my new brother," Jeffy announced.

Edith turned her attention back to the proud child. "What if you have a little sister?" she teased.

Jeffy shrugged his shoulders. "That'll be okay. We'll just call her Edith."

Dan flushed. "I guess the secret's out," he sighed. "We wanted to surprise you with the name if a girl was born."

Edith paused. She thought back through all the trials and tribulations she had shared with both Beth and Dan. "I'd be honored, but having a namesake carries a big responsibility to be a role model."

"We know," Dan replied. "Because you're a perfect example of compassion, if we have a girl, we want our daughter to bear your name."

Edith shook her head in amusement. "Surely after all these years you've seen my feet of clay."

"Yes, but we also know your feet are grounded on a solid Rock and you never waiver," Beth replied. "We just want to say thanks for all you've done for us throughout the years."

Edith's eyes misted. "I've grown to love you all as if you were my own flesh and blood." She paused a moment. "Speaking of flesh and blood, I have some other good news for you. Jean and Jim are expecting their second baby about the same time."

"That'll be fun, having the two exactly the same age," Beth beamed. "I'm sure Gloria is as excited about a sibling as Jeffy."

Edith spent the remainder of the afternoon visiting with Beth and Dan and reading stories to Jeffy. Jeffy was already able to identify most of the letters in the alphabet, and he enjoyed pointing them out to anyone who took the time to listen.

※

"I finally have Dick Reed locked in our jail," Phil Mooney exclaimed as he entered Chief Hatfield's office in the fire station. "It took the wheels of justice a long time to work, but the federal marshals flew in with him last night on the Treasure State Airlines."

"I imagine Dick wasn't very pleased to be back in Rocky Bluff," Andy replied dryly.

Phil grinned. "I think he was enjoying himself a little too much on

Saipan. It was about time his life of leisure ended. Seven months on the loose gave him a false sense of security."

"Stuart Leonard has been working on his prosecution for months. What attorney do you think will defend him?" Andy queried.

"Dick claims he doesn't have any money to hire a lawyer, so Judge Eubanks will have to appoint one," Phil responded. "My guess is that it will be Dave Wood. He's young and eager to get involved in heavy-duty cases."

Andy shook his head. "This would be his first major criminal case. I hope he doesn't get overwhelmed."

"I'm confident he'll do all right," Phil assured him. "He has some close attorney friends in Great Falls and Billings who'll be able to advise him if he gets into trouble."

"I'm glad it's him and not me," Andy retorted. "After all we've been through during the investigation, I don't think I could be very objective."

"That's what lawyers are paid for," Phil replied as he looked at his watch. "Guess it's time I get back to the station. They get extremely upset with me if I mess up their lunch schedules."

Andy could hardly wait for Saturday so he could call Rebecca. "Figuring out the time difference is such an inconvenience," he muttered to himself.

Saturday evening Andy dialed Rebecca's number on Guam and waited impatiently for the connection to be made.

"Hello."

"Hello, Rebecca. This is Andy. How are you doing?"

"Andy, it's good to hear your voice again. Until early Saturday morning I was doing great."

Wrinkles creased the fire chief's forehead. "And then what happened?"

"Some teachers and I decided to go boonie stomping through the jungles yesterday," Rebecca laughed. "The vegetation and view of the ocean was beautiful, but now I'm sunburned and covered with mosquito bites. I hurt so bad I couldn't get out of bed to go to church this morning."

Andy chuckled as he pictured her reddened face and arms.

"I hope you took lots of pictures. Times like those I'd like to be there to share them with you."

"I wish you were here, too. It'd be so much fun to explore the island together," Rebecca said as she rubbed more lotion on her sunburn. "There's so much to do and see, I don't know if I'll get it all taken in by the time my contract is up."

"Maybe you'll want to renew it," Andy teased.

"No way. I miss you and all my friends in Rocky Bluff too much. Don't prolong my suspense. What's the latest news from home?"

"Tuesday the federal marshals brought Dick Reed back to the local jail. It looks like Dave Wood will be defending him."

"Isn't he pretty young and inexperienced to handle a homicide case?" Rebecca queried.

"Few lawyers in this state are experienced with homicide cases. There's just not that many of them. I think he'll do a fine job."

A look of concern spread across Rebecca's face. "How soon will it get to trial?"

"Probably the first week of July. Will it be any problem for you to come back?"

"I'd love to, but I don't think I'll be able to afford it," Rebecca sighed.

"I imagine they'll subpoena you and then the court will pay your transportation. You'll be one of their key witnesses. I'll let you know when I have more of the details from Stuart Leonard."

Rebecca beamed. "I was planning on taking a few courses this summer at the University of Guam just to pass the time, but a trip back would be so much better. I'm getting so homesick I can hardly stand it."

"With that in mind, why don't you start marking your calendar? There are only nine weeks left of school and then you can come home for the summer. I'm sure the second school year will be much easier than the first."

"I'll need the second year to reap the fruits of my hard work of this year. I'm beginning to get used to hearing a mosaic of languages around me," Rebecca admitted. "Even my library automation project is progressing nicely."

"I always knew you could do it. When you started to get cold feet about your capabilities while we were in Hawaii, I realized how dedicated to quality library services you actually were."

Rebecca blushed under her sunburn. "I couldn't have done it without a lot of parent volunteers. Many of the military wives are immersed in their children's school and volunteer all their free time to help in the library."

"That could be either an asset or a liability, depending on their objectivity toward their own child," Andy chuckled.

Rebecca smiled. "Fortunately, most of our parents are just here to help and don't try to tell us how to do our jobs. As out of my own element as I am, I don't think I could stand any outside pressure."

"Hang in there," Andy replied. "You'll soon be home for good. Just savor each moment you have there. You may never be able to return once your contract is over."

"I know. That's why I try to go to as many cultural events as possible.

A couple weeks ago I went to the Discovery Day parade and fiesta. I really had a lot of fun and met a lot of the local people."

"I hate to show my ignorance as far as world history, but who did discover Guam?" Andy queried. "Obviously not Columbus."

"On March 6, 1521, Magellan first sighted Guam. Spain then dominated the island for nearly three hundred years." Rebecca hesitated. "I hate to waste your long-distance phone call giving you a history lesson. I'll write you a long letter and send you some informational brochures. This place is absolutely fascinating."

"I guess you're right," Andy sighed. "It's just so good to talk to you again. I'm looking forward to seeing you this summer."

"I can hardly wait," Rebecca replied. "Do take care of yourself."

"Good-bye, dear. I love you."

"I love you, too."

Rebecca hung up the phone. *I always thought that love would have to be exactly like what I had with Eric years ago, but love for Andy is so different, so relaxing. I think I'll write Edith a letter explaining my feelings toward Andy. She, more than anyone, will understand someone loving deeply and then having another love later in life.*

Dear Edith,

I just hung up from a long conversation with Andy. I miss him so much I can hardly stand it. It's strange how our friendship has developed into love while we're separated. I never thought I'd find anyone like Eric, so I figured I'd never fall in love again. Andy is so different from Eric and yet equally special. Now I can understand how you and George were so happy together all those years and yet when you met Roy you could again develop a loving relationship.

How is Roy doing? He was such a vivacious, outgoing person, it's hard to see him no longer able to communicate. I know he's getting excellent care, but I know it must be awfully hard for you to be separated.

There's a chance I'll be coming home this summer. Andy said that Dick Reed will be going to trial and I'll be one of the key witnesses. I hope I can see you then. I miss our long, heart-to-heart conversations.

Give my regards to Roy.

Love,
Rebecca

"Mom, Dad," Jay began as he lingered around the kitchen table after dinner. "The air force recruiter was at school today. I'm convinced that enlisting in the air force is what I want to do after high school."

"Are you sure you don't want to go to college?" Nancy Harkness protested. "If you majored in business, you'd be ready to take over the store when your dad retires."

"Dad and I have discussed this before," Jay reminded them. "I want to join the air force and see the world outside Montana."

"You could always join ROTC while you're in college and then you can go into the air force as an officer," Nancy continued.

"I know," Jay replied. "The recruiter explained all that to me, but I'd rather join the service now and take classes wherever I'm stationed. This is what I really want to do; I was hoping that I'd have your support."

Nancy looked chagrined. "Of course we'll support you in whatever you choose to do. It's just hard for me to think about you leaving home for good."

"We've got to accept the fact that our first baby has grown up," Bob snickered as he slapped his son on the shoulder. "When are you going to sign up?"

"There's a teachers' in-service day next Friday, so we don't have to go to class. I was wondering if you'd come with me to the air force recruiting station in Great Falls that day?" Jay queried.

Nancy and Bob exchanged questioning glances. "I think we could arrange that," Bob replied. "I'll call Larry Reynolds and see if he can take time from the Running Butte store for a couple days. We could spend the night and do some fun things while we're there. It might be the last time we'll get to take a trip together for some time."

"Thanks, Mom, Dad," Jay said as he got up to leave. "You're the greatest. Sorry I have to get back to the gym by seven-thirty. We have a late practice tonight."

As the back door slammed, Bob turned to his wife. Tears were building in Nancy's eyes.

"Nancy, the next few years will be as much a transition time for us as it will be for Jay and Dawn. The ones leaving home are too caught up in the adventure to be lonely; those of us left behind suffer the loneliness."

"I know," Nancy sighed. "I'll have to find another area to devote myself to. I remember how hard it was for your mother when she quit teaching. She struggled with it for several months before things came together for her. Through her searching, she became one of the most influential women in the community. Everyone seems to turn to her for guidance. If I could only obtain a fraction of her compassion, I'd be satisfied."

"Let's give Mom a call and see if she'd like to ride to Great Falls with us," Bob said as he reached for the kitchen phone.

Nancy nodded in agreement while Bob used the automatic dial on the phone and waited.

"Hello."

"Hello, Mother. How are you?"

"I'm doing fine. I'm just curled up with a new book from the library," Edith replied.

"Do you have any special plans for Friday and Saturday?" Bob queried.

Edith sounded puzzled. "That depends. What do you have in mind?"

"Nancy and I were going to take Jay to Great Falls, where he's going to enlist in the air force. We were going to spend the night and do the town up right. It'll probably be the last trip we'll get to take with him for a long time, and we were wondering if you'd like to join us."

"I'd love to," Edith replied and then she hesitated. "I'm afraid I'd better decline. I don't want to be that far away from Roy."

"Is something wrong?"

"It's not a crisis situation, but every time I go in, Roy seems to be weaker than the day before. He's losing a lot of weight and the nurses are now having to help feed him," Edith sighed.

"I'm sorry to hear that. The last few times Nancy and I have stopped to see him he was always sleeping, so we hadn't realized there was any change."

"I feel so helpless when I'm with him. I just want to share some of my limited strength with him."

"Mom, you're the most selfless person I know."

"Oh, no," Edith protested adamantly. "I struggle with selfishness just like everyone else." Edith paused. "What's amazed me in watching Roy's deteriorating health is the inner peace he's exhibiting. There always seems to be a smile on his face."

"I'm glad a failing body and mind can't take away the presence of our Lord," Bob replied as he remembered his stepfather during his more vibrant years. "That's the one thing I want to leave behind for my own children. Even when he doesn't realize it, Roy is still giving testimony to his faith in Christ."

Chapter 10

Mitzi Quinata burst into the library at Guam Christian Academy the following afternoon as soon as the students were dismissed for the day.

"Rebecca," she exclaimed. "What's this I hear about you going home for the summer?"

"The chances are pretty good," Rebecca replied. "But how did you hear so soon?"

"Angela said she heard you talking to the principal this morning," Mitzi giggled. "It pays to have a snoopy daughter in the same school. I don't know what I'll do for information when she graduates."

"It's still not certain, but I may get subpoenaed to testify at a murder trial," Rebecca stated matter-of-factly.

"Ooo. Sounds serious. What happened?"

"The guy next door decided he loved insurance money more than his wife and four kids. He set his house on fire and his wife and two of the children died."

Mitzi shook her head. "Sounds like a mean dude."

"Surprisingly enough, he was extremely soft-spoken." Rebecca sunk wearily into her chair. "He was the last person on earth I would have expected to do something like that."

"I guess one never knows what goes on in another's mind," Mitzi sighed, shaking her head. "Did you have nightmares about the fire after it happened or did coming to Guam help remove the memories?"

"I wish I could have left the memories behind, but during Christmas vacation on Saipan, I saw my neighbor working in one of the hotels. I reported him to the FBI and they arrested him. No matter where I go, I can't seem to get away from it."

"I hope it works out that you get to go home for the summer," Mitzi said, "but I'm afraid once you get home, you won't want to come back."

"No chance of that," Rebecca replied. "When I sign a contract and give my word, I have every intention of fulfilling it. Besides, it'll take at least another six months to finish automating the school library."

"I admire your dedication. The academy is fortunate to have you."

"It's been quite a learning experience for me. I'm glad I took the risk and came. It's been worth every minute of frustration that I've had."

The two women glanced at the clock while the janitor noisily pushed his cart into the library. "I better be getting home," Mitzi noted. "I don't have any idea what I'll fix for dinner and my family is used to eating at six o'clock sharp."

Rebecca finished shutting down the computers and locking the video cabinet and then said goodnight to the janitor. A warm tropical breeze blew against her face as she left the air-conditioned library. In the distance she could see the ocean waves lapping against the sandy beach. A surge of homesickness swept over her.

I can't begin to feel sorry for myself, she mused. *In just a few short weeks I'll be back in Montana. I'm sure I won't be nearly as lonely here during my second year.*

❧

The Lewistown High School gym was crowded with spectators from Lewistown and Rocky Bluff. The class A district basketball championship game was about to begin. "Daddy, do you think we'll win?" five-year-old Jeffy asked.

"I sure hope so," Dan Blair replied. "Last year we only lost by one point, so the team has vowed revenge for this game. They want to go to state in the worst way."

Just then Dan saw Larry and Libby Reynolds enter the gym. Dan stood and motioned for them to join him.

"You're a long ways from Running Butte," he chided as he reached out to shake Larry's hand.

"This is our big night out," Larry replied. "The kids are sleeping over at Jean and Jim's tonight. They wanted to be here to watch Jay play, but someone had to keep the store open."

"Only in Montana would someone drive one hundred and fifty miles one way to see a high school basketball game," Dan teased.

"They would if his kid brother was following in his footsteps and taking his team to the state championship," Larry chuckled.

Dan slapped his friend on the shoulder. "A lot has happened since you took Rocky Bluff High School to the state championship in Billings."

"A lot of it I'd like to forget," Larry replied. "I can't imagine that I ever thought playing basketball at the college level was so important that I'd shoot the principal when he disciplined me. I hope my little brother has better priorities than I had."

"You've come a long way since then and have become a model for the current team," Beth encouraged.

Larry nodded. "I owe a lot to the people of Rocky Bluff for forgiving me and accepting me for what I am today and not for what I used to be."

"Just listen to the crowd," Dan declared. "There's more pressure on those kids than on a professional team. The pros play for money while these kids play for community acceptance."

The roar of the crowd increased as the Lewistown High School band began to play their school song. The host team's fans cheered while the visiting team waiting politely for their school song. From the first tip-off, electricity filled the gym. By the end of the first quarter, it was obvious which team was dominating. Ryan Reynolds and Jay Harkness of Rocky Bluff were at their best. Even though they were both double-teamed most of the time, their accuracy at the hoop could not be matched.

The Lewistown fans became quieter and quieter as the point spread between the teams went from two to five. When the final buzzer sounded, the Rocky Bluff Rams led by ten points. The Rams lifted their leading scorer, Ryan Reynolds, to their shoulders while he cut the traditional victory net from the hoop. No one could have been prouder of their team than former star Larry Reynolds.

"Are you going to Billings next week for the championship games?" Larry asked Dan as the cheering began to subside and the crowd surged toward the exits.

"I'd like to," Dan replied, "but it's my turn to work the crisis lines. Will you be there?"

"I wouldn't miss it for the world. In fact, I'm planning to personally host a celebration for the team whether they win or lose. I don't want them to do what my team did after the final game. . .go out and party."

Dan smiled. "Sounds like a great idea. I'm sure the school officials will appreciate your efforts."

"It's the least I can do."

❧

"Mom, would you like to ride to Billings with us for the state tournaments?" Bob Harkness asked as Edith joined them for Sunday dinner the day after the district basketball finals. "Jay played a fabulous game last night and the state championship game is going to be even better."

Edith turned to her grandson. "Jay, you know how much I've enjoyed watching your sporting events through the years. I hate missing the biggest game of your high school career, but Roy is so bad now I'd hate to leave town for fear he'd take a turn for the worse. I'll be sure to listen to the game on the radio, and I hope I can get a copy of the coach's videotape and watch it when you get home."

Jay patted his grandmother's arm. "I understand, Grandma. I'm sure Beth Blair wouldn't mind making a duplicate of the video for you in the school library. She's getting pretty good with the audiovisual equipment."

"I'd appreciate it," Edith smiled. "I'll give Beth a blank tape to use. In the meantime, I'll keep you and the entire team in my prayers. We don't want any repeat of the championship game a few years ago."

Jay chuckled. "We could use all the prayers we can get, but thanks to Larry Reynolds, you don't have to worry about a repeat. He's planning a post-game victory dinner whether we win or lose. He's making sure we all keep our priorities straight."

"All the parents are breathing a sigh of relief," Nancy sighed. "We want our kids to have a good time without destroying their futures."

Wednesday afternoon the Rocky Bluff basketball team filled one school bus while the pep band filled another. A score of supporters lined their cars behind the buses. When everyone was ready, Philip Mooney led the procession to the city limits in his patrol car with its lights flashing and siren wailing. Passersby waved and motorists honked their horns. A spirit of jubilation and pride filled the city.

In the Billings Metra the Rocky Bluff Rams won the first three elimination games with ease. The combination of Jay and Ryan could not be stopped. Jay was high scorer in one game and Ryan led in the other two. In the championship game, the Rams were paired against the Miles City Bisons.

Larry and Libby Reynolds sat with Bob Harkness. "Did you remember to bring the sheet of team statistics from Sunday's paper?" Bob asked Larry.

"I have it in my pocket," Larry laughed, "but I don't need it. I've got the whole thing memorized. The Bisons' number fifty-five is their top scorer while number twenty-three is their best rebounder. Their point guard is the one to watch out for, though. He doesn't shoot much, but he's a magnificent ball handler."

"Sounds like our boys have their work cut out for them tonight," Bob observed.

"Yes, but I have confidence in them. They're on a roll and I don't think anything can stop them tonight."

The championship teams were evenly matched. First the Bisons led and then the Rams. The roar of the crowd in the Billings Metra was deafening. The pep bands and the cheerleaders helped keep the intensity at a high pitch. The score was tied at seventy-eight with thirty seconds left in the game.

The referee's whistle penetrated the roar of the crowd. He motioned that a foul was called against number twenty-three on the Bisons. Ryan Reynolds was on the free throw line for the Rams. His first shot hit the rim and bounced back. The Rams fans sighed and held their breath while their star took aim for the second shot. The ball teetered on the rim and fell through the net. The Metra was filled with cheers. The Bisons took the ball and raced down the court. The Rams used their best defense and kept their opponents midcourt. With five seconds left in the game, number fifty-five broke loose and shot. Everyone held their breath as the ball neared the hoop. It hit the rim and bounced down. Jay grabbed the rebound and was dribbling down the court when the final buzzer sounded. The Rocky Bluff Rams had won seventy-nine to seventy-eight.

"That was some game," Larry sighed as he relaxed back in his seat, "but it was a little too close for comfort."

"Well, at least we won," Bob shrugged. "Are you ready to go?"

"No way. They're going to have the presentation of the trophies in a few minutes," Larry replied. "The championship trophy will be a welcome addition to the school's trophy case."

The crowd became quiet as a middle-aged man dressed in a sports shirt and slacks walked to the center of the gym floor carrying a portable microphone. Behind him two teenagers pushed a cart bearing five trophies. One by one he called the teams to the floor. First the fourth place team, then the third place, the second place Miles City Bisons, and finally the Class A Montana State Champions—the Rocky Bluff Rams.

The Rocky Bluff pep band played the school song as their team ran onto the floor to accept the trophy. When the cheers subsided, the master of ceremonies again took the microphone. "And now for the most coveted honor of the tournament," he said, "the Most Valuable Player Award."

The crowd held their breath with anticipation. Each fan had their own selection. Would their favorite be the winner?

"And now the Most Valuable Class A Basketball Player by unanimous decision of the board is. . .Ryan Reynolds of the Rocky Bluff Rams."

Tears rolled unashamedly down Larry's cheeks as his younger brother went forward to accept the honor. His long road back to respectability had been worth it all. Larry's influence on his brother and teammates helped them taste the sweetness of victory while maintaining their priorities and integrity. Tonight Rocky Bluff had many things to celebrate. This night would be chiseled in the history book of Rocky Bluff, Montana.

∽

Attorney Dave Wood walked slowly back to his modest office at the edge of town. *Why did Judge Eubanks pick me to defend Dick Reed? There are several more experienced attorneys in Little Big Horn County. I've never handled a homicide case before. The biggest case I've had was the burglary at the lumberyard,* he mused. *Where should I begin?*

Dave turned the corner and walked toward the police station. Maybe Philip Mooney would be able to help him. Dave greeted the receptionist and dispatcher on duty and headed for Phil's office.

"Dave, come in," Phil greeted as he looked up from his pile of paperwork. "Have a seat. What brings you out on such a nice day?"

"I guess I need a little help," he sighed. "Judge Eubanks just appointed me as defense attorney for Dick Reed. I feel extremely inadequate for such a challenge."

"I'm sure you'll do a good job," Phil assured him. "Remember, not many attorneys in Montana have experience with homicide cases. I'll pull the file and you can begin familiarizing yourself with it. There's a little room in the back you can use."

"Thanks," Dave grinned. "I appreciate that. I want to read the file before I meet with Dick. I need to make sure I can make the best decisions for him, given the extreme circumstances and community sentiment."

Phil reached into the file cabinet and handed Dave a bulging manila folder. "Take your time. If you have any questions, be sure and ask."

Dave retreated to the back office furnished only with two straight back chairs and a desk. A small banker's lamp graced the desk. One hour passed and then two. Dave only left the desk to refill his coffee mug. The file was more fascinating than any mystery novel. *What motivates a person like this?* he mused. *My only hope is convincing Dick to plead innocent by reason of insanity.*

Two and a half hours later, Dave closed the folders and walked to the police captain's office.

"Thanks for letting me read the file. Would it be possible to talk with Dick now?"

"Sure," Phil agreed. "Let me get the keys."

Phil unlocked the iron gate. Dave shuddered as the metal door clanged shut behind them. *So this is what the inside of a jail looks like,* the young attorney pondered. *If this doesn't scare anyone straight, I don't know what will.*

"Wait here," Phil directed as he pointed to a chair in the jail interview room. "I'll bring Dick to you."

Dave paced around the narrow room until Phil appeared with Dick on the other side of the barred wall.

"Hello, Dick. I'm Dave Wood. How are you doing?"

"How would anyone be doing locked up like this?"

Dave took a deep breath. "I've been appointed as your defense attorney."

"You look awfully young. How many murder cases have you defended?"

"None, but I've done extensive research in criminal law and there are a number of experts I can call on for assistance."

"I hope so because I expect you to get me off the hook," Dick snapped.

"I'll do the best I can," Dave assured him. "Now can you tell me what happened the night of the fire?"

Dick recounted exactly the same story he told the investigating officers. . . . He had fallen asleep on the sofa and woke up when the house was engulfed in flames.

"I've read your file and the prosecution has a good case against you. It looks like your best option is to let me strike a deal with Stu Leonard for a guilty plea to the lesser charge of murder in the second degree. You'll get life, but seven to ten years down the road, you'll be eligible for parole."

"Huh, that's my best option? No way. Try again."

"Well, you can always plead guilty by reason of insanity."

Dick's face reddened. "I'll do no such thing. I didn't start the fire and I'm not insane."

"Dick, let's review the facts. A few months before the fire, you took out a huge insurance policy on your wife."

"And one on myself, too. Don't forget that," Dick interrupted.

"You also bought the electric space heater that caused the fire," Dave continued.

"So what!" snarled Dick.

"The state's arson investigator will testify that the thermostat was removed and that caused the heater to overheat. That fact goes to premeditation, and don't forget we're talking three counts of murder here."

"You can't prove I took that thermostat off the heater. Maybe there never was one on it."

"Oh, there was one all right. The signs of it having been removed are there, plain as day," Dave continued. "Your neighbors will also testify that they heard you and your wife arguing about money on numerous occasions and that you physically abused her."

"No law against that. The motel took every cent we made; there was never enough money to go around. Yeah, we argued about money. I could've told you that. You don't need testimony from my nosy neighbors. And I did slap her around a few times."

"Then there were your actions the night of the fire. Instead of trying to save your family, you ran next door and asked for help."

"I've explained that a dozen times. I couldn't get to them because of the smoke and the flames. I ran to Rebecca Sutherland's house and asked her to call the fire department."

"Dick, as your attorney I'm telling you that your chances of being acquitted on these charges are slim and none."

"Yeah, well, I still won't plead guilty or insane."

"Let me remind you that Montana ~~has the~~ death penalty and that's by hanging."

Dick's right hand automatically went to his neck; his face blanched white. "I'll think it over," he whispered.

"Well, don't think on it too long. I have a lot of work to do. First, I'm going to move the court for a change of venue. Sentiment is running so high against you in this town, I doubt if you could get a fair trial here."

"What do they say about me leaving Rocky Bluff?"

"At the time you left, the investigation was still open. No charges had been filed against you, nor were you a suspect. The prosecution will probably not try to draw any inferences from your departure. He really doesn't have to. He has all he needs to convict you without speculating why you left. Look, Dick, let me try to plea bargain with Stu Leonard. He'll accept a guilty plea to murder in the second degree."

"You're my lawyer. You're supposed to have my best interests at heart. Why are you trying to get me to plead guilty?"

"I do have your best interests at heart, Dick. I'm trying to save you from hanging. Again let me remind you: The prosecution's case against you is overwhelming. I'll do my level best for you, but I still believe your best defense is to seek a plea bargain of a guilty plea to the lesser charge of second degree murder."

Chapter 11

Good morning, Rebecca," Principal Diaz greeted as Rebecca signed the school register that she was on campus. "How are things going in the library?"

"Great, but I have a lot of things to get done before the last day of school. The students are extremely slow in getting their books returned, and I'm still working on the inventory."

"I'm sure everything will get done in the end," her principal assured her. "This is traditionally the most hectic time of the year for the librarian." He hesitated and took a deep breath. "I hate to ask you this on such a short notice, but I heard that you were able to play the piano."

A look of puzzlement spread across her face. "I used to play for personal enjoyment, but I'm pretty rusty. I haven't touched a piano since I came to Guam."

"I'm really in a bind," Mr. Diaz confided. "The band was going to play for graduation, but the band director has a death in the family and he left this morning for the mainland. There's only a week left before graduation, and with the director gone, the band is out. If you could play the piano for us at least we would have music. Could you play the processional for us?"

Rebecca paused, shrugged her shoulders, and then nodded. "I suppose I could practice after school and be able to have something worked up. It'll be far from perfect."

"No one will recognize perfection anyway," he grinned. "They're too excited with having their graduation before Memorial Day. The public schools don't get out until the second week of June. We're trying it this way so our students will have first crack at the summer jobs."

"Sounds like a good idea. I'll look around the music room later today and see if I can find some appropriate piano music," Rebecca replied as she turned to leave the office.

After school that day, Rebecca stayed in the music room and practiced traditional graduation marches. After an hour and a half, she became tired and hurried home for a light dinner. As she walked down the hall, she noticed the open door across the hall from her apartment and could hear the evening news on the TV.

430

"It's about time you're getting home," Ella Mae shouted. "Why don't you come in and have a cold drink with me?"

"Don't mind if I do," Rebecca replied. "We haven't had time to talk in a long time. How are things going at GW High School?"

"Busy as usual," Ella Mae sighed. "I'm glad the school year's about over. The kids are getting terribly restless. The hardest part for me is that Major Lee is going back to Georgia just as soon as school is out. GW won't be the same without him."

"You mean Ella Mae won't be the same without him," Rebecca teased.

The young teacher blushed. "Some of that, too. However, we plan to keep in touch. He wants me to come to Georgia to see him just as soon as I return to the States next summer. I don't know if we can sustain a relationship after a year of separation."

"I used to think the same thing," Rebecca admitted. "But I'm finding the longer I've been away from Andy, the closer we're becoming."

"They say absence makes the heart grow fonder." Ella Mae jiggled the ice cubes in her empty glass. "By the way, your phone's been ringing off the hook this afternoon. Someone seems desperate to talk to you."

Rebecca shrugged her shoulders. "If it's important, they'll call back."

The two continued their conversation for a few minutes and then Rebecca excused herself. Just as she was unlocking her apartment door, her telephone rang again.

"Hello," she said, laying her purse on the kitchen table.

"Hello," a familiar male voice greeted her. "Where have you been? I've been trying to get you for the last two hours."

"Hi, Andy. I had to work late at school. It seems that the music teacher had to return to the mainland for a funeral and they didn't have anyone to provide music for graduation. Somehow the principal found out that I used to play the piano."

"So you were drafted?" Andy teased.

"Something like that. He somehow made me feel like it was my patriotic duty."

"That's what you get for being multitalented," Andy reminded her. He paused, cleared his throat, and took a deep breath. "Rebecca, why I called is there has been an important development in Dick Reed's case."

"What's that?"

"Dick is maintaining his innocence, so there will be an emotional trial. Dave Wood, his attorney, filed for a change of venue because he didn't believe Dick could get a fair trial here. Judge Eubanks agreed, and the trial has been moved to Great Falls. The trial is scheduled to begin July fifteenth.

You'll be one of the primary witnesses."

"I was afraid of that," Rebecca sighed. "As much as I'll enjoy coming home for the summer, I'm not looking forward to a long, drawn-out trial. I don't function well under pressure."

"I saw you handle the immediate fallout from the fire and you were brilliant. The trial will be a piece of cake in comparison. Just tell them what happened."

"I guess you're right," Rebecca shrugged. "I just don't want to have to relive those tragic hours again."

"It'll be tough, but I'll be there with you every step of the way."

"Those are the most encouraging words I could hear. I've really missed being with you these last few months."

"Good," Andy chuckled. "Catch the first plane out of there when school is out and I'll meet you at the airport."

"The Blairs are comfortable in my house now and I promised they could stay there for two years, so I'll have to find someplace else to stay."

"I suppose you know Beth's baby is due the end of June?"

"Yes. She wrote me the nicest letter. They're so excited and I'm delighted for them. They deserve the best. I wonder if Edith Dutton would mind if I stayed with her for a couple months."

"I'm sure she'd be pleased to have you," Andy assured her. "I'll talk to her tomorrow and explain the circumstances. When is your school out?"

Rebecca thought a moment. "Graduation's May thirtieth. I could be back by the third of June."

Rebecca could not see the broad grin that spread across Andy's face. "That's terrific. Our seniors don't graduate until June fourth. I'm sure Jay and Ryan would like to have you at their graduation ceremonies."

"Those two were among my favorite students. I watched them change from rowdy freshman into well-mannered young gentleman. I know they'll go far in life," Rebecca responded.

"Two weeks after graduation Jay is leaving for Lackland Air Force Base in Texas for air force basic training. He's so excited about seeing the world he can hardly stand it. However, his parents are having a problem letting him go."

"That's understandable," Rebecca replied. "The Harknesses have always been a close-knit family."

The pair chatted for a few more minutes about the events in Rocky Bluff before they noticed the time and imagined dollar signs over the telephone lines. They hurriedly finalized their plans and bade each other good-bye, anticipating the time they would soon be together.

"It's so thoughtful of you to bring me here to meet Rebecca's plane," Edith Dutton said as she and Andy Hatfield stared through the plate-glass window, waiting for the evening Treasure State Airlines flight to arrive.

"You're the first one Rebecca wants to see," Andy replied. "Every time I've called her, she's always asked about you."

Edith smiled as she remembered her former coworker at the high school. "We've shared our lives with each other, both the good times and the bad. I'm glad she'll be able to stay with me. We have a lot of catching up to do."

A speck appeared in the western horizon and slowly grew larger. The dozen people gathered in the Rocky Bluff Airport waiting room rose to their feet as the twin-propeller, eighteen-seat Treasure State plane rolled to a stop.

"The evening flying culvert has arrived," one of the men said as the others roared with laughter. Even though the small airline was the brunt of many jokes, everyone in rural Montana realized its existence kept them from sheer isolation.

As the door opened, Rebecca Sutherland was the third passenger down the steps. Tears filled her eyes as she gazed upon the snowcapped mountains in the distance. She was finally home.

As she walked into the terminal, Andy grabbed her into his arms and held her tight. Their lips met before they realized where they were, and Rebecca pulled away. "Andy, it's so good to see you. You don't know how much I've missed you."

"The feeling is mutual," Andy replied. "I've been marking off the days until you returned."

Just then Rebecca spotted Edith standing a few feet away and extended both her arms.

"Edith, thanks for coming. I've so missed all our heart-to-heart chats."

Edith hugged her longtime friend.

"I have, too. I'm glad you're able to stay with me so we can visit undisturbed."

"How's Roy doing?" Rebecca queried.

"Not good," Edith sighed. "He's not able to feed himself anymore. He just lies on his bed barely aware when people come and go. Occasionally I can get a smile from him, but those times are becoming further and further apart."

Rebecca's smile faded. "I'm sorry to hear that. You both have been pillars of strength through extremely difficult times."

"I'll get your luggage," Andy offered. "How about dinner at the steak house? I'm sure they don't provide meals on the flying culvert."

"They don't even provide peanuts," Rebecca giggled as the trio headed for the baggage claim.

Two nights later the Rocky Bluff gymnasium was filled with family and friends of the graduating seniors. Frances and Donald Reynolds arrived early in order to get a front seat in the special section reserved for family members. Their older son, Larry, and his family from Running Butte sat beside them.

"Mom, it looks like Ryan is up for a lot of awards and honors tonight," Larry whispered. "His athletic scholarship to Montana A&M will come in handy. Those are hard to come by. You must be mighty proud of him."

Mrs. Reynolds nodded. "We are."

"I'm sorry I let you down when I graduated. It must have been a terrible embarrassment for you."

Mrs. Reynolds took her son's hand. "Yes, it was," she admitted, "but now I'm bursting with pride for both my sons. You made your share of mistakes in your younger years, but you turned your life around after you made friends with the Harknesses."

"They're one terrific family," Larry replied. "I'd hate to think what would have happened to me if Edith and Bob hadn't intervened."

Three rows behind the Reynoldses, Edith Dutton sat with her son and daughter-in-law.

"How does it feel to be father of the smartest kid in the class?" Nancy teased Bob.

"He must have gotten the brainy gene from you," Bob retorted, "or maybe it's a combination of you and Mother. It definitely didn't come from me."

Farther back in the gymnasium, Rebecca Sutherland was crowded tightly against Andy Hatfield in the bleachers. His arm was lightly across her back to support her. Rebecca studied the program in silence. Each name was familiar as former students of hers.

"Hmm, this is interesting. Jay Harkness will be giving the valedictorian address," she whispered to Andy. "I'm not surprised that he obtained the highest grades in his class. He's always been an excellent student."

The fire chief chuckled. "You've missed all the town chatter. Having a valedictorian leave immediately for the military instead of college is an unheard of thing in Rocky Bluff."

Rebecca joined Andy in laughter. "I've always been proud of Jay. From the day he entered high school, he's been his own person and thought for himself. Even when he was little, he never gave in to peer pressure."

Andy shook his head. "Some people are caught in their own paradigm, thinking that the only way to get an education is to go to a four-year college directly after high school."

Everyone rose as the band began to play "Pomp and Circumstance" and the senior class filed into the gymnasium. Dawn Harkness could scarcely play her saxophone as she kept one eye on her music and the other watching for her brother to come down the aisle.

Rebecca's eyes filled with tears as she thought about the changes she had seen in this class of students since she was librarian at Rocky Bluff High School. So much had happened to them and to herself during the last year.

The Harkness family stirred restlessly in their seats. Jay had refused to tell them what he was planning to say in his valedictorian speech.

"Jay's always been such a joker, I'm almost afraid what he'll say," Nancy whispered to her mother-in-law.

Edith patted her hand. "I'm sure we'll be proud of whatever he says. Jay knows when to tease and when to be serious. He's had a good set of parents."

Nancy smiled, relaxed, and leaned back in her chair. This was her son's big night. As class representative, he was giving the farewell address to Rocky Bluff.

After the traditional introductory speeches, Principal Grady Walker took the microphone. "The valedictorian of this class needs no introduction to the community of Rocky Bluff. He has not only excelled in academics and athletics but has also worked in the family business and has volunteered for numerous community projects. I'm proud to announce the valedictorian with a 3.97 grade point—Jay Harkness."

The roar was deafening as Jay walked to the podium. The clapping gradually subsided as Jay surveyed the crowd.

"Fellow classmates, teachers, parents, and friends," he began. "I feel extremely honored and humbled to stand here tonight as a spokesperson for my class. After thirteen years of being together, it is now time to say good-bye to each other and go our separate ways. Some we may never see again. Others will be constantly with us throughout our lives, but wherever we go and whatever we become, the community of Rocky Bluff, Montana, has given us a strong foundation. I'd like to say thank you to Mr. Walker, all the teachers and staff who have sacrificed of themselves for our entire class so that we would be grounded in truth, education, and the love of our country. Beyond that, I'd like to thank my family for being there for me when I needed them most. Many times I thought I could make it on my own, but in the end I found security and strength in their faith and confidence in me. My parents, Bob and Nancy Harkness, taught me the importance of honesty and integrity that I see slipping away from our society in general. My grandmother, Edith Dutton, and her husband, Roy, have demonstrated to me that life is not merely for the young. Education and love are intergenerational needs. I need the wisdom they have developed through their years of experience and I offer to them my youth and enthusiasm. When I become discouraged I need only remember my grandmother's struggle back from a near-fatal heart attack and Roy's struggles today while he is convalescing in the care center. Even through their physical pain, they could find inner strength to go on and face an uncertain future, knowing God was in charge of their lives. I want to thank each one of them for my strong foundation as I leave Rocky Bluff to serve my country in the United States Air Force. I want to give back to society some of what has been given to me during my growing-up years in Rocky Bluff. Thank you and may God bless each of you."

The audience sat in stunned silence as Jay left the podium. *They must not have liked my speech,* he thought dejectedly. Suddenly a spontaneous round of applause began as everyone in the gymnasium stood to cheer the moving words of a young man wise beyond his years.

The next morning as Edith and Rebecca lingered around Edith's kitchen table after their last cup of coffee, their conversation was interrupted by the ringing of the telephone. Edith reached for the phone.

"Hello."

"Hello, Edith. This is Bonnie Jenson, the head nurse at the care center. Roy has taken a turn for the worse and I was wondering if you could come to the care center right away."

Edith's face blanched. "Is he all right?"

"He's having a little difficulty breathing, so we thought you'd like to be here."

"I'll be right there. Thanks for calling." Edith hung up the phone and turned to her friend. "Roy has taken a turn for the worse and I need to get to the care center right away. Does Andy have the day off today?"

"Yes, he was planning on coming over later this morning. I'll give him a call," Rebecca replied as she reached for the phone and dialed the familiar number.

There was a flurry of activity in the Dutton home for the next few minutes. The two women hurriedly changed clothes, fixed their hair, and touched up their makeup. They were standing on the front steps waiting when Andy Hatfield's car pulled to a stop at the curb. Rebecca took Edith's arm as they hurried to the car. As Andy drove toward the care center, each sat in their own silence, afraid of giving false hopes.

As the trio turned down the corridor toward Roy's room, Dr. Brewer and Bonnie Jenson were coming out of his room. Edith's eyes searched their faces for answers.

"How is he?"

"Edith, let's go to the family room and talk," Dr. Brewer said as he took her gently by the arm and led her to the nearby lounge. He motioned for her to be seated on the sofa by the window. "I'm sorry. Roy passed away about ten minutes ago. He did not suffer in the end, but closed his eyes and slipped away."

Edith sat motionless. Her nearly six years of happiness with Roy were over. Rebecca put her arm around her friend and pulled her close. Edith buried her face on her friend's shoulder and began to sob. All during Roy's long illness, Edith had rarely shed a tear, and now all the built-up pressures were released. Words were not necessary to share their mutual grief.

After ten long minutes, Edith lifted her head, dried her eyes, and forced a smile. "Roy was such a good man. I'm thankful I was the one who got to share his latter years. Let's go to his room and say good-bye."

The three tiptoed solemnly into Roy's room. Edith took his lifeless hand in hers. "Farewell," she whispered. "I'll see you later. Thanks for a wonderful life together."

Edith turned to her companions. "I need to call Bob and Jean. They accepted and loved Roy as if he were their natural father. We'll need to contact relatives and make the final arrangements. Roy would want his memorial service to be one that brings glory to the God he loves. It should be a time to proclaim Christ's victory over death."

Chapter 12

Sunday morning Edith awoke with a dull headache. It had been over a year since she had been awaking alone in her bed, but this day was different. She did not have the anticipation of going to the care center to visit Roy. For the second time she was a widow. The smell of freshly brewed coffee drifted into her bedroom. Edith wrapped her satin robe around her waist and ambled to the kitchen.

"Good morning, Edith," Rebecca greeted. "Can I fix you some breakfast?"

"Thanks, dear. A couple of pieces of toast is all I can handle now," Edith replied as she sank onto a kitchen chair.

Rebecca popped a couple of pieces of bread into the toaster and took a cup and saucer from the cupboard. "Did you sleep well?"

Edith shook her head. "I must have," she replied. "But I have a terrible headache that won't quit."

Rebecca surveyed her friend's wrinkled forehead. "Just take it easy today and I'll take care of the cooking and hostessing for your family and friends."

"Thanks. I'd appreciate that," Edith sighed. "Jean and Jim and Gloria will be here by noon. Usually Jean takes over the meals, but she's eight months pregnant and the summer heat has been bothering her a lot lately."

"I'll have everything ready when they get here," Rebecca assured her. "I may have to make a few hurried trips to the deli in the next few days."

Edith forced a smile. "I hate to put you in such a position," she murmured. "You're here as my guest. You shouldn't have to take care of my family, but I don't know what else to do. Nancy has always been a big help when I've needed her, but she has a houseful of relatives who came for Jay's graduation."

Rebecca spread butter and jelly on the freshly toasted bread and set the plate before Edith. "That's what friends are for. You've helped me during difficult times, and now I'd like to help you."

"I appreciate that. Since he's been ill for so long I thought I was prepared for Roy's death, but I wasn't nearly as prepared as I thought. All I want is to see him and talk to him one more time. I'm every bit as numb as when George died suddenly."

"I'm sure losing Roy has triggered all kinds of memories and emotions," Rebecca noted.

"That it has," Edith admitted, taking a deep breath. "Before I met Roy I never dreamed that I would ever be able to love anyone as much as I loved George. But I soon learned that love is different later in life. I learned to savor every moment we had together and took nothing for granted. The few years of joy I had with Roy make the pain I feel now worth it all."

Rebecca nodded. "I'm glad to hear you say that. I'm beginning to wonder whether I should risk entering into a more permanent relationship later in life. No one could ever replace Eric."

"That's true," Edith reminded her. "Roy did not replace George; he complemented and added on to the relationship I once had. In fact, a second marriage gave me a second chance not to make some of the same mistakes I did in my younger years.

"Roy had so much maturity and depth of character. He'd been through so much losing his first wife and having to raise a handicapped son by himself. His ability to forgive Bob for the car accident that killed his son was an example for the entire community. I'm really going to miss him."

Just then the back door slammed. "Hello, Mom!" Bob shouted. "May I come in?"

"Come on in. The coffeepot's on."

"Nancy went to church with her family, but I wanted to spend the time with you. How are you doing?"

"I'm okay," Edith replied. "Everyone has been notified and the final arrangements have been made. Rebecca has promised to be hostess for whoever comes by the house."

Bob turned to Rebecca. "I don't know how I can thank you for all the help you've been for Mother. Your presence has taken a lot of pressure off the family."

"I'm glad I can help. You all have been a source of strength and encouragement to me throughout the years."

Bob stayed and reminisced with his mother about the good times he had shared with Roy. They talked about the beginning of the crisis center and how it had developed throughout the years.

As the clock tolled noon, Bob stood and pushed his chair under the table. "Nancy and the others will be home from church soon. I better leave now and let you get dressed. You're going to be having lots of company this afternoon."

"Thanks for stopping," Edith replied. "Rebecca is planning dinner around six. I hope you can bring your family over."

"Certainly," Bob smiled. "As long as the commotion won't be too much for you."

Wednesday afternoon Rocky Bluff Community Church was crowded with family and friends wishing to pay the final respects to one of the patriarchs of their community. The service for Roy had much the same bittersweet grief as the funeral for his son had had six years before. Pastor Rhodes again reminded them that because of Christ's sacrifice, death no longer held a sting over them. The music comforted their souls as the soloist sang, "Because He lives I can face tomorrow." The service was a celebration of the life of someone who had fought a good fight and kept the faith until the end.

An hour later Bob took his mother's arm as they approached the gravesite in Pine Hills Memorial Cemetery. Roy was to be buried next to his son. Edith dabbed her eyes with a tissue. A lump built in Bob's throat. *I have to be strong for Mother, but no one knows how difficult it is for me to come back to this spot. It was here at Pete's burial that I realized how selfish and misdirected my life had become. I fought Mother's remarriage every step of the way. And now, looking back, I'm so ashamed. Roy brought immeasurable happiness not only to her, but to the rest of the family as well. I hope I can lead a life of love and integrity until the end the way that Roy did.*

Six-year-old Jeffy Blair hurried past Edith and the rest of the Harkness family. In his chubby hand he clutched a long-stemmed red rose. Solemnly he laid it on the casket. "Good-bye, Grandpa Roy," he whispered. "I'll see you someday in heaven."

In the back of the crowd Andy Hatfield strolled across the lawn toward the gravesite with Rebecca Sutherland on his arm. "In spite of Edith's diminishing health and her tremendous loss, she's a pillar of strength," Andy noted.

"I've often wondered if marriage later in life is worth it when it's obvious that the human body is on a downhill slide," Rebecca replied, "but Edith has made it plain to me that mature love is stronger than failing health."

Andy nodded and chuckled softly. "They say loneliness is one of the greatest robbers of health among the elderly. Edith and Roy were a perfect example that love can lengthen your days on earth. As the days go by, I am beginning to experience moments of loneliness that I never felt as a young, active thirty year old."

Pastor Rhodes spoke the same words to the family and friends of Roy

Dutton as he did six years before at Pete Dutton's gravesite. Choosing words from Paul's letters to the Corinthians and Thessalonians, Pastor Rhodes's voice echoed across the hillside:

" 'Eye hath not seen, nor ear heard, neither have entered into the heart of man, the things which God hath prepared for them that love him.'

" 'For our light affliction, which is but for a moment, worketh for us a far more exceeding and eternal weight of glory.'

" 'For if we believe that Jesus died and rose again, even so them also which sleep in Jesus will God bring with him.' "

A week after his step-grandfather's funeral, Jay Harkness stopped by his grandmother's home to say good-bye before he left for basic training at Lackland Air Force Base in Texas. Edith and Rebecca relaxed on the sofa while Jay propped his feet on the chair beside Edith. Conversation flew easily. There was no generation gap as they exchanged their common interests and expectations. After half an hour Jay turned his attention to Rebecca.

"Tell me more about Guam. I've always wanted to see the tropics."

"It's a beautiful island with palm trees and sandy beaches," Rebecca replied. "But a tourist will never know what Guam is all about. A person must live there and get to know the people and the culture and it will have meaning for them."

"How's it different? Aren't they U.S. citizens?" Jay queried.

"Yes, they are. The American flag is large enough to cover all types and cultures of people," Rebecca explained. "They are South Sea Island people who have been thrust into the modern Western world in just three generations. Some have excelled in this new environment while others have become frustrated and have given up. Even the climate makes their attitudes different from us frozen Northerners. Their lifestyle is much more relaxed."

Jay sat entranced while Rebecca described the island and the people. "I'm glad there's an air force base on Guam. When I get done with basic training, I'm going to put Andersen Air Force Base down as my first choice for assignment."

Rebecca laughed affectionately. "I hope you get it while I'm still there. I'd love to show you the island."

Jay stood and hugged his grandmother. "Good-bye, Grandma, I'll see you in eight weeks after I've completed basic training." He then turned his attention to his former librarian. "I hope the next time I see you it'll be in Guam." With that Jay disappeared out the front door to begin a new life.

After two weeks of jury selection, July fifteenth finally arrived and the courtroom in the Cascade County Courthouse in Great Falls was packed. Stuart Leonard sat at the prosecutor's table with his paralegal, Libby Reynolds. In front of them was a laptop computer to record every word spoken and search for the context of any new laws that might surface.

Libby had worked for him in the Little Big Horn county attorney's office until her husband had been transferred to Running Butte. Stuart was never able to find a replacement of equal abilities, and when the triple homicide case became time consuming, he turned to his former employee. Libby worked closely with Stuart from Running Butte via fax and modem until she was totally familiar with the facts of the case and the laws involved.

Dave Wood sat nervously beside his client. He felt as if all eyes were upon him. *Whether I think Dick is guilty or not, he deserves the best defense possible. The outcome is up to the judge and jury,* he mused. *But how can I present a good defense when the supportive evidence is so weak?*

Rebecca Sutherland sat in the back row holding Andy's hand. "I don't know if I can go through with this," she whispered. "I've never been face-to-face with Dick since he was arrested."

"When you testify, don't think about Dick; think about Anita and the two children. Remember, this is not your decision. Your only responsibility is to tell the facts as you know them and leave the rest up to the judge and jury."

Rebecca grinned as she squeezed her friend's hand. "Thanks. I needed that. I'm glad you'll be by my side during this entire ordeal to give me moral support."

Suddenly the side door opened and the bailiff entered the courtroom. "Please rise," he ordered. "The District Court of Cascade County is now in session. The Honorable Herman Kessler presiding."

As soon as Judge Kessler took his seat on the bench, he pounded his gavel and commanded, "You may be seated. The court will come to order." He paused. "The clerk will call the first case."

The clerk rose and monotoned, "The State of Montana versus Richard Reed."

Judge Kessler looked down at the prosecutor's table and asked, "Mr. Leonard, are the people ready?"

"Ready, Your Honor."

He then looked to his right at Dave Wood. "Mr. Wood, is the defense ready?"

"Ready, Your Honor," Dave replied and then said, "Your Honor, I request that the rule be imposed."

Judge Kessler again turned to Stuart Leonard. "Mr. Leonard?"

"No objections, Your Honor."

"So ordered," Judge Kessler gaveled. "All persons who were subpoenaed as witnesses in this case will now retire to the witness room. You will remain there until you are either called or dismissed. You are ordered not to discuss this case with anyone."

A bailiff escorted Rebecca and Andy and the other witnesses from the courtroom.

Judge Kessler now directed his attention to the defendant: Richard Reed.

"Mr. Reed," he said as both Dick and Dave rose. "You are charged with three counts of murder in the first degree. Do you understand these charges against you, sir?

"Yes, I do Your Honor."

"Has your attorney explained the serious nature of these charges to you and their possible consequences?"

"Yes, he has, Your Honor."

"Very well then, understanding the seriousness of these charges to you and their possible consequences, as to the murder of Anita Reed, how do you plead?"

"Not guilty, Your Honor."

"As to the murder of Christopher Reed, how do you plead?"

"Not guilty, Your Honor."

"As to the murder of Richard Reed the Second, how do you plead?"

"Not guilty, Your Honor."

"Very well, your plea of not guilty is accepted."

With that Dave and Dick sat and Judge Kessler turned to Stuart Leonard. "Mr. Leonard, do you wish to make an opening statement?"

"Yes, Your Honor," Stu said as he rose and strolled to the jury box. Facing the jury, his opening statement of how the crime that took three innocent lives was perpetrated and how the state would prove the defendant committed the crimes was a masterpiece.

Dave Wood both admired and feared Stu's presentation. Dick Reed became visibly upset and whispered in Dave's ear, "Is it too late to cut a guilty plea for second degree murder?"

"I'll see what I can do as soon as Stu finishes his opening statement," said Dave, unable to conceal his disgust. *It's a little late for that*, he told himself.

When Stu finished and returned to his seat, Dave thought, *If this were not a courtroom, the audience would have applauded.* Judge Kessler interrupted his thoughts. "Mr. Wood, do you wish to make an opening statement?"

Dave rose and asked, "Your Honor, may we approach the bench?"

"You may," came the reply.

Dave motioned to Stu, and the two lawyers quickly moved to Judge Kessler's bench. Judge Kessler was slightly annoyed. "Mr. Wood, this is highly irregular. What's going on?"

"Your Honor, my client wants to change his plea. May I have an hour's recess to discuss this with Mr. Leonard?"

"Mr. Leonard, any objections?"

"None, Your Honor."

"Very well." With that Judge Kessler gaveled his annoyance. "The court will recess for one hour."

The two lawyers and the defendant met in Judge Kessler's anteroom. "Okay, Dave, you have the floor."

"Stu, Dick is willing to plead guilty to three counts of second degree murder and save the state the burden of a trial in exchange for a thirty-year sentence, ten years for each count."

"I don't consider this trial a burden, Dave. But I might agree to a plea of guilty of three counts of second degree murder in exchange for three life sentences. One life sentence for each of the innocents."

"But that means no chance of parole," said Dave.

"Take it or leave it," replied Stu.

"May I be alone with my client?"

"Sure," said Stu as he left the room.

As the door closed, Dick was furious. "You said you could swing it," he yelled. "You lied to me."

"I could have swung it back in Rocky Bluff before the court convened," Dave yelled back. "But you refused to even consider it. You are now facing three counts of murder in the first degree and Leonard will demand the death penalty. The choice is yours. I've done all I can do," said Dave as he sat down.

After a long silence a much subdued Dick said, "It beats hanging."

Dave rose from his chair, opened the door, and motioned for Stu. "Well?"

"We'll take it," said Dave.

The three then entered Judge Kessler's chambers and explained the plea bargain they had reached. It was all over but finalizing the nitty gritty details, reconvening the court to officially change the plea, and setting a date for officially handing down the agreed-upon sentence.

❧

Rebecca could not remember the dismissal of the court. She sat numbly in her chair as everyone filed out. As soon as the courtroom was empty, Rebecca burst into sobs. Andy wrapped his arms around her and held her close.

"It's okay," he whispered. "It's over. We can now go back to Rocky Bluff and start our lives over again."

"I don't know why I'm crying. I knew how this was going to end. Seeing Dick and worrying about testifying was difficult, but I should have been able to handle it. I've had a year in Guam to fill my mind with new adventures and thoughts."

"Now when you go back you'll not have nagging questions and fears hanging over you," Andy reminded her. "You can approach a new school year with freshness and certainty, which you never had during your first year on Guam. You can go back to Guam with the certainty that there is someone who loves you and is anxiously awaiting your return."

Chapter 13

The wind rustled through the pine trees as Andy and Rebecca strolled along Lone Mountain Trail to the peak of Old Baldy.

"Just think," Rebecca sighed. "In a week I'll be walking among palm trees instead of pine trees."

"It's going to be hard to say good-bye," Andy replied. "Nine and a half months without seeing you is just too long."

Rebecca nodded. "I know, but I'm bound to my two-year contract. Even if I wasn't under contract, I feel honor-bound to finish the library automation project."

Andy took Rebecca's hand as the trail became steeper.

"That's what I like about you the most," he said. "Your sense of dedication."

"I only do what I have to do. I'd much rather stay here in Rocky Bluff with you."

"This winter I'll have three weeks of vacation coming," Andy said as he gazed into the distance. "I think I'll check with the travel agency about a round-trip ticket to Guam."

Rebecca halted. A smile spread across her face. "Do you really mean you'd come to Guam?" Her voice faltered. "I. . .I'd love to show you the sights."

Andy pulled her next to him. "I'd follow you to the ends of the earth."

"And you think Guam is the end of the earth?" Rebecca teased as she snuggled against him.

"It's sure a long way from Montana," Andy retorted as his lips brushed hers.

As the pair reached the peak, they sat on a boulder to enjoy the view and a cold drink. Words were not necessary to share their mutual love and respect. They had both observed how rewarding love in later years could be by watching Roy and Edith Dutton. The same was happening to them, only their love had to grow over the distant seas.

꩜

A week later Rebecca Sutherland stepped off the plane at the Won Pat International Airport. *I wonder if Ella Mae got my letter asking if she could meet me at the airport?* Rebecca thought as she waited for her luggage in the baggage claim area. *If she's not here, I guess I could call a taxi, but the taxis here are so undependable.*

In the distance Rebecca spotted her young teacher friend. Beside her was Major Tom Lee. She hurried to embrace her. "Ella Mae, I'm glad you could come. How are you? How was your summer?"

"I'm great. This was the best summer ever. Tom has returned to Guam."

Rebecca turned to the retired army officer. "Tom, it's good to see you again," she said as she extended her hand. "What brought you back to Guam?"

"Love," he chuckled. "I went back to Georgia to work with my brother, but construction on our new building was delayed for several months. I couldn't get this little Southern belle out of my mind, so I came back until Ella Mae finishes her contract at George Washington High School."

Ella Mae and Tom helped Rebecca carry her luggage to their car. "How about dinner at the San Francisco House before we go home?" Tom asked.

"Sounds good. The meals on the flight over were pretty skimpy," Rebecca replied. "I want to catch up on all the latest news."

Within minutes the three were gathered in a corner booth in their favorite restaurant enjoying heaping plates of spaghetti with garlic toast. After a few minutes of small talk, Rebecca turned to Tom, who was sitting beside her. "So what are you doing with your time while you're waiting for Ella Mae to finish her contract?"

Tom squeezed Ella Mae's hand under the table as they exchanged knowing glances. "I'm a consultant for a local security firm. I've also been keeping busy planning our wedding."

Rebecca looked at Ella Mae quizzically.

Ella Mae nodded. "We're planning on getting married on Labor Day. We were waiting for you to get back so you could be my matron of honor."

Rebecca beamed. "This certainly has been a summer for romance. I'd be honored to stand up for you."

The rest of the evening the friends discussed wedding plans. As the sun began to sink over the Philippine Sea, the trio headed toward their apartment building in Dededo. Rebecca unlocked the front door of her one-bedroom apartment and a flood of emotions overcame her. . .relief to be back on Guam was mixed with fatigue and a loneliness for Andy Hatfield.

The morning sun was high in the tropical sky before Rebecca awoke. She showered and dressed and routinely walked to the kitchen. Reality hit her as she opened her refrigerator door. *What am I doing?* she scolded herself. *There isn't a bite of food in the house. I cleaned out the cupboards and refrigerator before I left for the summer.*

Rebecca grabbed her purse and walked to the parking lot. *I'm glad Ella Mae was here this summer to drive my car occasionally,* she mused. *At least there's a good chance it'll start.* She unlocked the door and slid behind the wheel. The scent of coconut air freshener greeted her nostrils. She chuckled as she read the note taped on the steering wheel.

"Welcome home." She turned the key in the ignition and the engine turned over on the first try. *What a dear to take care of my car this way,* she thought. *I've got to find a way to repay her.*

Rebecca turned off the side street onto Marine Drive and headed for McDonalds in spite of her dislike of fast food breakfasts. An egg sandwich sounded delicious. After eating alone, Rebecca stopped at the neighborhood supermarket. Within an hour she was back at her apartment in Dededo. She spent the rest of the day recuperating from jet lag. Crossing the international dateline always left her body clock totally confused.

Late that afternoon Ella Mae knocked on her neighbor's door. "Rebecca, I need to go to the florists and pick out flowers for the wedding. Would you like to come with me?"

"Sounds like fun. It's been a long time since I helped plan a wedding."

The two friends laughed and joked as they drove to Pacific Florist in downtown Agana. In one week they would both be back at work and they had to take advantage of every minute. "What colors have you chosen for your wedding?" Rebecca queried.

"Pink and white. I want to use as many tropical flowers as possible. After we get back I'll show you the spot on the beach where we'll say our vows. We're planning an evening wedding to take advantage of the setting sun."

"It sounds beautiful. Are you inviting many guests?"

"Hopefully most of the faculty from George Washington will be there," Ella Mae replied. Her eyes became distant before she continued. "I wish my parents could come, but it's too expensive and neither one of them could get the time off work."

"You'll have to have lots of pictures taken," Rebecca replied. "An island wedding will be a novelty for South Carolina. You'll be the talk of the town."

Ella Mae burst out laughing. "If you Yankees only knew how important romance was to those south of the Mason-Dixon line, you'd appreciate why

I'm having the entire ceremony videotaped. It's liable to be shown in the local theater."

Rebecca joined her laughter. "If that's the case and I'm going to be a movie star, I'd better look my best. When we get done let's stop at Ardiss's Dress Shop and see if I can find a suitable bridesmaid's dress."

Before the sun set that evening, every detail of the wedding that coming Saturday evening was finalized. The caterer agreed to provide a tent to shelter the wedding fiesta and guests who might linger long into the twilight hours.

The next few days flew by as Rebecca helped Ella Mae and Tom prepare their wedding. The day before the wedding, the trio moved a few of Tom's personal belongings into Ella Mae's apartment in Dededo. At the end of the day, they gathered in Rebecca's apartment to relax.

"I'm exhausted," Rebecca sighed as she collapsed onto her sofa. "Let's order out for pizza."

"I'm in favor of that," Tom grinned. "I'm tired myself and this will be the last time I'll see my bride before she walks down the beach tomorrow night."

Nothing could have been more picture perfect than Major and Mrs. Tom Lee's wedding the following evening. The band played traditional island music before the ceremony and during the festivities that followed. Ella Mae was radiant in her white dress with a lei of tropical flowers around her neck and one clipped to her hair.

"The people of Abbeville will be talking about this for years," Rebecca teased as she hugged the bride.

At the reception, Rebecca spotted her friend and coworker Mitzi Quinata and her daughter Angela among the guests. She weaved through the crowd until she was beside them.

"Hello," she greeted. "It's good to see you again."

Mitzi embraced her friend. "Rebecca, I'm glad you're back on the island. How was your summer?"

"Extremely eventful," Rebecca smiled. "Sometime when we have a couple hours, I'll tell you all about it."

"Have you been to the academy yet?"

"I've been so busy helping Ella Mae with her wedding that I haven't had a chance. I'm definitely not ready for school to start Tuesday."

"It's been entirely repainted, both inside and out," Mitzi explained. "I never expected such an elaborate change."

"Did they do the library?"

"You wouldn't believe how much bigger it looks with white walls instead of institutional green."

"I can hardly wait," Rebecca replied and then turned her attention to the attractive young woman. "Angela, how are you doing? How was your summer?"

"I went to summer school at Guam Community College and took several basic courses," Angela explained. "I've decided to get a degree in cosmetology. I've always enjoyed trying to make people look their best. It lifts their morale and they walk away with their heads held high."

Rebecca put her arm around her former student's shoulder. "Good for you. I know exactly where I'll go when I need to have my hair done."

It was a magical night on Guam. Chamorros, statesiders, and Filipinos mingled together to celebrate the love of a young couple far away from home.

This was the true island spirit.

≈

Airman Second Class Jay Harkness stepped off the Treasure State commuter plane in Rocky Bluff. His eyes feasted on the distant mountain peaks. After eight weeks of air force basic training, he walked tall and proud in his dress blues. He broke into a run when he spotted his sister, parents, and grandmother.

Jay picked up his sister and whirled her around. "Hi, Sis. Did you miss me?"

"Maybe a little," Dawn grinned. "It sounded impressive at school to say my brother's in the air force."

"I figured you'd milk it for all it's worth," he teased and then turned to his parents. He hugged his mother and kissed her on the cheek. Jay hugged his father, who was proudly slapping him on the back.

"Welcome home, Son. We're all proud of you."

"Thanks, Dad," he said as he looked at his grandmother beaming with pride. She looked older and more frail than what he remembered when he left. He gave her an extra long hug. "How are you doing, Grandma? I really missed you."

"I'm doing great, but life's getting pretty boring not having some kind of ball game of yours to go to," she chided.

The Harkness clan hurried to the baggage claim to pick up Jay's duffel bag. Everyone seemed to be talking at once. Jay had seen so much and had made so many new friends, he was anxious to provide every detail of the last eight weeks.

"I've made your favorite meal," Nancy said as they walked to their car

450

on the far side of the parking lot.

"Roast beef with potatoes and carrots, I hope," Jay smiled.

Nancy took her son's arm. "I wouldn't fix anything else for your first night home."

The family lingered around the dining room table long after the last bite of apple pie had been eaten. They basked in each moment they were together as a family.

Bob waited through minutes of small talk before asking what was paramount on everyone's mind.

"Jay, how long are you going to be home?"

"Two weeks," he replied seriously, "then off to Maxwell Air Force Base in Alabama for twelve weeks' advanced training. I've been accepted into computer services. When I complete that I'm being assigned to the 805 Computer Services Squadron at Anderson Air Force Base in Guam."

Edith beamed. "You got exactly what you wanted. Rebecca will be thrilled."

"I hope nobody lets her know I'm coming," Jay responded. "I want the pleasure of surprising her face-to-face. I've already started corresponding with my military host and they've clued me in on what to expect."

A twinkle come into Dawn's eyes. "Guam? Mmm. You won't be able to take your car."

"Sorry, Sis. You'll have to give the keys back," Jay chided. "We're allowed to ship our cars. Remember that was just a loan we agreed upon."

Dawn shrugged her shoulders. "I know, but it was fun while it lasted. I've been saving money from my after-school job and I almost have enough for a down payment on a car of my own."

Nancy turned to her son.

"What do you want to do while you're home? We'd like to spend as much time together as we can."

"I want to sleep a lot," Jay confessed with a grin. "Then I want to drive over to Montana A&M to see Ryan. His letters sound like things are going well for him there and he really likes it there."

"Would you like me to hold an open house for you Saturday night so all your friends can stop by and say 'hello'?" Nancy asked.

"Mom, that'd be super. It would save me a lot of running around. I'll get on the phone and let everyone know I'm back and that there'll be lots of food and soft drinks that night if they would like to stop by."

The lively family discussion continued for another hour when Bob looked over at his mother just as she was yawning.

"Getting tired, Mom?" he queried. "Maybe we should call it a day. I'll take you home if you'd like."

"I am getting a little weary," Edith responded as she pushed back her chair.

"Why don't you stay here, Dad," Jay offered. "I'll give Grandma a ride home. It'll give me an excuse to reclaim my car and see if I still remember how to drive."

"Now that's an unsettling offer," Edith teased as she walked toward the front door. "If there's a chance you've forgotten, I'd rather ride with your father."

"Grandma, driving my own car is something I'll never forget," Jay responded as Dawn handed him the keys.

The next afternoon Jay Harkness stopped by the fire station to visit Chief Hatfield. Andy was just finishing some paperwork when Jay tapped on the open door.

"Jay, come in. When did you get back?"

"Yesterday afternoon. It's good to be back in Rocky Bluff. I see you're taking good care of it and it hasn't burnt down."

Andy grinned. "We did have a major grass fire at the edge of town while you were gone, does that count?"

"Not much," Jay retorted and then turned serious. "Have you talked with Rebecca Sutherland lately?"

"I called her Labor Day and she was doing great. She had just been matron of honor at a wedding on the beach."

"Sounds like fun," Jay replied. "Please don't let Mrs. Sutherland know until I get there, but I'm leaving in three months for the air base on Guam."

Andy could not mask his pleasure as he tried to visualize the island he had heard so much about. "Great. I'll get to have Christmas with you."

"But I won't be able to come home for two years," Jay protested.

Andy grinned even wider. "I know, but I already have my tickets bought for the winter holidays on Guam."

The dashing airman studied the face of the most confirmed bachelor in Montana. "Hmmm. This sounds serious."

"It could be," Andy replied. "If you can keep this quiet, I'll let you in on my personal secret."

"My lips are sealed."

"I'm going to take a diamond ring with me to Guam and present it to Rebecca at the exact spot where she was the matron of honor at the wedding. She described it as the most beautiful place on earth."

"Whoever said that love is only for the young was dead wrong," Jay laughed. "Those of you over fifty seem to have more fun with your romances than the young could ever imagine."

Chapter 14

I am sure glad it's Friday, Rebecca thought as she shelved the last book of the day. *I'm ready for a day off, but ever since Ella Mae was married, I've had a lot of free time that I've had to spend by myself.*

Rebecca flinched as the silence was broken by the creaking of the library door. A striking young airman in full dress uniform entered.

"May I help you?" she said as she left the stack and hurried toward the front of the library. Halfway across the room she halted. Her chin dropped.

"Jay Harkness?" she nearly shouted.

Jay opened his arms as he hurried toward her. "Mrs. Sutherland, I've never hugged one of my teachers before, but it's so good to see you."

"Jay, what are you doing here?" she gasped.

"I got my dream assignment, Anderson Air Force Base Guam."

"Congratulations! When did you get here?"

"Tuesday afternoon, but they've kept me so busy I haven't had time to contact you. I'm off for the rest of the day. How about going to dinner with me?"

"Sounds good. Do you have a place in mind?"

"Mrs. Sutherland, you're familiar with the island. Where would you suggest?"

Rebecca squeezed his hand. "Jay, now that you've graduated from high school you may call me Rebecca like all my other friends do."

"Thanks. I guess we'll have an entirely different relationship from now on," Jay replied. "Now, where should we eat?"

"I've always liked the San Francisco House. It specializes in every kind of pasta imaginable. It's quite a ways from here. Would you like to follow me?"

"That would probably be best," Jay replied. "I still get lost as soon as I get off the base."

Rebecca reached in her desk for her keys. "I'll lock up and be right with you."

Jay followed Rebecca's red Toyota down Cross Island Road onto Marine Drive and then into Agana. The excitement of the sights and sounds of island life entranced him. He wanted to see and do everything. He was more fortunate than other military personnel in that he had a

454

familiar face from home to acquaint him with the island.

As Rebecca enjoyed a plate of lasagna and Jay devoured a huge order of ravioli, they updated each other on the events in their lives.

"It's too bad the air force sent you over just three weeks before Christmas," Rebecca noted. "It would have been nice to have another Christmas with your family."

"I know," Jay sighed, "but they needed someone in the position right away."

"Andy Hatfield is going to come for Christmas, so you can have Christmas with us," Rebecca offered.

Jay bit his lip, knowing he had a secret to protect. "You and Andy need time alone together," he protested. "I don't want to be a third wheel."

"Jay, don't be silly. We Rocky Bluffers have to stick together when we're out of Montana. How about me showing you the island tomorrow?"

"If you wouldn't mind. There's so much to see. The brochures the military gave me said that the southern part of the island is totally different from that around the base."

"You won't believe the difference," Rebecca replied. "Why don't you come to my apartment around nine o'clock? I'll make us some sandwiches and we can make a day of it."

"I'd love it. Before I leave base I'll stop by the commissary and get some ice and soft drinks."

The next day Rebecca took Jay to the same spots she visited during her introductory tour of the island. . .Talafofo Falls, Mount Lamlam, and the villages of Merizo, Inarajan, and Agat.

"Jay, I have a dear friend who lives just down the road in the village of Santa Rita. I'd love to have you meet her. I've told her all about the people of Rocky Bluff."

"Your friends are mine," Jay quipped.

Rebecca turned her car into a drive lined with banana trees. The cement house was a freshly painted white with green trim.

"Wait here and I'll see if she's home," Rebecca said as she slid from under the wheel.

Rebecca knocked on the screen door and within seconds a dark-haired Chamorro woman opened the door. "Rebecca, I'm glad you stopped by. Come in and relax. I just finished making a batch of cookies."

"I have a friend from Rocky Bluff with me who arrived this week for a two-year tour at Anderson Air Force Base. I'd love to have you meet him. He's a delightful young man."

Mitzi Quinata smiled as she looked over her shoulder at her daughter

Angela. "Invite him in," Mitzi urged. "Maybe we could coax you both to stay for dinner."

Rebecca motioned for Jay to join her. He quickly obeyed and Rebecca made the formal introductions. He politely greeted Mitzi and then turned to Angela. He blushed as he surveyed her natural beauty. For the remainder of the evening Jay's attention remained centered on the local girl who was studying cosmetology at Guam Community College. She was so different from the fair-skinned girls he'd known in Montana.

December twenty-third Rebecca was back at the Won Pat International Airport. She nervously paced inside the terminal as she waited for the plane from Hawaii to land. She watched the variety of races as they emerged from the covered ramp. Somewhere in the crowd, would be her best friend from Rocky Bluff.

"Rebecca."

There trying to work his way through a group of Japanese tourists was Andy. As soon as he had broken through the crowd, they were in each others' arms.

"Andy, I'm glad you finally got here. I've missed you so."

"I've missed you, too," he whispered as his lips brushed hers. "It seems like it's been forever since we were climbing Old Baldy together."

"Let's get your luggage and get out of here," Rebecca urged. "This place is too crowded for me."

Rebecca steered her Toyota toward her apartment in Dededo. Andy admired the waving coconut palms as they drove. "I always thought Hawaii was hot, but this is oppressive," he noted.

"What do you expect?" Rebecca chided. "Look at the way you're dressed. I hope you brought lighter clothes with you."

"I don't own many light clothes," Andy replied. "Remember, I'm from Montana where there's now two feet of snow on the ground."

Rebecca laughed. "I'll have to take you shopping for Guamanian clothes tomorrow." She paused a moment and peered into the distance. "We're almost to the beach where Ella Mae and Tom were married. It's beautiful there. Would you like to stop?"

Andy beamed. This was almost too good to be true.

"Please do. Your pictures of it were beautiful."

As Rebecca parked her car under a coconut palm, Andy reached for a small box in his carry-on bag. They locked hands and began strolling toward the water.

"Your pictures didn't do this place justice," Andy noted. "I've traveled a lot, but I've never seen anyplace that could compare with this."

"I know. This is my favorite spot on the entire island."

The couple halted and Andy reached into his pocket and took out the small box. "Rebecca, I love you and I hope you will accept this."

She looked puzzled as she opened the box, and then her face broke into a broad smile as tears welled in her eyes.

"It's beautiful," she whispered.

"Will you marry me as soon as you get back to Rocky Bluff? I've been so lonely without you."

Without hesitating Rebecca replied, "Yes, yes. Of course I will."

Andy took the quarter karat diamond ring out of the box and slipped it onto Rebecca's finger.

"It's a perfect fit," he said proudly.

The pair sat on the sand and watched the waves beat against the rocks. This was a sight so different from their home in Montana. Finally Rebecca looked at her watch.

"I've invited Jay Harkness over for dinner tonight," she said. "He was so excited about your coming."

"It'll be fun to see him again. I haven't seen him since he completed his basic training in Texas. How's he doing?"

"He loves the air force," Rebecca replied. "In fact, he was kind enough to arrange for housing for you with him at the base. It's beautiful out there."

"Thanks, I appreciate all you've done," Andy said as he took her hand.

Andy's vacation on Guam flew by. The happy couple viewed every part of the island. Jay was even able to convince him to try snorkeling with a group of his friends. Certain no one in Rocky Bluff would believe that their fire chief could possibly be that adventuresome, Rebecca was there with her camera to record the event.

The evening before Andy left Guam, he and Rebecca returned to their favorite beach. "This is a memory I want to take back to Montana with me," Andy said. "I want to remember the wind blowing through your hair underneath a coconut palm with the sun setting over the ocean behind you."

"I'll always remember this spot, not because of Ella Mae's wedding, but because it's the spot where you asked me to become Mrs. Andy Hatfield. Up until Edith married Roy Dutton, I never thought love over fifty was possible, but now I find it's even more precious than the first time around."

"I'll talk with Pastor Rhodes when I get back and schedule our wedding for the first open weekend in June. Don't worry about a thing. This will be a wedding ceremony planned exclusively by the groom."

The weeks after Andy left passed slowly for Rebecca. She felt a tremendous sense of accomplishment as she looked around her workplace. The library automation project was winding down and the students were thrilled to be able to use the computer instead of their old-fashioned card catalog to locate their books.

During Easter vacation Jay called Rebecca early in the morning. "Rebecca, have you been listening to the radio?"

"No, I've slept in. What's up?"

"There's a typhoon warning and it's already at condition two."

Rebecca sat erect. "What does that mean?"

"It means that destructive winds are anticipated within twenty-four hours. The winds could be over a hundred miles an hour. Do you have any provisions set aside?"

"I've never given it much thought," Rebecca confessed. "I didn't think this was even typhoon season."

"It's not, but they say typhoons can happen anytime. Why don't I come and take you to the store? If you don't mind, I'd like to stay with you until the storm is over. I don't like the idea of you being there alone."

"Thanks, Jay. I appreciate your concern. I'll begin getting prepared for a water and power outage."

The next few minutes Rebecca spent filling the bathtub and every possible container with water. *How silly of me to live in the prime typhoon belt and not be prepared for the inevitable,* she scolded herself.

A sharp knock on the door startled Rebecca and she hurried to open the door. "Jay, come in. Thanks for caring. How do you know so much about what to do during typhoons?"

"The air force required everyone assigned to Guam to attend a special training session on typhoons. They directed that we do our best to look out for the civilian population, so here I am," he chuckled. "Come with me and I'll take you to the store. We don't have any time at all to waste."

A light rain was already beginning to fall as the pair hurried to Jay's car. "Do you have a flashlight with batteries?" Jay queried.

"No," Rebecca replied meekly. "I've always relied on the electricity."

"Do you have a transistor radio with batteries?"

"No. I have an electric radio-alarm."

"Do you have enough canned food to last five days?"

"No. Most of my food is either fresh or frozen."

"Do you have candles or a hurricane lantern?"

"No. I guess I am in pretty bad shape."

"We can get all those things in Agana, but we're pushing our luck going shopping now. The stores are probably already packed with everyone looking for the same things," Jay noted.

Jay and Rebecca stopped at a combination grocery/variety store. They grabbed a cart and hurried down the aisles. They found everything they had talked about enroute plus a first aid kit and a manual can opener. Rebecca also bought a couple magazines from the rack along with a paperback book.

When they got to the checkout stands, they found the lines halfway down the aisles. It took nearly twenty minutes before they were checked out. As they stood nervously waiting, they could see the rain begin to pound upon the plate glass window of the store. The store owner locked the door so no one else could come in and then began pounding plywood over his windows.

As soon as Jay and Rebecca had paid for their supplies, they snatched their bags and ran into the torrential rain. The windshield wipers could not clear the windshield fast enough as they inched their way toward Rebecca's apartment. They got soaking wet running from the car to the apartment.

"That will teach me not to be prepared," Rebecca said as she locked the door behind them. "I have a sloppy shirt and an oversized pair of shorts if you'd like to go to the bathroom and change."

"Don't mind if I do," Jay replied.

Rebecca rummaged in her drawers until she found what she was looking for. She handed them to Jay along with a towel from the hall closet. She then went back to the bedroom to find something dry for herself. She had no sooner gotten out of her wet clothes when the lights went out.

"I've never used a hurricane lamp before," Rebecca said as she rustled through the sacks. "But there's always a first time for everything."

She read out the directions of the newly purchased kerosene lamp, which came as a kit. "I'm sure glad we remembered to pick up the wooden matches. I haven't used these things in years. I wasn't even aware they still made them."

"It looks like we'll be roughing it for awhile," Jay replied as he began going through the bags. "Let's turn on the radio and see what's happening. They update the warnings every two hours. It sounds like the wind is really picking up."

When they had finishing getting everything set up, Jay and Rebecca sat down to ride out the storm.

"Would you like a ham and cheese sandwich?" Rebecca asked. "We'd better eat them now because the refrigerator items won't be good much longer."

"Sounds good to me," Jay replied as he opened a couple cans of soft drinks.

As they waited through the storm, Rebecca and Jay could hear the palm tree across the street crash to the ground, crushing a car in its path. Trash cans went flying past the living room window.

"Jay, we've been so busy getting ready for the storm that we didn't do the most important thing," Rebecca said as they pulled their chairs into the corner of the kitchen away from the windows.

The young airman looked puzzled. "What's that? I think I've done everything the military class taught."

"We haven't prayed for God's protection."

Jay flushed with embarrassment. "You're right. After all Grandma taught me about prayer, I can't imagine I didn't stop to pray as soon as I learned there was a problem."

Rebecca and Jay took turns asking God for protection for themselves and for others on the island. The relaxing calm helped them refocus their thoughts and quiet their fears. They thumbed through the magazines to help pass the time and talked about the challenges of a Montana blizzard. They laughed at the irony of their conversation.

The night turned black as the wind began to subside.

"Maybe we should try to get some sleep," Rebecca suggested. "I'll get a pillow and you can stretch out on the sofa."

"I never thought I could sleep through a typhoon, but I feel secure in God's hands and I believe I could sleep for a week," Jay replied.

True to their expectations, they both slept soundly and did not awaken until the tropical sun was beating through their living room window. The apartment was unbearably hot as the electricity was still off and the air conditioner remained quiet in the window.

Rebecca pushed open the windows.

"The air is so heavy and humid," she said. "Even an electric fan would feel good now."

Jay stepped onto the patio. "There are power lines down all over the place. I don't think it would be wise to leave for the base yet. Turn on the radio and see if there's anything new."

Civil Defense Headquarters was still in control of the radio station and announced that all roads and streets were closed to vehicular traffic until further notice. Engineers from the army national guard and line crews from Guam Power were clearing debris and repairing downed power lines.

Jay picked up the phone. "The telephone lines are down as well. I guess you're stuck with me for awhile longer. I can't even call the base to let them know where I'm at."

"If that's the case, how about some breakfast?" Rebecca replied, trying to sound cheerful. "How do cold breakfast turnovers sound?"

"Right now anything would taste good," Jay chuckled.

The morning passed slowly for the pair as they sat glued to their transistor radio. After what seemed like an eternity, the radio spread the good news that the emergency was over. Jay breathed a sigh of relief, said goodbye to Rebecca, and headed back to the base. The crisis was over, but the cleanup would last for weeks.

Guam Christian Academy suffered mild damage from the typhoon, and several sections of the roof had to be repaired before the students could return to school. The added vacation made the days until Rebecca returned to Rocky Bluff drag by. She spent hours writing letters to Andy, Edith, and Beth describing the typhoon. Most importantly, she wrote to Bob and Nancy, thanking them for raising such a thoughtful son. She explained to them how prepared he was and concerned for her safety. The Montana spirit was not confined within the state boundaries.

Chapter 15

After the students left on the last day of school, friends and colleagues packed the cafeteria of Guam Christian Academy for a farewell fiesta honoring Rebecca Sutherland. Friends from the other schools and her church joined the GCA faculty in bringing their favorite dish so the serving table had a truly international flavor. Each person came to say good-bye to Rebecca and wish her well. Everyone at school praised her for the library automation project.

Principal Diaz took the microphone and thanked Rebecca for her contribution to the school. He asked her to come forward and then handed her a plaque from the entire school honoring her for outstanding service.

Choking back tears, Rebecca struggled for words. "I'd like to thank each one of you for helping make this such a rewarding two years for me," she began. "I feel that I have gained more by coming to Guam than I could ever contribute back. I'd especially like to thank Principal Diaz for his support and encouragement. Also, I'd like to say a big thanks to Mitzi Quinata, who made me feel welcome the first day I walked onto the campus of GCA. There are many others who have meant a lot to me during my stay here. Among those, Ella Mae and Tom Lee have made tremendous neighbors. I had the privilege of being matron of honor at their beautiful wedding on the beach."

Rebecca scanned the room and spotted Jay Harkness standing in the back with Angela Quinata. *They make a striking couple standing there. I wonder if their friendship will develop into something more,* she mused.

"I'd also like to thank a former student and friend from Rocky Bluff, Montana, for all his help. I hadn't the faintest idea what to do during a typhoon and he stepped right in and walked me through the process. It was a humbling experience to have a former student teach me basic survival skills. If any of you haven't met Airman Second Class Jay Harkness yet, I'd encourage you to do so. From the day he stepped off the plane, he fell in love with Guam and the island ways. He's the kind of person we can be proud of to represent and protect our country."

That night Rebecca tossed and turned in her bed. It was a bittersweet time. She looked forward to going home to Rocky Bluff and Andy Hatfield, but she was leaving so many friends and memories behind. Early in the morning she gave her apartment key to the building manager and Ella Mae drove her to the airport. As the pair was walking to the terminal, a male voice behind her said, "May I help you with your bags?"

A shot of adrenaline raced through Rebecca's body. *I've been on Guam for two years without being assaulted, it can't happen now.* She wheeled around.

"Jay! What are you doing here?"

"Angela and I wanted to come and see you off. I'm sorry we're so late, but I was detained on base."

Rebecca took a deep breath and then grinned. "You gave me such a start. I'm so glad you're here. I didn't get to talk to you alone or say good-bye the night of my going-away fiesta."

"I wanted to let you know how much it meant to me having you here and teaching me the ropes of adapting to the Guamanian culture. Most of all I wanted to thank you for introducing me to Angela."

Angela blushed. "I've never made close friendships with statesiders before. I always thought they were rich and arrogant and looked down on us, but Jay is different. He appreciates the relaxed island flavor."

"I'm glad I got to come to Guam. I learned to appreciate the differences in cultures along with the similarities of all being one of God's creations. You and your mother were special people and I'll never forget you."

"I'll never forget you. I wanted to give you a going-away present." Angela handed Rebecca a brightly colored box.

The four hurried inside and checked her luggage. While they were waiting, Angela insisted that Rebecca open her package. Inside the box was a beautifully sculpted wooden clock in the shape of the island of Guam.

"It's beautiful," Rebecca gasped. "I'll treasure it forever, but I've never seen this kind of wood before."

"It's ifil wood," Angela replied. "It's native to only this part of the world and is becoming very rare. It's so tough that it is often called iron wood."

The boarding announcement for the flight to Honolulu interrupted their well wishing. Rebecca hugged her friends and grabbed her present and carry-on luggage. Tears filled her eyes as she bravely walked toward her plane. The people of Guam were now a part of her history; she was soon to become Mrs. Andy Hatfield.

The Treasure State evening flight taxied to a stop in front of the airport of Rocky Bluff, Montana. An exhausted librarian entered the terminal. She had changed planes in Hawaii, Seattle, and Great Falls. It had been eighteen hours of flight time, not counting the three layovers.

Andy rushed toward her. "Welcome home," he whispered as he held her close. "I knew you'd be tired so I called Edith Dutton and she has a warm bath and a bed all ready for you. As soon as you wake up in the morning, call me and we can begin making our plans then."

"Andy, you're so considerate," Rebecca replied as she laid her tired head on his shoulder. "You think of everything."

"I've never had a woman to take care of before and I think I'm going to like it."

When Rebecca arrived at Edith's, Andy carried her suitcase into the guest room and bade the two friends goodnight. Rebecca chatted a few moments with Edith and then both women went to bed early. Tomorrow would be soon enough for serious conversation.

The next morning it was after eleven o'clock before Rebecca walked into Edith's living room.

"Good morning," Edith greeted. "I trust you slept well."

"It was the heaviest sleep I think I've ever had. I feel great today and anxious to talk to everyone in town."

"Would you like some breakfast first?" Edith queried.

"Don't go to any extra trouble," Rebecca protested. "I can fix some toast and coffee for myself."

The two friends sat around the kitchen table talking while Rebecca ate her breakfast. After finishing, she turned to Edith. "I think I better give Andy a call and let him know I'm up. We have a lot of planning to get done today."

"This is an exciting time for you," Edith noted. "Planning a marriage when you're over fifty is an entirely different experience. So much living goes into each decision."

Within minutes Andy joined Rebecca and Edith. "There's so much to do, I scarcely know where to begin," Rebecca said.

"Don't worry about a thing," Andy told her. "I've already done a lot of pre-work. First, where do we want to live? I assume you'll want to keep your home."

"You're right there," Rebecca nodded. "Since you were renting a small apartment, it would be much more comfortable in my place. I need to talk to Dan and Beth Blair about their moving plans."

"Dan stopped by the fire station the other day and we had a nice long talk. He's been offered a job at the crisis center in Missoula and was all excited about the possibilities there. It's a much larger center and Beth will be able to work on a bachelor's degree. I don't know when they plan to move."

"I'll go over and talk with them later today," Rebecca replied and then turned to her hostess. "Edith, would you mind if I stay here for a few more days so the Blairs can have some flexibility in their moving plans?"

"I'd love having you for as long as is necessary," Edith assured her. "This house gets plenty lonely at times."

"Next question you're going to ask is about the wedding date. Right?" Andy teased.

Rebecca's eyes twinkled. "You're reading my mind."

"I talked with Pastor Rhodes and he reserved the church for June twenty-seventh. I hope the date's suitable. There were a number of weddings this month that he had to work around," Andy explained.

"The date's fine," Rebecca replied. "However, it won't give me much time to plan the details."

"I thought next week Edith could come with us when we drive to Great Falls and find you a wedding dress. I've already had the invitations printed, so all we have to do is address them."

"You've thought of everything," Rebecca chided. "What else have you planned?"

"Teresa Lennon agreed to plan the reception. She wants to know your colors just as soon as you get home. I've met with the florist and she's waiting for your final stamp of approval."

"Andy, you don't waste any time at all, do you?"

"I sure don't," Andy chuckled. "I've never gotten married before and if I'd known it would be this much fun, I'd have done it a long time ago."

Rebecca grinned and shrugged her shoulders. "What else have you done?"

"Pastor Rhodes would like to meet with us a couple times before the wedding, so I scheduled that for the next two Thursday nights," Andy explained.

"What about the rehearsal dinner?" Rebecca queried. "I suppose you've taken care of that as well."

"I didn't miss a thing," Andy replied. "I reserved the banquet room at Beefy's Steak House for twenty-five people the evening before the wedding."

Rebecca shook her head in amazement. "I suppose you even have the guest list prepared?"

"Only part of it," Andy replied as he reached for a tattered sheet of paper in his pocket.

Rebecca giggled. "It looks like you're going to invite half the town."

"I would have invited the rest of them, but I don't know their names," Andy replied. "I also don't know the names of all your relatives."

"Looks like it's going to be a packed house," Edith inserted.

"That's what we want," Andy replied. "I want the whole world to celebrate with us." Andy suddenly became serious as he turned to Rebecca. "Kenneth and Laura Taylor were in town Memorial Day with Dick Reed's two children. They wanted to make sure their daughter's grave was decorated. When I told them we were getting married, they were so excited. They plan to drive back for the wedding."

"How sweet of them," Rebecca replied. "After all their heartaches, they're willing to come back and celebrate with us."

"The Taylors are tremendous people. They came through that tragedy with such grace and dignity," Edith said as she offered the happy couple another cold drink. "The children seem to be thriving under their care."

That afternoon Edith and Rebecca drove to Rebecca's home. As soon as they approached the front step, the door was flung open.

"Rebecca, I'm so glad to see you," Beth exclaimed as she hugged her former boss. "Come and see little Edith."

A sense of peace enveloped her as she entered the living room. She was finally home. Across the room a dark-haired baby girl crawled toward them. Rebecca reached over and picked her up. "She's beautiful. She looks just like you." The baby babbled her satisfaction.

"Thank you," Beth beamed. "She's been such a blessing. Jeffy's so proud of her that he's become my number one baby-sitter."

Rebecca scanned her home. "Speaking of Jeffy, where is he?"

"He has a Little League practice. He just loves it. He's going to be the next generation of Montana athletic stars."

"She's not exaggerating," Edith chimed in. "I went to his first game and he reminded me of Jay when he was that age."

"Dan contacted the Missoula Little League Association and they have already assigned Jeffy to a team."

Rebecca put her arm around the young mother and pulled her close. "Beth, I'm so proud of all you've accomplished. I hate to see you leave Rocky Bluff, but I'm glad that you've decided to get a degree in library science."

"Thanks. I had an excellent mentor." A look of chagrin covered Beth's face. "I tried to have all our things packed and out of here by the time you returned, but the moving company can't come until the fifteenth. I hope that won't be a problem for you."

"No problem at all. Edith said I could stay with her until you're able to move. Andy and I were planning to redecorate anyway."

Baby Edith became restless in Rebecca's arms and reached for her mother. "I hope you both are free Saturday night," Beth said as she surveyed the two women. "I want to throw a big celebration party. God has been so good to us. Dan obtained a prestigious job in Missoula and I was accepted into the University of Montana. We're going to have our second anniversary this month and little Edith is having her first birthday on the twenty-third. Jean and Jim Thompson are going to bring little Heidi so we can celebrate their first birthdays together. Larry and Libby Reynolds are going to bring their children as well."

"I wouldn't miss it for the world," Rebecca assured her as Edith nodded in agreement. "That would be the best welcome home I could ever have."

The next few weeks flew by for Rebecca. She and Andy finished their wedding plans and changed the decor of her home to blend both their tastes. Former students dropped by her home, anxious to hear her tales of the South Pacific. But Guam seemed a hundred years ago and an entirely different lifetime. Her life now consisted of becoming Mrs. Andrew Hatfield.

A week before her wedding, Rebecca was at the airport to meet her parents. "Mom, Dad!" she shouted as an elderly couple walked through the door. "I'm so glad you could come."

"Honey, we wouldn't have missed it for anything," Charles Harris replied. "You've waited much too long to find yourself another love."

"I know," Rebecca grinned, "but Andy is well worth the wait."

"I'm anxious to meet him," Maud said as she embraced her daughter.

Charles Harris became serious.

"Rebecca," he began. "My Parkinson's disease has really been giving me problems and my walk has become so unstable. Could you find someone else to escort you down the aisle?"

"I'll do no such thing," Rebecca protested. "I'll push you in a wheelchair if necessary."

Charles smiled. "Fortunately it's not that bad yet, but I just wanted to warn you."

"I'll tell you what, Dad," Rebecca suggested. "I'll take your arm as if you're escorting me. No one needs to be the wiser."

Tears filled Maud's eyes. "You've become such a sensitive woman, Rebecca. We're so proud of you."

"Thanks, Mom. Whatever I am is because of you and Dad."

June twenty-seventh dawned bright and clear. The temperature hovered in the mid-seventies, a perfect Montana day. Early in the afternoon Rebecca drove to the church to help Teresa, who was putting the final touches on the decorations in the fellowship hall.

"It's beautiful," Rebecca gasped. "You have such exquisite taste."

"I'm glad you like it," Teresa replied. "I'm so happy for you. Only you and Edith get an opportunity to have romance over fifty."

"I don't know about that," Rebecca protested. "I hear it's becoming more and more common. After I met Andy I realized that no aspect of life is limited to just the young."

Promptly at seven o'clock the organist in Rocky Bluff Community Church began to play the wedding march. There was scarcely a dry eye in the place as the maid of honor, Edith Dutton, strolled down the aisle carrying a bouquet of daisies. In the front she met the best man, Philip Mooney. The organist struck a chord and Maud Harris led the congregation in standing to respect the bride as she entered on the arm of her aging father.

Laura Taylor dabbed her eyes as Pastor Rhodes helped the happy couple recite the traditional wedding vows. He then addressed his words to the congregation, "Ladies and gentlemen, I'd like to present Mr. and Mrs. Andrew Hatfield. May their love continue to shine out to others, proving that distance and heartache cannot dampen a love that is guided from above. May God bless them with a long, happy life together. Amen and God bless you."

Two hours later the congregation gathered on the church steps waiting the departure of the bridal couple.

"I hope I catch the bridal bouquet," Dawn giggled to her best friend.

"No, several of the girls who graduated a couple years ago are sure to catch it. Most of them have serious boyfriends and it's a toss-up which one will be married first," the teenager replied.

A hush fell over the group while everyone reached for their packet of rice. Andy and Rebecca Hatfield stood at the steps and thanked everyone for their love and support. The single ladies giggled with anticipation.

468

Rebecca tossed her bouquet toward them just as a gust of wind blew across the town. The bouquet drifted directly into Teresa Lennon's hands.

Teresa turned to Nancy Harkness beside her. "I'm glad I'm not the superstitious type. Otherwise I'd start getting nervous. I'm the most confirmed old maid in town."

A Letter to Our Readers

Dear Readers:

In order that we might better contribute to your reading enjoyment, we would appreciate you taking a few minutes to respond to the following questions. When completed, please return to the following: Fiction Editor, Barbour Publishing, Inc., P.O. Box 719, Uhrichsville, OH 44683.

1. Did you enjoy reading *Montana?*
   □ Very much. I would like to see more books like this.
   □ Moderately—I would have enjoyed it more if _____

   _____

   _____

2. What influenced your decision to purchase this book?
   (Check those that apply.)
   □ Cover   □ Back cover copy   □ Title   □ Price
   □ Friends   □ Publicity   □ Other

3. Which story was your favorite?
   □ *Autumn Love*   □ *Contagious Love*
   □ *Inspired Love*   □ *Distant Love*

4. Please check your age range:
   □ Under 18   □ 18–24   □ 25–34
   □ 35–45   □ 46–55   □ Over 55

5. How many hours per week do you read? _____

Name _____

Occupation _____

Address _____

City_____ State _____ Zip _____

If you enjoyed

Montana

then read:

Getaways

*Four Inspirational Love Stories to
Sweep You Away on Romantic Excursions*

Spring in Paris
Wall of Stone
River Runners
Sudden Showers

If you enjoyed
Montana
then read:

LESSONS
of the
Heart

Four Novellas in Which
Modern Teachers Learn About Love

Love Lessons
Beauty for Ashes
Scrambled Eggs
Test of Time

If you enjoyed
Montana
then read:

Frontiers

Four Inspirational Love Stories
from America's Frontier by Colleen L. Reece

Flower of Seattle
Flower of the West
Flower of the North
Flower of Alaska

$\mathcal{H}$EARTSONG ❤ PRESENTS

Love Stories
Are Rated G!

That's for godly, gratifying, and of course, great! If you love a thrilling love story, but don't appreciate the sordidness of some popular paperback romances, **Heartsong Presents** is for you. In fact, **Heartsong Presents** is the only inspirational romance book club, the only one featuring love stories where Christian faith is the primary ingredient in a marriage relationship.

Sign up today to receive your first set of four, never-before-published Christian romances. Send no money now; you will receive a bill with the first shipment. You may cancel at any time without obligation, and if you aren't completely satisfied with any selection, you may return the books for an immediate refund!

Imagine. . .four new romances every four weeks—two historical, two contemporary—with men and women like you who long to meet the one God has chosen as the love of their lives. . .all for the low price of $9.97 postpaid.

To join, simply complete the coupon below and mail to the address provided. **Heartsong Presents** romances are rated G for another reason: They'll arrive Godspeed!

YES!   Sign me up for Heart❤ng!

NEW MEMBERSHIPS WILL BE SHIPPED IMMEDIATELY!
Send no money now. We'll bill you only $9.97 postpaid with your first shipment of four books. Or for faster action, call toll free 1-800-847-8270.

NAME _____

ADDRESS _____

CITY_____ STATE_____ ZIP_____

MAIL TO: HEARTSONG PRESENTS, P.O. Box 719, Uhrichsville, Ohio 44683